BROTHER CADFAEL OMNIBUS

ELLIS PETERS

BROTHER CADFAEL
OMNIBUS

DEAD MAN'S RANSOM

THE PILGRIM OF HATE

AN EXCELLENT MYSTERY

LITTLE, BROWN AND COMPANY

A *Little, Brown* Book

This first edition published in Great Britain in 1999 by
Little, Brown and Company.

Copyright © The Estate of Ellis Peters 1999
Dead Man's Ransom copyright © Elllis Peters 1984
The Pilgrim of Hate copyright © Ellis Peters 1984
An Excellent Mystery copyright © Ellis Peters 1985

The moral right of the author has been asserted.

A CIP catalogue for this book is available from the
British Library.

ISBN 0 316 85372 0

Printed and bound in Great Britain.

Little, Brown and Company (UK)
Brettenham House
Lancaster Place
London WC2E 7EN

DEAD MAN'S RANSOM

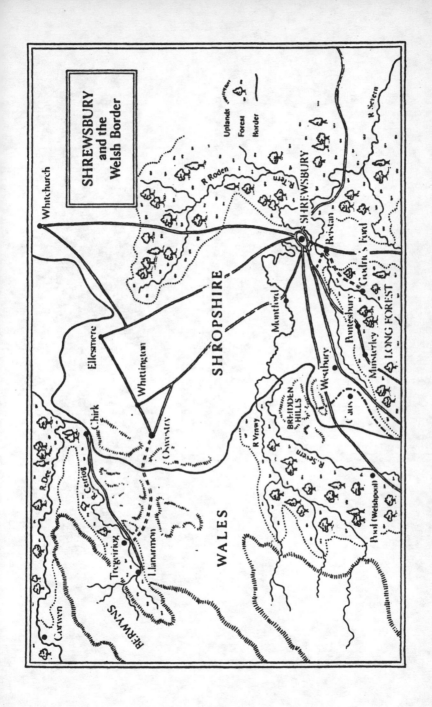

Chapter One

On that day, which was the seventh of
February of the year of Our Lord 1141,
they had offered special prayers at every
office, not for the victory of one party or the
defeat of another in the battlefields of the north,
but for better counsel, for reconciliation, for the
sparing of blood-letting and the respect of life
between men of the same country – all desirable
consummations, as Brother Cadfael sighed to
himself even as he prayed, but very unlikely to be
answered in this torn and fragmented land with
any but a very dusty answer. Even God needs
some consideration and support from his material
to make reasoning and benign creatures of men.

Shrewsbury had furnished King Stephen with a
creditable force to join his muster for the north,
where the earls of Chester and Lincoln, ambitious
half-brothers, had flouted the king's grace and
moved to set up their own palatine, and with
much in their favour, too. The parish part of the
great church was fuller than usual even at the
monastic offices, with anxious wives, mothers and
grandsires fervent in praying for their menfolk.
Not every man who had marched with Sheriff

7

Gilbert Prestcote and his deputy, Hugh Beringar, would come home again unscathed to Shrewsbury. Rumours flew, but news was in very poor supply. Yet word had filtered through that Chester and Lincoln, long lurking in neutrality between rival claimants for the crown, having ambitious plans of their own in defiance of both, had made up their minds in short order when menaced by King Stephen's approach, and sent hotfoot for help from the champions of his antagonist, the Empress Maud. Thus committing themselves for the future, perhaps, so deep that they might yet live to regret it.

Cadfael came out from Vespers gloomily doubting the force, and even the honesty of his own prayers, however he had laboured to give them heart. Men drunk with ambition and power do not ground their weapons, nor stop to recognise the fellow-humanity of those they are about to slay. Not here – not yet. Stephen had gone rampaging north with his muster, a huge, gallant, simple, swayable soul roused to rage by Chester's ungrateful treachery, and drawn after him many, and many a wiser and better balanced man who could have done his reasoning for him, had he taken a little more time for thought. The issue hung in the balance and the good men of Shropshire were committed with their lord. So was Cadfael's close friend, Hugh Beringar of Maesbury, deputy sheriff of the shire, and his wife must be anxiously waiting there in the town for news. Hugh's son, a year old now, was Cadfael's godson, and he had leave to visit him whenever he wished, a godfather's duties being important and sacred. Cadfael turned his back on supper in the refectory, and made his way out of the abbey gates, along the highway between the abbey mill and mill-pond on his left, and the belt of woodland sheltering the main abbey gardens of the Gaye on his right, over the bridge that spanned the Severn, glimmering in the wintry, starlit frost, and in through the great town gate.

There were torches burning at the door of Hugh's house by Saint Mary's church and beyond, at the High Cross, it seemed to Cadfael that there were more folk abroad and stirring than was usual at this hour of a winter evening. The faintest shiver of excitement hung in the air, and as soon as his foot touched the doorstone Aline came flying to the doorway with open arms. When she knew him her face remained pleased and welcoming, but nonetheless lost in an instant its special burning brightness.

'Not Hugh!' said Cadfael ruefully, knowing for whom the door had been thus thrown wide. 'Not yet. Is there news, then? Are they homing?'

'Will Warden sent word an hour ago, before the light was quite gone. They sighted steel from the towers, a good way off then, but by now they must be in the castle foregate. The gate's open for them. Come in to the fire, Cadfael, and stay for him.' She drew him in by the hands, and closed the door resolutely on the night and her own aching impatience. 'He is there,' she said, catching in Cadfael's face the reflection of 'her own partisan love and anxiety. 'They caught his colours. And the array in good order. Yet it cannot be quite as it went forth, that I know.'

9

No, never that. Those who go forth to the battle never return without holes in their ranks, like gaping wounds. Pity of all pities that those who lead never learn, and the few wise men among those who follow never quite avail to teach. But faith given and allegiance pledged are stronger than fear, thought Cadfael, and that, perhaps, is virtue, even in the teeth of death. Death, after all, is the common expectation from birth. Neither heroes nor cowards can escape it.

'He's sent no word ahead,' he asked, 'of how the day went?'

'None. But the rumour is it did not go well.' She said it firmly and freely, putting back with a small hand the pale gold hair from her forehead. A slender girl, still only twenty-one years old and mother of a year-old son and as fair as her husband was black-avised. The shy manner of her girlhood years had matured into a gentle dignity. 'This is a very wanton idea that flows and carries us all, here in England,' she said. 'It cannot always run one way, there must be an ebb.' She was brisk and practical about it, whatever that firm face cost her. 'You haven't eaten, you can't have stayed for supper,' she said, the housewife complete. 'Sit there and nurse your godson a little while, and I'll bring you meat and ale.'

The infant Giles, formidably tall for a year old when he was reared erect by holding to benches and trestles and chests to keep his balance, made his way carefully but with atonishing rapidity round the room to the stool by the fireside, and clambered unaided into Cadfael's rusty black lap. He had a flow of words, mostly of his own invention, though now and then a sound made sudden adult sense. His mother talked to him much, so did her woman Constance, his devoted slave, and this egg of the nobility listened and made voluble response. Of lordly scholars, thought Cadfael, rounding his arms to cradle the solid weight comfortably, we can never have too many. Whether he takes to the church or the sword, he'll never be the worse for a quick and ready mind. Like a pair of hound puppies nursed in the lap, Hugh's heir gave off glowing warmth, and the baked-bread scent of young and untainted flesh.

'He won't sleep,' said Aline, coming with a wooden tray to set it on the chest close to the fire, 'for he knows there's something in the wind. Never ask me how, I've said no word to him, but he knows. There, give him to me now, and take your meal. We may have a long wait, for they'll see all provided at the castle before ever Hugh comes to me.'

It was more than an hour before Hugh came. By then Constance had whisked away the remains of Cadfael's supper, and carried off a drooping princeling, who could not keep his eyes open any longer for all his contrivances, but slept in sprawled abandon in her arms as she lifted him. For all Cadfael's sharp hearing, it was Aline who first pricked up her head and rose, catching the light footsteps in the doorway. Her radiant smile faltered suddenly, for the feet trod haltingly.

'He's hurt!'

'Stiff from a long ride,' said Cadfael quickly. 'His legs serve him. Go, run, whatever's amiss will mend.'

She ran, and Hugh entered into her arms. As

11

soon as she had viewed him from head to foot, weary and weather-stained as he was, and found him whole, whatever lesser injuries he might be carrying, she became demure, brisk and calm, and would make no extravagant show of anxiety, though she watched him every moment from behind the fair shield of her wifely face. A small man, lightly built, not much taller than his wife, black-haired, black-browed. His movements lacked their usual supple ease, and no wonder after so long in the saddle, and his grin was brief and wry as he kissed his wife, drove a fist warmly into Cadfael's shoulder, and dropped with a great, hoarse sigh on to the cushioned bench beside the fire, stretching out his booted feet gingerly, the right decidedly with some pain. Cadfael kneeled, and eased off the stiff, ice-rimmed boots that dripped melting rivulets into the rushes.

'Good Christian soul!' said Hugh, leaning to clap a hand on his friend's tonsure. 'I could never have reached them myself. God, but I'm weary! No matter, that's the first need met – they're home and so am I.'

Constance came sailing in with food and a hot posset of wine, Aline with his gown and to rid him of his leather coat. He had ridden light the last stages, shedding his mail. He scrubbed with both hands at cheeks stiffened from the cold, twitched his shoulders pleasurably in the warmth of the fire, and drew in a great, easing breath. They watched him eat and drink with hardly a word spoken. Even the voice stiffens and baulks after long exertion and great weariness. When he was ready the cords of his throat would soften and warm, and words find their way out without creaking.

'Your man-child held open his eyelids,' said Aline cheerfully, eyeing his every least move as he ate and warmed, 'until he could prop them up no longer, even with his fingers. He's well and grown even in this short while – Cadfael will tell you. He goes on two feet now and makes nothing of a fall or two.' She did not offer to wake and bring him; clearly there was no place here tonight for matters of childhood, however dear.

Hugh sat back from his meal, yawned hugely, smiled upwards suddenly at his wife, and drew her down to him in his arm. Constance bore away the tray and refilled the cup, and closed the door quietly on the room where the boy slept.

'Never fret for me, love,' said Hugh, clasping Aline to his side. 'I'm saddle-sore and bruised, but nothing worse. But a fall or two we have certainly taken. No easy matter to rise, either. Oh, I've brought back most of the men we took north with us, but not all – not all! Not the chief – Gilbert Prestcote's gone. Taken, not dead, I hope and think, but whether it's Robert of Gloucester or the Welsh that hold him – I wish I knew.'

'The Welsh?' said Cadfael, pricking his ears. 'How's that? Owain Gwynedd has never put his hand in the fire for the empress? After all his careful holding off, and the gains it's brought him? He's no such fool! Why should he aid either of his enemies? He'd be more like to leave them free to cut each other's throats.'

'Spoke like a good Christian brother,' said

13

Hugh, with a brief, grey smile, and fetched a grunt and a blush out of Cadfael to his small but welcome pleasure. 'No, Owain has judgement and sense, but alas for him, he has a brother. Cadwaladr was there with a swarm of his archers, and Madog ap Meredith of Powys with him, hot for plunder, and they've sunk their teeth into Lincoln and swept the field clear of any prisoner who promises the means of ransom, even the half-dead. And I doubt they've got Gilbert among the rest.' He shifted, easing his stiff, sore body in the cushions. 'Though it's not the Welsh,' he said grimly, 'that have got the greatest prize. Robert of Gloucester is halfway to his own city this night with a prisoner worth this kingdom to deliver up to the Empress Maud. God knows what follows now, but I know what my work must be. My sheriff is out of the reckoning, and there's none now at large to name his successor. This shire is mine to keep, as best I may, and keep it I will, till fortune turns her face again. King Stephen is taken at Lincoln, and carried off prisoner to Gloucester.'

Once his tongue was loosed he had need to tell the whole of it, for his own enlightenment as much as theirs. He was the sole lord of a county now, holding and garrisoning it on the behalf of a king in eclipse, and his task was to nurse and guard it inviolate within its boundaries, until it could serve again beyond them for an effective lord.

'Ranulf of Chester slipped out of Lincoln castle and managed to get out of a hostile town before ever we got near, and off to Robert of Gloucester

14

in a great hurry, with pledges of allegiance to the empress in exchange for help against us. And Chester's wife is Robert's daughter, when all's said, and he'd left her walled up in the castle with the earl of Lincoln and his wife, and the whole town in arms and seething round them. That was a welcome indeed, when Stephen got his muster there, the city fawned on him. Poor wretches, they've paid for it since. Howbeit, there we were, the town ours and the castle under siege, and winter on our side, any man would have said, with the distance Robert had to come, and the snow and the floods to hold him. But the man's none so easily held.'

'I never was there in the north,' said Cadfael, with a glint in his eye and a stirring in his blood that he had much ado to subdue. His days in arms were over, forsworn long since, but he could not help prickling to the sting of battle, when his friends were still venturing. 'It's a hill city, Lincoln, so they say. And the garrison penned close. It should have been easy to hold the town, Robert or no Robert. What went astray?'

'Why, granted we under-valued Robert, as always, but that need not have been fatal. The rains there'd been up there, the river round the south and west of the town was up in flood, the bridge guarded, and the ford impassable. But Robert passed it, whether or no! Into the flood with him, and what could they do but come after? "A way forward, but no way back!" he says – so one of our prisoners told us. And what with the solid wall of them, they got across with barely a man swept away. Oh, surely they still had the uphill

15

way, out of that drowned plain to our hilltop – if Stephen were not Stephen! With the mass of them camped below in the wet fields and all the omens at Mass against him – you know he half-regards such warnings – what say you he'll do? Why, with that mad chivalry of his, for which God knows I love him though I curse him, he orders his array down from the height into the plain, to meet his enemy on equal terms.'

Hugh heaved his shoulders back against the solid brace of the wall, hoisted his agile brows and grinned, torn between admiration and exasperation.

'They'd drawn up on the highest and driest bit of land they could find, in what was a half-frozen marsh. Robert had all the disinherited, Maud's liegemen who had lost lands eastward for her sake, drawn up in the first line, horsed, with nothing to lose and all to gain, and vengeance the first of all. And our knights had every man his all to lose and nothing to gain, and felt themselves far from their homes and lands, and aching to get back and strengthen their own fences. And there were these hoards of Welsh, hungry for plunder, and their own goods and gear safe as sanctuary in the west, with no man threatening. What should we look for? When the disinherited hit our horse five earls broke under the shock and ran. On the left Stephen's Flemings drove the Welshmen back; but you know their way, they went but far enough and easily enough to mass again without loss, and back they came, archers almost to a man, able to pick their ground and their prey, and when the Flemish footmen ran, so did their captains – William of Ypres and Ten Eyck and all. Stephen was left unhorsed with us, the remnant of his horse and foot, around him. They rolled over us. It was then I lost sight of Gilbert. No marvel, it was hand to hand chaos, no man saw beyond the end of his sword or dagger, whatever he had in his hand to keep his head. Stephen still had his sword then. Cadfael, I swear to you, you never saw such a man in battle once roused, for all his easy goodwill takes so much rousing. It was rather the siege of a castle than the overcoming of a man. There was a wall round him of the men he had slain, those coming had to clamber over it, and went to build it higher. Chester came after him – give him his due, there's not much can frighten Ranulf – and he might have been another stone in the rampart, but that the king's sword shattered. There was one somewhere close to him thrust a Danish axe into his hand in its place, but Chester had leaped back out of reach. And then someone clear of the mêlée grubbed a great stone out of the ground, and hurled it at Stephen from aside. It struck him down flatlings, clean out of his wits, and they swarmed over him and pinned him hand and foot while he was senseless. And I went down under another wave,' said Hugh ruefully, 'and was trampled below better men's bodies, to come to myself in the best time to make vantage of it, after they'd dragged the king away and swarmed into the town to strip it bare, and before they came back to comb the battlefield for whatever was worth picking up. So I mustered what was left of our own, more than ever I expected, and hauled them off far enough

17

to be out of reach, while I and one or two with me looked for Gilbert. We did not find him and when they began to come back sated out of the city, scavenging, we drew off to bring back such as we had. What else could we have done?'

'Nothing to any purpose,' said Cadfael firmly. 'And thanks to God you were brought out man alive to do so much. If there's a place Stephen needs you now, it's here, keeping this shire for him.'

He was talking to himself, Hugh knew that already, or he would never have withdrawn from Lincoln. As for the slaughter there, no word was said. Better to make sure of bringing back all but a few of the solid townsfolk of Shrewsbury, his own special charge, and so he had done.

'Stephen's queen is in Kent and mistress of Kent, with a strong army, all the south and the east she holds,' said Hugh. 'She will shift every stone between her and London, but she'll get Stephen out of captivity somehow. It is not an ending. A reverse can be reversed. A prisoner can be loosed from prison.'

'Or exchanged,' said Cadfael, but very dubious. 'There's no great prize taken on the king's side? Though I doubt if the empress would let go of Stephen for any three of her best lords, even Robert himself, helpless as she'd be without him. No, she'll keep a fast hold of her prisoner, and make headlong for the throne. And do you see the princes of the church standing long in her way?'

'Well,' said Hugh, stretching his slight body wincingly, discovering new bruises, 'my part at

18

least I know. It's my writ that runs here in Shropshire now as the king's writ, and I'll see to it this shire, at least, is kept for the king.'

He came down to the abbey, two days later, to attend the Mass Abbot Radulfus had decreed for the souls of all those dead at Lincoln, on both parts, and for the healing of England's raw and festering wounds. In particular there were prayers to be offered for the wretched citizens of the northern city, prey to vengeful armies and plundered of all they had, many even of their lives, and many more fled into the wilds of the winter countryside. Shropshire stood nearer to the fighting now than it had been for three years, being neighbour to an earl of Chester elated by success and greedy for still more lands. Every one of Hugh's depleted garrison stood to arms, ready to defend its threatened security.

They were out from Mass, and Hugh had lingered in speech with the abbot in the great court, where there was sudden bustle in the arch of the gatehouse, and a small procession entered from the Foregate. Four sturdy countrymen in homespun came striding confidently, two with bows strung and slung ready for action, one shouldering a billhook, and the fourth a long-handled pikel. Between them, with two of her escort on either side, rode a plump middle-aged woman on a diminutive mule, and wearing the black habit of a Benedictine nun. The white bands of her wimple framed a rounded rosy face, well-fleshed and well-boned, and lit by a pair of bright brown eyes. She was booted like a man,

19

and her habit kilted for riding, but she swung it loose with one motion of a broad hand as she dismounted, and stood alert and discreet, looking calmly about her in search of someone in authority.

'We have a visiting sister,' said the abbot mildly, eyeing her with interest, 'but one that I do not know.'

Brother Cadfael, crossing the court without haste towards the garden and the herbarium, had also marked the sudden brisk bustle at the gate, and checked at the sight of a well-remembered figure. He had encountered this lady once before, and found her well worth remembering. And it seemed that she, also, recalled their meeting with pleasure, for the moment her eyes lit upon him the spark of recognition flashed in them, and she came at once towards him. He went to meet her gladly. Her rustic bodyguard, satisfied at having delivered her successfully where she would be, stood by the gatehouse, straddling the cobbles complacently, and by no means intimidated or impressed by their surroundings.

'I thought I should know that gait,' said the lady with satisfaction. 'You are Brother Cadfael, who came once on business to our cell. I'm glad to have found you to hand, I know no one else here. Will you make me known to your abbot?'

'Proudly,' said Cadfael, 'and he's regarding you this minute from the corner of the cloister. It's two years now ... Am I to tell him he's honoured by a visit from Sister Avice?'

'Sister Magdalen,' she said demurely and faintly smiled; and when she smiled, however briefly and

20

decorously, the sudden dazzling dimple he remembered flashed like a star in her weathered cheek. He had wondered then whether she had not better find some way of exorcising it in her new vocation, or whether it might not still be the most formidable weapon in her armoury. He was aware that he blinked, and that she noted it. There was always something conspiratorial in Avice of Thornbury that made every man feel he was the only one in whom she confided. 'And my errand,' she said practically, 'is really to Hugh Beringar, for I hear Gilbert Prestcote did not come back from Lincoln. They told us in the Foregate we should find him here, or we were bound up to the castle to look for him.'

'He is here,' said Cadfael, 'fresh from Mass, and talking with Abbot Radulfus. Over my shoulder you'll see them both.'

She looked, and by the expression of her face she approved. Abbot Radulfus was more than commonly tall, erect as a lance, and sinewy, with a lean hawk-face and a calmly measuring eye; and Hugh, if he stood a whole head shorter and carried but light weight, if he spoke quietly and made no move to call attention to himself, nevertheless seldom went unnoticed. Sister Magdalen studied him from head to heel with one flash of her brown eyes. She was a judge of a man, and knew one when she saw him.

'Very well so!' she said, nodding. 'Come, and I'll pay my respects.'

Radulfus marked their first move towards him and went to meet them, with Hugh at his shoulder.

'Father Abbot,' said Cadfael, 'here is come Sister Magdalen of our order, from the cell of Polesworth which lies some miles to the southwest, in the forest at Godric's Ford. And her business is also with Hugh Beringar as sheriff of this shire.'

She made a very graceful reverence and stooped to the abbot's hand. 'Truly, what I have to tell concerns all here who have to do with order and peace, Father. Brother Cadfael here has visited our cell, and knows how we stand in these troublous times, solitary and so close to Wales. He can advise and explain, if I fall short.'

'You are welcome, sister,' said Radulfus, measuring her as shrewdly as she had measured him. 'Brother Cadfael shall be of our counsel, I trust you will be my guest for dinner. And for your guards – for I see they are devoted in attendance on you – I will give orders for their entertainment. And if you are not so far acquainted, here at my side is Hugh Beringar, whom you seek.'

Though that cheek was turned away from him, Cadfael was certain that her dimple sparkled as she turned to Hugh and made her formal acknowledgement. 'My lord, I was never so happy,' she said – and whether that was high courtesy or mischief might still be questioned – 'as to meet with you before, it was with your sheriff I once had some speech. As I have heard he did not return with you and may be prisoner, and for that I am sorry.'

'I, too,' said Hugh. 'As I hope to redeem him, if chance offers. I see from your escort, sister, that you have had cause to move with caution through the forest. I think that is also my business, now I am back.'

'Let us go into my parlour,' said the abbot, 'and hear what Sister Magdalen has to tell us. And, Brother Cadfael, will you bear word to Brother Denis that the best of our house is at the disposal of our sister's guards? And then come to join us, for your knowledge may be needed.'

She was seated a little withdrawn from the fire when Cadfael entered the abbot's parlour some minutes later, her feet drawn trimly under the hem of her habit, her back erect against the panelled wall. The more closely and the longer he viewed her, the more warmly did he remember her. She had been for many years, from her beautiful youth, a baron's mistress, accepting that situation as an honest business agreement, a fair return for her body to give her escape from her poverty and cultivation for her mind. And she had held to her bargain loyally, even affectionately, as long as her lord remained alive. The loss of one profession offering scope for her considerable talents had set her looking about, with her customary resolution, for another as rewarding, at an age when such openings may be few indeed. The superior at Godric's Ford, first, and the prioress of Polesworth after, however astonished they might have been at being confronted with such a postulant, must have seen something in Avice of Thornbury well worth acquiring for the order. A woman of her word, ungrudging, to her first allegiance, she would be

23

as good as her word now to this new attachment. Whether it could have been called a vocation in the first place might seem very doubtful, but with application and patience she would make it so.

'When this matter of Lincoln blazed up as it did in January,' she said, 'we got rumour that certain of the Welsh were ready to rise in arms. Not, I suppose, for any partisan loyalty, but for plunder to be had when these two powers collided. Prince Cadwaladr of Gwynedd was mustering a war-band, and the Welsh of Powys rose to join him, and it was said they would march to aid the earl of Chester. So before the battle we had our warning.'

It was she who had heeded it. Who else, in that small nest of holy women, could have sensed how the winds blew between claimants for the crown, between Welsh and English, between ambitious earl and greedy tribesman?

'Therefore, Father, it was no great surprise to us, some four days ago, when a lad from an assart west of us came running in haste to tell us how his father's cot and holding was laid waste, his family fled eastward, and how a Welsh raiding party was drinking its fill in what remained of his home, and boasting how it would disembowel the nunnery of Godric's Ford. Huntsmen on their way home will not despise a few stray head of game to add to their booty. We had not the news of the defeat of Lincoln then,' she said, meeting Hugh's attentive gaze, 'but we made our judgements accordingly and took heed. Cadwaladr's shortest way home with his plunder to his castle at Aberystwyth skirts Shrewsbury close. Seemingly he still feared to come too near the town, even with the garrison

24

thinned as he knew it must be. But he felt safer with us in the forest. And with only a handful of women to deal with, it was worth his while to spend a day in sport, and strip us bare.'

'And this was four days ago?' asked Hugh, sharply intent.

'Four when the boy came. He's safe enough, and so is his sire, but their cattle are gone, driven off westward. Three days, when they reached us. We had a day to prepare.'

'This was a despicable undertaking,' said Radulfus with anger and disgust, 'to fasten like cowards upon a household of defenceless women. Great shame to the Welsh or any others who attempt such infamies. And we here knowing nothing of your need!'

'Never fear, Father, we have weathered this storm well enough. Our house yet stands, and has not been plundered, nor harm come to any of our women, and barely a scratch or two among the forest menfolk. And we were not quite defenceless. They came on the western side, and our brook runs between. Brother Cadfael knows the lie of the land there.'

'The brook would be a very frail barrier most of the year,' said Cadfael doubtfully. 'but we have had great rains this winter season. But there's both the ford and the bridge to guard.'

'True, but it takes no time there among good neighbours to raise a very fair muster. We are well thought of among the forest folk, and they are stout men.' Four of the stout men of her army were regaling themselves in the gatehouse with meat and bread and ale at this moment, proud

25

and content, set up in their own esteem, very properly, by their own exploits. 'The brook was high in flood already, but we contrived to pit the ford, in case they should still venture it, and then John Miller opened up all his sluices to swell the waters. As for the bridge, we sawed through the wood of the piers, leaving them only the last holt, and fastened ropes from them into the bushes. You'll recall the banks are well treed both sides. We could pluck the piers loose from cover whenever we saw fit. And all the men of the forest came with bills and dung-forks and bows to line our bank, and deal with any who did get over.'

No question who had generalled that formidable reception. There she sat, solid, placid and comely, like a well-blessed village matron talking of the doings of her children and grandchildren, fond and proud of their precocious achievements, but too wise to let them see it.

'The foresters,' she said, 'are as good archers as you will find anywhere, we had them spaced among the trees, all along our bank. And the men of the other bank were drawn aside in cover, to speed the enemy's going when he ran.'

The abbot was regarding her with a warily respectful face, and brows that signalled his guarded wonder. 'I recall,' he said, 'that Mother Mariana is old and frail. This attack must have caused her great distress and fear. Happy for her that she had you, and could delegate her powers to so stout and able a deputy.'

Sister Magdalen's benign smile might, Cadfael thought, be discreet cover for her memory of

Mother Mariana distracted and helpless with dread at the threat. But all she said was: 'Our superior was not well at that time, but praise be, she is now restored. We entreated her to take with her the elder sisters, and shut themselves up in the chapel, with such sacred valuables as we have, and there to pray for our safe deliverance. Which doubtless availed us above our bills and bows, for all passed without harm to us.'

'Yet their prayers did not turn the Welsh back short of the planned attempt, I doubt,' said Hugh, meeting her guileless eyes with an appreciative smile. 'I see I shall have to mend a few fences down there. What followed? You say all fell out well. You used those ropes of yours?'

'We did. They came thick and fast, we let them load the bridge almost to the near bank, and then plucked the piers loose. Their first wave went down into the flood, and a few who tried the ford lost their footing in our pits, and were swept away. And after our archers had loosed their first shafts, the Welsh turned tail. The lads we had in cover on the other side took after them and sped them on their way. John Miller has closed his sluices now. Give us a couple of dry weeks, and we'll have the bridge up again. The Welsh left three men dead, drowned in the brook, the rest they hauled out half-sodden, and dragged them away with them when they ran. All but one, and he's the occasion for this journey of mine. There's a very fine young fellow,' she said, 'was washed downstream, and we pulled him out bloated with water and far gone, if we had not emptied him, and pounded him alive to tell the tale. You may send and take him off our hands whenever you please. Things being as it seems they are, you may well have a use for him.'

'For any Welsh prisoner,' said Hugh, glowing. 'Where have you stowed him?'

'John Miller has him under lock and key and guarded. I did not venture to try and bring him to you, for good reason. He's sudden as a kingfisher and slippery as a fish, and short of tying him hand and foot I doubt if we could have held him.'

'We'll undertake to bring him away safely,' said Hugh heartily. 'What manner of man do you make of him? And has he given you a name?'

'He'll say no word but in Welsh, and I have not the knowledge of that tongue, nor has any of us. But he's young, princely provided, and lofty enough in his manner to be princely born, no common kern. He may prove valuable if it comes to an exchange.'

'I'll come and fetch him away tomorrow,' promised Hugh, 'and thank you for him heartily. By morning I'll have a company ready to ride. As well I should look to all that border, and if you can bide overnight, sister, we can escort you home in safety.'

'Indeed it would be wise,' said the abbot. 'Our guest-hall and all we have is open to you, and your neighbours who have done you such good service are equally welcome. Far better return with the assurance of numbers and arms. Who knows if there may not be marauding parties still lurking in the forest, if they're grown so bold?'

'I doubt it,' she said. 'We saw no sign of it on the way here. It was the men themselves would not let me venture alone. But I will accept your hospitality, Father, with pleasure, and be as grateful for your company, my lord,' she said, smiling thoughtfully at Hugh, 'on the way home.'

'Though, faith,' said Hugh to Cadfael, as they crossed the court together, leaving Sister Magdalen to dine as the abbot's guest, 'it would rather become me to give her the generalship of all the forest than offer her any protection of mine. We should have had her at Lincoln, where our enemies crossed the floods, as hers failed to do. Riding south with her tomorrow will certainly be pleasure, it might well be profit. I'll bend a devout ear to any counsel that lady chooses to dispense.'

'You'll be giving pleasure as well as receiving it,' said Cadfael frankly. 'She may have taken vows of chastity, and what she swears she'll keep. But she has not sworn never to take delight in the looks and converse and company of a proper man. I doubt they'll ever bring her to consent to that, she'd think it a waste and a shame, so to throw God's good gifts in his teeth.'

The party mustered after Prime next morning, Sister Magdalen and her four henchmen, Hugh and his half-dozen armed guards from the castle garrison. Brother Cadfael stood to watch them gather and mount, and took a warmly appreciative leave of the lady.

'I doubt I shall be hard put to it, though,' he admitted, 'to learn to call you by your new name.'

At that her dimple dipped and flashed, and

again vanished. 'Ah, that! You are thinking that I never yet repented of anything I did – and I confess I don't recall such a thing myself. No, but it was such a comfort and satisfaction to the women. They took me to their hearts so joyfully, the sweet things, a fallen sister retrieved. I couldn't forbear giving them what they wanted and thought fitting. I am their special pride, they boast of me.'

'Well they may,' said Cadfael, 'seeing you just drove back pillage, ravishment and probable murder from their nest.'

'Ah, that they feel to be somewhat unwomanly, though glad enough of the result. The doves were all aflutter – but then, I was never a dove,' said Sister Magdalen, 'and it's only the men truly admire the hawk in me.'

And she smiled, mounted her little mule and rode off homeward surrounded by men who already admired her, and men who were more than willing to offer admiration. In the court or in the cloister, Avice of Thornbury would never pass by without turning men's heads to follow her.

Chapter Two

Before nightfall Hugh was back with his prisoner, having prospected the western fringe of the Long Forest and encountered no more raiding Welshmen and no masterless men living wild. Brother Cadfael saw them pass by the abbey gatehouse on their way up through the town to the castle, where this possibly valuable Welsh youth could be held in safekeeping and, short of a credible parole, doubtless under lock and key in some sufficiently impenetrable cell. Hugh could not afford to lose him.

Cadfael caught but a passing glimpse of him as they rode by in the early dusk. It seemed he had given some trouble on the way, for his hands were tied, his horse on a leading rein, his feet roped into the stirrups and an archer rode suggestively close at his rear. If these precautions were meant to secure him, they had succeeded, but if to intimidate, as the young man himself appeared to suppose, they had signally failed, for he went with a high, disdainful impudence, stretching up tall and whistling as he went, and casting over his shoulder at the archer occasional volleys of Welsh,

31

which the man might not have endured so stolidly had he been able to understand their purport as well as Cadfael did. He was, in fact, a very forward and uppish young fellow, this prisoner, though it might have been partly bravado.

He was also a very well-looking young man, middling tall for a Welshman, with the bold cheekbones and chin and the ruddy colouring of his kind, and a thick tangle of black curls that fell very becomingly about his brow and ears, blown by the south-west wind, for he wore no cap. Tethered hands and feet did not hamper him from sitting his horse like a centaur, and the voice that teased his guards in insolent Welsh was light and clear. Sister Magdalen had said truly that his gear was princely, and his manner proclaimed him certainly proud and probably, thought Cadfael, spoiled to the point of ruin. Not a particularly rare condition in a well-made, personable and probably only son.

They passed, and the prisoner's loud, melodious whistle of defiance died gradually along the Foregate and over the bridge. Cadfael went back to his workshop in the herbarium, and blew up his brazier to boil a fresh elixir of horehound for the winter coughs and colds.

Hugh came down from the castle next morning with a request to borrow Brother Cadfael on his captive's behalf, for it seemed the boy had a raw gash in his thigh, ripped against a stone in the flood, and had gone to some pains to conceal it from the nuns.

'Ask me,' said Hugh, grinning, 'he'd have died rather than bare his hams for the ladies to poultice. And give him his due, though the tear is none so grave, the few miles he rode yesterday must have cost him dear in pain, and he never gave a sign. And blushed like a girl when we did notice him favouring the raw cheek, and made him strip.'

'And left his sore undressed overnight? Never tell me! So why do you need me?' asked Cadfael shrewdly.

'Because you speak good Welsh, and Welsh of the north, and he's certainly from Gwynedd, one of Cadwaladr's boys — though you may as well make the lad comfortable while you're about it. We speak English to him, and he shakes his head and answers with nothing but Welsh, but for all that, there's a saucy look in his eye that tells me he understands very well, and is having a game with us. So come and speak English to him, and trip the bold young sprig headlong when he thinks his Welsh insults can pass for civilities.'

'He'd have had short shrift from Sister Magdalen,' said Cadfael thoughtfully, 'if she'd known of his hurt. All his blushes wouldn't have saved him.' And he went off willingly enough to see Brother Oswin properly instructed as to what needed attention in the workshop, before setting out with Hugh to the castle. A fair share of curiosity, and a little over-measure, was one of the regular items of his confessions. And after all, he was a Welshman; somewhere in the tangled genealogies of his nation, this obdurate boy might be his distant kin.

They had a healthy respect for their prisoner's strength, wit and ingenuity, and had him in a windowless cell, though decently provided. Cadfael went in to him alone, and heard the door locked upon them. There was a lamp, a floating wick in a saucer of oil, sufficient for seeing, since the pale stone of the walls reflected the light from all sides. The prisoner looked askance at the Benedictine habit, unsure what this visit predicted. In answer to what was clearly a civil greeting in English, he replied as courteously in Welsh, but in answer to everything else he shook his dark head apologetically, and professed not to understand a word of it. He responded readily enough, however, when Cadfael unpacked his scrip and laid out his salves and cleansing lotions and dressings. Perhaps he had found good reason in the night to be glad of having submitted his wound to tending, for this time he stripped willingly, and let Cadfael renew the dressing. He had aggravated his hurt with riding, but rest would soon heal it. He had pure, spare flesh, lissome and firm. Under the skin the ripple of muscles was smooth as cream.

'You were foolish to bear this,' said Cadfael in casual English, 'when you could have had it healed and forgotten by now. Are you a fool? In your situation you'll have to learn discretion.'

'From the English,' said the boy in Welsh, and still shaking his head to show he understood no word of this, 'I have nothing to learn. And no, I am not a fool, or I should be as talkative as you, old shaven-head.'

'They would have given you good nursing at Godric's Ford,' went on Cadfael innocently. 'You wasted your few days there.'

'A parcel of silly women,' said the boy, brazen-faced, 'and old and ugly into the bargain.'

That was more than enough. 'A parcel of women,' said Cadfael in loud and indignant Welsh, 'who pulled you out of the flood and squeezed your lordship dry, and pummelled the breath back into you. And if you cannot find a civil word of thanks to them, in a language they'll understand, you are the most ungrateful brat who ever disgraced Wales. And that you may know it, my fine paladin, there's nothing older nor uglier than ingratitude. Nor sillier, either, seeing I'm minded to rip that dressing off you and let you burn for the graceless limb you are.'

The young man was bolt upright on his stone bench by this time, his mouth fallen open, his half-formed, comely face stricken into child-ishness. He stared and swallowed, and slowly flushed from breast to brow.

'Three times as Welsh as you, idiot child,' said Cadfael, cooling, 'being three times your age, as I judge. Now get your breath and speak, and speak English, for I swear if you ever speak Welsh to me again, short of extremes, I'll off and leave you to your own folly, and you'll find that cold company. Now, have we understood each other?'

The boy hovered for an instant on the brink of humiliation and rage, being unaccustomed to such falls, and then as abruptly redeemed himself by throwing back his head and bursting into a peal of laughter, both rueful for his own folly and appreciative of the trap into which he had stepped so blithely. Blessedly, he had the native good-nature that prevented his being quite spoiled.

'That's better,' said Cadfael disarmed. 'Fair enough to whistle and swagger to keep up your courage, but why pretend you know no English? So close to the border, how long before you were bound to be smoked out?'

'Even a day or two more,' sighed the young man resignedly, 'and I might have found out what's in store for me.' His command of English was fluent enough, once he had consented to use it. 'I'm new to this, I wanted to get my bearings.'

'And the impudence was to stiffen your sinews, I suppose. Shame to miscall the holy women who saved your saucy life for you.'

'No one was meant to hear and understand,' protested the prisoner, and in the next breath owned magnanimously: 'But I'm not proud of it, either. A bird in a net, pecking every way, as much for spite as for escape. And then I didn't want to give away any word of myself until I had my captor's measure.'

'Or to admit to your value,' Cadfael hazarded shrewdly, 'for fear you should be held against a high ransom. No name, no rank, no way of putting a price on you?'

The black head nodded. He eyed Cadfael, and visibly debated within himself how much to concede, even now he was found out, and then as impulsively flung open the floodgates and let the words come hurtling out. 'To tell truth, long before ever we made that assault on the nunnery I'd grown very uneasy about the whole wild affair. Owain Gwynedd knew nothing of his brother's muster, and he'll be displeased with us all, and when Owain's displeased I mind my walking very

36

carefully. Which is what I did *not* do when I went with Cadwaladr. I wish heartily that I had, and kept out of it. I never wanted to do harm to your ladies, but how could I draw back once I was in? And then to let myself be taken! By a handful of old women and peasants! I shall be in black displeasure at home, if not a laughing-stock.' He sounded disgusted rather than downcast, and shrugged and grinned good-naturedly at the thought of being laughed at, but for all that, the prospect was painful. 'And if I'm to cost Owain high, there's another black stroke against me. He's not the man to take delight in paying out gold to buy back idiots.'

Certainly this young man improved upon acquaintance. He turned honestly and manfully from wanting to kick everyone else to acknowledging that he ought to be kicking himself. Cadfael warmed to him.

'Let me drop a word in your ear. The higher your value, the more welcome will you be to Hugh Beringar, who holds you here. And not for gold, either. There's a lord, the sheriff of this shire, who is most likely prisoner in Wales as you are here, and Hugh Beringar wants him back. If you can balance him, and he is found to be there alive, you may well be on your way home. At no cost to Owain Gwynedd, who never wanted to dip his fingers into that trough, and will be glad to show it by giving Gilbert Prestcote back to us.'

'You mean it?' The boy had brightened and flushed, wide-eyed. 'Then I should speak? I'm in a fair way to get my release and please both Welsh and English? That would be better deliverance than ever I expected.'

'Or deserved!' said Cadfael roundly, and watched the smooth brown neck stiffen in offence, and then suddenly relax again, as the black curls tossed and the ready grin appeared. 'Ah, well, you'll do! Tell your tale now, while I'm here, for I'm mightily curious, but tell it once. Let me fetch in Hugh Beringar, and let's all come to terms. Why lie here on stone and all but in the dark, when you could be stretching your legs about the castle wards?'

'I'm won!' said the boy, hopefully shining. 'Bring me to confession, and I'll hold nothing back.'

Once his mind was made up he spoke up cheerfully and volubly, an outward soul by nature, and very poorly given to silence. His abstention must have cost him prodigies of self-control. Hugh listened to him with an unrevealing face, but Cadfael knew by now how to read every least twitch of those lean, live brows and every glint in the black eyes.

'My name is Elis ap Cynan, my mother was cousin to Owain Gwynedd. He is my overlord, and he has over-watched me in the fosterage where he placed me when my father died. That is, with my uncle Griffith ap Meilyr, where I grew up with my cousin Eliud as brothers. Griffith's wife is also distant kin to the prince, and Griffith ranks high among his officers. Owain values us. He will not willingly leave me in captivity,' said the young man sturdily.

'Even though you hared off after his brother to

38

a battle in which he wanted no part?' said Hugh, unsmiling but mild of voice.

'Even so,' persisted Elis firmly. 'Though if truth must out, I wish I never had, and am like to wish it even more earnestly when I must go back and face him. He'll have my hide, as like as not.' But he did not sound particularly depressed at the thought, and his sudden grin, tentative here in Hugh's untested presence, nevertheless would out for a moment. 'I was a fool. Not for the first time and I daresay not the last. Eliud had more sense. He's grave and deep, he thinks like Owain. It was the first time we ever went different ways. I wish now I'd listened to him. I never knew him to be wrong when it came to it. But I was greedy to see action, and pig-headed, and I went.'

'And did you like the action you saw?' asked Hugh drily.

Elis gnawed a considering lip. 'The battle, that was fair fight, all in arms on both parts. You were there? Then you know yourself it was a great thing we did, crossing the river in flood, and standing to it in that frozen marsh as we were, sodden and shivering ...' That exhilarating memory had suddenly recalled to him the second such crossing attempted, and its less heroic ending, the reverse of the dream of glory. Fished out like a drowning kitten, and hauled back to life face-down in muddy turf, hiccuping up the water he had swallowed, and being squeezed between the hands of a brawny forester. He caught Hugh's eye, and saw his own recollection reflected there, and had the grace to grin. 'Well, flood-water is on no man's side, it gulps down Welsh as readily as

39

English. But I was not sorry then, not at Lincoln. It was a good fight. Afterwards – no – the town turned my stomach. If I'd known before, I should not have been there. But I was there, and I couldn't undo it.'

'You were sick at what was done to Lincoln,' Hugh pointed out reasonably, 'yet you went with the raiders to sack Godric's Ford.'

'What was I to do? Draw out against the lot of them, my own friends and comrades, stick my nose in the air and tell them what they intended was vile? I'm no such hero!' said Elis openly and heartily. 'Still, you'll allow I did no harm there to anyone, as it fell out. I was taken, and if it please you to say, serve me right, I'll take no offence. The end of it is, here I am and at your disposal. And I'm kin to Owain and when he knows I'm living he'll want me back.'

'Then you and I may very well come to a sensible agreement,' said Hugh, 'for I think it very likely that my sheriff, whom I want back just as certainly, is prisoner in Wales as you are here, and if that proves true, an exchange should be no great problem. I've no wish to keep you under lock and key in a cell, if you'll behave yourself seemly and wait the outcome. It's your quickest way home. Give me your parole not to attempt escape, or to go outside the wards here, and you may have the run of the castle.'

'With all my heart!' said Elis eagerly. 'I pledge you my word to attempt nothing, and set no foot outside your gates, until you have your man again, and give me leave to go.'

*

Cadfael paid a second visit next day, to make sure that his dressing had drawn the Welsh boy's ragged scratch together with no festering; but that healthy young flesh sprang together like the matching of lovers, and the slash would vanish with barely a scar.

He was an engaging youth, this Elis ap Cynan, readable like a book, open like a daisy at noon. Cadfael lingered to draw him out, which was easy enough, and brought a lavish and guileless harvest. All the more with nothing now to lose, and no man listening but a tolerant elder of his own race, he unfolded his leaves in garrulous innocence.

'I fell out badly with Eliud over this caper,' he said ruefully. 'He said it was poor policy for Wales, and whatever booty we might bring back with us, it would not be worth half the damage done. I should have known he'd be proved right, he always is. And yet no offence in it, that's the marvel! A man can't be angry with him – at least I can't.'

'Kin by fostering can be as close as brothers by blood, I know,' said Cadfael.

'Closer far than most brothers. Like twins, as we almost could be. Eliud had half an hour's start of me into the world, and has acted the elder ever since. He'll be half out of his wits over me now, for all he'll hear is that I was swept away in the brook. I wish we might make haste with this exchange, and let him know I'm still alive to plague him.'

'No doubt there'll be others besides your friend and cousin,' said Cadfael, 'fretting over your absence. No wife as yet?'

Elis made an urchin's grimace. 'No more than threatened. My elders betrothed me long ago as a child, but I'm in no haste. The common lot, it's what men do when they grow to maturity. There are lands and alliances to be considered.' He spoke of it as of the burden of the years, accepted but not welcomed. Quite certainly he was not in love with the lady. Probably he had known and played with her from infancy, and scarcely gave her a thought now, one way or the other.

'She may yet be a deal more troubled for you than you are for her,' said Cadfael.

'Ha!' said Elis on a sharp bark of laughter. 'Not she! If I had drowned in the brook they'd have matched her with another of suitable birth, and he would have done just as well. She never chose me, nor I her. Mind, I don't say she makes any objections, more than I do, we might both of us do very much worse.'

'Who is this fortunate lady?' Cadfael wondered drily.

'Now you grow prickly, because I am honest,' Elis reproved him airily. 'Did I ever say I was any great bargain? The girl is very well, as a matter of fact, a small, sharp, dark creature, quite handsome in her way, and if I must, then she'll do. Her father is Tudur ap Rhys, the lord of Tregeiriog in Cynllaith – a man of Powys, but close friend to Owain and thinks like him, and her mother was a woman of Gwynedd. Cristina, the girl is called. Her hand is regarded as a great prize,' said the proposed beneficiary without enthusiasm. 'So it is, but one I could have done without for a while yet.'

They were walking the outer ward to keep warm, for though the weather had turned fine it was also frosty, and the boy was loth to go indoors until he must. He went with his face turned up to the clear sky above the towers, and his step as light and springy as if he trod turf already.

'We could save you yet a while,' suggested Cadfael slyly, 'by spinning out this quest for our sheriff, and keeping you here single and snug as long as you please.'

'Oh, no!' Elis loosed a shout of laughter. 'Oh, no, not that! Better a wife in Wales than that fashion of freedom here. Though best of all Wales and no wife,' admitted the reluctant bridegroom, still laughing at himself. 'Marry or avoid, I suppose, it's all one in the end. There'll still be hunting and arms and friends.'

A poor lookout, thought Cadfael, shaking his head, for that small, sharp, dark creature, Cristina daughter of Tudur, if she required more of her husband than a good-looking adolescent boy, willing to tolerate and accommodate her, but quite indisposed to love. Though many a decent marriage has started on no better ground, and burned into a glow later.

They had reached the archway into the inner ward in their circlings, and the slanting sunlight, chill and bright, shone through across their path. High in the corner tower within there, Gilbert Prestcote had made his family apartments, rather than maintain a house in the town. Between the merlons of the curtain wall the sun just reached the narrow doorway that led to the private rooms above, and the girl who emerged stepped full into

43

the light. She was the very opposite of small, sharp and dark, being tall and slender like a silver birch, delicately oval of face, and dazzlingly fair. The sun in her uncovered, waving hair glittered as she hesitated an instant on the doorstone, and shivered lightly at the embrace of the frosty air.

Elis had seen her shimmering pallor take the light, and stood stock-still, gazing through the archway with eyes rounded and fixed, and mouth open. The girl hugged her cloak about her, closed the door at her back, and stepped out briskly across the ward towards the arch on her way out to the town. Cadfael had to pluck Elis by the sleeve to bring him out of his daze, and draw him onward out of her path, recalling him to the realisation that he was staring with embarrassing intensity, and might well give her offence if she noticed him. He moved obediently, but in a few more paces his chin went round on to his shoulder, and he checked again and stood, and could not be shifted further.

She came through the arch, half-smiling for pleasure in the fine morning, but still with something grave, anxious and sad in her countenance. Elis had not removed himself far enough to pass unobserved, she felt a presence close, and turned her head sharply. There was a brief moment when their eyes met, hers darkly blue as periwinkle flowers. The rhythm of her gait was broken, she checked at his gaze, and it almost seemed that she smiled at him hesitantly, as at someone recognised. Fine rose-colour mounted softly in her face, before she recollected herself, tore her gaze away, and went on more hurriedly towards the barbican.

44

Elis stood looking after her until she had passed through the gate and vanished from sight. His own face had flooded richly red.

'Who was that lady?' he asked, at once urgent and in awe.

'That lady,' said Cadfael, 'is daughter to the sheriff, that very man we're hoping to find somewhere alive in Welsh hold, and buy back with your captive person. Prestcote's wife is come to Shrewsbury on that very matter, and brought her step-daughter and her little son with her, in hopes soon to greet her lord again. This is his second lady. The girl's mother died without bringing him a son.

'Do you know her name? The girl?'

'Her name,' said Cadfael, 'is Melicent.'

'Melicent!' the boy's lips shaped silently. Aloud he said, to the sky and the sun rather than to Cadfael: 'Did you ever see such hair, like sun silver, finer than gossamer! And her face all milk and rose ... How old can she be?'

'Should I know? Eighteen or so by the look of her. Much the same age as your Cristina, I suppose,' said Brother Cadfael, dropping a none too gentle reminder of the reality of things. 'You'll be doing her a great service and grace if you send her father back to her. And as I know, you're just as eager to get home yourself,' he said with emphasis.

Elis removed his gaze with an effort from the corner where Melicent Prestcote had disappeared and blinked uncomprehendingly, as though he had just been startled out of a deep sleep. 'Yes,' he said uncertainly, and walked on still in a daze.

*

In the middle of the afternoon, while Cadfael was busy about replenishing his stock of winter cordials in his workshop in the herb-garden, Hugh came in bringing a chilly draught with him before he could close the door against the east wind. He warmed his hands over the brazier, helped himself uninvited to a beaker from Cadfael's wine-flask, and sat down on the broad bench against the wall. He was at home in this dim, timber-scented, herb-rustling miniature world where Cadfael spent so much of his time, and did his best thinking.

'I've just come from the abbot,' said Hugh, 'and borrowed you from him for a few days.'

'And he was willing to lend me?' asked Cadfael with interest, busy stoppering a still-warm jar.

'In a good cause and for a sound reason, yes. In the matter of finding and recovering Gilbert he's as earnest as I am. And the sooner we know whether such an exchange is possible, the better for all.'

Cadfael could not but agree with that. He was thinking, uneasily but not too anxiously as yet, about the morning's visitation. A vision so far from everything Welsh and familiar might well dazzle young, impressionable eyes. There was a prior pledge involved, the niceties of Welsh honour, and the more bitter consideration that Gilbert Prestcote had an old and flourishing hatred against the Welsh, which certain of that race heartily reciprocated.

'I have a border to keep and a garrison to conserve,' said Hugh, nursing his beaker in both hands to warm it, 'and neighbours across the border drunk on their own prowess, and all too

46

likely to be running wild in search of more conquests. Getting word through to Owain Gwynedd is a risky business and we all know it. I would be dubious of letting a captain loose on that mission who lacks Welsh, for I might never see hide nor hair of him again. Even a well-armed party of five or six could vanish. You're Welsh, and have your habit for a coat of mail, and once across the border you have kin everywhere. I reckon you a far better hazard than any battle party. With a small escort, in case of masterless men, and your Welsh tongue and net of kindred to tackle any regular company that crosses you. What do you say?'

'I should be ashamed, as a Welshman,' said Cadfael comfortably, 'if I could not recite my pedigree back sixteen degrees, and some of my kin are here across the border of this shire, a fair enough start towards Gwynedd.'

'Ah, but there's word that Owain may not be so far distant as the wilds of Gwynedd. With Ranulf of Chester so set up in his gains, and greedy for more, the prince has come east to keep an eye on his own. So the rumours say. There's even a whisper he may be our side of the Berwyns, in Cynllaith or Glyn Ceiriog, keeping a close watch on Chester and Wrexham.'

'It would be like him,' agreed Cadfael. 'He thinks large and forwardly. What is the commission? Let me hear it?'

'To ask of Owain Gwynedd whether he has, or can take from his brother, the person of my sheriff, taken at Lincoln. And if he has him, or can find and possess him, whether he will exchange him for this young kinsman of his, Elis ap Cynan. You know, and can report best of any, that the boy is whole and well. Owain may have whatever safeguards he requires, since all men know that he's a man of his word, but regarding me he may not be certain of the same. He may not so much as know my name. Though he shall know me better, if he will have dealings over this. Will you go?'

'How soon?' asked Cadfael, putting his jar aside to cool, and sitting down beside his friend.

'Tomorrow, if you can delegate all here.'

'Mortal man should be able and willing to delegate at any moment,' said Cadfael soberly, 'since mortal he is. Oswin is grown wonderfully deft and exact among the herbs, more than I ever hoped for when he first came to me. And Brother Edmund is master of his own realm, and well able to do without me. If Father Abbot frees me, I'm yours. What I can, I'll do.'

'Then come up to the castle in the morning, after Prime, and you shall have a good horse under you.' He knew that would be a lure and a delight, and smiled at seeing it welcomed. 'And a few picked men for your escort. The rest is in your Welsh tongue.'

'True enough,' said Cadfael complacently, 'a fast word in Welsh is better than a shield. I'll be there. But have your terms drawn up fair on a parchment. Owain has a legal mind, he likes a bill well drawn.'

After Prime in the morning – a greyer morning than the one that went before – Cadfael donned boots and cloak, and went up through the town to

48

the castle wards, and there were the horses of his escort already saddled, and the men waiting for him. He knew them all, even to the youngster Hugh had chosen as a possible hostage for the desired prisoner, should all go well. He spared a few moments to say farewell to Elis, and found him sleepy and mildly morose at this hour in his cell.

'Wish me well, boy, for I'm away to see what can be done about this exchange for you. With a little goodwill and a morsel of luck, you may be on your way home within a couple of weeks. You'll be mightily glad to be back in your own country and a free man.'

Elis agreed that he would, since it was obviously expected of him, but it was a very lukewarm agreement. 'But it's not yet certain, is it, that your sheriff is there to be redeemed? And even if he is, it may take some time to find him and get him out of Cadwaladr's hands.'

'In that case,' said Cadfael, 'you will have to possess your soul in patience and in captivity a while longer.'

'If I must, I can,' agreed Elis, all too cheerfully and continently for one surely not hitherto accomplished at possessing his soul in patience. 'But I do trust you may go and return safe,' he said dutifully.

'Behave yourself, while I'm about your affairs,' Cadfael advised resignedly and turned to leave him. 'I'll bear your greetings to your foster-brother Eliud, if I should encounter him, and leave him word you've come to no harm.'

Elis embraced that offer gladly enough, but crassly failed to add another name that might

49

fittingly have been linked with the same message. And Cadfael refrained from mentioning it in his turn. He was at the door when Elis suddenly called after him: 'Brother Cadfael ...'

'Yes?' said Cadfael, turning.

'That lady ... the one we saw yesterday, the sheriff's daughter ...'

'What of her?'

'Is she spoken for?'

Ah well, thought Cadfael, mounting with his mission well rehearsed in his head, and his knot of light-armed men about him, soon on, soon off, no doubt, and she has never spoken word to him and most likely never will. Once home, he'll soon forget her. If she had not been so silver-fair, so different from the trim, dark Welsh girls, he would never have noticed her.

Cadfael had answered the enquiry with careful indifference, saying he had no notion what plans the sheriff had for his daughter, and forbore from adding the blunt warning that was on the tip of his tongue. With such a springy lad as this one, to put him off would only put him on the more resolutely. With no great obstacles in the way, he might lose interest. But the girl certainly had an airy beauty, all the more appealing for being touched with innocent gravity and sadness on her father's account. Only let this mission succeed, and the sooner the better!

They left Shrewsbury by the Welsh bridge, and made good speed over the near reaches of their way, north-west towards Oswestry.

*

Sybilla, Lady Prestcote, was twenty years younger than her husband, a pretty, ordinary woman of good intentions towards all, and notable chiefly for one thing, that she had done what the sheriff's first wife could not do, and borne him a son. Young Gilbert was seven years old, the apple of his father's eye and the core of his mother's heart. Melicent found herself indulged but neglected, but in affection to a very pretty little brother she felt no resentment. An heir is an heir; an heiress is a much less achievement.

The apartments in the castle tower, when the best had been done to make them comfortable, remained stony, draughty and cold, no place to bring a young family, and it was exceptional indeed for Sybilla and her son to come to Shrewsbury, when they had six far more pleasant manors at their disposal. Hugh would have offered the hospitality of his own town house on this anxious occasion, but the lady had too many servants to find accommodation there, and preferred the austerity of her bleak but spacious dwelling in the tower. Her husband was accustomed to occupying it alone, when his duties compelled him to remain with the garrison. Wanting him and fretting over him, she was content to be in the place which was his by right, however Spartan its appointments.

Melicent loved her little brother, and found no fault with the system which would endow him with all their father's possessions, and provide her with only a modest dowry. Indeed, she had had serious thoughts of taking the veil, and leaving the Prestcote inheritance as good as whole, having an

51

inclination towards altars, relics and devotional candles, though she had just sense enough to know that what she felt fell far short of a vocation. It had not that quality of overwhelming revelation it should have had.

The shock of wonder, delight and curiosity, for instance, that stopped her, faltering, in her steps when she sailed through the archway into the outer ward and glanced by instinct towards the presence she felt close and intent beside her, and met the startled dark eyes of the stranger, the Welsh prisoner. It was not even his youth and comeliness, but the spellbound stare he fixed on her, that pierced her to the heart.

She had always thought of the Welsh with fear and distrust, as uncouth savages; and suddenly here was this trim and personable young man whose eyes dazzled and whose cheeks flamed at meeting her gaze. She thought of him much. She asked questions about him, careful to dissemble the intensity of her interest. And on the same day that Cadfael set out to hunt for Owain Gwynedd, she saw Elis from an upper window, half-accepted already among the young men of the garrison, stripped to the waist and trying a wrestling-bout with one of the best pupils of the master-at-arms in the inner ward. He was no match for the English youth, who had the advantage in weight and reach, and he took a heavy fall that made her catch her breath in distressed sympathy, but he came to his feet laughing and blown, and thumped the victor amiably on the shoulder.

There was nothing in him, no movement, no glance, in which she did not find generosity and grace.

She took her cloak and slipped away down the stone stair, and out to the archway by which he must pass to his lodging in the outer ward. It was beginning to be dusk, they would all be putting away their work and amusement, and making ready for supper in hall. Elis came through the arch limping a little from his new bruises, and whistling, and the same quiver of awareness which had caused her to turn her head now worked the like enchantment upon him.

The tune died on his parted lips. He stood stock-still, holding his breath. Their eyes locked, and could not break free, nor did they try very hard.

'Sir,' she said, having marked the broken rhythm of his walk, 'I fear you are hurt.'

She saw the quiver that passed through him from head to foot as he breathed again. 'No,' he said, hesitant as a man in a dream, 'no, never till now. Now I am wounded to death.'

'I think,' she said, shaken and timorous, 'you do not yet know me …'

'I do know you,' he said. 'You are Melicent. It is your father I must buy back for you – at a price …'

At a price, at a disastrous price, at the price of tearing asunder this marriage of eyes that drew them closer until they touched hands, and were lost.

Chapter Three

Cadwaladr might have had his frolics on his way back to his castle at Aberystwyth with his booty and his prisoners, but to the north of his passage Owain Gwynedd had kept a fist clamped down hard upon disorder. Cadfael and his escort had had one or two brushes with trouble, after leaving Oswestry on their right and plunging into Wales, but on the first occasion the three masterless men who had put an arrow across their path thought better of it when they saw what numbers they had challenged, and took themselves off at speed into the brush; and on the second, an unruly patrol of excitable Welsh warmed into affability at Cadfael's unruffled Welsh greeting, and ended giving them news of the prince's movements, Cadfael's numerous kinsfolk, first and second cousins and shared forebears, were warranty enough over much of Clwyd and part of Gwynedd.

Owain, they said, had come east out of his eyrie to keep a weather eye upon Ranulf of Chester, who might be so blown up with his success as to mistake the mettle of the prince of Gwynedd. He was patrolling the fringes of Chester territory, and had reached Corwen on the Dee. So said the first informants. The second, encountered near Rhiwlas, were positive that he had crossed the Berwyns and come down into Glyn Ceiriog, and might at that moment be encamped near Llanarmon, or else with his ally and friend, Tudur ap Rhys, at his maenol at Tregeiriog. Seeing it was winter, however merciful at this moment, and seeing that Owain Gwynedd was considerably saner than most Welshmen, Cadfael chose to make for Tregeiriog. Why camp, when there was a close ally at hand, with a sound roof and a well-stocked larder, in a comparatively snug valley among these bleak central hills?

Tudur ap Rhys's maenol lay in a cleft where a mountain brook came down into the river Ceiriog, and his boundaries were well but unobtrusively guarded in these shaken days, for a two-man patrol came out on the path, one on either side, before Cadfael's party were out of the scrub forest above the valley. Shrewd eyes weighed up this sedate company, and the mind behind the eyes decided that they were harmless even before Cadfael got out his Welsh greeting. That and his habit were enough warranty. The young man bade his companion run ahead and acquaint Tudur that he had visitors, and himself conducted them at leisure the rest of the way. Beyond the river, with its fringes of forest and the few stony fields and huddle of wooden cots about the maenol, the hills rose again brown and bleak below, white and bleak above, to a round snow-summit against a leaden sky.

Tudur ap Rhys came out to welcome them and

exchange the civilities; a short, square man, very powerfully built, with a thick thatch of brown hair barely touched with grey, and a loud, melodious voice that ranged happily up and down the cadences of song rather than speech. A Welsh Benedictine was a novelty to him; a Welsh Benedictine sent as negotiator from England to a Welsh prince even more so, but he suppressed his curiosity courteously, and had his guest conducted to a chamber in his own house, where presently a girl came to him bearing the customary water for his feet, by the acceptance or rejection of which he would signify whether or not he intended to spend the night there.

It had not occurred to Cadfael, until she entered, that this same lord of Tregeiriog was the man of whom Elis had talked, when he poured out the tale of his boyhood betrothal to a little, sharp, dark creature who was handsome enough in her way, and who, if he must marry at all, would do. Now there she stood, with the gently steaming bowl in her hands, demure before her father's guest, by her dress and her bearing manifestly Tudur's daughter. Little she certainly was, but trimly made and carried herself proudly. Sharp? Her manner was brisk and confident, and though her approach was deferent and proper, there was an assured spark in her eyes. Dark, assuredly. Both eyes and hair fell just short of raven black by the faint, warm tint of red in them. And handsome? Not remarkably so in repose, her face was irregular in feature, tapering from wide-set eyes to pointed chin, but as soon as she spoke or moved there was such flashing life in her

56

that she needed no beauty.

'I take your service very kindly,' said Cadfael, 'and thank you for it. And you, I think, must be Cristina, Tudur's daughter. And if you are, then I have word for you and for Owain Gwynedd that should be heartily welcome to you both.'

'I am Cristina,' she said, burning into bright animation, 'but how did a brother of Shrewsbury learn my name?'

'From a young man by the name of Elis ap Cynan, whom you may have been mourning for lost, but who is safe and well in Shrewsbury castle this moment. What may you have heard of him, since the prince's brother brought his muster and his booty home again from Lincoln?'

Her alert composure did not quiver, but her eyes widened and glowed. 'They told my father he was left behind with some that drowned near the border,' she said, 'but none of them knew how he had fared. Is it true? He is alive? And prisoner?'

'You may be easy,' said Cadfael, 'for so he is, none the worse for the battle of the brook, and can be bought free very simply, to come back to you and make you, I hope, a good husband.'

You may cast your bait, he told himself watching her face, which was at once eloquent and unreadable, as though she even thought in a strange language, but you'll catch no fish here. This one has her own secrets, and her own way of taking events into her hands. What she wills to keep to herself you're never like to get out of her. And she looked him full in the eyes and said: 'Eliud will be glad. Did he speak of him, too?' But she knew the answer.

57

'A certain Eliud was mentioned,' Cadfael admitted cautiously, feeling shaky ground under them. 'A cousin, I gathered, but brought up like brothers.'

'Closer than brothers,' said the girl. 'Am I permitted to tell him this news? Or should it wait until you have supped with my father and told him your errand?'

'Eliud is here?'

'Not here at this moment, but with the prince, somewhere north along the border. They'll come with the evening. They are lodged here, and Owain's companies are encamped close by.'

'Good, for my errand is to the prince, and it concerns the exchange of Elis ap Cynan for one of comparable value to us, taken, as we believe, by Prince Cadwaladr at Lincoln. If that is as good news to Eliud as it is to you, it would be a Christian act to set his mind at rest for his cousin as soon as may be.'

She kept her face bright, mute and still as she said: 'I will tell him as soon as he alights. It would be a great pity to see such a comradely love blighted a moment longer than it need be.' But there was acid in the sweet, and her eyes burned. She made her courteous obeisance, and left him to his ablutions before the evening meal. He watched her go, and her head was high and her step fierce but soundless, like a hunting cat.

So that was how it went, here in this corner of Wales! A girl betrothed, and with a girl's sharp eye on her rights and privileges, while the boy went about whistling and obtuse, child to her woman, and had his arm about another youth's

58

neck, sworn pair from infancy, oftener than he even paid a compliment to his affianced wife. And she resented with all her considerable powers of mind and heart the love that made her only a third, and barely half-welcome.

Nothing here for her to mourn, if she could but know it. A maid is a woman far before a boy is a man, leaving aside the simple maturity of arms. All she need do was wait a little, and use her own arts, and she would no longer be the neglected third. But she was proud and fierce and not minded to wait.

Cadfael made himself presentable, and went to the lavish but simple table of Tudor ap Rhys. In the dusk torches flared at the hall door and up the valley from the north, from the direction of Llansantffraid, came a brisk bustle of horsemen back from their patrol. Within the hall the tables were spread and the central fire burned bright, sending up fragrant wood-smoke into the blackened roof, as Owain Gwynedd, lord of North Wales and much country beside, came content and hungry to his place at the high table.

Cadfael had seen him once before, a few years past, and he was not a man to be easily forgotten, for all he made very little ado about state and ceremony, barring the obvious royalty he bore about in his own person. He was barely thirty-seven years old, in his vigorous prime; very tall for a Welshman, and fair, after his grandmother Ragnhild of the Danish kingdom of Dublin, and his mother Angharad, known for her flaxen hair among the dark women of the south. His young men, reflecting his solid self-confidence, did it with a swagger of which their prince had no need. Cadfael wondered which of all these boisterous boys was Eliud ap Griffith, and whether Cristina had yet told him of his cousin's survival, and in what terms, and with what jealous bitterness at being still a barely-regarded hanger-on in this sworn union.

'And here is Brother Cadfael of the Shrewsbury Benedictines,' said Tudur heartily, placing Cadfael close at the high table, 'with an embassage to you, my lord, from that town and shire.'

Owain weighed and measured the stocky figure and weathered countenance with a shrewd blue gaze, and stroked his close-trimmed golden beard. 'Brother Cadfael is welcome, and so is any motion of amity from that quarter, where I can do with an assured peace.'

'Some of your countrymen and mine,' said Cadfael bluntly, 'paid a visit recently to Shropshire's borders with very little amity in mind, and left our peace a good deal less assured, even, than it could be said to be after Lincoln. You may have heard of it. Your princely brother did not come raiding himself, it may even be that he never sanctioned the frolic. But he left a few drowned men in one of our brooks in flood whom we have buried decently. And one,' he said, 'whom the good sisters took out of the water living, and whom your lordship may wish to redeem, for by his own tale he's of your kinship.'

'Do you tell me!' The blue eyes had widened and brightened. 'I have not been so busy about fencing out the earl of Chester that I have failed to go into matters with my brother. There was

60

more than one such frolic on the way home from Lincoln, and every one a folly that will cost me some pains to repair. Give your prisoner a name.'

'His name,' said Cadfael, 'is Elis ap Cynan.'

'Ah!' said Owain on a long, satisfied breath, and set down his cup ringing on the board. 'So the fool boy's alive yet to tell the tale, is he? I'm glad indeed to hear it, and thank God for the deliverance and you, brother, for the news. There was not a man of my brother's company could swear to how he was lost or what befell him.'

'They were running too fast to look over their shoulders,' said Cadfael mildly.

'From a man of our own blood,' said Owain grinning, 'I'll take that as it's meant. So Elis is live and prisoner! Has he come to much harm?'

'Barely a scratch. And he may have come by a measure of sense into the bargain. Sound as a well-cast bell, I promise you, and my mission is to offer an exchange with you, if by any chance your brother has taken among his prisoners one as valuable to us as Elis is to you. I am sent,' said Cadfael, 'by Hugh Beringar of Maesbury, speaking for Shropshire, to ask of you the return of his chief and sheriff, Gilbert Prestcote. With all proper greetings and compliments to your lordship, and full assurance of our intent to maintain the peace with you as hitherto.'

'The time's ripe for it,' acknowledged Owain drily, 'and it's to the vantage of both of us, things being as they are. Where is Elis now?'

'In Shrewsbury castle, and has the run of the wards on his parole.'

'And you want him off your hands?'

61

'No haste for that,' said Cadfael. 'We think well enough of him to keep him yet a while. But we do want the sheriff, if he lives, and if you have him. For Hugh looked for him after the battle, and found no trace, and it was your brother's Welsh who overran the place where he fought.'

'Bide here a night or two,' said the prince, 'and I will send to Cadwaladr, and find out if he holds your man. And if so, you shall have him.'

There was harping after supper, and singing, and drinking of good wine long after the prince's messenger had ridden out on the first stage of his long journey to Aberystwyth. There was also a certain amount of good-natured wrestling and horse-play between Owain's young cockerels and the men of Cadfael's escort, though Hugh had taken care to choose some who had Welsh kin to recommend them, no very hard task in Shrewsbury at any time.

'Which of all these,' asked Cadfael, surveying the hall, smoky now from the fire and the torches, and loud with voices, 'is Eliud ap Griffith?'

'I see Elis has chattered to you as freely as ever,' said Owain smiling, 'prisoner or no. His cousin and foster-brother is hovering this moment at the end of the near table, and eyeing you hard, waiting his chance to have speech with you as soon as I withdraw. The long lad in the blue coat.'

No mistaking him, once noticed, though he could not have been more different from his cousin: such a pair of eyes fixed upon Cadfael's face in implacable determination and eagerness and such a still, braced body waiting for the least encouragement to fly to respond. Owain, humouring him, lifted a beckoning finger, and he came like a lance launched, quivering. A long lad he was, and thin and intense, with bright hazel eyes in a grave oval face, featured finely enough for a woman, but with good lean bones in it, too. There was a quality of devotional anxiety about him that must be for Elis ap Cynan at this moment, but at another might be for Wales, for his prince, some day, no doubt, for a woman, but whatever its object it would always be there. This one would never be quite at rest.

He bent the knee eagerly to Owain, and Owain clouted him amiably on the shoulder and said: 'Sit down here with Brother Cadfael, and have out of him everything you want to know. Though the best you know already. Your other self is alive and can be bought back for you at a price.' And with that he left them together and went to confer with Tudur.

Eliud sat down willingly and spread his elbows on the board to lean ardently close. 'Brother, it *is* true, what Cristina told me? You have Elis safe in Shrewsbury? They came back without him ... I sent to know, but there was no one could tell me where he went astray or how. I have been hunting and asking everywhere and so has the prince, for all he makes a light thing of it. He is my father's fostering – you're Welsh yourself, so you know. We grew up together from babes, and there are no more brothers, either side ...'

'I do know,' agreed Cadfael, 'and I say again, as Cristina said to you, he is safe enough, man alive and as good as new.'

63

'You've seen him? Talked to him? You're sure it's Elis and no other? A well-looking man of his company,' explained Eliud apologetically, 'if he found himself a prisoner, might award himself a name that would stead him better than his own ...'

Cadfael patiently described this man, and told over the whole tale of the rescue from the flooded brook and Elis's obstinate withdrawal into the Welsh tongue until a Welshman challenged him. Eliud listened, his lips parted and his eyes intent, and was visibly eased into conviction.

'And was he so uncivil to those ladies who saved him? Oh, now I do know him for Elis, he'd be so shamed, to come back to life in such hands – like a babe being thumped into breathing!' No mistake, the solemn youth could laugh, and laughter lit up his grave face and made his eyes sparkle. It was no blind love he had for his twin who was no twin, he knew him through and through, scolded, criticised, fought with him, and loved him none the less. The girl Cristina had a hard fight on her hands. 'And so you got him from the nuns. And had he no hurts at all, once he was wrung dry?'

'Nothing worse than a gash in his hinder end, got from a sharp rock in the brook, while he was drowning. And that's salved and healed. His worst trouble was that you would be mourning him for dead, but my journey here eases him of that anxiety, as it does you of yours. No need to fret about Elis ap Cynan. Even in an English castle he is soon and easily at home.'

'So he would be,' agreed Eliud in the soft, musing voice of tolerant affection. 'So he always was and always will be. He has the gift. But so *free*

64

with it, sometimes I fret for him indeed!'

Always, rather than sometimes, thought Cadfael, after the young man had left him, and the hall was settling down for the night round the turfed and quiet fire. Even now, assured of his friend's safety and well-being, and past question or measure glad of that, even now he goes with locked brows and inward-gazing eyes. He had a troubled vision of those three young creatures bound together in inescapable strife, the two boys linked together from childhood, locked even more securely by the one's gravity and the other's innocent rashness, and the girl betrothed in infancy to half of an inseparable pair. Of the three the prisoner in Shrewsbury seemed to him the happiest by far, since he lived in the day, warming in its sunlight, taking cover from its storms, in every case finding by instinct the pleasant corner and the gratifying entertainment. The other two burned like candles, eating their own substance and giving an angry and vulnerable light.

He said prayers for all three before he slept, and awoke in the night to the uneasy reflection that somewhere, shadowy as yet, there might be a fourth to be considered and prayed for.

The next day was clear and bright, with light frost that lost its powdery sparkle as soon as the sun came up; and it was pleasure to have a whole day to spend in his own Welsh countryside with a good conscience and in good company. Owain Gwynedd again rode out eastward upon another patrol with a half-dozen of his young men, and again came back in the evening well content. It seemed that Ranulf of Chester was lying low for the moment, digesting his gains.

As for Cadfael, since word could hardly be expected to come back from Aberystwyth until the following day, he gladly accepted the prince's invitation to ride with them, and see for himself the state of readiness of the border villages that kept watch on England. They returned to the courtyard of Tudur's maenol in the early dusk, and beyond the flurry and bustle of activity among the grooms and the servants, the hall door hung open, and sharp and dark against the glow of the fire and the torches within stood the small, erect figure of Cristina, looking out for the guests returning, in order to set all forward for the evening meal. She vanished within for a few moments only, and then came forth to watch them dismount, her father at her side.

It was not the prince Cristina watched. Cadfael passed close by her as he went within, and saw by the falling light of the torches how her face was set, her lips taut and unsmiling, and her eyes fixed insatiably upon Eliud as he alighted and handed over his mount to the waiting groom. The glint of dark red that burned in the blackness of hair and eyes seemed by this light to have brightened into a deep core of anger and resentment.

What was no less noticeable, when Cadfael looked back in sheer human curiosity, was the manner in which Eliud, approaching the doorway, passed by her with an unsmiling face and a brief word, and went on his way with averted eyes. For was not she as sharp a thorn in his side as he in hers?

The sooner the marriage, the less the mischief, and the better prospect of healing it again, thought Cadfael, departing to his Vesper office, and instantly began to wonder whether he was not making far too simple a matter of this turmoil between three people, of whom only one was simple at all.

The prince's messenger came back late in the afternoon of the following day, and made report to his master, who called in Cadfael at once to hear the result of the quest.

'My man reports that Gilbert Prestcote is indeed in my brother's hands, and can and shall be offered in exchange for Elis. There may be a little delay, for it seems he was badly wounded in the fighting at Lincoln, and is recovering only slowly. But if you will deal directly with me, I will secure him as soon as he is fit to be moved, and have him brought by easy stages to Shrewsbury. We'll lodge him at Montford on the last night, where Welsh princes and English earls used to meet for parley, send Hugh Beringar word ahead, and bring him to the town. There your garrison may hand over Elis in exchange.'

'Content, indeed!' said Cadfael heartily, 'And so will Hugh Beringar be.'

'I shall require safeguards,' said Owain, 'and am willing to give them.'

'As for your good faith, nowhere in this land of Wales or my foster-land of England is it in question. But *my* lord you do not know, and he is content to leave with you a hostage, to be his guarantee until you have Elis safe in your hands again. From you he requires none. Send him Gilbert Prestcote, and you may have Elis ap Cynan, and send back the guarantor at your pleasure.'

'No,' said Owain firmly. 'If I ask warranty of a man, I also give it. Leave me your man here and now, if you will, and if he has his orders and is ready and willing, and when my men bring Gilbert Prestcote home I will send Eliud with him to remain with you as surety for his cousin's honour and mine until we again exchange hostages halfway – on the border dyke by Oswestry, shall we say, if I am still in these parts? – and conclude the bargain. There is virtue, sometimes, in observing the forms. And besides, I should like to meet your Hugh Beringar, for he and I have a common need to be on our guard against others you wot of.'

'The same thought has been much in Hugh's mind,' agreed Cadfael fervently, 'and trust me, he will take pleasure in coming to meet you wherever may be most suited to the time. He shall bring you Eliud again, and you shall restore him a young man who is his cousin on his mother's side, John Marchmain. You noted him this morning, the tallest among us. John came with me ready and willing to remain if things went well.'

'He shall be well entertained,' said Owain.

'Faith, he's been looking forward to it, though his knowledge of Welsh is small. And since we are agreed,' said Cadfael, 'I'll see him instructed in his duty tonight, and make an early start back to

Shrewsbury in the morning with the rest of my company.'

Before sleeping that night he went out from the smoke and warmth of the hall to take a look at the weather. The air was on the softer edge of frost, no wind stirring. The sky was clear and full of stars, but they had not the blaze and bite of extreme cold. A beautiful night, and even without his cloak he was tempted to go as far as the edge of the maenol, where a copse of bushes and trees sheltered the gate. He drew in deep, chill breaths, scented with timber, night and the mysterious sweetness of turf and leaf sleeping but not dead, and blew the smokiness of withindoors out of his nose.

He was about to turn back and compose his mind for the night prayers when the luminous darkness quickened around him, and two people came up from the shadowy buildings of the stables towards the hall, softly and swiftly, but with abrupt pauses that shook the air more than their motion. They were talking as they came, just above the betraying sibilance of whispers, and their conference had an edge and an urgency that made him freeze where he stood, covered by the bulk and darkness of the trees. By the time he was aware of them they were between him and his rest, and when they drew close enough he could not choose but hear. But man being what he is, it cannot be avowed that he would so have chosen, even if he could.

'—mean me no harm!' breathed the one, bitter and soft. 'And do you not harm me, do you not

69

rob me of what's mine by right, with every breath you draw? And now you will be off to him, as soon as this English lord can be moved ...'

'Have I a choice,' protested the other, 'when the prince sends me? And he is my foster-brother, can you change that? Why can you not let well alone?'

'It is *not* well, it is very ill! Sent, indeed!' hissed the girl's voice viciously. 'Ha! And you would murder any who took the errand from you, and well you know it. And I to sit here! While you will be together again, his arm around your neck, and never a thought for me!'

The two shadows glared in the muted gleam from the dying fire within, black in the doorway. Eliud's voice rose perilously. The taller shadow, head and shoulders taller, wrenched itself away.

'For God's love, woman, will you not hush, and let me be!'

He was gone, casting her off roughly, and vanishing into the populous murmur and hush of the hall. Cristina plucked her skirts about her with angry hands, and followed slowly, withdrawing to her own retiring place.

And so did Cadfael, as soon as he was sure there was none to be discomposed by his going. There went two losers in this submerged battle. If there was a winner, he slept with a child's abandon, as seemed to be his wont, in a stone cell that was no prison, in Shrewsbury castle. One that would always fall on his feet. Two that probably made a practice of falling over theirs, from too intense peering ahead, and too little watching where they trod.

Nevertheless, he did not pray for them that night. He lay long in thought instead, pondering how so complex a knot might be disentangled.

In the early morning he and his remaining force mounted and rode. It did not surprise him that the devoted cousin and foster-brother should be there to see him go, and send by him all manner of messages to his captive friend, to sustain him until his release. Most fitting that the one who was older and wiser should stand proxy to rescue the younger and more foolish. If folly can be measured so.

'I was not clever,' owned Eliud ruefully, holding Cadfael's stirrup as he mounted, and leaning on his horse's warm shoulder when he was up. 'I made too much of it that he should not go with Cadwaladr. I doubt I drove him the more firmly into it. But I *knew* it was mad!'

'You must grant him one grand folly,' said Cadfael comfortably. 'Now he's lived through it, and knows it was folly as surely as you do. He'll not be so hot after action again. And then,' he said, eyeing the grave oval countenance close, 'I understand he'll have other causes for growing into wisdom when he comes home. He's to be married, is he not?'

Eliud faced him a moment with great hazel eyes shining like lanterns. Then: 'Yes!' he said very shortly and forbiddingly, and turned his head away.

Chapter Four

The news went round in Shrewsbury —
abbey, castle and town — almost before
Cadfael had rendered account of his
stewardship to Abbot Radulfus, and reported his
success to Hugh. The sheriff was alive, and his
return imminent, in exchange for the Welshman
taken at Godric's Ford. In her high apartments in
the castle, Lady Prestcote brightened and grew
buoyant with relief. Hugh rejoiced not only in
having found and recovered his chief, but also in
the prospect of a closer alliance with Owain
Gwynedd, whose help in the north of the shire, if
ever Ranulf of Chester did decide to attack, might
very well turn the tide. The provost and
guildsmen of the town, in general, were well
pleased. Prestcote was a man who did not
encourage close friendships, but Shrewsbury had
found him a just and well-intentioned officer of
the crown, if heavy-handed at times, and was well
aware that it might have fared very much worse.
Not everyone, however, felt the same simple
pleasure. Even just men make enemies.

Cadfael returned to his proper duties well
content, and having reviewed Brother Oswin's

stewardship in the herbarium and found everything in good order, his next charge was to visit the infirmary and replenish the medicine-cupboard there.

'No new invalids since I left?'

'None. And two have gone out, back to the dortoir, Brother Adam and Brother Everard. Strong constitutions they have, both, in spite of age, and it was no worse than a chest cold, and has cleared up well. Come and see how they all progress. If only we could send out Brother Maurice with the same satisfaction as those two,' said Edmund sadly. 'He's eight years younger, strong and able, and barely sixty. If only he was as sound in mind as in body! But I doubt we'll never dare let him loose. It's the bent his madness has taken. Shame that after a blameless life of devotion he now remembers only his grudges, and seems to have no love for any man. Great age is no blessing, Cadfael, when the body's strength outlives the mind.'

'How do his neighbours bear with him?' asked Cadfael with sympathy.

'With Christian patience! And they need it. He fancies now that every man is plotting some harm against him. And says so, outright, besides any real and ancient wrongs he's kept in mind all too clearly.'

They came into the big, bare room where the beds were laid, handy to the private chapel where the infirm might repair for the offices. Those who could rise to enjoy the brighter part of the day sat by a large log fire, warming their ancient bones and talking by fits and starts, as they waited for

73

the next meal, the next office or the next diversion. Only Brother Rhys was confined to his bed, though most of those within here were aged, and spent much time there. A generation of brothers admitted in the splendid enthusiasm of an abbey's founding also comes to senility together, yielding place to the younger postulants admitted by ones and twos after the engendering wave. Never again, thought Cadfael, moving among them, would a whole chapter of the abbey's history remove thus into retirement and decay. From this time on they would come one by one, and be afforded each a death-bed reverently attended, single and in solitary dignity. Here were four or five who would depart almost together, leaving even their attendant brothers very weary, and the world indifferent.

Brother Maurice sat installed by the fire, a tall, gaunt, waxen-white old man of elongated patrician face and irascible manner. He came of a noble house, an oblate since his youth, and had been removed here some two years previously, when after a trivial dispute he had suddenly called out Prior Robert in a duel to the death, and utterly refused to be distracted or reconciled. In his more placid moments he was gracious, accommodating and courteous, but touch him in his pride of family and honour and he was an implacable enemy. Here in his old age he called up from the past, vivid as when they happened, every affront to his line, every lawsuit waged against them, back to his own birth and beyond, and brooded over every one that had gone unrevenged.

It was a mistake, perhaps, to ask him how he did, but his enthroned hauteur seemed to demand it. He raised his narrow hawk-nose, and tightened his bluish lips. 'None the better for what I hear, if it be true. They're saying that Gilbert Prestcote is alive and will soon be returning here. Is that truth?'

'It is,' said Cadfael. 'Owain Gwynedd is sending him home in exchange for the Welshman captured in the Long Forest a while since. And why should you be none the better for good news of a decent Christian man?'

'I had thought justice had been done,' said Maurice loftily, 'after all too long a time. But however long, divine justice should not fail in the end. Yet once again it has glanced aside and spared the malefactor.' The glitter of his eyes was grey as steel.

'You'd best leave divine justice to its own business,' said Cadfael mildly, 'for it needs no help from us. And I asked you how *you* did, my friend, so never put me off with others. How is it with that chest of yours, this wintry weather? Shall I bring you a cordial to warm you?'

It was no great labour to distract him, for though he was no complainer as to his health, he was open to the flattery of concerned attention and enjoyed being cosseted. They left him soothed and complacent, and went out to the porch very thoughtful.

'I knew he had these hooks in him,' said Cadfael when the door was closed between, 'but not that he had such a barb from the Prestcote family. What is it he holds against the sheriff?'

75

Edmund shrugged, and drew resigned breath. 'It was in his father's time, Maurice was scarcely born! There was a lawsuit over a piece of land and long arguments either side, and it went Prestcote's way. For all I know, as sound a judgement as ever was made, and Maurice was in his cradle, and Gilbert's father, good God, was barely a man, but here the poor ancient has dredged it up as a mortal wrong. And it is but one among a dozen he keeps burnished in his memory, and wants blood for them all. Will you believe it, he has never set eyes on the sheriff? Can you hate a man you've never seen or spoken to, because his grandsire beat your father at a suit at law? Why should old age lose everything but the all-present evil?'

A hard question, and yet sometimes it went the opposite way, kept the good, and let all the malice and spite be washed away. And why one old man should be visited by such grace, and another by so heavy a curse, Cadfael could not fathom. Surely a balance must be restored elsewhere.

'Not everyone, I know,' said Cadfael ruefully, 'loves Gilbert Prestcote. Good men can make as devoted enemies as bad men. And his handling of law has not always been light or merciful, though it never was corrupt or cruel.'

'There's one here has somewhat better cause than Maurice to bear him a grudge,' said Edmund. 'I am sure you know Anion's history as well as I do. He's on crutches, as you'll have seen before you left us on this journey, and getting on well, and we like him to go forth when there's no frost and the ground's firm and dry, but he's still bedded with us, within there. He says nothing,

76

while Maurice says too much, but you're Welsh, and you know how a Welshman keeps his counsel. And one like Anion, half-Welsh, half-English, how do you read such a one?'

'As best you can,' agreed Cadfael, 'bearing in mind both are humankind.'

He knew the man Anion, though he had never been brought close to him, since Anion was a lay servant among the livestock, and had been brought into the infirmary in late autumn from one of the abbey granges, with a broken leg that was slow to knit. He was no novelty in the district about Shrewsbury, offspring of a brief union between a Welsh wool-trader and an English maid-servant. And like many another of his kind, he had kept touch with his kin across the border, where his father had a proper wife, and had given her a legitimate son no long time after Anion was conceived.

'I do remember now,' said Cadfael, enlightened. 'There were two young fellows came to sell their fleeces that time, and drank too deep and got into a brawl, and one of the gate-keepers on the bridge was killed. Prestcote hanged them for it. I did hear tell at the time the one had a half-brother this side the border.'

'Griffri ap Griffri, that was the young man's name. Anion had got to know him, the times he came into town, they were on good terms. He was away among the sheep in the north when it happened or he might well have got his brother to bed without mischief. A good worker and honest, Anion, but a surly fellow and silent, and never forgets a benefit nor an injury.'

77

Cadfael sighed, having seen in his time a long line of decent men wiped out in alternate savageries as the result of just such a death. The blood-feud could be a sacred duty in Wales.

'Ah, well, it's to be hoped the English half of him can temper his memories. That must be two years ago now. No man can bear a grudge for ever.'

In the narrow, stone-cold chapel of the castle by the meagre light of the altar lamp, Elis waited in the gloom of the early evening, huddled into his cloak in the darkest corner, biting frost without and gnawing fire within. It was a safe place for two to meet who could otherwise never be alone together. The sheriff's chaplain was devout, but within limits, and preferred the warmth of the hall and the comforts of the table, once Vespers was disposed of, to this cold and draughty place.

Melicent's step on the threshold was barely audible, but Elis caught it, and turned eagerly to draw her in by both hands, and swing the heavy door closed to shut out the rest of the world.

'You've heard?' she said, hasty and low. 'They've found him, they're bringing him back. Owain Gwynedd has promised it ...'

'I know!' said Elis, and drew her close, folding the cloak about them both, as much to assert their unity as to shield her from the chill and the trespassing wind. For all that, he felt her slipping away like a wraith of mist out of his hold. 'I'm glad you'll have your father back safely.' But he could not sound glad, no matter how manfully he lied. 'We knew it must be so if he lived ...' His voice baulked there, trying not to sound as if he wished her father dead, one obstacle out of the way from between them, and himself still a prisoner, unransomed. Her prisoner, for as long as might be, long enough to work the needful miracle, break one tie and make another possible, which looked all too far out of reach now.

'When he comes back,' she said, her cold brow against his cheek, 'then you will have to go. How shall we bear it!'

'Don't I know it! I think of nothing else. It will all be vain, and I shall never see you again. I won't, I can't accept that. There *must* be a way ...'

'If you go,' she said, 'I shall die.'

'But I must go, we both know it. How else can I even do this one thing for you, to buy your father back?' But neither could he bear the pain of it. If he let her go now he was for ever lost, there would be no other to take her place. The little dark creature in Wales, so faded from his mind he could hardly recall her face, she was nothing, she had no claim on him. Rather a hermit's life, if he could not have Melicent. 'Do you not *want* him back?'

'Yes!' she said vehemently, torn and shivering, and at once took it back again: '*No!* Not if I must lose you! Oh, God, do I know what I want? I want both you and him – *but you most!* I do love my father, but as a father. I must love him, love is due between us, but ... Oh, Elis, I hardly know him, he never came near enough to be loved. Always duty and affairs taking him away, and my mother and I lonely, and then my mother dead ... He was never unkind, always careful of me, but always a long

79

way off. It is a kind of love, but not like this … not as I love you! It's no fair exchange …'

She did not say: 'Now if he had died …' but it was there stark at the back of her mind, horrifying her. If they had failed to find him, or found him dead, she would have wept for him, yes, but her stepmother would not have cared too much where she chose to marry. What would have mattered most to Sybilla was that her son should inherit all, and her husband's daughter be content with a modest dowry. And so she would have been content, yes, with none.

'But it must not be an end!' vowed Elis fiercely. 'Why should we submit to it? I won't give you up, I can't, I won't part from you.'

'Oh, foolish!' she said, her tears gushing against his cheek, 'The escort that brings him home will take you away. There's a bargain struck, and no choice but to keep it. You must go, and I must stay, and that will be the end. Oh, if he need never reach here …' Her own voice uttering such things terrified her, she buried her lips in the hollow of his shoulder to smother the unforgivable words.

'No, but listen to me, my heart, my dear! Why should I not go to him and offer for you? Why should he not give me fair hearing? I'm born princely, I have lands, I'm his equal, why should he refuse to let me have you? I can endow you well, and there's no man could ever love you more.'

He had never told her, as he had so light-heartedly told Brother Cadfael, of the girl in Wales, betrothed to him from childhood. But that agreement had been made over their heads, by consent of others, and with patience and goodwill it could be honourably dissolved by the consent of all. Such a reversal might be a rarity in Gwynedd, but it was not unheard of. He had done no wrong to Cristina, it was not too late to withdraw.

'Sweet fool innocent!' she said, between laughter and rage. 'You do not know him! Every manor he holds is a border manor, he has had to sweat and fight for them many a time. Can you not see that after the empress, his enemy is Wales? And he as good a hater as ever was born! He would as soon marry his daughter to a blind leper in St Giles as to a Welshman, if he were the prince of Gwynedd himself. Never go near him, you will but harden him, and he'll rend you. Oh, trust me, there's no hope there.'

'Yet I will not let you go,' vowed Elis into the cloud of her pale hair, that stirred and stroked against his face with a life of its own, in nervous, feathery caresses. 'Somehow, somehow, I swear I'll keep you, no matter what I must do to hold you, no matter how many I must fight to clear the way to you. I'll kill whoever comes between us, my love, my dear ...'

'Oh, hush!' she said. 'Don't talk so. That's not for you. There must, there must be some way for us ...'

But she could see none. They were caught in an inexorable process that would bring Gilbert Prestcote home, and sweep Elis ap Cynan away.

'We have still a little time,' she whispered, taking heart as best she could. 'They said he is not well, he had wounds barely healed. They'll be a week or two yet.'

81

'And you'll still come? You *will* come? Every day? How should I bear it if I could no longer see you?'

'I'll come,' she said, 'these moments are my life, too. Who knows, something may yet happen to save us.'

'Oh God, if we could but stop time! If we could hold back the days, make him take for ever on the journey, and never, never reach Shrewsbury!'

It was ten days before the next word came from Owain Gwynedd. A runner came in on foot, armed with due authorisation from Einon ab Ithel, who ranked second only to Owain's own *penteulu*, the captain of his personal guard. The messenger was brought to Hugh in the castle guardroom early in the afternoon; a border man, with some business dealings into England, and well acquainted with the language.

'My lord, I bring greetings from Owain Gwynedd through the mouth of his captain, Einon ab Ithel. I am to tell you that the party lies tonight at Montford, and tomorrow we shall bring you our charge, the lord Gilbert Prestcote. But there is more. The lord Gilbert is still very weak from his wounds and hardships, and for most of the way we have carried him in a litter. All went well enough until this morning, when we had hoped to reach the town and discharge our task in one day. Because of that, the lord Gilbert would ride the last miles, and not be carried like a sick man into his own town.'

The Welsh would understand and approve that, and not presume to deter him. A man's face

82

is half his armour, and Prestcote would venture any discomfort or danger to enter Shrewsbury erect in the saddle, a man master of himself even in captivity.

'It was like him and worthy of him,' said Hugh, but scenting what must follow. 'And he tried himself too far. What has happened?'

'Before we had gone a mile he swooned and fell. Not a heavy fall, but a healed wound in his side has started open again, and he lost some blood. It may be that there was some manner of fit or seizure, more than the mere exertion, for when we took him up and tended him he was very pale and cold. We wrapped him well – Einon ab Ithel swathed him further in his own cloak – and laid him again in the litter, and have carried him back to Montford.'

'Has he his senses? Has he spoken?' asked Hugh anxiously.

'As sound in his wits as any man, once he opened his eyes, and speaks clearly, my lord. We would keep him at Montford longer, if need be, but he is set to reach Shrewsbury now, being so near. He may take more harm, being vexed, than if we carry him here as he wishes, tomorrow.'

So Hugh thought, too, and gnawed his knuckles a while pondering what was best. 'Do you think this setback may be dangerous to him? Even mortal?'

The man shook his head decidedly. 'My lord, though you'll find him a sick man and much fallen and aged, I think he needs only rest and time and good care to be his own man again. But it will not be a quick or an easy return.'

'Then it had better be here, where he desires to be,' Hugh decided, 'but hardly in these cold, harsh chambers. I would take him to my own house, gladly, but the best nursing will surely be at the abbey, and there you can just as well bear him, and he may be spared being carried helpless through the town. I will bespeak a bed for him in the infirmary there, and see his wife and children into the guest-hall to be near him. Go back now to Einon ab Ithel with my greetings and thanks, and ask him to bring his charge straight to the abbey. I will see Brother Edmund and Brother Cadfael prepared to receive him, and all ready for his rest. At what hour may we expect your arrival? Abbot Radulfus will wish to have your captains be his guests before they leave again.'

'Before noon,' said the messenger, 'we should reach the abbey.'

'Good! Then there shall be places at table for all, for the midday meal, before you set forth with Elis ap Cynan in exchange for my sheriff.'

Hugh carried the news to the tower apartments, to Lady Prestcote, who received them with relief and joy, though tempered with some uneasiness when she heard of her husband's collapse. She made haste to collect her son and her maid, and make ready to move to the greater comfort of the abbey guest-hall, ready for her lord's coming, and Hugh conducted them there and went to confer with the abbot about the morrow's visit. And if he noted that one of the party went with them mute and pale, brilliant-eyed as much with tears as with eagerness, he thought little of it then. The

84

daughter of the first wife, displaced by the son of the second, might well be the one who missed her father most, and had worn her courage so threadbare with the grief of waiting that she could not yet translate her exhaustion into joy.

Meantime, there was hum and bustle about the great court. Abbot Radulfus issued orders, and took measures to furnish his own table for the entertainment of the representatives of the prince of Gwynedd. Prior Robert took counsel with the cooks concerning properly lavish provision for the remainder of the escort, and room enough in the stables to rest and tend their horses. Brother Edmund made ready the quietest enclosed chamber in the infirmary, and had warm, light covers brought, and a brazier to temper the air, while Brother Cadfael reviewed the contents of his workshop with the broken wound in mind, and the suggestion of something more than a swoon. The abbey had sometimes entertained much larger parties, even royalty, but this was the return of a man of their own, and the Welsh who had been courteous and punctilious in providing him his release and his safe-conduct must be honoured like princes, as they stood for a prince.

In his cell in the castle Elis ap Cynan lay face-down on his pallet, the heart in his breast as oppressive as a hot and heavy stone. He had watched her go, but from hiding, unwilling to cause her the same suffering and despair he felt. Better she should go without a last reminder, able at least to try to turn all her thoughts towards her father, and leave her lover out of mind. He had strained his eyes after her to the last, until she vanished down the ramp from the gatehouse, the silver-gold of her coiled hair the only brightness in a dull day. She was gone, and the stone that had taken the place of his heart told him that the most he could hope for now was a fleeting glimpse of her on the morrow, when they released him from the castle wards and conducted him down to the abbey, to be handed over to Einon ab Ithel; for after the morrow, unless a miracle happened, he might never see her again.

Chapter Five

Brother Cadfael was ready with Brother Edmund in the porch of the infirmary to see them ride in, as they did in the middle of the morning, just after High Mass was ended. Owain's trusted captain in the lead with Eliud ap Griffith, very solemn of face, close behind him as body-squire and two older officers following, and then the litter, carefully slung between two strong hill ponies, with attendants on foot walking alongside to steady the ride. The long form in the litter was so cushioned and swathed that it looked bulky, but the ponies moved smoothly and easily, as if the weight was very light.

Einon ab Ithel was a big, muscular man in his forties, bearded, with long moustaches and a mane of brown hair. His clothing and the harness of the fine horse under him spoke his wealth and importance. Eliud leaped down to take his lord's bridle, and walked the horse aside as Hugh Beringar came to greet the arrivals and after him, with welcoming dignity, Abbot Radulfus himself. There would be a leisurely and ceremonious meal in the abbot's lodging for Einon and the elder officers of his party, together with Lady Prestcote and her daughter and Hugh himself, as was due when two powers came together in civilised agreement. But the most urgent business fell to Brother Edmund and his helpers.

The litter was unharnessed, and carried at once into the infirmary, to the room already prepared and warmed for the sick man's reception. Edmund closed the door even against Lady Prestcote, who was blessedly delayed by the civilities, until they should have unwrapped, unclothed and installed the invalid, and had some idea of his state.

They unfastened from the high, close-drawn collar of the clipped sheepskin cloak that was his outer wrapping, a long pin with a large, chased gold head, secured by a thin gold chain. Everyone knew there was gold worked in Gwynedd, probably this came from Einon's own land for certainly this must be his cloak, added to pillow and protect his sacred charge. Edmund laid it aside, folded, on a low chest beside the bed, the great pin showing clearly, for fear someone should run his hand on to the point if it were hidden. Between them they unwound Gilbert Prestcote from the layers in which he was swathed, and as they handled him his eyes opened languidly, and his long, gaunt body made some feeble moves to help them. He was much fallen in flesh, and bore several scars, healed but angry, besides the moist wound in his flank which had gaped again with his fall. Carefully Cadfael dressed and covered the place. Even being handled exhausted the sick man. By the time they had lifted him into the warmed bed and covered him his eyes were again closed. As yet he had not tried to speak.

A marvel how he had ever ridden even a mile before foundering, thought Cadfael, looking down at the figure stretched beneath the covers, and the lean, livid face, all sunken blue hollows and staring, blanched bones. The dark hair of his head and beard was thickly sown with grey, and lay lank and lifeless. Only his iron spirit, intolerant of any weakness, most of all his own, had held him up in the saddle, and when even that failed he was lost indeed.

But he drew breath, he had moved to assert his rights in his own body, however weakly, and again he opened the dulled and sunken eyes and stared up into Cadfael's face. His grey lips formed, just audibly: 'My son?' Not: 'My wife?' Nor yet: 'My daughter?' Cadfael thought with rueful sympathy, and stooped to assure him: 'Young Gilbert is here, safe and well.' He glanced at Edmund, who signalled back agreement. 'I'll bring him to you.'

Small boys are very resilient, but for all that Cadfael said some words, both of caution and reassurance, as much for the mother as the child, before he brought them in and drew aside into a corner to leave them the freedom of the bedside. Hugh came in with them. Prestcote's first thought was naturally for his son, the second, no less naturally, would be for his shire. And his shire, considering all things, was in very good case to encourage him to live, mend and mind it again.

Sybilla wept, but quietly. The little boy stared in some wonder at a father hardly recognised, but let himself be drawn close by a gaunt, cold hand, and stared at hungrily by eyes like firelit caverns. His mother leaned and whispered to him, and obediently he stooped his rosy, round face and kissed a bony cheek. He was an accommodating child, puzzled but willing, and not at all afraid. Prestcote's eyes ranged beyond, and found Hugh Beringar.

'Rest content,' said Hugh, leaning close and answering what need not be asked, 'your borders are whole and guarded. The only breach has provided you your ransom, and even there the victory was ours. And Owain Gwynedd is our ally. What is yours to keep is in good order.'

The dulling glance faded beneath drooping lids, and never reached the girl standing stark and still in the shadows near the door. Cadfael had observed her, from his own retired place, and watched the light from brazier and lamp glitter in the tears flowing freely and mutely down her cheeks. She made no sound at all, she hardly drew breath. Her wide eyes were fixed on her father's changed, aged face, in the most grievous and desperate stare.

The sheriff had understood and accepted what Hugh said. Brow and chin moved slightly in a satisfied nod. His lips stirred to utter almost clearly: 'Good!' And to the boy, awed but curious, hanging over him: 'Good boy! Take care ... of your mother ...'

He heaved a shallow sigh and his eyes drooped closed. They held still for some time, watching and listening to the heave and fall of the covers over his sunken breast and the short, harsh in and out of his breath, before Brother Edmund stepped softly forward and said in a cautious whisper. 'He's sleeping. Leave him so, in quiet. There is nothing better or more needed any man can do for him.'

Hugh touched Sybilla's arm, and she rose obediently and drew her son up beside her. 'You see him well cared for,' said Hugh gently. 'Come to dinner, and let him sleep.'

The girl's eyes were quite dry, her cheeks pale but calm, when she followed them out to the great court, and down the length of it to the abbot's lodging, to be properly gracious and grateful to the Welsh guests, before they left again for Montford and Oswestry.

Over their midday meal, which was served before the brothers ate in the refectory, the inhabitants of the infirmary laid their ageing but inquisitive heads together to make out what was causing the unwonted stir about their retired domain. The discipline of silence need not be rigorously observed among the old and sick, and just as well, since they tend to be incorrigibly garrulous, from want of other active occupation.

Brother Rhys, who was bedridden and very old indeed, but sharp enough in mind and hearing even if his sight was filmed over, had a bed next to the corridor, and across from the retired room where some newcomer had been brought during the morning, with unusual to-do and ceremony. He took pleasure in being the member who knew what was going on. Among so few pleasures left to him, this was the chief, and not to be lightly spent.

91

He lay and listened. Those who sat at the table, as once in the refectory, and could move around the infirmary and sometimes the great court if the weather was right, nevertheless were often obliged to come to him for knowledge.

'Who should it be,' said Brother Rhys loftily, 'but the sheriff himself, brought back from being a prisoner in Wales.'

'Prestcote?' said Brother Maurice, rearing his head on its stringy neck like a gander giving notice of battle. 'Here? In our infirmary? Why should they bring him here?'

'Because he's a sick man, what else? He was wounded in the battle, and in no shape to shift for himself yet, or trouble any other man. I heard their voices in there – Edmund, Cadfael and Hugh Beringar – and the lady, too, and the child. It's Gilbert Prestcote, take my word.'

'There is justice,' said Maurice with sage satisfaction, and the gleam of vengeance in his eye, 'though it be too long delayed. So Prestcote is brought low, neighbour to the unfortunate. The wrong done to my line finds a balance at last, I repent that ever I doubted.'

They humoured him, being long used to his obsessions. They murmured variously, most saying reasonably enough that the shire had not fared badly in Prestcote's hands, though some had old grumbles to vent and reservations about sheriffs in general, even if this one of theirs was not by any means the worst of his kind. On the whole they wished him well. But Brother Maurice was not to be reconciled.

'There was a wrong done,' he said implacably,

'which even now is not fully set right. Let the false pleader pay for his offence, I say, to the bitter end.'

The stockman Anion, at the end of the table, said never a word, but kept his eyes lowered to his trencher, his hip pressed against the crutch he was almost ready to discard, as though he needed a firm contact with the reality of his situation, and the reassurance of a weapon to hand in the sudden presence of his enemy. Young Griffri had killed, yes, but in drink, in hot blood, and in fair fight man against man. He had died a worse death, turned off more casually than wringing a chicken's neck. And the man who had made away with him so lightly lay now barely twenty yards away, and at the very sound of his name every drop of blood in Anion ran Welsh, and cried out to him of the sacred duty of *galanas*, the blood-feud for his brother.

Eliud led Einon's horse and his own down the great court into the stable-yard, and the men of the escort followed with their own mounts, and the shaggy hill ponies that had carried the litter. An easy journey those two would have on the way back to Montford. Einon ab Ithel, when representing his prince on a ceremonial occasion, required a squire in attendance, and Eliud undertook the grooming of the tall bay himself. Very soon now he would be changing places with Elis, and left to chafe here while his cousin rode back to his freedom in Wales. In silence he hoisted off the heavy saddle, lifted aside the elaborate harness, and draped the saddle-cloth over his arm. The bay tossed his head with pleasure in his freedom, and blew great misty breaths. Eliud caressed him absently; his mind was not wholly on what he was doing, and his companions had found him unusually silent and withdrawn all that day. They eyed him cautiously and let him alone. It was no great surprise when he suddenly turned and tramped away out of the stable-yard, back to the open court.

'Gone to see whether there's any sign of his cousin yet,' said his neighbour tolerantly, rubbing down one of the shaggy ponies. 'He's been like a man maimed and out of balance ever since the other one went off to Lincoln. He can hardly believe it yet that he'll turn up here without a scratch on him.'

'He should know his Elis better than that,' grunted the man beside him. 'Never yet did that one fall anywhere but on his feet.'

Eliud was away perhaps ten minutes, long enough to have been all the way to the gatehouse and peered anxiously along the Foregate towards the town, but he came back in dour silence, laid aside the saddle-cloth he was still carrying, and went to work without a word or a look aside.

'Not come yet?' asked his neighbour with careful sympathy.

'No,' said Eliud shortly, and continued working vigorously on the bright bay hide.

'The castle's the far side of the town, they'll have kept him there until they were sure of our man. They'll bring him. He'll be at dinner with us.'

Eliud said nothing. At this hour the monks

themselves were at their meal in the refectory, and the abbot's guests with him at his own table in his lodging. It was the quietest hour of the day; even the comings and goings about the guest-hall were few at this time of year, though with the spring the countryside would soon be on the move again.

'Never show him so glum a face,' said the Welshman, grinning, 'even if you must be left here in his place. Ten days or so, and Owain and this young sheriff will be clasping hands on the border, and you on your way home to join him.'

Eliud muttered a vague agreement, and turned a forbidding shoulder on further talk. He had Einon's horse stalled and glossy and watered by the time Brother Denis the hospitaller came to bid them to the refectory, newly laid and decked for them after the brothers had ended their repast, and dispersed to enjoy their brief rest before the afternoon's work began. The resources of the house were at their disposal, warmed water brought to the lavatorium for their hands, towels laid out and their table, when they entered the refectory, graced with more dishes than the brothers had enjoyed. And there waiting, somewhat in the manner of a nervous host, was Elis ap Cynan, freshly brushed and spruced for the occasion, and on his most formal behaviour.

The awe of the exchange, himself the unwise cause of it and to some extent already under censure for his unwisdom, or something else of like weight, had had its effect upon Elis, for he came with stiff bearing and very sombre face, who was known rather for his hearty cheerfulness in and out of season. Certainly his eyes shone at the sight of Eliud entering, and he came with open arms to embrace him, but thereafter shoved free again. The grip of his hand had some unaccountable tension about it, and though he sat down to table beside his cousin, the talk over that meal was general and restrained. It caused some mild wonder among their companions. There were these two inseparables, together again after long and anxious separation, and both as mute as blocks, and as pale and grave of face as men arraigned for their lives.

It was very different when the meal was over, the grace said, and they were free to go forth into the court. Elis caught his cousin by the arm and hauled him away into the cloister, where they could take refuge in one of the carrels where no monk was working or studying, and go to earth there like hunted foxes, shoulder warm for comfort against shoulder, as when they were children and fled into sanctuary from some detected misdeed. And now Eliud could recognise his foster-brother as he had always been, as he always would be, and marvelled fondly what misdemeanour or misfortune he could have to pour out here, where he had been so loftily on his dignity.

'Oh, Eliud!' blurted Elis, hugging him afresh in arms which had certainly lost none of their heedless strength. 'For God's sake, what am I to do? How shall I tell you! I can't go back! If I do, I've lost all. Oh, Eliud, I must have her! If I lose her I shall die! You haven't seen her? Prestcote's daughter?'

96

'His daughter?' whispered Eliud, utterly dazed. 'There was a lady, with a grown girl and a young boy ... I hardly noticed.'

'For God's sake, man, how could you *not* notice her? Ivory and roses, and her hair all pale, like spun silver ... I love her!' proclaimed Elis in high fever. 'And she is just as fain, I swear it, and we've pledged ourselves. Oh, Eliud, if I go now I shall never have her. If I leave her now, I'm lost. And he's an enemy, she warned me, he hates the Welsh. Never go near him, she said ...'

Eliud, who had sat stunned and astray, roused himself to take his friend by the shoulders and shake him furiously until he fell silent for want of breath, staring astonished.

'*What* are you telling me? You have a girl here? You *love* her? You no longer want to make any claim on Cristina? Is *that* what you're saying?'

'Were you not listening? Haven't I told you?' Elis, unsubdued and unchastened, heaved himself free and grappled in his turn. 'Listen, let me tell you how it fell. What pledge did I myself ever give Cristina? Is it her fault or mine if we're tied like tethered cattle? She cares no more for me than I for her. I'd brother the girl and dance at her wedding, and kiss her and wish her well heartily. But this ... this is another matter! Oh, Eliud, hush and hear me!'

It poured forth like music, the whole story from his first glimpse of her, the silver maiden at the door, blue-eyed, magical. Plenty of bards had issued from the stock to which Elis belonged, he had both the gift of words and the eloquent tune. Eliud sat stricken mute, gaping at him in blanched

97

astonishment and strange dismay, his hands gripped and wrung in Elis's persuading hands.

'And I was frantic for you!' he said softly and slowly, almost to himself. 'If I had but known …'

'But Eliud, he's here!' Elis held him by the arms, peering eagerly into his face. 'He *is* here? You brought him, you must know. She says, don't go, but how can I lose this chance? I'm noble, I pledge the girl my whole heart, all my goods and lands, where will he find a better match? And she is not spoken for. I can, I must win him, he must listen to me … why should he not?' He flashed one sweeping glance about the most vacant court. 'They're not yet ready, they haven't called us. Eliud, you know where he's laid. I'm going to him! I must, I will! Show me the place!'

'He's in the infirmary.' Eliud was staring at him with open mouth and wide, shocked eyes. 'But you can't, you mustn't … He's sick and weary, you can't trouble him now.'

'I'll be gentle, humble, I'll kneel to him. I'll put my life in his hands. The infirmary – which is it? I never was inside these walls until now. Which door?' He caught Eliud by the arm and dragged him to the archway that looked out on the court. 'Show me, quickly!'

'*No!* Don't go! Leave him be! For shame to rush in on his rest …'

'*Which door?*' Elis shook him fiercely. 'You brought him, you saw!'

'There! The building drawn back to the precinct wall, to the right from the gatehouse. But don't do it! Surely the girl knows her father best. Wait, don't harry him now – an old, sick man!'

'You think I'd offer any hardihood to *her father*?

All I want is to tell him my heart, and that I have her favour. If he curses me, I'll bear it. But I must put it to the test. What chance shall I ever have again?' He made to pull clear, and Eliud held him convulsively, then as suddenly heaved a great sigh and loosed his hold.

'Go, then, try your fortune! I can't keep you.'

Elis was away, without the least caution or dissembling, out into the court and straight as an arrow across it to the door of the infirmary. Eliud stood in shadow to watch him vanish within, and leaned his forehead against the stone and waited with eyes closed some while before he looked again.

The abbot's guests were just emerging from the doorway of his lodging. The young man who was now virtually sheriff set off with the lady and her daughter, to conduct them again to the porch of the guest-hall. Einon ab Ithel lingered in talk with the abbot, his two companions, having less English, waited civilly a pace aside. Very soon he would be ordering the saddling of the horses, and the ceremonious leave-taking.

From the doorway of the infirmary two figures emerged, Elis first, stiffly erect, and after him one of the brothers. At the head of the few stone steps the monk halted, and stood to watch Elis stalk away across the great court, taut with offence, quenched in despair, like our first forefather expelled from Eden.

'He's sleeping,' he said, coming in crestfallen. 'I couldn't speak with him, the infirmarer turned me away.'

*

99

Barely half an hour now, and they would be on their way back to Montford, there to spend the first night of their journey into Wales. In the stables Eliud led out Einon's tall bay, and saddled and bridled him, before turning his attention to the horse he himself had ridden, which now Elis must ride in his place, while he lingered here.

The brothers had roused themselves after their customary rest, and were astir about the court again, on their way to their allotted labours. Some days into March, there was already work to be done in field and garden, besides the craftsmen who had their workshops in cloister and scriptorium. Brother Cadfael, crossing at leisure towards the garden and the herbarium, was accosted suddenly by an Eliud evidently looking about him for a guide, and pleased to recognise a face he knew.

'Brother, if I may trouble you – I've been neglecting my duty, there's something I had forgotten. My lord Einon left his cloak wrapping the lord Gilbert in the litter, for an extra covering. Of sheared sheepskins – you'll have seen it? I must reclaim it, but I don't want to disturb the lord Gilbert. If you will show me the place, and hand it forth to me ...'

'Very willingly,' said Cadfael, and led the way briskly. He eyed the young man covertly as they walked together. That passionate, intense face was closed and sealed, but trouble showed in his eyes. He would always be carrying half the weight of that easy foster-brother of his who went so light through the world. And a fresh parting imminent, after so brief a reunion; and that

100

marriage waiting to make parting inevitable and lifelong. 'You'll know the place,' said Cadfael, 'though not the room. He was deep asleep when we all left him. I hope he is still. Sleep in his own town, with his family by and his charge in good heart, is all he needs.'

'There was no mortal harm, then?' asked Eliud, low-voiced.

'None that time should not cure. And here we are. Come in with me. I remember the cloak. I saw Brother Edmund fold it aside on the chest.'

The door of the narrow chamber had been left ajar, to avoid the noise of the iron latch, but it creaked on being opened far enough to admit entrance. Cadfael slipped through the opening sidewise, and paused to look attentively at the long, still figure in the bed, but it remained motionless and oblivious. The brazier made a small, smokeless eye of gold in the dimness within. Reassured, Cadfael crossed to the chest on which the clothes lay folded and gathered up the sheepskin cloak. Unquestionably it was the one Eliud sought, and yet even at this moment Cadfael was oddly aware that it did not answer exactly to his recollection of it, though he did not stop to try and identify what was changed about it. He had turned back to the door, where Eliud hovered half-in, half-out, peering anxiously, when the young man made a step aside to let him go first into the passage, and knocked over the stool that stood in the corner. It fell with a loud wooden clap and rolled. Eliud bent to arrest its flight and snatch it up from the tiled floor and Cadfael, waving a hand furiously at him for silence, whirled round to see if the noise had startled the sleeper awake.

Not a movement, not a sharp breath, not a sigh. The long body, scarcely lifting the bedclothes, lay still as before. Too still. Cadfael went close, and laid a hand to draw down the brychan that covered the grizzled beard and hid the mouth. The bluish eyelids in their sunken hollows stared up like carven eyes in a tomb sculpture. The lips were parted and drawn a little back from clenched teeth, as if in some constant and customary pain. The gaunt breast did not move at all. No noise could ever again disturb Gilbert Prestcote's sleep.

'What is it?' whispered Eliud, creeping close to gaze.

'Take this,' ordered Cadfael, thrusting the folded cloak into the boy's hands. 'Come with me to your lord and Hugh Beringar, and God grant the women are safe indoors.'

He need not have been in immediate anxiety for the women, he saw as he emerged into the open court with Eliud mute and quivering at his heels. It was chilly out there, and this was men's business now the civilities were properly attended to, and Lady Prestcote had made her farewells and withdrawn with Melicent into the guest-hall. The Welsh party were waiting with Hugh in an easy group near the gatehouse, ready to mount and ride, the horses saddled and tramping the cobbles with small, ringing sounds. Elis stood docile and dutiful at Einon's stirrup, though he did not look overjoyed at being on his way home. His face was overcast like the sky. At the sound of

102

Cadfael's rapid steps approaching, and the sight of his face, every eye turned to fasten on him.

'I bring black news,' said Cadfael bluntly. 'My lord, your labour has been wasted, and I doubt your departure must wait yet a while. We are just come from the infirmary. Gilbert Prestcote is dead.'

Chapter Six

hey went with him, Hugh Beringar and
Einon ab Ithel, jointly responsible here for
this exchange of prisoners which had
suddenly slithered away out of their control. They
stood beside the bed in the dim, quiet room, the
little lamp a mild yellow eye on one side, the
brazier a clear red one on the other. They gazed
and touched, and held a bright, smooth blade to
the mouth and nose, and got no trace of breath.
The body was warm and pliable, no long time
dead; but dead indeed.

'Wounded and weak, and exhausted with
travelling,' said Hugh wretchedly. 'No blame to
you, my lord, if he had sunk too far to climb back
again.'

'Nevertheless, I had a mission,' said Einon. 'My
charge was to bring you one man, and take
another back from you in exchange. This matter
is void, and cannot be completed.'

'So you did bring him, living, and living you
delivered him over. It is in our hands his death
came. There is no bar but you should take your
man and go, according to the agreement. Your
part was done, and done well.'

'Not well enough. The man is dead. My prince does not countenance the exchange of a dead man for one living,' said Einon haughtily. 'I split no hairs, and will have none split in my favour. Nor will Owain Gwynedd. We have brought you, however innocently, a dead man. I will not take a live one for him. This exchange cannot go forward. It is null and void.'

Brother Cadfael, though with one ear pricked and aware of these meticulous exchanges, which were no more than he had foreseen, had taken up the small lamp, shielding it from draughts with his free hand, and held it close over the dead face. No very arduous or harsh departure. The man had been deeply asleep, and very much enfeebled, to slip over a threshold would be all too easy. Not, however, unless the threshold were greased or had too shaky a doorstone. This mute and motionless face, growing greyer as he gazed, was a face familiar to him for some years, fallen and aged though it might be. He searched it closely, moving the lamp to illumine every plane and every cavernous hollow. The pitted places had their bluish shadows, but the full lips, drawn back a little, should not have shown the same livid tint, nor the pattern of the large, strong teeth within, and the staring nostrils should not have gaped so wide and shown the same faint bruising.

'You will do what seems to you right,' said Hugh at his back, 'but I, for my part, make plain that you are free to depart in company as you came, and take both your young men with you. Send back mine, and I consider the terms will have been faithfully observed. Or if Owain

Gwynedd still wants a meeting, so much the better, I will go to him on the border, wherever he may appoint, and take my hostage from him there.'

'Owain will speak his own mind,' said Einon, 'when I have told him what has happened. But without his word I must leave Elis ap Cynan unredeemed, and take Eliud back with me. The price due for Elis has not been paid, not to my satisfaction. He stays here.'

'I am afraid,' said Cadfael, turning abruptly from the bed, 'Elis will not be the only one constrained to remain here.' And as they fixed him with two blank and questioning stares: 'There is more here than you know. Hugh said well, there was no mortal harm to him, all he needed was time, rest and peace of mind, and he would have come back to himself. An older self before his time, perhaps, but he would have come. This man did not simply drown in his own weakness and weariness. There was a hand that held him under.'

'You are saying,' said Hugh, after a bleak silence of dismay and doubt, 'that this was murder?'

'I am saying so. There are the signs on him clear.'

'Show us,' said Hugh.

He showed them, one intent face stooped on either side to follow the tracing of his finger. 'It would not take much pressure, there would not be anything to be called a struggle. But see what signs there are. These marks round nose and mouth, faint though they are, are bruises he had

106

not when we bedded him. His lips are plainly bruised, and if you look closely you will see the shaping of his teeth in the marks on the upper lip. A hand was clamped over his face to cut off breath. I doubt if he awoke, in his deep sleep and low state it would not take long.'

Einon looked at the furnishings of the bed, and asked, low-voiced: 'What was used to muffle nose and mouth, then? These covers?'

'There's no knowing yet. I need better light and time enough. But as sure as God sees us, the man was murdered.'

Neither of them raised a word to question further. Einon had experience of many kinds of dying, and Hugh had implicit trust by now in Brother Cadfael's judgement. They looked wordlessly at each other for a long, thinking while.

'The brother here is right,' said Einon then, 'I cannot take away any of my men who may by the very furthest cast have any part in this killing. Not until truth is shown openly can they return home.'

'Of all your party,' said Hugh, 'you, my lord, and your two captains are absolutely clear of any slur. You never entered the infirmary until now, they have not entered it at all, and all three have been in my company and in the abbot's company every minute of this visit, besides the witness of the women. There is no one can keep you, and it is well you should return to Owain Gwynedd, and let him know what has happened here. In the hope that truth may out very soon, and set all the guiltless free.'

'I will so return, and they with me. But for the

rest …' They were both considering that, recalling how the party had separated to its several destinations, the abbot's guests with him to his lodging, the rest to the stables to tend their horses, and after that to wander where they would and talk to whom they would until they were called to the refectory for their dinner. And that half-hour before the meal saw the court almost empty.

'There is not one other among us,' said Einon, 'who could not have entered here. Six men of my own, and Eliud. Unless some of them were in company with men of this household, or within sight of such, throughout. That I doubt, but it can be examined.'

'There are also all within here to be considered. Of all of us, surely your Welshmen had the least cause to wish him dead, having carried and cared for him all this way. It is madness to think it. Here are the brothers, such wayfarers as they have within the precinct, the lay servants, myself, though I have been with you the whole while, my men who brought Elis from the castle … Elis himself …'

'He was taken straight to the refectory,' said Einon. 'However, he above all stays here. We had best be about sifting out any of mine who can be vouched for throughout, and if there are such I will have them away with me, for the sooner Owain Gwynedd knows of this, the better.'

'And I,' said Hugh ruefully, 'must go break the news to his widow and daughter, and make report to the lord abbot, and a sorry errand that will be. Murder in his own enclave!'

*

Abbot Radulfus came, grimly composed, looked long and grievously at the dead face, heard what Cadfael had to tell, and covered the stark visage with a linen cloth. Prior Robert came, jolted out of his aristocratic calm, shaking his silver head over the iniquity of the world and the defilement of holy premises. There would have to be ceremonies of re-consecration to make all pure again, and that could not be done until truth was out and justice vindicated. Brother Edmund came, distressed beyond all measure at such a happening in his province and under his devoted and careful rule, as though the guilt of it fouled his own hands and set a great black stain against his soul. It was hard to comfort him. Over and over he lamented that he had not placed a constant watch by the sheriff's bed, but how could any man have known that there would be need? Twice he had looked in, and found all quiet and still, and left it so. Quietness and stillness, time and rest, these were what the sick man most required. The door had been left ajar, any brother passing by could have heard if the sleeper had awakened and wanted for any small service.

'Hush you, now!' said Cadfael sighing. 'Take to yourself no more than your due, and that's small enough. There's no man takes better care of his fellows, as well you know. Keep your balance, for you and I will have to question all those within here, if they heard or saw anything amiss.'

Einon ab Ithel was gone by then, with only his two captains to bear him company, his hill ponies on a leading rein, back to Montford for the night, and then as fast as might be to wherever Owain Gwynedd now kept his border watch in the north.

There was not one of his men could fill up every moment of his time within here, and bring witnesses to prove it. Here or in the closer ward of the castle they must stay, until Prestcote's murderer was found and named.

Hugh, wisely enough, had gone first to the abbot, and only after speeding the departing Welsh did he go to perform the worst errand of all.

Edmund and Cadfael withdrew from the bedside when the two women came in haste and tears from the guest-hall, Sybilla stumbling blindly on Hugh's arm. The little boy they had managed to leave in happy ignorance with Sybilla's maid. There would be a better time than this to tell him he was fatherless.

Behind him, as he drew the door quietly to, Cadfael heard the widow break into hard and painful weeping, as quickly muffled in the coverings of her husband's bed. From the girl not a sound. She had walked into the room stiffly, with blanched, icy face and eyes fallen empty with shock.

In the great court the little knot of Welshmen hung uneasily together, with Hugh's guards unobtrusive but watchful on all sides, and in particular between them and the closed wicket in the gate. Elis and Eliud, struck silent and helpless in this disaster, stood a little apart, not touching, not looking at each other. Now for the first time Cadfael could see a family resemblance in them, so tenuous that in normal times it would never be noticed, while the one went solemn and thoughtful, and the other as blithe and

110

untroubled as a bird. Now they both wore the same shocked visage, the one as lost as the other, and they could almost have been twin brothers.

They were still standing there waiting to be disposed of, and shifting miserably from foot to foot in silence, when Hugh came back across the court with the two women. Sybilla had regained a bleak but practical control over her tears, and showed more stiffening in her backbone than Cadfael, for one, had expected. Most likely she had already turned a part of her mind and energy to the consideration of her new situation, and what it meant for her son, who was now the lord of six valuable manors, but all of them in this vulnerable border region. He would need either a very able steward or a strong and well-disposed step-father. Her lord was dead, his overlord the king a prisoner; there was no one to force her into an unwelcome match. She was many years younger than her lost husband, and had a dower of her own, and good enough looks to make her a fair bargain. She would live, and do well enough.

The girl was another matter. Within her frosty calm a faint fire had begun to burn again, deep sparks lurked in the quenched eyes. She turned one unreadable glance upon Elis, and then looked straight before her.

Hugh checked for a moment to commit the Welshmen of the escort to his sergeants, and have them led away to the security of the castle, with due civility, since all of them might be entirely innocent of wrong, but into close and vigilant guard. He would have passed on, to see the women into their apartments before attempting

111

any further probing, but Melicent suddenly laid a hand upon his arm.

'My lord, since Brother Edmund is here, may I ask him a question, before we leave this in your hands?' She was very still but the fire in her was beginning to burn through, and her pallor to show sharp edges of steel. 'Brother Edmund, you best know your own domain, and I know you watch over it well. There is no blame falls upon you. But tell us, who, if anyone, entered my father's chamber after he was left there asleep?'

'I was not constantly by,' said Edmund unhappily. 'God forgive me, I never dreamed there could be any need. Anyone could have gone in to him.'

'But you know of one who certainly did go in?'

Sybilla had plucked her step-daughter by the sleeve, distressed and reproving, but Melicent shook her off without a glance. 'And only one?' she said sharply.

'To my knowledge, yes,' agreed Edmund, uncomprehendingly, 'but surely no harm. It was shortly before you all returned from the abbot's lodging. I had time then to make a round, and I saw the sheriff's door opened, and found a young man beside the bed, as though he meant to disturb his sleep. I could not have that, so I took him by the shoulder and turned him about, and pointed him out of the room. And he went obediently and made no protest. There was no word spoken,' said Edmund simply, 'and no harm done. The patient had not awakened.'

'No,' said Melicent, her voice shaken at last out of its wintry calm, 'nor never did again, nor never

112

will. Name him, this *one*.'

And Edmund did not even know the boy's name, so little had he had to do with him. He indicated Elis with a hesitant hand. 'It was our Welsh prisoner.'

Melicent let out a strange, grievous sound of anger, guilt and pain, and whirled upon Elis. Her marble whiteness had become incandescent, and the blue of her eyes was like the blinding fire sunlight strikes from ice. 'Yes, *you*! None but you! None but you went in there. Oh, God, what have you and I done between us! And I, fool, fool, I never believed you could mean it, when you told me, many times over, you'd kill for me, kill whoever stood between us. Oh, God, and I *loved* you! I may even have invited you, urged you to the deed. I never understood. Anything, you said, to keep us together a while longer, anything to prevent your being sent away, back to Wales. *Anything*! You said you would kill, and now you have killed, and God forgive me, I am guilty along with you.'

Elis stood facing her, the poor lucky lad suddenly most unlucky and defenceless as a babe. He stared with dropped jaw and startled, puzzled, terrified face, struck clean out of words and wits, open to any stab. He shook his head violently from side to side, as if dreamers who use their fingers to prise open eyelids beset by unbearable dreams. He could not get out a word or a sound.

'I take back every evidence of love,' raged Melicent, her voice like a cry of pain. 'I hate you, I loathe you … I hate myself for ever loving you. You have so mistaken me, you have killed my father.'

He wrenched himself out of his stupor then, and made a wild move towards her. 'Melicent! For God's sake, what are you saying?'

She drew back violently out of his reach. 'No, don't touch me, don't come near me. Murderer!'

'This shall end,' said Hugh, and took her by the shoulders and put her into Sybilla's arms. 'Madam, I had thought to spare you any further distress today, but you see this will not wait. Bring her! And sergeant, have these two put into the gatehouse, where we may be private. Edmund and Cadfael, go with us, we may well need you.'

'Now,' said Hugh, when he had herded them all, accused, accuser and witnesses, into the anteroom of the gatehouse out of the cold and out of the public eye, 'now let us get to the heart of this. Brother Edmund, you say you found this man in the sheriff's chamber, standing beside his bed. How did you read it? Did you think, by appearances, he had been long in there? Or that he had but newly come?'

'I thought he had but just crept in,' said Edmund. 'He was close to the foot of the bed, a little stooped, looking down as though he wondered whether he dared wake the sleeper.'

'Yet he could have been here longer? He could have been standing over a man he had smothered, to assure himself it was thoroughly done?'

'It might be interpretable so,' agreed Edmund very dubiously, 'but the thought did not enter my mind. If there had been anything so sinister in him, would it not have shown? It's true he started

114

when I touched him, and looked guilty – but I mean as a boy caught in mischief, nothing that caused me an ill thought. And he went, when I ordered him, as biddable as a child.'

'Did you look again at the bed, after he was gone? Can you say if the sheriff was still breathing then? And the coverings of the bed, were they disarranged?'

'All was smooth and quiet as when we left him sleeping. But I did not look more closely,' said Edmund sadly. 'I wish to God I had.'

'You knew of no cause, and his best cure was to be let alone to sleep. One more thing – had Elis anything in his hands?'

'No, nothing. Nor had he on the cloak he has on his arm now.' It was of a dark red cloth, smooth-surfaced and close-woven.

'Very well. And you have no knowledge of any other who may have made his way into the room?'

'No knowledge, no. But at any time entry was possible. There may well have been others.'

Melicent said with deadly bitterness: 'One was enough! And that one we do know.' She shook Sybilla's hand from her arm, refusing any restraint but her own. 'My lord Beringar, hear me speak. I say again, he has killed my father. I will not go back from that.'

'Have your say,' said Hugh shortly.

'My lord, you must know that this Elis and I learned to know each other in your castle where he was prisoner, but with the run of the wards on his parole, and I was with my mother and brother in my father's apartments waiting for news of him. We came to see and touch – my bitter regret

115

that I am forced to say it, we loved. It was not our fault, it happened to us, we had no choice. We came to extreme dread that when my father came home we must be parted, for then Elis must leave in his place. And you, my lord, who best knew my father, know that he would never countenance a match with a Welshman. Many a time we talked of it, many a time we despaired. And he said – I swear he said so, he dare not deny it! – he said he would kill for me if need be, kill any man who stood between us. Anything, he said, to hold us together, even murder. In love men say wild things. I never thought of harm, and yet I am to blame, for I was as desperate for love as he. And now he has done what he threatened, for he has surely killed my father.'

Elis got his breath, coming out of his stunned wretchedness with a heave that almost lifted him out of his boots. 'I did not! I swear to you I never laid hand on him, never spoke word to him. I would not for any gain have hurt your father, even though he barred you from me. I would have reached you somehow, there would have been a way ... You do me terrible wrong!'

'But you did go to the room where he lay?' Hugh reminded him equably. 'Why?'

'To make myself known to him, to plead my cause with him, what else? It was the only present hope I had, I could not let it slip through my fingers. I wanted to tell him that I love Melicent, that I am a man of lands and honour, and desire nothing better than to serve her with all my goods and gear. He might have listened! I knew, she had told me, that he was sworn enemy to the Welsh, I knew it was a poor hope, but it was all the hope I had. But I never got the chance to speak. He was deep asleep, and before I ventured to disturb him the good brother came and banished me. This is the truth, and I will swear to it on the altar.'

'It *is* truth!' Eliud spoke up vehemently for his friend. He stood close, since Elis had refused a seat, his shoulder against Elis's shoulder for comfort and assurance. He was as pale as if the accusation had been made against him, and his voice was husky and low. 'He was with me in the cloister, he told me of his love, and said he would go to the lord Gilbert and speak to him man to man. I thought it unwise, but he would go. It was not many minutes before I saw him come forth, and Brother Infirmarer making sure he departed. And there was no manner of stealth in his dealings,' insisted Eliud stoutly, 'for he crossed the court straight and fast, not caring who might see him go in.'

'That may well be true,' agreed Hugh thoughtfully, 'but for all that, even if he went in with no ill intent, and no great hope, once he stood there by the bedside it might come into his mind how easy, and how final, to remove the obstacle – a man sleeping and already very low.'

'He never would!' cried Eliud. 'His is no such mind.'

'I did not,' said Elis, and looked helplessly at Melicent, who stared back at him stonily and gave him no aid. 'For God's sake, believe me! I think I could not have touched or roused him, even if there had been no one to send me away. To see a fine, strong man so – quite defenceless ...'

'Yet no one entered there but you,' she said mercilessly.

'That cannot be proved!' flashed Eliud. 'Brother Infirmarer has said that the way was open, anyone might have gone in.'

'Nor can it be proved that anyone did,' she said with aching bitterness.

'But I think it can,' said Brother Cadfael.

He had all eyes on him in an instant. All this time some morsel of his memory had been worrying at the flaw he could not quite identify. He had picked up the folded sheepskin cloak from the chest, where he had watched Edmund lay it, and there had been something different about it, though he could not think what it could be. And then the encounter with death had driven the matter to the back of his mind, but it had lodged there ever since, like chaff in the throat after eating porridge. And suddenly he had it. The cloak was gone now, gone with Einon ab Ithel back to Wales, but Edmund was there to confirm what he had to say. And so was Eliud, who would know his lord's belongings.

'When we disrobed and bedded Gilbert Prestcote,' he said, 'the cloak that wrapped him, which belonged to Einon ab Ithel, was folded and laid by – Brother Edmund will remember it – in such case as to leave plain to be seen in the collar a great gold pin that fastened it. When Eliud, here, came to ask me to show him the room and hand out his lord's cloak to him and I did so, the cloak was folded as before, but the pin was gone. Small wonder if we forgot the matter, seeing what else we found. But I knew there was something I

118

should have noted, and now I have recalled what it was.'

'It is truth!' cried Eliud, his face brightening eagerly. 'I never thought! And I have let my lord go without it, never a word said. I fastened the collar of the cloak with it myself, when we laid him in the litter, for the wind blew cold. But with this upset, I never thought to look for it again. Here is Elis and has never been out of men's sight since he came from the infirmary – ask all here! If he took it, he has it on him still. And if he has it not, then someone else has been in there before him and taken it. My foster-brother is no thief and no murderer – but if you doubt, you have your remedy.'

'What Cadfael says is truth,' said Edmund. 'The pin was there plain to be seen. If it is gone, then someone went in and took it.'

Elis had caught the fierce glow of hope, in spite of the unchanging bitterness and grief of Melicent's face. 'Strip me!' he demanded, glittering. 'Search my body! I won't endure to be thought thief and murderer both.'

In justice to him, rather than having any real doubts in the matter, Hugh took him at his word, but allowed only Cadfael and Edmund to be witnesses with him in the borrowed cell where Elis, with sweeping, arrogant, hurt gestures, tore off his clothes and let them fall about him, until he stood naked with braced feet astride and arms outspread, and dragged disdainful fingers painfully through his thick thatch of curls and shook his head violently to show there was

119

nothing made away there. Now that he was safe from the broken, embittered stare of Melicent's eyes the tears he had defied came treacherously into his own, and he blinked and shook them proudly away.

Hugh let him cool gradually and in considerate silence.

'Are you content?' the boy demanded stiffly, when he had his voice well in rein.

'Are *you*?' said Hugh, and smiled.

There was a brief, almost consoling silence. Then Hugh said mildly: 'Cover yourself, then. Take your time.' And while Elis was dressing, with hands that shook now in reaction: 'You do understand that I must hold you in close guard, you and your foster-brother and the others alike. As at this moment, you are no more in suspicion than many who belong here within the pale, and will not be let out of it until I know to the last moment where they spent this morn and noon. This is no more than a beginning, and you but one of many.'

'I do understand,' said Elis and wavered, hesitant to ask a favour. 'Need I be separated from Eliud?'

'You shall have Eliud,' said Hugh.

When they went out again to those who still waited in the anteroom, the two women were on their feet, and plainly longing to withdraw. Sybilla had but half her mind here in support of her step-daughter, the better half was with her son; and if she had been a faithful and dutiful wife to her older husband and mourned him truly now

120

after her fashion, love was much too large a word for what she had felt for him and barely large enough for what she felt for the boy he had given her. Sybilla's thoughts were with the future, not the past.

'My lord,' she said, 'you know where.we may be found for the days to come. Let me take my daughter away now, we have things which must be done.'

'At your pleasure, madam,' said Hugh. 'You shall not be troubled more than is needful.' And he added only: 'But you should know that the matter of this missing pin remains. There has been more than one intruder into your husband's privacy. Bear it in mind.'

'Very gladly I leave it all in your hands,' said Sybilla fervently. And forth she went, her hand imperative at Melicent's elbow. They passed close by Elis in the doorway, and his starving stare fastened on the girl's face. She passed him by without a glance, she even drew aside her skirts for fear they should brush him in departing. He was too young, too open, too simple to understand that more than half the hatred and revulsion she felt for him belonged rather to herself, and her dread that she had gone far towards desiring the death she now so desperately repented.

Chapter Seven

In the death-chamber, with the door closed fast, Hugh Beringar and Brother Cadfael stood beside Gilbert Prestcote's body and turned back the brychan and sheet to the sunken breast. They had brought in lamps to set close where they would burn steadily and cast a strong light on the dead face. Cadfael took the smaller saucer lamp in his hand and moved it slowly across the bruised mouth and nostrils and the grizzled beard, to catch every angle of vision and pick out every mote of dust or thread.

'No matter how feeble, no matter how deep asleep, a man will fight as best as he can for his breath, and whatever is clamped over his face, unless so hard and smooth it lacks any surface pile, he will inhale. And so did this one.' The dilated nostrils had fine hairs within, a trap for tiny particles of thread. 'Do you see colour there?'

In an almost imperceptible current of air a gossamer wisp quivered, taking the light. 'Blue,' said Hugh, peering close, and his breath caused the cobweb strand to dance. 'Blue is a difficult and expensive dye. And there's no such tint in these brychans.'

'Let's have it forth,' said Cadfael, and advanced his small tweezers, used for extracting thorns and splinters from unwary labouring fingers, to capture a filament almost too delicate to be seen. There was more of it, however, when it emerged, two or three fine strands that had the springy life of wool.

'Hold your breath,' said Cadfael, 'till I have this safe under a lid from being blown away.' He had brought one of the containers in which he stored his tablets and lozenges when he had moulded and dried them, a little polished wooden box, almost black in colour, and against the glossy dark surface the shred of wool shone brightly, a full, clear blue. He shut the lid upon it carefully, and probed again with the tweezers. Hugh shifted the lamp to cast its light at a new angle, and there was a brief gleam of red, the soft pale red of late summer roses past their prime. It winked and vanished. Hugh moved the light to find it again. Barely two frail, curling filaments of the many that must have made up this wool that had woven the cloth, but wool carries colour bravely.

'Blue and rose. Both precious colours, not for the furnishings of a bed.' Cadfael captured the elusive thing after two or three casts, and imprisoned it with the blue. The light, carefully deployed, found no more such traces in the stretched nostrils. 'Well, he also wore a beard. Let us see!'

There was a clear thread of the blue fluttering in the greying beard. Cadfael extracted it, and carefully combed the grizzled strands out into order to search for more. When he shook and stroked out the dust and hairs from the comb into his box, two or three points of light glimmered and vanished, like motes of dust lit by the sun. He tilted the box from side to side to recover them, for they were invisible once dimmed, and one single gold spark rewarded him. He found what he sought caught between the clenched teeth. One strand had frayed from age or use, and the spasm of death had bitten and held it. He drew it forth and held it to the light in his tweezers. A first finger-joint long, brittle and bright, glinting in the lamplight, the gold thread that had shed those invisible, scintillating particles.

'Expensive indeed!' said Cadfael, shutting it carefully into his box. 'A princely death, to be smothered under cloth of fine wool embroidered with thread of gold. Tapestry? Altar-cloth? A lady's brocaded gown? A piece from a worn vestment? Certainly nothing here within the infirmary, Hugh. Whatever it may have been, some man brought it with him.'

'So it would seem,' agreed Hugh, brooding.

They found nothing more, but what they had found was puzzling enough.

'So where is the cloth that smothered him?' wondered Cadfael, fretting. 'And where is the gold pin that fastened Einon ab Ithel's cloak?'

'Search for the cloth,' said Hugh, 'since it has a richness that could well be found somewhere within the abbey walls. And I will search for the pin. I have six Welshmen of the escort and Eliud yet to question and strip, and if that fails, we'll burrow our way through the entire enclave as best we can. If they are here, we'll find them.'

*

They searched, Cadfael for a cloth, any cloth which could show the rich colours and the gold thread he was seeking, Hugh for the gold pin. With the abbot's leave and the assistance of Prior Robert, who had the most comprehensive knowledge of the riches of the house and demonstrated its treasures with pride, Cadfael examined every hanging, tapestry and altar-cloth the abbey possessed, but none of them matched the quivering fragments he brought to the comparison. Shades of colour are exact and consistent. This rose and this blue had no companions here.

Hugh, for his part, thoroughly searched the clothing and harness of all the Welshmen made prisoner by this death, and Prior Robert, though with disapproval, sanctioned the extension of the search into the cells of the brothers and novices, and even the possessions of the boys, for children may be tempted by a bright thing, without realising the gravity of what they do. But nowhere did they find any trace of the old and massive pin that had held the collar of Einon's cloak close to keep the cold away from Gilbert Prestcote on his journey.

The day was spent by then and the evening coming on, but after Vespers and supper Cadfael returned to the quest. The inhabitants of the infirmary were quite willing to talk; they had not often so meaty a subject on which to debate. Yet neither Cadfael nor Edmund got much information out of them. Whatever had happened had happened during the half-hour or more when the brothers were at dinner in the refectory, and at that time the infirmary, already

125

fed, was habitually asleep. There was one, however, who, being bedridden, slept a great deal at odd times, and was well able to remain wakeful if something more interesting than usual was going on.

'As for seeing,' said Brother Rhys ruefully, 'I'm as little profit to you, brother, as I am to myself. I know if another inmate passes by me and I know which of them it is, and I know light from dark, but little more. But my ears, I dare swear, have grown sharper as my eyes have grown dimmer. I heard the door of the chamber opposite, where the sheriff lay, open twice, now you ask me to cudgel my memory. You know it creaks, opening. Closing, it's silent.'

'So someone entered there or at least opened the door. What more did you hear? Did anyone speak?'

'No, but I heard a stick tapping – very lightly – and then the door creaked. I reckoned it must be Brother Wilfred, who helps here when he's needed, for he's the only brother who walks with a stick, being lame from a young man.'

'Did he go in?'

'That you may better ask him, for I can't tell you. All was quiet a while, and then I heard him tap away along the passage to the outer door. He may only have pushed the door open to look and listen if all was well in there.'

'He must have drawn the door to again after him,' said Cadfael, 'or you would not have heard it creak again the second time. When was it Brother Wilfred paid his visit?'

But Rhys was vague about time. He shook his

head and pondered. 'I did drowse for a while after my dinner. How should I know for how long? But they must have been still in the refectory some time after that, for it wasn't until later that Brother Edmund came back.'

'And the second time?'

'That must have been some while later, it might be as much as a quarter-hour. The door creaked again. He had a light step, whoever came, I just caught the fall of his foot on the threshold, and then nothing. The door making no sound, drawn to, I don't know how long he was within there, but I fancy he did go in. Brother Wilfred might have a proper call to peer inside to see all was well, but this other one had none.'

'How long was he within there? How long *could* he have been? Did you hear him leave?'

'I was in a doze again,' admitted Rhys regretfully. 'I can't tell you. And he did tread very soft, a young man's tread.'

So the second could have been Elis, for there had been no word spoken when Edmund followed him in and expelled him, and Edmund from long sojourning among the sick trod as silently as a cat. Or it might have been someone else, someone unknown, coming and going undisturbed and deadly, before ever Elis intruded with his avowedly harmless errand.

Meantime, he could at least find out if Brother Wilfred had indeed been left here to keep watch, for Cadfael had not numbered the brothers in the refectory at dinner, or noticed who was present and who absent. He had another thought.

'Did anyone from within here leave this room

127

during all that time? Brother Maurice, for one, seldom sleeps much during the day, and when others are sleeping he may well be restless, wanting company.'

'None of them passed by me to the door while I was waking,' said Rhys positively. 'And I was not so deep asleep but I think I should have awakened if they had.'

Which might very well be true, yet could not be taken for granted. But of what he had heard he was quite certain. Twice the door had creaked open wide enough to let somebody in.

Brother Maurice had spoken up for himself without even being asked, as soon as the sheriff's death was mentioned, as daily it would be now until the truth was known and the sensation allowed to fade away into oblivion. Brother Edmund reported it to Cadfael after Compline, in the half-hour of repose before bed.

'I had prayers said for his soul, and told them tomorrow we should say a Mass for him – an honourable officer who died here among us and had been a good patron of our house. Up stands Maurice and says outright that he will faithfully put up prayers for the man's salvation, for now at last his debts are fully paid, and divine justice has been done. I asked him by whose hand, seeing he knew so much,' said Edmund with uncharacteristic bitterness, but even more resignation, 'and he reproved me for doubting that the hand was God's. Sometimes I question whether his ailment of the mind is misfortune or cunning. But try to pin him down and he'll slip through your fingers every time. He is certainly very content with this death. God forgive us all our backslidings and namely those into which we fall unwitting.'

'Amen!' said Cadfael fervently. 'And he's a strong, able man, and always in the right, even if it came to murder. But where would he lay hands on such a cloth as I have in mind?' He remembered to ask: 'Did you leave Brother Wilfred to keep a close eye on things here, when you went to dinner in the refectory?'

'I wish I had,' owned Edmund sadly. 'There might have been no such evil then. No, Wilfred was at dinner with us, did you never see him? I wish I had set a watch, with all my heart. But that's hindsight. Who was ever to suppose that murder would walk in and let loose chaos on us? There was nothing to give me warning.'

'Nothing,' agreed Cadfael and brooded, considering. 'So Wilfred is out of the reckoning. Who else among us walks with a stick? None that I know of.'

'There's Anion is still on a crutch,' said Edmund, 'though he's about ready to discard it. He rather flies with it now than hobbles, but for the moment it's grown a habit with him, after so stubborn a break. Why, are you looking for a man with a prop?'

Now there, thought Cadfael, going wearily to his bed at last, is a strange thing. Brother Rhys, hearing a stick tapping, looks for the source of it only among the brothers; and I, making my way round the infirmary, never give a thought to any but those who are brothers, and am likely to be blind and deaf to what any other may be up to even in my presence. For it had only now dawned on him that when he and Brother Edmund entered the long room, already settling for the evening, one younger and more active soul had risen from the corner where he sat and gone quietly out by the door to the chapel, the leather-shod tip of his crutch so light upon the stones that it seemed he hardly needed it, and could only have taken it away with him, as Edmund said, out of habit or in order to remove it from notice.

Well, Anion would have to wait until tomorrow. It was too late to trouble the repose of the ageing sick tonight.

In a cell of the castle, behind a locked door, Elis and Eliud shared a bed no harder than many they had shared before and slept like twin babes, without a care in the world. They had care enough now. Elis lay on his face, sure that his life was ended, that he would never love again, that nothing was left to him, even if he escaped this coil alive, but to go on Crusade or take the tonsure or undergo some barefoot pilgrimage to the Holy Land from which he would certainly never return. And Eliud lay patient and agonising at his back, with an arm wreathed over the rigid, rejecting shoulders, fetching up comfort from where he himself had none. This cousin-brother of his was far too vehemently alive to die for love, or to succumb for grief because he was accused of an infamy he had not committed. But his pain, however curable, was extreme while it lasted.

130

'She never loved me,' lamented Elis, tense and quivering under the embracing arm. 'If she had, she would have trusted me, she would have known me better. If ever she'd loved me, how could she believe I would do murder?' As indignantly as if he had never in his transports sworn that he would! That or *anything*.

'She's shocked to the heart for her father,' pleaded Eliud stoutly. 'How can you ask her to be fair to you? Only wait, give her time. If she loved you, then she still does. Poor girl, she can't choose. It's for her you should be sorry. She takes this death to her own account – have you not told me? You've done no wrong and so it will be proved.'

'No, I've lost her, she'll never let me near her again, never believe a word I say.'

'She will, for it will be proven you're blameless. I swear to you it will! Truth will come out, it must, it will.'

'If I don't win her back,' Elis vowed, muffled in his cradling arms, 'I shall die.'

'You won't die, you won't fail to win her back,' promised Eliud in desperation. 'Hush, hush and sleep!' He reached out a hand and snuffed out the flailing flame of their tiny lamp. He knew the tensions and releases of this body he had slept beside from childhood, and knew that sleep was already a weight on Elis's smarting eyelids. There are those who come brand-new into the new day and have to rediscover their griefs. Eliud was no such person. He nursed his griefs, unsleeping into the small hours, with the chief of them fathoms deep under his protecting arm.

131

Chapter Eight

Anion the cattle-man, for want of calf or lamb to keep his hand in within the abbey enclave, had taken to spending much of his time in the stables, where at least there was horseflesh to be tended and enjoyed. Very soon now he would be fit to be sent back to the grange where he served, but he could not go until Brother Edmund discharged him. He had a gifted hand with animals, and the grooms were on familiar and friendly terms with him.

Brother Cadfael approached him somewhat sidelong, unwilling to startle or dismay him too soon. It was not difficult. Horses and mules had their sicknesses and injuries, as surely as men, and called frequently for remedies from Cadfael's store. One of the ponies the lay servants used as pack-horses had fallen lame and was in need of Cadfael's rubbing oils to treat the strain, and he brought the flask himself to the stable-yard, as good as certain he would find Anion there. It was easy enough to entice the practised stockman into taking over the massage, and to linger to watch and admire as he worked his thick but agile fingers into the painful muscles. The pony stood

132

like a statue for him, utterly trusting. That in itself had something eloquent to say.

'You spend less and less time in the infirmary now,' said Cadfael, studying the dour, dark profile under the fall of straight black hair. 'Very soon we shall be losing you at this rate. You're as fast on a crutch as many of us are with two sturdy legs that never suffered a break. I fancy you could throw the prop away anytime you pleased.'

'I'm told to wait,' said Anion shortly. 'Here I do what I'm told. It's some men's fate in life, brother, to take orders.'

'Then you'll be glad to be back with your cattle again, where they do obedience to you for a change.'

'I tend and care for them and mean them well,' said Anion, 'and they know it.'

'So does Edmund to you, and you know it.' Cadfael sat down on a saddle beside the stooping man, to come down to his level and view him on equal terms. Anion made no demur, it might even have been the faint shadow of a smile that touched his firmly-closed mouth. Not at all an ill-looking man, and surely no more than twenty-seven or twenty-eight years old. 'You know the thing that happened there in the infirmary,' said Cadfael. 'You may well have been the most active man in there that dinner time. Though I doubt if you stayed long after you'd eaten. You're over-young to be shut in there with the ailing old. I've asked them all, did they hear or see any man go in there, by stealth or any other way, but they slept after they'd eaten. That's for the aged, not for you. You'd be up and about while they drowsed.'

133

'I left them snoring,' said Anion, turning the full stare of his deep-set eyes on Cadfael. He reached for a rag to wipe his hands, and rose nimbly enough, the still troublesome leg drawn up after him.

'Before we were all out of the refectory? And the Welsh lads led in to their repast?'

'While it was all quiet. I reckon you brothers were in the middle of your meal. Why?' demanded Anion pointblank.

'Because you might be a good witness, what else? Do you know of anyone who made his way into the infirmary about that time that you left it? Did you see or hear aught to give you pause? Any man lurking who should not have been there? The sheriff had his enemies,' said Cadfael firmly, 'like the rest of us mortals, and one of them deadly. Whatever he owed is paid now, or shortly to pay. God send none of us may take with him a worse account.'

'Amen!' said Anion. 'When I came forth from the infirmary, brothers, I met no man, I saw no man, friend or enemy, anywhere near that door.'

'Where were you bound? Down here to view the Welsh horses? If so,' explained Cadfael easily, warding off the sharp glance Anion gave him, 'you'd be a witness if any of those lads went off and left his fellows about that time.'

Anion shrugged that off disdainfully. 'I never came near the stables, not then. I went through the garden and down to the brook. With a west wind it smells of the hills down there,' said Anion. 'I grow sick of the shut-in smell of tired old men, and their talk that goes round and round.'

134

'Like mine!' said Cadfael tolerantly, and rose from the saddle. His eye lingered upon the crutch that was laid carelessly aside against the open door of a stall, a good fifty paces from where its owner was working. 'Yes, I see you're about ready to throw it away. You were still using it yesterday, though, unless Brother Rhys was mistaken. He heard you tap your way out for your walk in the garden, or thought he did.'

'He well might,' said Anion, and shook back his shaggy black mane from his round brown forehead. 'It's habit with me, after so long, even after the need's gone. But when there's a beast to see to, I forget, and leave it behind me in corners.'

He turned deliberately, laid an arm over the pony's neck, and led him slowly round on the cobbles, to mark his gait. And that was the end of the colloquy.

Brother Cadfael was fully occupied with his proper duties all that day, but that did not prevent him from giving a great deal of thought to the matter of Gilbert Prestcote's death. The sheriff had long ago requested space for his tomb in the abbey church of which he had been a steady patron and benefactor, and the next day was to see him laid to rest there. But the manner of his death would not allow any rest to those who were left behind him. From his distracted family to the unlucky Welsh suspects and prisoners in the castle, there was no one who did not find his own life disrupted and changed by this death.

The news was surely making its way about the countryside by this time, from village to village

135

and assart to manor round the shire, and no doubt men and women in the streets of Shrewsbury were busily allotting the blame to this one and that one, with Elis ap Cynan their favourite villain. But they had not seen the minute, bright fragments Cadfael nursed in his little box, or hunted in vain through the precinct for any cloth that could show the identical tints and the twisted gold thread. They knew nothing about the massive gold pin that had vanished from Gilbert's death-chamber and could not be found within the pale.

Cadfael had caught glimpses of Lady Prestcote about the court, moving between the guest-hall and the church, where her husband lay in the mortuary chapel, swathed for his burial. But the girl had not once shown her face. Gilbert the younger, a little bewildered but oblivious of misfortune, played with the child oblates and the two young pupils, and was tenderly shepherded by Brother Paul, the master of the children. At seven years old he viewed with untroubled tolerance the eccentricities of grown-up people, and could make himself at home wherever his mother unaccountably conveyed him. As soon as his father was buried she would certainly take him away from here, to her favourite among her husband's manors, where his life would resume its placid progress untroubled by bereavement.

A few close acquaintances of the sheriff had begun to arrive and take up residence ready for the morrow. Cadfael lingered to watch them, and fit noble names to the sombre faces. He was thus occupied, on his way to the herbarium, when he observed one unexpected but welcome face entering. Sister Magdalen, on foot and alone, stepped briskly through the wicket, and looked about her for the nearest known face. To judge by her brightening eye and prompt advice, she was pleased that it should be Cadfael's.

'Well, well!' said Cadfael, going to meet her with equal pleasure. 'We had no thought of seeing you again so soon. Is all well in your forest? No more raiders?'

'Not so far,' said Sister Magdalen cautiously, 'but I would not say they might not try again, if ever they see Hugh Beringar looking the other way. It must have gone much against the grain with Madog ap Meredith to be bested by a handful of foresters and cottars, he may well want his revenge when he feels it safe to bid for it. But the forest men are keeping a good watch. It's not we who are in turmoil now, it seems. What's this I've been hearing in the town? Gilbert Prestcote dead, and that Welsh youngster I sent you blamed for the deed?'

'You've been in the town, then? And no stout escort with you this time?'

'Two,' she said, 'but I've left them up in the Wyle, where we shall lie overnight. If it's true the sheriff is to be buried tomorrow I must stay to do him honour among the rest. I'd no thought of such a thing when we set out this morning. I came on quite different business. There's a great-niece of Mother Mariana, daughter to a cloth-merchant here in Shrewsbury, who's coming to take the veil among us. A plain child, none too bright, but willing, and knows she has small hopes of a pleasing marriage. Better with us than sold off

137

like an unpromising heifer to the first that makes a grudging offer for her. I've left my men and horses in their yard, where I heard tell of what had happened here. Better to get the tale straight – there are any number of versions up there in the streets.'

'If you have an hour to spare,' said Cadfael heartily, 'come and share a flask of wine of my own making in the herb-garden, and I'll tell you the whole truth of it, so far as any man knows what's truth. Who knows, you may find a pattern in it that I have failed to find.'

In the wood-scented dimness of the workshop in the herbarium he told her, at leisure and in detail, everything he knew or had gathered concerning the death of Gilbert Prestcote, everything he had observed or thought concerning Elis ap Cynan. She listened, seated with spread knees and erect back on the bench against the wall, with her cup nursed in both hands to warm it, for the wine was red and full. She no longer exerted herself to be graceful, if ever she had, but her composed heaviness had its own impressive grace.

'I would not say but that boy *might* kill,' she said at the end of it. 'They act before they think and regret only too late. But I don't think he would kill his girl's father. Very easy, you say, and I believe it, to ease the man out of the world, so that even one not given to murder might do it before ever he realised. Yes, but those a man kills easily are commonly strangers to him. Hardly people at all. But this one would be armoured in identity – her father, no less, the man that begot her. And

138

yet,' she owned, shaking her head, 'I may be wrong about him. He may be the one of his kind who does what his kind does not do. There is always one.'

'The girl believes absolutely that he is guilty,' said Cadfael thoughtfully, 'perhaps because she is all too well aware of what she feels to be her own guilt. The sire returns and the lovers are to be torn apart — no great step to dream of his failure to return, and only one more leap to see death as the final and total cause of that failure. But dreams they surely were, never truly even wished. The boy is on firmer ground when he swears he went to try and win her father to look kindly on his suit. For if ever I saw a lad sunlit and buoyed up with hope by nature, Elis is the one.'

'And this girl?' wondered Sister Magdalen, twirling her wine-cup between nursing palms. 'If they're of an age, then she must be the more mature by some years. So it goes! Is it anyway possible that *she* ...?'

'No,' said Cadfael with certainty. 'She was with the lady, and Hugh, and the Welsh princelings, throughout. I know she left her father living, and never came near him again until he was dead, and then in Hugh's company. No, she torments herself vainly. If you had her in your hands,' said Cadfael with conviction, 'you would soon find her out for the simple, green child she is.'

Sister Magdalen was in the act of saying philosophically: 'I'm hardly likely to get the chance,' when the tap on the door came. So light and tentative a sound, and yet so staunchly repeated, they fell silent and still to make sure of it.

Cadfael rose to open it and peer out through the

narrowest possible chink, convinced there was no one there; and there she stood, her hand raised to knock again, pallid, wretched and resolute, half a head taller than he, the simple, green child of his description, with a steely core of Norman nobility forcing her to transcend herself. Hastily he flung the door wide. 'Come within from the cold. How can I serve you?'

'The porter told me,' said Melicent, 'that the sister from Godric's Ford came a while ago, and might be here wanting remedies from your store. I should like to speak with her.'

'Sister Magdalen is here,' said Cadfael. 'Come, sit with her by the brazier, and I'll leave you to talk with her in private.'

She came in half afraid, as though this small, unfamiliar place held daunting secrets. She stepped with fastidious delicacy, almost inch by inch, and yet with that determination in her that would not let her turn back. She looked at Sister Magdalen eye to eye, fascinated, doubtless having heard her history both ancient and recent, and found some difficulty in reconciling the two.

'Sister,' said Melicent, going arrow-straight to the point, 'when you go back to Godric's Ford, will you take me with you?'

Cadfael, as good as his word, withdrew softly and with alacrity, drawing the door to after him, but not so quickly that he did not hear Sister Magdalen reply simply and practically: 'Why?'

She never did or said quite what was expected of her, and it was a good question. It left Melicent in the delusion that this formidable woman knew little or nothing about her, and necessitated the

140

entire re-telling of the disastrous story, and in the re-telling it might fall into truer proportion, and allow the girl to reconsider her sitution with somewhat less desperate urgency. So, at any rate, Brother Cadfael hoped, as he trotted away through the garden to go and spend a pleasant half-hour with Brother Anselm, the precentor, in his carrel in the cloister, where he would certainly be compiling the sequence of music for the burial of Gilbert Prestcote.

'I intend,' said Melicent, rather grandly because of the jolt the blunt question had given her, 'to take the veil, and I would like it to be among the Benedictine sisters of Polesworth.'

'Sit down here beside me,' said Sister Magdalen comfortably, 'and tell me what has turned you to this withdrawal, and whether your family are in your confidence and approve your choice. You are very young, and have the world before you ...'

'I am done with the world,' said Melicent.

'Child, as long as you live and breathe you will not have done with this world. We within the pale live in the same world as all poor souls without. Come, you have your reasons for wishing to enter the conventual life. Sit and tell me, let me hear them. You are young and fair and nobly born, and you wish to abandon marriage, children, position, honours, all ... Why?'

Melicent, yielding, sank beside her on the bench, hugged her slenderness in the warmth of the brazier, and let fall the barriers of her bitterness to loose the flood. What she had vouchsafed to the preoccupied ears of Sybilla was

141

no more than the thread on which this confession was strung. All that heady dream of minstrels' love-tales poured out of her.

'Even if you are right in rejecting one man,' said Magdalen mildly, 'you may be most unjust in rejecting all. Let alone the possibility that you mistake even this Elis ap Cynan. For until it is proved he lies, you must bear in mind he *may* be telling truth.'

'He said he would kill for me,' said Melicent, relentless, 'he went to where my father lay, and my father is dead. There was no other known to have gone near. As for me, I have no doubts. I wish I had never seen his face, and I pray I never may again.'

'And you will not wait to make your peace with one betrayal, and still show your countenance to others who do not betray?'

'At least I do know,' said Melicent bitterly, 'that God does not betray. And I am done with men.'

'Child,' said Sister Magdalen, sighing, 'not until the day of your death will you have done with men. Bishops, abbots, priests, confessors, all are men, blood-brothers to the commonest of sinful mankind. While you live, there is no way of escape from your part in humanity.'

'I have finished, then, with love,' said Melicent, all the more vehemently because a morsel of her heart cried out to her that she lied.

'Oh, my dear soul, love is the one thing with which you must never dispense. Without it, what use are you to us or to any? Granted there are ways and ways of loving,' said the nun come late to her celibacy, recalling what at the time she had hardly recognised as deserving the title, but knew now for one aspect of love, 'yet for all there is a warmth needed, and if that fire goes out it cannot be rekindled. Well,' she said, considering, 'if your stepmother approve your going with me, then you may come, and welcome. Come and be quiet with us for a while, and we shall see.'

'Will you come with me to my mother, then, and hear me ask her leave?'

'I will,' said Sister Magdalen, and rose and plucked her habit about her ready to set forth.

She told Brother Cadfael the gist of it when she stayed to attend Vespers before going back to the cloth-merchant's house in the town.

'She'll be better out of here, away from the lad, but left with the image of him she already carries about with her. Time and truth are what the pair of them most need, and I'll see she takes no vows until this whole matter is resolved. The boy is better left to you, if you can keep an eye on him now and then.'

'You don't believe,' said Cadfael with certainty, 'that he ever did violence to her father.'

'Do I know? Is there man or woman who might not kill given the driving need? A proper, upstanding, impudent, open-hearted lad, though,' said Sister Magdalen, who had never repented anything she did, 'one that I might have fancied, when my fancying days were.'

Cadfael went to supper in the refectory, and then to Collations in the chapter-house, which he often missed if he had vulnerable preparations brewing

143

in his workshop. In thinking over such slight gains as he had made in his quest for the truth, he had got nowhere, and it was good to put all that aside and listen with good heart to the lives of saints who had shrugged off the cares of the world to let in the promises of a world beyond and viewed earthly justice as no more than a futile shadow-play obscuring the absolute justice of heaven, for which no man need wait longer than the life-span of mortality.

They were past St Gregory and approaching St Edward the Confessor and St Benedict himself – the middle days of March, and the blessed works of spring beginning, with everything hopeful and striving ahead. A good time. Cadfael had spent the hours before Sister Magdalen came digging and clearing the fresh half of his mint-bed, to give it space to proliferate new and young and green, rid of the old and debilitated. He emerged from the chapter-house feeling renewed, and it came at first as no more than a mild surprise when Brother Edmund came seeking him before Compline, looking almost episcopal as he brandished in one hand what at first sight might have been a crozier but when lowered to the ground reached no higher than his armpit, and was manifestly a crutch.

'I found it lying in a corner of the stable-yard. Anion's! Cadfael, he did not come for his supper tonight and he is nowhere in the infirmary – neither in the common room, nor in his bed, nor in the chapel. Have you seen him anywhere this day?'

'Not since morning,' said Cadfael, thinking

144

back with something of an effort from the peace of the chapter-house. 'He came to dinner at midday?'

'So he did, but I find no man who has seen him since. I've looked for him everywhere, asked every man, and found nothing more of him than this, discarded. Anion is gone! Oh, Cadfael, I doubt he has fled his mortal guilt. Why else should he run from us?'

It was well past Compline when Hugh Beringar entered his own hall, empty-handed and disconcerted from his enquiries among the Welshmen, and found Brother Cadfael sitting by the fireside with Aline, waiting for him with a clouded brow.

'What brings you here so late?' wondered Hugh. 'Out without leave again?' It had been known to happen, and the recollection of one such expedition, before the austere days of Abbot Radulfus, was an old and private joke between them.

'That I am not,' said Cadfael firmly. 'There's a piece of unexpected news even Prior Robert thought had better come to your ears as soon as possible. We had in our infirmary, with a broken leg mending and all but ready to leave us, a fellow named Anion. I doubt if the name means much to you, it was not you had to do with his brother. But do you remember a brawl in the town, two years ago now, when a gate-keeper on the bridge was knifed? Prestcote hanged the Welshman that did it – well, whether he did it or not, and naturally he'd say he didn't, but he was blind drunk at the time and probaby never knew the truth of it himself. However it was, he was hanged for it. A young fellow who used to trade in fleeces to the town market from somewhere in Mechain. Well, this Anion is his brother born the wrong side of the brychan, when the father was doing the trading, and there was no bad blood between the two. They got to know each other and there was a fondness.'

'If ever I knew of this,' said Hugh, drawing up to the fire with him, 'I had forgot it.'

'So had not Anion. He's said little, but it's known he nursed his grudge, and there's enough Welsh in him to make him look upon revenge as a duty, if ever the chance came his way.'

'And what of him now?' Hugh was studying his friend's face intently, foreseeing what was to come. 'Are you telling me this fellow was within the pale now, when the sheriff was brought there helpless?'

'He was, and only a door ajar between him and his enemy – if so he held him, as rumour says he did. Not the only one with a grudge, either, so that's no proof of anything more than this, that the opportunity was there. But tonight there's another mark against him. The man's gone. He did not come for his supper, he's not in his bed, and no man has seen him since dinner. Edmund missed him at the meal and has been looking for him ever since, but never a sign. And the crutch he was still using, though more from habit than need, was lying in the stable-yard. Anion has taken to his heels. And the blame, if blame there is,' said Cadfael honestly, 'is mine. Edmund and I

146

have been asking every man in the infirmary if he saw or heard anything of note about the sheriff's chamber, any traffic in or out. It was but the same asking with Anion, indeed I was more cautious with him than with any when I spoke with him this morning in the stables. But for all that, no question, I've frightened him away.'

'Not necessarily a proof of guilt, to take fright and run,' said Hugh reasonably. 'Men without privilege are apt to suppose they'll be blamed for whatever's done amiss. Is it certain he's gone? A man just healed of a broken leg? Has he taken horse or mule? Nothing stolen?'

'Nothing. But there's more to tell. Brother Rhys, whose bed is by the door, across the passage from where the sheriff lay, heard the door creak twice and the first time he says someone entered, or at least pushed the door open, who walked with a stick. The second time came later, and may have been the time the Welsh boy went in there. Rhys is hazy about time, and slept before and after, but both visitors came while the court was quiet – he says, while we of the house were in the refectory. With that, and now he's run – even Edmund is taking it for granted Anion is your murderer. They'll be crying his guilt in the town by morning.'

'But you are not so sure,' said Hugh, eyeing him steadily.

'Something he had on his mind, surely, something he saw as guilt, or knew others would call guilt, or he would not have run. But murderer ...? Hugh, I have in that pill-box of mine certain proof of dyed wools and gold thread

147

in whatever cloth was used to kill. *Certain* – whereas flight is uncertain proof of anything worse than fear. You know as I know that there was no such woven cloth anywhere in that room, or in the infirmary, or in the entire pale so far as we can discover. Whoever used it brought it with him. Where would Anion get hold of any such rich material? He can never have handled anything better than drab homespun and unbleached flax in his life. It casts great doubt on his guilt, though it does not utterly rule it out. It's why I did not press him too far – or thought I had not!' he added ruefully.

Hugh nodded guarded agreement, and put the point away in his mind. 'But for all that, tomorrow at dawn I must send out search parties between here and Wales, for surely that's the way he'll go. A border between him and his fear will be his first thought. If I can take him, I must and will. Then we may get out of him whatever it is he does know. A lame man cannot yet have got very far.'

'But remember the cloth. For those threads do not lie, though a mortal man may, guilty or innocent. The instrument of death is what we have to find.'

The hunt went forth at dawn, in small parties filtering through the woods by all the paths that led most directly to Wales, but they came back with the dark, empty-handed. Lame or no, Anion had contrived to vanish within half a day.

The tale had gone forth through the town and the Foregate by then, every shop had it and every customer, the ale-houses discussed it avidly, and the general agreement was that neither Hugh Beringar nor any other man need look further for the sheriff's murderer. The dour cattle-man with a grudge had been heard going into and leaving the death-chamber, and on being questioned had fled. Nothing could be simpler.

And that was the day when they buried Gilbert Prestcote, in the tomb he had had made for himself in a transept of the abbey church. Half the nobility of the shire was there to do him honour, and Hugh Beringar with an escort of his officers, and the provost of Shrewsbury, Geoffrey Corviser, with his son Philip and his son's wife Emma, and all the solid merchants of the town guild. The sheriff's widow came in deep mourning, with her small son round-eyed and awed at the end of her arm. Music and ceremony, and the immensity of the vault, and the candles and the torches, all charmed and fascinated him, he was good as gold throughout the service.

And whatever personal enemies Gilbert Prestcote might have had, he had been a fair and trusted sheriff to this county in general, and the merchant princes were well aware of the relative security and justice they had enjoyed under him, where much of England suffered a far worse fate.

So in his passing Gilbert had his due, and his people's weighty and deserved intercession for him with his God.

'No,' said Hugh, waiting for Cadfael as the brothers came out from Vespers that evening, 'nothing as yet. Crippled or not, it seems young Anion has got clean away. I've set a watch along

149

the border, in case he's lying in covert this side till the hunt is called off, but I doubt he's already over the dyke. And whether to be glad or sorry for it, that's more than I know. I have Welsh in my own manor, Cadfael, I know what drives them, and the law that vindicates them where ours condemns. I've been a frontiersman all my life, tugged two ways.'

'You must pursue it,' said Cadfael with sympathy. 'You have no choice.'

'No, none. Gilbert was my chief,' said Hugh, 'and had my loyalty. Very little we two had in common, I don't know that I even liked him overmuch. But respect – yes, that we had. His wife is taking her son back to the castle tonight, with what little she brought here. I'm waiting now to conduct her.' Her step-daughter was already departed with Sister Magdalen and the cloth-merchant's daughter, to the solitude of Godric's Ford. 'He'll miss his sister,' said Hugh, diverted into sympathy for the little boy.

'So will another,' said Cadfael, 'when he hears of her going. And the news of Anion's flight could not change her mind?'

'No, she's marble, she's damned him. Scold if you will,' said Hugh, wryly smiling, 'but I've let fall the word in his ear already that she's off to study the nun's life. Let him stew for a while – he owes us that, at least. And I've accepted his parole, his and the other lad's, Eliud. Either one of them has gone bail for himself *and* his cousin, not to stir a foot beyond the barbican, not to attempt escape, if I let them have the run of the wards. They've pledged their necks, each for the other. Not that I want to wring either neck, they suit very well as they are, untwisted, but no harm in accepting their pledges.'

'And I make no doubt,' said Cadfael, eyeing him closely, 'that you have a very sharp watch posted on your gates, and a very alert watchman on your walls, to see whether either of the two, or which of the two, breaks and runs for it.'

'I should be ashamed of my stewardship,' said Hugh candidly, 'if I had not.'

'And do they know, by this time, that a bastard Welsh cowman in the abbey's service has cast his crutch and run for his life?'

'They know it. And what do they say? They say with one voice, Cadfael, that such a humble soul and Welsh into the bargain, without kin or privilege here in England, would run as soon as eyes were cast on him, sure of being blamed unless he could show he was a mile from the matter at the fatal time. And can you find fault with that? It's what I said myself when you brought me the same news.'

'No fault,' said Cadfael thoughtfully. 'Yet matter for consideration, would you not say? From the threatened to the threatened, that's large grace.'

151

Chapter Nine

Owain Gwynedd sent back his response to the events at Shrewsbury on the day after Anion's flight, by the mouth of young John Marchmain, who had remained in Wales to stand surety for Gilbert Prestcote in the exchange of prisoners. The half-dozen Welsh who had escorted him home came only as far as the gates of the town, and there saluted and withdrew again to their own country.

John, son to Hugh's mother's younger sister, a gangling youth of nineteen, rode into the castle stiff with the dignity of the embassage with which he was entrusted, and reported himself ceremoniously to Hugh.

'Owain Gwynedd bids me to say that in the matter of a death so brought about, his own honour is at stake, and he orders his men here to bear themselves in patience and give all possible aid until the truth is known, the murderer uncovered, and they vindicated and free to return. He sends me back as freed by fate. He says he has no other prisoner to exchange for Elis ap Cynan, nor will he lift a finger to deliver him until both guilty and innocent are known.'

Hugh, who had known him from infancy, hoisted impressed eyebrows into his dark hair, whistled and laughed. 'You may stoop now, you're flying too high for me.'

'I speak for a high-flying hawk,' said John, blowing out a great breath and relaxing into a grin as he leaned back against the guard-room wall. 'Well, you've understood him. That's the elevated tenor of it. He says hold them and find your man. But there's more. How recent is the news you have from the south? I fancy Owain has his eyes and ears alert up and down the borders, where your writ can hardly go. He says that the empress is likely to win her way and be crowned queen, for Bishop Henry has let her into Winchester cathedral, where the crown and the treasure are guarded, and the archbishop of Canterbury is dilly-dallying, putting her off with – he can't well acknowledge her until he's spoken with the King. And by God, so he has, for he's been to Bristol and taken a covey of bishops with him, and been let in to speak with Stephen in his prison.'

'And what says King Stephen?' wondered Hugh.

'He told them, in that large way of his, that they kept their own consciences, that they must do, of course, what seemed to them best. And so they will, says Owain, what seems to them best for their own skins! They'll bend their necks and go with the victor. But here's what counts and what Owain has in mind. Ranulf of Chester is well aware of all this, and knows by now that Gilbert Prestcote is dead and this shire, he thinks, is in confusion, and

153

the upshot is he's probing south, towards Shropshire and over into Wales, pouring men into his forward garrisons and feeling his way ahead by easy stages.'

'And what does Owain ask of us?' questioned Hugh, with kindling brightness.

'He says, if you will come north with a fair force, show your hand all along the Cheshire border, and reinforce Oswestry and Whitchurch and every other fortress up there, you will be helping both yourself and him, and he will do as much for you against the common enemy. And he says he'll come to the border at Rhyd-y-Croesau by Oswestry two days from now, about sunset, if you're minded to come and speak with him there.'

'Very firmly so minded!' said Hugh heartily, and rose to embrace his glowing cousin round the shoulders and haul him out about the business of meeting Owain's challenge and invitation, with the strongest force possible from a beleaguered shire.

That Owain had given them only two and a half days in which to muster, provide cover for the town and castle with a depleted garrison, and get their host into the north of the shire in time for the meeting on the border, was rather an earnest of the ease and speed with which Owain could move about his own mountainous land than a measure of the urgency of their mutual watch. Hugh spent the rest of that day making his dispositions in Shrewsbury and sending out his call for men to those who owed service. At dawn the next day his advance party would leave, and

154

he himself with the main body by noon. There was much to be done in a matter of hours.

Lady Prestcote was also marshalling her servants and possessions in her high, bleak apartments, ready to leave next morning for the most easterly and peaceful of her manors. She had already sent off one string of pack-ponies with three of her men-servants. But while she was in town it was sensible to purchase such items as she knew to be in short supply where she was bound, and among other commodities she had requested a number of dried herbs from Cadfael's store. Her lord might be dead and in his tomb, but she had still an honour to administer, and for her son's sake had every intention of proving herself good at it. Men might die, but the meats necessary to the living would still require preservatives, salts and spices to keep them good and palatable. The boy was given, also, to a childish cough in spring, and she wanted a jar of Cadfael's herbal rub for his chest. Between them, Gilbert Prestcote the younger and domestic cares would soon fill up the gap, already closing, where Gilbert Prestcote the elder had been.

There was no real need for Cadfael to deliver the herbs and medicines in person, but he took advantage of the opportunity as much to satisfy his curiosity as to enjoy the walk and the fresh air on a fine, if blustery, March day. Along the Foregate, over the bridge spanning a Severn muddied and turgid from the thaw in the mountains, in through the town gate, up the long, steep curve of the Wyle, and gently downhill from the High Cross to the castle gatehouse, he went with eyes and ears alert, stopping many times to exchange greetings and pass the time of day. And everywhere men were talking of Anion's flight, and debating whether he would get clean away or be hauled back before night in a halter.

Hugh's muster was not yet common gossip in the town, though by nightfall it surely would be. But as soon as Cadfael entered the castle wards it was plain, by the purposeful bustle everywhere, that something of importance was in hand. The smith and the fletchers were hard at work, so were the grooms, and store-wagons were being loaded to follow stolidly after the faster horse- and foot-men. Cadfael delivered his herbs to the maid who came down to receive them, and went looking for Hugh. He found him directing the stalling of commandeered horses in the stables.

'You're moving, then? Northward?' said Cadfael, watching without surprise. 'And making quite a show, I see.'

'With luck, it need be only a show,' said Hugh, breaking his concentration to give his friend a warm sidelong smile.

'Is it Chester feeling his oats?'

Hugh laughed and told him. 'With Owain one side of the border and me the other, he should think twice. He's no more than trying his arm. He knows Gilbert is gone, but me he does not know. Not yet!'

'High time he should know Owain,' observed Cadfael. 'Men of sense have measured and valued him some while since, I fancy. And Ranulf is no fool, though I wouldn't say he's not capable of folly, blown up by success as he is. The wisest man

in his cups may step too large and fall on his face.'
And he asked, alert to all the sounds about him,
and all the shadows that patterned the cobbles:
'Do your Welsh pair know where you're bound,
and why, and who sent you word?'

He had lowered his voice to ask it, and Hugh,
without need of a reason, did the same. 'Not from
me. I've had no time to spare for civilities. But
they're at large. Why?' He did not turn his head;
he had noted where Cadfael was looking.

'Because they're bearing down on us, the pair in
harness. And in anxiety.'

Hugh made their approach easier, waving into
the groom's hands the thickset grey he had been
watching about the cobbles, and turning naturally
to withdraw from the stables as from a job
finished for the present. And there they were, Elis
and Eliud, shoulders together as though they had
been born in one linked birth, moving in on him
with drawn brows and troubled eyes.

'My lord Beringar ...' It was Eliud who spoke
for them, the quiet, the solemn, the earnest one.
'You're moving to the border? There's threat of
war? Is it with Wales?'

'To the border, yes,' said Hugh easily, 'there to
meet with the prince of Gwynedd. The same that
bade you and all your company here bear your
souls in patience and work with me for justice
concerning the matter you know of. No, never
fret! Owain Gwynedd lets me know that both he
and I have a common interest in the north of this
shire, and a common enemy trying his luck there.
Wales is in no danger from me and my shire, I
believe, in no danger from Wales. At least,' he

added, reconsidering briskly, 'not from Gwynedd.'

The cousins looked along wide, straight shoulders at each other, measuring thoughts. Elis said abruptly: 'My lord, but keep an eye to Powys. They ... *we*,' he corrected in a gasp of disgust, '*we* went to Lincoln under the banner of Chester. If it's Chester now, they'll know in Caus as soon as you move north. They may think it time ... think it safe ... The ladies there at Godric's Ford ...'

'A parcel of silly women,' said Cadfael musingly into his cowl, but audibly, 'and old and ugly into the bargain.'

The round, ingenuous face under the tangle of black curls flamed from neck to brow, but did not lower its eyes or lose its fixed intensity. 'I'm confessed and shriven of all manner of follies,' said Elis sturdily, 'that among them. Only do keep a watch on them! I mean it! That failure will rankle, they may still venture.'

'I had thought of it,' said Hugh patiently. 'I have no mind to strip this border utterly of men.'

The boy's blush faded and flamed anew. 'Pardon!' he said. 'It is your field. Only I do know ... It will have gone deep, that rebuff.'

Eliud plucked at his cousin's arm, drawing him back. They withdrew some paces without withdrawing their twin, troubled gaze. At the gate of the stables they turned, still with one last glance over their shoulders, and went away still linked, as one disconsolate creature.

'Christ!' said Hugh on a blown breath, looking after them. 'And I with less men than I should like, if truth be told, and that green child to warn

158

me! As if I do not know I take chances now with every breath I draw and every archer I move. Should I ask him how a man spreads half a company across three times a company's span?'

'Ah, but he would have your whole force drawn up between Godric's Ford and his own countrymen,' said Cadfael tolerantly. 'The girl he fancies is there. I doubt if he cares so much what happens to Oswestry or Whitchurch, provided the Long Forest is left undisturbed. They've neither of them given you any trouble?'

'Good as gold! Not a step even into the shadow of the gate.' It was said with casual certainty. Cadfael drew his own conclusions. Hugh had someone commissioned to watch every move the two prisoners made, and knew all that they did, if not all that they said, from dawn to dark, and if ever one of them did advance a foot over the threshold, his toes would be promptly and efficiently trampled on. Unless, of course, it was more important to follow, and find out with what intent he broke his parole. But when Hugh was in the north, who was to say his deputy would maintain the same unobtrusive watch?

'Who is it you're leaving in charge here?'

'Young Alan Herbard. But Will Warden will have a hand on his shoulder. Why, do you expect a bolt for it as soon as my back's turned?' By the tone of his voice Hugh was in no great anxiety on that score. 'There's no absolute certainty in any man, when it comes to it, but those two have been schooled under Owain, and measure themselves by him, and by and large I'd take their word.'

So thought Cadfael, too. Yet it's truth that to

159

any man may come the one extreme moment when he turns his back on his own nature and goes the contrary way. Cadfael caught one more glimpse of the cousins as he turned for home and passed through the outer ward. They were up on the guard-walk of the curtain wall, leaning together in one of the wide embrasures between the merlons, and gazing clean across the busy wards of the castle into the hazy distance beyond the town, on the road to Wales. Eliud's arm was about Elis's shoulders, to settle them comfortably into the space, and the two faces were close together and equally intent and reticent. Cadfael went back through the town with that dual likeness before his mind's eye, curiously memorable and deeply disturbing. More than ever they looked to him like mirror images, where left and right were interchangeable, the bright side and the dark side of the same being.

Sybilla Prestcote departed, her son on his stout brown pony at her elbow, her train of servants and pack-horses stirring the March mire which the recent east winds were drying into fine dust. Hugh's advance party had left at dawn, he and his main body of archers and men-at-arms followed at noon, and the commissariat wagons creaked along the northern road between the two groups, soon overhauled and left behind on the way to Oswestry. In the castle a somewhat nervous Alan Herbard, son of a knight and eager for office, mounted scrupulous guard and made every round of his responsibilities twice, for fear he had missed something the first time. He was athletic,

160

fairly skilled in arms, but of small experience as yet, and well aware that any one of the sergeants Hugh had left behind was better equipped for the task in hand than he. They knew it, too, but spared him the too obvious demonstration of it.

A curious quiet descended on town and abbey with the departure of half the garrison, as though nothing could now happen here. The Welsh prisoners were condemned to boredom in captivity, the quest for Gilbert's murderer was at a standstill, there was nothing to be done but go on with the daily routine of work and leisure and worship, and wait.

And think, since action was suspended. Cadfael found himself thinking all the more steadily and deeply about the two missing pieces that held the whole puzzle together. Einon ab Ithel's gold pin, which he remembered very clearly, and that mysterious cloth which he had never seen, but which had stifled a man and urged him out of the world.

But was it so certain that he had never seen it? Never consciously, yet it had been here, here within the enclave, within the infirmary, within that room. It had been here, and now was not. And the search for it had been begun the same day, and the gates had been closed to all men attempting departure from the moment the death was discovered. How long an interval did that leave? Between the withdrawl of the brothers into the refectory and the finding of Gilbert dead, any man might have walked out by the gatehouse unquestioned. A matter of nearly two hours. That was one possibility.

161

The second possibility, thought Cadfael honestly, is that both cloth and pin are still here, somewhere within the enclave, but so well hidden that all our searching has not uncovered them.

And the third – he had been mulling it over in his mind all day, and repeatedly discarding it as a pointless aberration, but still it came back insistently, the one loophole. Yes, Hugh had put a guard on the gate from the moment the crime was known, but three people had been let out, all the same, the three who could not possibly have killed, since they had been in the abbot's company and Hugh's throughout. Einon ab Ithel and his two captains had ridden back to Owain Gwynedd. They had not taken any particle of guilt with them, yet they might unwittingly have taken evidence.

Three possibilities, and surely it might be worth examining even the third and most tenuous. He had lived with the other two for some days, and pursued them constantly, and all to no purpose. And for those countrymen of his penned in the castle, and for abbot and prior and brothers here, and for the dead man's family, there would be no true peace of mind until the truth was known.

Before Compline Cadfael took his trouble, as he had done many times before, to Abbot Radulfus.

'Either the cloth is still here among us, Father, but so well hidden that all our searching has failed to find it, or else it has been taken out of our walls by someone who left it in the short time between the hour of dinner and the discovery of the sheriff's

162

death, or by someone who left, openly and with sanction, after that discovery. From that time Hugh Beringar has had a watch kept on all who left the enclave. For those who may have passed through the gates before the death was known, I think they must be few indeed, for the time was short, and the porter did name three, all good folk of the Foregate on parish business, and all have been visited and are clearly blameless. That there may be others I do concede, but he has called no more to mind.'

'We know,' said the abbot thoughtfully, 'of three who left that same afternoon, to return to Wales, being by absolute proof clear of all blame. Also of one, the man Anion, who fled after being questioned. It is known to you, as it is to me, that for most men Anion's guilt is proven by his flight. It is not so to you?'

'No, Father, or at least not that mortal guilt. Something he surely knows, and fears, and perhaps has cause to fear. But not that. He has been in our infirmary for some weeks, his every possession is known to all those within – he has little enough, the list is soon ended – and if ever he had had in his hands such a cloth as I seek, it would have been noticed and questioned.'

Radulfus nodded agreement. 'You have not mentioned, though that also is missing, the gold pin from the lord Einon's cloak.'

'That,' said Cadfael, understanding the allusion, 'is possible. It would account for his flight. And he has been sought, and still is. But if he took the one thing, he did not bring the other. Unless he had in his hands such a cloth as I have shadowed for you, Father, then he is no murderer. And that little he had, many men here have seen and known. Nor, so far as ever we can discover, had this house ever such a weave within its store, to be pilfered and so misused.'

'Yet if this cloth came and went in that one day,' said Radulfus, 'are you saying it went hence with the Welsh lords? We know they did no wrong. If they had cause to think anything in their baggage, on returning, had to do with this matter, would they not have sent word?'

'They would have no such cause, Father, they would not know it had any importance to us. Only after they were gone did we recover those few frail threads I have shown you. How should they know we were seeking such a thing? Nor have we had any word from them, nothing but the message from Owain Gwynedd to Hugh Beringar. If Einon ab Ithel valued and has missed his jewel, he has not stopped to think he may have lost it here.'

'And you think,' asked the abbot, considering, 'that it might be well to speak with Einon and his officers, and examine these things?'

'At your will only,' said Cadfael. 'There is no knowing if it will lead to more knowledge than we have. Only, it *may*! And there are so many souls who need for their comfort to have this matter resolved. Even the guilty.'

'He most of all,' said Radulfus, and sat a while in silence. There in the parlour the light was only now beginning to fade. A cloudy day would have brought the dusk earlier. About this time, perhaps a little before, Hugh would have been waiting on the great dyke at Rhyd-y-Croesau by Oswestry for Owain Gwynedd. Unless, of course, Owain was like him in coming early to any meeting. Those two would understand each other without too many words. 'Let us go to Compline,' said the abbot, stirring, 'and pray for enlightenment. Tomorrow after Prime we will speak again.'

The Welsh of Powys had done very well out of their Lincoln venture, undertaken rather for plunder than out of any desire to support the earl of Chester, who was more often enemy than ally. Madog ap Meredith was quite willing to act in conjunction with Chester again, provided there was profit in it for Madog, and the news of Ranulf's probes into the borders of Gwynedd and Shropshire alerted him to pleasurable possibilities. It was some years since the men of Powys had captured and partially burned the castle of Caus, after the death of William Corbett and in the absence of his brother and heir, and they had held on to this advanced outpost ever since, a convenient base for further incursions. With Hugh Beringar gone north, and half the Shrewsbury garrison with him, the time seemed ripe for action.

The first thing that happened was a lightning raid from Caus along the valley towards Minsterley, the burning of an isolated farmstead and the driving off of a few cattle. The raiders drew off as rapidly as they had advanced, when the men of Minsterley mustered against them, and vanished into Caus and through the hills into

165

Wales with their booty. But it was indication enough that they might be expected back and in greater strength, since this first assay had passed off so easily and without loss. Alan Herbard sweated, spared a few men to reinforce Minsterley, and waited for worse.

News of this tentative probe reached the abbey and the town next morning. The deceptive calm that followed was too good to be true, but the men of the borders, accustomed to insecurity as the commonplace of life, stolidly picked up the pieces and kept their billhooks and pitchforks ready to hand.

'It would seem, however,' said Abbot Radulfus, pondering the situation without surprise or alarm, but with concern for a shire threatened upon two fronts, 'that this conference in the north would be the better informed, on both parts, if they knew of this raid. There is a mutual interest. However short-lived it may prove,' he added drily, and smiled. A stranger to the Welsh, he had learned a great deal since his appointment in Shrewsbury. 'Gwynedd is close neighbour to Chester, as Powys is not, and their interests are very different. Moreover, it seems the one is to be trusted to be both honourable and sensible. The other – no, I would not say either wise or stable by our measure. I do not want these western people of ours harried and plundered, Cadfael. I have been thinking of what we said yesterday. If you return once again to Wales, to find these lords who visited us, you will also be close to where Hugh Beringar confers with the prince.'

'Certainly,' said Cadfael, 'for Einon ab Ithel is

next in line to Owain Gwynedd's *penteulu*, the captain of his own guard. They will be together.'

'Then if I send you, as my envoy, to Einon, it would be well if you should also go to the castle, and make known to this young deputy there that you intend this journey, and can carry such messages as he may wish to Hugh Beringar. You know, I think,' said Radulfus with his dark smile, 'how to make such a contact discreetly. The young man is new to office.'

'I must, in any case, pass through the town,' said Cadfael mildly, 'and clearly I ought to report my errand to the authorities at the castle, and have their leave to pass. It is a good opportunity, where men are few and needed.'

'True,' said Radulfus, thinking how acutely men might shortly be needed down the border. 'Very well! Choose a horse to your liking. You have leave to deal as you think best. I want this death reconciled and purged, I want God's peace on my infirmary and within my walls, and the debt paid. Go, do what you can.'

There was no difficulty at the castle. Herbard needed only to be told that an envoy from the abbot was bound into Oswestry and beyond, and he added an embassage of his own to his sheriff. Raw and uneasy though he might be, he was braced and steeled to cope with whatever might come, but it was an additional snell of armour to have informed his chief. He was frightened but resolute; Cadfael thought he shaped well, and might be a useful man to Hugh, once blooded. And that might be no long way off.

'Let the lord Beringar know,' said Herbard, 'that I intend a close watch on the border by Caus. But I desire he should know the men of Powys are on the move. And if there are further raids, I will send word.'

'He shall know,' said Cadfael, and forthwith rode back a short spell through the town, down from the high cross to the Welsh bridge, and so north-west for Oswestry.

It was two days later that the next thrust came. Madog ap Meredith had been pleased with his first probe, and brought more men into the field before he launched his attack in force. Down the Rea valley to Minsterley they swarmed, burned and looted, wheeled both ways round Minsterley, and flowed on towards Pontesbury.

In Shrewsbury castle Welsh ears, as well as English, stretched and quivered to the bustle and fever of rumours.

'They are out!' said Elis, tense and sleepless beside his cousin in the night. 'Oh God, and Madog with this grudge to pay off! And *she* is there! Melicent is there at Godric's Ford. Oh, Eliud, if he should take it into his head to take revenge!'

'You're fretting for nothing,' Eliud insisted passionately. 'They know what they're doing here, they're on the watch, they'll not let any harm come to the nuns. Besides, Madog is not aiming there, but along the valley, where the pickings are best. And you saw yourself what the forest men can do. Why should he try that a second time? It wasn't his own nose was put out of joint there,

168

either, you told me who led that raid. What plunder is there at Godric's Ford for such as Madog, compared with the fat farms in the Minsterley valley? No, surely she's safe there.'

'*Safe*! How can you say it? Where is there any safety? They should never have let her go.' Elis ground angry fists in the rustling straw of their palliasse, and heaved himself round in the bed. 'Oh, Eliud, if only I were out of here and free ...'

'But you're not,' said Eliud, with the exasperated sharpness of one racked by the same pain, 'and neither am I. We're bound, and nothing we can do about it. For God's sake, do some justice to these English, they're neither fools nor cravens, they'll hold their city and their ground, and they'll take care of their women, without having to call on you or me. What right have you to doubt them? And you to talk so, who went raiding there yourself!'

Elis subsided with a defeated sigh and a drear smile. 'And got my come-uppance for it! Why did I ever go with Cadwaladr? God knows how often and how bitterly I've repented it since.'

'You would not be told,' said Eliud sadly, ashamed at having salted the wound. 'But she will be safe, you'll see, no harm will come to her, no harm will come to the nuns. Trust these English to look after their own. You must! There's nothing else we can do.'

'If I were free,' Elis agonised helplessly, 'I'd fetch her away from there, take her somewhere out of all danger ...'

'She would not go with you,' Eliud reminded him bleakly. 'You, of all people! Oh, God, how did we ever get into this quagmire, and how are we ever to get out of it?'

'If I could reach her, I could persuade her. In the end she would listen. She'll have remembered me better by now, she'll know she wrongs me. She'd go with me. If only I could reach her ...'

'But you're pledged, as I am,' said Eliud flatly. 'We've given our word, and it was freely accepted. Neither you nor I can stir a foot out of the gates without being dishonoured.'

'No,' agreed Elis miserably, and fell silent and still, staring into the darkness of the shallow vault over them.

Chapter Ten

Brother Cadfael arrived in Oswestry by evening, to find town and castle alert and busy, but Hugh Beringar already departed. He had moved east after his meeting with Owain Gwynedd, they told him, to Whittington and Ellesmere, to see his whole northern border stiffened and call up fresh levies as far away as Whitchurch. While Owain had moved north on the border to meet the constable of Chirk and see that corner of the confederacy secure and well-manned. There had been some slight brushes with probing parties from Cheshire, but so tentative that it was plain Ranulf was feeling his way with caution, testing to see how well organised the opposition might prove to be. So far he had drawn off at the first encounter. He had made great gains at Lincoln and had no intention of endangering them now, but a very human desire to add to them if he found his opponents unprepared.

'Which he will not,' said the cheerful sergeant who received Cadfael into the castle and saw his horse stabled and the rider well entertained. 'The earl is no madman to shove his fist into a hornets' nest. Leave him one weak place he can gnaw wider and he'd be in, but we're leaving him none. He thought he might do well, knowing Prestcote was gone. He thought our lad would be green and easy. He's learning different! And if these Welsh of Powys have an ear pricked this way, they should also take the omens. But who's to reason what the Welsh will do? This Owain, now, he's a man on his own. Straw-gold like a Saxon, and big! What's such a one doing in Wales?'

'He came here?' asked Cadfael, feeling his Cambrian blood stir in welcome.

'Last night, to sup with Beringar, and rode for Chirk at dawn. Welsh and English will man that fortress instead of fighting over it. There's a marvel!'

Cadfael pondered his errands and considered time. 'Where would Hugh Beringar be this night, do you suppose?'

'At Ellesmere, most like. And tomorrow at Whitchurch. The next day before we should look for him back here. He means to meet again with Owain, and make his way down the border after, if all goes well here.'

'And if Owain lies at Chirk tonight, where will he be bound tomorrow?'

'He has his camp still at Tregeiriog, with his friend Tudur ap Rhys. It's there he's called whatever new levies come in to his border service.'

So he must keep touch there always, in order to deploy his forces wherever they might be needed. And if he returned there the next night, so would Einon ab Ithel.

'I'll sleep the night here,' said Cadfael, 'and

tomorrow I'll also make for Tregeiriog. I know the maenol and its lord. I'll wait for Owain there. And do you let Hugh Beringar know that the Welsh of Powys are in the field again, as I've told you. Small harm yet, and should there be worse, Herbard will send word here. But if this border holds fast, and bloodies Chester's nose wherever he ventures it, Madog ap Meredith will also learn sense.'

This extreme border castle of Oswestry, with its town, was the king's, but the manor of Maesbury, of which it had become the head, was Hugh's own native place, and there was no man here who did not hold with him and trust him. Cadfael felt the solid security of Hugh's name about him, and a garrison doubly loyal – to Stephen and to Hugh. It was a good feeling, all the more now that Owain Gwynedd spread the benign shadow of his hand over a border that belonged by location to Powys. Cadfael slept well after hearing Compline in the castle chapel, rose early, took food and drink, and crossed the great dyke into Wales.

He had all but ten miles to go to Tregeiriog, winding all the way through the enclosing hills, always with wooded slopes one side or the other or both, and in open glimpses the bald grass summits leaning to view, and a sky veiled and still and mild overhead. Not mountain country, not the steel-blue rocks of the north-west, but hill-country always, with limited vistas, leaning hangers of woodland, closed valleys that opened only at the last moment to permit another curtained view. Before he drew too close to

173

Tregeiriog the expected pickets heaved out of the low brush, to challenge, recognise and admit him. His Welsh tongue was the first safe-conduct, and stood him in good stead.

All the colours had changed since last he rode down the steep hillside into Tregeiriog. Round the brown, timbered warmth of maenol and village beside the river, the trees had begun to soften their skeletal blackness with a delicate pale-green froth of buds, and on the lofty, rounded summits beyond the snow was gone, and the bleached pallor of last year's grass showed the same elusive tint of new life. Through the browned and rotting bracken the first fronds uncurled. Here it was already Spring.

At the gate of Tudur's maenol they knew him, and came readily to lead him in and take charge of his horse. Not Tudur himself, but his steward, came to welcome the guest and do the honours of the house. Tudur was with the prince, doubtless at this hour on his way back from Chirk. In the cleft of the tributary brook behind the maenol the turfed camp-fires of his border levies gave off blue wisps of smoke on the still air. By evening the hall would again be Owain's court, and all his chief captains in this border patrol mustered about his table.

Cadfael was shown to a small chamber within the house, and offered the ceremonial water to wash off the dust of travel from his feet. This time it was a maid-servant who waited upon him, but when he emerged into the court it was to see Cristina advancing upon him in a flurry of blown skirts and flying hair from the kitchens.

'Brother Cadfael ... it *is* you! They told me,' she said, halting before him breathless and intent, 'there was a brother come from Shrewsbury, I hoped it might be you. You know them – you can tell me the truth ... about Elis and Eliud ...'

'What have they already told you?' asked Cadfael. 'Come within, where we can be quiet, and what I can tell you, that I will, for I know you must have been in bitter anxiety.' But for all that, he thought ruefully, as she turned willingly and led the way into the hall, if he made that good, and told all he knew, it would be little to her comfort. Her betrothed, for whom she was contending so fiercely with so powerful a rival, was not only separated from her until proven innocent of murder, but disastrously in love with another girl as he had never been with her. What can you say to such a misused lady? Yet it would be infamous to lie to Cristina, just as surely as it would be cruel to bludgeon her with the blunt truth. Somewhere between the two he must pick his way.

She drew him with her into a corner of the hall, remote and shadowed at this hour when most of the men were out about their work, and there they sat down together against smoky tapestries, her black hair brushing his shoulder as she poured out what she knew and begged for what she needed to know.

'The English lord died, that I know, before ever Einon ab Ithel was ready to leave, and they are saying it was no simple death from his wounds, and all those who are not proven blameless must stay there as prisoners and suspect murderers,

175

until the guilt is proven on some one man –
English or Welsh, lay or brother, who knows?
And here we must wait also. But what is being
done to set them free? How are you to find the
guilty one? Is all this true? I know Einon came
back and spoke with Owain Gwynedd, and I know
the prince will not receive his men back until they
are cleared of all blame. He says he sent back a
dead man, and a dead man cannot buy back one
living. And moreover, that your dead man's
ransom must be a life – the life of his murderer.
Do *you* believe any man of ours owes that debt?'

'I dare not say there is any man who might not
kill, given some monstrous, driving need,' said
Cadfael honestly.

'Or any woman, either,' she said with a fierce,
helpless sigh. 'But you have not fixed on any one
man for this deed? No finger has been pointed?
Not yet?'

No, of course she did not know. Einon had left
before ever Melicent cried out both her love and
her hatred, accusing Elis. No further news had yet
reached these parts. Even if Hugh had now
spoken of this matter with the prince, no such
word had yet found its way back here to
Tregeiriog. But surely it would, when Owain
returned. In the end she would hear how her
betrothed had fallen headlong in love with
another woman, and been accused by her of her
father's murder, murder for love that put an end
to love. And where did that leave Cristina?
Forgotten, eclipsed, but still in tenuous possession
of a bridegroom who did not want her, and could
not have the bride he did want! Such a tangled

coil enmeshing all these four hapless children!

'Fingers have been pointed, more than one way,' said Cadfael, 'but there is no proof against one man more than another. No one is yet in danger of his life, and all are in health and well enough treated, even if they must be confined. There is no help for it but to wait and believe in justice.'

'Believing in justice is not always so easy,' she said tartly. 'You say they are well? And they are together, Elis and Eliud?'

'They are. They have that comfort. And within the castle wards they have their liberty. They have given their word not to try to escape, and it has been accepted. They are well enough, you may believe that.'

'But you can give me no hope, set me no period, when he will come home?' She sat confronting Cadfael with great, steady eyes, and in her lap her fingers were knotted so tightly that the knuckles shone white as naked bone. 'Even if he does come home, living and justified,' she said.

'That I can tell no more than you,' Cadfael owned wryly. 'But I will do what I can to shorten the time. This waiting is hard upon you, I know it.' But how much harder would the return be, if ever Elis came back vindicated, only to pursue his suit for Melicent Prestcote, and worm his way out of his Welsh betrothal. It might even be better if she had warning now, before the blow fell. Cadfael was pondering what he could best do for her, and with only half an ear tuned to what she was saying.

'At least I have purged my own soul,' she said,

as much to herself as to him. 'I have always known how well he loves me, if only he did not love his cousin as well or better. Fosterlings are like that – you are Welsh, you know it. But if he could not bring himself to undo what was done so ill, I have done it for him now. I tired of silence. Why should we bleed without a cry? I have done what had to be done. I've spoken with my father and with his. In the end I shall have my way.'

She rose, giving him a pale but resolute smile. 'We shall be able to speak again, brother, before you leave us. I must go and see how things fare in the kitchen, they'll be home with the evening.'

He gave her an abstracted farewell, and watched her cross the hall with her free, boy's stride and straight, proud carriage. Not until she had reached the door did he realise the meaning of what she had said. 'Cristina!' he called in startled enlightenment, but the door had closed and she was gone.

There was no error, he had heard aright. *She knew how well he loved her, if only he did not love his cousin as well or better, in the way of fosterlings!* Yes, all that he had known before, he had seen it manifested in their warring exchanges, and misread it utterly. How a man can be deceived, where every word, every aspect, confirms him in his blindness! Not a single lie spoken or intended, yet the sum total a lie.

She had spoken with her father – *and with his!*

Cadfael heard in his mind's ear Elis ap Cynan's blithe voice accounting for himself when first he came to Shrewsbury. Owain Gwynedd was his

178

overlord, and had overseen him in the fosterage where he had placed him when his father died ...

' ... with my uncle Griffith ap Meilyr, where I grew up with my cousin Eliud as brothers ...'

Two young men, close as twins, far too close to make room for the bride destined for one of them. Yes, and she fighting hard for what she claimed as her rights, and knowing there was love deep enough and wild enough to match her love, *if only* ... If only a mistaken bond made in infancy could be honourably dissolved. If only those two could be severed, that dual creature staring into a mirror, the left-handed image and the right-handed, and which of them the reality? How is a stranger to tell?

But now he knew. She had not used the word loosely, of the kinsman who had reared them both. No, she meant just what she had said. An uncle may also be a foster-father, but only a natural father is a father.

They came, as before, with the dusk. Cadfael was still in a daze when he heard them come, and stirred himself to go out and witness the torchlit bustle in the court, the glimmer on the coats of the horses, the jingle of harness, bit and spur, the cheerful and purposeful hum of entwining voices, the hissing and crooning of the grooms, the trampling of hooves and the very faint mist of warm breath in the chilling but frostless air. A grand, vigorous pattern of lights and shadows, and the open door of the hall glowing warmly for welcome.

Tudur ap Rhys was the first down from the

saddle, and himself strode to hold his prince's stirrup. Owain Gwynedd's fair hair gleamed uncovered in the ruddy light of the torches as he sprang down, a head taller than his host. Man after man they came, chieftain after chieftain, the princelings of Gwynedd's nearer commoes, the neighbours of England. Cadfael stood to survey each one as he dismounted, and lingered until all were on foot, and their followers dispersed into the camps beyond the maenol. But he did not find among them Einon ab Ithel, whom he sought.

'Einon?' said Tudur, questioned. 'He's following, though he may come late to table. He had a visit to pay in Llansantffraid, he has a daughter married there, and his first grandson is come new into the world. Before the evening's out he'll be with us. You're heartily welcome to my roof again, brother, all the more if you bring news to please the prince's ear. It was an ill thing that happened there with you, he feels it as a sad stain on a clean acquaintance.'

'I'm rather seeking than bringing enlightenment,' Cadfael confessed. 'But I trust one man's ill deed cannot mar these meetings between your prince and our sheriff. Owain Gwynedd's goodwill is gold to us in Shropshire, all the more since Madog ap Meredith is showing his teeth again.'

'Do you tell me so? Owain will want to hear of it, but after supper will be the fitting time. I'll make you a place at the high table.'

Since he had in any case to wait for the arrival of Einon, Cadfael sat back to study and enjoy the gathering in Tudur's hall over supper, the warmth of the central fire, the torches, the wine, and the harping. A man of Tudur's status was privileged to possess a harp and maintain his own harper, in addition to his duty to be a generous patron to travelling minstrels. And with the prince here to praise and be praised, they had a rivalry of singers that lasted throughout the meal. There was still a deal of coming and going in the courtyard, late-comers riding in, officers from the camps patrolling their bounds and changing pickets, and the womenfolk fetching and carrying, and loitering to talk to the archers and men-at-arms. For the time being this was the court of Gwynedd, where petitioners, bringers of gifts, young men seeking office and favour, all must come.

The dishes had been removed, and the mead and wine were circulating freely, when Tudur's steward came into the hall and made for the high table.

'My lord, there's one here asks leave to present to you his natural son, whom he has acknowledged and admitted to his kinship only two days ago. Griffri ap Llywarch, from close by Meifod. Will you hear him?'

'Willingly,' said Owain, pricking up his fair head to stare down through the smoke and shadows of the hall with some curiosity. 'Let Griffri ap Llywarch come in and be welcome.'

Cadfael had not paid due attention to the name, and might not even have recognised it if he had, nor was he likely to recognise a man he had never seen before. The newcomer followed the steward into the hall, and up between the tables to

181

the high place. A lean, sinewy man, perhaps fifty years old, balding and bearded, with a hillman's gait, and the weathered face and wrinkled, far-seeing eyes of the shepherd. His clothing was plain and brown, but good homespun. He came straight to the dais, and made the Welshman's brisk, unservile reverence to the prince.

'My lord Owain, I have brought you my son, that you may know and approve him. For the only son I had by my wife is two years and more dead, and I was without children, until this my son by another woman came to me declaring his birth and proving it. And I have acknowledged him mine and brought him into my kinship, and as mine he is accepted. Now I ask your countenance also.'

He stood proudly, glad of what he had to say and of the young man he had to present; and Cadfael would have had neither eyes nor ears for any other man present, if it had not been for the courteous silence that had followed him up the hall, and the one clear sound that carried in it. Shadows and smoke veiled the figure that followed respectfully at some yards distance, but the sound of its steps was plainly audible, and went haltingly, lighter and faster upon one foot. Cadfael's eyes were upon the son when he came hesitantly into the torchlight from the high table. This one he knew, though the black hair was trimmed and thrown proudly back from a face not now sullen and closed, but open, hopeful and eager, and there was no longer a crutch under the leaning armpit.

Cadfael looked back from Anion ap Griffri to

182

Griffri ap Llywarch, to whose drear and childless middle age this unlooked-for son had suddenly supplied a warm heart of hope and content. The homespun cloak hanging loose upon Griffri's shoulders bore in its folds a long pin with a large, chased gold head secured with a thin gold chain. And that, too, Cadfael had seen before, and knew only too well.

So did another witness. Einon ab Ithel had come in, as one familiar with the household and desirous of making no inconvenient stir, by the high door from the private chamber, and emerged behind the prince's table unnoticed. The man who was holding all attention naturally drew his. The red of torchlight flashed from the ornament worn openly and proudly. Its owner had the best reason to know there could not be two such, not of that exact and massive size and ornamentation.

'God's breath!' swore Einon ab Ithel in a great bellow of astonishment and indignation. 'What manner of thief have we here, wearing my gold under my very eyes?'

Silence fell as ominously as thunder, and every head whirled from prince and petitioner to stare at this loud accuser. Einon came round the high table in a few long strides, dropped from the dais so close as to send Griffri lurching back in alarm, and stabbed a hard brown finger at the pin that glowed in the drab cloak.

'My lord, *this* – is mine! Gold out of my earth, I had it mined, I had it made for me, there is not another exactly like it in this or any land. When I

183

came back from Shrewsbury, on that errand you know of, it was not in my collar, nor have I seen it since that day. I thought it fallen somewhere on the road, and made no ado about it. What is it to mourn for, gold! Now I see it again and marvel. My lord, it is in your hands. Demand of this man how he comes to be wearing what is mine.'

Half the hall was on its feet, and rumbling with menace, for theft, unmitigated by circumstances, was the worst crime they acknowledged, and the thief caught red-handed could be killed on sight by the wronged man. Griffri stood stricken dumb, staring in bewilderment. Anion flung himself with stretched arms and braced body between his father and Einon.

'My lord, my lord, I gave it, I bought it to my father. I did not steal … I took a price! Hold my father blameless, if there is blame it is mine only …'

He was sweating with terror, great sudden gouts that ran on his forehead and were snared in his thick brows. And if he knew a little Welsh, in this extremity it did not serve him, he had cried out in English. That gave them all a moment of surprise. And Owain swept a hand over the hall and brought silence.

They murmured, but they obeyed. In the ensuing hush Brother Cadfael rose unobtrusively to his feet and made his way round the table and down to the floor of the hall. His movements, however discreet, drew the prince's eye.

'My lord,' said Cadfael deprecatingly, 'I am of Shrewsbury, I know and am known to this man Anion ap Griffri. He was raised English, no fault

184

of his. Should he need one to interpret, I can do that service, so that he may be understood by all here.'

'A fair offer,' said Owain, and eyed him thoughtfully. 'Are you also empowered, brother, to speak for Shrewsbury, since it seems this accusation goes back to that town, and the business of which we know? And if so, for shire and town or for abbey?'

'Here and now,' said Cadfael boldly, 'I will venture for both. And if you find fault hereafter, let it fall on me.'

'You are here, I fancy,' said Owain, considering, 'over this very matter.'

'I am. In part to look for this same jewel. For it vanished from Gilbert Prestcote's chamber in our infirmary on the day that he died. The cloak that had been added to the sick man's wrappings in the litter was handed back to Einon ab Ithel without it. Only after he had left did we remember and look for the brooch. And only now do I see it again.'

'From the room where a man died by murder,' said Einon. 'Brother, you have found more than the gold. You may send our men home.'

Anion stood fearful but steadfast between his father and the accusing stare of a hall full of eyes. He was white as ice, translucent, as though all the blood had left his veins. 'I did not kill,' he said hoarsely, and heaved hard to get breath enough to speak. 'My lord, I never knew ... I thought the pin was his, Prestcote's. I took it from the cloak, yes –'

'After you had killed him,' said Einon harshly.

185

'No! I swear it! I never touched the man.' He turned in desperate appeal to Owain, who sat listening dispassionately at the table, his fingers easy round the stem of his wine-cup, but his eyes very bright and aware. 'My lord, only hear me! And hold my father clear of all, for all he knows is what I have told him, and the same I shall tell you, and as God sees me, I do not lie.'

'Hand up to me,' said Owain, 'that pin you wear.' And as Griffri hurried with trembling fingers to detach it, and reached up to lay it in the prince's hand: 'So! I have known this too long and seen it worn too often to be in any doubt whose it is. From you, Brother, as from Einon here, I know how it came to be lying open to hand by the sheriff's bed. Now you may tell, Anion, how you came by it. English I can follow, you need not fear being misunderstood. And Brother Cadfael will put what you say into Welsh, so that all here may understand you.'

Anion gulped air and found a creaky voice had contracted his throat, but the flow of words washed constraint away. 'My lord, until these last days I never saw my father, nor he me, but I had a brother, as he has said, and by chance I got to know him when he came into Shrewsbury with wool to sell. There was a year between us, and I am the elder. He was my kin, and I valued him. And once when he visited the town and I was not by, there was a fight, a man was killed and my brother was blamed for it. Gilbert Prestcote hanged him!'

Owain glanced aside at Cadfael, and waited until this speech had been translated for the

Welshmen. Then he asked: 'You know of this case? Was it fairly done?'

'Who knows which hand did the killing?' said Cadfael. 'It was a street brawl, the young men were drunk. Gilbert Prestcote was hasty by nature, but just. But this is certain, here in Wales the young man would not have hanged. A blood-price would have paid it.'

'Go on,' said Owain.

'I carried that grudge on my heart from that day,' said Anion, gathering passion from old bitterness. 'But when did I ever come within reach of the sheriff? Never until your men brought him into Shrewsbury wounded and housed him in the infirmary. And I was there with this broken leg of mine all but healed, and that man only twenty paces from me, only a wall between us, my enemy at my mercy. While it was all still and the brothers at dinner, I went into the room where he was. He owed my house a life – even if I was mongrel, I felt Welsh then, and I meant to take my due revenge – I meant to kill! The only brother ever I had, and he was merry and good to look upon, and then to hang for an unlucky blow when he was full of ale! I went in there to kill. But I could not do it! When I saw my enemy brought down so low, so old and weary, hardly blood or breath in him … I stood by him and watched, and all I could feel was sadness. It seemed to me that there was no call there for vengeance, for all was already avenged. So I thought on another way. There was no court to set a blood-price or enforce payment, but there was the gold pin in the cloak beside him. I thought it was his. How could I

187

know? So I took it as *galanas*, to clear the debt and the grudge. But by the end of that day I knew, we all knew, that Prestcote was dead and dead by murder, and when they began to question even me, I knew that if ever it came out what I had done it would be said I had also killed him. So I ran. I meant, in any case, to come and seek my father some day, and tell him my brother's death was paid for, but because I was afraid I had to run in haste.'

'And come to me he did,' said Griffri earnestly, his hand upon his son's shoulder, 'and showed me by way of warranty the yellow mountain stone I gave his mother long ago. But by his face I knew him, for he's like the brother he lost. And he gave me that thing you hold, my lord, and told me that young Griffri's death was requited, and this was the token price exacted, and the grudge buried, for our enemy was dead. I did not well understand him then, for I told him if he had slain Griffri's slayer, then he had no right to take a price as well. But he swore to me by most solemn oath that it was not he who had killed and I believe him. And judge if I am glad to have a son restored me in my middle years, to be the prop of my old age. For God's sake, my lord, do not take him from me now!'

In the dour, considering hush that followed Cadfael completed his translation of what Anion had said, and took his time about it to allow him to study the prince's impassive face. At the end of it the silence continued still for a long minute, since no one would speak until Owain made it possible. He, too, was in no hurry. He looked at father and son, pressed together there below the dais in apprehensive solidarity, he looked at Einon, whose face was as unrevealing as his own, and last at Cadfael.

'Brother, you know more of what has gone forward in Shrewsbury abbey than any of us here. You know this man. How do you say? Do you believe his story?'

'Yes,' said Cadfael, with grave and heartfelt gratitude, 'I do believe it. It fits with all I know. But I would ask Anion one question.'

'Ask it.'

'You stood beside the bed, Anion, and watched the sleeper. Are you sure that he was then alive?'

'Yes, surely,' said Anion wondering. 'He breathed, he moaned in his sleep. I saw and heard. I know.'

'My lord,' said Cadfael, watching Owain's enquiring eye, 'there was another heard to enter and leave that room, some little while later, someone who went not haltingly, as Anion did, but lightly. That one did not take anything, unless it was a life. Moreover, I believe what Anion has told us because there is yet another thing I have to find before I shall have found Gilbert Prestcote's murderer.'

Owain nodded comprehension, and mused for a while in silence. Then he picked up the gold pin with a brisk movement, and held it out to Einon. 'How say you? Was this theft?'

'I am content,' said Einon and laughed, releasing the tension in the hall. In the general stir and murmur of returning ease, the prince turned to his host.

'Make a place below there, Tudur, for Griffri ap Llywarch, and his son Anion.'

Chapter Eleven

So there went Shrewsbury's prime suspect, the man gossip had already hanged and buried, down the hall on his father's heels, stumbling a little and dazed like a man in a dream, but beginning to shine as though a torch had been kindled within him; down to a place with his father at one of the tables, equal among equals. From a serving-maid's by-blow, without property or privilege, he was suddenly become a free man, with a rightful place of his own in a kindred, heir to a respected sire, accepted by his prince. The threat that had forced him to take to his heels had turned into the greatest blessing of his life and brought him to the one place that was his by right in Welsh law, true son to a father who acknowledged him proudly. Here Anion was no bastard.

Cadfael watched the pair of them to their places, and was glad that something good, at least, should have come out of the evil. Where would that young man have found the courage to seek out his father, distant, unknown, speaking another language, if fear had not forced his hand, and made it easy to leap across a frontier? The ending was well worth the terror that had gone before. He could forget Anion now. Anion's hands were clean.

'At least you've sent me one man,' observed Owain, watching thoughtfully as the pair reached their places, 'in return for my eight still in bond. Not a bad figure of a man, either. But no training in arms, I doubt.'

'An excellent cattle-man,' said Cadfael. 'He has an understanding with all animals. You may safely put your horses in his care.'

'And you lose, I gather, your chief contender for a halter. You have no after-thoughts concerning him?'

'None. I am sure he did as he says he did. He dreamed of avenging himself on a strong and overbearing man, and found a broken wreck he could not choose but pity.'

'No bad ending,' said Owain. 'And now I think we might withdraw to some quieter place, and you shall tell us whatever you have to tell, and ask whatever you need to ask.'

In the prince's chamber they sat about the small, wire-guarded brazier, Owain, Tudur, Einon ab Ithel and Cadfael. Cadfael had brought with him the little box in which he had preserved the wisps of wool and gold thread. Those precise shades of deep blue and soft rose could not be carried accurately in the mind, but must continually be referred to the eye, and matched against whatever fabric came to light. He had the box in the scrip at his girdle, and was wary of opening it where there might be even the faintest draught,

191

for fear the frail things within would be blown clean away. A breath from a loophole could whisk his ominous treasures out of reach in an instant.

He had debated within himself how much he should tell, but in the light of Cristina's revelation, and since her father was here in conference, he told all he knew, how Elis in his captivity had fallen haplessly in love with Prestcote's daughter, and how the pair of them had seen no possible hope of gaining the sheriff's approval for such a match, hence providing reason enough why Elis should attempt to disturb the invalid's rest — whether to remove by murder the obstacle to his love, as Melicent accused, or to plead his forlorn cause, as Elis himself protested.

'So that was the way of it,' said Owain, and exchanged a straight, hard look with Tudur, unsurprised, and forbearing from either sympathy or blame. Tudur was on close terms of personal friendship with his prince, and had surely spoken with him of Cristina's confidences. Here was the other side of the coin. 'And this was after Einon had left you?'

'It was. It came out that the boy had tried to speak with Gilbert, and been ordered out by Brother Edmund. When the girl heard of it, she turned on him for a murderer.'

'But you do not altogether accept that. Nor, it seems, has Beringar accepted it.'

'There is no more proof of it than that he was there, beside the bed, when Edmund came and drove him out. It could as well have been for the boy's declared purpose as for anything worse. And then, you'll understand, there was the matter of the gold pin. We never realised it was missing, my lord, until you had ridden for home. But very certainly Elis neither had it on him, nor had had any opportunity to hide it elsewhere before he was searched. Therefore someone else had been in that room, and taken it away.'

'But now that we know what befell my pin,' said Einon, 'and are satisfied Anion did not murder, does not that leave that boy again in danger of being branded for the killing of a sick and sleeping man? Though it sorts very poorly,' he added, 'with what I know of him.'

'Which of us,' said Owain sombrely, 'has never been guilty of some unworthiness that sorts very ill with what our friends know of us? Even with what we know, or think we know of ourselves! I would not rule out any man from being capable once in his life of a gross infamy.' He looked up at Cadfael. 'Brother, I recall you said, within there, that there was yet one more thing you must find, before you would have found Prestcote's murderer. What is that thing?'

'It is the cloth that was used to smother Gilbert. By its traces it will be known, once found. For it was pressed down over his nose and mouth, and he breathed it into his nostrils and drew it into his teeth, and a thread or two of it we found in his beard. No ordinary cloth. Elis had neither that nor anything else in his hands when he came from the infirmary. Once I had found and preserved the filaments from it, we searched for it throughout the abbey precincts, for it could have been a hanging or an altar-cloth, but we have found nothing to match these fragments. Until we

193

know what it was, and what became of it, we shall not know who killed Gilbert Prestcote.'

'This is certain?' asked Owain. 'you drew these threads from the dead man's nostrils and mouth? You think you will know, when you find it, the very cloth that was used to stifle him?'

'I do think so, for the colours are clear, and not common dyes. I have the box here. But open it with care. What's within is fine as cobweb.' Cadfael handed the little box across the brazier. 'But not here. The up-draught from the warmth could blow them away.'

Owain took the box aside, and held it low under one of the lamps, where the light would play into it. The minute threads quivered faintly, and again were still. 'Here's gold thread, that's plain, a twisted strand. The rest – I see it's wool, by the many hairs and the live texture. A darker colour and a lighter.' He studied them narrowly, but shook his head. 'I could not say what tints are here, only that the cloth had a good gold thread woven into it. And I fancy it would be thick, a heavy weave, by the way the wool curls and crimps. Many more such fine hairs went to make up this yarn.'

'Let me see,' said Einon, and narrowed his eyes over the box. 'I see the gold, but the colours ... No, it means nothing to me.'

Tudur peered, and shook his head. 'We have not the light for this, my lord. By day these would show very differently.'

It was true, by the mellow light of these oil-lamps the prince's hair was deep harvest-gold, almost brown. By daylight it was the yellow of primroses. 'It might be better,' agreed Cadfael, 'to leave the matter until morning. Even had we better vision, what could be done at this hour?'

'This light foils the eye,' said Owain. He closed the lid over the airy fragments. 'Why did you think you might find what you seek here?'

'Because we have not found it within the pale of the abbey, so we must look outside, wherever men have dispersed from the abbey. The lord Einon and two captains beside had left us before ever we recovered these threads, it was a possibility, however frail, that unknowingly this cloth had gone with them. By daylight the colours will show for what they truly are. You may yet recall seeing such a weave.'

Cadfael took back the box. It had been a fragile hope at best, but the morrow remained. There was a man's life, a man's soul's health, snared in those few quivering hairs, and he was their custodian.

'Tomorrow,' said the prince emphatically, 'we will try what God's light can show us, since ours is too feeble.'

In the deep small hours of that same night Elis awoke in the dark cell in the outer ward of Shrewsbury castle, and lay with stretched ears, struggling up from the dullness of sleep and wondering what had shaken him out of so profound a slumber. He had grown used to all the daytime sounds native to this place, and to the normal unbroken silence of the night. This night was different, or he would not have been heaved so rudely out of the only refuge he had from his

195

daytime miseries. Something was not as it should have been, someone was astir at a time when there was always silence and stillness. The air quivered with soft movements and distant voices.

They were not locked in, their word had been accepted without question, bond enough to hold them. Elis raised himself cautiously on an elbow, and leaned to listen to Eliud's breathing in the bed beside him. Deep asleep, if not altogether at peace. He twitched and turned without awaking, and the measure of his breathing changed uneasily, shortening and shallowing sometimes, then easing into a long rhythm that promised better rest. Elis did not want to disturb him. It was all due to him, to his pig-headed folly in joining Cadwaladr, that Eliud was here a prisoner beside him. He must not be drawn still deeper into question and danger, whatever happened to Elis.

There were certainly voices, at some small distance but muffled and made to sound infinitely more distant by the thick stone walls. And though at this remove there could not possibly be distinguishable words, yet there, was an indefinable agitation about the exchanges, a quiver of panic on the air. Elis slid carefully from the bed, halted and held his breath a moment to make sure that Eliud had not stirred, and felt for his coat, thankful that he slept in shirt and hose, and need not fumble in the dark to dress. With all the grief and anxiety he carried about with him night and day, he must discover the reason of this added and unforeseen alarm. Every divergence from custom was a threat.

The door was heavy but well hung, and swung

196

without a sound. Outside the night was moonless but clear, very faint starlight patterned the sky between the walls and towers that made a shell of total darkness. He drew the door closed after him, and eased the heavy latch into its socket gingerly. Now the murmur of voices had body and direction, it came from the guard-room within the gatehouse. And that crisp, brief clatter that struck a hidden spark on the ground was hooves on the cobbles. A rider at this hour?

He felt his way along the wall towards the sound, at every angle flattening himself against the stones to listen afresh. The horse shifted and blew. Shapes grew gradually out of the solid darkness, the twin turrets of the barbican showed their teeth against a faintly lighter sky, and the flat surface of the closed gate beneath had a tall, narrow slit of pallor carved through it, tall as a man on horse-back, and wide enough for a horse to pass in haste. The rider's wicket was open. Open because someone had entered by it with urgent news only minutes since, and no one had yet thought to close it.

Elis crept nearer. The door of the guard-room was ajar, a long sliver of light from torches within quivered across the dark cobbles. The voices emerged by fits and starts, as they were raised and again lowered, but he caught words clearly here and there.

'... burned a farm west of Pontesbury,' reported a messenger, still breathless from his haste, 'and never withdrew ... They're camped overnight ... and another party skirting Minsterley to join them.'

197

Another voice, sharp and clear, most likely one of the experienced sergeants: 'What numbers?'

'In all ... if they foregather ... I was told it might be as many as a hundred and fifty ...'

'Archers? Lancers? Foot or horse?' That was not the sergeant, that was a young voice, a shade higher than it should have been with alarm and strain. They had got Alan Herbard out of bed. This was a grave matter.

'My lord, far the greater part on foot. Lancers and archers both. They may try to encircle Pontesbury ... they know Hugh Beringar is in the north ...'

'Halfway to Shrewsbury!' said Herbard's voice, taut and jealous for his first command.

'They'll not dare that,' said the sergeant. 'Plunder's the aim. Those valley farms ... with new lambs ...'

'Madog ap Meredith has a grudge to settle,' ventured the messenger, still short of breath, 'for that raid in February. They're close ... but the pickings are smaller, there in the forest ... I doubt ...'

Halfway to Shrewsbury was more than halfway to the ford in the forest where that grudge had come to birth. And the pickings ... Elis turned his forehead into the chill of the stone against which he leaned and swallowed terror. A parcel of women! He was more than paid for that silly flaunt, who had a woman of his own there to sweat and bleed for, young, beautiful, fair as flax, tall like a willow. The square dark men of Powys would come to blows over her, kill one another for her, kill her when they were done.

198

He had started out of his shelter under the wall before he even knew what he intended. The patient, drooping horse might have given him away, but there was no groom holding it, and it stood its ground silently, unstartled, as he stole past, a hand raised to caress and beseech acceptance. He did not dare take it, the first clatter of hooves would have brought them out like hornets disturbed, but as least it let him pass unbetrayed. The big body steamed gently, he felt its heat. The tired head turned and nuzzled his hand. He drew his fingers away with stealthy gentleness, and slid past towards the elongated wicket that offered a way out into the night.

He was through, he had the descent to the castle Foregate on his right, and the way up into the town on his left. But he was out of the castle, he who had given his word not to pass the threshold, he who was forsworn from this moment, false to his word, outcast. Not even Eliud would speak for him when he knew.

The town gates would not open until dawn. Elis turned left, into the town, and groped his way by unknown lanes and passages to find some corner where he could hide until the morning. He was none too sure of his best way out, and did not stop to wonder if he would ever manage to pass unnoticed. All he knew was that he had to get to Godric's Ford before his countrymen reached it. He got his bearings by instinct, blundering blindly round towards the eastward gates. In Saint Mary's churchyard, though he did not know it for that, he shrank into the shelter of a porch from the chill of the wind. He had left his cloak behind in his dishonoured cell, he was half-naked to shame and the night, but he was free and on his way to deliver her. What was his honour, more than his life, compared to her safety.

The town woke early. Tradesmen and travellers rose and made their way down to the gates before full daylight, to be out and about their proper business betimes. So did Elis ap Cynan, going with them discreetly down the Wyle, cloakless, weaponless, desperate, heroic and absurd, to the rescue of his Melicent.

Eliud put out his hand, before he was fully awake, to feel for his cousin, and sat up in abrupt shock to find Elis's side of the bed empty and cold. But the dark red cloak was still draped over the foot of the bed, and Eliud's sense of loss was utterly irrational. Why should not Elis rise early and go out into the wards before his bedfellow was awake? Without his cloak he could not be far away. But for all that, and however brief the separation, it troubled Eliud like a physical pain. Here in their imprisonment they had hardly been a moment out of each other's company, as if for each of them faith in a final happy delivery depended upon the presence of the other.

Eliud rose and dressed, and went out to the trough by the well, to wash himself fully awake in the shock of the cold water. There was an unusual stir about the stables and the armoury, but he saw no sign of Elis anywhere in either place, nor was he brooding on the walls with his face towards Wales. The want of him began to ache like an amputation.

They took their meals in hall among their English peers, but on this clear morning Elis did not come to break his fast. And by this time others had remarked his absence.

One of the sergeants of the garrison stopped Eliud as he was leaving the hall. 'Where is your cousin? Is he sick?'

'I know no more than you,' said Eliud. 'I've been looking for him. He was out before I awoke, and I've seen nothing of him since.' And he added in jealous haste, seeing the man frown and give him the first hard stare of suspicion: 'But he can't be far. His cloak is still in the cell. There's so much stirring here, I thought he might have risen early to find out what was all the to-do.'

'He's pledged not to set foot out of the gates,' said the sergeant. 'But do you tell me he's given up eating? You must know more than you pretend.'

'No! But he's here within, he must be. He would not break his word, I promise you.'

The man eyed him hard, and turned abruptly on his heel to make for the gatehouse and question the guards. Eliud caught him entreatingly by the sleeve. 'What is brewing here? Is there news? Such activity in the armoury and the archers drawing arrows ... What's happened overnight?'

'What's happened? Your countrymen are swarming in force along the Minsterley valley, if you want to know, burning farmsteads and moving in on Pontesbury. Three days ago it was a handful, it's past a hundred tribesmen now.' He swung back suddenly to demand: 'Did you hear aught in the night? Is that it? Has that cousin of yours run, broke out to join his ragamuffin kin and help in the killing? The sheriff was not enough for him?'

'No!' cried Eliud. 'He would not! It's impossible!'

'It's how we got him in the first place, a murdering, looting raid the like of these. It suited him then, it comes very timely for him now. His neck out of a noose and his friends close by to bring him off safely.'

'You cannot say so! You don't yet know but he's here within, true to his word.'

'No, but soon we shall,' said the sergeant grimly, and took Eliud firmly by the arm. 'Into your cell and wait. The lord Herbard must know of this.'

He flung away at speed and Eliud, in desolate obedience, trudged back to his cell and sat there upon the bed with only Elis's cloak for company. By then he was certain what the result of any search must be. Only an hour or two of daylight gone and there were endless places a man could be, if he felt no appetite either for food or for the company of his fellowmen, and yet the castle felt empty of Elis, as cold and alien as if he had never been there. And a courier had come in the night, it seemed, with news of stronger forces from Powys plundering closer to Shrewsbury, and closer still to the forest grange of the abbey of Polesworth at Godric's Ford. Where all this heavy burden had begun and where, perhaps, it must end. If Elis had heard that nocturnal arrival and gone out to discover the cause – yes, then he might in desperation forget oath and honour and all. Eliud waited wretchedly until Alan Herbard came, with two sergeants at his heels. A long wait it had been. They would have scoured the castle by now. By their grim faces it was clear they had not found Elis.

Eliud rose to his feet to face them. He would need all his powers and all his dignity now if he was to speak for Elis. This Alan Herbard was surely no more than a year or two his senior, and being as harshly tested as he.

'If you know the manner of your cousin's flight,' said Herbard bluntly, 'you would be wise to speak. You shared this narrow space. If he rose in the night, surely you would know. For I tell you plainly, he is gone. He has run. In the night the wicket was opened for a man to enter. It's no secret now that it let out a man-renegade, forsworn, self-branded murderer. Why else should he so seize this chance?'

'No!' said Eliud. 'You wrong him and in the end it will be shown you wrong him. He is no murderer. If he has run, that is not the reason.'

'There is no *if*. He is gone. You know nothing of it? You slept through his flight?'

'I missed him when I awoke,' said Eliud. 'I know nothing of how he went or when. But I know *him*. If he rose in the night because he heard your man arriving and if he heard then – is it so? – that the Welsh of Powys are coming too close and in dangerous numbers, then I swear to you he had fled only out of dread for Gilbert Prestcote's daughter. She is there with the sisters at Godric's Ford and Elis loves her. Whether she has discarded him or no, he has not ceased to love

203

her, and if she is in danger, he will venture life, yes and his honour with it, to bring her to safety. And when that is done,' said Eliud passionately, 'he will return here, to suffer whatever fate may await him. He is no renegade! He has broken his oath only for Melicent's sake. He will come back and give himself up. I pledge my own honour for him! My own life!'

'I would remind you,' said Herbard grimly, 'you have already done so. Either one of you gave his word for both. At this moment you stand attainted as his surety for his treachery. I could hang you, and be fully justified.'

'Do so!' said Eliud, blanched to the lips, his eyes dilated into a blaze of green. 'Here am I, still his warranty. I tell you, this neck is yours to wring if Elis proves false. I give you leave freely. You are mustering to ride, I've seen it. You go against these Welsh of Powys. Take me with you! Give me a horse and a weapon, and I will fight for you, and you may have an archer at my back to strike me dead if I make a false step, and a halter about my neck ready for the nearest tree after the Powysmen are hammered, if Elis does not prove to you the truth of every word I say.'

He was shaking with fervour, strung taut like a bowstring. Herbard opened his eyes wide at such open passion, and studied him in wary surprise a long moment. 'So be it!' he said then abruptly, and turned to his men. 'See to it! Give him a horse and a sword, and a rope about his neck, and have your best shot follow him close and be ready to spit him if he plays false. He says he is a man of his word, that even this defaulting fellow of his is such. Very well, we'll take him at his word.'

He looked back from the doorway. Eliud had taken up Elis's red cloak and was holding it in his arms. 'If your cousin had been half the man you are,' said Herbard, 'your life would be safe enough.'

Eliud whirled, hugging the folded cloak to him as if applying balm to an unendurable ache. 'Have you not understood even yet? He is *better* than I, a thousand times better!'

Chapter Twelve

I n Tregeiriog, too, they were up with the first blush of light, barely two hours after Elis's flight through the wicket at Shrewsbury. For Hugh Beringar had ridden through half the night, and arrived with the dove-grey hush of pre-dawn. Sleepy grooms rose, blear-eyed, to take the horses of their English guests, a company of twenty men. The rest Hugh had left distributed across the north of the shire, well armed, well supplied, and so far proof against the few and tentative tests to which they had been subjected.

Brother Cadfael, as sensitive to nocturnal arrivals as Elis, had started out of sleep when he caught the quiver and murmur on the air. There was much to be said for the custom of sleeping in the full habit, apart from the scapular, a man could rise and go, barefoot or staying to reclaim his sandals, as complete and armed as in the middle of the day. No doubt the discipline had originated where monastic houses were located in permanently perilous places, and time had given it the blessing of tradition. Cadfael was out, and halfway to the stables, when he met Hugh coming thence in the pearly twilight, and Tudur equally wide awake and alert beside his guest.

'What brings you so early?' asked Cadfael. 'Is there fresh news?'

'Fresh to me, but for all I know stale already in Shrewsbury.' Hugh took him by the arm, and turned him back with them towards the hall. 'I must make my report to the prince, and then we're off down the border by the shortest way. Madog's castellan from Caus is pouring more men into the Minsterley valley. There was a messenger waiting for me when we rode into Oswestry or I'd meant to stay the night there.'

'Herbard sent the word from Shrewsbury?' asked Cadfael. 'It was no more than a handful of raiders when I left, two days ago.'

'It's a war-party of a hundred or more now. They hadn't moved beyond Minsterley when Herbard got wind of the muster, but if they've brought out such a force as that, they mean worse mischief. And you know them better than I – they waste no time. They may be on the move this very dawn.'

'You'll be needing fresh horses,' said Tudor practically.

'We got some remounts at Oswestry, they'll be fit for the rest of the way. But I'll gladly borrow from you for the rest, and thank you heartily. I've left all quiet and every garrison on the alert across the north, and Ranulf seems to have pulled back his advance parties towards Wrexham. He made a feint at Whitchurch and got a bloody nose, and it's my belief he's drawn in his horns for this while. Whether or no, I must break off to attend to Madog.'

'You may make your mind easy about Chirk,'

Tudur assured him. 'We'll see to that. Have your men in for a meal, at least, and give the horses a breather. I'll get the womenfolk out of their beds to see to the feeding of you, and have Einon rouse Owain, if he's not already up.'

'What do you intend?' Cadfael asked. 'Which way shall you head?'

'For Llansilin and down the border. We'll pass to east of the Breiddens, and down by Westbury to Minsterley, and cut them off, if we can, from getting back to their base in Caus. I tire of having men of Powys in that castle,' said Hugh, setting his jaw. 'We must have it back and make it habitable, and keep a garrison there.'

'You'll be few for such a muster as you report,' said Cadfael. 'Why not aim at getting to Shrewsbury first for more men, and westward to meet them from there?'

'The time's too short. And besides, I credit Alan Herbard with sense and stomach enough to field a good force of his own to mind the town. If we move fast enough we may take them between the two prongs and crack them like a nut.'

They had reached the hall. Word had gone before, the sleepers within were rolling out of the rushes in haste, servants were setting tables, and the maids ran with new loaves from the bakery, and great pitchers of ale.

'If I can finish my business here,' said Cadfael tempted, 'I'll ride with you, if you'll have me.'

'I will so and heartily welcome.'

'Then I'd best be seeing to what's left undone here, when Owain Gwynedd is free. While you're closeted with him, I'll see my own horse readied for the journey.'

He was so preoccupied with thoughts of the coming clash, and of what might already be happening in Shrewsbury, that he turned back towards the stables without at first noticing the light footsteps that came flying after him from the direction of the kitchens, until a hand clutched at his sleeve, and he turned to find Cristina confronting him and peering intently up into his face with dilated dark eyes.

'Brother Cadfael, is it true, what my father says? He says I need fret no longer, for Elis has found some girl in Shrewsbury, and wants nothing better now than to be rid of me. He says it can be ended with goodwill on both sides. That I'm free, and Eliud is free! Is it true?' She was grave, and yet she glowed. Elis's desertion was hope and help to her. The tangled knot could indeed be undone by consent, without grudges.

'It is true,' said Cadfael. 'But beware of building too high on his prospects as yet, for it's no way certain he'll get the lady he wants. Did Tudur also tell you it is she who accuses Elis of being her father's murderer? No very hopeful way to set up a marriage.'

'But he's in earnest? He loves the girl? Then he'll not turn back on me, whether he wins his way with her or no. He never wanted me. Oh, I would have done well enough for him,' she said, hoisting eloquent shoulders and curling a tolerant lip, 'as any girl his match in age and rank would have done, but all I ever was to him was a child he grew up with, and was fond of after a fashion. Now,' she said feelingly, 'he knows what it is to want.

209

God knows I wish him his happiness as I hope for mine.'

'Walk with me down to the stables,' said Cadfael, 'and keep me company, these few minutes we have. For I'm away with Hugh Beringar as soon as his men have broken their fast and rested their horses, and I've had a word again with Owain Gwynedd and Einon ab Ithel. Come, and tell me plainly how things stand between you and Eliud, for once before when I saw you together I misread you utterly.'

She went with him gladly, her face clear and pure in the pearly light just flushing into rose. Her voice was tranquil as she said: 'I loved Eliud from before I knew what love was. All I knew was how much it hurt, that I could not endure to be away from him, that I followed and would be with him, and he would not see me, would not speak with me, put me roughly from his side as often as I clung. I was already promised to Elis, and Elis was more than half Eliud's world, and not for anything would he have touched or coveted anything that belonged to his foster-brother. I was too young then to know that the measure of his rejection of me was the measure of how much he wanted me. But when I came to understand what it was that tortured me, then I knew that Eliud went daily in the selfsame pain.'

'You are quite sure of him,' said Cadfael, stating, not doubting.

'I am sure. From the time I understood, I have tried to make him acknowledge what I know and he knows to be truth. The more I pursue and plead, the more he turns away and will not speak

210

or listen. But ever the more he wants me. I tell you truth, when Elis went away, and was made prisoner, I began to believe I had almost won Eliud, almost brought him to admit to love and join with me to break this threatened marriage, and speak for me himself. Then he was sent to be surety for this unhappy exchange and all went for nothing. And now it's Elis who cuts the knot and frees us all.'

'Too early yet to speak of being free,' warned Cadfael seriously. 'Neither of those two is yet out of the wood — none of us is, until the matter of the sheriff's death is brought to a just end.'

'I can wait,' said Cristina.

Pointless, thought Cadfael, to attempt to cast any doubt over this new radiance of hers. She had lived in shadow far too long to be intimidated. What was a murder unsolved to her? He doubted if guilt or innocence would make any difference. She had but one aim, nothing would deflect her from it. No question but from childhood she had read her playfellows rightly, known the one who contained the gnawing grief of loving her and knowing her to be pledged to the foster-brother he loved only a little less. Perhaps no less at all, until he grew into the pain of manhood. Girl children are always years older than their brothers at the same age in years, and see more accurately and jealously.

'Since you are going back,' said Cristina, viewing the activity in the stables with a kindling eye, 'you will see him again. Tell him I am my own woman now, or soon shall be, and can give myself where I will. And I will give myself to no one but him.'

'I will tell him so,' said Cadfael.

211

The yard was alive with men and horses, harness and gear slung on every staple and trestle down the line of stalls. The morning light rose clear and pale over the timber buildings, and the greens of the valley forest were stippled with the pallor of new leaf-buds like delicate green veils among the darkness of fir. There was a small wind, enough to refresh without troubling. A good day for riding.

'Which of these horses is yours?' she asked.

Cadfael led him forth to be seen, and surrendered him to the groom who came at once to serve.

'And that great raw-boned grey beast? I never saw him before. He should go well, even under a man in armour.'

'That is Hugh Beringar's favourite,' said Cadfael, recognising the dapple with pleasure. 'And a very ill-conditioned brute towards any other rider. Hugh must have left him resting in Oswestry, or he would not be riding him now.'

'I see they're saddling up for Einon ab Ithel, too,' she said. 'I fancy he'll be going back to Chirk, to keep an eye on your Beringar's northern border while he's busy elsewhere.'

A groom had come out across their path with a draping of harness on one arm and a saddle-cloth over the other, and tossed them over a rail while he went back to lead out the horse that would wear them. A very handsome beast, a tall, bright bay that Cadfael remembered seeing in the great court at Shrewsbury. He watched its lively gait with pleasure as the groom hoisted the saddle-cloth and flung it over the broad, glossy

212

back, so taken with the horse that he barely noticed the quality of its gear. Fringes to the soft leather bridle; and a tooled brow-band with tiny studs of gold. There was gold on Einon's land, he recalled. And the saddle-cloth itself …

He fixed and stared, motionless, for an instant holding his breath. A thick, soft fabric of dyed woollens, woven from heavy yarns in a pattern of twining, blossomy sprays, muted red roses, surely faded to that gentle shade, and deep blue irises. Through the centre of the flowers and round the border ran thick, crusted gold threads. It was not new, it had seen considerable wear, the wool had rubbed into tight balls here and there, some threads had frayed, leaving short, fine strands quivering.

No need even to bring out for comparison the little box in which he kept his captured threads. Now that he saw these tints at last he knew them past any doubt. He was looking at the very thing he had sought, too well known here, too often seen and too little regarded, to stir any man's memory.

He knew, moreover, instantly and infallibly, the meaning of what he saw.

He said never a word to Cristina of what he knew, as they walked back together. What could he say? Better by far keep all to himself until he could see his way ahead, and knew what he must do. Not one word to any, except to Owain Gwynedd, when he took his leave.

'My lord,' he said then, 'I have heard it reported

213

of you that you have said, concerning the death of Gilbert Prestcote, that the only ransom for a murdered man is the life of the murderer. Is that truly reported? Must there be another death? Welsh law allows for the paying of a blood-price, to prevent the prolonged bloodshed of a feud. I do not believe you have forsaken Welsh for Norman law.'

'Gilbert Prestcote did not live by Welsh law,' said Owain, eyeing him very keenly. 'I cannot ask him to die by it. Of what value is a payment in goods or cattle to his widow and children?'

'Yet I think *galanas* can be paid in other mintage,' said Cadfael. 'In penitence, grief and shame, as high as the highest price judge ever set. What then?'

'I am not a priest,' said Owain, 'nor any man's confessor. Penance and absolution are not within my writ. Justice is.'

'And mercy also,' said Cadfael.

'God forbid I should order any death wantonly. Deaths atoned for, whether by goods or grief, pilgrimage or prison, are better far than deaths prolonged and multiplied. I would keep alive all such as have value to this world and to those who rub shoulders with them here in this world. Beyond that it is God's business.' The prince leaned forward, and the morning light through the embrasure shone on his flaxen head. 'Brother,' he said gently, 'had you not something we should have looked at again this morning by a better light? Last night we spoke of it.'

'That is of small importance now,' said Brother Cadfael, 'if you will consent to leave it in my hands

214

some brief while. There shall be account rendered.'

'I will well!' said Owain Gwynedd, and suddenly smiled, and the small chamber was filled with the charm of his presence. 'Only, for my sake – and others, doubtless? – carry it carefully.'

Chapter Thirteen

Elis had more sense than to go rushing straight to the enclosure of the Benedictine sisters, all blown and mired as he was from his run, and with the dawn only just breaking. So few miles from Shrewsbury here, and yet so lonely and exposed! Why, he had wondered furiously as he ran, why had those women chosen to plant their little chapel and garden in so perilous a place? It was provocation! The abbess at Polesworth should be brought to realise her error and withdraw her threatened sisters. This present danger could be endlessly repeated, so near so turbulent a border.

He made rather for the mill on the brook, upstream, where he had been held prisoner, under guard by a muscular giant named John, during those few February days. He viewed the brook with dismay, it was so fallen and tamed, for all its gnarled and stony bed, no longer the flood he remembered. But if they came they would expect to wade across merrily where the bed opened out into a smooth passage, and would scarcely wet them above the knee. Those stretches, at least, could be pitted and sown with spikes or caltrops. And the wooded banks at least still offered good cover for archers.

John Miller, sharpening stakes in the mill-yard, dropped his hatchet and reached for his pitch-fork when the hasty, stumbling feet thudded on the boards. He whirled with astonishing speed and readiness for a big man, and gaped to see his sometime prisoner advancing upon him empty-handed and purposeful, and to be greeted in loud, demanding English by one who had professed total ignorance of that language only a few weeks previously.

'The Welsh of Powys — a war-party not two hours away! Do the women know of it? We could still get them away towards the town — they're surely mustering there, but *late* ...'

'Easy, easy!' said the miller, letting his weapon fall, and scooping up his pile of murderous, pointed poles. 'You've found your tongue in a hurry, seemingly! And whose side may you be on this time, and who let you loose? Here, carry these, if you're come to make yourself useful.'

'The women must be got away,' persisted Elis feverishly. 'It's not too late, if they go at once ... Get me leave to speak to them, surely they'll listen. If *they* were safe, we could stand off even a war-band. I came to warn them ...'

'Ah, but they know. We've kept good watch since the last time. And the women won't budge, so you may spare your breath to make one man more, and welcome,' said the miller, 'if you're so minded. Mother Mariana holds it would be want of faith to shift an ell, and Sister Magdalen reckons she can be more use where she is, and most of the folks hereabouts would say that's no more than truth. Come on, let's get these planted – the ford's pitted already.'

Elis found himself running beside the big man, his arms full. The smoothest stretch of the brook flanked the chapel wall of the grange, and he realised as he fed out stakes at the miller's command that there was a certain amount of activity among the bushes and coppice-woods on both sides of the water. The men of the forest were well aware of the threat, and had made their own preparations, and by her previous showing, Sister Magdalen must also be making ready for battle. To have Mother Mariana's faith in divine protection is good, but even better if backed by the practical assistance heaven has a right to expect from sensible mortals. But a war-party of a hundred or more – and with one ignominious rout to avenge! Did they understand what they were facing?

'I need a weapon,' said Elis, standing aloft on the bank with feet solidly spread and black head reared towards the north-west, from which the menace must come. 'I can use sword, lance, bow, whatever's to spare ... That hatchet of yours, on a long haft ...' He had another chance weapon of his own, he had just realised it. If only he could get wind in time, and be the first to face them when they came, he had a loud Welsh tongue where they would be looking only for terrified English, he had the fluency of bardic stock, all the barbs of surprise, vituperation and scarifying mockery, to loose in a flood against the cowardly paladins who came preying on holy women. A

218

tongue like a whip-lash! Better still drunk, perhaps, to reach the true heights of scalding invective, but even in this state of desperate sobriety, it might still serve to unnerve and delay.

Elis waded into the water, and selected a place for one of his stakes, hidden among the water-weed with its point sharply inclined to impale anyone crossing in unwary haste. By the careful way John Miller was moving, the ford had been pitted well out in midstream. If the attackers were horsed, a step astray into one of those holes might at once lame the horse and toss the rider forward on to the pales. If they came afoot, at least some might fall foul of the pits, and bring down their fellows with them, in a tangle very vulnerable to archery.

The miller, knee-deep in midstream, stood to look on critically as Elis drove in his murderous stake, and bedded it firmly through the tenacious mattress of weed into the soil under the bank. 'Good lad!' he said with mild approval. 'We'll find you a pikel, or the foresters may have an axe to spare among them. You shan't go weaponless if your will's good.'

Sister Magdalen, like the rest of the household, had been up since dawn, marshalling all the linens, scissors, knives, lotions, ointments and stunning draughts that might be needed within a matter of hours, and speculating how many beds could be made available with decorum and where, if any of the men of her forest army should be too gravely hurt to be moved. Magdalen had given serious thought to sending away the two young

219

postulants eastward to Beistan, but decided against it, convinced in the end that they were safer where they were. The attack might never come. If it did, at least here there was readiness, and enough stout-hearted forest folk to put up a good defence. But if the raiders moved instead towards Shrewsbury, and encountered a force they could not match, then they would double back and scatter to make their way home, and two girls hurrying through the woods eastward might fall foul of them at any moment on the way. No, better hold together here. In any case, one look at Melicent's roused and indignant face had given her due warning that that one, at any rate, would not go even if she was ordered.

'I am not afraid,' said Melicent disdainfully.

'The more fool you,' said Sister Magdalen simply. 'Unless you're lying, of course. Which of us doesn't, once challenged with being afraid! Yet it's generations of being afraid, with good reason, that have caused us to think out these defences.'

She had already made all her dispositions within. She climbed the wooden steps into the tiny bell-turret and looked out over the exposed length of the brook and the rising bank beyond, thickly lined with bushes, and climbing into a slope once coppiced but now run to neglected growth. Countrymen who have to labour all the hours of daylight to get their living cannot, in addition, keep up a day-and-night vigil for long. Let them come today, if they're coming at all, thought Sister Magdalen, now that we're at the peak of resolution and readiness, can do no more, and can only grow stale if we must wait too long.

From the opposite bank she drew in her gaze to the brook itself, the deep-cut and rocky bed smoothing out under her walls to the broad stretch of the ford. And there John Miller was just wading warily ashore, the water turgid after his passage and someone else, a young fellow with a thatch of black curls, was bending over the last stake, vigorous arms and shoulders driving it home, low under the bank and screened by reeds. When he straightened up and showed a flushed face, she knew him.

She descended to the chapel very thoughtfully. Melicent was busy putting away, in a coffer clamped to the wall and strongly banded, the few valuable ornaments of the altar and the house. At least it should be made as difficult as possible to pillage this modest church.

'You have not looked out to see how the men progress?' said Sister Magdalen mildly. 'It seems we have one ally more than we knew. There's a young Welshman of your acquaintance and mine hard at work out there with John Miller. A change of allegiance for him, but by the look of him he relishes this cause more than when he came the last time.'

Melicent turned to stare, her eyes very wide and solemn. '*He?*' she said, in a voice brittle and low. 'He was prisoner in the castle. How can he be here?'

'Plainly he has slipped his collar. And been through a bog or two on his way here,' said Sister Magdalen placidly, 'by the state of his boots and hose, and I fancy fallen in at least one by his dirty face.'

'But why make this way? If he broke loose ... what is he doing here?' demanded Melicent feverishly.

'By all the signs he's making ready to do battle with his own countrymen. And since I doubt if he remembers me warmly enough to break out of prison in order to fight for me,' said Sister Magdalen with a small, reminiscent smile, 'I take it he's concerned with *your* safety. But you may ask him by leaning over the fence.'

'No!' said Melicent in sharp recoil, and closed down the lid of the coffer with a clash. 'I have nothing to say to him.' And she folded her arms and hugged herself tightly as if cold, as if some traitor part of her might break away and scuttle furtively into the garden.

'Then if you'll give me leave,' said Sister Magdalen serenely, 'I think I have.' And out she went, between newly-dug beds and first salad sowings in the enclosed garden, to mount the stone block that made her tall enough to look over the fence. And suddenly there was Elis ap Cynan almost nose to nose with her, stretching up to peer anxiously within. Soiled and strung and desperately in earnest, he looked so young that she, who had never borne children, felt herself grandmotherly rather than merely maternal. The boy recoiled, startled, and blinked as he recognised her. He flushed beneath the greenish smear the marsh had left across his cheek and brow, and reached a pleading hand to the crest of the fence between them.

'Sister, is she – is Melicent within there?'

'She is, safe and well,' said Sister Magdalen,

'and with God's help and yours, and the help of all the other stout souls busy on our account like you, safe she'll remain. How you got here I won't enquire, boy, but whether let out or broken out you're very welcome.'

'I wish to God,' said Elis fervently, 'that she was back in Shrewsbury this minute.'

'So do I, but better here than astray in between. And besides, she won't go.'

'Does she know,' he asked humbly, 'that I am here?'

'She does, and what you're about, too.'

'Would she not – could you not persuade her? – to speak to me?'

'That she refuses to do. But she may think the more,' said Sister Magdalen encouragingly. 'If I were you, I'd let her alone to think the while. She knows you're here to fight for us – there's matter for thought there. Now you'd best go to ground soon and keep in cover. Go and sharpen whatever blade they've found for you and keep yourself whole. These flurries never take long,' she said, resigned and tolerant, 'but what comes after lasts a lifetime, yours and hers. You take care of Elis ap Cynan, and I'll take care of Melicent.'

Hugh and his twenty men had skirted the Breidden hills before the hour of Prime, and left those great, hunched outcrops on the right as they drove on towards Westbury. A few remounts they got there, not enough to relieve all the tired beasts. Hugh had held back to a bearable pace for that very reason, and allowed a halt to give men and horses time to breathe. It was the first opportunity there had been even to speak a word, and now that it came no man had much to say. Not until the business on which they rode was tackled and done would tongues move freely again. Even Hugh, lying flat on his back for ease beside Cadfael under the budding trees, did not question him concerning his business in Wales.

'I'll ride with you, if I can finish my business here,' Cadfael had said. Hugh had asked him nothing then, and did not ask him now. Perhaps because his mind was wholly engrossed in what had to be done to drive the Welsh of Powys back into Caus and beyond. Perhaps because he considered this other matter to be very much Cadfael's business, and was willing to wait for enlightenment until it was offered, as at the right time it would be.

Cadfael braced his aching back against the bole of an oak just forming its tight leaf-buds, eased his chafed feet in his boots, and felt his sixty-one years. He felt all the older because all these troubled creatures pulled here and there through this tangle of love and guilt and anguish were so young and vulnerable. All but the victim, Gilbert Prestcote, dead in his helpless weakness – for whom Hugh would, because he must, take vengeance. There could be no clemency, there was no room for it. Hugh's lord had been done to death, and Hugh would exact payment. In iron duty, he had no choice.

'Up!' said Hugh, standing over him, smiling the abstracted but affectionate smile that flashed like a reflection from the surface of his mind when his entire concern was elsewhere. 'Get your eyes open! We're off again.' and he reached a hand to grip Cadfael's wrist and hoist him to his feet, so smoothly and carefully that Cadfael was minded to take offence. He was not so old as all that, nor so stiff! But he forgot his mild grievance when Hugh said: 'A shepherd from Pontesbury brought word. They're up from their night camp and making ready to move.'

Cadfael was wide awake instantly. 'What will you do?'

'Hit the road between them and Shrewsbury and turn them back. Alan will be up and alert, we may meet him along the way.'

'Dare they attempt the town?' wondered Cadfael, astonished.

'Who knows? They're blown up with success, and I'm thought to be far off. And our man says they've avoided Minsterley but brought men round it by night. It seems they may mean a foray into the suburbs, at least, even if they draw off after. Town pickings would please them. But we'll be faster, we'll make for Hanwood or thereabouts and be between.'

Hugh made a gentle joke of hoisting Cadfael into the saddle, but for all that, Cadfael set the pace for the next mile, ruffled at being humoured and considered like an old man. Sixty-one was not old, only perhaps a little past a man's prime. He had, after all, done a great deal of hard riding these last few days, he had a right to be stiff and sore.

They came over a hillock into view of the Shrewsbury road, and beheld, thin and languid in the air above the distant trees beyond, a faint

225

column of smoke rising. 'From their douted fires,' said Hugh, reining in to gaze. 'And I smell older burning than that. Somewhere near the rim of the forest, someone's barns have gone up in flames.'

'More than a day old and the smoke gone,' said Cadfael, sniffing the air. 'Better make straight for them, while we know where they are, for there's no telling which way they'll strike next.'

Hugh led his party down to the road and across it, where they could deploy in the fringes of woodland, going fast but quietly in thick turf. For a while they kept within view of the road, but saw no sign of the Welsh raiders. It began to seem that their present thrust was not aimed at the town after all, or even the suburbs, and Hugh led his force deeper into the woodland, striking straight at the deserted night camp. Beyond that trampled spot there were traces enough for eyes accustomed to reading the bushes and grass. A considerable number of men had passed through here on foot, and not so long ago, with a few ponies among them to leave droppings and brush off budding twigs from the tender branches. The ashen, blackened ruin of a cottage and its clustering sheds showed where their last victim had lost home, living and all, if not his life, and there was blood dried into the soil where a pig had been slaughtered. They spurred fast along the trail the Welsh had left, sure now where they were bound, for the way led deeper into the northern uplands of the Long Forest, and it could not be two miles now to the cell at Godric's Ford.

That ignominious rout at the hands of Sister Magdalen and her rustic army had indeed rankled. The men of Caus were not averse to driving off a few cattle and burning a farm or two by the way, but what they wanted above all, what they had come out to get, was revenge.

Hugh set spurs to his horse and began to thread the open woodland at a gallop, and after him his company spurred in haste. They had gone perhaps a mile more when they heard before them, distant and elusive, a voice raised high and bellowing defiance.

It was almost the hour of High Mass when Alan Herbard got his muster moving out of the castle wards. He was hampered by having no clear lead as to which way the raiders planned to move, and there was small gain in careering aimlessly about the western border hunting for them. For want of knowledge he had to stake on his reasoning. When the company rode out of the town they aimed towards Pontesbury itself, prepared to swerve either northward, to cut across between the raiders and Shrewsbury, or south-west towards Godric's Ford, according as they got word on the way from scouts sent out before daylight. And this first mile they took at speed, until a breathless countryman started out of the bushes to arrest their passage, when they were scarcely past the hamlet of Beistan.

'My lord, they've turned away from the road. From Pontesbury they're making eastward into the forest towards the high commons. They've turned their backs on the town for other game. Bear south at the fork.'

'How many?' demanded Herbard, already wheeling his horse in haste.

'A hundred at least. They're holding all together, no rogue stragglers left loose behind. They expect a fight.'

'They shall have one!' promised Herbard and led his men south down the track, at a gallop wherever the going was fairly open.

Eliud rode among the foremost, and found even that pace too slow. He had in full all the marks of suspicion and shame he had invited, the rope to hang him coiled about his neck for all to see, the archer to shoot him down if he attempted escape close at his back, but also he had a borrowed sword at his hip, a horse under him and was on the move. He fretted and burned, even in the chill of the March morning. Here Elis had at least the advantage of having ridden these paths and penetrated these woodlands once before. Eliud had never been south of Shrewsbury, and though the speed they were making seemed to his anxious heart miserably inadequate, he could gain nothing by breaking away, for he did not know exactly where Godric's Ford lay. The archer who followed him, however good a shot he might be, was no very great horseman, it might be possible to put on speed, make a dash for it and elude him, but what good would it do? Whatever time he saved he would inevitably waste by losing himself in these woods. He had no choice but to let them bring him there, or at least near enough to the place to judge his direction by ear or eye. There would be signs. He strained for any betraying sound as he rode, but there was nothing but the swaying and cracking of brushed branches, and the thudding rumble of their hooves in the deep turf, and now and again the call of a bird, undisturbed by this rough invasion, and startlingly clear.

The distance could not be far now. They were threading rolling uplands of heath, to drop lower again into thick woodland and moist glades. All this way Elis must have run afoot in the night hours, splashing through these hollows of stagnant green and breasting the sudden rises of heather and scrub and outcrop rock.

Herbard checked abruptly in open heath, waving them all to stillness. 'Listen! Ahead on our right – men on the move.'

They sat straining their ears and holding their breath. Only the softest and most continuous whisper of sounds, compounded of the swishing and brushing of twigs, the rustle of last autumn's leaves under many feet, the snap of a dead stick, the brief and soft exchange of voices, a startled bird rising from underfoot in shrill alarm and indignation. Signs enough of a large body of men moving through woods almost stealthily, without noise or haste.

'Across the brook and very near the ford,' said Herbard sharply. And he shook his bridle, spurred and was away, his men hard on his heels. Before them a narrow ride opened between well-grown trees, a long vista with a glimpse of low timber buildings, weathered dark brown, distant at the end of it, and a sudden lacework of daylight beyond, between the trees, where the channel of the brook crossed.

They were halfway down the ride when the boiling murmur of excited men breaking out of

229

cover eddied up from the invisible waterside, and then, soaring loudly above, a single voice shouting defiance, and even more strangely, an instant's absolute hush after the sound.

The challenge had meant nothing to Herbard. It meant everything to Eliud. For the words were Welsh, and the voice was the voice of Elis, high and imperious, honed sharp by desperation, bidding his fellow-countrymen: 'Stand and turn! For shame on your fathers, to come whetting your teeth on holy women! Go back where you came from and find a fight that does you some credit!' And higher and more peremptorily: 'The first man ashore I spit on this pikel, Welsh or no, he's no kinsman of mine!'

This to a war-band roused and happy and geared for killing!

'Elis!' cried Eliud in a great howl of anger and dismay, and he lay forward over his horse's neck and drove in his heels, shaking the bridle wild. He heard the archer at his back shout an order to halt, heard and felt the quivering thrum of the shaft as it skimmed his right shoulder, tore away a shred of cloth, and buried itself vibrating in the turf beyond. He paid no heed, but plunged madly ahead, down the steep green ride and out on to the bank of the brook.

They had come by way of the thicker cover a little downstream, to come at the grange and the ford before they were detected, and leave aimless and out of range any defenders who might be stationed at the mill, where there was a better field for archery. The little footbridge had not yet been repaired, but with a stream so fallen from its winter spate there was no need of a bridge. From stone to stone the water could be leaped in two or three places, but the attackers favoured the ford, because so many could cross there shoulder to shoulder and bring a battering-ram of lances in one sweep to drive along the near bank. The forest bowmen lay in reeds and bushes, dispersed along the brink, but such a spearhead, with men and weight enough behind it, could cleave through and past them and be into the precinct within moments.

They were deceived if they thought the forest men had not detected their approach, but there was no sign of movement as the attackers threaded their way quietly between the trees to mass and sweep across the brook. Perhaps twenty cottars, woodsmen and hewers of laborious assarts from the forest lay in cover against more than a hundred Welsh, and every man of the twenty braced himself, and knew only too well how great a threat he faced. They knew how to keep still until the proper moment to move. But as the lurkers in the trees signalled along their half-seen ranks and closed all together in a sudden surge into the open at the edge of the ford, one man rose out of the bushes opposite and bestrode the grassy shelf of the shore, brandishing a long, two-tined pikel lashed to a six-foot pole, and sweeping the ford with it at breast-height.

That was enough to give them an instant's pause out of sheer surprise. But what stopped them mid-stride and set them back on their heels was the indignant Welsh trumpet blaring: 'Stand and turn! For shame on your fathers, to come whetting your teeth on holy women!'

He had not done, there was more, rolling off the inspired tongue in dread of a pause, or in such flight as to be unable to pause. 'Cowards of Powys, afraid to come north and meddle with men! They'll sing you in Gwynedd for this noble venture, how you jumped a brook and showed yourselves heroes against women older than your mothers, and a world more honest. Even your drabs of dams will disown you for this. You and your mongrel pedigrees shall be known for ever by the songs we'll make ...'

They had begun to stir out of their astonishmnent, to scowl and to grin. And still the hidden bowmen in the bushes held their hands, willing to wait the event, though their shafts were fitted and their bows partly drawn, ready to brace and loose. If by some miracle this peril might dissolve in withdrawal and conciliation, why lose arrows or blunt blades?

'*You*, is it?' shouted a Welshman scornfully. 'Cynan's pup, that we left spewing water and being pumped dry by the nuns. He, to halt us! A lickspit of the English now!'

'A match for you and better!' flashed Elis, and swung the pikel towards the voice. 'And with grace enough to let the sisters here alone, and to be grateful to them, too, for a life they could as well have let go down the stream, for all they owed me. What are you looking for here? What plunder is there, here among the willing poor? And for God's sake and your Welsh fathers' sake, what glory?'

He had done all he could, perhaps provided a few minutes of time, but he could do little more, and it was not enough. He knew it. He even saw the archer in the fringe of the trees opposite fit his shaft without haste, and draw very steadily and deliberately. He saw it out of the corner of his eye, while he continued to confront the lances levelled against him, but there was nothing he could do to deflect or elude, he was forced to stand and hold them as long as he could, shifting neither foot nor eye.

Behind him there was a rush of hooves, stamping deep into the turf, and someone flung himself sobbing out of the saddle in one vaulting bound, and along the shelf of grass above the water, just as the forest bowmen drew and loosed their first shafts, every man for himself, and the archer on the opposite shore completed his easy draw, and loosed full at Elis's breast. Welsh of Powys striking coldly at Welsh of Gwynedd. Eliud vented a scream of anger and defiance, and hurled himself between, embracing Elis breast to breast and covering him with his own body, sending them both reeling a pace backwards into the turf, to crash against a corner of the sisters' garden fence. The pikel with its long handle was jerked out of Elis's hand, and slashed into the stream in a great fan of water. The Welshman's arrow jutted from under Eliud's right shoulder-blade, transfixing his body and piercing through the under-flesh of Elis's upper arm, pinning the two together inseparably. They slid down the fence and lay in the grass locked in each other's arms, and their blood mingled and made one, closer even than fostering.

And then the Welsh were over and ashore, floundering in the pits of the ford, ripped on the stakes among the reeds, trampling the two fallen bodies, and battle was joined along the banks of the brook.

Almost at the same moment, Alan Herbard deployed his men along the eastern bank and waded into the fighting, and Hugh Beringar swept through the trees on the western bank, and drove the Welsh outposts into the churned and muddied ford.

The clang of hammer on anvil, with themselves cracked between, demoralised the Welsh of Powys, and the battle of Godric's Ford did not last long. The din and fury was out of proportion to the damage done, when once they had leisure to assess it. The Welsh were ashore when their enemies struck from both sides, and had to fight viciously and hard to get out of the trap and melt away man by man into cover, like the small forest predators whose kinship with the earth and close understanding of it they shared. Beringar, once he had shattered the rear of the raiders, herded them like sheep but held his hand from unnecessary killing as soon as they fled into cover and made for home. Alan Herbard, younger and less experienced, gritted his teeth and thrust in with all his weight, absolute to make a success of his first command, and perhaps did more execution than was heedful out of pure anxiety.

However it was, within half an hour it was over.

What Brother Cadfael most keenly remem-

bered, out of all that clash, was the apparition of a
tall girl surging out of the fenced enclosure of the
grange, her black habit kilted in both hands, the
wimple torn from her head and her fair hair
streaming silvery in sudden, sunlight, a long,
fighting scream of defiance trailing like a
bannerole from her drawn-back lips, as she
evaded a greedy Welsh hand grasping at her, and
flung herself on her knees beside the trampled,
bruised, bleeding bodies of Elis and Eliud, still
clamped in each other's arms against the bloodied
fence.

Chapter Fourteen

I t was done, they were gone, vanishing very rapidly and quietly, leaving only the rustling of bushes behind them on the near side of the brook, to make for some distant place where they could cross unseen and unpursued. On the further side, where the bulk of their numbers fled, the din of their flight subsided gradually into the depths of the neglected coppices, seeking thicker cover into which they could scatter and be lost. Hugh was in no haste, he let them salvage their wounded and hustle them away with them, several among them who might, indeed, be dead. There would be cuts and grazes and wounds enough among the defenders, by all means let the Welsh tend their own and bury their own. But he deployed his men, and a dozen or so of Herbard's party, like beaters after game, to herd the Welshmen back methodically into their own country. He had no wish to start a determined blood-feud with Madog ap Meredith, provided this lesson was duly learned.

The defenders of the grange came out of hiding, and the nuns out of their chapel, all a little dazed, as much by the sudden hush as by the violence that had gone before. Those who had escaped hurt dropped their bows and forks and axes, and turned to help those who were wounded. And Brother Cadfael turned his back on the muddy ford and the bloodied stakes, and knelt beside Melicent in the grass.

'I was in the bell-turret,' she said in a dry whisper. 'I saw how splendid ... He for us and his friend for him. They will live, they *must* live, both ... we can't lose them. Tell me what I must do.'

She had done well already, no tears, no shaking, no outcry after that first scream that had carried her through the ranks of the Welsh like the passage of a lance. She had slid an arm carefully under Elis's shoulders to raise him, and prevent the weight of the two of them from falling on the head of the arrow that had pinned them together. That spared them at least the worst agony and aggravated damage of being impaled. And she had wrapped the linen of her wimple round the shaft beneath Elis's arm to stem the bleeding as best she could.

'The iron is clean through,' she said. 'I can raise them more, if you can reach the shaft.'

Sister Magdalen was at Cadfael's shoulder by then, as sturdy and practical as ever, but having taken a shrewd look at Melicent's intent and resolute face she left the girl the place she had chosen, and went off placidly to salve others. Folly to disturb either Melicent or the two young men she nursed on her arm and her braced knee, when shifting them would only be worse pain. She went, instead, to fetch a small saw and the keenest

237

knife to be found, and linen enough to stem the first bursts of bleeding when the shaft should be withdrawn. It was Melicent who cradled Elis and Eliud as Cadfael felt his way about the head of the shaft, sawed deeply into the wood, and then braced both hands to snap off the head with the least movement. He brought it out, barely dinted from its passage through flesh and bone, and dropped it aside in the grass.

'Lay them down now – so! Let them lie a moment.' The solid slope, cushioned by turf, received the weight gently as Melicent lowered her burden. 'That was well done,' said Cadfael. She had bunched the blood-stained wimple and held it under the wound as she drew aside, freeing a cramped and aching arm. 'Now do you rest, too. The one of these is shorn through the flesh of his arm, and has let blood enough, but his body is sound, and his life safe. The other – no blinking it, his case is grave.'

'I know it,' she said, staring down at the tangled embrace that bound the pair of them fast. 'He made his body a shield,' she said softly, marvelling. 'So much he loved him!'

And so much *she* loved him, Cadfael thought, that she had blazed forth out of shelter in much the same way, shrieking defiance and rage. To the defence of her father's murderer? Or had she long since discarded that belief, no matter how heavily circumstances might tell against him? Or had she simply forgotten everything else, when she heard Elis yelling his solitary challenge? Everything but his invited peril and her anguish for him?

No need for her to have to see and hear the worst moment of all. 'Go fetch my scrip from the saddle yonder,' said Cadfael, 'and bring more cloth, padding and wrapping both, we shall need plenty.'

She was gone long enough for him to lay firm hold on the impaling shaft, rid now of its head, and draw it fast and forcefully out from the wound, with a steadying hand spread against Eliud's back. Even so it fetched a sharp, whining moan of agony, that subsided mercifully as the shaft came free. The spurt of blood that followed soon flowed; the wound was neat, a mere slit, and healthy flesh closes freely over narrow lesions, but there was no certainty what damage had been done within. Cadfael lifted Eliud's body carefully aside, to let both breathe more freely, though the entwined arms relinquished their hold very reluctantly. He enlarged the slit the arrow had made in the boy's clothing, wadded a clean cloth against the wound, and turned him gently on his back. By that time Melicent was back with all that he had asked; a wild, soiled figure with a blanched and resolute face. There was blood drying on her hands and wrists, the skirts of her habit at the knee were stiffening into a hard, dark crust, and her wimple lay on the grass, a stained ball of red. It hardly mattered. She was never going to wear that or any other in earnest.

'Now, we'd best get these two indoors, where I can strip and cleanse their injuries properly,' said Cadfael, when he was assured the worst of the bleeding was checked. 'Go and ask Sister Magdalen where we may lay them, while I find

239

some stout men to help me carry them in.'

Sister Magdalen had made provision for more than one cell to be emptied within the grange, and Mother Mariana and the nuns of the house were ready to fetch and carry, heat water and bandage minor injuries with very good will, relieved now of the fear of outrage. They carried Elis and Eliud within and lodged them in neighbouring cells, for the space was too small to allow free movement to Cadfael and those helping him, if both cots were placed together. All the more since John Miller, who had escaped without a scratch from the mêlée, was one of the party. The gentle giant could not only heft sturdy young men as lightly as babies, he also had a deft and reassuring hand with injuries.

Between the two of them they stripped Eliud, slitting the clothes from him to avoid racking him with worse pain, washed and dressed the wounds in back and breast, and laid him in the cot with his right arm padded and cradled to lie still. He had been trampled in the rush of the Welshmen crossing to shore, bruises were blackening on him, but he had no other wound, and it seemed the tramping feet had broken no bones. The arrowhead had emerged well to the right, through his shoulder, to pierce the flesh of Elis's upper arm. Cadfael considered the line the shot had taken, and shook his head doubtfully but not quite hopelessly over the chances of life and death. With this one he would stay, sit with him the evening through – the night if need be – wait the return of sense and wit. There were things

240

they had to say to each other, whether the boy was to live or die.

Elis was another matter. He would live, his arm would heal, his honour would be vindicated, his name cleared, and for all Cadfael could see, there was no reason in the world why he should not get his Melicent. No father to deny him, no overlord at liberty to assert his rights in the girl's marriage, and Lady Prestcote would be no bar at all. And if Melicent had flown to his side before ever the shadow was lifted from him, how much more joyfully would she accept him when he emerged sunlit from head to foot. Happy innocent, with nothing left to trouble him but a painful arm, some weakness from loss of blood, a wrenched knee that gave him pain at an incautious movement, and a broken rib from being trampled. Troubles that might keep him from riding for some time, but small grievances indeed, now he had opened dazed dark eyes on the unexpected vision of a pale, bright face stooped close to his, and heard a remembered voice, one hard and cold as ice, saying very softly and tenderly: 'Elis … Hush, lie still! I'm here, I won't leave you.'

It was another hour and more before Eliud opened his eyes, unfocussed and feverish, glittering greenly in the light of the lamp beside his bed, for the cell was very dim. Even then he roused to such distress that Cadfael eased him out of it again with a draught of poppy syrup, and watched the drawn lines of pain gradually smooth out from the thin, intense face, and the large

241

eyelids close again over the distracted gleam. No point in adding further trouble to one so troubled in body and soul. When he revived so far as to draw the garment of his own dignity about him, then his time would come.

Others came in to look down at him for a moment, and as quietly depart. Sister Magdalen came to bring Cadfael food and ale, and stood a while in silence watching the shallow, painful heave and fall of Eliud's breast, and the pinched flutter of his nostrils on whistling breath. All her volunteer army of defenders had dispersed about its own family business, every hurt tended, the stakes uprooted from the ford, the pitted bed raked smooth again, a day's work very well done. If she was tired, she gave no sign of it. Tomorrow there would be a number of the injured to visit again, but there had been few serious hurts, and no deaths. Not yet! Not unless this boy slipped through their fingers.

Hugh came back towards evening, and sought out Cadfael in the silent cell. 'I'm off back to the town now,' he said in Cadfael's ear. 'We've shepherded them more than halfway home, you'll see no more of them here. You'll be staying?'

Cadfael nodded towards the bed.

'Yes – a great pity! I'll leave you a couple of men, send by them for whatever you need. And after this,' said Hugh grimly, 'we'll have them out of Caus. They shall know whether there's still a sheriff in the shire.' He turned to the bedside and stood looking down sombrely at the sleeper. 'I saw what he did. Yes, a pity ...' Eliud's soiled and dismembered clothing had been removed; he

242

retained nothing but the body in which he had been born into the world, and the means by which he had demanded to be ushered out of it, if Elis proved false to his word. The rope was coiled and hung over the bracket that held the lamp. 'What is this?' asked Hugh, as his eye lit upon it, and as quickly understood. 'Ah! Alan told me. This I'll take away, let him read it for a sign. This will never be needed. When he wakes, tell him so.'

'I pray God!' said Cadfael, so low that not even Hugh heard.

And Melicent came, from the cell where Elis lay sore with trampling, but filled and overfilled with unexpected bliss. She came at his wish, but most willingly, saw Cadfael to all appearances drowsing on his stool against the wall, signed Eliud's oblivious body solemnly with the cross, and stooped suddenly to kiss his furrowed forehead and hollow cheek before stealing silently away to her own chosen vigil.

Brother Cadfael opened one considerate eye to watch her draw the door to softly after her, and could not take great comfort. But with all his heart he hoped and prayed that God was watching with him.

In the pallid first light before dawn Eliud stirred and quivered, and his eyelids began to flutter stressfully as though he laboured hard to open them and confront the day, but had not yet the strength. Cadfael drew his stool close, leaning to wipe the seamed brow and working lips, and having an eye to the ewer he had ready to hand

243

for when the tormented body needed it. But that was not the unease that quickened Eliud now, rousing out of his night's respite. His eyes opened wide, staring into the wooden roof of the cell and beyond, and shortened their range only when Cadfael leaned down to him braced to speak, seeing desperate intelligence in the hazel stare, and having something ripe within him that must inevitably be said.

He never needed to say it. It was taken out of his mouth.

'I have got my death,' said the thread of a voice that issued from Eliud's dry lips, 'get me a priest. I have sinned – I must deliver all those who suffer doubt ...'

Not his own deliverance, not that first, only the deliverance of all who laboured under the same suspicion.

Cadfael stooped closer. The gold-green eyes were straining too far, they had not recognised him. They did so now and lingered, wondering. 'You are the brother who came to Tregeiriog. Welsh?' Something like a sorrowful smile mellowed the desperation of his face. 'I do remember. It was you brought word of him ... Brother, I have my death in my mouth, whether he take me now of this grief or leave me for worse ... A debt ... I pledged it ...' He essayed, briefly, to raise his right hand, being strongly right-handed, and gave up the attempt with a whining intake of breath at the pain it cost him and shifted, pitiless, to the left, feeling at his neck where the coiled rope should have been. Cadfael laid a hand to the lifted wrist, and eased it back into the covers of the bed.

244

'Hush, lie still! I am here to command, there's no haste. Rest, take thought, ask of me what you will, bid me whatever you will. I'm here, I shan't leave you.'

He was believed. The slight body under the brychans seemed to sink and slacken in one great sigh. There was a small silence. The hazel eyes hung upon him with a great weight of trust and sorrow, but without fear. Cadfael offered a drop of wine laced with honey, but the braced head turned aside. 'I want confession,' said Eliud faintly but clearly, 'of my mortal sin. Hear me!'

'I am no priest,' said Cadfael. 'Wait, he shall be brought to you.'

'I cannot wait. Do I know my time? If I live,' he said simply, 'I will tell it again and again – as long as there's need – I am done with all conceal.'

They had neither of them observed the door of the cell slowly opening, it was done so softly and shyly, by one troubled with dawn voices, but as hesitant to disturb those who might wish to be private as unwilling to neglect those who might be in need. In her own as yet unreasoned and unquestioned happiness Melicent moved as one led by angelic inspiration, exalted and humbled, requiring to serve. Her bloodied habit was shed, she had a plain woollen gown on her. She hung in the half-open doorway, afraid to advance or withdraw, frozen into stillness and silence because the voice from the bed was so urgent and uncomforted.

'I have killed,' said Eliud clearly. 'God knows I am sorry! I had ridden with him, cared for him, watched him founder and urged his rest ... And if

245

ever he came home alive, then Elis was free … to go back to Cristina, to marry …' A great shudder went through him from head to foot, and fetched a moan of pain out of him. 'Cristina … I loved her always … from when we were children, but I did not, I did not speak of it, never, never … She was promised to him before ever I knew her, in her cradle. How could I touch, how could I covet what was his?'

'She also loved,' said Cadfael, nursing him along the way. 'She let you know of it …'

'I would not hear, I dared not, I had no right … And all the while she was so dear, I could not bear it. And when they came back without Elis, and we thought him lost … Oh, God, can you conceive such trouble as was mine, half-praying for his safe return, half wishing him dead, for all I loved him, so that at last I might speak out without dishonour, and ask for my love … And then – you know it, it was you brought word … and I was sent here, my mouth stopped just when it was so full of words … And all that way I thought, I could not stop thinking, the old man is so sick, so frail, if he dies there'll be none to exchange for Elis … If he dies I can return and Elis must stay … Even a little time and I could still speak … All I needed was a little time, now I was resolved. And that last day when he foundered … I did all I could, I kept him man alive, and all the time, all the time it was clamouring in me, let him die! I did not do it, we brought him still living …'

He lay still for a minute to draw breath, and Cadfael wiped the corners of the lips that laboured against exhaustion to heave the worst

246

burden from heart and conscience. 'Rest a little. You try yourself too hard.'

'No, let me end it. Elis … I loved him, but I loved Cristina more. And he would have wed her, and been content, but she … He did not know the burning we knew. He knows it now. I never willed it … it was not planned, what I did. All I did was to remember the lord Einon's cloak and I went, just as I was, to fetch it. I had his saddle-cloth on my arm –' He closed his eyes against what he remembered all too clearly, and tears welled out from under the bruised lids and ran down on either cheek. 'He was so still, hardly breathing at all – so like death. And in an hour Elis would have been on his way home and I left behind in his place. So short a step to go! I did the thing I wish to God I had cut off my hands rather than do, I held the saddle-cloth over his face. There has not been a waking moment since when I have not wished it undone,' whispered Eliud, 'but to undo is not so easy as to do. As soon as I understood my own evil I snatched my hands away, but he was gone. And I was cowardly afraid and left the cloak lying, for if I'd taken it, it would have been known I'd been there. And that was the quiet hour and no one saw me, going or coming.'

Again he waited, gathering strength with a terrible, earnest patience to continue to the end. 'And all for nothing – for nothing! I made myself a murderer for nothing. For Elis came and told me how he loved the lord Gilbert's daughter and willed to be released from his bond with Cristina, as bitterly as she willed it, and I also. And he would go to make himself known to her father …

247

I tried to stop him ... I needed someone to go there and find my dead man, and cry it aloud, but not Elis, oh, not Elis! But he would go. And even then they still thought the lord Gilbert alive, only sleeping. So I had to fetch the cloak, if no one else would cry him dead – but not alone ... a witness, to make the discovery. I still thought Elis would be held and I should go home. He longed to stay and I to go ... This knot some devil tied,' sighed Eliud, 'and only I have deserved it. All they three suffer because of me. And you, brother, I did foully by you ...'

'In choosing me to be your witness?' said Cadfael gently. 'And you had to knock over the stool to make me look closely enough, even then. Your devil still had you by the hand, for if you had chosen another there might never have been the cry of murder that kept you both prisoners.'

'It was my angel, then, no devil. For I am glad to be rid of all lies and known for what I am. I would never have let it fall on Elis – nor on any other man. But I am human and fearful,' he said inflexibly, 'and I hoped to go free. Now that is solved. One way or another, I shall give a life for a life. I would not have let Elis bear it ... Tell her so!'

There was no need, she already knew. But the head of the cot was towards the door, and Eliud had seen nothing but the rough vault of the cell, and Cadfael's stooping face. The lamp had not wavered, and did not waver now, as Melicent withdrew from the threshold very softly and carefully, drawing the door to by inches after her.

'They have taken away my halter,' said Eliud,

248

his eyes wandering languidly over the bare little room. 'They'll have to find me another one now.'

When it was all told he lay drained, very weak and utterly biddable, eased of hope and grateful for contrition. He let himself be handled for healing, though with a drear smile that said Cadfael wasted his pains on a dead man. He did his best to help the handling, and bore pain without a murmur when his wounds were probed and cleansed and dressed afresh. He tried to swallow the draughts that were held to his lips, and offered thanks for even the smallest service. When he drifted into an uneasy sleep, Cadfael went to find the two men Hugh had left to run his errands, and sent one of them riding to Shrewsbury with the news that would bring Hugh back again in haste. When he returned into the precinct, Melicent was waiting for him in the doorway. She read in his face the mixture of dismay and resignation he felt at having to tell over again what had been ordeal enough to listen to in the first place, and offered instant and firm reassurance.

'I know. I heard. I heard you talking, and his voice … I thought you might need someone to fetch and carry for you, so I came to ask, I heard what Eliud said. What is to be done now?' For all her calm, she was bewildered and lost between father killed and lover saved, and the knowledge of the fierce affection those two foster-brothers had for each other, and every way was damage and every escape was barred. 'I have told Elis,' she said. 'Better we should all know what we are

249

about. God knows I am so confused now, I doubt if I know right from wrong. Will you come to Elis? He's fretting for Eliud.'

Cadfael went with her in perplexity as great as hers. Murder is murder, but if a life can pay the debt for a life, there was Elis to level the account. Was yet another life demanded? Another death justifiable? He sat down with her beside the bed, confronted by an Elis wide awake and in full possession of his senses, for all he hesitated on the near edge of fever.

'Melicent has told me,' said Elis, clutching agitatedly at Cadfael's sleeve. '*But is it true*? You don't know him as I do! Are you sure he is not making up this story, because he fears I may yet be charged? May he not even believe I did it? It would be like him to shoulder all to cover me. So he has done in old times when we were children, so he might even now. You saw, you saw what he has already done for me! Should I be here alive now but for Eliud? I can't believe so easily ...'

Cadfael went about hushing him the most practical way, by examining the dressing on his arm and finding it dry, unstained and causing him no pain, let well alone for the time being. The tight binding round his damaged rib had caused him some discomfort and shortness of breath, and might be slightly slackened to ease him. And whatever dose was offered him he swallowed almost absently, his eyes never shifting from Cadfael's face, demanding answers to desperate questions. And there would be small comfort for him in the naked truth.

'Son,' said Cadfael, 'there's no virtue in fending

250

off truth. The tale Eliud has told fits in every particular and it is truth. Sorry I am to say it, but true it is. Put all doubts out of your head.'

They received that with the same white calm and made no further protest. After a long silence Melicent said: 'I think you knew it before.'

'I did know it, from the moment I set eyes on Einon ab Ithel's brocaded saddle-cloth. That, and nothing else, could have killed Gilbert, and it was Eliud whose duty it was to care for Einon's horse and harness. Yes, I knew. But he made his confession willingly, eagerly, before I could question or accuse him. That must count to him for virtue, and speak on his side.'

'God knows,' said Melicent, shutting her pale face hard between her hands, as if to hold her wits together, 'on what side I dare speak, who am so torn. All I know is that Eliud cannot, does not carry all the guilt. In this matter, which of us is innocent?'

'*You* are!' said Elis fiercely. 'How did you fail? But if I had taken a little thought to see how things were with him and with Cristina ... I was too easy, too light, too much in love with myself to take heed. I'd never dreamed of such a love, I didn't know ... I had all to learn.' It had been no easy lesson for him, but he had it by heart now.

'If only I had had more faith in myself and my father,' said Melicent, 'we could have sent word honestly into Wales, to Owain Gwynedd and to my father, that we two loved and entreated leave to marry ...'

'If only I had been as quick to see what ailed Eliud as he always was to put trouble away from me ...'

'If none of us ever fell short, or put a foot astray,' said Cadfael sadly, 'everything would be good in this great world, but we stumble and fall, every one. We must deal with what we have. He did it, and all we must share the gall.'

Out of a drear hush Elis asked: 'What will become of him? Will there be mercy? Surely he need not die?'

'It rests with the law, and with the law I have no weight.'

'Melicent relented to me,' said Elis, 'before ever she knew I was clean of her father's blood ...'

'Ah, but I did know!' she said quickly. 'I was sick in mind that ever I doubted.'

'And I love her the more for it. And Eliud has made confession when no man was accusing, and that must count for virtue to him, as you said, and speak on his side.'

'That and all else that speaks for him,' promised Cadfael fervently, 'shall be urged in his defence, I will see to that.'

'But you are not hopeful,' said Elis bleakly, watching his face with eyes all too sharp.

He would have liked to deny it, but to what end, when Eliud himself had accepted and embraced, with resignation and humility, the inevitable death? Cadfael made what comfort he could, short of lying, and left them together. The last glimpse, as he closed the door, was of two braced, wary faces following his going with a steady, veiled stare, their minds shuttered and secret. Only the fierce alliance of hand clasping hand on the brychan betrayed them.

*

Hugh Beringar came next day in a hurry, listened in dour silence as Eliud laboured with desolate patience through the story yet again, as he had already done for the old priest who said Mass for the sisters. As Eliud's soul faced humbly toward withdrawal from the world, Cadfael noted his misused body began to heal and find ease, very slowly, but past any doubt. His mind consented to dying, his body resolved to live. The wounds were clean, his excellent youth and health fought hard, whether for or against him who could say?

'Well, I am listening,' said Hugh somewhat wearily, pacing the bank of the brook with Cadfael at his side. 'Say what you have to say.' But Cadfael had never seen his face grimmer.

'He made full and free confession,' said Cadfael, 'before ever a finger was pointed at him, as soon as he felt he might die. He was in desperate haste to do justice to all, not merely Elis, who might lie under the shadow of suspicion because of him. You know me, I know you. I have said honestly, I was about to tell him that I knew he had killed. I swear to you he took that word clean out of my mouth. He wanted confession, penance, absolution. Most of all he wanted to lift the threat from Elis and any other who might be overcast.'

'I take your word absolutely,' said Hugh, 'and it is something. But enough? This was no hot-blood squall blown up in a moment before he could think, it was an old man, wounded and sick, sleeping in his bed.'

'It was not planned. He went to reclaim his lord's cloak. That I am sure is true. But if you

253

think the blood was cold, dear God, how wrong you are! The boy was half-mad with the long bleeding of hopeless love, and had just come to the point of rebellion, and the thread of a life – one he had been nursing in duty! – cut him off from the respite his sudden courage needed. God forgive him, he had hoped Gilbert would die! He has said so honestly. Chance showed him a thread so thin it could be severed by a breath, and before ever he took thought, he blew! He says he has repented of it every moment that has passed since that moment, and I believe it. Did you never, Hugh, do one unworthy thing on impulse, that grieved and shamed you ever after?'

'Not to the length of killing an old man in his bed,' said Hugh mercilessly.

'No! Nor nothing to match it,' said Cadfael with a deep sigh and briefer smile. 'Pardon me, Hugh! I am Welsh and you are English. We Welsh recognise degrees. Theft, theft absolute, without excuse, is our most mortal offence, and therefore we hedge it about with degrees, things which are not theft absolute – taking openly by force, taking in ignorance, taking without leave, providing the offender owns to it, and taking to stay alive, where a beggar has starved three days – no man hangs in Wales for these. Even in dying, even in killing, we acknowledge degrees. We make a distinction between homicide and murder, and even the worst may sometimes be compounded for a lesser price than hanging.'

'So might I make distinctions,' said Hugh, brooding over the placid ford. 'But this was my lord, into whose boots I step, for want of my king

254

to give orders. He was no close friend of mine, but he was fair to me always, he had an ear to listen, if I was none too happy with some of his more austere judgments. He was an honourable man and did his duty by this shire of mine as he best knew, and his death fetters me.'

Cadfael was silent and respectful. It was a discipline removed now from his, but once there had been such a tie, such a fealty, and he remembered it, and they were none so far apart.

'God forbid,' said Hugh, 'that I should hurl out of the world any but such as are too vile to be let live in it. And this is no such monster. One mortal error, one single vileness, and a creature barely – what's his age? Twenty-one? And driven hard, but which of us is not? He shall have his trial and I shall do what I must,' said Hugh hardly. 'But I would to God it was taken out of my hands!'

Chapter Fifteen

Before he left that evening he made his will clear for the others. 'Owain may be pressed, if Chester moves again, he wants his men. I have sent to say that all who are clear now shall leave here the day after tomorrow. I have six good men-at-arms belonging to him in Shrewsbury. They are free, and I shall equip them for their journey home. The day after tomorrow as early as may be, around dawn, they will be here to take Elis ap Cynan with them, back to Tregeiriog.'

'Impossible,' said Cadfael flatly. 'He cannot yet ride. He has a twisted knee and a cracked rib, besides the arm wound, though that progresses well. He will not ride in comfort for three or four weeks. He will not ride hard or into combat for longer.'

'He need not,' said Hugh shortly. 'You forget we have horses borrowed from Tudur ap Rhys, rested and ready for work now, and Elis can as well ride in a litter as could Gilbert in far worse condition. I want all the men of Gwynedd safely out of here before I move against Powys, as I mean to. Let's have one trouble finished and put by before we face another.'

So that was settled and no appeal. Cadfael had expected the order to be received with consternation by Elis, both on Eliud's account and his own, but after a brief outcry of dismay, suddenly checked, there was a longer pause for thought, while Elis put the matter of his own departure aside, not without a hard, considering look, and turned only to confirm that there was no chance of Eliud escaping trial for murder and very little of any sentence but death being passed upon him. It was a hard thing to accept, but in the end it seemed Elis had no choice but to accept it. A strange, embattled calm had taken possession of the lovers, they had a way of looking at each other as though they shared thoughts that needed no words to be communicated, but were exchanged in a silent code no one else could read. Unless, perhaps, Sister Magdalen understood the language. She herself went about in thoughtful silence and with a shrewd eye upon them both.

'So I am to be fetched away early, the day after tomorrow,' said Elis. He cast one brief glance at Melicent and she at him. 'Well, I can and will send in proper form from Gwynedd, it's as well the thing should be done openly and honestly when I pay my suit to Melicent. And there will be things to set right at Tregeiriog before I shall be free.' He did not speak of Cristina, but the thought of her was there, desolate and oppressive in the room with them. To win her battle, only to see the victory turn to ash and drift through her fingers. 'I'm a sound sleeper,' said Elis with a sombre smile, 'they may have to roll me in my blankets

257

and carry me out snoring, if they come too early.'
And he ended with abrupt gravity: 'Will you ask
Hugh Beringar if I may have my bed moved into
the cell with Eliud these last two nights? It is not a
great thing to ask of him.'

'I will,' said Cadfael, after a brief pause to get
the drift of that, for it made sense more ways than
one. And he went at once to proffer the request.
Hugh was already preparing to mount and ride
back to the town, and Sister Magdalen was in the
yard to see him go. No doubt she had been
deploying for him, in her own way, all the
arguments for mercy which Cadfael had already
used, and perhaps others of which he had not
thought. Doubtful if there would be any harvest
even from her well-planted seed, but if you never
sow you will certainly never reap.

'Let them be together by all means,' said Hugh,
shrugging morosely, 'if it can give them any
comfort. As soon as the other one is fit to be
moved I'll take him off your hands, but until then
let him rest. Who knows, that Welsh arrow may
yet do the solving for us, if God's kind to him.'

Sister Magdalen stood looking after him until
the last of the escort had vanished up the forested
ride.

'At least,' she said then, 'it gives him no
pleasure. A pity to proceed where nobody's the
gainer and every man suffers.'

'A great pity! He said himself,' reported
Cadfael, equally thoughtfully, 'he wished to God
it could be taken out of his hands.' And he looked
along his shoulder at Sister Magdalen, and found
her looking just as guilelessly at him. He suffered

a small, astonished illusion that they were even beginning to resemble each other, and to exchange glances in silence as eloquently as did Elis and Melicent.

'Did he so?' said Sister Magdalen in innocent sympathy. 'That might be worth praying for, I'll have a word said in chapel at every office tomorrow. If you ask for nothing, you deserve nothing.'

They went in together, and so strong was this sense of an agreed understanding between them, though one that had better not be acknowledged in words, that he went so far as to ask her advice on a point which was troubling him. In the turmoil of the fighting and the stress of tending the wounded he had had no chance to deliver the message with which Cristina had entrusted him, and after Eliud's confession he was divided in mind as to whether it would be a kindness to do so now, or the most cruel blow he could strike.

'This girl of his in Tregeiriog – the one for whom he was driving himself mad – she charged me with a message to him and I promised her he should be told. But now, with this hanging over him ... Is it well to give him everything to live for, and when there may be no life for him? Should we make the world, if he's to leave it, a thousand times more desirable? What sort of kindness would that be?'

He told her, word for word, what the message was. She pondered, but not long.

'Small choice if you promised the girl. And truth should never be feared as harm. But besides – from all I see, he is willing himself to die, though his body is determined on life, and without every spur he may win the fight over his body, turn his face to the wall, and slip away. As well, perhaps, if the only other way is the gallows. But if – I say *if* – the times relent and let him live, then pity not to give him every armour and every weapon to survive to hear the good news.' She turned her head and looked at him again with the deep, calculating glance he had observed before, and then she smiled. 'It is worth a wager,' she said.

'I begin to think so, too,' said Cadfael and went in to see the wager laid.

They had not yet moved Elis and his cot into the neighbouring cell; Eliud still lay alone. Sometimes, marking the path the arrow had taken clean through his right shoulder, but a little low, Cadfael doubted if he would ever draw bow again, even if at some future time he could handle a sword. That was the least of his threatened harms now. Let him be offered as counterbalance the greatest promised good.

Cadfael sat down beside the bed, and told how Elis had asked leave to join him and been granted what he asked. That brought a strange, forlorn brightness to Eliud's thin, vulnerable face. Cadfael refrained from saying a word about Elis's imminent departure, however, and wondered briefly why he kept silent on that matter, only to realise hurriedly that it was better not even to wonder, much less question. Innocence is an infinitely fragile thing and thought can sometimes injure, even destroy it.

'And there is also a word I promised to bring

you and have had no quiet occasion until now. From Cristina when I left Tregeiriog.' Her name caused all the lines of Eliud's face to contract into a tight, wary pallor, and his eyes to dilate in sudden bright green like stormy sunlight through June leaves. 'Cristina sends to tell you, by me, that she has spoken with her father and with yours and soon, by consent, she will be her own woman to give herself where she will. And she will give herself to none but you.'

An abrupt and blinding flood drowned the green and sent the sunlight sparkling in sudden fountains, and Eliud's good left hand groped lamely after anything human he might hold by for comfort, closed hungrily on the hand Cadfael offered, and drew it down against his quivering face, and lower into the bed, against his frantically beating heart. Cadfael let him alone thus for some moments, until the storm passed. When the boy was still again, he withdrew his hand gently.

'But she does not know,' whispered Eliud wretchedly, 'what I am ... what I have done ...'

'What she knows of you is all she needs to know, that she loves you as you love her, and there is not nor ever could be any other. I do not believe that guilt or innocence, good or evil can change Cristina towards you. Child, by the common expectation of man you have some thirty years at least of your life to live, which is room for marriage, children, fame, atonement, sainthood. What is done matters, but what is yet to do matters far more. Cristina has that truth in her. When she does know all, she will be grieved, but she will not be changed.'

261

'My expectation,' said Eliud faintly through the covers that hid his ravaged face, 'is in weeks, months at most, not thirty years.'

'It is God fixes the term,' said Cadfael, 'not men, not kings, not judges. A man must be prepared to face life, as well as death, there's no escape from either. Who knows the length of the penance, or the magnitude of the reparation, that may be required of you?'

He rose from his place then, because John Miller and a couple of other neighbours, nursing the small scars of the late battle, carried in Elis, cot and all, from the next cell and set him down beside Eliud's couch. It was a good time to break off, the boy had the spark of the future already alive in him, however strongly resignation prompted him to quench it, and now this reunion with the other half of his being came very aptly, Cadfael stood by to see them settled and watch John Miller strip down the covers from Eliud and lift and replace him bodily, as lightly as an infant and as deftly as if handled by a mother. John had been closeted with Elis and Melicent, and was grown fond of Elis as of a bold and promising small boy from among his kin. A useful man, with his huge and balanced strength, able to pick up a sick man from his sleep – provided he cared enough for the man! – and carry him hence without disturbing his rest. And devoted to Sister Magdalen, whose writ ran here firm as any king's.

Yes, a useful ally.

Well ...

The next day passed in a kind of deliberate hush,

as if every man and every woman walked delicately, with bated breath, and kept the ritual of the house with particular awe and reverence warding off all mischance. Never had the horarium of the order been more scrupulously observed at Godric's Ford. Mother Mariana, small, wizened and old, presided over a sisterhood of such model devotion as to disarm fate. And her enforced guests in their twin cots in one cell were quiet and private together, and even Melicent, now a lay guest of the house and no postulant, went about the business of the day with a pure, still face, and left the two young men to their own measures.

Brother Cadfael observed the offices, made some fervent prayers of his own, and went out to help Sister Magdalen tend the few injuries still in need of supervision among the neighbours.

'You're worn out,' said Sister Magdalen solicitously, when they returned for a late bite of supper and Compline. 'Tomorrow you should sleep until Prime, you've had no real rest for three nights now. Say your farewell to Elis tonight, for they'll be here at first light in the morning. And now I think of it,' she said, 'I could do with another flask of that syrup you brew from poppies, for I've emptied my bottle, and I have one patient to see tomorrow who gets little sleep from pain. Will you refill the flask if I bring it?'

'Willingly,' said Cadfael, and went to fetch the jar he had had sent from Brother Oswin in Shrewsbury after the battle. She brought a large green glass flask, and he filled it to the brim without comment.

Nor did he rise early in the morning, though he was awake in good time; he was as good at interpreting a nudge in the ribs as the next man. He heard the horsemen when they came, and the voice of the portress and other voices, Welsh and English both, and among them, surely, the voice of John Miller. But he did not rise and go out to speed them on their way.

When he came forth for Prime, the travellers, he reckoned, must be two hours gone on their way into Wales, armed with Hugh's safe-conduct to cover the near end of the journey, well mounted and provided. The portress had conducted them to the cell where their charge, Elis ap Cynan, would be found in the nearer bed, and John Miller had carried him out in his arms, warmly swathed, and bestowed him in the litter sent to bear him home. Mother Mariana herself had risen to witness and bless their going.

After Prime Cadfael went to tend his remaining patient. As well to continue just as in the previous days. Two clear hours should be ample start, and someone had to be the first to go in – no, not the first, for certainly Melicent was there before him, but the first of the others, the potential enemy, the uninitiated.

He opened the door of the cell, and halted just within the threshold. In the dim light two roused, pale faces confronted him, almost cheek to cheek. Melicent sat on the edge of the bed, supporting the occupant in her arms, for he had raised himself to sit upright, with a cloak draped round his naked shoulders, to meet this moment erect. The bandage swathing his cracked rib heaved to a

264

quickened and apprehensive heartbeat, and the eyes that fixed steadily upon Cadfael were not greenish hazel, but almost as dark as the tangle of black curls.

'Will you let the lord Beringar know,' said Elis ap Cynan, 'that I have sent away my foster-brother out of his hands, and am here to answer for all that may be held against him. He put his neck in a noose for me, so do I now for him. Whatever the law wills can be done to me in his place.'

It was said. He drew a deep breath, and winced at the stab it cost him, but the sharp expectancy of his face eased and warmed now the first step was taken, and there was no more need of any concealment.

'I am sorry I had to deceive Mother Mariana,' he said. 'Say I entreat her forgiveness, but there was no other way in fairness to all here. I would not have any other blamed for what I have done.' And he added with sudden impulsive simplicity: 'I'm glad it was you who came. Send to the town quickly, I shall be glad to have this over. And Eliud will be safe now.'

'I'll do your errand,' said Cadfael gravely, 'both your errands. And ask no questions.' Not even whether Eliud had been in the plot, for he already knew the answer. From all those who had found it necessary to turn a blind eye and a deaf ear, Eliud stood apart in his despairing innocence and lamentable guilt. Someone among those bearers of his on the road to Wales might have a frantically distressed invalid on his hands when the long, deep sleep drew to a close. But at the end of the enforced flight, whatever measures Owain Gwynedd took in the matter, there was Cristina waiting.

'I have provided as well as I could,' said Elis earnestly. 'They'll send word ahead, she'll come to meet him. It will be a hard enough furrow, but it will be life.'

A deal of growing up seemed to have been done since Elis ap Cynan first came raiding to Godric's Ford. This was not the boy who had avenged his nervous fears in captivity by tossing Welsh insults at his captors with an innocent face, nor the girl who had cherished dreamy notions of taking the veil before ever she knew what marriage or vocation meant.

'The affair seems to have been well managed,' said Cadfael judicially. 'Very well, I'll go and make it known – here and in Shrewsbury.'

He had the door half-closed behind him when Elis called: 'And then will you come and help me do on my clothes? I would like to meet Hugh Beringar decent and on my feet.'

And that was what he did, when Hugh came in the afternoon, grim-faced and black-browed, to probe the loss of his felon. In Mother Mariana's tiny parlour, dark-timbered and bare, Elis and Melicent stood side by side to face him. Cadfael had got the boy into his hose and shirt and coat, and Melicent had combed out the tangles from his hair, since he could not do it himself without pain. Sister Magdalen, after one measuring glance as he took his first unsteady steps, had provided him a staff to reinforce his treacherous knee, which would not go fairly under him as yet, but threatened to double all ways to let him fall. When he was ready he looked very young, neat and solemn, and understandably afraid. He stood twisted a little sideways, favouring the knitting rib that shortened his breath. Melicent kept a hand ready, close to his arm, but held off from touching.

'I have sent Eliud back to Wales in my place,' said Elis, stiff as much with apprehension as with resolve, 'since I owe him a life. But here am I, at your will and disposal, to do with as you see fit. Whatever you hold due to him, visit upon me.'

'For God's sake sit down,' said Hugh shortly and disconcertingly. 'I object to being made the target of your self-inflicted suffering. If you're offering me your neck, that's enough. I have no need of your present pains. Sit and take ease. I am not interested in heroes.'

Elis flushed, winced and sat obediently, but he did not take his eyes from Hugh's grim countenance.

'Who helped you?' demanded Hugh with chilling quietness.

'No one. I alone made this plan. Owain's men did as they were ordered by me.' That could be said boldly, they were well away in their own country.

'*We* made the plan,' said Melicent firmly.

Hugh ignored her, or seemed to. 'Who helped you?' he repeated forcibly.

'No one. Melicent knew, but she took no part. The sole blame is mine. Deal with me!'

'So alone you moved your cousin into the other bed. That was marvel enough, for a man crippled

267

himself and unable to walk, let alone lift another man's weight. And as I hear, a certain miller of these parts carried Eliud ap Griffith to the litter.'

'It was dark within, and barely light without,' said Elis steadily, 'and I ...'

'*We*,' said Melicent.

' ... I had already wrapped Eliud well, there was little of him to see. John did nothing but lend his strong arms in kindness to me.'

'Was Eliud party to this exchange?'

'*No!*' they said together, loudly and fiercely.

'No! repeated Elis, his voice shaking with the fervour of his denial. 'He knew nothing. I gave him in his last drink a great draught of the poppy syrup that Brother Cadfael used on us to dull the pain, that first day. It brings on deep sleep. Eliud slept through all. He never knew! He never would have consented.'

'And how did you, bed-held as you were, come by that syrup?'

'*I* stole the flask from Sister Magdalen,' said Melicent. 'Ask her! She will tell you what a great dose has been taken from it.' So she would, with all gravity and concern. Hugh never doubted it, nor did he mean to put her to the necessity of answering. Nor Cadfael either. Both had considerately absented themselves from this trial, judge and culprits held the whole matter in their hands.

There was a brief, heavy silence that weighed distressfully on Elis, while Hugh eyed the pair of them from under knitted brows, and fastened at last with frowning attention upon Melicent.

'You of all people,' he said, 'had the greatest right to require payment from Eliud. Have you so

268

soon forgiven him? Then who else dare gainsay?'

'I am not even sure,' said Melicent slowly, 'that I know what forgiveness is. Only it seems a sad waste that all a man's good should not be able to outweigh one evil, however great. That is the world's loss. And I wanted no more deaths. One was grief enough, the second would not heal it.'

Another silence, longer than the first. Elis burned and shivered, wanting to hear his penalty, whatever it might be, and know the best and the worst. He quaked when Hugh rose abruptly from his seat.

'Elis ap Cynan, I have no charge to make in law against you. I want no exaction from you. You had best rest here a while yet. Your horse is still in the abbey stables. When you are fit to ride, you may follow your foster-brother home.' And before they had breath to speak, he was out of the room, and the door closing after him.

Brother Cadfael walked a short way beside his friend when Hugh rode back to Shrewsbury in the early evening. The last days had been mild, and in the long green ride the branches of the trees wore the first green veil of the spring budding. The singing of the birds, likewise, had begun to throb with the yearly excitement and unrest before mating and nesting and rearing the young. A time for all manner of births and beginnings, and for putting death out of mind.

'What else could I have done?' said Hugh. 'This one has done no murder, never owed me that very comely neck he insists on offering me. And if I had hanged him I should have been hanging both, for God alone knows how even so resolute a girl as Melicent – or the one you spoke of in Tregeiriog for that matter – is ever going to part the two halves of that pair. Two lives for one is no fair bargain.' He looked down from the saddle of the raw-boned grey which was his favourite mount, and smiled at Cadfael, and it was the first time for some days that he had been seen to smile utterly without irony or reserve. 'How much did you know?'

'Nothing,' said Cadfael simply. 'I guessed at much, but I can fairly say I knew nothing and never lifted finger.' In silence and deafness and blindness he had connived, but no need to say that, Hugh would know it, Hugh, who could not have connived. Nor was there any need for Hugh ever to say with what secret gratitude he relinquished the judgement he would never have laid down of his own will.

'What will become of them all?' Hugh wondered. 'Elis will go home as soon as he's well enough, I suppose, and send formally to ask for his girl. There's no man of her kin to ask but her own mother's brother, and he's far off with the queen in Kent and out of reach. I fancy Sister Magdalen will advise the girl to go back to her step-mother for the waiting time, and have all done in proper form, and she has sense enough to listen to advice, and the patience to wait for what she wants, now she's assured of getting it in the end. But what of the other pair?'

Eliud and his companions would be well into Wales by this time and need not hurry, to tire the invalid too much. The draught of forgetfulness they had given him might dull his senses for a while even when he awoke, and his fellows would do their best to ease his remorse and grief, and his fear for Elis. But that troubled and passionate spirit would never be quite at rest.

'What will Owain do with him?'

'Neither destroy nor waste him,' said Cadfael, 'provided you cede your rights in him. He'll live, he'll marry his Cristina – there'll be no peace for prince or priest or parent until she gets her way. As for his penance, he has it within him, he'll carry it lifelong. There is nothing but death itself you or any man could lay upon him that he will not lay upon himself. But God willing, he will not have to carry it alone. There is no crime and no failure can drive Cristina from him.'

They parted at the head of the ride. It was premature dusk under the trees, but still the birds sang with the extreme and violent joy that seemed loud enough to shake such fragile instruments into dust or burst the hearts in their breasts. There were windflowers quivering in the grass.

'I go lighter than I came,' said Hugh, reining in for a moment before he took the homeward road.

'As soon as I see that lad walking upright and breathing deep, I shall follow. And glad to be going home.' Cadfael looked back at the low timber roofs of Mother Mariana's grange, where the silvery light through gossamer branches reflected the ceaseless quivering of the brook. 'I hope we have made, between us all, the best of a great ill, and who could do more? Once, I remember, Father Abbot said that our purpose is justice, and with God lies the privilege of mercy. But even God, when he intends mercy, needs tools to his hand.'

271

THE PILGRIM OF HATE

CHAPTER ONE

They were together in Brother Cadfael's hut in the herbarium, in the afternoon of the twenty-fifth day of May, and the talk was of high matters of state, of kings and empresses, and the unbalanced fortunes that plagued the irreconcilable contenders for thrones.

'Well, the lady is not crowned yet!' said Hugh Beringar, almost as firmly as if he saw a way of preventing it.

'She is not even in London yet,' agreed Cadfael, stirring carefully round the pot embedded in the coals of his brazier, to keep the brew from boiling up against the sides and burning. 'She cannot well be crowned until they let her in to Westminster. Which it seems, from all I gather, they are in no hurry to do.'

'Where the sun shines,' said Hugh ruefully, 'there whoever's felt the cold will gather. My cause, old friend, is out of the sun. When Henry of Blois shifts, all men shift with him, like starvelings huddled in one bed. He heaves the coverlet, and they go with him, clinging by the hems.'

'Not all,' objected Cadfael, briefly smiling as he stirred. 'Not you. Do you think you are the only one?'

'God forbid!' said Hugh, and suddenly laughed, shaking off his gloom. He came back from the open doorway, where the pure light spread a soft golden sheen over the bushes and beds of the herb-garden and the moist noon air drew up a heady languor of spiced and drunken odours, and plumped his slender person down again on the bench against the timber wall, spreading his booted feet on the earth floor. A small man in one sense only, and even so trimly made. His modest stature and light weight had deceived many a man to his undoing. The sunshine from without, fretted by the breeze that swayed the bushes, was reflected from one of Cadfael's great glass flagons to illuminate by flashing glimpses a lean, tanned face, clean shaven, with a quirky mouth, and agile black eyebrows that could twist upward sceptically into cropped black hair. A face at once eloquent and inscrutable. Brother Cadfael was one of the few who knew how to read it. Doubtful if even Hugh's wife Aline understood him better. Cadfael was in his sixty-second year, and Hugh still a year or two short of thirty but, meeting thus in easy companionship in Cadfael's workshop among the herbs, they felt themselves contemporaries.

'No,' said Hugh, eyeing circumstances narrowly, and taking some cautious comfort, 'not all. There are a few of us yet, and not so badly placed to hold on to what we have. There's the queen in Kent with her army. Robert of Gloucester is not going to turn his back to come hunting us here while she hangs on the southern fringes of London. And with the Welsh of Gwynedd keeping our backs against the earl of Chester, we can hold this shire for King Stephen and wait out the time. Luck that turned once can turn again. And the empress is not queen of England yet.'

But for all that, thought Cadfael, mutely stirring his brew for Brother Aylwin's scouring calves, it began to look as though she very soon would be. Three years of civil war between cousins fighting for the sovereignty of England had done nothing to reconcile the factions, but much to sicken the general populace with insecurity, rapine and killing. The craftsman in the town, the cottar in the village, the serf on the demesne, would be only too glad of any monarch who could guarantee him a quiet and orderly country in which to carry on his modest business. But to a man like Hugh it was no such indifferent matter. He was King Stephen's liege man, and now King Stephen's sheriff of Shropshire, sworn to hold the shire for his cause. And his king was a prisoner in Bristol castle since the lost battle of Lincoln. A single February day of this year had seen a total reversal of the fortunes of the two claimants to the throne. The Empress Maud was up in the clouds, and Stephen, crowned and anointed though he might be, was down in the midden, close-bound and close-guarded, and his

7

brother Henry of Blois, bishop of Winchester and papal legate, far the most influential of the magnates and hitherto his brother's supporter, had found himself in a dilemma. He could either be a hero, and adhere loudly and firmly to his allegiance, thus incurring the formidable animosity of a lady who was in the ascendant and could be dangerous, or trim his sails and accommodate himself to the reverses of fortune by coming over to her side. Discreetly, of course, and with well-prepared arguments to render his about-face respectable. It was just possible, thought Cadfael, willing to do justice even to bishops, that Henry also had the cause of order and peace genuinely at heart, and was willing to back whichever contender could restore them.

'What frets me,' said Hugh restlessly, 'is that I can get no reliable news. Rumours enough and more than enough, every new one laying the last one dead, but nothing a man can grasp and put his trust in. I shall be main glad when Abbot Radulfus comes home.'

'So will every brother in this house,' agreed Cadfael fervently. 'Barring Jerome, perhaps, he's in high feather when Prior Robert is left in charge, and a fine time he's had of it all these weeks since the abbot was summoned to Winchester. But Robert's rule is less favoured by the rest of us, I can tell you.'

'How long is it he's been away now?' pondered Hugh. 'Seven or eight weeks! The legate's keeping his court well stocked with mitres all this

8

time. Maintaining his own state no doubt gives him some aid in confronting hers. Not a man to let his dignity bow to princes, Henry, and he needs all the weight he can get at his back.'

'He's letting some of his cloth disperse now, however,' said Cadfael. 'By that token, he may have got a kind of settlement. Or he may be deceived into thinking he has. Father Abbot sent word from Reading. In a week he should be here. You'll hardly find a better witness.'

Bishop Henry had taken good care to keep the direction of events in his own hands. Calling all the prelates and mitred abbots to Winchester early in April, and firmly declaring the gathering a legatine council, no mere church assembly, had ensured his supremacy at the subsequent discussions, giving him precedence over Archbishop Theobald of Canterbury, who in purely English church matters was his superior. Just as well, perhaps. Cadfael doubted if Theobald had greatly minded being outflanked. In the circumstances a quiet, timorous man might be only too glad to lurk peaceably in the shadows, and let the legate bear the heat of the sun.

'I know it. Once let me hear his account of what's gone forward, down there in the south, and I can make my own dispositions. We're remote enough here, and the queen, God keep her, has gathered a very fair array, now she has the Flemings who escaped from Lincoln to add to her force. She'll move heaven and earth to get Stephen out of hold, by whatever means, fair or

9

foul. She is,' said Hugh with conviction, 'a better soldier than her lord. Not a better fighter in the field – God knows you'd need to search Europe through to find such a one, I saw him at Lincoln – a marvel! But a better general, that she *is*. She holds to her purpose, where he tires and goes off after another quarry. They tell me, and I believe it, she's drawing her cordon closer and closer to London, south of the river. The nearer her rival comes to Westminster, the tighter that noose will be drawn.'

'And is it certain the Londoners have agreed to let the empress in? We hear they came late to the council, and made a faint plea for Stephen before they let themselves be tamed. It takes a very stout heart, I suppose, to stand up to Henry of Winchester face to face, and deny him,' allowed Cadfael, sighing.

'They've agreed to admit her, which is as good as acknowledging her. But they're arguing terms for her entry, as I heard it, and every delay is worth gold to me and to Stephen. If only,' said Hugh, the dancing light suddenly sharpening every line of his intent and eloquent face, 'if only I could get a good man into Bristol! There are ways into castles, even into the dungeons. Two or three good, secret men might do it. A fistful of gold to a malcontent gaoler … Kings have been fetched off before now, even out of chains, and he's not chained. She has not gone so far, not yet. Cadfael, I dream! My work is here, and I am but barely equal to it. I have no means of carrying off Bristol, too.'

10

'Once loosed,' said Cadfael, 'your king is going to need this shire ready to his hand.'

He turned from the brazier, hoisting aside the pot and laying it to cool on a slab of stone he kept for the purpose. His back creaked a little as he straightened it. In small ways he was feeling his years, but once erect he was spry enough.

'I'm done here for this while,' he said, brushing his hands together to get rid of the hollow worn by the ladle. 'Come into the daylight, and see the flowers we're bringing on for the festival of Saint Winifred. Father Abbot will be home in good time to preside over her reception from Saint Giles. And we shall have a houseful of pilgrims to care for.'

They had brought the reliquary of the Welsh saint four years previously from Gwytherin, where she lay buried, and installed it on the altar of the church at the hospital of Saint Giles, at the very edge of Shrewsbury's Foregate suburb, where the sick, the infected, the deformed, the lepers, who might not venture within the walls, were housed and cared for. And thence they had borne her casket in splendour to her altar in the abbey church, to be an ornament and a wonder, a means of healing and blessing to all who came reverently and in need. This year they had undertaken to repeat that last journey, to bring her from Saint Giles in procession, and open her altar to all who came with prayers and offerings. Every year she had drawn many pilgrims. This

11

year they would be legion.

'A man might wonder,' said Hugh, standing spread-footed among the flower beds just beginning to burn from the soft, shy colours of spring into the blaze of summer, 'whether you were not rather preparing for a bridal.'

Hedges of hazel and may-blossom shed silver petals and dangled pale, silver-green catkins round the enclosure where they stood, cowslips were rearing in the grass of the meadow beyond, and irises were in tight, thrusting bud. Even the roses showed a harvest of buds, erect and ready to break and display the first colour. In the walled shelter of Cadfael's herb-garden there were fat globes of peonies, too, just cracking their green sheaths. Cadfael had medicinal uses for the seeds, and Brother Petrus, the abbot's cook, used them as spices in the kitchen.

'A man might not be so far out, at that,' said Cadfael, viewing the fruits of his labours complacently. 'A perpetual and pure bridal. This Welsh girl was virgin until the day of her death.'

'And you have married her off since?'

It was idly said, in revulsion from pondering matters of state. In such a garden a man could believe in peace, fruitfulness and amity. But it encountered suddenly so profound and pregnant a silence that Hugh pricked up his ears, and turned his head almost stealthily to study his friend, even before the unguarded answer came. Unguarded either from absence of mind, or of design, there was no telling.

'Not wedded,' said Cadfael, 'but certainly bedded. With a good man, too, and her honest champion. He deserved his reward.'

Hugh raised quizzical brows, and cast a glance over his shoulder towards the long roof of the great abbey church, where reputedly the lady in question slept in a sealed reliquary on her own altar. An elegant coffin just long enough to contain a small and holy Welshwoman, with the neat, compact bones of her race.

'Hardly room within there for two,' he said mildly.

'Not two of our gross make, no, not there. There was space enough where we put them.' He knew he was listened to, now, and heard with sharp intelligence, if not yet understood.

'Are you telling me,' wondered Hugh no less mildly, 'that she is *not* there in that elaborate shrine of yours, where everyone else *knows* she is?'

'Can I tell? Many a time I've wished it could be possible to be in two places at once. A thing too hard for me, but for a saint, perhaps, possible? Three nights and three days she was in there, that I do know. She may well have left a morsel of her holiness within – if only by way of thanks to us who took her out again, and put her back where I still, and always shall, believe she wished to be. But for all that,' owned Cadfael, shaking his head, 'there's a trailing fringe of doubt that nags at me. How if I read her wrong?'

'Then your only resort is confession and penance,' said Hugh lightly.

13

'Not until Brother Mark is full-fledged a priest!'
Young Mark was gone from his mother-house
and from his flock at Saint Giles, gone to the
household of the bishop of Lichfield, with Leoric
Aspley's endowment to see him through his
studies, and the goal of all his longings shining
distant and clear before him, the priesthood for
which God had designed him. 'I'm saving for
him,' said Cadfael, 'all those sins I feel, perhaps
mistakenly, to be no sins. He was my right hand
and a piece of my heart for three years, and
knows me better than any man living. Barring, it
may be, yourself?' he added, and slanted a
guileless glance at his friend. 'He will know the
truth of me, and by his judgement and for his
absolution I'll embrace any penance. You might
deliver the judgement, Hugh, but you cannot
deliver the absolution.'

'Nor the penance, neither,' said Hugh, and
laughed freely. 'So tell it to me, and go free
without penalty.'

The idea of confiding was unexpectedly
pleasing and acceptable. 'It's a long story,'* said
Cadfael warningly.

'Then now's your time, for whatever I can do
here is done, nothing is asked of me but
watchfulness and patience, and why should I wait
unentertained if there's a good story to be heard?
And you are at leisure until Vespers. You may

*See *A Morbid Taste for Bones*, Futura 1984.

even get merit,' said Hugh, composing his face into priestly solemnity, 'by unburdening your soul to the secular arm. And I can be secret,' he said, 'as any confessional.'

'Wait, then,' said Cadfael, 'while I fetch a draught of that maturing wine, and come within to the bench under the north wall, where the afternoon sun falls. We may as well be at ease while I talk.'

'It was a year or so before I knew you,' said Cadfael, bracing his back comfortably against the warmed, stony roughness of the herb-garden wall. 'We were without a tame saint to our house, and somewhat envious of Wenlock, where the Cluny community had discovered their Saxon foundress Milburga, and were making great play with her. And we had certain signs that sent off an ailing brother of ours into Wales, to bathe at Holywell, where this girl Winifred died her first death, and brought forth her healing spring. There was her own patron, Saint Beuno, ready and able to bring her back to life, but the spring remained, and did wonders. So it came to Prior Robert that the lady could be persuaded to leave Gwytherin, where she died her second death and was buried, and come and bring her glory to us here in Shrewsbury. I was one of the party he took with him to deal with the parish there, and bring them to give up the saint's bones.'

'All of which,' said Hugh, warmed and attentive

15

beside him, 'I know very well, since all men here know it.'

'Surely! But you do not know to the end what followed. There was one Welsh lord in Gwytherin who would not suffer the girl to be disturbed, and would not be persuaded or bribed or threatened into letting her go. And he died, Hugh – murdered. By one of us, a brother who came from high rank, and had his eyes already set on a mitre. And when we came near to accusing him, it was his life or a better. There were certain young people of that place put in peril by him, the dead lord's daughter and her lover. The boy lashed out in anger, with good reason, seeing his girl wounded and bleeding. He was stronger than he knew. The murderer's neck was broken.'

'How many knew of this?' asked Hugh, his eyes narrowed thoughtfully upon the glossy-leaved rose-bushes.

'When it befell, only the lovers, the dead man and I. And Saint Winifred, who had been raised from her grave and laid in that casket of which you and all men know. *She* knew. She was there. From the moment I raised her,' said Cadfael, 'and by God, it was I who took her from the soil, and I who restored her – and still that makes me glad – from the moment I uncovered those slender bones, I felt in mine they wished only to be left in peace. It was so little and so wild and quiet a graveyard there, with the small church long out of use, meadow flowers growing over all, and the mounds so modest and green. And Welsh soil!

16

The girl was Welsh, like me, her church was of the old persuasion, what did she know of this alien English shire? And I had those young things to keep. Who would have taken their word or mine against all the force of the church? They would have closed their ranks to bury the scandal, and bury the boy with it, and he guilty of nothing but defending his dear. So I took measures.'

Hugh's mobile lips twitched. 'Now indeed you amaze me! And what measures were those? With a dead brother to account for, and Prior Robert to keep sweet ...'

'Ah, well, Robert is a simpler soul than he supposes, and then I had a good deal of help from the dead brother himself. He'd been busy building himself such a reputation for sanctity, delivering messages from the saint herself – it was he told us she was offering the grave she'd left to the murdered man – and going into trance-sleeps, and praying to leave this world and be taken into bliss living ... So we did him that small favour. He'd been keeping a solitary night-watch in the old church, and in the morning when it ended, there were his habit and sandals fallen together at his prayer-stool, and the body of him lifted clean out of them, in sweet odours and a shower of may-blossom. That was how he claimed the saint had already visited him, why should not Robert recall it and believe? Certainly he was gone. Why look for him? Would a modest brother of our house be running through the Welsh woods mother-naked?'

17

'Are you telling me,' asked Hugh cautiously, 'that what you have there in the reliquary is *not* ... Then the casket had not yet been sealed?' His eyebrows were tangling with his black forelock, but his voice was soft and unsurprised.

'Well ...' Cadfael twitched his blunt brown nose bashfully between finger and thumb. 'Sealed it was, but there are ways of dealing with seals that leave them unblemished. It's one of the more dubious of my remembered skills, but for all that I was glad of it then.'

'And you put the lady back in the place that was hers, along with her champion?'

'He was a decent, good man, and had spoken up for her nobly. She would not grudge him house-room. I have always thought,' confided Cadfael, 'that she was not displeased with us. She has shown her power in Gwytherin since that time, by many miracles, so I cannot believe she is angry. But what a little troubles me is that she has not so far chosen to favour us with any great mark of her patronage here, to keep Robert happy, and set my mind at rest. Oh, a few little things, but nothing of unmistakable note. How if I have displeased her, after all? Well for me, who *know* what we have within there on the altar – and *mea culpa* if I did wrongly! But what of the innocents who do *not* know, and come in good faith, hoping for grace from her? What if I have been the means of their deprivation and loss?'

'I see,' said Hugh with sympathy, 'that Brother Mark had better make haste through the degrees

18

of ordination, and come quickly to lift the load from you. Unless,' he added with a flashing sidelong smile, 'Saint Winifred takes pity on you first, and sends you a sign.'

'I still do not see,' mused Cadfael, 'what else I could have done. It was an ending that satisfied everyone, both here and there. The children were free to marry and be happy, the village still had its saint, and she had her own people round her. Robert had what he had gone to find – or thought he had, which is the same thing. And Shrewsbury abbey has its festival, with every hope of a full guest-hall, and glory and gain in good measure. If she would but just cast an indulgent look this way, and wink her eye, to let me know I understood her aright.'

'And you've never said word of this to anyone?'

'Never a word. But the whole village of Gwytherin knows it,' admitted Cadfael with a remembering grin. 'No one told, no one had to tell, but they knew. There wasn't a man missing when we took up the reliquary and set out for home. They helped to carry it, whipped together a little chariot to bear it. Robert thought he had them nicely tamed, even those who'd been most reluctant from the first. It was a great joy to him. A simple soul at bottom! It would be great pity to undo him now, when he's busy writing his book about the saint's life, and how he brought her to Shrewsbury.'

'I would not have the heart to put him to such distress,' said Hugh. 'Least said, best for all.

Thanks be to God, I have nothing to do with canon law, the common law of a land almost without law costs me enough pains.' No need to say that Cadfael could be sure of his secrecy, that was taken for granted on both sides. 'Well, you speak the lady's own tongue, no doubt she understood you well enough, with or without words. Who knows? When this festival of yours takes place – the twenty-second day of June, you say? – she may take pity on you, and send you a great miracle to set your mind at rest.'

And so she might, thought Cadfael an hour later, on his way to obey the summons of the Vesper bell. Not that he had deserved so signal an honour, but there surely must be one somewhere among the unceasing stream of pilgrims who did deserve it, and could not with justice be rejected. He would be perfectly and humbly and cheerfully content with that. What if she was eighty miles or so away, in what was left of her body? It had been a miraculous body in this life, once brutally dead and raised alive again, what limits of time or space could be set about such a being? If it so pleased her she could be both quiet and content in her grave with Rhisiart, lulled by bird-song in the hawthorn trees, and here attentive and incorporeal, a little flame of spirit in the coffin of unworthy Columbanus, who had killed not for her exaltation but for his own.

Brother Cadfael went to Vespers curiously relieved at having confided to his friend a secret from before the time when they had first known each other, in the beginning as potential antagonists stepping subtly to outwit each other, then discovering how much they had in common, the old man – alone with himself Cadfael admitted to being somewhat over the peak of a man's prime – and the young one, just setting out, exceedingly well-equipped in shrewdness and wit, to build his fortune and win his wife. And both he had done, for he was now undisputed sheriff of Shropshire, if under a powerless and captive king, and up there in the town, near St Mary's church, his wife and his year-old son made a nest for his private happiness when he shut the door on his public burdens.

Cadfael thought of his godson, the sturdy imp who already clutched his way lustily round the rooms of Hugh's town house, climbed unaided into a godfather's lap, and began to utter human sounds of approval, enquiry, indignation and affection. Every man asks of heaven a son. Hugh had his, as promising a sprig as ever budded from the stem. So, by proxy, had Cadfael, a son in God.

There was, after all, a great deal of human happiness in the world, even a world so torn and mangled with conflict, cruelty and greed. So it had always been, and always would be. And so be it, provided the indomitable spark of joy never went out.

In the refectory, after supper and grace, in the grateful warmth and lingering light of the end of May, when they were shuffling their benches to

21

rise from table, Prior Robert Pennant rose first in his place, levering erect his more than six feet of lean, austere prelate, silver-tonsured and ivory-featured.

'Brothers, I have received a further message from Father Abbot. He has reached Warwick on his way home to us, and hopes to be with us by the fourth day of June or earlier. He bids us be diligent in making proper preparation for the celebration of Saint Winifred's translation, our most gracious patroness.' Perhaps the abbot had so instructed, in duty bound, but it was Robert himself who laid such stress on it, viewing himself, as he did, as the patron of their patroness. His large patrician eye swept round the refectory tables, settling upon those heads most deeply committed. 'Brother Anselm, you have the music already in hand?'

Brother Anselm the precentor, whose mind seldom left its neums and instruments for many seconds together, looked up vaguely, awoke to the question, and stared, wide-eyed. 'The entire order of procession and office is ready,' he said, in amiable surprise that anyone should feel it necessary to ask.

'And Brother Denis, you have made all the preparations necessary for stocking your halls to feed great numbers? For we shall surely need every cot and every dish we can muster.'

Brother Denis the hospitaller, accustomed to outer panics and secure ruler of his own domain, testified calmly that he had made the fullest

22

provision he considered needful, and further, that he had reserves laid by to tap at need.

'There will also be many sick persons to be tended, for that reason they come.'

Brother Edmund the infirmarer, not waiting to be named, said crisply that he had taken into account the probable need, and was prepared for the demands that might be made on his beds and medicines. He mentioned also, being on his feet, that Brother Cadfael had already provided stocks of all the remedies most likely to be wanted, and stood ready to meet any other needs that should arise.

'That is well,' said Prior Robert. 'Now, Father Abbot has yet a special request to make until he comes. He asks that prayers be made at every High Mass for the repose of the soul of a good man, treacherously slain in Winchester as he strove to keep the peace and reconcile faction with faction, in Christian duty.'

For a moment it seemed to Brother Cadfael, and perhaps to most of the others present, that the death of one man, far away in the south, hardly rated so solemn a mention and so signal a mark of respect, in a country where deaths had been commonplace for so long, from the field of Lincoln strewn with bodies to the sack of Worcester with its streets running blood, from the widespread baronial slaughters by disaffected earls to the sordid village banditries where law had broken down. Then he looked at it again, and with the abbot's measuring eyes. Here was a good man cut down in the very city where prelates and barons were parleying over matters of peace and sovereignty, killed in trying to keep one faction from the throat of the other. At the very feet, as it were, of the bishop-legate. As black a sacrilege as if he had been butchered on the steps of the altar. It was not one man's death, it was a bitter symbol of the abandonment of law and the rejection of hope and reconciliation. So Radulfus had seen it, and so he recorded it in the offices of his house. There was a solemn acknowledgement due to the dead man, a memorial lodged in heaven.

'We are asked,' said Prior Robert, 'to offer thanks for the just endeavour and prayers for the soul of one Rainald Bossard, a knight in the service of the Empress Maud.'

'One of the enemy,' said a young novice doubtfully, talking it over in the cloisters afterwards. So used were they, in this shire, to thinking of the king's cause as their own, since it had been his writ which had run here now in orderly fashion for four years, and kept off the worst of the chaos that troubled so much of England elsewhere.

'Not so,' said Brother Paul, the master of the novices, gently chiding. 'No good and honourable man is an enemy, though he may take the opposing side in this dissension. The fealty of this world is not for us, but we must bear it ever in mind as a true value, as binding on those who owe it as our vows are on us. The claims of these two

24

cousins are both in some sort valid. It is no reproach to have kept faith, whether with king or empress. And this was surely a worthy man, or Father Abbot would not thus have recommended him to our prayers.'

Brother Anselm, thoughtfully revolving the syllables of the name, and tapping the resultant rhythm on the stone of the bench on which he sat, repeated to himself softly: 'Rainald Bossard, Rainald Bossard ...'

The repeated iambic stayed in Brother Cadfael's ear and wormed its way into his mind. A name that meant nothing yet to anyone here, had neither form nor face, no age, no character; nothing but a name, which is either a soul without a body or a body without a soul. It went with him into his cell in the dortoir, as he made his last prayers and shook off his sandals before lying down to sleep. It may even have kept a rhythm in his sleeping mind, without the need of a dream to house it, for the first he knew of the thunderstorm was a silent double-gleam of lightning that spelled out the same iambic, and caused him to start awake with eyes still closed, and listen for the answering thunder. It did not come for so long that he thought he had dreamed it, and then he heard it, very distant, very quiet, and yet curiously ominous. Beyond his closed eyelids the quiet lightnings flared and died, and the echoes answered so late and so softly, from so far away ...

As far, perhaps, as that fabled city of Winchester, where momentous matters had been decided, a place Cadfael had never seen, and probably never would see. A threat from a town so distant could shake no foundations here, and no hearts, any more than such far-off thunders could bring down the walls of Shrewsbury. Yet the continuing murmur of disquiet was still in his ears as he fell asleep.

CHAPTER TWO

Abbot Radulfus rode back into his abbey of Saint Peter and Saint Paul on the third day of June, escorted by his chaplain and secretary, Brother Vitalis, and welcomed home by all the fifty-three brothers, seven novices and six schoolboys of his house, as well as all the lay stewards and servants.

The abbot was a long, lean, hard man in his fifties, with a gaunt, ascetic face and a shrewd, scholar's eye, so vigorous and able of body that he dismounted and went straight to preside at High Mass, before retiring to remove the stains of travel or take any refreshment after his long ride. Nor did he forget to offer the prayer he had enjoined upon his flock, for the repose of the soul of Rainald Bossard, slain in Winchester on the evening of Wednesday, the ninth day of April of this year of Our Lord 1141. Eight weeks dead, and half the length of England away, what meaning could Rainald Bossard have for this indifferent town of Shrewsbury, or the members of this far-distant Benedictine house?

Not until the next morning's chapter would the

household hear its abbot's account of that momentous council held in the south to determine the future of England; but when Hugh Beringar waited upon Radulfus about mid-afternoon, and asked for audience, he was not kept waiting. Affairs demanded the close co-operation of the secular and the clerical powers, in defence of such order and law as survived in England.

The abbot's private parlour in his lodging was as austere as its presiding father, plainly furnished, but with sunlight spilled across its flagged floor from two open lattices at this hour of the sun's zenith, and a view of gracious greenery and glowing flowers in the small walled garden without. Quiverings of radiance flashed and vanished and recoiled and collided over the dark panelling within, from the new-budded life and fresh breeze and exuberant light outside. Hugh sat in shadow, and watched the abbot's trenchant profile, clear, craggy and dark against a ground of shifting brightness.

'My allegiance is well known to you, Father,' said Hugh, admiring the stillness of the noble mask thus framed, 'as yours is to me. But there is much that we share. Whatever you can tell me of what passed in Winchester, I do greatly need to know.'

'And I to understand,' said Radulfus, with a tight and rueful smile. 'I went as summoned, by him who has a right to summon me, and I went knowing how matters then stood, the king a

28

prisoner, the empress mistress of much of the south, and in due position to claim sovereignty by right of conquest. We knew, you and I both, what would be in debate down there. I can only give you my own account as I saw it. The first day that we gathered there, a Monday it was, the seventh of April, there was nothing done by way of business but the ceremonial of welcoming us all, and reading out – there were many of these! – the letters sent by way of excuse from those who remained absent. The empress had a lodging in the town then, though she made several moves about the region, to Reading and other places, while we debated. She did not attend. She has a measure of discretion.' His tone was dry. It was not clear whether he considered her measure of that commodity to be adequate or somewhat lacking. 'The second day ...' He fell silent, remembering what he had witnessed. Hugh waited attentively, not stirring.

'The second day, the eighth of April, the legate made his great speech ...'

It was no effort to imagine him. Henry of Blois, bishop of Winchester, papal legate, younger brother and hitherto partisan of King Stephen, impregnably ensconced in the chapter house of his own cathedral, secure master of the political pulse of England, the cleverest manipulator in the kingdom, and on his own chosen ground – and yet hounded on to the defensive, in so far as that could ever happen to so expert a practitioner. Hugh had never seen the man, never been near

29

the region where he ruled, had only heard him described, and yet could see him now, presiding with imperious composure over his half-unwilling assembly. A difficult part he had to play, to extricate himself from his known allegiance to his brother, and yet preserve his face and his status and influence with those who had shared it. And with a tough, experienced woman narrowly observing his every word, and holding in reserve her own new powers to destroy or preserve, according to how he managed his ill-disciplined team in this heavy furrow.

'He spoke a tedious while,' said the abbot candidly, 'but he is a very able speaker. He put us in mind that we were met together to try to salvage England from chaos and ruin. He spoke of the late King Henry's time, when order and peace was kept throughout the land. And he reminded us how the old king, left without a son, commanded his barons to swear an oath of allegiance to his only remaining child, his daughter Maud the empress, now widowed, and wed again to the count of Anjou.'

And so those barons had done, almost all, not least this same Henry of Winchester. Hugh Beringar, who had never come to such a test until he was ready to choose for himself, curled a half-disdainful and half-commiserating lip, and nodded understanding. 'His lordship had somewhat to explain away.'

The abbot refrained from indicating, by word or look, agreement with the implied criticism of his brother cleric. 'He said that the long delay which might then have arisen from the empress's being in Normandy had given rise to natural concern for the well-being of the state. An interim of uncertainty was dangerous. And thus, he said, his brother Count Stephen was accepted when he offered himself, and became king by consent. His own part in this acceptance he admitted. For he it was who pledged his word to God and men that King Stephen would honour and revere the Holy Church, and maintain the good and just laws of the land. In which undertaking, said Henry, the king has shamefully failed. To his great chagrin and grief he declared it, having been his brother's guarantor to God.'

So that was the way round the humiliating change of course, thought Hugh. All was to be laid upon Stephen, who had so deceived his reverend brother and defaulted upon all his promises, that a man of God might well be driven to the end of his patience, and be brought to welcome a change of monarch with relief tempering his sorrow.

'In particular,' said Radulfus, 'he recalled how the king had hounded certain of his bishops to their ruin and death.'

There was more than a grain of truth in that, though the only death in question, of Robert of Salisbury, had resulted naturally from old age, bitterness and despair, because his power was gone.

'Therefore, *he said*,' continued the abbot with chill deliberation, 'the judgement of God had been manifested against the king, in delivering him up prisoner to his enemies. And he, devout in the service of the Holy Church, must choose between his devotion to his mortal brother and to his immortal father, and could not but bow to the edict of heaven. Therefore he had called us together, to ensure that a kingdom lopped of its head should not founder in utter ruin. And this very matter, he told the assembly, had been discussed most gravely on the day previous among the greater part of the clergy of England, who – *he said*! – had a prerogative surmounting others in the election and consecration of a king.'

There was something in the dry, measured voice that made Hugh prick up his ears. For this was a large and unprecedented claim, and by all the signs Abbot Radulfus found it more than suspect. The legate had his own face to save, and a well-oiled tongue with which to wind the protective mesh of words before it.

'Was there such a meeting? Were you present at such, Father?'

'There was a meeting,' said Radulfus, 'not prolonged, and by no means very clear in its course. The greater part of the talking was done by the legate. The empress had her partisans there.' He said it sedately and tolerantly, but clearly he had not been one. 'I do not recall that he then claimed this prerogative for us. Nor that there was ever a count taken.'

'Nor, as I guess, declared. It would not come to a numbering of heads or hands.' Too easy, then,

32

to start a counter-count of one's own, and confound the reckoning.

'He continued,' said Radulfus coolly and drily, 'by saying that we had chosen as Lady of England the late king's daughter, the inheritor of his nobility and his will to peace. As the sire was unequalled in merit in our times, so might his daughter flourish and bring peace, as he did, to this troubled country, where we now offer her – *he said*! – our whole-hearted fealty.'

So the legate had extricated himself as adroitly as possible from his predicament. But for all that, so resolute, courageous and vindictive a lady as the empress was going to look somewhat sidewise at a whole-hearted fealty which had already once been pledged to her, and turned its back nimbly under pressure, and might as nimbly do so again. If she was wise she would curb her resentment and take care to keep on the right side of the legate, as he was cautiously feeling his way to the right side of her; but she would not forget or forgive.

'And there was no man raised a word against it?' asked Hugh mildly.

'None. There was small opportunity, and even less inducement. And with that the bishop announced that he had invited a deputation from the city of London, and expected them to arrive that day, so that it was expedient we should adjourn our discussion until the morrow. Even so, the Londoners did not come until next day, and we met again somewhat later than on the days previous. Howbeit, they did come. With somewhat dour faces and stiff necks. They said that they represented the whole commune of London, into which many barons had also entered as members after Lincoln, and that they all, with no wish to challenge the legitimacy of our assembly, yet desired to put forward with one voice the request that the lord king should be set at liberty.'

'That was bold,' said Hugh with raised brows. 'How did his lordship counter it? Was he put out of countenance?'

'I think he was shaken, but not disastrously, not then. He made a long speech – it is a way of keping others silent, at least for a time – reproving the city for taking into its membership men who had abandoned their king in war, after leading him astray by their evil advice, so grossly that he forsook God and right, and was brought to the judgement of defeat and captivity, from which the prayers of those same false friends could not now reprieve him. These men do but flatter and favour you now, he said, for their own advantage.'

'If he meant the Flemings who ran from Lincoln,' Hugh allowed, 'he told no more than truth there. But for what other end is the city ever flattered and wooed? What then? Had they the hardihood to stand their ground against him?'

'They were in some disarray as to what they should reply, and went apart to confer. And while there was quiet, a man suddenly stepped forward from among the clerks, and held out a parchment

34

to Bishop Henry, asking him to read it aloud, so confidently that I wonder still he did not at once comply. Instead, he opened and began to read it in silence, and in a moment more he was thundering in a great rage that the thing was an insult to the reverend company present, its matter disgraceful, its witnesses attainted enemies of Holy Church, and not a word of it would he read aloud to us in so sacred a place as his chapter house. Whereupon,' said the abbot grimly, 'the clerk snatched it back from him, and himself read it aloud in a great voice, riding above the bishop when he tried to silence him. It was a plea from Stephen's queen to all present, and to the legate in especial, own brother to the king, to return to fealty and restore the king to his own again from the base captivity into which traitors had betrayed him. And I, said the brave man who read, am a clerk in the service of Queen Matilda, and if any ask my name, it is Christian, and true Christian I am as any here, and true to my salt.'

'Brave, indeed!' said Hugh, and whistled softly. 'But I doubt it did him little good.'

'The legate replied to him in a tirade, much as he had spoken already to us the day before, but in a great passion, and so intimidated the men from London that they drew in their horns, and grudgingly agreed to report the council's election to their citizens, and support it as best they could. As for the man Christian, who had so angered Bishop Henry, he was attacked that same evening in the street, as he set out to return to the queen

35

empty-handed. Four or five ruffians set on him in the dark, no one knows who, for they fled when one of the empress's knights and his men came to the rescue and beat them off, crying shame to use murder as argument in any cause, and against an honest man who had done his part fearlessly in the open. The clerk got no worse than a few bruises. It was the knight who got the knife between his ribs from behind and into the heart. He died in the gutter of a Winchester street. A shame to us all, who claim to be making peace and bringing enemies into amity.'

By the shadowed anger of his face it had gone deep with him, the single wanton act that denied all pretences of good will and justice and conciliation. To strike at a man for being honestly of the opposite persuasion, and then to strike again at the fair-minded and chivalrous who sought to prevent the outrage – very ill omens, these, for the future of the legate's peace.

'And no man taken for the killing?' demanded Hugh, frowning.

'No. They fled in the dark. If any creature knows name or hiding-place, he has spoken no word. Death is so common a matter now, even by stealth and treachery in the darkness, this will be forgotten with the rest. And the next day our council closed with sentence of excommunication against a great number of Stephen's men, and the legate pronounced all men blessed who would bless the empress, and accursed those who cursed her. And so dismissed us,' said Radulfus. 'But that we monastics were not dismissed, but kept to attend on him some weeks longer.'

'And the empress?'

'Withdrew to Oxford, while these long negotiations with the city of London went on, how and when she should be admitted within the gates, on what terms, what numbers she might bring in with her to Westminster. On all which points they have wrangled every step of the way. But in nine or ten days now she will be installed there, and soon thereafter crowned.' He lifted a long, muscular hand, and again let it fall into the lap of his habit. 'So, at least, it seems. What more can I tell you of her?'

'I meant, rather,' said Hugh, 'how is she bearing this slow recognition? How is she dealing with her newly converted barons? And how do they rub, one with another? It's no easy matter to hold together the old and the new liegemen, and keep them from each other's throats. A manor in dispute here and there, a few fields taken from one and given to another ... I think you know the way of it, Father, as well as I.'

'I would not say she is a wise woman,' said Radulfus carefully. 'She is all too well aware how many swore allegiance to her at her father's order, and then swung to King Stephen, and now as nimbly skip back to her because she is in the ascendant. I can well understand she might take pleasure in pricking into the quick where she can, among these. It is not wise, but it is human. But that she should become lofty and cold to those who never wavered – for there are some,' said the

37

abbot with respectful wonder, 'who have been faithful throughout at their own great loss, and will not waver even now, whatever she may do. Great folly and great injustice to use them so high-handedly, who have been her right hand and her left all this while.'

You comfort me, thought Hugh, watching the lean, quiet face intently. The woman is out of her wits if she flouts even the like of Robert of Gloucester, now she feels herself so near the throne.

'She has greatly offended the bishop-legate,' said the abbot, 'by refusing to allow Stephen's son to receive the rights and titles of his father's honours of Boulogne and Mortain, now that his father is a prisoner. It would have been only justice. But no, she would not suffer it. Bishop Henry quit her court for some while, it took her considerable pains to lure him back again.'

Better and better, thought Hugh, assessing his position with care. If she is stubborn enough to drive away even Henry, she can undo everything he and others do for her. Put the crown in her hands and she may, not so much drop it, as hurl it at someone against whom she has a score to settle. He set himself to extract every detail of her subsequent behaviour, and was cautiously encouraged. She had taken land from some who held it and given it to others. She had received her naturally bashful new adherents with arrogance, and reminded them ominously of their past hostility. Some she had even repulsed with anger, recalling old injuries. Candidates for a disputed crown should be more accommodatingly for-getful. Let her alone, and pray! She, if anyone, could bring about her own ruin.

At the end of a long hour he rose to take his leave, with a very fair picture in his mind of the possibilities he had to face. Even empresses may learn, and she might yet inveigle herself safely into Westminster and assume the crown. It would not do to underestimate William of Normandy's grand-daughter and Henry the First's daughter. Yet that very stock might come to wreck on its own unforgiving strength.

He was never afterwards sure why he turned back at the last moment to ask: 'Father Abbot, this man Rainald Bossard, who died … A knight of the empress, you said. In whose following?'

All that he had learned he confided to Brother Cadfael in the hut in the herb-garden, trying out upon his friend's unexcitable solidity his own impressions and doubts, like a man sharpening a scythe on a good memorial stone. Cadfael was fussing over a too-exuberant wine, and seemed not to be listening, but Hugh remained undeceived. His friend had a sharp ear cocked for every intonation, even turned a swift glance occasionally to confirm what his ear heard, and reckon up the double account.

'You'd best lean back, then,' said Cadfael finally, 'and watch what will follow. You might also, I suppose, have a good man take a look at Bristol? He is the only hostage she has. With the

39

king loosed, or Robert, or Brian FitzCount, or some other of sufficient note made prisoner to match him, you'd be on secure ground. God forgive me, why am I advising you, who have no prince in this world!' But he was none too sure about the truth of that, having had brief remembered dealings with Stephen himself, and liked the man, even at his ill-advised worst, when he had slaughtered the garrison of Shrewsbury castle, to regret it as long as his ebullient memory kept nudging him with the outrage. By now, in his dungeon in Bristol, he might well have forgotten the uncharacteristic savagery.

'And do you know,' asked Hugh with deliberation, 'whose man was this knight Rainald Bossard, left bleeding to death in the lanes of Winchester? He for whom your prayers have been demanded?'

Cadfael turned from his boisterously bubbling jar to narrow his eyes on his friend's face. 'The empress's man is all we've been told. But I see you're about to tell me more.'

'He was in the following of Laurence d'Angers.'

Cadfael straightened up with incautious haste, and grunted at the jolt to his ageing back. It was the name of a man neither of them had ever set eyes on, yet it started vivid memories for them both.

'Yes, *that* Laurence! A baron of Gloucestershire, and liegeman to the empress. One of the few who has not once turned his coat yet in this to-ing and fro-ing, and uncle to those two children you

40

helped away from Bromfield to join him, when they went astray after the sack of Worcester. Do you still remember the cold of that winter? And the wind that scoured away hills of snow overnight, and laid them down in fresh places before morning? I still feel it, clean through flesh and bone ...'

There was nothing about that winter journey that Cadfael would ever forget.* It was hardly a year and a half past, the attack on the city of Worcester, the flight of brother and sister northwards towards Shrewsbury, through the worst weather for many a year. Laurence d'Angers had been but a name in the business, as he was now in this. An adherent of the Empress Maud, he had been denied leave to enter King Stephen's territory to search for his young kin, but he had sent a squire in secret to find and fetch them away. To have borne a hand in the escape of those three was something to remember lifelong. All three arose living before Cadfael's mind's eye, the boy Yves, thirteen years old then, ingenuous and gallant and endearing, jutting a stubborn Norman chin at danger, his elder sister Ermina, newly shaken into womanhood and resolutely shouldering the consequences of her own follies. And the third ...

'I have often wondered,' said Hugh thoughtfully, 'how they fared afterwards. I knew you would get them off safely, if I left it to you,

*See *The Virgin in the Ice*, Futura 1984.

41

but it was still a perilous road before them. I wonder if we shall ever get word. Some day the world will surely hear of Yves Hugonin.' At the thought of the boy he smiled with affectionate amusement. 'And that dark lad who fetched them away, he who dressed like a woodsman and fought like a paladin ... I fancy you knew more of him than ever I got to know.'

Cadfael smiled into the glow of the brazier and did not deny it. 'So his lord is there in the empress's train, is he? And this knight who was killed was in d'Angers' service? That was a very ill thing, Hugh.'

'So Abbot Radulfus thinks,' said Hugh sombrely.

'In the dusk and in confusion – and all got clean away, even the one who used the knife. A foul thing, for surely that was no chance blow. The clerk Christian escaped out of their hands, yet one among them turned on the rescuer before he fled. It argues a deal of hate at being thwarted, to have ventured that last moment before running. And is it left so? And Winchester full of those who should most firmly stand for justice?'

'Why, some among them would surely have been well enough pleased if that bold clerk had spilled his blood in the gutter, as well as the knight. Some may well have set the hunt on him.'

'Well for the empress's good name,' said Cadfael, 'that there was one at least of her men stout enough to respect an honest opponent, and stand by him to the death. And shame if that

42

death goes unpaid for.'

'Old friend,' said Hugh ruefully, rising to take his leave, 'England has had to swallow many such a shame these last years. It grows customary to sigh and shrug and forget. At which, as I know, you are a very poor hand. And I have seen you overturn custom more than once, and been glad of it. But not even you can do much now for Rainald Bossard, bar praying for his soul. It is a very long way from here to Winchester.'

'It is not so far,' said Cadfael, as much to himself as to his friend, 'not by many a mile, as it was an hour since.'

He went to Vespers, and to supper in the refectory, and thereafter to Collations and Compline, and all with one remembered face before his mind's eye, so that he paid but fractured attention to the readings, and had difficulty in concentrating his thoughts on prayer. Though it might have been a kind of prayer he was offering throughout, in gratitude and praise and humility.

So suave, so young, so dark and vital a face, startling in its beauty when he had first seen it over the girl's shoulder, the face of the young squire sent to bring away the Hugonin children to their uncle and guardian. A long, spare, wide-browed face, with a fine scimitar of a nose and a supple bow of a mouth, and the fierce, fearless, golden eyes of a hawk. A head capped closely with curving, blue-black hair, coiling

43

crisply at his temples and clasping his cheeks like folded wings. So young and yet so formed a face, east and west at home in it, shaven clean like a Norman, olive-skinned like a Syrian, all his memories of the Holy Land in one human countenance. The favourite squire of Laurence d'Angers, come home with him from the Crusade. Olivier de Bretagne.

If his lord was here in the south with his following, in the empress's retinue, where else would Olivier be? The abbot might even have rubbed shoulders with him, unbeknown, or seen him ride past at his lord's elbow, and for one absent moment admired his beauty. Few such faces blaze out of the humble mass of our ordinariness, thought Cadfael, the finger of God cannot choose but mark them out for notice, and his officers here will be the first to recognise and own them.

And this Rainald Bossard who is dead, an honourable man doing right by an honourable opponent, was Olivier's comrade, owning the same lord and pledged to the same service. His death will be grief to Olivier. Grief to Olivier is grief to me, a wrong done to Olivier is a wrong done to me. As far away as Winchester may be, here am I left mourning in that dark street where a man died for a generous act, in which, by the same token, he did not fail, for the clerk Christian lived on to return to his lady, the queen, with his errand faithfully done.

The gentle rustlings and stirrings of the dortoir

44

sighed into silence outside the frail partitions of Cadfael's cell long before he rose from his knees, and shook off his sandals. The little lamp by the night stairs cast only the faintest gleam across the beams of the roof, a ceiling of pearly grey above the darkness of his cell, his home now for – was it eighteen years or nineteen? – he had difficulty in recalling. It was as if a part of him, heart, mind, soul, whatever that essence might be, had not so much retired as come home to take seisin of a heritage here, his from his birth. And yet he remembered and acknowledged with gratitude and joy the years of his sojourning in the world, the lusty childhood and venturous youth, the taking of the Cross and the passion of the Crusade, the women he had known and loved, the years of his sea-faring off the coast of the Holy Kingdom of Jerusalem, all that pilgrimage that had led him here at last to his chosen retreat. None of it wasted, however foolish and amiss, nothing lost, nothing vain, all of it somehow fitting him to the narrow niche where now he served and rested. God had given him a sign, he had no need to regret anything, only to lay all open and own it his. For God's viewing, not for man's.

He lay quiet in the darkness, straight and still like a man coffined, but easy, with his arms lax at his sides, and his half-closed eyes dreaming on the vault above him, where the faint light played among the beams.

There was no lightning that night, only a

consort of steady rolls of thunder both before and after Matins and Lauds, so unalarming that many among the brothers failed to notice them. Cadfael heard them as he rose, and as he returned to his rest. They seemed to him a reminder and a reassurance that Winchester had indeed moved nearer to Shrewsbury, and consoled him that his grievance was not overlooked, but noted in heaven, and he might look to have his part yet in collecting the debt due to Rainald Bossard. Upon which warranty, he fell asleep.

CHAPTER THREE

On the seventeenth day of June Saint Winifred's
elaborate oak coffin, silver-ornamented and lined
with lead behind all its immaculate seals, was
removed from its place of honour and carried
with grave and subdued ceremony back to its
temporary resting-place in the chapel of the
hospital of Saint Giles, there to wait, as once
before, for the auspicious day, the twenty-second
of June. The weather was fair, sunny and still,
barely a cloud in the sky, and yet cool enough for
travelling, the best of weather for pilgrims. And
by the eighteenth day the pilgrims began to
arrive, a scattering of fore-runners before the full
tide began to flow.

Brother Cadfael had watched the reliquary
depart on its memorial journey with a slightly
guilty mind, for all his honest declaration that he
could hardly have done otherwise than he had
done, there in the summer night in Gwytherin. So
strongly had he felt, above all, her Welshness, the
feeling she must have for the familiar tongue
about her, and the tranquil flow of the seasons in

47

her solitude, where she had slept so long and so well in her beatitude, and worked so many small, sweet miracles for her own people. No, he could not believe he had made a wrong choice there. If only she would glance his way, and smile, and say, well done!

The very first of the pilgrims came probing into the walled herb-garden, with Brother Denis's directions to guide him, in search of a colleague in his own mystery. Cadfael was busy weeding the close-planted beds of mint and thyme and sage late in the afternoon, a tedious, meticulous labour in the ripeness of a favourable June, after spring sun and shower had been nicely balanced, and growth was a green battlefield. He backed out of a cleansed bed, and backed into a solid form, rising startled from his knees to turn and face a rusty black brother shaped very much like himself, though probably fifteen years younger. They stood at gaze, two solid, squarely built brethren of the Order, eyeing each other in instant recognition and acknowledgement.

'You must be Brother Cadfael,' said the stranger-brother in a broad, melodious bass voice. 'Brother Hospitaller told me where to find you. My name is Adam, a brother of Reading. I have the very charge there that you bear here, and I have heard tell of you, even as far south as my house.'

His eye was roving, as he spoke, towards some of Cadfael's rarer treasures, the eastern poppies he had brought from the Holy Land and reared here with anxious care, the delicate fig that still contrived to thrive against the sheltering north wall, where the sun nursed it. Cadfael warmed to him for the quickening of his eye, and the mild greed that flushed the round, shaven face. A sturdy, stalwart man, who moved as if confident of his body, one who might prove a man of his hands if challenged. Well-weathered, too, a genuine outdoor man.

'You're more than welcome, brother,' said Cadfael heartily. 'You'll be here for the saint's feast? And have they found you a place in the dortoir? There are a few cells vacant, for any of our own who come, like you.'

'My abbot sent me from Reading with a mission to our daughter house of Leominster,' said Brother Adam, probing with an experimental toe into the rich, well-fed loam of Brother Cadfael's bed of mint, and raising an eyebrow respectfully at the quality he found. 'I asked if I might prolong the errand to attend on the translation of Saint Winifred, and I was given the needful permission. It's seldom I could hope to be sent so far north, and it would be pity to miss such an opportunity.'

'And they've found you a brother's bed?' Such a man, Benedictine, gardener and herbalist, could not be wasted on a bed in the guest-hall. Cadfael coveted him, marking the bright eye with which the newcomer singled out his best endeavours.

'Brother Hospitaller was so gracious. I am placed in a cell close to the novices.'

'We shall be near neighbours,' said Cadfael

contentedly. 'Now come, I'll show you whatever we have here to show, for the main garden is on the far side of the Foregate, along the bank of the river. But here I keep my own herber. And if there should be anything here that can be safely carried to Reading, you may take cuttings most gladly before you leave us.'

They fell into a very pleasant and voluble discussion, perambulating all the walks of the closed garden, and comparing experiences in cultivation and use. Brother Adam of Reading had a sharp eye for rarities, and was likely to go home laden with spoils. He admired the neatness and order of Cadfael's workshop, the collection of rustling bunches of dried herbs hung from the roof-beams and under the eaves, and the array of bottles, jars and flagons along the shelves. He had hints and tips of his own to propound, too, and the amiable contest kept them happy all the afternoon. When they returned together to the great court before Vespers it was to a scene notably animated, as if the bustle of celebration was already beginning. There were horses being led down into the stableyard, and bundles being carried in at the guest-hall. A stout elderly man, well equipped for riding, paced across towards the church to pay his first respects on arrival, with a servant trotting at his heels.

Brother Paul's youngest charges, all eyes and curiosity, ringed the gatehouse to watch the early arrivals, and were shooed aside by Brother Jerome, very busy as usual with all the prior's errands. Though the boys did not go very far, and formed their ring again as soon as Jerome was out of sight. A few of the citizens of the Foregate had gathered in the street to watch, excited dogs running among their legs.

'Tomorrow,' said Cadfael, eyeing the scene, 'there will be many more. This is but the beginning. Now if the weather stays fair we shall have a very fine festival for our saint.'

And she will understand that all is in her honour, he thought privately, even if she does lie very far from here. And who knows whether she may not pay us a visit, out of the kindness of her heart? What is distance to a saint, who can be where she wills in the twinkling of an eye?

The guest-hall filled steadily on the morrow. All day long they came, some singly, some in groups as they had met and made comfortable acquaintance on the road, some afoot, some on ponies, some whole and hearty and on holiday, some who had travelled only a few miles, some who came from far away, and among them a number who went on crutches, or were led along by better-sighted friends, or had grievous deformities or skin diseases, or debilitating illnesses; and all these hoping for relief.

Cadfael went about the regular duties of his day, divided between church and herbarium, but with an interested eye open for all there was to see whenever he crossed the great court, boiling now with activity. Every arriving figure, every face, engaged his notice, but as yet distantly, none being provided with a name, to make him individual. Such of them as needed his services for relief would be directed to him, such as came his way by chance would be entitled to his whole attention, freely offered.

It was the woman he noticed first, bustling across the court from the gatehouse to the guest-hall with a basket on her arm, fresh from the Foregate market with new-baked bread and little cakes, soon after Prime. A careful housewife, to be off marketing so early even on holiday, decided about what she wanted, and not content to rely on the abbey bakehouse to provide it. A sturdy, confident figure of a woman, perhaps fifty years of age but in full rosy bloom. Her dress was sober and plain, but of good material and proudly kept, her wimple snow-white beneath her head-cloth of brown linen. She was not tall, but so erect that she could pass for tall, and her face was round, wide-eyed and broad-cheeked, with a determined chin to it.

She vanished briskly into the guest-hall, and he caught but a glimpse of her, but she was positive enough to stay with him through the offices and duties of the morning, and as the worshippers left the church after Mass he caught sight of her again, arms spread like a hen-wife driving her birds, marshalling two chicks, it seemed, before her, both largely concealed beyond her ample width and bountiful skirts. Indeed she had a general largeness about her, her head-dress surely taller and broader than need, her hips

52

bolstered by petticoats, the aura of bustle and command she bore about with her equally generous and ebullient. He felt a wave of warmth go out to her for her energy and vigour, while he spared a morsel of sympathy for the chicks she mothered, stowed thus away beneath such ample, smothering wings.

In the afternoon, busy about his small kingdom and putting together the medicaments he must take along the Foregate to Saint Giles in the morning, to be sure they had provision enough over the feast, he was not thinking of her, nor of any of the inhabitants of the guest-hall, since none had as yet had occasion to call for his aid. He was packing lozenges into a small box, soothing tablets for scoured, dry throats, when a bulky shadow blocked the open door of his workshop, and a brisk, light voice said, 'Pray your pardon, brother, but Brother Denis advised me to come to you, and sent me here.'

And there she stood, filling the doorway, shoulders squared, hands folded at her waist, head braced and face full forward. Her eyes, wide and wide-set, were bright blue but meagrely supplied with pale lashes, yet very firm and fixed in their regard.

'It's my young nephew you see, brother,' she went on confidently, 'my sister's son, that was fool enough to go off and marry a roving Welshman from Builth, and now her man's gone, and so is she, poor lass, and left her two children orphan, and nobody to care for them but me. And me with

53

my own husband dead, and all his craft fallen to me to manage, and never a chick of my own to be my comfort. Not but what I can do very well with the work and the journeymen, for I've learned these twenty years what was what in the weaving trade, but still I could have done with a son of my own. But it was not to be, and a sister's son is dearly welcome, so he is, whether he has his health or no, for he's the dearest lad ever you saw. And it's the pain, you see, brother. I don't like to see him in pain, though he doesn't complain. So I'm come to you.'

Cadfael made haste to wedge a toe into this first chink in her volubility, and insert a few words of his own into the gap.

'Come within, mistress, and welcome. Tell me what's the nature of your lad's pain, and what I can do for you and him I'll do. But best I should see him and speak with him, for he best knows where he hurts. Sit down and be easy, and tell me about him.'

She came in confidently enough, and settled herself with a determined spreading of ample skirts on the bench against the wall. Her gaze went round the laden shelves, the stored herbs dangling, the brazier and the pots and flasks, interested and curious, but in no way awed by Cadfael or his mysteries.

'I'm from the cloth country down by Campden, brother, Weaver by name and by trade was my man, and his father and grandfather before him, and Alice Weaver is my name, and I keep up the work just as he did. But this young sister of mine, she went off with a Welshman, and the pair of them are dead now, and the children I sent for to live with me. The girl is eighteen years old now, a good, hard-working maid, and I daresay we shall contrive to find a decent match for her in the end, though I shall miss her help, for she's grown very handy, and is strong and healthy, not like the lad. Named for some outlandish Welsh saint, she is, Melangell, if ever you heard the like!'

'I'm Welsh myself,' said Cadfael cheerfully. 'Our Welsh names do come hard on your English tongues, I know.'

'Ah well, the boy brought a name with him that's short and simple enough. Rhun, they named him. Sixteen he is now, two years younger than his sister, but wants her heartiness, poor soul. He's well-grown enough, and very comely, but from a child something went wrong with his right leg, it's twisted and feebled so he can put but the very toe of it to the ground at all, and even that turned on one side, and can lay no weight on it, but barely touch. He goes on two crutches. And I've brought him here in the hope good Saint Winifred will do something for him. But it's cost him dear to make the walk, even though we started out three weeks ago, and have taken it by easy shifts.'

'He walked the whole way?' asked Cadfael, dismayed.

'I'm not so prosperous I can afford a horse, more than the one they need for the business at home. Twice on the way a kind carter did give him a ride as far as he was bound, but the rest he's hobbled on his crutches. Many another at this feast, brother, will have done as much, in as bad case or worse. But he's here now, safe in the guest-hall, and if my prayers can do anything for him, he'll walk home again on two sound legs as ever held up a hale and hearty man. But now for these few days he suffers as bad as before.'

'You should have brought him here with you,' said Cadfael. 'What's the nature of his pain? Is it in moving, or when he lies still? Is it the bones of the leg that ache?'

'It's worst in his bed at night. At home I've often heard him weeping for pain in the night, though he tries to keep it so silent we need not be disturbed. Often he gets little or no sleep. His bones do ache, that's truth, but also the sinews of his calf knot into such cramps it makes him groan.'

'There can be something done about that,' said Cadfael, considering. 'At least we may try. And there are draughts can dull the pain and help him to a night's sleep, at any rate.'

'It isn't that I don't trust to the saint,' explained Mistress Weaver anxiously. 'But while he waits for her, let him be at rest if he can, that's what I say. Why should not a suffering lad seek help from ordinary decent mortals, too, good men like you who have faith and knowledge both?'

'Why not, indeed!' agreed Cadfael. 'The least of us may be an instrument of grace, though not by

56

his own deserving. Better let the boy come to me here, where we can be private together. The guest-hall will be busy and noisy, here we shall have quiet.'

She rose, satisfied, to take her leave, but she had plenty yet to say even in departing of the long, slow journey, the small kindnesses they had met with on the way, and the fellow pilgrims, some of whom had passed them and arrived here before them.

'There's more than one in there,' said she, wagging her head towards the lofty rear wall of the guest-hall, 'will be needing your help, besides my Rhun. There were two young fellows we came along with the last days, we could keep pace with them, for they were slowed much as we were. Oh, the one of them was hale and lusty enough, but would not stir a step ahead of his friend, and that poor soul had come barefoot more miles even than Rhun had come crippled, and his feet a sight for pity, but would he so much as bind them with rags? Not he! He said he was under vow to go unshod to his journey's end. And a great heavy cross on a string round his neck, too, and he rubbed raw with the chafing of it, but that was part of his vow, too. I see no reason why a fine young fellow should choose such a torment of his own will, but there, folk do strange things, I daresay he hopes to win some great mercy for himself with his austerities. Still, I should think he might at least get some balm for his feet, while he's here at rest? Shall I bid him come to you? I'd

57

gladly do a small service for that pair. The other one, Matthew, the sturdy one, he hefted my girl safe out of the way of harm when some mad horsemen in a hurry all but rode us down into the ditch, and he carried our bundles for her after, for she was well loaded, I being busy helping Rhun along. Truth to tell, I think the young man was taken with our Melangell, for he was very attentive to her once we joined company. More than to his friend, though indeed he never stirred a step away from him. A vow is a vow, I suppose, and if a man's taken all that suffering on himself of his own will, what can another do to prevent it? No more than bear him company, and that the lad is doing, faithfully, for he never leaves him.'

She was out of the door and spreading appreciative nostrils for the scent of the sunlit herbs, when she looked back to add: 'There's others among them may call themselves pilgrims as loud and often as they will, but I wouldn't trust one or two of them as far as I could throw them. I suppose rogues will make their way everywhere, even among the saints.'

'As long as the saints have money in their purses, or anything about them worth stealing,' agreed Cadfael wryly, 'rogues will never be far away.'

Whether Mistress Weaver did speak to her strange travelling companion or not, it was he who arrived at Cadfael's workshop within half an hour, before ever the boy Rhun showed his face.

Cadfael was back at his weeding when he heard them come, or heard, rather, the slow, patient footsteps of the sturdy one stirring the gravel of his pathways. The other made no sound in walking, for he stepped tenderly and carefully in the grass border, which was cool and kind to his misused feet. If there was any sound to betray his coming it was the long, effortful sighing of his breath, the faint, indrawn hiss of pain. As soon as Cadfael straightened his back and turned his head, he knew who came.

They were much of an age, and even somewhat alike in build and colouring, above middle height but that the one stooped in his laboured progress, brown-haired and dark of eye, and perhaps twenty-five or twenty-six years old. Yet not so like that they could have been brothers or close kin. The hale one had the darker complexion, as though he had been more in the air and the sun, and broader bones of cheek and jaw, a stubborn, proud, secret face, disconcertingly still, confiding nothing. The sufferer's face was long, mobile and passionate, with high cheekbones and hollow cheeks beneath them, and a mouth tight-drawn, either with present pain or constant passion. Anger might be one of his customary companions, burning ardour another. The young man Matthew stalked at his heels mute and jealously watchful in attendance on him.

Mindful of Mistress Weaver's loquacious confidences, Cadfael looked from the scarred and swollen feet to the chafed neck. Within the collar

59

of his plain dark coat the votary had wound a length of linen cloth, to alleviate the rubbing of the thin cord from which a heavy cross of iron, chaced in a leaf pattern with what looked like gold, hung down upon his breast. By the look of the seam of red that marked the linen, either this padding was new, or else it had not been effective. The cord was mercilessly thin, the cross certainly heavy. To what desperate end could a young man choose so to torture himself? And what pleasure did he think it could give to God or Saint Winifred to contemplate his discomfort?

Eyes feverishly bright scanned him. A low voice asked: 'You are Brother Cadfael? That is the name Brother Hospitaller gave me. He said you would have ointments and salves that could be of help to me. So far,' he added, eyeing Cadfael with glittering fixity, 'as there is any help anywhere for me.'

Cadfael gave him a considering look for that, but asked nothing until he had marshalled the pair of them into his workshop and sat the sufferer down to be inspected with due care. The young man Matthew took up his stand beside the open door, careful to avoid blocking the light, but would not come further within.

'You've come a fairish step unshod,' said Cadfael, on his knees to examine the damage. 'Was such cruelty needful?'

'It was. I do not hate myself so much as to bear this to no purpose.' The silent youth by the door stirred slightly, but said no word. 'I am under vow,' said his companion, 'and will not break it.' It seemed that he felt a need to account for himself, forestalling questioning. 'My name is Ciaran, I am of a Welsh mother, and I am going back to where I was born, there to end my life as I began it. You see the wounds on my feet, brother, but what most ails me does not show anywhere upon me. I have a fell disease, no threat to any other, but it must shortly end me.'

And it could be true, thought Cadfael, busy with a cleansing oil on the swollen soles, and the toes cut by gravel and stones. The feverish fire of the deep-set eyes might well mean an even fiercer fire within. True, the young body, now eased in repose, was well-made and had not lost flesh, but that was no sure proof of health. Ciaran's voice remained low, level and firm. If he knew he had his death, he had come to terms with it.

'So I am returning in penitential pilgrimage, for my soul's health, which is of greater import. Barefoot and burdened I shall walk to the house of canons at Aberdaron, so that after my death I may be buried on the holy isle of Ynys Enlli, where the soil is made up of the bones and dust of thousands upon thousands of saints.'

'I should have thought,' said Cadfael mildly, 'that such a privilege could be earned by going there shod and tranquil and humble, like any other man.' But for all that, it was an understandable ambition for a devout man of Welsh extraction, knowing his end near. Aberdaron, at the tip of the Lleyn peninsula, fronting the wild sea and the holiest island of the Welsh church, had been the last resting place of many, and the hospitality of the canons of the house was never refused to any man. 'I would not cast doubt on your sacrifice, but self-imposed suffering seems to me a kind of arrogance, and not humility.'

'It may be so,' said Ciaran remotely. 'No help for it now, I am bound.'

'That is true,' said Matthew from his corner by the door. A measured and yet an abrupt voice, deeper than his companion's. 'Fast bound! So are we both, I no less than he.'

'Hardly by the same vows,' said Cadfael drily. For Matthew wore good, solid shoes, a little down at heel, but proof against the stones of the road.

'No, not the same. But no less binding. And I do not forget mine, any more than he forgets his.'

Cadfael laid down the foot he had anointed, setting a folded cloth under it, and lifted its fellow into his lap. 'God forbid I should tempt any man to break his oath. You will both do as you must do. But at least you may rest your feet here until after the feast, which will give you three days for healing, and here within the pale the ground is not so harsh. And once healed, I have a rough spirit that will help to harden your soles for when you take to the road again. Why not, unless you have forsworn all help from men? And since you came to me I take it you have not yet gone so far. There, sit a while longer, and let that dry.'

He rose from his knees, surveying his work critically, and turned his attention next to the linen wrapping about Ciaran's neck. He laid both

62

hands gently on the cord by which the cross depended, and made to lift it over the young man's head.

'No, no, let be!' It was a soft, wild cry of alarm, and Ciaran clutched at cross and cord, one with either hand, and hugged his burden to him fiercely. 'Don't touch it! Let it be!'

'Surely,' said Cadfael, startled, 'you may lift it off while I dress the wound it's cost you? Hardly a moment's work, why not?'

'*No!*' Ciaran fastened both hands upon the cross and hugged it to his breast. 'No, never for a moment, night or day! No! Let it alone!'

'Lift it, then,' said Cadfael resignedly, 'and hold it while I dress this cut. No, never fear, I'll not cheat you. Only let me unwind this cloth, and see what damage you have there, hidden.'

'Yet he should doff it, and so I have prayed him constantly,' said Matthew softly. 'How else can he be truly rid of his pains?'

Cadfael unwound the linen, viewed the scored line of half-dried blood, still oozing, and went to work on it with a stinging lotion first to clean it of dust and fragments of frayed skin, and then with a healing ointment of cleavers. He refolded the cloth, and wound it carefully under the cord. 'There, you have not broken faith. Settle your load again. If you hold up the weight in your hands as you go, and loosen it in your bed, you'll be rid of your gash before you depart.'

It seemed to him that they were both of them in haste to leave him, for the one set his feet tenderly

63

to ground as soon as he was released, holding up the weight of his cross obediently with both hands, and the other stepped out through the doorway into the sunlit garden, and waited on guard for his friend to emerge. The one owed no special thanks, the other offered only the merest acknowledgement.

'But I would remind you both,' said Cadfael, and with a thoughtful eye on both, 'that you are now present at the feast of a saint who has worked many miracles, even to the defiance of death. One who may have life itself within her gift,' he said strongly, 'even for a man already condemned to death. Bear it in mind, for she may be listening now!'

They said never a word, neither did they look at each other. They stared back at him from the scented brightness of the garden, with startled, wary eyes, and then they turned abruptly as one man, and limped and strode away.

CHAPTER FOUR

There was so short an interval, and so little weeding done, before the second pair appeared, that Cadfael could not choose but reason that the two couples must have met at the corner of his herber, and perhaps exchanged at least a friendly word or two, since they had travelled side by side the last miles of their road here.

The girl walked solicitously beside her brother, giving him the smoothest part of the path, and keeping a hand supportingly under his left elbow, ready to prop him at need, but barely touching. Her face was turned constantly towards him, eager and loving. If he was the tended darling, and she the healthy beast of burden, certainly she had no quarrel with the division. Though just once she did look back over her shoulder, with a different, a more tentative smile. She was neat and plain in her homespun country dress, her hair austerely braided, but her face was vivid and glowing as a rose, and her movements, even at her brother's pace, had a spring and grace to them that spoke of a high and ardent spirit. She was fair for a Welsh girl, her hair a coppery gold, her brows darker, arched hopefully above wide blue eyes. Mistress Weaver could not be far out in supposing that a young man who had hefted this neat little woman out of harm's way in his arms might well remember the experience with pleasure, and not be averse to repeating it. If he could take his eyes from his fellow-pilgrim long enough to attempt it!

The boy came leaning heavily on his crutches, his right leg dangling inertly, turned with the toe twisted inward, and barely brushing the ground. If he could have stood erect he would have been a hand's-breadth taller than his sister, but thus hunched he looked even shorter. Yet the young body was beautifully proportioned, Cadfael judged, watching his approach with a thoughtful eye, wide-shouldered, slim-flanked, the one good leg long, vigorous and shapely. He carried little flesh, indeed he could have done with more, but if he spent his days habitually in pain it was unlikely he had much appetite.

Cadfael's study of him had begun at the twisted foot, and travelling upward, came last to the boy's face. He was fairer than the girl, wheat-gold of hair and brows, his thin, smooth face like ivory, and the eyes that met Cadfael's were a light, brilliant grey-blue, clear as crystal between long, dark lashes. It was a very still and tranquil face, one that had learned patient endurance, and expected to have need of it lifelong. It was clear to Cadfael, in that first exchange of glances, that

Rhun did not look for any miraculous deliverance, whatever Mistress Weaver's hopes might be.

'If you please,' said the girl shyly, 'I have brought my brother, as my aunt said I should. And his name is Rhun, and mine is Melangell.'

'She has told me about you,' said Cadfael, beckoning them with him towards his workshop. 'A long journey you've had of it. Come within, and let's make you as easy as we may, while I take a look at this leg of yours. Was there ever an injury brought this on? A fall, or a kick from a horse? Or a bout of the bone-fever?' He settled the boy on the long bench, took the crutches from him and laid them aside, and turned him so that he could stretch out his legs at rest.

The boy, with grave eyes steady on Cadfael's face, slowly shook his head. 'No such accident,' he said in a man's low, clear voice. 'It came, I think, slowly, but I don't remember a time before it. They say I began to falter and fall when I was three or four years old.'

Melangell, hesitant in the doorway – strangely like Ciaran's attendant shadow, thought Cadfael – had her chin on her shoulder now, and turned almost hastily to say: 'Rhun will tell you all his case. He'll be better private with you. I'll come back later, and wait on the seat outside there until you need me.'

Rhun's light, bright eyes, transparent as sunlit ice, smiled at her warmly over Cadfael's shoulder. 'Do go,' he said. 'So fine and sunny a day, you should make good use of it, without me dangling about you.'

She gave him a long, anxious glance, but half her mind was already away; and satisfied that he was in good hands, she made her hasty reverence, and fled. They were left looking at each other, strangers still, and yet in tentative touch.

'She goes to find Matthew,' said Rhun simply, confident of being understood. 'He was good to her. And to me, also – once he carried me the last piece of the way to our night's lodging on his back. She likes him, and he would like her, if he could truly see her, but he seldom sees anyone but Ciaran.'

This blunt simplicity might well get him the reputation of an innocent, though that would be the world's mistake. What he saw, he said – provided, Cadfael hoped, he had already taken the measure of the person to whom he spoke – and he saw more than most, having so much more need to observe and record, to fill up the hours of his day.

'They were here?' asked Rhun, shifting obediently to allow Cadfael to strip down the long hose from his hips and his maimed leg.

'They were here. Yes, I know.'

'I would like her to be happy.'

'She has it in her to be very happy,' said Cadfael, answering in kind, almost without his will. The boy had a quality of dazzle about him that made unstudied answers natural, almost inevitable. There had been, he thought, the slightest of stresses on 'her'. Rhun had little enough expectation that he could ever be happy, but he wanted happiness for his sister. 'Now pay heed,' said Cadfael, bending to his own duties, 'for this is important. Close your eyes and be at ease as far as you can, and tell me where I find a spot that gives pain. First, thus at rest, is there any pain now?'

Docilely Rhun closed his eyes and waited, breathing softly. 'No, I am quite easy now.'

Good, for all his sinews lay loose and trustful, and at least in that state he felt no pain. Cadfael began to finger his way, at first very gently and soothingly, all down the thigh and calf of the helpless leg, probing and manipulating. Thus stretched out at rest, the twisted limb partially regained its proper alignment, and showed fairly formed, though much wasted by comparison with the left, and marred by the inturned toe and certain tight, bunched knots of sinew in the calf. He sought out these, and let his fingers dig deep there, wrestling with hard tissue.

'There I feel it,' said Rhun, breathing deep. 'It doesn't feel like pain – yes, it hurts, but not for crying. A good hurt ...'

Brother Cadfael oiled his hands, smoothed a palm over the shrunken calf, and went to work with firm fingertips, working tendons unexercised for years, beyond that tensed touch of toe upon ground. He was gentle and slow, feeling for the hard cores of resistance. There were unnatural tensions there, that would not melt to him yet. He let his fingers work softly, and his mind probed elsewhere.

'You were orphaned early. How long have you been with your Aunt Weaver?'

'Seven years now,' said Rhun almost drowsily, soothed by the circling fingers. 'I know we are a burden to her, but she never says it, nor she would never let any other say it. She has a good business, but small, it provides her needs and keeps two men at work, but she is not rich. Melangell works hard keeping the house and the kitchen, and earns her keep. I have learned to weave, but I am slow at it. I can neither stand for long nor sit for long, I am no profit to her. But she never speaks of it, for all she has an edge to her tongue when she pleases.'

'She would,' agreed Cadfael peacefully. 'A woman with many cares is liable to be short in her speech now and again, and no ill meant. She has brought you here for a miracle. You know that? Why else would you all three have walked all this way, measuring out the stages day by day at your pace? And yet I think you have no expectation of grace. Do you not believe Saint Winifred can do wonders?'

'I?' The boy was startled, he opened great eyes clearer than the clear waters Cadfael had navigated long ago, in the eastern fringes of the Midland Sea, over pale and glittering sand. 'Oh, you mistake me, I *do* believe. But why for me? In case like mine we come by our thousands, in worse case by the hundred. How dare I ask to be among the first? Besides, what I have I can bear. There are some who cannot bear what they have. The saint will know where to choose. There is no reason her choice should fall on me.'

'Then why did you consent to come?' Cadfael asked.

Rhun turned his head aside, and eyelids blue-veined like the petals of anemones veiled his eyes. 'They wished it, I did what they wanted. And there was Melangell ...'

Yes, Melangell who was altogether comely and bright and a charm to the eye, thought Cadfael. Her brother knew her dowryless, and wished her a little of joy and a decent marriage, and there at home, working hard in house and kitchen, and known for a penniless niece, suitors there were none. A venture so far upon the roads, to mingle with so various a company, might bring forth who could tell what chances?

In moving Rhun had plucked at a nerve that gripped and twisted him, he eased himself back against the timber wall with aching care. Cadfael drew up the homespun hose over the boy's nakedness, knotted him decent, and gently drew down his feet, the sound and the crippled, to the beaten earth floor.

'Come again to me tomorrow, after High Mass, for I think I can help you, if only a little. Now sit until I see if that sister of yours is waiting, and if not, you may rest easy until she comes. And I'll give you a single draught to take this night when you go to your bed. It will ease your pain and help

71

you to sleep.'

The girl was there, still and solitary against the sun-warmed wall, the brightness of her face clouded over, as though some eager expectation had turned into a grey disappointment; but at the sight of Rhun emerging she rose with a resolute smile for him, and her voice was as gay and heartening as ever as they moved slowly away.

He had an opportunity to study all of them next day at High Mass, when doubtless his mind should have been on higher things, but obstinately would not rise above the quivering crest of Mistress Weaver's head-cloth, and the curly dark crown of Matthew's thick crop of hair. Almost all the inhabitants of the guest-halls, the gentles who had separate apartments as well as the male and female pilgrims who shared the two common dortoirs, came in their best to this one office of the day, whatever they did with the rest of it. Mistress Weaver paid devout attention to every word of the office, and several times nudged Melangell sharply in the ribs to recall her to duty, for as often as not her head was turned sidewise, and her gaze directed rather at Matthew than at the altar. No question but her fancy, if not her whole heart, was deeply engaged there. As for Matthew, he stood at Ciaran's shoulder, always within touch. But twice at least he looked round, and his brooding eyes rested, with no change of countenance, upon Melangell. Yet on the one occasion when their glances met, it was Matthew

72

who turned abruptly away.

That young man, thought Cadfael, aware of the broken encounter of eyes, has a thing to do which no girl must be allowed to hinder or spoil: to get his fellow safely to his journey's end at Aberdaron.

He was already a celebrated figure in the enclave, this Ciaran. There was nothing secret about him, he spoke freely and humbly of himself. He had been intended for ordination, but had not yet gone beyond the first step as sub-deacon, and had not reached, and now never would reach, the tonsure. Brother Jerome, always a man to insinuate himself as close as might be to any sign of superlative virtue and holiness, had cultivated and questioned him, and freely retailed what he had learned to any of the brothers who would listen. The story of Ciaran's mortal sickness and penitential pilgrimage home to Aberdaron was known to all. The austerities he practised upon himself made a great impression. Brother Jerome held that the house was honoured in receiving such a man. And indeed that lean, passionate face, burning-eyed beneath the uncropped brown hair, had a vehement force and fervour.

Rhun could not kneel, but stood steady and stoical on his crutches throughout the office, his eyes fixed, wide and bright, upon the altar. In this soft, dim light within, already reflecting from every stone surface the muted brightness of a cloudless day outside, Cadfael saw that the boy was beautiful, the planes of his face as suave and graceful as any girl's, the curving of his fair hair round ears and cheeks angelically pure and chaste. If the woman with no son of her own doted on him, and was willing to forsake her living for a matter of weeks on the off-chance of a miracle that would heal him, who could wonder at her?

Since both his attention and his eyes were straying, Cadfael gave up the struggle and let them stray at large over all those devout heads, gathered in a close assembly and filling the nave of the church. An important pilgrimage has much of the atmosphere of a public fair about it, and brings along with it all the hangers-on who frequent such occasions, the pickpockets, the plausible salesmen of relics, sweetmeats, remedies, the fortune-tellers, the gamblers, the swindlers and cheats of all kinds. And some of these cultivate the most respectable of appearances, and prefer to work from within the pale rather than set up in the Foregate as at a market. It was always worth running an eye over the ranks within, as Hugh's sergeants were certainly doing along the ranks without, to mark down probable sources of trouble before ever the trouble began.

This congregation certainly looked precisely what it purported to be. Nevertheless, there were a few there worth a second glance. Three modest, unobtrusive tradesmen who had arrived closely one after another and rapidly and openly made acquaintance, to all appearances until then strangers: Walter Bagot, glover; John Shure, tailor; William Hales, farrier. Small craftsmen making this their summer holiday, and modestly out to enjoy it. And why not? Except that Cadfael had noted the tailor's hands devoutly folded, and observed that he cultivated the long, well-tended nails of a fairground sharper, hardly suitable for a tailor's work. He made a mental note of their faces, the glover rounded and glossy, as if oiled with the same dressing he used on his leathers, the tailor lean-jowled and sedate, with lank hair curtaining a lugubrious face, the farrier square, brown and twinkling of eye, the picture of honest good-humour.

They might be what they claimed. They might not. Hugh would be on the watch, so would the careful tavern-keepers of the Foregate and the town, by no means eager to hold their doors open to the fleecers and skinners of their own neighbours and customers.

Cadfael went out from Mass with his brethren, very thoughtful, and found Rhun already waiting for him in the herbarium.

The boy sat passive and submitted himself to Cadfael's handling, saying no word beyond his respectful greeting. The rhythm of the questing fingers, patiently coaxing apart the rigid tissues that lamed him, had a soothing effect, even when they probed deeply enough to cause pain. He let his head lean back against the timbers of the wall, and his eyes gradually closed. The tension of his cheeks and lips showed that he was not sleeping, but Cadfael was able to study the boy's face closely as he worked on him, and note his pallor, and the dark rings round his eyes.

'Well, did you take the dose I gave you for the night?' asked Cadfael, guessing at the answer.

'No.' Rhun opened his eyes apprehensively, to see if he was to be reproved for it, but Cadfael's face showed neither surprise nor reproach.

'Why not?'

'I don't know. Suddenly I felt there was no need. I was happy,' said Rhun, his eyes again closed, the better to examine his own actions and motives. 'I had prayed. It's not that I doubt the saint's power. Suddenly it seemed to me that I need not even wish to be healed … that I ought to offer up my lameness and pain freely, not as a price for favour. People bring offerings, and I have nothing else to offer. Do you think it might be acceptable? I meant it humbly.'

There could hardly be, thought Cadfael, among all her devotees, a more costly oblation. He has gone far along a difficult road who has come to the point of seeing that deprivation, pain and disability are of no consequence at all, beside the inward conviction of grace, and the secret peace of the soul. An acceptance which can only be made for a man's own self, never for any other. Another's grief is not to be tolerated, if there can be anything done to alleviate it.

'And did you sleep well?'

'No. But it didn't matter. I lay quiet all night

76

long. I tried to bear it gladly. And I was not the only one there wakeful.' He slept in the common dormitory for the men, and there must be several among his fellows there afflicted in one way or another, besides the sick and possibly contagious whom Brother Edmund had isolated in the infirmary. 'Ciaran was restless, too,' said Rhun reflectively. 'When it was all silent, after Lauds, he got up very quietly from his cot, trying not to disturb anyone, and started towards the door. I thought then how strange it was that he took his belt and scrip with him ...'

Cadfael was listening intently enough by this time. Why, indeed, if a man merely needed relief for his body during the night, should he burden himself with carrying his possessions about with him? Though the habit of being wary of theft, in such shared accommodation, might persist even when half-asleep, and in monastic care into the bargain.

'Did he so, indeed? And what followed?'

'Matthew has his own pallet drawn close beside Ciaran's, even in the night he lies with a hand stretched out to touch. Besides, you know, he seems to know by instinct whatever ails Ciaran. He rose up in an instant, and reached out and took Ciaran by the arm. And Ciaran started and gasped, and blinked round at him, like a man startled awake suddenly, and whispered that he'd been asleep and dreaming, and had dreamed it was time to start out on the road again. So then Matthew took the scrip from him and laid it aside,

77

and they both lay down in their beds again, and all was quiet as before. But I don't think Ciaran slept well, even after that, his dream had disturbed his mind too much, I heard him twisting and turning for a long time.'

'Did they know,' asked Cadfael, 'that you were also awake, and had heard what passed?'

'I can't tell. I made no pretence, and the pain was bad, I think they must have heard me shifting … I couldn't help it. But of course I made no sign, it would have been discourteous.'

So it passed as a dream, perhaps for the benefit of Rhun, or any other who might be wakeful as he was. True enough, a sick man troubled by night might very well rise by stealth to leave his friend in peace, out of consideration. But then, if he needed ease, he would have been forced to explain himself and go, when his friend nevertheless started awake to restrain him. Instead, he had pleaded a deluding dream, and lain down again. And men rousing in dreams do move silently, almost as if by stealth. It could be, it must be, simply what it seemed.

'You travelled some miles of the way with those two, Rhun. How did you all fare together on the road? You must have got to know them as well as any here.'

'It was their being slow, like us, that kept us all together, after my sister was nearly ridden down, and Matthew ran and caught her up and leaped the ditch with her. They were just slowly overtaking us then, after that we went on all together for company. But I wouldn't say we got to know them – they are so rapt in each other. And then, Ciaran was in pain, and that kept him silent, though he did tell us where he was bound, and why. It's true Melangell and Matthew took to walking last, behind us, and he carried our few goods for her, having so little of his own to carry. I never wondered at Ciaran being so silent,' said Rhun simply, 'seeing what he had to bear. And my Aunt Alice can talk for two,' he ended guilelessly.

So she could, and no doubt did, all the rest of the way into Shrewsbury.

'That pair, Ciaran and Matthew,' said Cadfael, still delicately probing, 'they never told you how they came together? Whether they were kin, or friends, or had simply met and kept company on the road? For they're much of an age, even of a kind, young men of some schooling, I fancy, bred to clerking or squiring, and yet not kin, or don't acknowledge it, and after their fashion very differently made. A man wonders how they ever came to be embarked together on this journey. It was south of Warwick when you met them? I wonder from how far south they came.'

'They never spoke of such things,' owned Rhun, himself considering them for the first time. 'It was good to have company on the way, one stout young man at least. The roads can be perilous for two women, with only a cripple like me. But now you speak of it, no, we did not learn much of where they came from, or what bound

79

them together. Unless my sister knows more. There were days,' said Rhun, shifting to assist Brother Cadfael's probings into the sinews of his thigh, 'when she and Matthew grew quite easy and talkative behind us.'

Cadfael doubted whether the subject of their conversation then had been anything but their two selves, brushing sleeves pleasurably along the summer highways, she in constant recall of the moment when she was snatched up bodily and swung across the ditch against Matthew's heart, he in constant contemplation of the delectable creature dancing at his elbow, and recollection of the feel of her slight, warm, frightened weight on his breast.

'But he'll hardly look at her now,' said Rhun regretfully. 'He's too intent on Ciaran, and Melangell will come between. But it costs him a dear effort to turn away from her, all the same.'

Cadfael stroked down the misshapen leg, and rose to scrub his oily hands. 'There, that's enough for today. But sit quiet a while and rest before you go. And will you take the draught tonight? At least keep it by you, and do what you feel to be right and best. But remember it's a kindness sometimes to accept help, a kindness to the giver. Would you wilfully inflict torment on yourself as Ciaran does? No, not you, you are too modest by far to set yourself up for braver and more to be worshipped than other men. So never think you do wrong by sparing yourself discomfort. Yet it's your choice, make it as you see fit.'

80

When the boy took up his crutches again and tapped his way out along the path towards the great court, Cadfael followed him at a distance, to watch his progress without embarrassing him. He could mark no change as yet. The stretched toe still barely dared touch ground, and still turned inward. And yet the sinews, cramped as they were, had some small force in them, instead of being withered and atrophied as he would have expected. If I had him here long enough, he thought, I could bring back some ease and use into that leg. But he'll go as he came. In three days now all will be over, the festival ended for this year, the guest-hall emptying. Ciaran and his guardian shadow will pass on northwards and westwards into Wales, and Dame Weaver will take her chicks back home to Campden. And those two, who might very well have made a fair match if things had been otherwise, will go their separate ways, and never see each other again. It's in the nature of things that those who gather in great numbers for the feasts of the church should also disperse again to their various duties afterwards. Still they need not all go away unchanged.

CHAPTER FIVE

Brother Adam of Reading, being lodged in the dortoir with the monks of the house, had had leisure to observe his fellow pilgrims of the guest-hall only at the offices of the church, and in their casual comings and goings about the precinct; and it happened that he came from the garden towards mid-afternoon, with Cadfael beside him, just as Ciaran and Matthew were crossing the court towards the cloister garth, there to sit in the sun for an hour or two before Vespers. There were plenty of others, monks, lay servants and guests, busy on their various occasions, but Ciaran's striking figure and painfully slow and careful gait marked him out for notice.

'Those two,' said Brother Adam, halting, 'I have seen before. At Abingdon, where I spent the first night after leaving Reading. They were lodged there the same night.'

'At Abingdon!' Cadfael echoed thoughtfully. 'So they came from far south. You did not cross them again after Abingdon, on the way here?'

'It was not likely. I was mounted. And then, I

had my abbot's mission to Leominster, which took me out of the direct way. No, I saw no more of them, never until now. But they can hardly be mistaken, once seen.'

'In what sort of case were they at Abingdon?' asked Cadfael, his eyes following the two inseparable figures until they vanished into the cloister. 'Would you say they had been long on the road before that night's halt? The man is pledged to go barefoot to Aberdaron, it would not take many miles to leave the mark on him.'

'He was going somewhat lamely, even then. They had both the dust of the roads on them. It might have been their first day's walking that ended there, but I doubt it.'

'He came to me to have his feet tended, yesterday,' said Cadfael, 'and I must see him again before evening. Two or three days of rest will set him up for the next stage of his walk.' From more than a day's going south of Abingdon to the remotest tip of Wales, a long, long walk. 'A strange, even a mistaken, piety it seems to me, to take upon oneself ostentatious pains, when there are poor fellows enough in the world who are born to pain they have not chosen, and carry it with humility.'

'The simple believe it brings merit,' said Brother Adam tolerantly. 'It may be he has no other claim upon outstanding virtue, and clutches at this.'

'But he's no simple soul,' said Cadfael with conviction, 'whatever he may be. He has, he tells me, a mortal disease, and is going to end his days in blessedness and peace at Aberdaron, and have his bones laid in Ynys Enlli, which is a noble ambition in a man of Welsh blood. The voluntary assumption of pain beyond his doom may even be a pennon of defiance, a wag of the hand against death. That I could understand. But I would not approve it.'

'It's very natural you should frown on it,' agreed Adam, smiling indulgence upon his companion and himself alike, 'seeing you are schooled to the alleviation of pain, and feel it to be a violator and an enemy. By the very virtue of these plants we have learned to use.' He patted the leather scrip at his girdle, and the soft rustle of seeds within answered him. They had been sorting over Cadfael's clay saucers of new seed from this freshly ripening year, and he had helped himself to two or three not native in his own herbarium. 'It is as good a dragon to fight as any in this world, pain.'

They had gone some yards more towards the stone steps that led up to the main door of the guest-hall, in no hurry, and taking pleasure in the contemplation of so much bustle and motion, when Brother Adam checked abruptly and stood at gaze.

'Well, well, I think you may have got some of our southern sinners as well as our would-be saints!'

Cadfael, surprised, followed where Adam was gazing, and stood to hear what further he would have to say, for the individual in question was the

84

least remarkable of men at first glance. He stood close to the gatehouse, one of a small group constantly on hand there to watch the new arrivals and the general commerce of the day. A big man, but so neatly and squarely built that his size was not wholly apparent, he stood with his thumbs in the belt of his plain but ample gown, which was nicely cut and fashioned to show him no nobleman, and no commoner, either, but a solid, respectable, comfortably provided fellow of the middle kind, merchant or tradesman. One of those who form the backbone of many a township in England, and can afford the occasional pilgrimage by way of a well-earned holiday. He gazed benignly upon the activity around him from a plump, shrewd, well-shaven face, favouring the whole creation with a broad, contented smile.

'That,' said Cadfael, eyeing his companion with bright enquiry, 'is, or so I am informed, one Simeon Poer, a merchant of Guildford, come on pilgrimage for his soul's sake, and because the summer chances to be very fine and inviting. And why not? Do you know of a reason?'

'Simeon Poer may well be his name,' said Brother Adam, 'or he may have half a dozen more ready to trot forward at need. I never knew a name for him, but his face and form I do know. Father Abbot uses me a good deal on his business outside the cloister and I have occasion to know most of the fairs and markets in our shire and beyond. I've seen that fellow — not gowned like a provost, as he is now, I grant you, but by the look of him he's been doing well lately – round every fairground, cultivating the company of those young, green roisterers who frequent every such gathering. For the contents of their pockets, surely. Most likely, dice. Even more likely, loaded dice. Though I wouldn't say he might not pick a pocket here and there, if business was bad. A quicker means to the same end, if a riskier.'

So knowing and practical a brother Cadfael had not encountered for some years among the innocents. Plainly Brother Adam's frequent sallies out of the cloister on the abbot's business had broadened his horizons. Cadfael regarded him with respect and warmth, and turned to study the smiling, benevolent merchant more closely.

'You're sure of him?'

'Sure that he's the same man, yes. Sure enough of his practices to challenge him openly, no, hardly, since he has never yet been taken up but once, and then he proved so slippery he slithered through the bailiff's fingers. But keep a weather eye on him, and this may be where he'll make the slip every rogue makes in the end, and get his comeuppance.'

'If you're right,' said Cadfael, 'has he not strayed rather far from his own haunts? In my experience, from years back I own, his kind seldom left the region where they knew their way about better than the bailiffs. Has he made the south country so hot for him that he must run for a fresh territory? That argues something worse

86

than cheating at dice.'

Brother Adam hoisted dubious shoulders. 'It could be. Some of our scum have found the disorders of faction very profitable, in their own way, just as their lords and masters have in theirs. Battles are not for them – far too dangerous to their own skins. But the brawls that blow up in towns where uneasy factions come together are meat and drink to them. Pockets to be picked, riots to be started – discreetly from the rear – unoffending elders who look prosperous to be knocked on the head or knifed from behind or have their purse-strings cut in the confusion ... Safer and easier than taking to the woods and living wild for prey, as their kind do in the country.'

Just such gatherings, thought Cadfael, as that at Winchester, where at least one man was knifed in the back and left dying. Might not the law in the south be searching for this man, to drive him so far from his usual hunting-grounds? For some worse offence than cheating silly young men of their money at dice? Something as black as murder itself?

'There are two or three others in the common guest-hall,' he said, 'about whom I have my doubts, but this man has had no truck with them so far as I've seen. But I'll bear it in mind, and keep a watchful eye open, and have Brother Denis do the same. And I'll mention what you say to Hugh Beringar, too, before this evening's out. Both he and the town provost will be glad to have fair warning.'

Since Ciaran was sitting quietly in the cloister garth, it seemed a pity he should be made to walk through the gardens to the herbarium, when Cadfael's broad brown feet were in excellent condition, and sensibly equipped with stout sandals. So Cadfael fetched the salve he had used on Ciaran's wounds and bruises, and the spirit that would brace and toughen his tender soles, and brought them to the cloister. It was pleasant there in the afternoon sun, and the turf was thick and springy and cool to bare feet. The roses were coming into full bloom, and their scent hung in the warm air like a benediction. But two such closed and sunless faces! Was the one truly condemned to an early death, and the other to lose and mourn so close a friend?

Ciaran was speaking as Cadfael approached, and did not at first notice him, but even when he was aware of the visitor bearing down on them he continued steadily to the end, ' ... you do but waste your time, for it will not happen. Nothing will be changed, don't look for it. Never! You might far better leave me and go home.'

Did the one of them believe in Saint Winifred's power, and pray and hope for a miracle? And was the other, the sick man, all too passionately of Rhun's mind, and set on offering his early death as an acceptable and willing sacrifice, rather than ask for healing?

Matthew had not yet noticed Cadfael's approach. His deep voice, measured and resolute, said just audibly, 'Save your breath! For I will go with you, step for step, to the very end.'

Then Cadfael was close, and they were both aware of him, and stirred defensively out of their private anguish, heaving in breath and schooling their faces to confront the outer world decently. They drew a little apart on the stone bench, welcoming Cadfael with somewhat strained smiles.

'I saw no need to make you come to me,' said Cadfael, dropping to his knees and opening his scrip in the bright green turf, 'when I am better able to come to you. So sit and be easy, and let me see how much work is yet to be done before you can go forth in good heart.'

'This is kind, brother,' said Ciaran, rousing himself with a sigh. 'Be assured that I do go in good heart, for my pilgrimage is short and my arrival assured.'

At the other end of the bench Matthew's voice said softly, 'Amen!'

After that it was all silence as Cadfael anointed the swollen soles, kneading spirit vigorously into the misused skin, surely heretofore accustomed always to going well shod, and soothed the ointment of cleavers into the healing grazes.

'There! Keep off your feet through tomorrow, but for such offices as you feel you must attend. Here there's no need to go far. And I'll come to you tomorrow and have you fit to stand somewhat longer the next day, when the saint is brought home.' When he spoke of her now, he hardly knew whether he was truly speaking of the mortal substance of Saint Winifred, which was generally believed to be in that silver-chaced reliquary, or of some hopeful distillation of her spirit which could fill with sanctity even an empty coffin, even a casket containing pitiful, faulty human bones, unworthy of her charity but subject, like all mortality, to the capricious, smiling mercies of those above and beyond question. If you could reason by pure logic for the occurrence of miracles, they would not be miracles, would they?

He scrubbed his hands on a handful of wool, and rose from his knees. In some twenty minutes or so it would be time for Vespers.

He had taken his leave, and almost reached the archway into the great court, when he heard rapid steps at his heels, a hand reached deprecatingly for his sleeve, and Matthew's voice said in his ear, 'Brother Cadfael, you left this lying.'

It was his jar of ointment, of rough, greenish pottery, almost invisible in the grass. The young man held it out in the palm of a broad, strong, workmanlike hand, long-fingered and elegant. Dark eyes, reserved but earnestly curious, searched Cadfael's face.

Cadfael took the jar with thanks, and put it away in his scrip. Ciaran sat where Matthew had left him, his face and burning gaze turned towards them; they stood at a distance between him and the outer day, and he had, for one moment, the look of a soul abandoned to absolute solitude in a populous world.

Cadfael and Matthew stood gazing in speculation and uncertainty into each other's eyes. This was that able, ready young man who had leaped into action at need, upon whom Melangell had fixed her young, unpractised heart, and to whom Rhun had surely looked for a hopeful way out for his sister, whatever might become of himself. Good, cultivated stock, surely, bred of some small gentry and taught a little Latin as well as his schooling in arms. How, except by the compulsion of inordinate love, did this one come to be ranging the country like a penniless vagabond, without root or attachment but to a dying man?

'Tell me truth,' said Cadfael. 'Is it indeed true — is it *certain* — that Ciaran goes this way towards his death?'

There was a brief moment of silence, as Matthew's wide-set eyes grew larger and darker. Then he said very softly and deliberately, 'It is truth. He is already marked for death. Unless your saint has a miracle for us, there is nothing can save him. Or me!' he ended abruptly, and wrenched himself away to return to his devoted watch.

Cadfael turned his back on supper in the refectory, and set off instead along the Foregate towards the town. Over the bridge that spanned the Severn, in through the gate, and up the curving slope of the Wyle to Hugh Beringar's town house. There he sat and nursed his godson Giles, a large, comely self-willed child, fair like his mother, and long of limb, some day to dwarf his small, dark, sardonic

91

father. Aline brought food and wine for her husband and his friend, and then sat down to her needlework, favouring her menfolk from time to time with a smiling glance of serene contentment. When her son fell asleep in Cadfael's lap she rose and lifted the boy away gently. He was heavy for her, but she had learned how to carry him lightly balanced on arm and shoulder. Cadfael watched her fondly as she bore the child away into the next room to his bed, and closed the door between.

'How is it possible that that girl can grow every day more radiant and lovely? I've known marriage rub the fine bloom off many a handsome maid. Yet it suits her as a halo does a saint.'

'Oh, there's something to be said for marriage,' said Hugh idly. 'Do I look so poorly on it? Though it's an odd study for a man of your habit, after all these years of celibacy ... And all the stravagings about the world before that! You can't have thought too highly of the wedded state, or you'd have ventured on it yourself. You took no vows until past forty, and you a well-set-up young fellow crusading all about the east with the best of them. How do I know you have not an Aline of your own locked away somewhere, somewhere in your re-membrance, as dear as mine is to me? Perhaps even a Giles of your own,' he added, whimsically smiling, 'a Giles God knows where, grown a man now ...'

Cadfael's silence and stillness, though perfectly easy and complacent, nevertheless sounded a mute warning in Hugh's perceptive senses. On the edge of drowsiness among his cushions after a long day out of doors, he opened a black, considering eye to train upon his friend's musing face, and withdrew delicately into practical business.

'Well, so this Simeon Poer is known in the south. I'm grateful to you and to Brother Adam for the nudge, though so far the man has set no foot wrong here. But these others you've pictured for me … At Wat's tavern in the Foregate they've had practice in marking down strangers who come with a fair or a feast, and spread themselves large about the town. Wat tells my people he has a group moving in, very merry, some of them strangers. They could well be these you name. Some of them, of course, the usual young fellows of the town and the Foregate with more pence than sense. They've been drinking a great deal, and throwing dice. Wat does not like the way the dice fall.'

'It's as I supposed,' said Cadfael, nodding. 'For every Mass of ours they'll be celebrating the Gamblers' Mass elsewhere. And by all means let the fools throw their money after their sense, so the odds be fair. But Wat knows a loaded throw when he sees one.'

'He knows how to rid his house of the plague, too. He has hissed in the ears of one of the strangers that his tavern is watched, and they'd be wise to take their school out of there. And for tonight he has a lad on the watch, to find out where they'll meet. Tomorrow night we'll have at them, and rid you of them in good time for the feast day, if all goes well.'

Which would be a very welcome cleansing, thought Cadfael, making his way back across the bridge in the first limpid dusk, with the river swirling its coiled currents beneath him in gleams of reflected light, low summer water leaving the islands outlined in swathes of drowned, browning weed. But as yet there was nothing to shed light, even by reflected, phantom gleams, upon that death so far away in the south country, whence the merchant Simeon Poer had set out. On pilgrimage for his respectable soul? Or in flight from a law aroused too fiercely for his safety, by something graver than the cozening of fools? Though Cadfael felt too close to folly himself to be loftily complacent even about that, however much it might be argued that gamblers deserved all they got.

The great gate of the abbey was closed, but the wicket in it stood open, shedding sunset light through from the west. In the mild dazzle Cadfael brushed shoulders and sleeves with another entering, and was a little surprised to be hoisted deferentially through the wicket by a firm hand at his elbow.

'Give you goodnight, brother!' sang a mellow voice in his ear, as the returning guest stepped within on his heels. And the solid, powerful, woollen-gowned form of Simeon Poer, self-styled merchant of Guildford, rolled vigorously past him, and crossed the great court to the stone steps of the guest-hall.

CHAPTER SIX

They were emerging from High Mass on the morning of the twenty-first day of June, the eve of Saint Winifred's translation, stepping out into a radiant morning, when the abbot's sedate progress towards his lodging was rudely disrupted by a sudden howl of dismay among the dispersing multitude of worshippers, a wild ripple of movement cleaving a path through their ranks, and the emergence of a frantic figure lurching forth on clumsy, naked feet to clutch at the abbot's robe, and appeal in a loud, indignant cry, 'Father Abbot, stand my friend and give me justice, for I am robbed! A thief, there is a thief among us!'

The abbot looked down in astonishment and concern into the face of Ciaran, convulsed and ablaze with resentment and distress.

'Father, I beg you, see justice done! I am helpless unless you help me!'

He awoke, somewhat late, to the unwarranted violence of his behaviour, and fell on his knees at the abbot's feet. 'Pardon, pardon! I am too loud and troublous, I hardly know what I say!'

The press of gossiping, festive worshippers just

95

loosed from Mass had fallen quiet all in a moment, and instead of dispersing drew in about them to listen and stare, avidly curious. The monks of the house, hindered in their orderly departure, hovered in quiet deprecation. Cadfael looked beyond the kneeling, imploring figure of Ciaran for its inseparable twin, and found Matthew just shouldering his way forward out of the crowd, open-mouthed and wide-eyed in patent bewilderment, to stand and gaze a few paces apart, and frown helplessly from the abbot to Ciaran and back again, in search of the cause of this abrupt turmoil. Was it possible that something had happened to the one that the other of the matched pair did not know?

'Get up!' said Radulfus, erect and calm. 'No need to kneel. Speak out whatever you have to say, and you shall have right.'

The pervasive silence spread, grew, filled even the most distant reaches of the great court. Those who had already scattered to the far corners turned and crept unobtrusively back again, large-eyed and prick-eared, to hang upon the fringes of the crowd already assembled.

Ciaran clambered to his feet, voluble before he was erect. 'Father, I had a ring, the copy of one the lord bishop of Winchester keeps for his occasions, bearing his device and inscription. Such copies he uses to afford safe-conduct to those he sends forth on his business or with his blessing, to open doors to them and provide protection on the road. Father, the ring is gone!'

'This ring was given to you by Henry of Blois himself?' asked Radulfus.

'No, Father, not in person. I was in the service of the prior of Hyde Abbey, a lay clerk, when this mortal sickness came on me, and I took this vow of mine to spend my remaining days in the canonry of Aberdaron. My prior – you know that Hyde is without an abbot, and has been for some years – my prior asked the lord bishop, of his goodness, to give me what protection he could for my journey ...'

So that had been the starting point of this barefoot journey, thought Cadfael, enlightened. Winchester itself, or as near as made no matter, for the New Minster of that city, always a jealous rival of the Old, where Bishop Henry presided, had been forced to abandon its old home in the city thirty years ago, and banished to Hyde Mead, on the north-western outskirts. There was no love lost between Henry and the community at Hyde, for it was the bishop who had been instrumental in keeping them deprived of an abbot for so long, in pursuit of his own ambition of turning them into an episcopal monastery. The struggle had been going on for some time, the bishop deploying various schemes to get the house into his own hands, and the prior using every means to resist these manipulations. It seemed Henry had still the grace to show compassion even on a servant of the hostile house, when he fell under the threat of disease and death. The traveller over whom the bishop-legate spread his protecting hand would pass unmolested wherever law retained its validity. Only those irreclaimably outlaw already would dare interfere with him.

'Father, the ring is gone, stolen from me this very morning. See here, the slashed threads that held it!' Ciaran heaved forward the drab linen scrip that rode at his belt, and showed two dangling ends of cord, very cleanly severed. 'A sharp knife – someone here has such a dagger. And my ring is gone!'

Prior Robert was at the abbot's elbow by then, agitated out of his silvery composure. 'Father, what this man says is true. He showed me the ring. Given to ensure him aid and hospitality on his journey, which is of most sad and solemn import. If now it is lost, should not the gate be closed while we enquire?'

'Let it be so,' said Radulfus, and stood silent to see Brother Jerome, ever ready and assiduous on the prior's heels, run to see the order carried out. 'Now, take breath and thought, for your loss cannot be lost far. You did not wear the ring, then, but carried it knotted securely by this cord, within your scrip?'

'Yes, Father. It was beyond words precious to me.'

'And when did you last ascertain that it was still there, and safe?'

'Father, this very morning I know I had it. Such few things as I possess, here they lie before you. Could I fail to see if this cord had been cut in the night while I slept? It is not so. This morning all was as I left it last night. I have been bidden to rest, by reason of my barefoot vow. Today I ventured out only for Mass. Here in the very church, in this great press of worshippers, some malevolent has broken every ban, and slashed loose my ring from me.'

And indeed, thought Cadfael, running a considering eye round all the curious, watching faces, it would not be difficult, in such a press, to find the strings that anchored the hidden ring, flick it out from its hiding-place, cut the strings and make away with it, discreetly between crowding bodies, and never be seen by a soul or felt by the victim. A neat thing, done so privately and expertly that even Matthew, who missed nothing that touched his friend, had missed this impudent assault. For Matthew stood there staring, obviously taken by surprise, and unsure as yet how to take this turn of events. His face was unreadable, closed and still, his eyes narrowed and bright, darting from face to face as Ciaran or abbot or prior spoke. Cadfael noted that Melangell had stolen forward close to him, and taken him hesitantly by the sleeve. He did not shake her off. By the slight lift of his head and widening of his eyes he knew who had touched him, and he let his hand feel for hers and clasp it, while his whole attention seemed to be fixed on Ciaran. Somewhere not far behind them Rhun leaned on his crutches, his fair face frowning in anxious dismay, Aunt Alice attendant at his shoulder, bright with curiosity. Here are we all, thought Cadfael, and not one of us knows what is in any other mind, or who has done what has been done, or what will come of it for any of those who look on and marvel.

'You cannot tell,' suggested Prior Robert, agitated and grieved, 'who stood close to you during the service? If indeed some ill-conditioned person has so misused the holy office as to commit theft in the very sacredness of the Mass ...'

'Father, I was intent only upon the altar.' Ciaran shook with fervour, holding the ravished scrip open before him with his sparse possessions bared to be seen. 'We were close pressed, so many people ... as is only seemly, in such a shrine ... Matthew was close at my back, but so he ever is. Who else there may have been by me, how can I say? There was no man or woman among us who was not hemmed in every way.'

'It is truth,' said Prior Robert, who had been much gratified at the large attendance. 'Father, the gate is now closed, we are all here who were present at Mass. And surely we all have a desire to see this wrong righted.'

'All, as I suppose,' said Radulfus drily, 'but one. One, who brought in here a knife or dagger sharp enough to slice through these tough cords cleanly. What other intents he brought in with him, I bid him consider and tremble for his soul. Robert, this ring must be found. All men of goodwill here will offer their aid, and show freely what they have. So will every guest who has not theft and sacrilege to hide. And see to it also that enquiry be

100

made, whether other articles of value have not been missed. For one theft means one thief, here within.'

'It shall be seen to, Father,' said Robert fervently. 'No honest, devout pilgrim will grudge to offer his aid. How could he wish to share his lodgings here with a thief?'

There was a stir of agreement and support, perhaps slightly delayed, as every man and woman eyed a neighbour, and then in haste elected to speak first. They came from every direction, hitherto unknown to one another, mingling and forming friendships now with the abandon of holiday. But how did they know who was immaculate and who was suspect, now the world had probed a merciless finger within the fold?

'Father,' pleaded Ciaran, still sweating and shaking with distress, 'here I offer in this scrip all that I brought into this enclave. Examine it, show that I have indeed been robbed. Here I came without even shoes to my feet, my all is here in your hands. And my fellow Matthew will open to you his own scrip as freely, an example to all these others that they may deliver themselves pure of blame. What we offer, they will not refuse.'

Matthew had withdrawn his hand from Melangell's sharply at this word. He shifted the unbleached cloth scrip, very like Ciaran's, round upon his hip. Ciaran's meagre travelling equipment lay open in the prior's hands. Robert slid them back into the pouch from which they had

101

come, and looked where Ciaran's distressed gaze guided him.

'Into your hands, Father, and willingly,' said Matthew, and stripped the bag from its buckles and held it forth.

Robert acknowledged the offering with a grave bow, and opened and probed it with delicate consideration. Most of what was there within he did not display, though he handled it. A spare shirt and linen drawers, crumpled from being carried so, and laundered on the way, probably more than once. The means of a gentleman's sparse toilet, razor, morsel of lye soap, a leather-bound breviary, a lean purse, a folded trophy of embroidered ribbon. Robert drew forth the only item he felt he must show, a sheathed dagger, such as any gentleman might carry at his right hip, barely longer than a man's hand.

'Yes, that is mine,' said Matthew, looking Abbot Radulfus straightly in the eyes. 'It has not slashed through those cords. Nor has it left my scrip since I entered your enclave, Father Abbot.'

Radulfus looked from the dagger to its owner, and briefly nodded. 'I well understand that no young man would set forth on these highroads today without the means of defending himself. All the more if he had another to defend, who carried no weapons. As I understand is your condition, my son. Yet within these walls you should not bear arms.'

'What, then, should I have done?' demanded Matthew, with a stiffening neck, and a note in his voice that just fell short of defiance.

'What you must do now,' said Radulfus firmly. 'Give it into the care of Brother Porter at the gatehouse, as others have done with their weapons. When you leave here you may reclaim it freely.'

There was nothing to be done but bow the head and give way gracefully, and Matthew managed it decently enough, but not gladly. 'I will do so, Father, and pray your pardon that I did not ask advice before.'

'But, Father,' Ciaran pleaded anxiously, 'my ring ... How shall I survive the way if I have not that safe-conduct to show?'

'Your ring shall be sought throughout this enclave, and every man who bears no guilt for its loss,' said the abbot, raising his voice to carry to the distant fringes of the silent crowd, 'will freely offer his own possessions for inspection. See to it, Robert!'

With that he proceeded on his way, and the crowd, after some moments of stillness as they watched him out of sight, dispersed in a sudden murmur of excited speculation. Prior Robert took Ciaran under his wing, and swept away with him towards the guest-hall, to recruit help from Brother Denis in his enquiries after the bishop's ring; and Matthew, not without one hesitant glance at Melangell, turned on his heel and went hastily after them.

A more innocent and co-operative company than

the guests at Shrewsbury abbey that day it would have been impossible to find. Every man opened his bundle or box almost eagerly, in haste to demonstrate his immaculate virtue. The quest, conducted as delicately as possible, went on all the afternoon, but they found no trace of the ring. Moreover, one or two of the better-off inhabitants of the common dormitory, who had had no occasion to penetrate to the bottom of their baggage so far, made grievous discoveries when they were obliged to do so. A yeoman from Lichfield found his reserve purse lighter by half than when he had tucked it away. Master Simeon Poer, one of the first to fling open his possessions, and the loudest in condemning so blasphemous a crime, claimed to have been robbed of a silver chain he had intended to present at the altar next day. A poor parish priest, making this pilgrimage the one fulfilled dream of his life, was left lamenting the loss of a small casket, made by his own hands over more than a year, and decorated with inlays of silver and glass, in which he had hoped to carry back with him some memento of his visit, a dried flower from the garden, even a thread or two drawn from the fringe of the altar-cloth under Saint Winifred's reliquary. A merchant from Worcester could not find his good leather belt to his best coat, saved up for the morrow. One or two others had a suspicion that their belongings had been fingered and scorned, which was worst of all.

It was all over, and fruitless, when Cadfael at

last repaired to his workshop in time to await the coming of Rhun. The boy came prompt to his hour, great-eyed and thoughtful, and lay submissive and mute under Cadfael's ministrations, which probed every day a little deeper into his knotted and stubborn tissues.

'Brother,' he said at length, looking up, 'you did not find a dagger in any man's pouch, did you?'

'No, no such thing.' Though there had been, understandably, a number of small, homely knives, the kind a man needs to hack his bread and meat in lodgings along the way, or meals under a hedge. Many of them were sharp enough for most everyday purposes, but not sharp enough to leave stout cords sheared through without a twitch to betray the assault. 'But men who go shaven carry razors, too, and a blunt razor would be an abomination. Once a thief comes into the pale, child, it's hard for honest men to be a match for him. He who has no scruple has always the advantage of those who keep to rule. But you need not trouble your heart, you've done no wrong to any man. Never let this ill thing spoil tomorrow for you.'

'No,' agreed the boy, still preoccupied. 'But, brother, there *is* another dagger – one, at least. Sheath and all, a good length – I know, I was pressed close against him yesterday at Mass. You know I have to hold fast by my crutches to stand for long, and he had a big linen scrip on his belt, hard against my hand and arm, where we were crowded together. I felt the shape of it, cross-hilt and all. I know! But you did not find it.'

105

'And who was it,' asked Cadfael, still carefully working the tissues that resisted his fingers, 'who had his armoury about him at Mass?'

'It was that big merchant with the good gown – made from valley wool. I've learned to know cloth. They call him Simeon Poer. But you didn't find it. Perhaps he's handed it to Brother Porter, just as Matthew has had to do now.'

'Perhaps,' said Cadfael. 'When was it you discovered this? Yesterday? And what of today? Was he again close to you?'

'No, not today.'

No, today he had stood stolidly to watch the play, eyes and ears alert, ready to open his pouch there before all if need be, smiling complacently as the abbot directed the disarming of another man. He had certainly had no dagger on him then, however he had disposed of it in the meantime. There were hiding-places enough here within the walls, for a dagger and any amount of small, stolen valuables. To search was itself only a pretence, unless authority was prepared to keep the gates closed and the guests prisoned within until every yard of the gardens had been dug up, and every bed and bench in dortoir and hall pulled to pieces. The sinners have always the start of the honest men.

'It was not fair that Matthew should be made to surrender his dagger,' said Rhun, 'when another man had one still about him. And Ciaran already so terribly afraid to stir, not having his ring. He won't even come out of the dortoir until tomorrow. He is sick for loss of it.'

106

Yes, that seemed to be true. And how strange, thought Cadfael, pricked into realisation, to see a man sweating for fear, who has already calmly declared himself as one condemned to death? Then why fear? Fear should be dead.

Yet men are strange, he thought in revulsion. And a blessed and quiet death in Aberdaron, well-prepared, and surrounded by the prayers and compassion of like-minded votaries, may well seem a very different matter from crude slaughter by strangers and footpads somewhere in the wilder stretches of the road.

But this Simeon Poer – say he had such a dagger yesterday, and therefore may well have had it on him today, in the crowded array of the Mass. Then what did he do with it so quickly, before Ciaran discovered his loss? And how did he know he must perforce dispose of it quickly? Who had such fair warning of the need, if not the thief?

'Trouble your head no more,' said Cadfael, looking down at the boy's beautiful, vulnerable face, 'for Matthew nor for Ciaran, but think only of the morrow, when you approach the saint. Both she and God see you all, and have no need to be told of what your needs are. All you have to do is wait in quiet for whatever will be. For whatever it may be, it will not be wanton. Did you take your dose last night?'

Rhun's pale, brilliant eyes were startled wide open, sunlight and ice, blindingly clear. 'No. It was a good day, I wanted to give thanks. It isn't that I don't value what you can do for me. Only I wished also to give something. And I did sleep, truly I slept well ...'

'So do tonight also,' said Cadfael gently, and slid an arm round the boy's body to hoist him steadily upright. 'Say your prayers, think quietly what you should do, do it, and sleep. There is no man living, neither king nor emperor, can do more or better, or trust in a better harvest.'

Ciaran did not stir from within the guest-hall again that day. Matthew did, against all precedent emerging from the arched doorway without his companion, and standing at the head of the stone staircase to the great court with hands spread to touch the courses of the deep doorway, and head drawn back to heave in great breaths of evening air. Supper was eaten, the milder evening stir of movement threaded the court, in the cool, grateful lull before Compline.

Brother Cadfael had left the chapter-house before the end of the readings, having a few things to attend to in the herbarium, and was crossing towards the garden when he caught sight of the young man standing there at the top of the steps, breathing in deeply and with evident pleasure. For some reason Matthew looked taller for being alone, and younger, his face closed but tranquil in the soft evening light. When he moved forward and began to descend to the court, Cadfael looked instinctively for the other figure that should have been close behind him, if not in its usual place a step before him, but no Ciaran emerged. Well, he had been urged to rest, and presumably was glad to comply, but never before had Matthew left his side, by night or day, resting or stirring. Not even to follow Melangell, except broodingly with his eye and against his will.

People, thought Cadfael, going on his way without haste, people are endlessly mysterious, and I am endlessly curious. A sin to be confessed, no doubt, and well worth a penance. As long as man is curious about his fellowman, that appetite alone will keep him alive. Why do folk do the things they do? Why, if you know you are diseased and dying, and wish to reach a desired haven before the end, why do you condemn yourself to do the long journey barefoot, and burden yourself with a weight about your neck? How are you thus rendered more acceptable to God, when you might have lent a hand to someone on the road crippled not by perversity but from birth, like the boy Rhun? And why do you dedicate your youth and strength to following another man step by step the length of the land, and why does he suffer you to be his shadow, when he should be composing his mind to peace, and taking a decent leave of his friends, not laying his own load upon them?

There he checked, rounding the corner of the yew hedge into the rose garden. It was not his fellow-man he beheld, sitting in the turf on the far side of the flower beds, gazing across the slope of the pease fields beyond and the low, stony, silvery summer waters of the Meole brook, but his fellow-woman, solitary and still, her knees drawn up under her chin and encircled closely by her folded arms. Aunt Alice Weaver, no doubt, was deep in talk with half a dozen worthy matrons of her own generation, and Rhun, surely, already in his bed. Melangell had stolen away alone to be quiet here in the garden and nurse her lame dreams and indomitable hopes. She was a small, dark shape, gold-haloed against the bright west. By the look of that sky tomorrow, Saint Winifred's day, would again be cloudless and beautiful.

The whole width of the rose garden was between them, and she did not hear him come and pass by on the grassy path to his final duties of the day in his workshop, seeing everything put away tidily, checking the stoppers of all his flagons and flasks, and making sure the brazier, which had been in service earlier, was safely quenched and cooled. Brother Oswin, young, enthusiastic and devoted, was nonetheless liable to overlook details, though he had now outlived his tendency to break things. Cadfael ran an eye over everything, and found it good. There was no hurry now, he had time before Compline to sit down here in the wood-scented dimness and think. Time for others to lose and find one another, and use or waste these closing moments of the day. For those three blameless tradesmen, Walter Bagot, glover; John Shure, tailor; William Hales, farrier; to betake themselves to wherever their dice school was to meet this night, and run their necks into Hugh's trap. Time for that more ambiguous character, Simeon Poer, to evade or trip into the same snare, or go the other way about some other nocturnal business of his own. Cadfael had seen two of the former three go out from the gatehouse, and the third follow some minutes later, and was sure in his own mind that the self-styled merchant of Guildford would not be long after them. Time, too, for that unaccountably solitary young man, somehow loosed off his chain, to range this whole territory suddenly opened to him, and happen upon the solitary girl.

Cadfael put up his feet on the wooden bench, and closed his eyes for a brief respite.

Matthew was there at her back before she knew it. The sudden rustle as he stepped into sun-dried long grass at the edge of the field startled her, and she swung round in alarm, scrambling to her knees and staring up into his face with dilated eyes, half-blinded by the blaze of the sunset into which she had been steadily staring. Her face was utterly open, vulnerable and childlike. She looked as she had looked when he had swept her up in his arms and leaped the ditch with her, clear of the galloping horses. Just so she had opened her eyes and looked up at him, still dazed and frightened, and just so had her fear melted away into wonder and pleasure, finding in him nothing but reassurance, kindness and admiration.

111

That pure, paired encounter of eyes did not last long. She blinked, and shook her head a little to clear her dazzled vision, and looked beyond him, searching, not believing he could be here alone.

'Ciaran ...? Is there something you need for him?'

'No,' said Matthew shortly, and for a moment turned his head away. 'He's in his bed.'

'But you never leave his bed!' It was said in innocence, even in anxiety. Whatever she grudged to Ciaran, she still pitied and understood him.

'You see I have left it,' said Matthew harshly. 'I have needs, too ... a breath of air. And he is very well where he is, and won't stir.'

'I was well sure,' she said with resigned bitterness, 'that you had not come out to look for me.' She made to rise, swiftly and gracefully enough, but he put out a hand, almost against his will, as it seemed, to take her under the wrist and lift her. It was withdrawn as abruptly when she evaded his touch, and rose to her feet unaided. 'But at least,' she said deliberately, 'you did not turn and run from me when you found me. I should be grateful, even for that.'

'I am not free,' he protested, stung. 'You know it better than any.'

'Then neither were you free when we kept pace along the road,' said Melangell fiercely, 'when you carried my burden, and walked beside me, and let Ciaran hobble along before, where he could not see how you smiled on me then and were gallant and cherished me when the road was rough, and spoke softly, as if you took delight in being beside me. Why did you not give me warning then that you were not free? Or better, take him some other way, and leave us alone? Then I might have taken good heed in time, and in time forgotten you. As now I never shall! Never, to my life's end!'

All the flesh of his lips and cheeks shrank and tightened before her eyes, in a contortion of either rage or pain, she could not tell which. She was staring too close and too passionately to see very clearly. He turned his head sharply away, to evade her eyes.

'You charge me justly,' he said in a harsh whisper, 'I was at fault. I never should have believed there could be so clean and sweet a happiness for me. I should have left you, but I could not ... Oh, God! You think I could have turned him? He clung to you, to your good aunt ... Yet I should have been strong enough to hold off from you and let you alone ...' As rapidly as he had swung away from her he swung back again, reaching a hand to take her by the chin and hold her face to face with him, so ungently that she felt the pressure of his fingers bruising her flesh. 'Do you know how hard a thing you are asking? No! This countenance you never saw, did you, never but through someone else's eyes. Who would provide you a mirror to see yourself? Some pool, perhaps, if ever you had the leisure to lean over and look. How should you know what this face can do to a man already lost? And you marvel I took what I could get for water in a drought, when it walked beside me? I should rather have died than stay beside you, to trouble your peace. God forgive me!'

She was five years nearer childhood than he, even taking into account the two years or more a girl child has advantage over the boys of her own age. She stood entranced, a little frightened by his intensity, and inexpressibly moved by the anguish she felt emanating from him like a raw, drowning odour. The long-fingered hand that held her shook terribly, his whole body quivered. She put up her own hand gently and closed it over his, uplifted out of her own wretchedness by his greater and more inexplicable distress.

'I dare not speak for God,' she said steadily, 'but whatever there may be for me to forgive, that I dare. It is not your fault that I love you. All you ever did was be kinder to me than ever man was since I left Wales. And I did know, love, you did tell me, if I had heeded then, you did tell me you were a man under vow. What it was you never told me, but never grieve, oh, my own soul, never grieve so ...'

While they stood rapt, the sunset light had deepened, blazed and burned silently into glowing ash, and the first feathery shade of twilight, like the passing of a swift's wings, fled across their faces and melted into sudden pearly, radiant light. Her wide eyes were brimming with tears, almost the match of his. When he stooped to her, there was no way of knowing which of them had begun the kiss.

The little bell for Compline sounded clearly through the gardens on so limpid an evening, and stirred Brother Cadfael out of his half-doze at once. He was accustomed, in this refuge of his maturity as surely as in the warfaring of his youth, to awake fresh and alert, as he fell asleep, making the most of the twin worlds of night and day. He rose and went out into the earliest glowing image of evening, and closed the door after him.

It was but a few moments back to church through the herbarium and the rose garden. He went briskly, happy with the beauty of the evening and the promise for the morrow, and never knew why he should look aside to westward in passing, unless it was that the whole expanse of the sky on that side was delicate, pure and warming, like a girl's blush. And there they were, two clear shadows clasped together in silhouette against the fire of the west, outlined on the crest above the slope to the invisible brook. Matthew and Melangell, unmistakable, constrained still but in each other's arms, linked in a kiss that lasted while Brother Cadfael came, passed and slipped away to his different devotions, but with that image printed indelibly on his eyes, even in his prayers.

CHAPTER SEVEN

The outrider of the bishop-legate's envoy — or should he rather be considered the empress's envoy? — arrived within the town and was directed through to the gatehouse of the castle in mid-evening of that same twenty-first day of June, to be presented to Hugh Beringar just as he was marshalling a half-dozen men to go down to the bridge and take an unpredicted part in the plans of Master Simeon Poer and his associates. Who would almost certainly be armed, being so far from home and in hitherto unexplored territory. Hugh found the visitor an unwelcome hindrance, but was too well aware of the many perils hemming the king's party on every side to dismiss the herald without ceremony. Whatever this embassage might be, he needed to know it, and make due preparation to deal with it.

In the gatehouse guard-room he found himself facing a stolid middle-aged squire, who delivered his errand word perfect.

'My lord sheriff, the Lady of the English and the lord bishop of Winchester entreat you to receive in peace their envoy, who comes to you with offerings of peace and good order in their name, and in their name asks your aid in resolving the griefs of the kingdom. I come before to announce him.'

So the empress had assumed the traditional title of a queen-elect before her coronation! The matter began to look final.

'The lord bishop's envoy will be welcome,' said Hugh, 'and shall be received with all honour here in Shrewsbury. I will lend an attentive ear to whatever he may have to say to me. As at this moment I have an affair in hand which will not wait. How far ahead of your lord do you ride?'

'A matter of two hours, perhaps,' said the squire, considering.

'Good, then I can set forward all necessary preparations for his reception, and still have time to clear up a small thing I have in hand. With how many attendants does he come?'

'Two men-at-arms only, my lord, and myself.'

'Then I will leave you in the hands of my deputy, who will have lodgings made ready for you and your two men here in the castle. As for your lord, he shall come to my own house, and my wife shall make him welcome. Hold me excused if I make small ceremony now, for this business is a twilight matter, and will not wait. Later I will see amends made.'

The messenger was well content to have his horse stabled and tended, and be led away by Alan Herbard to a comfortable lodging where he

117

could shed his boots and leather coat, and be at his ease, and take his time and his pleasure over the meat and wine that was presently set before him. Hugh's young deputy would play the host very graciously. He was still new in office, and did everything committed to him with a flourish. Hugh left them to it, and took his half-dozen men briskly out through the town.

It was past Compline then, neither light nor dark, but hesitant between. By the time they reached the High Cross and turned down the steep curve of the Wyle they had their twilight eyes. In full darkness their quarry might have a better chance of eluding them, by daylight they would themselves have been too easily observed from afar. If these gamesters were experts they would have a lookout posted to give fair warning.

The Wyle, uncoiling eastward, brought them down to the town wall and the English gate, and there a thin, leggy child, shaggy-haired and bright-eyed, started out of the shadows under the gate to catch at Hugh's sleeve. Wat's boy, a sharp urchin of the Foregate, bursting with the importance of his errand and his own wit in managing it, had pinned down his quarry, and waited to inform and advise.

'My lord, they're met – all the four from the abbey, and a dozen or more from these parts, mostly from the town.' His note of scorn implied that they were sharper in the Foregate. 'You'd best leave the horses and go afoot. Riders out at this hour – they'd break and run as soon as you set hooves on the bridge. The sound carries.'

118

Good sense, that, if the meeting-place was close by. 'Where are they, then?' asked Hugh, dismounting.

'Under the far arch of the bridge, my lord – dry as a bone it is, and snug.' So it would be, with this low summer water. Only in full spate did the river prevent passage beneath that arch. In this fine season it would be a nest of dried-out grasses.

'They have a light, then?'

'A dark lantern. There's not a glimmer you'll see from either side unless you go down to the water, it sheds light only on the flat stone where they're throwing.'

Easily quenched, then, at the first alarm, and they would scatter like startled birds, every way. The fleecers would be the first and fleetest. The fleeced might well be netted in some numbers, but their offence was no more than being foolish at their own expense, not theft nor malpractice on any other.

'We leave the horses here,' said Hugh, making up his mind. 'You heard the boy. They're under the bridge, they'll have used the path that goes down to the Gaye, along the riverside. The other side of the arch is thick bushes, but that's the way they'll break. Three men to either slope, and I'll bear with the western three. And let our own young fools by, if you can pick them out, but hold fast the strangers.'

In this fashion they went to their raiding. They crossed the bridge by ones and twos, above the Severn water green with weedy shallows and

119

shimmering with reflected light, and took their places on either side, spaced among the fringing bushes of the bank. By the time they were in place the afterglow had dissolved and faded into the western horizon, and the night came down like a velvet hand. Hugh drew off to westward along the by-road until at length he caught the faint glimmer of light beneath the stone arch. They were there. If in such numbers, perhaps he should have held them in better respect and brought more men. But he did not want the townsmen. By all means let them sneak away to their beds and think better of their dreams of milking cows likely to prove drier than sand. It was the cheats he wanted. Let the provost of the town deal with his civic idiots.

He let the sky darken somewhat before he took them in. The summer night settled, soft wings folding, and no moon. Then, at his whistle, they moved down from either flank.

It was the close-set bushes on the bank, rustling stealthily in a windless night, that betrayed their coming a moment too soon. Whoever was on watch, below there, had a sharp ear. There was a shrill whistle, suddenly muted. The lantern went out instantly, there was black dark under the solid stonework of the bridge. Down went Hugh and his men, abandoning stealth for speed. Bodies parted, collided, heaved and fled, with no sound but the panting and gasping of scared breath. Hugh's officers waded through bushes, closing down to seal the archway. Some of those thus penned beneath the bridge broke to left, some to right, not venturing to climb into waiting arms, but wading through the shallows and floundering even into deeper water. A few struck out for the opposite shore, local lads well acquainted with their river and its reaches, and water-borne, like its fish, almost from birth. Let them go, they were Shrewsbury born and bred. If they had lost money, more fools they, but let them get to their beds and repent in peace. If their wives would let them!

But there were those beneath the arch of the bridge who had not Severn water in their blood, and were less ready to wet more than their feet in even low water. And suddenly these had steel in their hands, and were weaving and slashing and stabbing their way through into the open as best they could, and without scruple. It did not last long. In the quaking dark, sprawled among the trampled grasses up the riverside, Hugh's six clung to such captives as they could grapple, and shook off trickles of blood from their own scratches and gashes. And diminishing in the darkness, the thresh and toss of bushes marked the flight of those who had got away. Unseen beneath the bridge, the deserted lantern and scattered dice, grave loss to a trickster who must now prepare a new set, lay waiting to be retrieved.

Hugh shook off a few drops of blood from a grazed arm, and went scrambling through the rough grass to the path leading up from the Gaye to the highroad and the bridge. Before him a shadowy body fled, cursing. Hugh launched a shout to reach the road ahead of them: 'Hold him! The law wants him!' Foregate and town might be on their way to bed, but there were always late strays, both lawful and unlawful, and some on both sides would joyfully take up such an invitation to mischief or justice, whichever way the mind happened to bend.

Above him, in the deep, soft summer night that now bore only a saffron thread along the west, an answering hail shrilled, startled and merry, and there were confused sounds of brief, breathless struggle. Hugh loped up to the highroad to see three shadowy horsemen halted at the approach to the bridge, two of them closed in to flank the first, and that first leaning slightly from his saddle to grip in one hand the collar of a panting figure that leaned against his mount heaving in breath, and with small energy to attempt anything besides.

'I think, sir,' said the captor, eyeing Hugh's approach, 'this may be what you wanted. It seemed to me that the law cried out for him? Am I then addressing the law in these parts?'

It was a fine, ringing voice, unaccustomed to subduing its tone. The soft dark did not disclose his face clearly, but showed a body erect in the saddle, supple, shapely, unquestionably young. He shifted his grip on the prisoner, as though to surrender him to a better claim. Thus all but released, the fugitive did not break free and run for it, but spread his feet and stood his ground, half-defiant, eyeing Hugh dubiously.

'I'm in your debt for a minnow, it seems,' said Hugh, grinning as he recognised the man he had been chasing. 'But I doubt I've let all the salmon get clear away up-river. We were about breaking up a parcel of cheating rogues come here looking for prey, but this young gentleman you have by the coat turns out to be merely one of the simpletons, our worthy goldsmith out of the town. Master Daniel, I doubt there's more gold and silver to be lost than gained, in the company you've been keeping.'

'It's no crime to make a match at dice,' muttered the young man, shuffling his feet sullenly in the dust of the road. 'My luck would have turned ...'

'Not with the dice they brought with them. But true it's no crime to waste your evening and go home with empty pockets, and I've no charge to make against you, provided you go back now, and hand yourself over with the rest to my sergeant. Behave yourself prettily, and you'll be home by midnight.'

Master Daniel Aurifaber took his dismissal thankfully, and slouched back towards the bridge, to be gathered in among the captives. The sound of hooves crossing the bridge at a trot indicated that someone had run for the horses, and intended a hunt to westward, in the direction the birds of prey had taken. In less than a mile they would be safe in woodland, and it would take hounds to run them to earth. Small chance of hunting them down by night. On the morrow something might be attempted.

'This is hardly the welcome I intended for you,' said Hugh, peering up into the shadowy face above him. 'For you, I think, must be the envoy sent from the Empress Maud and the bishop of Winchester. Your herald arrived little more than an hour ago, I did not expect you quite so soon. I had thought I should be done with this matter by the time you came. My name is Hugh Beringar, I stand here as sheriff for King Stephen. Your men are provided for at the castle, I'll send a guide with them. You, sir, are my own guest, if you will do my house that honour.'

'You're very gracious,' said the empress's messenger blithely, 'and with all my heart I will. But had you not better first make up your accounts with these townsmen of yours, and let them creep away to their beds? My business can well wait a little longer.'

'Not the most successful action ever I planned,' Hugh owned later to Cadfael. 'I under-estimated both their hardihood and the amount of cold steel they'd have about them.'

There were four guests missing from Brother Denis's halls that night: Master Simeon Poer, merchant of Guildford; Walter Bagot, glover; John Shure, tailor; William Hales, farrier. Of these, William Hales lay that night in a stone cell in Shrewsbury castle, along with a travelling pedlar who had touted for them in the town, but the other three had all broken safely away, bar a few scratches and bruises, into the woods to

124

westward, the most northerly outlying spinneys of the Long Forest, there to bed down in the warm night and count their injuries and their gains, which were considerable. They could not now return to the abbey or the town; the traffic would in any case have stood only one more night at a profit. Three nights are the most to be reckoned on, after that some aggrieved wretch is sure to grow suspicious. Nor could they yet venture south again. But the man who lives on his wits must keep them well honed and adaptable, and there are more ways than one of making a dishonest living.

As for the young rufflers and simple tradesmen who had come out with visions of rattling their winnings on the way home to their wives, they were herded into the gatehouse to be chided, warned, and sent home chapfallen, with very little in their pockets.

And there the night's work would have ended, if the flare of the torch under the gateway had not caught the metal gleam of a ring on Daniel Aurifaber's right hand, flat silver with an oval bezel, for one instant sharply defined. Hugh saw it, and laid a hand on the goldsmith's arm to detain him.

'That ring – let me see it closer!'

Daniel handed it over with a hint of reluctance, though it seemed to stem rather from bewilderment than from any feeling of guilt. It fitted closely, and passed over his knuckle with slight difficulty, but the finger bore no sign of having worn it regularly.

'Where did you get this?' asked Hugh, holding it under the flickering light to examine the device and inscription.

'I bought it honestly,' said Daniel defensively.

'That I need not doubt. But from whom? From one of those gamesters? Which one?'

'The merchant – Simeon Poer he called himself. He offered it, and it was a good piece of work. I paid well for it.'

'You have paid double for it, my friend,' said Hugh, 'for you bid fair to lose ring and money and all. Did it never enter your mind that it might be stolen?'

By the single nervous flutter of the goldsmith's eyelids the thought had certainly occurred to him, however hurriedly he had put it out of his mind again. 'No! Why should I think so? He seemed a stout, prosperous person, all he claimed to be ...'

'This very morning,' said Hugh, 'just such a ring was taken during Mass from a pilgrim at the abbey. Abbot Radulfus sent word up to the provost, after they had searched thoroughly within the pale, in case it should be offered for sale in the market. I had the description of it in turn from the provost. This is the device and inscription of the bishop of Winchester, and it was given to the bearer to secure him safe-conduct on the road.'

'But I bought it in good faith,' protested Daniel, dismayed. 'I paid the man what he asked, the ring is mine, honestly come by.'

'From a thief. Your misfortune, lad, and it may

teach you to be more wary of sudden kind acquaintances in the future who offer you rings to buy – wasn't it so? – at somewhat less than you know to be their value? Travelling men rattling dice give nothing for nothing, but take whatever they can get. If they've emptied your purse for you, take warning for the next time. This must go back to the lord abbot in the morning. Let him deal with the owner.' He saw the goldsmith draw angry breath to complain of his deprivation, and shook his head to ward off the effort, not unkindly. 'You have no remedy. Bite your tongue, Daniel, and go make your peace with your wife.'

The empress's envoy rode gently up the Wyle in the deepening dark, keeping pace with Hugh's smaller mount. His own was a fine, tall beast, and the young man in the saddle was long of body and limb. Afoot, thought Hugh, studying him sidelong, he will top me by a head. Very much of an age with me, I might give him a year or two, hardly more.

'Were you ever in Shrewsbury before?'

'Never. Once, perhaps, I was just within the shire, I am not sure how the border runs. I was near Ludlow once. This abbey of yours, I marked it as I came by, a very fine, large enclosure. They keep the Benedictine Rule?'

'They do.' Hugh expected further questions, but they did not come. 'You have kinsmen in the Order?'

127

Even in the dark he was aware of his companion's grave, musing smile. 'In a manner of speaking, yes, I have. I think he would give me leave to call him so, though there is no blood-kinship. One who used me like a son. I keep a kindness for the habit, for his sake. And did I hear you say there are pilgrims here now? For some particular feast?'

'For the translation of Saint Winifred, who was brought here four years ago from Wales. Tomorrow is the day of her arrival.' Hugh had spoken by custom, quite forgetting what Cadfael had told him of that arrival, but the mention of it brought his friend's story back sharply to mind. 'I was not in Shrewsbury then,' he said, withholding judgement. 'I brought my manors to King Stephen's support the following year. My own country is the north of the shire.'

They had reached the top of the hill, and were turning towards Saint Mary's church. The great gate of Hugh's courtyard stood wide, with torches at the gateposts, waiting for them. His message had been faithfully delivered to Aline, and she was waiting for them with all due ceremony, the bedchamber prepared, the meal ready to come to table. All rules, all times, bow to the coming of a guest, the duty and privilege of hospitality.

She met them at the door, opening it wide to welcome them in. They stepped into the hall, and into a flood of light from torches at the walls and candles on the table, and instinctively they turned to face each other, taking the first long look. It grew ever longer as their intent eyes grew wider. It was a question which of them groped towards recognition first. Memory pricked and realisation awoke almost stealthily. Aline stood smiling and wondering, but mute, eyeing first one, then the other, until they should stir and shed a clearer light.

'But I know you!' said Hugh. 'Now I see you, I do know you.'

'I have seen you before,' agreed the guest. 'I was never in this shire but the once, and yet ...'

'It needed light to see you by,' said Hugh, 'for I never heard your voice but the once, and then no more than a few words. I doubt if you even remember them, but I do. Six words only. "Now have ado with a man!" you said. And your name, your name I never heard but in a manner I take as it was meant. You are Robert, the forester's son who fetched Yves Hugonin out of that robber fortress up on Titterstone Clee. And took him home with you, I think, and his sister with him.'

'And you are that officer who laid the siege that gave me the cover I needed,' cried the guest, gleaming. 'Forgive me that I hid from you then, but I had no warranty there in your territory. How glad I am to meet you honestly now, with no need to take to flight.'

'And no need now to be Robert, the forester's son,' said Hugh, elated and smiling. 'My name I have given you, and the freedom of this house I offer with it. Now may I know yours?'

'In Antioch, where I was born,' said the guest, 'I

was called Daoud. But my father was an Englishman of Robert of Normandy's force, and among his comrades in arms I was baptised a Christian, and took the name of the priest who stood my godfather. Now I bear the name of Olivier de Bretagne.'

They sat late into the night together, savouring each other now face to face, after a year and a half of remembering and wondering. But first, as was due, they made short work of Olivier's errand here.

'I am sent,' he said seriously, 'to urge all sheriffs of shires to consider, whatever their previous fealty, whether they should not now accept the proffered peace under the Empress Maud, and take the oath of loyalty to her. This is the message of the bishop and the council: This land has all too long been torn between two factions, and suffered great damage and loss through their mutual enmity. And here *I* say that I lay no blame on that party which is not my own, for there are valid claims on both sides, and equally the blame falls on both for failing to come to some agreement to end these distresses. The fortune at Lincoln might just as well have fallen the opposing way, but it fell as it did, and England is left with a king made captive, and a queen-elect free and in the ascendant. Is it not time to call a halt? For the sake of order and peace and the sound regulation of the realm, and to have a government in command which can and must put down the many injustices and tyrannies which you know, as well as I, have set themselves up outside all law. Surely any strong rule is better than no rule at all. For the sake of peace and order, will you not accept the empress, and hold your county in allegiance to her? She is already in Westminster now, the preparations for her coronation go forward. There is a far better prospect of success if all sheriffs come in to strengthen her rule.'

'You are asking me,' said Hugh gently, 'to go back on my sworn fealty to King Stephen.'

'Yes,' agreed Olivier honestly, 'I am. For weighty reasons, and in no treasonous mind. You need not love, only forbear from hating. Think of it rather as keeping your fealty to the people of this county of yours, and this land.'

'That I can do as well or better on the side where I began,' said Hugh, smiling. 'It is what I am doing now, as best I can. It is what I will continue to do while I have breath. I am King Stephen's man, and I will not desert him.'

'Ah, well!' said Olivier, smiling and sighing in the same breath. 'To tell you truth, now I've met you, I expected nothing less. I would not go from my oath, either. My lord is the empress's man, and I am my lord's man, and if our positions were changed round, my answer would be the same as yours. Yet there is truth in what I have pleaded. How much can a people bear? Your labourer in the fields, your little townsman with a bare living to be looted from him, these would be glad to settle for Stephen or for Maud, only to be rid of the other. And I do what I am sent out to do, as well as I can.'

'I have no fault to find with the matter or the manner,' said Hugh. 'Where next do you go? Though I hope you will not go for a day or two, I would know you better, and we have a great deal to talk over, you and I.'

'From here north-east to Stafford, Derby, Nottingham, and back by the eastern parts. Some will come to terms, as some lords have done already. Some will hold to their own king, like you. And some will do as they have done before, go back and forth like a weather-cock with the wind, and put up their price at every change. No matter, we have done with that now.'

He leaned forward over the table, setting his wine-cup aside. 'I had – I have – another errand of my own, and I should be glad to stay with you a few days, until I have found what I'm seeking, or made certain it is not here to be found. Your mention of this flood of pilgrims for the feast gives me a morsel of hope. A man who wills to be lost could find cover among so many, all strangers to one another. I am looking for a young man called Luc Meverel. He has not, to your knowledge, made his way here?'

'Not by that name,' said Hugh, interested and curious. 'But a man who willed to be lost might choose to doff his own name. What's your need of him?'

'Not mine. It's a lady who wants him back. You may not have got word, this far north,' said

Oliver, 'of everything that happened in Winchester during the council. There was a death there that came all too near to me. Did you hear of it? King Stephen's queen sent her clerk there with a bold challenge to the legate's authority, and the man was attacked for his audacity in the street by night, and got off with his life only at the cost of another life.'

'We have indeed heard of it,' said Hugh with kindling interest. 'Abbot Radulfus was there at the council, and brought back a full report. A knight by the name of Rainald Bossard, who came to the clerk's aid when he was set upon. One of those in the service of Laurence d'Angers, so we heard.'

'Who is my lord, also.'

'By your good service to his kin at Bromfield that was plain enough. I thought of you when the abbot spoke of d'Angers, though I had no name for you then. Then this man Bossard was well known to you?'

'Through a year of service in Palestine, and the voyage home together. A good man he was, and a good friend to me, and struck down in defending his honest opponent. I was not with him that night, I wish I had been, he might yet be alive. But he had only one or two of his own people, not in arms. There were five or six set on the clerk, it was a wretched business, confused and in the dark. The murderer got clean away, and has never been traced. Rainald's wife ... Juliana ... I did not know her until we came with our lord to Winchester, Rainald's chief manor is nearby. I

133

have learned,' said Olivier very gravely, 'to hold her in the highest regard. She was her lord's true match, and no one could say more or better of any lady.'

'There is an heir?' asked Hugh. 'A man grown, or still a child?'

'No, they never had children. Rainald was nearly fifty, she cannot be many years younger. And very beautiful,' said Olivier with solemn consideration, as one attempting not to praise, but to explain. 'Now she's widowed she'll have a hard fight on her hands to evade being married off again – for she'll want no other after Rainald. She has manors of her own to bestow. They had thought of the inheritance, the two of them together, that's why they took into their household this young man Luc Meverel, only a year ago. He is a distant cousin of Dame Juliana, twenty-four or twenty-five years old, I suppose, and landless. They meant to make him their heir.'

He fell silent for some minutes, frowning past the guttering candles, his chin in his palm. Hugh studied him, and waited. It was a face worth studying, clean-boned, olive-skinned, fiercely beautiful, even with the golden falcon's eyes thus hooded. The blue-black hair that clustered thickly about his head, clasping like folded wings, shot sullen bluish lights back from the candle's waverings. Daoud, born in Antioch, son of an English crusading soldier in Robert of Normandy's following, somehow blown across the world in the service of an Angevin baron, to fetch up here almost more Norman than the Normans

... The world, thought Hugh, is not so great, after all, but a man born to venture may bestride it.

'I have been three times in that household,' said Olivier, 'but I never knowingly set eyes on this Luc Meverel. All I know of him is what others have said, but among the others I take my choice which voice to believe. There is no one, man or woman, in that manor but agrees he was utterly devoted to Dame Juliana. But as to the manner of his devotion ... There are many who say he loved her far too well, by no means after the fashion of a son. Again, some say he was equally loyal to Rainald, but their voices are growing fainter now. Luc was one of those with his lord when Rainald was stabbed to death in the street. And two days later he vanished from his place, and has not been seen since.'

'Now I begin to see,' said Hugh, drawing in cautious breath. 'Have they gone so far as to say this man slew his lord in order to gain his lady?'

'It is being said now, since his flight. Who began the whisper there's no telling, but by this time it's grown into a bellow.'

'Then why should he run from the prize for which he had played? It makes poor sense. If he had stayed there need have been no such whispers.'

'Ah, but I think there would have been, whether he went or stayed. There were those who grudged him his fortune, and would have welcomed any means of damaging him. They are finding two good reasons, now, why he should break and run. The first, pure guilt and remorse, too late to save any one of the three of them. The second, fear – fear that someone had got wind of his act, and meant to fetch out the truth at all costs. Either way, a man might break and take to his heels. What you kill for may seem even less attainable,' said Olivier with rueful shrewdness, 'once you have killed.'

'But you have not yet told me,' said Hugh, 'what the lady says of him. Hers is surely a voice that should be heeded.'

'She says that such a vile suspicion is impossible. She did, she does, value her young cousin, but not in the way of love, nor will she have it that he has ever entertained such thoughts of her. She says he would have died for his lord, and that it is his lord's death which has driven him away, sick with grief, a little mad – who knows how deluded and haunted? For he was there that night, he saw Rainald die. She is sure of him. She wants him found and brought back to her. She looks upon him as a son, and now more than ever she needs him.'

'And it's for her sake you're seeking him. But why look for him here, northwards? He may have gone south, west, across the sea by the Kentish ports. Why to the north?'

'Because we have just one word of him since he was lost from his place, and that was going north on the road to Newbury. I came by that same way, by Abingdon and Oxford, and I have enquired for him everywhere, a young man travelling alone. But I can only seek him by his own name, for I know no other for him. As you say, who knows what he may be calling himself now!'

'And you don't even know what he looks like – nothing but merely his age? You're hunting for a spectre!'

'What is lost can always be found, it needs only enough patience.' Olivier's hawk's face, beaked and passionate, did not suggest patience, but the set of his lips was stubborn and pure in absolute resolution.

'Well, at least,' said Hugh, considering, 'we may go down to see Saint Winifred brought home to her altar, tomorrow, and Brother Denis can run through the roster of his pilgrims for us, and point out any who are of the right age and kind, solitary or not. As for strangers here in the town, I fancy Provost Corviser should be able to put his finger on most of them. Every man knows every man in Shrewsbury. But the abbey is the more likely refuge, if he's here at all.' He pondered, gnawing a thoughtful lip. 'I must send the ring down to the abbot at first light, and let him know what's happened to his truant guests, but before I may go down to the feast myself I must send out a dozen men and have them beat the near reaches of the woods to westward for our game birds. If they're over the border, so much the worse for Wales, and I can do no more, but I doubt if they intend to live wild any longer than they need. They may not go far. How if I should leave you with the provost, to pick his brains for your quarry here within the town, while I go hunting for mine? Then we'll go down together to see the brothers bring their saint home, and talk to Brother Denis concerning the list of his guests.'

'That would suit me well,' said Olivier gladly. 'I should like to pay my respects to the lord abbot, I do recall seeing him in Winchester, though he would not notice me. And there was a brother of that house, if you recall,' he said, his golden eyes veiled within long black lashes that swept his fine cheekbones, 'who was with you at Bromfield and up on Clee, that time ... You must know him well. He is still here at the abbey?'

'He is. He'll be back in his bed now after Lauds. And you and I had better be thinking of seeking ours, if we're to be busy tomorrow.'

'He was good to my lord's young kinsfolk,' said Olivier. 'I should like to see him again.'

No need to ask for a name, thought Hugh, eyeing him with a musing smile. And indeed, should he know the name? He had not mentioned any, when he spoke of one who was no blood-kin, but who had used him like a son, one for whose sake he kept a kindness for the Benedictine habit.

'You shall!' said Hugh, and rose in high content to marshal his guest to the bedchamber prepared for him.

CHAPTER EIGHT

Abbot Radulfus was up long before Prime on the festal morning, and so were his obedientiaries, all of whom had their important tasks in preparation for the procession. When Hugh's messenger presented himself at the abbot's lodging the dawn was still fresh, dewy and cool, the light lying brightly across the roofs while the great court lay in lilac-tinted shadow. In the gardens every tree and bush cast a long band of shade, striping the flower-beds like giant brush-strokes in some gilded illumination.

The abbot received the ring with astonished pleasure, relieved of one flaw that might have marred the splendour of the day. 'And you say these malefactors were guests in our halls, all four? We are well rid of them, but if they are armed, as you say, and have taken to the woods close by, we shall need to warn our travellers, when they leave us.'

'My lord Beringar has a company out beating the edges of the forest for them this moment,' said the messenger. 'There was nothing to gain by following them in the dark, once they were in cover. But by daylight we'll hope to trace them. One we have safe in hold, he may tell us more about them, where they're from, and what they have to answer for elsewhere. But at least now they can't hinder your festivities.'

'And for that I'm devoutly thankful. As this man Ciaran will certainly be for the recovery of his ring.' He added, with a glance aside at the breviary that lay on his desk, and a small frown for the load of ceremonial that lay before him for the next few hours: 'Shall we not see the lord sheriff here for Mass this morning?'

'Yes, Father, he does intend it, and he brings a guest also. He had first to set this hunt in motion, but before Mass they will be here.'

'He has a guest?'

'An envoy from the empress's court came last night, Father. A man of Laurence d'Angers' household, Olivier de Bretagne.'

The name that had meant nothing to Hugh meant as little to Radulfus, though he nodded recollection and understanding at mention of the young man's overlord. 'Then will you say to Hugh Beringar that I beg he and his guest will remain after Mass, and dine with me here. I should be glad to make the acquaintance of Messire de Bretagne, and hear his news.'

'I will so tell him, Father,' said the messenger, and forthwith took his leave.

Left alone in his parlour, Abbot Radulfus stood for a moment looking down thoughtfully at the ring in his palm. The sheltering hand of the bishop-legate would certainly be a powerful protection to any traveller so signally favoured, wherever there existed any order or respect for law, whether in England or Wales. Only those already outside the pale of law, with lives or liberty already forfeit if taken, would defy so strong a sanction. After this crowning day many of the guests here would be leaving again for home. He must not forget to give due warning, before they dispersed, that malefactors might be lurking at large in the woods to westward, and that they were armed, and all too handy at using their daggers. Best that the pilgrims should make sure of leaving in companies stout enough to discourage assault.

Meantime, there was satisfaction in returning to one pilgrim, at least, his particular armour.

The abbot rang the little bell that lay upon his desk, and in a few moments Brother Vitalis came to answer the summons.

'Will you enquire at the guest-hall, brother, for the man called Ciaran, and bid him here to speak with me?'

Brother Cadfael had also risen well before Prime, and gone to open his workshop and kindle his brazier into cautious and restrained life, in case it should be needed later to prepare tisanes for some ecstatic souls carried away by emotional excitement, or warm applications for weaker vessels trampled in the crowd. He was used to the transports of simple souls caught up in far from simple raptures.

He had a few things to tend to, and was happy to deal with them alone. Young Oswin was entitled to his fill of sleep until the bell awoke him. Very soon now he would graduate to the hospital of Saint Giles, where the reliquary of Saint Winifred now lay, and the unfortunates who carried their contagion with them, and might not be admitted into the town, could find rest, care and shelter for as long as they needed it. Brother Mark, that dearly-missed disciple, was gone from there now, already ordained deacon, his eyes fixed ahead upon his steady goal of priesthood. If ever he cast a glance over his shoulder, he would find nothing but encouragement and affection, the proper harvest of the seed he had sown. Oswin might not be such another, but he was a good enough lad and would do honestly by the unfortunates who drifted into his care.

Cadfael went down to the banks of the Meole brook, the westward boundary of the enclave, where the pease-fields declined to the sunken summer water. The rays from the east were just being launched like lances over the high roofs of the monastic buildings, and piercing the scattered copses beyond the brook, and the grassy banks on the further side. This same water, drawn off much higher in its course, supplied the monastery fish-ponds, the hatchery, and the mill and millpond beyond, and was fed back into the brook just before it entered the Severn. It lay low enough now, an archipelago of shoals, half sand, half grass and weed, spreading smooth islands across its breadth. After this spell, thought Cadfael, we shall need plenty of rain. But let that wait a day or two.

He turned back to climb the slope again. The earlier field of pease had already been gleaned, the second would be about ready for harvesting after the festival. A couple of days, and all the excitement would be over, and the horarium of the house and the cycle of the seasons would resume their imperturbable progress, two enduring rhythms in the desperately variable fortunes of mankind. He turned along the path to his workshop, and there was Melangell hesitating before its closed door.

She heard his step in the gravel behind her, and looked round with a bright, expectant face. The pearly morning light became her, softened the coarseness of her linen gown, and smoothed cool lilac shadows round the childlike curves of her face. She had gone to great pains to prepare herself fittingly for the day's solemnities. Her skirts were spotless, crisped out with care, her dark-gold hair, burning with coppery lustre, braided and coiled on her head in a bright crown, its tight plaits drawing up the skin of her temples and cheeks so strongly that her brows were pulled aslant, and the dark-lashed blue eyes elongated and made mysterious. But the radiance that shone from her came not from the sun's caresses, but from within. The blue of those eyes burned as

143

brilliantly as the blue of the gentians Cadfael had seen long ago in the mountains of southern France, on his way to the east. The ivory and rose of her cheeks glowed. Melangell was in the highest state of hope, happiness and expectation.

She made him a very pretty reverence, flushing and smiling, and held out to him the little vial of poppy-syrup he had given to Rhun three days ago. Still unopened!

'If you please, Brother Cadfael, I have brought this back to you. And Rhun prays that it may serve some other who needs it more, and with the more force because he has endured without it.'

He took it from her gently and held it in his cupped hand, a crude little vial stopped with a wooden stopper and a membrane of very thin parchment tied with a waxed thread to seal it. All intact. The boy's third night here, and he had submitted to handling and been mild and biddable in all, but when the means of oblivion was put into his hand and left to his private use, he had preserved it, and with it some core of his own secret integrity, at his own chosen cost. God forbid, thought Cadfael, that I should meddle there. Nothing short of a saint should knock on that door.

'You are not angry with him?' asked Melangell anxiously, but smiling still, unable to believe that any shadow should touch the day, now that her love had clasped and kissed her. 'Because he did not drink it? It was not that he ever doubted *you*. He said so to me. He said – I never quite understand him! – he said it was a time for offering, and he had his offering prepared.'

Cadfael asked: 'Did he sleep?' To have deliverance in hand, even unopened, might well bring peace. 'Hush, now, no, how could I be angry! But *did* he sleep?'

'He says that he did. I think it must be true, he looks so fresh and young. I prayed hard for him.' With all the force of her new happiness, loaded with bliss she felt the need to pour out upon all those near to her. In the conveyance of blessedness by affection Cadfael firmly believed.

'You prayed well,' said Cadfael. 'Never doubt he has gained by it. I'll keep this for some soul in worse need, as Rhun says. It will have the virtue of his faith to strengthen it. I shall see you both during the day.'

She went away from him with a light, springing step and a head reared to breathe in the very space and light of the sky. And Cadfael went in to make sure he had everything ready to provide for a long and exhausting day.

So Rhun had arrived at the last frontier of belief, and fallen, or emerged, or soared into the region where the soul realises that pain is of no account, that to be within the secret of God is more than well being, and past the power of the tongue to utter. To embrace the decree of pain is to translate it, to shed it like a rain of blessing on others who have not yet understood.

Who am I, thought Cadfael, alone in the solitude of his workshop, that I should dare to ask for a sign? If he can endure and ask nothing, must not I be ashamed of doubting?

Melangell passed with a dancing step along the path from the herbarium. On her right hand the western sky soared, in such reflected if muted brightness that she could not forbear from turning to stare into it. A counter-tide of light flowed in here from the west, surging up the slope from the brook and spilling over the crest into the garden. Somewhere on the far side of the entire monastic enclave the two tides would meet, and the light of the west falter, pale and die before the onslaught from the east; but here the bulk of guest-hall and church cut off the newly-risen sun, and left the field to this hesitant and soft-treading antidawn.

There was someone labouring along the far border of the flower-garden, going delicately on still tender feet, watching where he trod. He was alone. No attendant shadow appeared at his back, yesterday's magic still held. She was staring at Ciaran, Ciaran without Matthew. That in itself was a minor miracle, to bring in this day made for miracles.

Melangell watched him begin to descend the slope towards the brook, and when he was no more than a head and shoulders black against the brightness, she suddenly turned and went after him. The path down to the water skirted the growing pease, keeping close to a hedge of thick bushes above the mill-pool. Halfway down the slope she halted, uncertain whether to intrude on his solitude. Ciaran had reached the waterside, and stood surveying what looked like a safe green floor, dappled here and there with the bleached islands of sand, and studded with a few embedded rocks that stood dry from three weeks of fine weather. He looked upstream and down, even stepped into the shallow water that barely covered his naked feet, and surely soothed and refreshed them. Yet how strange, that he should be here alone! Never, until yesterday, had she seen either of these two without the other, yet now they went apart.

She was on the point of stealing away to leave him undisturbed when she saw what he was doing. He had some tiny thing in his hand, into which he was threading a thin cord, and knotting the cord to hold it fast. When he raised both hands to make fast the end of his cord to the tether that held the cross about his neck, the small talisman swung free into the light and glimmered for an instant in silver, before he tucked it away within the neck of his shirt, out of sight against his breast. Then she knew what it was, and stirred in pure pleasure for him, and uttered a small, breathless sound. For Ciaran had his ring again, the safe-conduct that was to ensure him passage to his journey's end.

He had heard her, and swung about, startled and wary. She stood shaken and disconcerted, and then, knowing herself discovered, ran down the last slope of grass to his side. 'They've found it

147

for you!' she said breathlessly, in haste to fill the silence between them and dispel her own uneasiness at having seemed to spy upon him. 'Oh, I am glad! Is the thief taken, then?'

'Melangell!' he said. 'You're early abroad, too? Yes, you see I am blessed, after all, I have it again. The lord abbot restored it to me only some minutes ago. But no, the thief is not caught, he and some fellow-rogues are fled into the woods, it seems. But I can go forth again without fear now.'

His dark eyes, deep-set under thick brows, opened wide upon her, smiling, holding her charmed in the abrupt discovery that he was, despite his disease, a young and comely man, who should have been in the fulness of his powers. Either she was imagining it, or he stood a little straighter, a little taller, than she had ever yet seen him, and the burning intensity of his face had mellowed into a brighter, more human ardour, as if some foreglow of the day's spiritual radiance had given him new hope.

'Melangell,' he said in a soft, vehement rush of words, 'you can't guess how glad I am of this meeting, it was God sent you here to me. I've long wanted to speak to you alone. Never think that because I myself am doomed, I can't see what's before my eyes concerning others who are dear to me. I have something to ask of you, to beg of you, most earnestly. Don't tell Matthew that I have my ring again!'

'Does he not know?' she asked, astray.

'No, he was not by when the abbot sent for me.

148

He must not know! Keep my secret, if you love him – if you have some pity, at least for me. I have told no one, and you must not. The lord abbot is not likely to speak of it to any other, why should he? That he would leave to me. If you and I keep silent, there's no need for anyone else to find out.'

Melangell was lost. She saw him through a rainbow of starting tears, for very pity of his long face hollowed in shade, his eyes glowing like the quiet, living heart of a banked fire.

'But why? Why do you want to keep it from him?'

'For his sake and yours – yes, and mine! Do you think I have not understood long ago that he loves you? – that you feel as much also for him? Only I stand in the way! It's bitter to know it, and I would have it changed. My one wish now is that you and he should be happy together. If he loves me so faithfully, may not I also love him? You know him! He will sacrifice himself, and you, and all things beside, to finish what he has undertaken, and see me safe into Aberdaron. I don't accept his sacrifice, I won't endure it! Why should you both be wretched, when my one wish is to go to my rest in peace of mind and leave my friend happy? Now, while he feels secure that I dare not set out without the ring, for God's sake, girl, leave him in innocence. *And I will go*, and leave you both my blessing.'

Melangell stood quivering, like a leaf shaken by the soft, vehement wind of his words, uncertain even of her own heart. 'Then what must I do? What is it you want of me?'

149

'Keep my secret,' said Ciaran, 'and go with Matthew in this holy procession. Oh, he'll go with you, and be glad. He won't wonder that I should stay behind and wait the saint's coming here within the pale. And while you're gone, I'll go on my way. My feet are almost healed, I have my ring again, I shall reach my haven. You need not be afraid for me. Only keep him happy as long as you may, and even when my going is known, then use your arts, keep him, hold him fast. That's all I shall ever ask of you.'

'But he'll know,' she said, alert to dangers. 'The porter will tell him you're gone, as soon as he looks for you and asks.'

'No, for I shall go by this way, across the brook and out to the west, for Wales. The porter will not see me go. See, it's barely ankle-deep in this season. I have kinsmen in Wales, the first miles are nothing. And among so great a throng, if he does look for me, he'll hardly wonder at not finding me. Not for hours need he so much as think of me, if you do your part. You take care of Matthew, I will absolve both you and him of all care of me, for I shall do well enough. All the better for knowing I leave him safe with you. For you do love him,' said Ciaran softly.

'Yes,' said Melangell in a long sigh.

'Then take and hold him, and my blessing on you both. You may tell him – but well afterwards! – that it is what I designed and intended,' he said, and suddenly and briefly smiled at some unspoken thought he did not wish to share with her.

150

'You will really do this for him and for me? You mean it? You would go on alone for his sake ... Oh, you are good!' she said passionately, and caught at his hand and pressed it to her heart for an instant, for he was giving her the whole world at his own sorrowful cost, and for selfless love of his friend, and there might never be any time but this one moment even to thank him. 'I'll never forget your goodness. All my life long I shall pray for you.'

'No,' said Ciaran, the same dark smile plucking at his lips as she released his hand, 'forget me, and help him to forget me. That is the best gift you can make me. And better you should not speak to me again. Go and find him. That's your part, and I depend on you.'

She drew back from him a few paces, her eyes still fixed on him in gratitude and worship, made him a strange little reverence with head and hands, and turned obediently to climb the field into the garden. By the time she reached level ground and began to thread the beds of the rose garden she was breaking into a joyous run.

They gathered in the great court as soon as everyone, monk, lay servant, guest and townsman, had broken his fast. Seldom had the court seen such a crowd, and outside the walls the Foregate was loud with voices, as the guildsmen of Shrewsbury, provost, elders and all, assembled to join the solemn procession that would set out for Saint Giles. Half of the choir monks, led by Prior

151

Robert, were to go in procession to fetch home the reliquary, while the abbot and the remaining brothers waited to greet them with music and candles and flowers on their return. As for the devout of town and Foregate, and the pilgrims within the walls, they might form and follow Prior Robert, such of them as were able-bodied and eager, while the lame and feeble might wait with the abbot, and prove their devotion by labouring out at least a little way to welcome the saint on her return.

'I should so much like to go with them all the way,' said Melangell, flushed and excited among the chattering, elbowing crowd in the court. 'It is not far. But too far for Rhun – he could not keep pace.'

He was there beside her, very silent, very white, very fair, as though even his flaxen hair had turned paler at the immensity of this experience. He leaned on his crutches between his sister and Dame Alice, and his crystal eyes were very wide, and looked very far, as though he was not even aware of their solicitude hemming him in on either side. Yet he answered simply enough, 'I should like to go a little way, at least, until they leave me behind. But you need not wait for me.'

'As though I would leave you!' said Mistress Weaver, comfortably clucking. 'You and I will keep together and see the pilgrimage out to the best we can, and heaven will be content with that. But the girl has her legs, she may go all the way and put up a few prayers for you going and returning, and we'll none of us be the worse for it.'

She leaned to twitch the neck of his shirt and the collar of his coat into immaculate neatness, and to fuss over his extreme pallor, afraid he was coming down with illness from over-excitement, though he seemed tranquil as ivory, and serenely absent in spirit, gone somewhere she could not follow. Her hand, rough-fingered from weaving, smoothed his well-brushed hair, teasing every tendril back from his tall forehead.

'Run off, then, child,' she said to Melangell, without turning from the boy. 'But find someone we know. There'll be riffraff running alongside, I dare say – no escaping them. Stay by Mistress Glover, or the apothecary's widow ...'

'Matthew is going with them,' said Melangell, flushing and smiling at his very name. 'He told me so. I met him when we came from Prime.'

It was only half-true. She had rather confided boldly to him that she wished to tread every step of the way, and at every step remember and intercede for the souls she most loved on earth. No need to name them. He, no doubt, thought with reflected tenderness of her brother; but she was thinking no less of this anguished pair whose fortunes she now carried delicately and fearfully in her hands. She had even said, greatly venturing, 'Ciaran cannot keep pace, poor soul, he must wait here, like Rhun. But can't we make our steps count for them?'

But for all that, Matthew had looked over his

shoulder, and hesitated a sharp instant before he turned his face fully to her, and said abruptly: 'Yes, we'll go, you and I. Yes, let's go that short way together, surely I have the right, this once … I'll make my prayers for Rhun every step of the way.'

'Trot and find him, then, girl,' said Dame Alice, satisfied. 'Matthew will take good care of you. See, they're forming up, you'd best hurry. We'll be here to watch you come in.'

Melangell fled, elated. Prior Robert had drawn up his choir, with Brother Anselm the precentor at their head, facing the gate. The shifting, murmuring, excited column of pilgrims formed up at his rear, twitching like a dragon's tail, a long, brightly-coloured, volatile train, brave with flowers, lighted tapers, offerings, crosses and banners. Matthew was waiting to reach out an eager hand to her and draw her in beside him. 'You have leave? She trusts you to me …?'

'You're not troubled about Ciaran?' she could not forbear asking anxiously. 'He's right to stay here, he couldn't manage the walk.'

The choir monks before them began their processional psalm, Prior Robert led the way through the open gate, and after him went the brothers in their ordered pairs, and after them the notabilities of the town, and after them the long retinue of pilgrims, crowding forward eagerly, picking up the chant where they had knowledge of it or a sensitive ear, pouring out

154

past the gatehouse and turning right towards Saint Giles.

Brother Cadfael went with Prior Robert's party, with Brother Adam of Reading walking beside him. Along the broad road by the enclave wall, past the great triangle of trodden grass at the horse-fair ground, and again bearing right with the road, between scattered houses and sun-bleached pastures and fields to the very edge of the suburb, where the squat tower of the hospital church, the roof of the hospice, and the long wattle fence of its garden showed dark against the bright eastern sky, slightly raised from the road on a gentle green mound. And all the way the long train of followers grew longer and more gaily-coloured, as the people of the Foregate in their best holiday clothes came out from their dwellings and joined the procession.

There was no room in the small, dark church for more than the brothers and the civic dignitaries of the town. The rest gathered all about the doorway, craning to get a glimpse of the proceedings within. With his lips moving almost soundlessly on the psalms and prayers, Cadfael watched the play of candle-light on the silver tracery that ornamented Saint Winifred's elegant oak coffin, elevated there on the altar as when they had first brought it from Gwytherin, four years earlier. He wondered whether his motive in securing for himself a place among the eight

brothers who would bear her back to the abbey
had been as pure as he had hoped. Had he been
staking a proprietory claim on her, as one who
had been at her first coming? Or had he meant it
as a humble and penitential gesture? He was,
after all, past sixty, and as he recalled, the oak
casket was heavy, its edges sharp on a creaky
shoulder, and the way back long enough to bring
out all the potential discomforts. She might yet
find a way of showing him whether she approved
his proceedings or no, by striking him helpless
with rheumatic pains!

The office ended. The eight chosen brothers,
matched in height and pace, lifted the reliquary
and settled it upon their shoulders. The prior
stooped his lofty head through the low doorway
into the mid-morning radiance, and the crowd
clustered about the church opened to make way
for the saint to ride to her triumph. The
procession reformed, Prior Robert before with
the brothers, the coffin with its bearers, flanked
by crosses and banners and candles, and eager
women bringing garlands of flowers. With
measured pace, with music and solemn joy, Saint
Winifred – or whatever represented her there in
the sealed and secret place – was borne back to
her own altar in the abbey church.

Curious, thought Cadfael, carefully keeping
the step by numbers, it seems lighter than I
remember. Is that possible? In only four years?
He was familiar with the curious propensities of
the body, dead or alive, he had once been led into

156

a gallery of caverns in the desert where ancient Christians had lived and died, he knew what dry air can do to flesh, preserving the light and shrivelled shell while the juice of life was drawn off into spirit. Whatever was there in the reliquary, it rode tranquilly upon his shoulder, like a light hand guiding him. It was not heavy at all!

CHAPTER NINE

Something wonderful happened along the way to Matthew and Melangell, hemmed in among the jostling, singing, jubilant train. Somewhere along that half-mile of road they were caught up in the fever and joy of the day, borne along on the tide of music and devotion, forgetting all others, forgetting even themselves, drawn into one without any word or motion of theirs. When they turned their heads to look at each other, they saw only mated eyes and a halo of sunshine. They did not speak at all, not once along the way. They had no need of speech. But when they had turned the corner of the precinct wall by the horse-fair, and drew near to the gatehouse, and heard and saw the abbot leading his own party out to meet them, splendidly vested and immensely tall under his mitre; when the two chants found their measure while yet some way apart, and met and married in a triumphant, soaring cry of worship, and all the ardent followers drew gasping breaths of exultation, Melangell heard beside her a broken breath drawn, like a soft sob, that turned as suddenly

158

into a peal of laughter, out of pure, possessed joy. Not a loud sound, muted and short of breath because the throat that uttered it was clenched by emotion, and the mind and heart from which it came quite unaware of what it shed upon the world. It was a beautiful sound, or so Melangell thought, as she raised her head to stare at him with wide eyes and parted lips, in dazzled and dazzling delight. Matthew's wry and rare smile she had seen sometimes, and wondered and grieved at its brevity, but never before had she heard him laugh.

The two processions merged. The cross-bearers walked before, Abbot Radulfus, prior and choir monks came after, and Cadfael and his peers with their sacred burden followed, hemmed in on both sides by worshippers who reached and leaned to touch even the sleeve of a bearer's habit, or the polished oak of the reliquary as it passed. Brother Anselm, in secure command of his choir, raised his own fine voice in the lead as they turned in at the gatehouse, bringing Saint Winifred home.

Brother Cadfael, by then, was moving like a man in a dual dream, his body keeping pace and time with his fellows, in one confident rhythm, while his mind soared in another, carried aloft on the cushioned cloud of sounds, compounded of the eager footsteps, exalted murmurs and shrill acclamations of hundreds of people, with the chant borne above it, and the voice of Brother Anselm soaring over all. The great court was crowded with people to watch them enter, the way

159

into the cloister, and so into the church, had to be cleared by slow, shuffling paces, the ranks pressing back to give them passage, Cadfael came to himself with some mild annoyance when the reliquary was halted in the court, to wait for a clear path ahead. He braced both feet almost aggressively into the familiar soil, and for the first time looked about him. He saw, beyond the throng already gathered, the saint's own retinue melting and flowing to find a place where eye might see all, and ear hear all. In this brief halt he saw Melangell and Matthew, hand in hand, hunt round the fringes of the crowd, and find a place to gaze.

They looked to Cadfael a little tipsy, like unaccustomed drinkers after strong wine. And why not? After long abstention he had felt the intoxication possessing his own feet, as they held the hypnotic rhythm, and his own mind, as it floated on the cadences of song. Those ecstasies were at once native and alien to him, he could both embrace and stand clear of them, feet firmly planted, gripping the homely earth, to keep his balance and stand erect.

They moved forward again into the nave of the church, and then to the right, towards the bared and waiting altar. The vast, dreaming, sun-warmed bulk of the church enclosed them, dim, silent and empty, since no other could enter until they had discharged their duty, lodged their patroness and retired to their own insignificant places. Then they came, led by abbot and prior, first the brothers to fill up their stalls in the choir, then the provost and guildsmen of the town and the notables of the shire, and then all that great concourse of people, flooding in from hot mid-morning sunlight to the cool dimness of stone, and from the excited clamour of festival to the great silence of worship, until all the space of the nave was filled with the colour and warmth and breath of humanity, and all as still as the candle-flames on the altar. Even the reflected gleams in the silver chacings of the casket were fixed and motionless as jewels.

Abbot Radulfus stood forth. The sobering solemnity of the Mass began.

For the very intensity of all that mortal emotion gathered thus between confining walls and beneath one roof, it was impossible to withdraw the eyes for an instant from the act of worship on which it was centred, or the mind from the words of the office. There had been times, through the years of his vocation, when Cadfael's thoughts had strayed during Mass to worrying at other problems, and working out other intents. It was not so now. Throughout, he was unaware of a single face in all that throng, only of the presence of humankind, in whom his own identity was lost; or, perhaps, into whom his own identity expanded like air, to fill every part of the whole. He forgot Melangell and Matthew, he forgot Ciaran and Rhun, he never looked round to see if Hugh had come. If there was a face before his mind's eye at all it was one he had never seen, though he well remembered the slight and fragile bones he had lifted with such care and awe out of the earth, and with so much better heart again laid beneath the same soil, there to resume her hawthorn-scented sleep under the sheltering trees. For some reason, though she had lived to a good old age, he could not imagine her older than seventeen or eighteen, as she had been when the king's son Cradoc pursued her. The slender little bones had cried out of youth, and the shadowy face he had imagined for her was fresh and eager and open, and very beautiful. But he saw it always half turned away from him. Now, if ever, she might at last look round, and show him fully that reassuring countenance.

At the end of Mass the abbot withdrew to his own stall, to the right of the entrance from nave to choir, round the parish altar, and with lifted voice and open arms bade the pilgrims advance to the saint's altar, where everyone who had a petition to make might make it on his knees, and touch the reliquary with hand and lip. And in orderly and reverent silence they came. Prior Robert took his stand at the foot of the three steps that led up to the altar, ready to offer a hand to those who needed help to mount or kneel. Those who were in health and had no pressing requirements to advance came through from the nave on the other side, and found corners where they might stand and watch, and miss nothing of this memorable day. They had faces again, they spoke in whispers, they were as various as an hour since they had been one.

162

On his knees in his stall, Brother Cadfael looked on, knowing them one from another now as they came, kneeled and touched. The long file of petitioners was drawing near its end when he saw Rhun approaching. Dame Alice had a hand solicitously under his left elbow, Melangell nursed him along on his right, Matthew followed close, no less anxious than they. The boy advanced with his usual laborious gait, his dragging toe just scraping the tiles of the floor. His face was intensely pale, but with a brilliant pallor that almost dazzled the watching eyes, and the wide gaze he fixed steadily upon the reliquary shone translucent, like ice with a bright bluish light behind it. Dame Alice was whispering low, encouraging entreaties into one ear, Melangell into the other, but he was aware of nothing but the altar towards which he moved. When his turn came, he shook off his supporters, and for a moment seemed to hesitate before venturing to advance alone.

Prior Robert observed his condition, and held out a hand. 'You need not be abashed, my son, because you cannot kneel. God and the saint will know your goodwill.'

The softest whisper of a voice, though clearly audible in the waiting silence, said tremulously: 'But, Father, I can! I will!'

Rhun straightened up, taking his hands from his crutches, which slid from under his armpits and fell. That on the left crashed with an unnerving clatter upon the tiles, on the right

Melangell started forward and dropped to her knees, catching the falling prop in her arms with a faint cry. And there she crouched, embracing the discarded thing desperately, while Rhun set his twisted foot to the ground and stood upright. He had but two or three paces to go to the foot of the altar steps. He took them slowly and steadily, his eyes fixed upon the reliquary. Once he lurched slightly, and Dame Alice made a trembling move to run after him, only to halt again in wonder and fear, while Prior Robert again extended his hand to offer aid. Rhun paid no attention to them or to anyone else, he did not seem to see or hear anything but his goal, and whatever voice it might be that called him forward. For he went with held breath, as a child learning to walk ventures across perilous distances to reach its mother's open arms and coaxing, praising blandishments that wooed it to the deed.

It was the twisted foot he set first on the lowest step, and now the twisted foot, though a little awkward and unpractised, was twisted no longer, and did not fail him, and the wasted leg, as he put his weight on it, seemed to have smoothed out into shapeliness, and bore him up bravely.

Only then did Cadfael become aware of the stillness and the silence, as if every soul present held his breath with the boy, spellbound, not yet ready, not yet permitted to acknowledge what they saw before their eyes. Even Prior Robert stood charmed into a tall, austere statue, frozen at gaze. Even Melangell, crouching with the crutch

164

hugged to her breast, could not stir a finger to help or break the spell, but hung upon every deliberate step with agonised eyes, as though she were laying her heart under his feet as a voluntary sacrifice to buy off fate.

He had reached the third step, he sank to his knees with only the gentlest of manipulations, holding by the fringes of the altar frontal, and the cloth of gold that was draped under the reliquary. He lifted his joined hands and starry face, white and bright even with eyes now closed, and though there was hardly any sound they saw his lips moving upon whatever prayers he had made ready for her. Certainly they contained no request for his own healing. He had put himself simply in her hands, submissively and joyfully, and what had been done to him and for him surely she had done, of her own perfect will.

He had to hold by her draperies to rise, as babes hold by their mothers' skirts. No doubt but she had him under the arms to raise him. He bent his fair head and kissed the hem of her garment, rose erect and kissed the silver rim of the reliquary, in which, whether she lay or not, she alone commanded and had sovereignty. Then he withdrew from her, feeling his way backward down the three steps. Twisted foot and shrunken leg carried him securely. At the foot he made obeisance gravely, and then turned and went briskly, like any other healthy lad of sixteen, to smile reassurance on his trembling womenfolk, take up gently the crutches for which he had no further use, and carry them back to lay them tidily under the altar.

The spell broke, for the marvellous thing was done, and its absolute nature made manifest. A great, shuddering sigh went round nave, choir, transepts and all, wherever there were human creatures watching and listening. And after the sigh the quivering murmur of a gathering storm, whether of tears or laughter there was no telling, but the air shook with its passion. And then the outcry, the loosing of both tears and laughter, in a gale of wonder and praise. From stone walls and lofty, arched roof, from rood-loft and transept arcades, the echoes flew and rebounded, and the candles that had stood so still and tall shook and guttered in the gale. Melangell hung weak with weeping and joy in Matthew's arms, Dame Alice whirled from friend to friend, spouting tears like a fountain, and smiling like the most blessed of women. Prior Robert lifted his hands in vindicated stewardship, and his voice in the opening of a thanksgiving psalm, and Brother Anselm took up the chant.

A miracle, a miracle, a miracle ...

And in the midst Rhun stood erect and still, even a little bewildered, braced sturdily on his two long, shapely legs, looking all about him at the shouting, weeping, exulting faces, letting the meaningless sounds wash over him in waves, wanting the quiet he had known when there had been no one here in this holy place but himself and his saint, who had told him, in how

166

sweet and private conference, all that he had to do.

Brother Cadfael rose with his brothers after the church was cleared of all others, after all that jubilant, bubbling, boiling throng had gone forth to spill its feverish excitement in open summer air, to cry the miracle aloud, carry it out into the Foregate, beyond into the town, buffet it back and forth across the tables at dinner in the guest-hall, and return to extol it at Vespers with what breath was left. When they dispersed the word would go with them wherever they went, sounding Saint Winifred's praises, inspiring other souls to take to the roads and bring their troubles to Shrewsbury. Where healing was proven, and attested by hundreds of voices.

The brothers went to their modest, accustomed dinner in the refectory, and observed, whatever their own feelings were, the discipline of silence. They were very tired, which made silence welcome. They had risen early, worked hard, been through fire and flood body and soul, no wonder they ate humbly, thankfully, in silence.

CHAPTER TEN

It was not until dinner was almost over in the guest-hall that Matthew, seated at Melangell's side and still flushed and exalted from the morning's heady wonders, suddenly bethought him of sterner matters, and began to look back with a thoughtful frown which as yet only faintly dimmed the unaccustomed brightness of his face. Being in attendance on Mistress Weaver and her young people had made him a part, for a while, of their unshadowed joy, and caused him to forget everything else. But it could not last, though Rhun sat there half-lost in wonder still, with hardly a word to say, and felt no need of food or drink, and his womenfolk fawned on him unregarded. So far away had he been that the return took time.

'I haven't seen Ciaran,' said Matthew quietly in Melangell's ear, and he rose a little in his place to look round the crowded room. 'Did you catch ever a glimpse of him in the church?'

She, too, had forgotten until then, but at sight of his face she remembered all too sharply, with a sickening lurch of her heart. But she kept her countenance, and laid a persuasive hand on his arm to draw him down again beside her. 'Among so many? But he surely would be there. He must have been among the first, he stayed here, he would find a good place. We didn't see all those who went to the altar – we all stayed with Rhun, and his place was far back.' Such a mingling of truth and lies, but she kept her voice confident, and clung to her shaken hope.

'But where is he now? I don't see him within here.' Though there was so much excitement, so much moving about from table to table to talk with friends, that one man might easily avoid detection. 'I must find him,' said Matthew, not yet greatly troubled but wanting reassurance, and rose.

'No, sit down! You know he must be here somewhere. Let him alone, and he'll appear when he chooses. He may be resting on his bed, if he has to go forth again barefoot tomorrow. Why look for him now? Can you not do without him even one day? And such a day?'

Matthew looked down at her with a face from which all the openness and joy had faded, and freed his sleeve from her grasp gently enough, but decidedly. 'Still, I must find him. Stay here with Rhun, I'll come back. All I want is to see him, to be sure ...'

He was away, slipping quietly out between the festive tables, looking sharply about him as he went. She was in two minds about following him, but then she thought better of it, for while he hunted time would be slipping softly away, and Ciaran would be dwindling into distance, as later she prayed he could fade even out of mind, and be forgotten. So she remained with the happy company, but not of it, and with every passing moment hesitated whether to grow more reassured or more uneasy. At last she could not bear the waiting any longer. She rose quietly and slipped away. Dame Alice was in full spate, torn between tears and smiles, sitting proudly by her prodigy, and surrounded by neighbours as happy and voluble as herself, and Rhun, still somehow apart though he was the centre of the group, sat withdrawn into his revelation, even as he answered eager questions, lamely enough but as well as he could. They had no need of Melangell, they would not miss her for a little while.

When she came out into the great court, into the brilliance of the noonday sun, it was the quietest hour, the pause after meat. There never was a time of day when there was no traffic about the court, no going and coming at the gatehouse, but now it moved at its gentlest and quietest. She went down almost fearfully into the cloister, and found no one there but a single copyist busy reviewing what he had done the previous day, and Brother Anselm in his workshop going over the music for Vespers; into the stable-yard, though there was no reason in the world why Matthew should be there, having no mount, and no expectation that his companion would or

170

possibly could acquire one; into the gardens, where a couple of novices were clipping back the too exuberant shoots of a box hedge; even into the grange court, where the barns and storehouses were, and a few lay servants were taking their ease, and harrowing over the morning's marvel, like everyone else within the enclave, and most of Shrewsbury and the Foregate into the bargain. The abbot's garden was empty, neat, glowing with carefully-tended roses, his lodging showed an open door, and some ordered bustle of guests within.

She turned back towards the garden, now in deep anxiety. She was not good at lying, she had no practice, even for a good end she could not but botch the effort. And for all the to and fro of customary commerce within the pale, never without work to be done, she had seen nothing of Matthew. But he could not be gone, no, the porter could tell him nothing, Ciaran had not passed there; and she would not, never until she must, never until Matthew's too fond heart was reconciled to loss, and open and receptive to a better gain.

She turned back, rounding the box hedge and out of sight of the busy novices, and walked breast to breast into Matthew.

They met between the thick hedges, in a terrible privacy. She started back from him in a brief revulsion of guilt, for he looked more distant and alien than ever before, even as he recognised her, and acknowledged with a contortion of his

171

troubled face her right to come out in search of him, and almost in the same instant frowned her off as irrelevant.

'He's gone!' he said in a chill and grating voice, and looked through her and far beyond. 'God keep you, Melangell, you must fend for yourself now, sorry as I am. He's gone – fled while my back was turned. I've looked for him everywhere, and never a trace of him. Nor has the porter seen him pass the gate, I've asked there. But he's gone! Alone! And I must go after him. God keep you, girl, as I cannot, and fare you well!'

And he was going so, with so few words and so cold and wild a face! He had turned on his heel and taken two long steps before she flung herself after him, caught him by the arms in both hands, and dragged him to a halt.

'No, no, *why*? What need has he of you, to match with my need? He's gone? Let him go! Do you think your life belongs to him? He doesn't want it! He wants you free, he wants you to live your own life, not die his death with him. He knows, he knows you love me! Dare you deny it? He knows I love you. He wants you happy! Why should not a friend want his friend to be happy? Who are you to deny him his last wish?'

She knew by then that she had said too much, but never knew at what point the error had become mortal. He had turned fully to her again, and frozen where he stood, and his face was like chiselled marble. He tugged his sleeve out of her grasp this time with no gentleness at all.

'*He wants*!' hissed a voice she had never heard before, driven through narrowed lips. 'You've spoken with him! You speak *for* him! *You knew*! You knew he meant to go, and leave me here bewitched, damned, false to my oath. *You knew*! When? When did you speak with him?'

He had her by the wrists, he shook her mercilessly, and she cried out and fell to her knees.

'You knew he meant to go?' persisted Matthew, stooping over her in a cold frenzy.

'Yes – yes! This morning he told me ... he wished it ...'

'*He wished it*! How dared he wish it? How could he dare, robbed of his bishop's ring as he was? He dared not stir without it, he was terrified to set foot outside the pale ...'

'He has the ring,' she cried, abandoning all deceit. 'The lord abbot gave it back to him this morning, you need not fret for him, he's safe enough, he has his protection ... He doesn't need you!'

Matthew had fallen into a deadly stillness, stooping above her. '*He has the ring*? And you knew it, and never said word! If you know so much, how much more do you know. Speak! *Where is he*?'

'Gone,' she said in a trembling whisper, 'and wished you well, wished us both well ... wished us to be happy ... Oh, let him go, let him go, he sets you free!'

Something that was certainly a laugh convulsed

Matthew, she heard it with her ears and felt it shiver through her flesh, but it was like no other laughter she had ever heard, it chilled her blood. '*He* sets *me* free! And you must be his confederate! Oh, God! He never passed the gate. If you know all, then tell all – how did he go?'

She faltered, weeping: 'He loved you, he willed you to live and forget him, and be happy ...'

'*How did he go?*' repeated Matthew, in a voice so ill-supplied with breath it seemed he might strangle on the words.

'Across the brook,' she said in a broken whisper, 'making the quickest way for Wales. He said ... he has kin there ...'

He drew in hissing breath and took his hands from her, leaving her drooping forward on her face as he let go of her wrists. He had turned his back and flung away from her, all they had shared forgotten, his obsession plucking him away. She did not understand, there was no way she could come to terms so rapidly with all that had happened, but she knew she had loosed her hold of her love, and he was in merciless flight from her in pursuit of some incomprehensible duty in which she had no part and no right. She sprang up and ran after him, caught him by the arm, wound her own arms about him, lifted her imploring face to his stony, frantic stare, and prayed him passionately: 'Let him go! Oh, let him go! He wants to go alone and leave you to me ...'

Almost silently above her the terrible laughter, so opposed to that lovely sound as he followed the reliquary with her, boiled like some thick, choking syrup in his throat. He struggled to shake off her clinging hands, and when she fell to her knees again and hung upon him with all her despairing weight he tore loose his right hand, and struck her heavily in the face, sobbing, and so wrenched himself loose and fled, leaving her face-down on the ground.

In the abbot's lodging Radulfus and his guests sat long over their meal, for they had much to discuss. The topic which was on everyone's lips naturally came first.

'It would seem,' said the abbot, 'that we have been singularly favoured this morning. Certain motions of grace we have seen before, but never yet one so public and so persuasive, with so many witnesses. How do you say? I grow old in experience of wonders, some of which turn out to fall somewhat short of their promise. I know of human deception, not always deliberate, for sometimes the deceiver is himself deceived. If saints have power, so have demons. Yet this boy seems to me as crystal. I cannot think he either cheats or is cheated.'

'I have heard,' said Hugh, 'of cripples who discarded their crutches and walked without them, only to relapse when the fervour of the occasion was over. Time will prove whether this one takes to his crutches again.'

'I shall speak with him later,' said the abbot, 'after the excitement has cooled. I hear from

Brother Edmund that Brother Cadfael has been treating the boy these three days he has been here. That may have eased his condition, but it can scarcely have brought about so sudden a cure. No, I must say it, I truly believe our house has been the happy scene of divine grace. I will speak also with Cadfael, who must know the boy's condition.'

Olivier sat quiet and deferential in the presence of so reverend a churchman as the abbot, but Hugh observed that his arched lids lifted and his eyes kindled at Cadfael's name. So he knew who it was he sought, and something more than a distant salute in action had passed between that strangely assorted pair.

'And now I should be glad,' said the abbot, 'to hear what news you bring from the south. Have you been in Westminster with the empress's court? For I hear she is now installed there.'

Olivier gave his account of affairs in London readily, and answered questions with goodwill. 'My lord has remained in Oxford, it was at his wish I undertook this errand. I was not in London, I set out from Winchester. But the empress is in the palace of Westminster, and the plans for her coronation go forward – admittedly very slowly. The city of London is well aware of its power, and means to exact due recognition of it, or so it seems to me.' He would go no nearer than that to voicing whatever qualms he felt about his liege lady's wisdom or want of it, but he jutted a dubious underlip, and momentarily frowned.

'Father, you were there at the council, you know all that happened. My lord lost a good knight there, and I a valued friend, struck down in the street.'

'Rainald Bossard,' said Radulfus sombrely. 'I have not forgotten.'

'Father, I have been telling the lord sheriff here what I should like to tell also to you. For I have a second errand to pursue, wherever I go on the business of the empress, an errand for Rainald's widow. Rainald had a young kinsman in his household, who was with him when he was killed, and after that death this young man left the lady's service without a word, secretly. She says he had grown closed and silent even before he vanished, and the only trace of him afterwards was on the road to Newbury, going north. Since then, nothing. So knowing I was bound north, she begged me to enquire for him wherever I came, for she values and trusts him, and needs him at her side. I may not deceive you, Father, there are those who say he has fled because he is guilty of Rainald's death. They claim he was besotted with Dame Juliana, and may have seized his chance in this brawl to widow her, and get her for himself, and then taken fright because these things were so soon being said. But *I* think they were not being said at all until after he had vanished. And Juliana, who surely knows him better than any, and looks upon him as a son, for want of children of her own, she is quite sure of him. She wants him home and vindicated, for whatever reason he

177

left her as he did. And I have been asking at every lodging and monastery along the road for word of such a young man. May I also ask here? Brother Hospitaller will know the names of all his guests. Though a name,' he added ruefully, 'is almost all I have, for if ever I saw the man it was without knowing it was he. And the name he may have left behind him.'

'It is not much to go on,' said Abbot Radulfus with a smile, 'but certainly you may enquire. If he has done no wrong, I should be glad to help you to find him and bring him off without reproach. What is his name?'

'Luc Meverel. Twenty-four years old, they tell me, middling tall and well made, dark of hair and eye.'

'It could fit many hundreds of young men,' said the abbot, shaking his head, 'and the name I doubt he will have put off if he has anything to hide, or even if he fears it may be unfairly besmirched. Yet try. I grant you in such a gathering as we have here now a young man who wished to be lost might bury himself very thoroughly. Denis will know which of his guests is of the right age and quality. For clearly your Luc Meverel is well-born, and most likely tutored and lettered.'

'Certainly so,' said Olivier.

'Then by all means, and with my blessing, go freely to Brother Denis, and see what he can do to help you. He has an excellent memory, he will be able to tell you which, among the men here, is of suitable years, and gentle. You can but try.'

On leaving the lodging they went first, however, to look for Brother Cadfael. And Brother Cadfael was not so easily found. Hugh's first resort was the workshop in the herbarium, where they habitually compounded their affairs. But there was no Cadfael there. Nor was he with Brother Anselm in the cloister, where he might well have been debating some nice point in the evening's music. Nor checking the medicine cupboard in the infirmary, which must surely have been depleted during these last few days, but had clearly been restocked in the early hours of this day of glory. Brother Edmund said mildly: 'He was here. I had a poor soul who bled from the mouth – too gorged, I think, with devotion. But he's quiet and sleeping now, the flux has stopped. Cadfael went away some while since.'

Brother Oswin, vigorously fighting weeds in the kitchen garden, had not seen his superior since dinner. 'But I think,' he said, blinking thoughtfully into the sun in the zenith, 'he may be in the church.'

Cadfael was on his knees at the foot of Saint Winifred's three-tread stairway to grace, his hands not lifted in prayer but folded in the lap of his habit, his eyes not closed in entreaty but wide open to absolution. He had been kneeling there for some time, he who was usually only too glad to rise from knees now perceptibly stiffening. He

179

felt no pains, no griefs of any kind, nothing but an immense thankfulness in which he floated like a fish in an ocean. An ocean as pure and blue and drowningly deep and clear as that well-remembered eastern sea, the furthest extreme of the tideless midland sea of legend, at the end of which lay the holy city of Jerusalem, Our Lord's burial-place and hard-won kingdom. The saint who presided here, whether she lay here or no, had launched him into a shining infinity of hope. Her mercies might be whimsical, they were certainly magisterial. She had reached her hand to an innocent, well deserving her kindness. What had she intended towards this less innocent but no less needy being?

Behind him, approaching quietly from the nave, a known voice said softly: 'And are you demanding yet a second miracle?'

He withdrew his eyes reluctantly from the reflected gleams of silver along the reliquary, and turned to look towards the parish altar. He saw the expected shape of Hugh Beringar, the thin dark face smiling at him. But over Hugh's shoulder he saw a taller head and shoulders loom, emerging from dimness in suave, resplendent planes, the bright, jutting cheekbones, the olive cheeks smoothly hollowed below, the falcon's amber eyes beneath high-arched black brows, the long, supple lips tentatively smiling upon him.

It was not possible. Yet he beheld it. Olivier de Bretagne came out of the shadows and stepped unmistakable into the light of the altar candles.

And that was the moment when Saint Winifred turned her head, looked fully into the face of her fallible but faithful servant, and also smiled.

A second miracle! Why not? When she gave she gave prodigally, with both hands.

CHAPTER ELEVEN

They went out into the cloister all three together, and that in itself was memorable and good, for they had never been together before. Those trusting intimacies which had once passed between Cadfael and Olivier, on a winter night in Bromfield priory, were unknown still to Hugh, and there was a mysterious constraint still that prevented Olivier from openly recalling them. The greetings they exchanged were warm but brief, only the reticence behind them was eloquent, and no doubt Hugh understood that well enough, and was willing to wait for enlightenment, or courteously to make do without it. For that there was no haste, but for Luc Meverel there might be.

'Our friend has a quest,' said Hugh, 'in which we mean to enlist Brother Denis's help, but we shall also be very glad of yours. He is looking for a young man by the name of Luc Meverel, strayed from his place and known to be travelling north. Tell him the way of it, Olivier.'

Olivier told the story over again, and was

listened to with close attention. 'Very gladly,' said Cadfael then, 'would I do whatever man can do not only to bring off an innocent man from such a charge, but also to bring the charge home to the guilty. We know of this murder, and it sticks in every gullet that a decent man, protecting his honourable opponent, should be cut down by one of his own faction …'

'Is that certain?' wondered Hugh sharply.

'As good as certain. Who else would so take exception to the man standing up for his lady and doing his errand without fear? All who still held to Stephen in their hearts would approve, even if they dared not applaud him. And as for a chance attack by sneak-thieves – why choose to prey on a mere clerk, with nothing of value on him but the simple needs of his journey, when the town was full of nobles, clerics and merchants far better worth robbing? Rainald died only because he came to the clerk's aid. No, an adherent of the empress, like Rainald himself but most unlike, committed that infamy.'

'That's good sense,' agreed Olivier. 'But my chief concern now is to find Luc, and send him home again if I can.'

'There must be twenty or more young fellows in that age here today,' said Cadfael, scrubbing thoughtfully at his blunt brown nose, 'but I dare wager most of them can be pricked out of the list as well known to some of their companions by their own right names, or by reason of their calling or condition. Solitaries may come, but they're few and far between. Pilgrims are like starlings, they thrive on company. We'd best go and talk to Brother Denis. He'll have sorted out most of them by now.'

Brother Denis had a retentive memory and an appetite for news and rumours that usually kept him the best-informed person in the enclave. The fuller his halls, the more pleasure he took in knowing everything that went on there, and the name and vocation of every guest. He also kept meticulous books to record the visitations.

They found him in the narrow cell where he kept his accounts and estimated his future needs, thoughtfully reckoning up what provisions he still had, and how rapidly the demands on them were likely to dwindle from the morrow. He took his mind from his store-book courteously in order to listen to what Brother Cadfael and the sheriff required of him, and produced answers with exemplary promptitude when asked to sieve out from his swollen household males of about twenty-five years, bred gentle or within modest reach of gentility, lettered, of dark colouring and medium tall build, answering to the very bare description of Luc Meverel. As his forefinger flew down the roster of his guests the numbers shrank remarkably. It seemed to be true that considerably more than half of those who went on pilgrimage were women, and that among the men the greater part were in their forties or fifties, and of those remaining, many would be in minor orders, either monastics or secular priests or

184

would-be priests. And Luc Meverel was none of these.

'Are there any here,' asked Hugh, viewing the final list, which was short enough, 'who came solitary?'

Brother Denis cocked his round, rosy, tonsured head aside and ran a sharp brown eye, very remiscent of a robin's, down the list. 'Not one. Young squires of that age seldom go as pilgrims, unless with an exigent lord – or an equally exigent lady. In such a summer feast as this we might have young friends coming together, to take the fill of the time before they settle down to sterner disciplines. But alone ... Where would be the pastime in that?'

'Here are two, at any rate,' said Cadfael, 'who came together, but surely not for pastime. They have puzzled me, I own. Both are of the proper age, and such word as we have of the man we're looking for would fit either. You know them, Denis – that youngster who's on his way to Aberdaron, and his friend who bears him company. Both lettered, both bred to the manor. And certainly they came from the south, beyond Abingdon, according to Brother Adam of Reading, who lodged there the same night.'

'Ah, the barefoot traveller,' said Denis, and laid a finger on Ciaran in the shrunken toll of young men, 'and his keeper and worshipper. Yes, I would not put half a year beween them, and they have the build and colouring, but you needed only one.'

185

'We could at least look at two,' said Cadfael. 'If neither of them is what we're seeking, yet coming from that region they may have encountered such a single traveller somewhere on the road. If we have not the authority to question them closely about who they are and whence they come, and how and why thus linked, then Father Abbot has. And if they have no reason to court concealment, then they'll willingly declare to him what they might not as readily utter to us.'

'We may try it,' said Hugh, kindling. 'At least it's worth the asking, and if they have nothing to do with the man we are looking for, neither they nor we have lost more than half an hour of time, and surely they won't grudge us that.'

'Granted what is so far related of these two hardly fits the case,' Cadfael acknowledged doubtfully, 'for the one is said to be mortally ill and going to Aberdaron to die, and the other is resolute to keep him company to the end. But a young man who wishes to disappear may provide himself with a circumstantial story as easily as with a new name. And at all events, between Abingdon and Shrewsbury it's possible they may have encountered Luc Meverel alone and under his own name.'

'But if one of these two, either of these two, should truly be the man I want,' said Olivier doubtfully, 'then who, in the name of God, is the other?'

'We ask each other questions,' said Hugh practically, 'which either of these two could answer in a moment. Come, let's leave Abbot

Radulfus to call them in, and see what comes of it.'

It was not difficult to induce the abbot to have the two young men sent for. It was not so easy to find them and bring them to speak for themselves. The messenger, sent forth in expectation of prompt obedience, came back after a much longer time than had been expected, and reported ruefully that neither of the pair could be found within the abbey walls. True, the porter had not actually seen either of them pass the gatehouse. But what had satisfied him that the two were leaving was that the young man Matthew had come, no long time after dinner, to reclaim his dagger, and had left behind him a generous gift of money to the house, saying that he and his friend were already bound away on their journey, and desired to offer thanks for their lodging. And had he seemed – it was Cadfael who asked it, himself hardly knowing why – had he seemed as he always was, or in any way disturbed or alarmed or out of countenance and temper, when he came for his weapon and paid his and his friend's score?

The messenger shook his head, having asked no such question at the gate. Brother Porter, when enquiry was made direct by Cadfael himself, said positively: 'He was like a man on fire. Oh, as soft as ever in voice, and courteous, but pale and alight, you'd have said his hair stood on end. But what with every soul within here wandering in a dream, since this wonder, I never

187

thought but here were some going forth with the news while the furnace was still white-hot.'

'Gone?' said Olivier, dismayed, when this word was brought back to the abbot's parlour. 'Now I begin to see better cause why one of these two, for all they come so strangely paired, and so strangely account for themselves, may be the man I'm seeking. For if I do not know Luc Meverel by sight, I have been two or three times his lord's guest recently, and he may well have taken note of me. How if he saw me come, today, and is gone hence thus in haste because he does not wish to be found? He could hardly know I am sent to look for him, but he might, for all that, prefer to put himself clean out of sight. And an ailing companion on the way would be good cover for a man wanting a reason for his wanderings. I wish I might yet speak with these two. How long have they been gone?'

'It cannot have been more than an hour and a half after noon,' said Cadfael, 'according to when Matthew reclaimed his dagger.'

'And afoot!' Olivier kindled hopefully. 'And even unshod, the one of them! It should be no great labour to overtake them, if it's known what road they will have taken.'

'By far their best way is by the Oswestry road, and so across the dyke into Wales. According to Brother Denis, that was Ciaran's declared intent.'

'Then, Father Abbot,' said Olivier eagerly, 'with your leave I'll mount and ride after them, for they cannot have got far. It would be a pity to miss the chance, and even if they are not who I'm seeking, neither they nor I will have lost anything. But with or without my man, I shall return here.'

'I'll ride through the town with you,' said Hugh, 'and set you on your way, for this will be new country to you. But then I must be about my own business, and see if we've gathered any harvest from this morning's hunt. I doubt they've gone deeper into the forest, or I should have had word by now. We shall look for you back before night, Olivier. One more night at the least we mean to keep you and longer if we can.'

Olivier took his leave hastily but gracefully, made a dutiful reverence to the abbot, and turned upon Brother Cadfael a brief, radiant smile that shattered his preoccupation for an instant like a sunburst through clouds. 'I will not leave here,' he said in simple reassurance, 'without having quiet conference with you. But this I must see finished, if I can.'

They were gone away briskly to the stables, where they had left their horses before Mass. Abbot Radulfus looked after them with a very thoughtful face.

'Do you find it surprising, Cadfael, that these two young pilgrims should leave so soon, and so abruptly? Is it possible the coming of Messire de Bretagne can have driven them away?'

Cadfael considered, and shook his head. 'No, I think not. In the great press this morning, and the excitement, why should one man among the many be noticed, and one not looked for at all in

189

these parts? But, yes, their going does greatly surprise me. For the one, he should surely be only too glad of an extra day or two of rest before taking barefoot to the roads again. And for the other – Father, there is a girl he certainly admires and covets, whether he yet knows it to the full or no, and with her he spent this morning, following Saint Winifred home, and I am certain there was then no other thought in his mind but of her and her kin, and the greatness of this day. For she is sister to the boy Rhun, who came by so great a mercy and blessing before our eyes. It would take some very strong compulsion to drag him away suddenly like this.'

'The boy's sister, you say?' Abbot Radulfus recalled an intent which had been shelved in favour of Olivier's quest. 'There is still an hour or more before Vespers. I should like to talk with this youth. You have been treating his condition, Cadfael. Do you think your handling has had anything to do with what we witnessed today? Or could he – though I would not willingly attribute falsity to one so young – could he have made more of his distress than it was, in order to produce a prodigy?'

'No,' said Cadfael very decidedly. 'There is no deceit at all in him. And as for my poor skills, they might in a long time of perseverance have softened the tight cords that hampered the use of his limb, and made it possible to set a little weight on it – but straighten that foot and fill out the sinews of the leg – never! The greatest doctor in the world could not have done it. Father, on the day he came I gave him a draught that should have eased his pain and brought him sleep. After three nights he sent it back to me untouched. He saw no reason why he should expect to be singled out for healing, but he said that he offered his pain freely, who had nothing else to give. Not to buy grace, but of his goodwill to give and want nothing in return. And further, it seems that thus having accepted his pain out of love, his pain left him. After Mass we saw that deliverance completed.'

'Then it was well deserved,' said Radulfus, pleased and moved. 'I must indeed talk with this boy. Will you find him for me, Cadfael, and bring him here to me now?'

'Very gladly, Father,' said Cadfael, and departed on his errand. Dame Alice was sitting in the sunshine of the cloister garth, the centre of a voluble circle of other matrons, her face so bright with the joy of the day that it warmed the very air; but Rhun was not with them. Melangell had withdrawn into the shadow of the arcade, as though the light was too bright for her eyes, and kept her face averted over the mending of a frayed seam in a linen shirt which must belong to her brother. Even when Cadfael addressed her she looked up only very swiftly and timidly, and again stooped into shadow, but even in that glimpse he saw that the joy which had made her shine like a new rose in the morning was dimmed and pale now in the lengthening afternoon. And was he merely imagining that her left cheek showed the faint bluish tint of a bruise? But at the mention of Rhun's name she smiled, as though at the recollection of happiness rather than its presence.

'He said he was tired, and went away into the dortoir to rest. Aunt Weaver thinks he is lying down on his bed, but I think he wanted only to be left alone, to be quiet and not have to talk. He is tired by having to answer things he seems not to understand himself.'

'He speaks another tongue today from the rest of mankind,' said Cadfael. 'It may well be we who don't understand, and ask things that have no meaning for him.' He took her gently by the chin and turned her face up to the light, but she twisted nervously out of his hold. 'You have hurt yourself?' Certainly it was a bruise beginning there.

'It's nothing,' she said. 'My own fault. I was in the garden, I ran too fast and I fell. I know it's unsightly, but it doesn't hurt now.'

Her eyes were very calm, not reddened, only a little swollen as to the lids. Well, Matthew had gone, abandoned her to go with his friend, letting her fall only too disastrously after the heady running together of the morning hours. That could account for tears now past. But should it account for a bruised cheek? He hesitated whether to question further, but clearly she did not wish it. She had gone back doggedly to her work, and would not look up again.

Cadfael sighed, and went out across the great court to the guest-hall. Even a glorious day like this one must have its vein of bitter sadness.

In the men's dortoir Rhun sat alone on his bed, very still and content in his blissfully restored body. He was deep in his own rapt thoughts, but readily aware when Cadfael entered. He looked round and smiled.

'Brother, I was wishing to see you. You were there, you know. Perhaps you even heard ... See, how I'm changed!' The leg once maimed stretched out perfect before him, he bent and stamped the boards of the floor. He flexed ankle and toes, drew up his knee to his chin, and everything moved as smoothly and painlessly as his ready tongue. 'I am whole! I never asked it, how dared I? Even then, I was praying not for this, and yet this was given ...' He went away again for a moment into his tranced dream.

Cadfael sat down beside him, noting the exquisite fluency of those joints hitherto flawed and intransigent. The boy's beauty was perfected now.

'You were praying,' said Cadfael gently, 'for Melangell.'

'Yes. And Matthew, too. I truly thought ... But you see he is gone. They are both gone, gone together. Why could I not bring my sister into bliss? I would have gone on crutches all my life for that, but I couldn't prevail.'

'That is not yet determined,' said Cadfael firmly. 'Who goes may also return. And I think

193

your prayers should have strong virtue, if you do not fall into doubt now, because heaven has need of a little time. Even miracles have their times. Half our lives in this world are spent in waiting. It is needful to wait with faith.'

Rhun sat listening with an absent smile, and at the end of it he said: 'Yes, surely, and I will wait. For see, one of them left this behind in his haste when he went away.'

He reached down between the close-set cots, and lifted to the bed between them a bulky but lightweight scrip of unbleached linen, with stout leather straps for the owner's belt. 'I found it dropped between the two beds they had, drawn close together. I don't know which of them owned this one, the two they carried were much alike. But one of them doesn't expect or want ever to come back, does he? Perhaps Matthew does, and has forgotten this, whether he meant it or no, as a pledge.'

Cadfael stared and wondered, but this was a heavy matter, and not for him. He said seriously: 'I think you should bring this with you, and give it into the keeping of Father Abbot. For he sent me to bring you to him. He wants to speak with you.'

'With me?' wavered Rhun, stricken into a wild and rustic child again. 'The lord abbot himself?'

'Surely, and why not? You are Christian soul as he is, and may speak with him as equal.'

The boy faltered: 'I should be afraid ...'

'No, you would not. You are not afraid of anything, nor need you ever be.'

194

Rhun sat for a moment with fists doubled into the blanket of his bed; then he lifted his clear, ice-blue gaze and blanched, angelic face and smiled blindingly into Cadfael's eyes. 'No, I need not. I'll come.' And he hoisted the linen scrip and stood up stately on his two long, youthful legs, and led the way to the door.

'Stay with us,' said Abbot Radulfus, when Cadfael would have presented his charge and left the two of them together. 'I think he might be glad of you.' Also, said his eloquent, austere glance, your presence may be of value to me as witness. 'Rhun knows you. Me he does not yet know, but I trust he shall, hereafter.' He had the drab, brownish scrip on the desk before him, offered on entry with a word to account for it, until the time came to explore its possibilities further.

'Willingly, Father,' said Cadfael heartily, and took his seat apart on a stool withdrawn into a corner, out of the way of those two pairs of formidable eyes that met, and wondered, and probed with equal intensity across the small space of the parlour. Outside the windows the garden blossomed with drunken exuberance, in the burning colours of summer, and the blanched blue sky, at its loftiest in the late afternoon, showed the colour of Rhun's eyes, but without their crystal blaze. The day of wonders was drawing very slowly and radiantly towards its evening.

'Son,' said Radulfus at his gentlest, 'you have

195

been the vessel for a great mercy poured out here. I know, as all know who were there, what we saw, what we felt. But I would know also what you passed through. I know you have lived long with pain, and have not complained. I dare guess in what mind you approached the saint's altar. Tell me, what was it happened to you then?'

Rhun sat with his empty hands clasped quietly in his lap, and his face at once remote and easy, looking beyond the walls of the room. All his timidity was lost.

'I was troubled,' he said carefully, 'because my sister and my Aunt Alice wanted so much for me, and I knew I needed nothing. I would have come, and prayed, and passed, and been content. But then I heard her call.'

'Saint Winifred spoke to you?' asked Radulfus softly.

'She called me to her,' said Rhun positively.

'In what words?'

'No words. What need had she of words? She called me to go to her, and I went. She told me, here is a step, and here, and here, come, you know you can. And I knew I could, so I went. When she told me, kneel, for so you can, then I kneeled, and I could. Whatever she told me, that I did. And so I will still,' said Rhun, smiling into the opposing wall with eyes that paled the sun.

'Child,' said the abbot, watching him in solemn wonder and respect, 'I do believe it. What skills you have, what gifts to stead you in your future life, I scarcely know. I rejoice that you have to the

196

full the blessing of your body, and the purity of your mind and spirit. I wish you whatever calling you may choose, and the virtue of your resolve to guide you in it. If there is anything you can ask of this house, to aid you after you go forth from here, it is yours.'

'Father,' said Rhun earnestly, withdrawing his blinding gaze into shadow and mortality, and becoming the child he was, 'need I go forth? She called me to her, how tenderly I have no words to tell. I desire to remain with her to my life's end. She called me to her, and I will never willingly leave her.'

CHAPTER TWELVE

'And will you keep him?' asked Cadfael, when the boy had been dismissed, made his deep reverence, and departed in his rapt, unwitting perfection.

'If his intent holds, yes, surely. He is the living proof of grace. But I will not let him take vows in haste, to regret them later. Now he is transported with joy and wonder, and would embrace celibacy and seclusion with delight. If his will is still the same in a month, then I will believe in it, and welcome him gladly. But he shall serve his full novitiate, even so. I will not let him close the door upon himself until he is sure. And now,' said the abbot, frowning down thoughtfully at the linen scrip that lay upon his desk, 'what is to be done with this? You say it was fallen between the two beds, and might have belonged to either?'

'So the boy said. But, Father, if you remember, when the bishop's ring was stolen, both those young men gave up their scrips to be examined. What each of them carried, apart from the dagger that was duly delivered over at the gatehouse, I cannot say with certainty, but Father Prior, who handled them, will know.'

'True, so he will. But for the present,' said Radulfus, 'I cannot think we have any right to probe into either man's possessions, nor is it of any great importance to discover to which of them this belongs. If Messire de Bretagne overtakes them, as he surely must, we shall learn more, he may even persuade them to return. We'll wait for his word first. In the meantime, leave it here with me. When we know more we'll take whatever steps we can to restore it.'

The day of wonders drew in to its evening as graciously as it had dawned, with a clear sky and soft, sweet air. Every soul within the enclave came dutifully to Vespers, and supper in the guest-hall as in the refectory was a devout and tranquil feast. The voices hasty and shrill with excitement at dinner had softened and eased into the grateful languor of fulfilment.

Brother Cadfael absented himself from Collations in the chapter house, and went out into the garden. On the gentle ridge where the gradual slope of the pease fields began he stood for a long while watching the sky. The declining sun had still an hour or more of its course to run before its rim dipped into the feathery tops of the copses across the brook. The west which had reflected the dawn as this day began triumphed now in pale gold, with no wisp of cloud to dye it deeper or mark its purity. The scent of the herbs within the walled garden rose in a heady cloud of sweetness and spice. A good place, a resplendent day – why should any man slip away and run from it?

A useless question. Why should any man do the things he does? Why should Ciaran submit himself to such hardship? Why should he profess such piety and devotion, and yet depart without leave-taking and without thanks in the middle of so auspicious a day? It was Matthew who had left a gift of money on departure. Why could not Matthew persuade his friend to stay and see out the day? And why should he, who had glowed with excited joy in the morning, and run hand in hand with Melangell, abandon her without remorse in the afternoon, and resume his harsh pilgrimage with Ciaran as if nothing had happened?

Were they two men or three? Ciaran, Matthew and Luc Meverel? What did he know of them, all three, if three they were? Luc Meverel had been seen for the last time south of Newbury, walking north towards that town, and alone. Ciaran and Matthew were first reported, by Brother Adam of Reading, coming from the south into Abingdon for their night's lodging, two together. If one of them was Luc Meverel, then where and why had he picked up his companion, and above all, *who was his companion*?

By this time, surely Olivier should have overhauled his quarry, and found the answers to some of these questions. And he had said he would return, that he would not leave Shrewsbury without having some converse with a man remembered as a good friend. Cadfael took that assurance to his heart, and was warmed.

It was not the need to tend any of his herbal potions or bubbling wines that drew him to walk on to his workshop, for Brother Oswin, now in the chapter house with his fellows, had tidied everything for the night, and seen the brazier safely out. There was flint and tinder there in a box, in case it should be necessary to light it again in the night or early in the morning. It was rather that Cadfael had grown accustomed to withdrawing to his own special solitude to do his best thinking, and this day had given him more than enough cause for thought, as for gratitude. For where were his qualms now? Miracles may be spent as frequently on the undeserving as on the deserving. What marvel that a saint should take the boy Rhun to her heart, and reach out her sustaining hand to him? But the second miracle was doubly miraculous, far beyond her sorry servant's asking, stunning in its generosity. To bring him back Olivier, whom he had resigned to God and the great world, and made himself content never to see again! And then Hugh's voice, unwitting herald of wonders, said out of the dim choir, 'And are you demanding yet a second miracle?' He had rather been humbling himself in wonder and thanks for one, demanding nothing more; but he had turned his head, and beheld Olivier.

The western sky was still limpid and bright,

201

liquid gold, the sun still clear of the treetops, when he opened the door of his workshop and stepped within, into the timber-warm, herb-scented dimness. He thought and said afterwards that it was at that moment he saw the inseparable relationship between Ciaran and Matthew suddenly overturned, twisted into its opposite, and began, in some enclosed and detached part of his intelligence, to make sense of the whole matter, however dubious and flawed the revelation. But he had no time to catch and pin down the vision, for as his foot crossed the threshold there was a soft gasp somewhere in the shadowy corner of the hut, and a rustle of movement, as if some wild creature had been disturbed in its lair, and shrunk into the last fastness to defend itself.

He halted, and set the door wide open behind him for reassurance that there was a possibility of escape. 'Be easy!' he said mildly. 'May I not come into my own workshop without leave? And should I be entering here to threaten any soul with harm?'

His eyes, growing accustomed rapidly to the dimness, which seemed dark only by contrast with the radiance outside, scanned the shelves, the bubbling jars of wine in a fat row, the swinging, rustling swathes of herbs dangling from the beams of the low roof. Everything took shape and emerged into view. Stretched along the broad wooden bench against the opposite wall, a huddle of tumbled skirts stirred slowly and reared itself upright, to show him the spilled ripe-corn gold of a girl's hair, and the tear-stained, swollen-lidded countenance of Melangell.

She said no word, but she did not drop blindly into her sheltering arms again. She was long past that, and past being afraid to show herself so to one secret, quiet creature whom she trusted. She set down her feet in their scuffed leather shoes to the floor, and sat back against the timbers of the wall, bracing slight shoulders to the solid contact. She heaved one enormous, draining sigh that was dragged up from her very heels, and left her weak and docile. When he crossed the beaten earth floor and sat down beside her, she did not flinch away.

'Now,' said Cadfael, settling himself with deliberation, to give her time to compose at least her voice. The soft light would spare her face. 'Now, child dear, there is no one here who can either save you or trouble you, and therefore you can speak freely, for everything you say is between us two only. But we two together need to take careful counsel. So what is it you know that I do not know?'

'Why should we take counsel?' she said in a small, drear voice from below his solid shoulder. 'He is gone.'

'What is gone may return. The roads lead always two ways, hither as well as yonder. What are you doing out here alone, when your brother walks erect on two sound feet, and has all he wants in this world, but for your absence?'

He did not look directly at her, but felt the stir

of warmth and softness through her body, which must have been a smile, however flawed. 'I came away,' she said, very low, 'not to spoil his joy. I've borne most of the day. I think no one has noticed half my heart was gone out of me: Unless it was you,' she said, without blame, rather in resignation.

'I saw you when we came from Saint Giles,' said Cadfael, 'you and Matthew. Your heart was whole then, so was his. If yours is torn in two now, do you suppose his is preserved without wound? No! So what passed, afterwards? What was this sword that shore through your heart and his? You know! You may tell it now. They are gone, there is nothing left to spoil. There may yet be something to save.'

She turned her forehead into his shoulder and wept in silence for a little while. The light within the hut grew rather than dimming, now that his eyes were accustomed. She forgot to hide her forlorn and bloated face, he saw the bruise on her cheek darkening into purple. He laid an arm about her and drew her close for the comfort of the flesh. That of the spirit would need more of time and thought.

'He struck you?'

'I held him,' she said, quick in his defence. 'He could not get free.'

'And he was so frantic? He *must* go?'

'Yes, whatever it cost him or me. Oh, Brother Cadfael, why? I thought, I believed he loved me, as I do him. But see how he used me in his anger!'

'Anger?' said Cadfael sharply, and turned her by the shoulders to study her more intently. 'Whatever the compulsion on him to go with his friend, why should he be angry with you? The loss was yours, but surely no blame.'

'He blamed me for not telling him,' she said drearily. 'But I did only what Ciaran asked of me. For his sake and yours, he said, yes, and for mine, too, let me go, but hold him fast. Don't tell him I have the ring again, he said, and I will go. Forget me, he said, and help him to forget me. He wanted us to remain together and be happy ...'

'Are you telling me,' demanded Cadfael sharply, 'that *they did not go together*? That Ciaran made off without him?'

'It was not like that,' sighed Melangell. 'He meant well by us, that's why he stole away alone ...'

'When was this? When? When did you have speech with him? *When* did he go?'

'I was here at dawn, you'll remember. I met Ciaran by the brook ...' She drew a deep, desolate breath and loosed the whole flood of it, every word she could recall of that meeting in the early morning, while Cadfael gazed appalled, and the vague glimpse he had had of enlightenment awoke and stirred again in his mind, far clearer now.

'Go on! Tell me what followed between you and Matthew. You did as you were bidden, I know, you drew him with you, I doubt he ever gave a thought to Ciaran all those morning hours,

205

believing him still penned within doors, afraid to stir. When was it he found out?'

'After dinner it came into his mind that he had not seen him. He was very uneasy. He went to look for him everywhere ... He came to me here in the garden. "God keep you, Melangell," he said, "you must fend for yourself now, sorry as I am ..." ' Almost every word of that encounter she had by heart, she repeated them like a tired child repeating a lesson. 'I said too much, he knew I had spoken with Ciaran ... he knew that I knew he'd meant to go secretly ...'

'And then, after you had owned as much?'

'He laughed,' she said, and her very voice froze into a despairing whisper. 'I never heard him laugh until this morning, and then it was such a sweet sound. But this laughter was not so! Bitter and raging.' She stumbled through the rest of it, every word another fine line added to the reversed image that grew in Cadfael's mind, mocking his memory. '*He* sets *me* free!' And '*You* must be his confederate!' The words were so burned on her mind that she even reproduced the savagery of their utterance. And how few words it took, in the end, to transform everything, to turn devoted attendance into remorseless pursuit, selfless love into dedicated hatred, noble self-sacrifice into calculated flight, and the voluntary mortification of the flesh into body armour which must never be doffed.

He heard again, abruptly and piercingly, Ciaran's wild cry of alarm as he clutched his cross to him, and Matthew's voice saying softly: 'Yet he should doff it. How else can he truly be rid of his pains?'

How else, indeed! Cadfael recalled, too, how he had reminded them both that they were here to attend the feast of a saint who might have life itself within her gift – 'even for a man already condemned to death!' Oh Saint Winifred, stand by me now, stand by us all, with a third miracle to better the other two!

He took Melangell brusquely by the chin, and lifted her face to him. 'Girl, look to yourself now for a while, for I must leave you. Do up your hair and keep a brave face, and go back to your kin as soon as you can bear their eyes on you. Go into the church for a time, it will be quiet there now, and who will wonder if you give a longer time to your prayers? They will not even wonder at past tears, if you can smile now. Do as well as you can, for I have a thing I must do.'

There was nothing he could promise her, no sure hope he could leave with her. He turned from her without another word, leaving her staring after him between dread and reassurance, and went striding in haste through the gardens and out across the court, to the abbot's lodging.

If Radulfus was surprised to have Cadfael ask audience again so soon, he gave no sign of it, but had him admitted at once, and put aside his book to give his full attention to whatever this fresh business might be. Plainly it was something very much to the current purpose and urgent.

'Father,' said Cadfael, making short work of explanations, 'there's a new twist here. Messire de Bretagne has gone off on a false trail. Those two young men did not leave by the Oswestry road, but crossed the Meole brook and set off due west to reach Wales the nearest way. Nor did they leave together. Ciaran slipped away during the morning, while his fellow was with us in the procession, and Matthew has followed him by the same way as soon as he learned of his going. And, Father, there's good cause to think that the sooner they're overtaken and halted, the better surely for one, and I believe for both. I beg you, let me take a horse and follow. And send word of this to Hugh Beringar in the town, to come after us on the same trail.'

Radulfus received all this with a grave but calm face, and asked no less shortly: 'How did you come by this word?'

'From the girl who spoke with Ciaran before he departed. No need to doubt it is all true. And, Father, one more thing before you bid me go. Open, I beg you, that scrip they left behind, let me see if it has anything more to tell us of this pair – at the least, of one of them.'

Without a word or an instant of hesitation, Radulfus dragged the linen scrip into the light of his candles, and unbuckled the fastening. The contents he drew out fully upon the desk, sparse enough, what the poor pilgrim would carry, having few possessions and desiring to travel light.

'You know, I think,' said the abbot, looking up sharply, 'to which of the two this belonged?'

'I do not know, but I guess. In my mind I am sure, but I am also fallible. Give me leave!'

With a sweep of his hand he spread the meagre belongings over the desk. The purse, thin enough when Prior Robert had handled it before, lay flat and empty now. The leather-bound breviary, well-used, worn but treasured, had been rolled into the folds of the shirt, and when Cadfael reached for it the shirt slid from the desk and fell to the floor. He let it lie as he opened the book. Within the cover was written, in a clerk's careful hand, the name of its owner: 'Juliana Bossard'. And below, in newer ink and a less practised hand: *Given to me, Luc Meverel, this Christmastide, 1140. God be with us all!*

'So I pray, too,' said Cadfael, and stooped to pick up the fallen shirt. He held it up to the light, and his eye caught the thread-like outline of a stain that rimmed the left shoulder. His eye followed the line over the shoulder, and found it continued down and round the left side of the breast. The linen, otherwise, was clean enough, bleached by several launderings from its original brownish natural colouring. He spread it open, breast up, on the desk. The thin brown line, sharp on its outer edge, slightly blurred within, hemmed a great space spanning the whole left part of the chest and the upper part of the left sleeve. The space within the outline had been washed clear of any stain, even the rim was pale, but it stood clear to be seen, and the scattered shadowings of colour within it preserved a faint hint of what had been there.

Radulfus, if he had not ventured as far afield in the world as Cadfael, had nevertheless stored up some experience of it. He viewed the extended evidence and said composedly, 'This was blood.'

'So it was,' said Cadfael, and rolled up the shirt.

'And whoever owned this scrip came from where a certain Juliana Bossard was chatelaine.' His deep eyes were steady and sombre on Cadfael's face. 'Have we entertained a murderer in our house?'

'I think we have,' said Cadfael, restoring the scattered fragments of a life to their modest lodging. A man's life, shorn of all expectation of continuance, even the last coin gone from the purse. 'But I think we may have time yet to prevent another killing – if you give me leave to go.'

'Take the best of what may be in the stable,' said the abbot simply, 'and I will send word to Hugh Beringar, and have him follow you, and not alone.'

CHAPTER THIRTEEN

Several miles north on the Oswestry road, Olivier drew rein by the roadside where a wiry, bright-eyed boy was grazing goats on the broad verge, lush in summer growth and coming into seed. The child twitched one of his long leads on his charges, to bring him along gently where the early evening light lay warm on the tall grass. He looked up at the rider without awe, half-Welsh and immune from servility. He smiled and gave an easy good evening.

The boy was handsome, bold, unafraid; so was the man. They looked at each other and liked what they saw.

'God be with you!' said Olivier. 'How long have you been pasturing your beasts along here? And have you in all that time seen a lame man and a well man go by, the pair of them much of my age, but afoot?'

'God be with you, master,' said the boy cheerfully. 'Here along this verge ever since noon, for I brought my bit of dinner with me. But I've seen none such pass. And I've had a word by the road with every soul that did go by, unless he were galloping.'

'Then I waste my hurrying,' said Olivier, and idled a while, his horse stooping to the tips of the grasses. 'They cannot be ahead of me, not by this road. See, now, supposing they wished to go earlier into Wales, how may I bear round to pick them up on the way? They went from Shrewsbury town ahead of me, and I have word to bring to them. Where can I turn west and fetch a circle about the town?'

The young herdsman accepted with open arms every exchange that refreshed his day's labour. He gave his mind to the best road offering, and delivered judgement: 'Turn back but a mile or more, back across the bridge at Montford, and then you'll find a well-used cart-track that bears off west, to your right hand it will be. Bear a piece west again where the paths first branch, it's no direct way, but it does go on. It skirts Shrewsbury a matter of above four miles outside the town, and threads the edges of the forest, but it cuts across every path out of Shrewsbury. You may catch your men yet. And I wish you may!'

'My thanks for that,' said Olivier, 'and for your advice also.' He stooped to the hand the boy had raised, not for alms but to caress the horse's chestnut shoulder with admiration and pleasure, and slipped a coin into the smooth palm. 'God be with you!' he said, and wheeled his mount and set off back along the road he had travelled.

'And go with you, master!' the boy called after him, and watched until a curve of the road took horse and rider out of sight beyond a stand of trees. The goats gathered closer; evening was near, and they were ready to turn homeward, knowing the hour by the sun as well as did their herd. The boy drew in their tethers, whistled to them cheerily, and moved on along the road to his homeward path through the fields.

Olivier came for the second time to the bridge over the Severn, one bank a steep, tree-clad escarpment, the other open, level meadow. Beyond the first plane of fields a winding track turned off to the right, between scattered stands of trees, bearing at this point rather south than west, but after a mile or more it brought him on to a better road that crossed his track left and right. He bore right into the sun, as he had been instructed, and at the next place where two dwindling paths divided he turned left, and keeping his course by the sinking sun on his right hand, now just resting upon the rim of the world and glimmering through the trees in sudden blinding glimpses, began to work his way gradually round the town of Shrewsbury. The tracks wound in and out of copses, the fringe woods of the northern tip of the Long Forest, sometimes in twilight among dense trees, sometimes in open heath and scrub, sometimes past islets of cultivated fields and glimpses of hamlets. He rode with ears pricked for any promising sound, pausing wherever his labyrinthine path crossed a track bearing westward out of Shrewsbury, and wherever he met with cottage or assart he asked after his two travellers. No one had seen such a pair pass by. Olivier took heart.

They had had some hours start of him, but if they had not passed westward by any of the roads he had yet crossed, they might still be within the circle he was drawing about the town. The barefoot one would not find these ways easy going, and might have been forced to take frequent rests. At the worst, even if he missed them in the end, this meandering route must bring him round at last to the highroad by which he had first approached Shrewsbury from the south-east, and he could ride back into the town to Hugh Beringar's welcome, none the worse for a little exercise in a fine evening.

Brother Cadfael had wasted no time in clambering into his boots, kilting his habit, and taking and saddling the best horse he could find in the stables. It was not often he had the chance to indulge himself with such half-forgotten delights, but he was not thinking of that now. He had left considered word with the messenger who was already hurrying across the bridge and into the town, to alert Hugh; and Hugh would ask no questions, as the abbot had asked none, recognising the grim urgency there was no leisure now to explain.

'Say to Hugh Beringar,' the order ran, 'that Ciaran will make for the Welsh border the nearest way, but avoiding the too open roads. I think he'll bear south a small way to the old road the Romans made, that we've been fools enough to let run wild, for it keeps a steady level and makes straight for the border north of Caus.'

That was drawing a bow at a venture, and he

knew it, none better. Ciaran was not of these parts, though he might well have some knowledge of the borderland if he had kin on the Welsh side. But more than that, he had been here these three days past, and if he had been planning some such escape all that time, he could have picked the brains of brothers and guests, on easily plausible ground. Time pressed, and sound guessing was needed. Cadfael chose his way, and set about pursuing it.

He did not waste time in going decorously out at the gatehouse and round by the road to take up the chase westward, but led his horse at a trot through the gardens, to the blank astonishment of Brother Jerome, who happened to be crossing to the cloisters a good ten minutes early for Compline. No doubt he would report, with a sense of outrage, to Prior Robert. Cadfael as promptly forgot him, leading the horse round the unharvested pease-field and down to the quiet green stretches of the brook, and across to the narrow meadow, where he mounted. The sun was dipping its rim beyond the crowns of the trees to westward. Into that half-shine half-shadow Cadfael spurred, and made good speed while the tracks were familiar to him as his own palm. Due west until he hit the road, a half-mile on the road at a canter, until it turned too far to the south, and then westward again for the setting sun. Ciaran had a long start, even of Matthew, let alone of all those who followed now. But Ciaran was lame, burdened and afraid. Almost he was to be pitied.

Half a mile further on, at an inconspicuous

track which he knew, Cadfael again turned to bear south-west, and burrowed into deepest shade, and into the northernmost woodlands of the Long Forest. No more than a narrow forest ride, this, between sweeping branches, a fragment of ancient wood not worth clearing for an assart, being bedded on rock that broke surface here and there. This was not yet border country, but close kin to it, heaving into fretful outcrops that broke the thin soil, bearing heather and coarse upland grasses, scrub bushes and sparsity trees, then bringing forth prodigal life roofed by very old trees in every wet hollow. A little further on this course, and the close, dark woods began, tall top cover, heavy interweaving of middle growth, and a tangle of bush and bramble and ground-cover below. Undisturbed forest, though there were rare islands of tillage bright and open within it, every one an astonishment.

Then he came to the old, old road, that sliced like a knife across his path, heading due east, due west. He wondered about the men who had made it. It was shrunken now from a soldiers' road to a narrow ride, mostly under thin turf, but it ran as it had always run since it was made, true and straight as a lance, perfectly levelled where a level was possible, relentlessly climbing and descending where some hummock barred the way. Cadfael turned west into it, and rode straight for the golden upper arc of sun that still glowed between the branches.

*

In the parcel of old forest north and west of the hamlet of Hanwood there were groves where stray outlaws could find ample cover, provided they stayed clear of the few settlements within reach. Local people tended to fence their holdings and band together to protect their own small ground. The forest was for plundering, poaching, pasturing of swine, all with secure precautions. Travellers, though they might call on hospitality and aid where needed, must fend for themselves in the thicker coverts, if they cared to venture through them. By and large, safety here in Shropshire under Hugh Beringar was as good as anywhere in England, and encroachment by vagabonds could not survive long, but for brief occupation the cover was there, and unwanted tenants might take up occupation if pressed.

Several of the lesser manors in these border regions had declined by reason of their perilous location, and some were half-deserted, leaving their fields untilled. Until April of this year the border castle of Caus had been in Welsh hands, an added threat to peaceful occupation, and there had not yet been time since Hugh's reclamation of the castle for the depleted hamlets to re-establish themselves. Moreover, in this high summer it was no hardship to live wild, and skilful poaching and a little profitable thievery could keep two or three good fellows in meat while they allowed time for their exploits in the south to be forgotten, and made up their minds where best to pass the time until a return home seemed possible.

Master Simeon Poer, self-styled merchant of Guildford, was not at all ill-content with the pickings made in Shrewsbury. In three nights, which was the longest they dared reckon on operating unsuspected, they had taken a fair amount of money from the hopeful gamblers of the town and Foregate, besides the price Daniel Aurifaber had paid for the stolen ring, the various odds and ends William Hales had abstracted from market stalls, and the coins John Shure had used his long, smooth, waxed finger-nails to extract from pocket and purse in the crowds. It was a pity they had had to leave William Hales to his fate during the raid, but all in all they had done well to get out of it with no more than a bruise or two, and one man short. Bad luck for William, but it was the way the lot had fallen. Every man knew it could happen to him.

They had avoided the used tracks, refraining from meddling with any of the local people going about their business, and done their plundering by night and stealthily, after first making sure where there were dogs to be reckoned with. They even had a roof of sorts, for in the deepest thickets below the old road, overgrown and well-concealed, they had found the remains of a hut, relic of a failed assart abandoned long ago. After a few days more of this easy living, or if the weather should change, they would set off to make their way somewhat south, to be well clear of Shrewsbury before moving across to the east, to shires where they were not yet known.

When the rare traveller came past on the road, it was almost always a local man, and they let him alone, for he would be missed all too soon, and the hunt would be up in a day. But they would not have been averse to waylaying any solitary who was clearly a stranger and on his way to more distant places, since he was unlikely to be missed at once, and further, he was likely to be better worth robbing, having on him the means to finance his journey, however modestly. In these woods and thickets, a man could vanish very neatly, and for ever.

They had made themselves comfortable that night outside their hut, with the embers of their fire safe in the clay-lined hollow they had made for it, and the grease of the stolen chicken still on their fingers. The sunset of the outer world was already twilight here, but they had their night eyes, and were wide awake and full of restless energy after an idle day. Walter Bagot was charged with keeping such watch as they thought needful, and had made his way in cover some distance along the narrow track towards the town. He came sliding back in haste, but shining with anticipation instead of alarm.

'Here's one coming we may safely pick off. The barefoot fellow from the abbey ... well back as yet, and lame as ever, he's been among the stones, surely. Not a soul will know where he went to.'

'He?' said Simeon Poer, surprised. 'Fool, he has always his shadow breathing down his neck. It would mean both – if one got away he'd raise the hunt on us.'

'He has not his shadow now,' said Bagot glee-fully. 'Alone, I tell you, he's shaken him off, or else they've parted by consent. Who else cares a groat what becomes of him?'

'And a groat's his worth,' said Shure scornfully. 'Let him go. It's never worth it for his hose and shirt, and what else can he have on him?'

'Ah, but he has! Money, my friend!' said Bagot, glittering. 'Make no mistake, that one goes very well provided, if he takes good care not to let it be known. I know! I've felt my way about him every time I could get crowded against him in church, he has a solid, heavy purse belted about him inside coat, hose, shirt and all, but I never could get my fingers into it without using the knife, and that was too risky. He can pay his way wherever he goes. Come, rouse, he'll be an easy mark now.'

He was certain, and they were heartily willing to pick up an extra purse. They rose merrily, hands on daggers, worming their way quietly through the underbrush towards the thin thread of the track, above which the ribbon of clear sky showed pale and bright still. Shure and Bagot lurking invisible on the near side of the path, Simeon Poer across it, behind the lush screen of bushes that took advan-tage of the open light to grow leafy and tall. There were very old trees in their tract of forest, enor-mous beeches with trunks so gnarled and thick three men with arms outspread could hardly clip them. Old woodland was being cleared, assarted and turned into hunting-grounds in many places,

220

but the Long Forest still preserved large tracts of virgin growth untouched. In the green dimness the three masterless men stood still as the trees, and waited.

Then they heard him. Dogged, steady, laborious steps that stirred the coarse grasses. In the turfed verge of a highroad he could have gone with less pain and covered twice the miles he had accomplished on these rough ways. They heard his heavy breathing while he was still twenty yards away from them, and saw his tall, dark figure stir the dimness, leaning forward on a long, knotty staff he had picked up somewhere from among the debris of the trees. It seemed that he favoured the right foot, though both trod with wincing tenderness, as though he had trodden askew on a sharp-edged stone, and either cut his sole or twisted his ankle-joint. He was piteous, if there had been anyone to pity him.

He went with ears pricked, and the very hairs of his skin erected, in as intense wariness as any of the small nocturnal creatures that crept and quaked in the underbrush around him. He had walked in fear every step of the miles he had gone in company, but now, cast loose to his own dreadful company, he was even more afraid. Escape was no escape at all.

It was the extremity of his fear that saved him. They had let him pass slowly by the first covert, so that Bagot might be behind him, and Poer and Shure one on either side before him. It was not so much his straining ears as the prickly sensitivity of

221

his skin that sensed the sudden rushing presence at his back, the shifting of the cool evening air, and the weight of body and arm launched at him almost silently. He gave a muted shriek and whirled about, sweeping the staff around him, and the knife that should have impaled him struck the branch and sliced a ribbon of bark and wood from it. Bagot reached with his left hand for a grip on sleeve or coat, and struck again as nimbly as a snake, but missed his hold as Ciaran leaped wildly back out of reach, and driven beyond himself by terror, turned and plunged away on his lacerated feet, aside from the path and into the deepest and thickest shadows among the tangled trees. He hissed and moaned with pain as he went, but he ran like a startled hare.

Who would have thought he could still move so fast, once pushed to extremes? But he could not keep it up long, the spur would not carry him far. The three of them went after, spreading out a little to hem him from three sides when he fell exhausted. They were giggling as they went, and in no special haste. The mingled sounds of his crashing passage through the bushes and his uncontrollable whining with the pain of it, rang unbelievably strangely in the twilit woods.

Branches and brambles lashed Ciaran's face. He ran blindly, sweeping the long staff before him, cutting a noisy swathe through the bushes and stumbling painfully in the thick ground-debris of dead branches and soft, treacherous pits of the leaves of many years. They followed at leisure,

222

aware that he was slowing. The lean, agile tailor had drawn level with him, somewhat aside, and was bearing round to cut him off, still with breath enough to whistle to his fellows as they closed unhurriedly, like dogs herding a stray sheep. Ciaran fell out into a more open glade, where a huge old beech had preserved its own clearing, and with what was left of his failing breath he made a last dash to cross the open and vanish again into the thickets beyond. The dry silt of leaves among the roots betrayed him. His footing slid from under him, and fetched him down heavily against the bole of the tree. He had just time to drag himself up and set his back to the broad trunk before they were on him.

He flailed about him with the staff, screaming for aid, and never even knew on what name he was calling in his extremity.

'Help! Murder! Matthew, Matthew, help me!'

There was no answering shout, but there was an abrupt thrashing of branches, and something hurtled out of cover and across the grass, so suddenly that Bagot was shouldered aside and stumbled to his knees. A long arm swept Ciaran back hard against the solid bole of the tree, and Matthew stood braced beside him, his dagger naked in his hand. What remained of the western light showed his face roused and formidable, and gleamed along the blade.

'Oh, no!' he challenged loud and eager, lips drawn back from bared teeth. 'Keep your hands off! This man is mine!'

CHAPTER FOURTEEN

The three attackers had drawn off instinctively, before they realised that this was but one man erupting in their midst, but they were quick to grasp it, and had not gone far. They stood, wary as beasts of prey but undeterred, weaving a little in a slow circle out of reach, but with no thought of withdrawing. They watched and considered, weighing up coldly these altered odds. Two men and a knife to reckon with now, and this second one they knew as well as the first. They had been some days frequenting the same enclave, using the same dortoir and refectory. They reasoned without dismay that they must be known as well as they knew their prey. The twilight made faces shadowy, but a man is recognised by more things than his face.

'I said it, did I not?' said Simeon Poer, exchanging glances with his henchmen, glances which were understood even in the dim light. 'I said he would not be far. No matter, two can lie as snug as one.'

Once having declared his claim and his rights, Matthew said nothing. The tree against which they braced themselves was so grown that they could not be attacked from close behind. He circled it steadily when Bagot edged round to the far side, keeping his face to the enemy. There were three to watch, and Ciaran was shaken and lame, and in no case to match any of the three if it came to action, though he kept his side of the trunk with his staff gripped and ready, and would fight if he must, tooth and claw, for his forfeit life. Matthew curled his lips in a bitter smile at the thought that he might be grateful yet for that strong appetite for living.

Round the bole of the tree, with his cheek against the bark, Ciaran said, low-voiced: 'You'd have done better not to follow me.'

'Did I not swear to go with you to the very end?' said Matthew as softly. 'I keep my vows. This one above all.'

'Yet you could still have crept away safely. Now we are two dead men.'

'Not yet! If you did not want me, why did you call me?'

There was a bewildered silence. Ciaran did not know he had uttered a name.

'We are grown used to each other,' said Matthew grimly. 'You claimed me, as I claim you. Do you think I'll let any other man have you?'

The three watchers had gathered in a shadowy group, conferring with heads together, and faces still turned towards their prey.

'Now they'll come,' said Ciaran in the dead voice of despair.

'No, they'll wait for darkness.'

They were in no hurry. They made no loose, threatening moves, wasted no breath on words.

They bided their time as patiently as hunting animals. Silently they separated, spacing themselves round the clearing, and backing just far enough into cover to be barely visible, yet visible all the same, for their presence and stillness were meant to unnerve. Just so, motionless, relentless and alert, would a cat sit for hours outside a mousehole.

'This I cannot bear,' said Ciaran in a faint whisper, and drew sobbing breath.

'It is easily cured,' said Matthew through his teeth. 'You have only to lift off that cross from your neck, and you can be loosed from all your troubles.'

The light faded still. Their eyes, raking the smoky darkness of the bushes, were beginning to see movement where there was none, and strain in vain after it where it lurked and shifted to baffle them more. This waiting would not be long. The attackers circled in cover, watching for the unguarded moment when one or other of their victims would be caught unawares, staring in the wrong direction. Past all question they would expect that failure first from Ciaran, half-foundering as he already was. Soon now, very soon.

Brother Cadfael was some half-mile back along the ride when he heard the cry, ahead and to the right of the path, loud, wild and desperate. The words were indistinguishable, but the panic in the sound there was no mistaking. In this woodland silence, without even a wind to stir the branches or flutter the leaves, every sound carried clearly. Cadfael spurred ahead in haste, with all too dire a conviction of what he might find when he reached the source of that lamentable cry. All those miles of pursuit, patient and remorseless, half the length of England, might well be ending now, barely a quarter of an hour too soon for him to do anything to prevent. Matthew had overtaken, surely, a Ciaran grown weary of his penitential austerities, now there was no one by to see. He had said truly enough that he did not hate himself so much as to bear his hardships to no purpose. Now that he was alone, had he felt safe in discarding his heavy cross, and would he next have been in search of shoes for his feet? If Matthew had not come upon him thus recreant and disarmed.

The second sound to break the stillness almost passed unnoticed because of the sound of his own progress, but he caught some quiver of the forest's unease, and reined in to listen intently. The rush and crash of something or someone hurtling through thick bushes, fast and arrow-straight, and then, very briefly, a confusion of cries, not loud but sharp and wary, and a man's voice loud and commanding over all. Matthew's voice, not in triumph or terror, rather in short and resolute defiance. There were more than the two of them, there ahead, and not so far ahead now.

He dismounted, and led his horse at an anxious trot as far as he dared along the path, towards the spot from which the sounds had come. Hugh could move very fast when he saw reason, and in

Cadfael's bare message he would have found reason enough. He would have left the town by the most direct way, over the western bridge and so by a good road south west, to strike this old path barely two miles back. At this moment he might be little more than a mile behind. Cadfael tethered his horse at the side of the track, for a plain sign that he had found cause to halt here and was somewhere close by.

All was quiet about him now. He quested along the fringe of bushes for a place where he might penetrate without any betraying noise, and began to work his way by instinct and touch towards the place whence the cries had come, and where now all was almost unnaturally silent. In a little while he was aware of the last faint pallor of the afterglow glimmering between the branches. There was a more open glade ahead of him.

He froze and stood motionless, as a shadow passed silently between him and this lingering glimpse of light. Someone tall and lean, slithering snake-like through the bushes. Cadfael waited until the faint pattern of light was restored, and then edged carefully forward until he could see into the clearing.

The great bole of a beech-tree showed in the centre, a solid mass beneath its spread of branches. There was movement there in the dimness. Not one man, but two, stood pressed against the bole. A brief flash of steel caught just light enough to show what it was, a dagger naked and ready. Two at bay here, and surely more than one pinning them thus helpless until they could be safely pulled down. Cadfael stood still to survey the whole of the darkening clearing, and found, as he had expected, another quiver of leaves that hid a man, and then, on the opposite side, yet another. Three, probably all armed, certainly up to no good, thus furtively prowling the woods by night, going nowhere, waiting to make the kill. Three had vanished from the dice school under the bridge at Shrewsbury, and fled in this direction. Three reappeared here in the forest, still doing after their disreputable kind.

Cadfael stood hesitant, pondering how best to deal, whether to steal back to the path and wait and hope for Hugh's coming, or attempt something alone, at least to distract and dismay, to bring about a delay that might afford time for help to come. He had made up his mind to return to his horse, mount, and ride in here with as much noise and turmoil as he could muster, trying to sound like six mounted men instead of one, when with shattering suddenness the decision was taken out of his hands.

One of the three besiegers sprang out of cover with a startling shout, and rushed at the tree on the side where the momentary flash of steel had shown one of the victims, at least, to be armed. A dark figure leaned out from the darkness under the branches to meet the onslaught, and Cadfael knew him then for Matthew. The attacker swerved aside, still out of reach, in a calculated feint, and at the same moment both the other lurking shadows burst out of cover and bore down upon the other side of the tree, falling as one upon the weaker opponent. There was a confusion of violence, and a wild, tormented scream, and Matthew whirled about, slashing round him and stretching a long arm across his companion, pinning him back against the tree. Ciaran hung half-fainting, slipping down between the great, smooth bastions of the bole, and Matthew bestrode him, his dagger sweeping great swathes before them both.

Cadfael saw it, and was held mute and motionless, beholding this devoted enemy. He got his breath only as all three of the predators closed upon their prey together, slashing, mauling, by sheer weight bearing them down under them.

Cadfael filled his lungs full, and bellowed to the shaken night: 'Hold, there! On them, hold them all three. These are our felons!' He was making so much noise that he did not notice or marvel that the echoes, which in his fury he heard but did not heed, came from two directions at once, from the path he had left, and from the opposite point, from the north. Some corner of his mind knew he had roused echoes, but for his part he felt himself quite alone as he kept up his roaring, spread his sleeves like the wings of a bat, and surged headlong into the mêlée about the tree.

Long, long ago he had forsworn arms, but what of it? Barring his two stout fists, still active but somewhat rheumatic now, he was unarmed. He flung himself into the tangle of men and weapons under the beech, laid hands on the back of a dangling capuchon, hauled its wearer bodily backwards, and twisted the cloth to choke the throat that howled rage and venom at him. But his voice had done more than his martial progress. The black huddle of humanity burst into its separate beings. Two sprang clear and looked wildly about them for the source of the alarm, and Cadfael's opponent reached round, gasping, with a long arm and a vicious dagger, and sliced a dangling streamer out of a rusty black sleeve. Cadfael lay on him with all his weight, held him by the hair, and ground his face into the earth, shamelessly exulting. He would do penance for it some day soon, but now he rejoiced, all his crusader blood singing in his veins.

Distantly he was aware that something else was happening, more than he had reckoned on. He heard and felt the unmistakable quiver and thud of the earth reacting to hooves, and heard a peremptory voice shouting orders, the purport of which he did not release his grip to decypher or attend to. The glade was filled with motion as it filled with darkness. The creature under him gathered itself and heaved mightily, rolling him aside. His hold on the folds of the hood relaxed, and Simeon Poer tore himself free and scrambled clear. There was running every way, but none of the fugitives got far.

Last of the three to roll breathless out of hold, Simeon groped about him vengefully in the roots of the tree, touched a cowering body, found the cord of some dangling relic, possibly precious, in his hand, and hauled with all his strength before he gathered himself up and ran for cover. There was a wild scream of pain, and the cord broke, and the thing, whatever it was, came loose in his hand. He got his feet under him, and charged head-down for the nearest bushes, hurtled into them and ran, barely a yard clear of hands that stooped from horse-back to claw at him.

Cadfael opened his eyes and hauled in breath. The whole clearing was boiling with movement, the darkness heaved and trembled, and the violence had ordered itself into purpose and meaning. He sat up, and took his time to look about him. He was sprawled under the great beech, and somewhere before him, towards the path where he had left his horse, someone with flint and dagger and tinder, was striking sparks for a torch, very calmly. The sparks caught, glowed, and were gently blown into flame. The torch, well primed with oil and resin, sucked in the flame and gave birth to a small, shapely flame of its own, that grew and reared, and was used to kindle a second and a third. The clearing took on a small, confined, rounded shape, walled with close growth, roofed with the tree.

Hugh came out of the dark, smiling, and reached a hand to haul him to his feet. Someone else came running light-footed from the other side, and stooped to him a wonderful, torch-lit face, high-boned, lean-cheeked, with eager golden eyes, and blue-black raven wings of hair curving to cup his cheeks.

'Olivier?' said Cadfael, marvelling. 'I thought

232

you were astray on the road to Oswestry. How did you ever find us here?'

'By grace of God and a goat-herd,' said the warm, gay, remembered voice, 'and your bull's bellowing. Come, look round! You have won your field.'

They were gone, Simeon Poer, merchant of Guildford, Walter Bagot, glover, John Shure, tailor, all fled, but with half a dozen of Hugh's men hard on their heels, all to be brought in captive, to answer for more, this time, than a little cheating in the marketplace. Night stooped to enfold a closed arena of torchlight, very quiet now and almost still. Cadfael rose, his torn sleeve dangling awkwardly. The three of them stood in a half-circle about the beech-tree.

The torchlight was stark, plucking light and shadow into sharp relief. Matthew stirred out of his colloquy between life and death very slowly as they watched him, heaved his wide shoulders clear of the tree, and stood forth like a sleeper roused before his time, looking about him as if for something by which he might hold, and take his bearings. Between his feet, as he emerged, the coiled, crumpled form of Ciaran came into view, faintly stirring, his head huddled into his close-folded arms.

'Get up!' said Matthew. He drew back a little from the tree, his naked dagger in his hand, a slow drop gathering at its tip, more drops falling steadily from the hand that held it. His knuckles were sliced raw. 'Get up!' he said. 'You are not harmed.'

233

Ciaran gathered himself very slowly, and clambered to his knees, lifting to the light a face soiled and leaden, gone beyond exhaustion, beyond fear. He looked neither at Cadfael nor at Hugh, but stared up into Matthew's face with the helpless intensity of despair. Hugh felt the clash of eyes, and stirred to make some decisive movement and break the tension, but Cadfael laid a hand on his arm and held him still. Hugh gave him a sharp sidelong glance, and accepted the caution. Cadfael had his reasons.

There was blood on the torn collar of Ciaran's shirt, a stain that grew sluggishly before their eyes. He put up hands that seemed heavy as lead, and fumbled aside the linen from throat and breast. All round the left side of his neck ran a raw, bleeding slash, thin as a knife-cut. Simeon Poer's last blind clutch for plunder had torn loose the cross to which Ciaran had clung so desperately. He kneeled in the last wretched extreme of submission, baring a throat already symbolically slit.

'Here am I,' he said in a toneless whisper. 'I can run no further, I am forfeit. Now take me!'

Matthew stood motionless, staring at that savage cut the cord had left before it broke. The silence grew too heavy to be bearable, and still he had no word to say, and his face was a blank mask in the flickering light of the torches.

'He says right,' said Cadfael, very softly and reasonably. 'He is yours fairly. The terms of his penance are broken, and his life is forfeit. Take him!'

There was no sign that Matthew so much as heard him, but for the spasmodic tightening of his lips, as if in pain. He never took his eyes from the wretch kneeling humbly before him.

'You have followed him faithfully, and kept the terms laid down,' Cadfael urged gently. 'You are under vow. Now finish the work!'

He was on safe enough ground, and sure of it now. The act of submission had already finished the work, there was no more to be done. With his enemy at his mercy, and every justification for the act of vengeance, the avenger was helpless, the prisoner of his own nature. There was nothing left in him but a drear sadness, a sick revulsion of disgust, and self-disgust. How could he kill a wretched, broken man, kneeling here unresisting, waiting for his death? Death was no longer relevant.

'It is over, Luc,' said Cadfael softly. 'Do what you must.'

Matthew stood mute a moment longer, and if he had heard his true name spoken, he gave no sign, it was of no importance. After the abandonment of all purpose came the awful sense of loss and emptiness. He opened his blood-stained hand and let the dagger slip from his fingers into the grass. He turned away like a blind man, feeling with a stretched foot for every step, groped his way through the curtain of bushes, and vanished into the darkness.

Olivier drew in breath sharply, and started out of his tranced stillness to catch eagerly at Cadfael's

235

arm. 'Is it true? You have found him out? *He* is Luc Meverel?' He accepted the truth of it without another word said, and sprang ardently towards the place where the bushes still stirred after Luc's passing, and he would have been off in pursuit at a run if Hugh had not caught at his arm to detain him.

'Wait but one moment! You also have a cause here, if Cadfael is right. This is surely the man who murdered your friend. He owes you a death. He is yours if you want him.'

'That is truth,' said Cadfael. 'Ask him! He will tell you.'

Ciaran crouched in the grass, drooping now, bewildered and lost, no longer looking any man in the face, only waiting without hope or understanding for someone to determine whether he was to live or die, and on what abject terms. Olivier cast one wondering glance at him, shook his head in emphatic rejection, and reached for his horse's bridle. 'Who am I,' he said, 'to exact what Luc Meverel has remitted? Let this one go on his way with his own burden. My business is with the other.'

He was away at a run, leading the horse briskly through the screen of bushes, and the rustling of their passage gradually stilled again into silence. Cadfael and Hugh were left regarding each other mutely across the lamentable figure crouched upon the ground.

Gradually the rest of the world flowed back into Cadfael's ken. Three of Hugh's officers stood aloof with the horses and the torches, looking on in silence; and somewhere not far distant sounded a brief scuffle and outcry, as one of the fugitives was overpowered and made prisoner. Simeon Poer had been pulled down barely fifty yards in cover, and stood sullenly under guard now, with his wrists secured to a sergeant's stirrup-leather. The third would not be a free man long. This night's ventures were over. This piece of woodland would be safe even for barefoot and unarmed pilgrims to traverse.

'What is to be done with him?' demanded Hugh openly, looking down upon the wreckage of a man with some distaste.

'Since Luc has waived his claim,' said Cadfael, 'I would not dare meddle. And there is something at least to be said for him, he did not cheat or break his terms voluntarily, even when there was no one by to accuse him. It is a small virtue to have to advance for the defence of a life, but it is something. Who else has the right to foreclose on what Luc has spared?'

Ciaran raised his head, peering doubtfully from one face to the other, still confounded at being so spared, but beginning to believe that he still lived. He was weeping, whether with pain, or relief, or something more durable than either, there was no telling. The blood was blackening into a dark line about his throat.

'Speak up and tell truth,' said Hugh with chill gentleness. 'Was it you who stabbed Bossard?'

Out of the pallid disintegration of Ciaran's face

a wavering voice said: 'Yes.'

'Why did you so? Why attack the queen's clerk, who did nothing but deliver his errand faithfully?'

Ciaran's eyes burned for an instant, and a fleeting spark of past pride, intolerance and rage showed like the last glow of a dying fire. 'He came high-handed, shouting down the lord bishop, defying the council. My master was angry and affronted ...'

'Your master,' said Cadfael, 'was the prior of Hyde Mead. Or so you claimed.'

'How could I any longer claim service with one who had discarded me? I lied! The lord bishop himself – I served Bishop Henry, had his favour. Lost, lost now! I could not brook the man Christian's insolence to him ... he stood against everything my lord planned and willed. I hated him! I thought then that I hated him,' said Ciaran, drearily wondering at the recollection. 'And I thought to please my lord!'

'A calculation that went awry,' said Cadfael, 'for whatever he may be, Henry of Blois is no murderer. And Rainald Bossard prevented your mischief, a man of your own party, held in esteem. Did that make him a traitor in your eyes – that he should respect an honest opponent? Or did you strike out at random, and kill without intent?'

'No,' said the level, lame voice, bereft of its brief spark. 'He thwarted me, I was enraged. I knew what I did. I was glad ... *then*!' he said, and drew bitter breath.

'And who laid upon you this penitential jour-

238

ney?' asked Cadfael, 'and to what end? Your life was granted you, upon terms. What terms? Someone in the highest authority laid that load upon you.'

'My lord the bishop-legate,' said Ciaran, and wrung wordlessly for a moment at the pain of an old devotion, rejected and banished now for ever. 'There was no other soul knew of it, only to him I told it. He would not give me up to law, he wanted this thing put by, for fear it should threaten his plans for the empress's peace. But he would not condone. I am from the Danish kingdom of Dublin, my other half Welsh. He offered me passage under his protection to Bangor, to the bishop there, who would see me to Caergybi in Anglesey, and have me put aboard a ship for Dublin. But I must go barefoot all that way, and wear the cross round my neck, and if ever I broke those terms, even for a moment, my life was his who cared to take it, without blame or penalty. And I could never return.' Another fire, of banished love, ruined ambition, rejected service, flamed through the broken accents for a moment, and died of despair.

'Yet if this sentence was never made public,' said Hugh, seizing upon one thing still unexplained, 'how did Luc Meverel ever come to know of it and follow you?'

'Do I know?' The voice was flat and drear, worn out with exhaustion. 'All I know is that I set out from Winchester, and where the roads joined, near Newbury, this man stood and waited for me, and fell in beside me, and every step of my way on this journey he has gone on my heels like a demon, and waited for me to play false to my sentence – for there was no point of it he did not know! – to take my life without guilt, without a qualm, as so he might. He trod after me wherever I trod, he never let me from his sight, he made no secret of his wants, he tempted me to go aside, to put on shoes, to lay by the cross – and sirs, it was deathly heavy! Matthew, he called himself ... Luc, you say he is? You know him? I never knew ... He said I had killed his lord, whom he loved, and he would follow me to Bangor, to Caergybi, even to Dublin if ever I got aboard ship without putting off the cross or putting on shoes. But he would have me in the end. He had what he lusted for – why did he turn away and spare?' The last words ached with his uncomprehending wonder.

'He did not find you worth the killing,' said Cadfael, as gently and mercifully as he could, but honestly. 'Now he goes in anguish and shame because he spent so much time on you that might have been better spent. It is a matter of values. Study to learn what is worth and what is not, and you may come to understand him.'

'I am a dead man while I live,' said Ciaran, writhing, 'without master, without friends, without a cause ...'

'All three you may find, if you seek. Go where you were sent, bear what you were condemned to bear, and look for the meaning,' said Cadfael. 'For so must we all.'

He turned away with a sigh. No way of knowing how much good words might do, or the lessons of life, no telling whether any trace of compunction moved in Ciaran's bludgeoned mind, or whether all his feeling was still for himself. Cadfael felt himself suddenly very tired. He looked at Hugh with a somewhat lopsided smile. 'I wish I were home. What now, Hugh? Can we go?'

Hugh stood looking down with a frown at the confessed murderer, sunken in the grass like a broken-backed serpent, submissive, tear-stained, nursing minor injuries. A piteous spectacle, though pity might be misplaced. Yet he was, after all, no more than twenty-five or so years old, able-bodied, well-clothed, strong, his continued journey might be painful and arduous, but it was not beyond his powers, and he had his bishop's ring still, effective wherever law held. These three footpads now tethered fast and under guard would trouble his going no more. Ciaran would surely reach his journey's end safely, however long it might take him. Not the journey's end of his false story, a blessed death in Aberdaron and burial among the saints of Ynys Ennli, but a return to his native place, and a life beginning afresh. He might even be changed. He might well adhere to his hard terms all the way to Caergybi, where Irish ships plied, even as far as Dublin, even to his ransomed life's end. How can you tell?

'Make your own way from here,' said Hugh, 'as well as you may. You need fear nothing now from footpads here, and the border is not far. What you have to fear from God, take up with God.'

He turned his back, with so decisive a movement that his men recognised the sign that all was over, and stirred willingly about the captives and the horses.

'And those two?' asked Hugh. 'Had I not better leave a man behind on the track there, with a spare horse for Luc? He followed his quarry afoot, but no need for him to foot it back. Or ought I to send men after them?'

'No need for that,' said Cadfael with certainty. 'Olivier will manage all. They'll come home together.'

He had no qualms at all, he was beginning to relax into the warmth of content. The evil he had dreaded had been averted, however narrowly, at whatever cost. Olivier would find his stray, bear with him, follow if he tried to avoid, wrung and ravaged as he was, with the sole obsessive purpose of his life for so long ripped away from him, and within him only the aching emptiness where that consuming passion had been. Into that barren void Olivier would win his way, and warm the ravished heart to make it habitable for another love. There was the most comforting of messages to bring from Juliana Bossard, the promise regained of a home and a welcome. There was a future. How had Matthew-Luc seen his future when he emptied his purse of the last coin at the abbey, before taking up the pursuit of his enemy? Surely he had been contemplating the end of the person he had hitherto been, a total ending, beyond which he could not see. Now he was young again, there was a life before him, it needed only a little time to make him whole again.

Olivier would bring him back to the abbey, when the worst desolation was over. For Olivier had promised that he would not leave without spending some time leisurely with Cadfael, and upon Olivier's promise the heart could rest secure.

As for the other ... Cadfael looked back from the saddle, after they had mounted, and saw the last of Ciaran, still on his knees under the tree, where they had left him. His face was turned to them, but his eyes seemed to be closed, and his hands were wrung tightly together before his breast. He might have been praying, he might have been simply experiencing with every particle of his flesh the life that had been left to him. When we are all gone, thought Cadfael, he will fall asleep there where he lies, he can do no other, for he is far gone in something beyond exhaustion. Where he falls asleep, there he will have died. But when he awakes, I trust he may understand that he has been born again.

The slower cortège that would bring the prisoners into the town began to assemble, making the tethering thongs secure, and the torch-bearers crossed the clearing to mount, withdrawing their yellow light from the kneeling figure, so that Ciaran vanished gradually, as though he had been absorbed into the bole of the beech-tree.

Hugh led the way out to the track, and turned homeward. 'Oh, Hugh, I grow old!' said Cadfael, hugely yawning. 'I want my bed.'

CHAPTER FIFTEEN

It was past midnight when they rode in at the gatehouse, into a great court awash with moonlight, and heard the chanting of Matins within the church. They had made no haste on the way home, and said very little, content to ride companionably together as sometimes before, through summer night or winter day. It would be another hour or more yet before Hugh's officers got their prisoners back to Shrewsbury Castle, since they must keep a foot-pace, but before morning Simeon Poer and his henchmen would be safe in hold, under lock and key.

'I'll wait with you until Lauds is over,' said Hugh, as they dismounted at the gatehouse. 'Father Abbot will want to know how we've sped. Though I hope he won't require the whole tale from us tonight.'

'Come down with me to the stables, then,' said Cadfael, 'and I'll see this fellow unsaddled and tended, while they're still within. I was always taught to care for my beast before seeking my own rest. You never lose the habit.'

In the stable-yard the moonlight was all the light they needed. The quietness of midnight and the stillness of the air carried every note of the office to them softly and clearly. Cadfael unsaddled his horse and saw him settled and provided in his stall, with a light rug against any possible chill, rites he seldom had occasion to perform now. They brought back memories of other mounts and other journeys, and battlefields less happily resolved than the small but desperate skirmish just lost and won.

Hugh stood watching with his back turned to the great court, but his head tilted to follow the chant. Yet it was not any sound of an approaching step that made him look round suddenly, but the slender shadow that stole along the moonlit cobbles beside his feet. And there hesitant in the gateway of the yard stood Melangell, startled and startling, haloed in that pallid sheen.

'Child,' said Cadfael, concerned, 'what are you doing out of your bed at this hour?'

'How could I rest?' she said, but not as one complaining. 'No one misses me, they are all sleeping.' She stood very still and straight, as if she had spent all the hours since he had left her in earnest endeavour to put away for ever any memories he might have of the tear-stained, despairing girl who had sought solitude in his workshop. The great sheaf of her hair was braided and pinned up on her head, her gown was trim, and her face resolutely calm as she asked, 'Did you find him?'

A girl he had left her, a woman he came back to her. 'Yes,' said Cadfael, 'we found them both. There has nothing ill happened to either. The two

245

of them have parted. Ciaran goes on his way alone.'

'And Matthew?' she asked steadily.

'Matthew is with a good friend, and will come to no harm. We two have outridden them, but they will come.' She would have to learn to call him by another name now, but let the man himself tell her that. Nor would the future be altogether easy, for her or for Luc Meverel, two human creatures who might never have been brought within hail of each other but for freakish circumstance. Unless Saint Winifred had had a hand in that, too? On this night Cadfael could believe it, and trust her to bring all to a good end. 'He will come back,' said Cadfael, meeting her candid eyes, that bore no trace of tears now. 'You need not fear. But he has suffered a great turmoil of the mind, and he'll need all your patience and wisdom. Ask him nothing. When the time is right he will tell you everything. Reproach him with nothing –'

'God forbid,' she said, 'that I should ever reproach him. It was I who failed him.'

'No, how could you know? But when he comes, wonder at nothing. Be like one who is thirsty and drinks. And so will he.'

She had turned a little towards him, and the moonlight blanched wonderfully over her face, as if a lamp within her had been newly lighted. 'I will wait,' she said.

'Better go to your bed and sleep, the waiting may be longer than you think, he has been wrung. But he will come.'

But at that she shook her head. 'I'll watch till he comes,' she said, and suddenly smiled at them, pale and lustrous as pearl, and turned and went away swiftly and silently towards the cloister.

'That is the girl you spoke of?' asked Hugh, looking after her with somewhat frowning interest. 'The lame boy's sister? The girl that young man fancies?'

'That is she,' said Cadfael, and closed the half-door of the stall.

'The weaver-woman's niece?'

'That, too. Dowerless and from common stock,' said Cadfael, understanding but untroubled. 'Yes, true! I'm from common stock myself. I doubt if a young fellow who has been torn apart and remade as Luc has tonight will care much about such little things. Though I grant you others may! I hope the lady Juliana has no plans yet for marrying him off to some heiress from a neighbour manor, for I fancy things have gone so far now with these two that she'll be forced to abandon her plans. A manor or a craft – if you take pride in them, and run them well, where's the difference?'

'Your common stock,' said Hugh heartily, 'gave growth to a most uncommon shoot! And I wouldn't say but that young thing would grace a hall better than many a highbred dame I've seen. But listen, they're ending. We'd best present ourselves.'

Abbot Radulfus came from Matins and Lauds with his usual imperturbable stride, and found

247

them waiting for him as he left the cloister. This day of miracles had produced a fittingly glorious night, incredibly lofty and deep, coruscating with stars, washed white with moonlight. Coming from the dimness within, this exuberance of light showed him clearly both the serenity and the weariness on the two faces that confronted him.

'You are back!' he said, and looked beyond them. 'But not all! Messire de Bretagne – you said he had gone by a wrong way. He has not returned here. You have not encountered him?'

'Yes, Father, we have,' said Hugh. 'All is well with him, and he has found the young man he was seeking. They will return here, all in good time.'

'And the evil you feared, Brother Cadfael? You spoke of another death ...'

'Father,' said Cadfael, 'no harm has come tonight to any but the masterless men who escaped into the forest there. They are now safe in hold, and on their way under guard to the castle. The death I dreaded has been averted, no threat remains in that quarter to any man. I said, if the two young men could be overtaken, the better surely for one, and perhaps for both. Father, they were overtaken in time, and better for both it surely must be.'

'Yet there remains,' said Radulfus, pondering, 'the print of blood, which both you and I have seen. You said – you will recall – that, yes, we have entertained a murderer among us. Do you still say so?'

'Yes, Father. Yet not as you suppose. When

248

Olivier de Bretagne and Luc Meverel return, then all can be made plain, for as yet,' said Cadfael, 'there are still certain things we do not know. But we do know,' he said firmly, 'that what has passed this night is the best for which we could have prayed, and we have good need to give thanks for it.'

'So all is well?'

'All is very well, Father.'

'Then the rest may wait for morning. You need rest. But will you not come in with me and take some food and wine, before you sleep?'

'My wife,' said Hugh, gracefully evading, 'will be in some anxiety for me. You are kind, Father, but I would not have her fret longer than she need.'

The abbot eyed them both, and did not press them.

'And God bless you for that!' sighed Cadfael, toiling up the slight slope of the court towards the dortoir stair and the gatehouse where Hugh had hitched his horse. 'For I'm asleep on my feet, and even a good wine could not revive me.'

The moonlight was gone, and there was as yet no sunlight, when Olivier de Bretagne and Luc Meverel rode slowly in at the abbey gatehouse. How far they had wandered in the deep night neither of them knew very clearly, for this was strange country to both. Even when overtaken, and addressed with careful gentleness, Luc had still gone forward blindly, hands hanging slack at his sides or vaguely parting the bushes, saying nothing, hearing nothing, unless some core of feeling within him was aware of this calm, relentless pursuit by a tolerant, incurious kindness, and distantly wondered at it. When he had dropped at last and lain down in the lush grass of a meadow at the edge of the forest, Olivier had tethered his horse a little apart and lain down beside him, not too close, yet so close that the mute man knew he was here, waiting without impatience. Past midnight Luc had fallen asleep. It was his greatest need. He was a man ravished and emptied of every impulse that had held him alive for the past two months, a dead man still walking and unable quite to die. Sleep was his ransom. Then he could truly die to this waste of loss and bitterness, the awful need that had driven him, the corrosive grief that had eaten his heart out for his lord, who had died in his arms, on his shoulder, on his heart. The bloodstain that would not wash out, no matter how he laboured over it, was his witness. He had kept it to keep the fire of his hatred white-hot. Now in sleep he was delivered from all.

And he had awakened in the first mysterious pre-dawn stirring of the earliest summer birds, beginning to call tentatively into the silence, to open his eyes upon a face bending over him, a face he did not know, but remotely desired to know, for it was vivid, friendly and calm, waiting courteously on his will.

'Did I kill him?' Luc had asked, somehow aware that the man who bore this face would know the answer.

'No,' said a voice clear, serene and low. 'There was no need. But he's dead to you. You can forget him.'

He did not understand that, but he accepted it. He sat up in the cool, ripe grass, and his senses began to stir again, and record distantly that the earth smelled sweet, and there were paling stars in the sky over him, caught like stray sparks in the branches of the trees. He stared intently into Olivier's face, and Olivier looked back at him with a slight, serene smile, and was silent.

'Do I know you?' asked Luc wonderingly.

'No. But you will. My name is Olivier de Bretagne, and I serve Laurence d' Angers, just as your lord did. I knew Rainald Bossard well, he was my friend, we came from the Holy Land together in Laurence's train. And I am sent with a message to Luc Meverel, and that, I am sure, is your name.'

'A message to me?' Luc shook his head.

'From your cousin and lady, Juliana Bossard. And the message is that she begs you to come home, for she needs you, and there is no one who can take your place.'

He was slow to believe, still numbed and hollow within; but there was no impulsion for him to go anywhere or do anything now of his own will, and he yielded indifferently to Olivier's promptings. 'Now we should be getting back to the abbey,' said Olivier practically, and rose, and Luc responded, and rose with him. 'You take the horse, and I'll walk,' said Olivier, and Luc did as he was bidden. It was like nursing a simpleton gently along the way he must go, and holding him by the hand at every step.

They found their way back at last to the old track, and there were the two horses Hugh had left behind for them, and the groom fast asleep in the grass beside them. Olivier took back his own horse, and Luc mounted the fresh one, with the lightness and ease of custom, his body's instincts at least reawakening. The yawning groom led the way, knowing the path well. Not until they were halfway back towards the Meole brook and the narrow bridge to the highroad did Luc say a word of his own volition.

'You say she wants me to come back,' he said abruptly, with quickening pain and hope in his voice. 'Is it true? I left her without a word, but what else could I do? What can she think of me now?'

'Why, that you had your reasons for leaving her, as she has hers for wanting you back. Half the length of England I have been asking after you, at her entreaty. What more do you need?'

'I never thought to return,' said Luc, staring back down that long, long road in wonder and doubt.

No, not even to Shrewsbury, much less to his home in the south. Yet here he was, in the cool, soft morning twilight well before Prime, riding beside this young stranger over the wooden bridge that crossed the Meole brook, instead of wading through the shrunken stream to the pease-fields, the way by which he had left the enclave. Round to the highroad, past the mill and the pond, and in at

252

the gatehouse to the great court. There they lighted down, and the groom took himself and his two horses briskly away again towards the town.

Luc stood gazing about him dully, still clouded by the unfamiliarity of everything he beheld, as if his senses were still dazed and clumsy with the effort of coming back to life. At this hour the court was empty. No, not quite empty. There was someone sitting on the stone steps that climbed to the door of the guest-hall, sitting there alone and quite composedly, with her face turned towards the gate, and as he watched she rose and came down the wide steps, and walked towards him with a swift, light step. Then he knew her for Melangell.

In her at least there was nothing unfamiliar. The sight of her brought back colour and form and reality into the very stones of the wall at her back, and the cobbles under her feet. The elusive grey between-light could not blur the outlines of head and hand, or dim the brightness of her hair. Life came flooding back into Luc with a shock of pain, as feeling returns after a numbing wound. She came towards him with hands a little extended and face raised, and the faintest and most anxious of smiles on her lips and in her eyes. Then, as she hesitated for the first time, a few paces from him, he saw the dark stain of the bruise that marred her cheek.

It was the bruise that shattered him. He shook from head to heels in a great convulsion of shame and grief, and blundered forward blindly into her arms, which reached gladly to receive him. On his knees, with his arms wound about her and his face buried in her breast, he burst into a storm of tears, as spontaneous and as healing as Saint Winifred's own miraculous spring.

He was in perfect command of voice and face when they met after chapter in the abbot's parlour, abbot, prior, Brother Cadfael, Hugh Beringar, Olivier and Luc, to set right in all its details the account of Rainald Bossard's death, and all that had followed from it.

'Unwittingly I deceived you, Father,' said Cadfael, harking back to the interview which had sent him forth in such haste. 'When you asked if we had entertained a murderer unawares, I answered truly that I did think so, but that we might yet have time to prevent a second death. I never realised until afterwards how you might interpret that, seeing we had just found the blood-stained shirt. But see, the man who struck the blow might be spattered as to sleeve or collar, but he would not be marked by this great blot that covered breast and shoulder over the heart. No, that was rather the sign of one who had held a wounded man, a man wounded to death, in his arms as he died. Nor would the slayer, if his clothing was blood-stained, have kept and carried it with him, but burned or buried it, or somehow rid himself of it. But this shirt, though washed most carefully, still bore the outline of the stain clear to be seen, and it was carried as a sacred relic is carried, perhaps as a pledge to exact vengeance. So I knew that this same Luc whom we knew as Matthew, and in whose scrip the talisman was found, was not the murderer. But when I recalled all the words I had heard those two young men speak, and all the evidence of devoted attendance, the one on the other, then suddenly I saw that pairing in the utterly opposed way, as a pursuit. And I feared it must be to the death.'

The abbot looked at Luc and asked simply: 'Is that a true reading?'

'Father, it is.' Luc set forth with deliberation the progress of his own obsession, as though he discovered it and understood it only in speaking. 'I was with my lord that night, close to the Old Minster it was, when four or five set on the clerk, and my lord ran, and we with him, to beat them off. And then they fled, but one turned back and struck. I saw it done, and it was done of intent! I had my lord in my arms – he had been good to me, and I loved him,' said Luc with grimly measured moderation and burning eyes as he remembered. 'He was dead in a mere moment, in the twinkling of an eye ... And I had seen where the murderer fled, into the passage by the chapter house. I went after him, and I heard their voices in the sacristy – Bishop Henry had come from the chapter house after the council ended for the night, and there Ciaran had found him and fell on his knees to him, blurting out all. I lay in hiding, and heard every word. I think he even hoped for praise,' said Luc with bitter deliberation.

'Is it possible?' wondered Prior Robert, shocked

to the heart. 'Bishop Henry could not for one moment connive at or condone an act so evil.'

'No, he did not condone. But neither would he deliver over one of his own intimate servants as a murderer. To do him justice,' said Luc, but with plain distaste, 'his concern was not to cause further anger and quarrelling, but to put away and smooth over everything that threatened the empress's fortunes and the peace he was trying to make. But condone murder – no, that he would not. Therefore I overheard the sentence he laid upon Ciaran – though then I did not know who he was, nor that Ciaran was his name. He banished him back to his Dublin home, for ever, and condemned him to go every step of the way to Bangor and to the ship at Caergybi barefoot, and carrying that heavy cross. And if ever he put on shoes or laid by the cross from round his neck, then his forfeit life was no longer spared, but might be taken by whoever willed, without sin or penalty. But see,' said Luc, merciless in judgement, 'how he cheated! For not only did he give his creature the ring that would ensure him the protection of the church to Bangor, but also, mark, not one word was ever made public of this guilt or this sentence, so how was that forfeit life in danger? No one was to know of it but they two, if God had not prevented and brought there a witness to hear the sentence and take upon himself the vengeance due.'

'As you did,' said the abbot, and his voice was even and calm, avoiding judgement.

'As I did, Father. For as Ciaran swore to keep the

terms laid down on pain of death, so did I swear an oath as solemn to follow him the length of the land, and if ever he broke his terms for a moment, to have his life as payment for my lord.'

'And how,' asked Radulfus in the same mild tone, 'did you know what man you were thus to hunt to his death? For you say you did not see his face clearly or know his name then.'

'I knew the way he was bound to go, and the day of his setting out. I waited by the roadside for one walking north, barefoot — and one not used to going barefoot, but very well shod,' said Luc with a brief, wry smile. 'I saw the cross at his neck. I fell in at his side, and I told him, not who I was, but what. I took another name, so that no failure nor shame of mine should ever cast a shadow on my lady or her house. One Evangelist in exchange for another! Step for step with him I went all this way, here to this place, and never let him from my sight and reach, night or day, and never let him forget that I meant to be his death. He could not ask help to rid himself of me, since I could then as easily strip him of his pilgrim holiness and show what he really was. And I could not denounce him — partly for fear of Bishop Henry, partly because neither did I want more feuding between factions — my feud was between two men! — but chiefly because he was mine, mine, and I would not let any other vengeance or danger reach him. So we kept together, he trying to elude me — but he was court-bred and tender and crippled by the miles — and I holding fast to him, and waiting.'

He looked up suddenly and caught the abbot's compassionate but calm eyes upon him, and his own eyes were wide, dark and clear. 'It is not beautiful, I know. Neither was murder beautiful. And this blotch was only mine – my lord went to his grave immaculate, defending one opposed to him.'

It was Olivier, silent until now, who said softly: '*And so did you!*'

The grave, thought Cadfael at the height of the Mass, had closed firmly to deny Luc entrance, but that arm outstretched between his enemy and the knives of three assailants must never be forgotten. Hell had also shut its mouth and refused to devour him. He was young, clean, alive again after a kind of death. Yes, Olivier had uttered truth. His own life ventured, his enemy's life defended, what was there beween Luc and his lord but the accident, the vain and random accident of the death itself?

He recalled also, when he was most diligent in prayer, that these few days while Saint Winifred was manifesting her virtue in disentangling the troubled lives of some half-dozen people in Shrewsbury, were also the vital days when the fates of Englishmen in general were being determined, perhaps with less compassion and wisdom. For by this time the date of the empress's coronation might well be settled, the crown even now placed upon her head. No doubt God and the saints had that consideration in mind, too.

*

Matthew-Luc came once again to ask audience of the abbot, a little before Vespers. Radulfus had him admitted without question, and sat with him alone, divining his present need.

'Father, will you hear me my confession? For I need absolution from the vow I could not keep. And I do earnestly desire to be clean of the past before I undertake the future.'

'It is a right and a wise desire,' said Radulfus. 'One thing tell me – are you asking absolution for failing to fulfil the oath you swore?'

Luc, already on his knees, raised his head for a moment from the abbot's knee, and showed a face open and clear. 'No, Father, but for ever swearing such an oath. Even grief has its arrogance.'

'Then you have learned, my son, that vengeance belongs only to God?'

'More than that, Father,' said Luc. 'I have learned that in God's hands vengeance is safe. However long delayed, however strangely manifested, the reckoning is sure.'

When it was done, when he had raked out of his heart, with measured voice and long pauses for thought, every drifted grain of rancour and bitterness and impatience that fretted him, and received absolution, he rose with a great sigh, and raised a bright and resolute face.

'Now, Father, if I may pray of you one more grace, let me have one of your priests to join me to a wife before I go from here. Here, where I am made clean and new, I would have love and life begin together.'

CHAPTER SIXTEEN

On the next morning, which was the twenty-fourth day of June, the general bustle of departure began. There was packing of belongings, buying and parcelling of food and drink for the journey, and much leave-taking from friends newly made and arranging of company for the road. No doubt the saint would have due regard for her own reputation, and keep the June sun shining until all her devotees were safely home, and with a wonderful tale to tell. Most of them knew only half the wonder, but even that was wonder enough.

Among the early departures went Brother Adam of Reading, in no great hurry along the way, for today he would go no farther than Reading's daughter-house of Leominster, where there would be letters waiting for him to carry home to his abbot. He set out with a pouch well filled with seeds of species his garden did not yet possess, and a scholarly mind still pondering the miraculous healing he had witnessed from every theological angle, in order to be able to expound its full significance when he reached his own monastery. It had been a most instructive and enlightening festival.

'I'd meant to start for home today, too,' said Mistress Weaver to her cronies Mistress Glover and the apothecary's widow, with whom she had formed a strong matronly alliance during these memorable days, 'but now there's such work doing, I hardly know whether I'm waking or sleeping, and I must stay over yet a night or two. Who'd ever have thought what would come of it, when I told my lad we ought to come and make our prayers here to the good saint, and have faith that she'd be listening? Now it seems I'm to lose the both of them, my poor sister's chicks; for Rhun, God bless him, is set on staying here and taking the cowl, for he says he won't ever leave the blessed girl who healed him. And truly I don't wonder at it, and won't stand in his way, for he's too good for this wicked world outside, so he is! And now comes young Matthew – no, but it seems we must call him Luc, now, and he's well-born, if from a poor landless branch, and will come in for a manor or two in time, by his good kinswoman's taking him in ...'

'Well, and so did you take the boy and girl in,' pointed out the apothecary's widow warmly, 'and gave them a roof and a living. There's good sound justice there.'

'Well, so Matthew, I mean Luc, he comes to me and asks for my girl for his wife, last night it was, and when I answered honestly, for honest I am

261

and always will be, that my Melangell has but a meagre dowry, though the best I can give her I will, what says he? That as at this moment he himself has not one penny to his name in this world, but must go debtor to the young lord's charity that came to find him, and as for the future, if fortune favours him he'll be thankful, and if not, he has hands and a will and can make a way for two to live. Provided the other is my girl, he says, for there's none other for him. So what can I say but God bless them both, and stay to see them wedded?'

'It's a woman's duty,' said Mistress Glover heartily, 'to make sure all's done properly, when she hands over a young girl to a husband. But sure, you'll miss the two of them.'

'So I will,' agreed Dame Alice, shedding a few tears rather of pride and joy than of grief, at the advancement to semi-sainthood and promising matrimony of the charges who had cost her dear enough, and could now be blessed and sped on their respective and respectable ways with a quiet mind. 'So I will! But to see them both set up where they would be ... And good children both, that will take pains for me when I come to need, as I have for them.'

'And they're to marry here, tomorrow?' asked the apothecary's widow, visibly considering putting off her own departure for another day.

'They are indeed, before Mass in the morning. So it seems I'll have none to take home but my sole self,' said Dame Alice, dropping another proud tear or two, and wearing her reflected glory with admirable grace, 'when I take to the road again. But the day after tomorrow there's a sturdy company leaving southward, and with them I'll go.'

'And duty well done, my dear soul,' said Mistress Glover, embracing her friend in a massive arm, 'duty very well done!'

They were married in the privacy of the Lady Chapel, by Brother Paul, who was not only master of the novices, but the chief of their confessors, too, and already had Rhun under his care and instruction, and felt a fatherly interest in him, which the boy's affection very readily extended to embrace the sister. No one else was present but the family and their witnesses, and the bridal pair wore no festal garments, for they had none. Luc was in the serviceable brown cotte and hose he had slept in, out in the fields, and the same crumpled shirt, though newly washed and smoothed. Melangell was neat and modest in her homespun, proudly balancing her coronal of braided, deep-gold hair. They were pale as lilies, bright as stars, and solemn as the grave.

After high and moving events, daily life must still go on. Cadfael went to his work that afternoon well content. With the meadow grasses in ripe seed and the harvest imminent he had preparations to make for two seasonal ailments which could be relied upon to recur every year. There were some who suffered with eruptions on their hands when working in the harvest, and others who took to sneezing and wheezing, with running eyes, and needed lotions to help them.

He was busy bruising fresh leaves of dock and mandrake in a mortar for a soothing ointment, when he heard light, long-striding steps approaching along the gravel of the path, and then half the sunlight from the wide-open door was cut off, as someone hesitated in the doorway. He turned with the mortar hugged to his chest, and the green-stained wooden pestle arrested in his hand, and there stood Olivier, dipping his tall head to evade the hanging bunches of herbs, and asking, in the mellow, confident voice of one assured of the answer, 'May I come in?'

He was in already, smiling, staring about him with a boy's candid curiosity, for he had never been here before. 'I've been a truant, I know, but with two days to wait before Luc's marriage I thought best to get on with my errand to the sheriff of Stafford, being so close, and then come back here. I was back, as I said I'd be, in time to see them wedded. I thought you would have been there.'

'So I would, but I was called out to Saint Giles. Some poor soul of a beggar stumbled in there overnight covered with sores, they were afraid of a contagion, but it's no such matter. If he'd had treatment earlier it would have been an easy matter to cure him, but a week or so resting in the hospital will do him no harm. Our pair of youngsters here had no need of me. I'm a part of what's over and done with for them, you're a part of what's beginning.'

'Melangell told me where I should find you, however, you were missed. And here I am.'

'And as welcome as the day,' said Cadfael, laying his mortar aside. Long, shapely hands gripped both his hands heartily, and Olivier stooped his olive cheek for the greeting kiss, as simply as for the parting kiss when they had separated at Bromfield. 'Come, sit, let me offer you wine – my own making. You knew, then, that those two would marry?'

'I saw them meet, when I brought him back here. Small doubt how it would end. Afterwards he told me his intent. When two are agreed, and know their own minds,' said Olivier blithely, 'everything else will give way. I shall see them both properly provided for the journey home, since I must go by a more roundabout way.'

When two are agreed, and know their own minds! Cadfael remembered confidences now a year and a half past. He poured wine carefully, his hand being a shade less steady than usual, and sat down beside his visitor, the young, wide shoulder firm and vital against his elderly and stiff one, the clear, elegant profile close, and a pleasure to his eyes. 'Tell me,' he said, 'about Ermina,' and was sure of the answer even before Olivier turned on him his sudden blinding smile.

'If I had known my travels would bring me to you, I should have had so many messages to bring you, from both of them. From Yves – and from my wife!'

'Aaaah!' breathed Cadfael, on a deep, delighted sigh. 'So, as I thought, as I hoped! You have made good, then, what you told me, that they would acknowledge your worth and give her to you.' Two, there, who had indeed known their own minds, and been invincibly agreed! 'When was this match made?'

'This Christmas past, in Gloucester. She is there now, so is the boy. He is Laurence's heir – just fifteen now. He wanted to come to Winchester with us, but Laurence wouldn't let him be put in peril. They are safe, I thank God. If ever this chaos is ended,' said Olivier very solemnly, 'I will bring her to you, or you to her. She does not forget you.'

'Nor I her, nor I her! Nor the boy. He rode with me twice, asleep in my arms, I still recall the warmth and the shape and the weight of him. A good boy as ever stepped!'

'He'd be a load for you now,' said Olivier, laughing. 'This year past, he's shot up like a weed, he'll be taller than you.'

'Ah, well, I'm beginning to shrink like a spent weed. And you are happy?' asked Cadfael, thirsting for more blessedness even than he already had. 'You and she both?'

'Beyond what I know how to express,' said Olivier no less gravely. 'How glad I am to have seen you again, and been able to tell you so! Do you remember the last time? When I waited with you in Bromfield to take Ermina and Yves home? And you drew me maps on the floor to show me the ways?'

There is a point at which joy is only just bearable. Cadfael got up to refill the wine-cups, and turn his face away for a moment from a brightness almost too bright. 'Ah, now, if this is to be a contest in "do-you-remembers" we shall be at it until Vespers, for not one detail of that time have I forgotten. So let's have this flask here within reach, and settle down to it in comfort.'

But there was an hour and more left before Vespers when Hugh put an abrupt end to remembering. He came in haste, with a face blazingly alert, and full of news. Even so he was slow to speak, not wishing to exult openly in what must be only shock and dismay to Olivier.

'There's news. A courier rode in from Warwick just now, they're passing the word north by stages as fast as horse can go.' They were both on their feet by then, intent upon his face, and waiting for good or evil, for he contained it well. A good face for keeping secrets, and under strong control now out of courteous consideration. 'I fear,' he said, 'it will not come as gratefully to you, Olivier, as I own it does to me.'

'From the south ...' said Olivier, braced and still. 'From London? The empress?'

'Yes, from London. All is overturned in a day. There'll be no coronation. Yesterday as they sat at dinner in Westminster, the Londoners suddenly rang the tocsin – all the city bells. The entire town came out in arms, and marched on Westminster. They're fled, Olivier, she and all her court, fled in the clothes they wore and with very little else, and the city men have plundered the palace and driven out even the last hangers-on. She never made move to win them, nothing but threats and reproaches and demands for money ever since she entered. She's let the crown slip through her fingers for want of a few soft words and a queen's courtesy. For your part,' said Hugh, with real compunction, 'I'm sorry! For mine, I find it a great deliverance.'

'With that I find no fault,' said Olivier simply. 'Why should you not be glad? But she … she's safe? They have not taken her?'

'No, according to the messenger she's safely away, with Robert of Gloucester and a few others as loyal, but the rest, it seems, scattered and made off for their own lands, where they'd feel safe. That's the word as he brought it, barely a day old. The city of London was being pressed hard from the south,' said Hugh, somewhat softening the load of folly that lay upon the empress's own shoulders, 'with King Stephen's queen harrying their borders. To get relief their only way was to drive the empress out and let the queen in, and their hearts were on her side, no question, of the two they'd liefer have her.'

'I knew,' said Olivier, 'she was not wise – the Empress Maud. I knew she could not forget grudges, no matter how sorely she needed to close

268

her eyes to them. I have seen her strip a man's dignity from him when he came submissive, offering support ... Better at making enemies than friends. All the more she needs,' he said, 'the few she has. Where is she gone? Did your messenger know?'

'Westward for Oxford. And they'll reach it safely. The Londoners won't follow so far, their part was only to drive her out.'

'And the bishop? Is he gone with her?' The entire enterprise had rested upon the efforts of Henry of Blois, and he had done his best for her, not entirely creditably but understandably and at considerable cost, and his best she herself had undone. Stephen was a prisoner in Bristol, but Stephen was still crowned and anointed king of England. No wonder Hugh's eyes shone.

'Of the bishop I know nothing as yet. But he'll surely join her in Oxford. Unless ...'

'Unless he changes sides again,' Olivier ended for him, and laughed. 'It seems I shall have to leave you in more haste than I expected,' he said with regret. 'One fortune rises, another falls. No sense in quarrelling with the lot.'

'What will you do?' asked Hugh, watching him steadily. 'You know, I think, that whatever you may ask of us here, is yours, and the choice is yours. Your horses are fresh. Your men will not yet have heard the news, they'll be waiting on your word. If you need stores for a journey, take whatever you will. Or if you choose to stay ...'

Olivier shook his blue-black head, and the

269

clasping curves of glossy hair danced on his cheeks. 'I must go. Not north, where I was sent. What use in that, now? South for Oxford. Whatever she may be else, she is my liege lord's liege lady, where she is he will be, and where he is, I go.'

They eyed each other silently for a moment, and Hugh said softly, quoting remembered words: 'To tell you truth, now I've met you I expected nothing less.'

'I'll go and rouse my men, and we'll get to horse. You'll follow to your house, before I go? I must take leave of Lady Beringar.'

'I'll follow you,' said Hugh.

Olivier turned to Brother Cadfael without a word but with the brief golden flash of a smile breaking through his roused gravity for an instant, and again vanishing. 'Brother ... remember me in your prayers!' He stooped his smooth cheek yet again in farewell, and as the elder's kiss was given he embraced Cadfael vehemently, with impulsive grace. 'Until a better time!'

'God go with you!' said Cadfael.

And he was gone, striding rapidly along the gravel path, breaking into a light run, in no way disheartened or down, a match for disaster or for triumph. At the corner of the box hedge he turned in flight to look back, and waved a hand before he vanished.

'I wish to God,' said Hugh, gazing after him, 'he was of our party! There's an odd thing, Cadfael! Will you believe, just then, when he looked round,

I thought I saw something of you about him. The set of the head, something …'

Cadfael, too, was gazing out from the open doorway to where the last sheen of blue had flashed from the burnished hair, and the last echo of the light foot on the gravel died into silence. 'Oh, no,' he said absently, 'he is altogether the image of his mother.'

An unguarded utterance. Unguarded from absence of mind, or design?

The following silence did not trouble him, he continued to gaze, shaking his head gently over the lingering vision, which would stay with him through all his remaining years, and might even, by the grace of God and the saints, be made flesh for him yet a third time. Far beyond his deserts, but miracles are neither weighed nor measured, but as uncalculated as the lightnings.

'I recall,' said Hugh with careful deliberation, perceiving that he was permitted to speculate, and had heard only what he was meant to hear, 'I do recall that he spoke of one for whose sake he held the Benedictine order in reverence … one who had used him like a son …'

Cadfael stirred, and looked round at him, smiling as he met his friend's fixed and thoughtful eyes. 'I always meant to tell you, some day,' he said tranquilly, 'what he does not know, and never will from me. He *is* my son.'

AN EXCELLENT MYSTERY

Chapter One

AUGUST CAME in, that summer of 1141, tawny as a lion and somnolent and purring as a hearthside cat. After the plenteous rains of the spring the weather had settled into angelic calm and sunlight for the feast of Saint Winifred, and preserved the same benign countenance throughout the corn harvest. Lammas came for once strict to its day, the wheat-fields were already gleaned and white, ready for the flocks and herds that would be turned into them to make use of what aftermath the season brought. The loaf-Mass had been celebrated with great contentment, and the early plums in the orchard along the riverside were darkening into ripeness. The abbey barns were full, the well-dried straw bound and stacked, and if there was still no rain to bring on fresh green fodder in the reaped fields for the sheep, there were heavy morning dews. When this golden weather broke at last, it might well break in violent storms, but as yet the skies remained bleached and clear, the palest imaginable blue.

'Fat smiles on the faces of the husbandmen,' said Hugh Beringar, fresh from his own harvest in the north of the shire, and burned nut-brown from his

5

work in the fields, 'and chaos among the kings. If they had to grow their own corn, mill their own flour and bake their own bread they might have no time left for all the squabbling and killing. Well, thank God for present mercies, and God keep the killing well away from us here. Not that I rate it the less ill-fortune for being there in the south, but this shire is my field, and my people, mine to keep. I have enough to do to mind my own, and when I see them brown and rosy and fat, with full byres and barns, and a high wool tally in good quality fleeces, I'm content.'

They had met by chance at the corner of the abbey wall, where the Foregate turned right towards Saint Giles, and beside it the great grassy triangle of the horse-fair ground opened, pallid and pockmarked in the sun. The three-day annual fair of Saint Peter was more than a week past, the stalls taken down, the merchants departed. Hugh sat aloft on his raw-boned and cross-grained grey horse, tall enough to carry a heavyweight instead of this light, lean young man whose mastery he tolerated, though he had precious little love for any other human creature. It was no responsibility of the sheriff of Shropshire to see that the fairground was properly vacated and cleared after its three-day occupation, but for all that Hugh liked to view the ground for himself. It was his officers who had to keep order there, and make sure the abbey stewards were neither cheated of their fees nor robbed or otherwise abused in collecting them. That was over now for another year. And here were the signs of it, the dappling of post-holes, the pallid oblongs of the stalls, the green fringes, and the trampled, bald paths between the booths. From sun-starved

6

bleach to lush green, and back to the pallor again, with patches of tough, flat clover surviving in the trodden paths like round green footprints of some strange beast.

'One good shower would put all right,' said Brother Cadfael, eyeing the curious chessboard of blanched and bright with a gardener's eye. 'There's nothing in the world so strong as grass.'

He was on his way from the abbey of Saint Peter and Saint Paul to its chapel and hospital of Saint Giles, half a mile away at the very rim of the town. It was one of his duties to keep the medicine cupboard there well supplied with all the remedies the inmates might require, and he made this journey every couple of weeks, more often in times of increased habitation and need. On this particular early morning in August he had with him young Brother Oswin, who had worked with him among the herbs for more than a year, and was now on his way to put his skills into practice among the most needy. Oswin was sturdy, well-grown, glowing with enthusiasm. Time had been when he had cost plenty in breakages, in pots burned beyond recovery, and deceptive herbs gathered by mistake for others only too like them. Those times were over. All he needed now to be a treasure to the hospital was a cool-headed superior who would know when to curb his zeal. The abbey had the right of appointment, and the lay head they had installed would be more than proof against Brother Oswin's too exuberant energy.

'You had a good fair, after all,' said Hugh.

'Better than ever I expected, with half the south cut off by the trouble in Winchester. They got here from Flanders,' said Cadfael appreciatively. East

7

Anglia was no very peaceful ground just now, but the wool merchants were a tough breed, and would not let a little bloodshed and danger bar them off from a good profit.

'It was a fine wool clip.' Hugh had flocks of his own on his manor of Maesbury, in the north, he knew about the quality of the year's fleeces. There had been good buying in from Wales, too, all along this border. Shrewsbury had ties of blood, sympathy and mutual gain with the Welsh of both Powys and Gwynedd, whatever occasional explosions of racial exuberance might break the guarded peace. In this summer the peace with Gwynedd held firm, under the capable hand of Owain Gwynedd, since they had a shared interest in containing the ambitions of Earl Ranulf of Chester. Powys was less predictable, but had drawn in its horns of late after several times blunting them painfully on Hugh's precautions.

'And the corn harvest the best for years. As for the fruit . . . It *looks* well,' said Cadfael cautiously, 'if we get some good rains soon to swell it, and no thunderstorms before it's gathered. Well, the corn's in and the straw stacked, and as good a hay crop as we've had since my memory holds. You'll not hear me complain.'

But for all that, he thought, looking back in mild surprise, it had been an unchancy sort of year, overturning the fortunes of kings and empresses not once, but twice, while benignly smiling upon the festivities of the church and the hopeful labours of ordinary men, at least here in the midlands. February had seen King Stephen made prisoner at the disastrous battle of Lincoln, and swept away into close confinement in Bristol castle by his arch-enemy, cousin and rival claimant to the throne of England, the Empress Maud. A good many coats had been changed in haste after that reversal, not least that of Stephen's brother and Maud's cousin, Henry of Blois, Bishop of Winchester and papal legate, who had delicately hedged his wager and come round to the winning side, only to find that he would have done well to drag his feet a little longer. For the fool woman, with the table spread for her at Westminster and the crown all but touching her hair, had seen fit to conduct herself in so arrogant and overbearing a manner towards the citizens of London that they had risen in fury to drive her out in ignominious flight, and let King Stephen's valiant queen into the city in her place.

Not that this last spin of the wheel could set King Stephen free. On the contrary, report said it had caused him to be loaded with chains by way of extra security, he being the one formidable weapon the empress still had in her hand. But it had certainly snatched the crown from Maud's head, most probably for ever, and it had cost her the not inconsiderable support of Bishop Henry, who was not the man to be over-hasty in his alliances twice in one year. Rumour said the lady had sent her half-brother and best champion, Earl Robert of Gloucester, to Winchester to set things right with the bishop and lure him back to her side, but without getting a straight answer. Rumour said also, and probably on good grounds, that Stephen's queen had already forestalled her, at a private meeting with Henry at Guildford, and got rather more sympathy from him than the empress had succeeded in getting. And doubtless Maud had heard of it. For

9

the latest news, brought by latecomers from the south to the abbey fair, was that the empress with a hastily gathered army had marched to Winchester and taken up residence in the royal castle there. What her next move was to be must be a matter of anxious speculation to the bishop, even in his own city.

And meantime, here in Shrewsbury the sun shone, the abbey celebrated its maiden saint with joyous solemnity, the flocks flourished, the harvest whitened and was gathered in exemplary weather, the annual fair took its serene course through the first three days of August, and traders came from far and wide, conducted their brisk business, took their profits, made their shrewd purchases, and scattered again in peace to return to their own homes, as though neither king nor empress existed, or had any power to hamper the movements or threaten the lives of ordinary, sensible men.

'You'll have heard nothing new since the merchants left?' Cadfael asked, scanning the blanched traces their stalls had left behind.

'Nothing yet. It seems they're eyeing each other across the city, each waiting for the other to make a move. Winchester must be holding its breath. The last word is that the empress sent for Bishop Henry to come to her at the castle, and he has sent a soft answer that he is preparing himself for the meeting. But stirred not a foot, so far, to move within reach of her. But for all that,' said Hugh thoughtfully, 'I dare wager he's preparing, sure enough. She has mustered her forces, he'll be calling up his before ever he goes near her – *if* he does!'

'And while they hold their breath, you may breathe more freely,' said Cadfael shrewdly.

Hugh laughed. 'While my enemies fall out, at least it keeps their minds off me and mine. Even if they come to terms again, and she wins him back, there's at least a few weeks' delay gained for the king's party. If not – why, better they should tear each other than save their arrows for us.'

'Do you think he'll stand out against her?'

'She has treated him as haughtily as she does every man, when he did her good menial service. Now he has half-defied her he may well be reflecting that she takes very unkindly to being thwarted, and that a bishop can be clapped in chains as easily as a king, once she lays hands on him. No, I fancy his lordship is stocking his own castle of Wolvesey to withstand a siege, if it comes to that, and calling up his men in haste. Who bargains with the empress had better bargain from behind an army.'

'The queen's army?' demanded Cadfael, sharp-eyed.

Hugh had begun to wheel his horse back towards the town, but he looked round over a bare brown shoulder with a flashing glint of black eyes. 'That we shall see! I would guess the first courier ever he sent out for aid went to Queen Matilda.'

'Brother Cadfael . . .' began Oswin, trotting jauntily beside him as they walked on towards the rim of the town, where the hospital and its chapel rose plain and grey within their long wattle fence.

'Yes, son?'

'Would even the empress really dare lay hands on the Bishop of Winchester? The Holy Father's legate here?'

11

'Who can tell? But there's not much she will not dare.'

'But . . . That there could be fighting between them . . .'

Oswin puffed out his round young cheeks in a great breath of wonder and deprecation. Such a thing seemed to him unimaginable. 'Brother, you have been in the world and have experience of wars and battles. And I know that there were bishops and great churchmen went to do battle for the Holy Sepulchre, as you did, but should they be found in arms for any lesser cause?'

Whether they should, thought Cadfael, is for them to take up with their judge in the judgement, but that they are so found, have been aforetime and will be hereafter, is beyond doubt. 'To be charitable,' he said cautiously, 'in this case his lordship may consider his own freedom, safety and life to be a very worthy cause. Some have been called to accept martyrdom meekly, but that should surely be for nothing less than their faith. And a dead bishop could be of little service to his church, and a legate mouldering in prison little profit to the Holy Father.'

Brother Oswin strode beside for some moments judicially mute, digesting that plea and apparently finding it somewhat dubious, or else suspecting that he had not fully comprehended the argument. Then he asked ingenuously: 'Brother, would *you* take arms again? Once having renounced them? For *any* cause?'

'Son,' said Cadfael, 'you have the knack of asking questions which cannot be answered. How do I know what I would do, in extreme need? As a brother of the Order I would wish to keep my

12

hands from violence against any, but for all that, I hope I would not turn my back if I saw innocence or helplessness being abused. Bear in mind even the bishops carry a crook, meant to protect the flock as well as guide it. Let princes and empresses and warriors mind their own duties, you give all your mind to yours, and you'll do well.'

They were nearing the trodden path that led up a grassy slope to the open gate in the wattle fence. The modest turret of the chapel eyèd them over the roof of the hospice. Brother Oswin bounded up the slope eagerly, his cherubic face bright with confidence, bound for a new field of endeavour, and certain of mastering it. There was probably no pitfall here he would evade, but none of them would hold him for long, or damp his unquenchable ardour.

'Now remember all I've taught you,' said Cadfael. 'Be obedient to Brother Simon. You will work for a time under him, as he did under Brother Mark. The superior is a layman from the Foregate, but you'll see little of him between his occasional visitations and inspections, and he's a good soul and listens to counsel. And I shall be in attendance every now and again, should you ever need me. Come, and I'll show you where everything is.'

Brother Simon was a comfortable, round man in his forties. He came out to meet them at the porch, with a gangling boy of about twelve by the hand. The child's eyes were white with the caul of blindness, but otherwise he was whole and comely, by no means the saddest sight to be found here, where the infected and diseased might find at once a refuge and a prison for their contagion, since they were not permitted to carry it into the streets of the town, among the uncorrupted. There were cripples sunning themselves in the little orchard behind the hospice, old, pox-riddled men, and faded women in the barn plaiting bands for the straw stooks as they were stacked. Those who could work a little were glad to do so for their keep, those who could not were passive in the sun, unless they had skin rashes which the heat only aggravated. These kept under the shade of the fruit-trees, or those most fevered in the chill of the chapel.

'As at present,' said Brother Simon, 'we have eighteen, which is not so ill, for so hot a season. Three are able-bodied, and mending of their sickness, which was not contagious, and they'll be on their way within days now. But there'll be others, young man, there'll always be others. They come and go. Some by the roads, some out of this world's bane. None the worse, I hope, for passing through that door in this place.'

He had a slightly preaching style which caused Cadfael to smile inwardly, remembering Mark's lovely simplicity, but he was a good man, hardworking, compassionate, and very deft with those big hands of his. Oswin would drink in his solemn homilies with reverence and wonder, and go about his work refreshed and unquestioning.

'I'll see the lad round myself, if you'll let me,' said Cadfael, hitching forward the laden scrip at his girdle. 'I've brought you all the medicaments you asked for, and some I thought might be needed, besides. We'll find you when we're done.'

'And the news of Brother Mark?' asked Simon.

'Mark is already deacon. I have but to save my

most fearful confession a few more years, then, if need be, I'll depart in peace.'

'According to Mark's word?' wondered Simon, revealing unsuspected depths, and smiling to gloss them over. It was not often he spoke at such a venture.

'Well,' said Cadfael very thoughtfully, 'I've always found Mark's word good enough for me. You may well be right.' And he turned to Oswin, who had followed this exchange with a face dutifully attentive and bewilderedly smiling, earnest to understand what evaded him like thistledown. 'Come on, lad, let's unload these and be rid of the weight first, and then I'll show you all that goes on here at Saint Giles.'

They passed through the hall, which was for eating and for sleeping, except for those too sick to be left among their healthier fellows. There was a large locked cupboard, to which Cadfael had his own key, and its shelves within were full of jars, flasks, bottles, wooden boxes for tablets, ointments, syrups, lotions, all the products of Cadfael's workshop. They unloaded their scrips and filled the gaps along the shelves. Oswin enlarged with the importance of this mystery into which he had been initiated, and which he was now to practise in earnest.

There was a small kitchen garden behind the hospice, and an orchard, and barns for storage. Cadfael conducted his charge round the entire enclave, and by the end of the circuit they had three of the inmates in close and curious attendance, the old man who tended the cabbages and showed off his produce with pride, a lame youth herpling along nimbly enough on two crutches, and the blind

15

child, who had forsaken Brother Simon to attach himself to Cadfael's girdle, knowing the familiar voice.

'This is Warin,' said Cadfael, taking the boy by the hand as they made their way back to Brother Simon's little desk in the porch. 'He sings well in chapel, and knows the office by heart. But you'll soon know them all by name.'

Brother Simon rose from his accounts at sight of them returning. 'He's shown you everything? It's no great household, ours, but it does a great work. You'll soon get used to us.'

Oswin beamed and blushed, and said that he would do his best. It was likely that he was waiting impatiently for his mentor to depart, so that he could begin to exercise his new responsibility without the uneasiness of a pupil performing before his teacher. Cadfael clouted him cheerfully on the shoulder, bade him be good, in the tones of one having no doubts on that score, and turned towards the gate. They had moved out into the sunlight from the dimness of the porch.

'You've heard no fresh news from the south?' The denizens of Saint Giles, being encountered at the very edge of the town, were usually beforehand with news.

'Nothing to signify. And yet a man must wonder and speculate. There was a beggar, able-bodied but getting old, who came in three days ago, and stayed only overnight to rest. He was from the Staceys, near Andover, a queer one, perhaps a mite touched in his wits, who can tell? He gets notions, it seems, that move him on into fresh pastures, and when they come to him he must go. He said he got word in his head that he had best get away northwards while

16

there was time.'

'A man of those parts who had no property to tie him might very well get the same notion now,' said Cadfael ruefully, 'without being in want of his wits. Indeed, it might be his wits that advised him to move on.'

'So it might. But this fellow said – if he did not dream it – that the day he set out he looked back from a hilltop, and saw smoke in clouds over Winchester, and in the night following there was a red glow all above the city, that flickered as if with still quick flames.'

'It could be true,' said Cadfael, and gnawed a considering lip. 'It would come as no great surprise. The last firm news we had was that empress and bishop were holding off cautiously from each other, and shifting for position. A little patience . . . But she was never, it seems, a patient woman. I wonder, now, I wonder if she has laid him under siege. How long would your man have been on the road?'

'I fancy he made what haste he could,' said Simon, 'but four days at least, surely. That sets his story a week back, and no word yet to confirm it.'

'There will be, if it's true,' said Cadfael grimly, 'there will be! Of all the reports that fly about the world, ill news is the surest of all to arrive!'

He was still pondering this ominous shadow as he set off back along the Foregate, and his preoccupation was such that his greetings to acquaintances along the way were apt to be belated and absentminded. It was mid-morning, and the dusty road brisk with traffic, and there were few inhabitants of this parish of Holy Cross outside the town walls

17

that he did not know. He had treated many of
them, or their children, at some time in these his
cloistered years; even, sometimes, their beasts, for
he who learns about the sicknesses of men cannot
but pick up, here and there, some knowledge of the
sicknesses of their animals, creatures with as great
a capacity for suffering as their masters, and much
less means of complaining, together with far less
inclination to complain. Cadfael had often wished
that men would use their beasts better, and tried to
show them that it would be good husbandry. The
horses of war had been part of that curious, slow
process within him that had turned him at length
from the trade of arms into the cloister.

Not that all abbots and priors used their mules
and stock beasts well, either. But at least the best
and wisest of them recognised it for good policy, as
well as good Christianity.

But now, what could really be happening in
Winchester, to turn the sky over it black by day
and red by night? Like the pillars of cloud and
fire that marked the passage of the elect through
the wilderness, these had signalled and guided
the beggar's flight from danger. He saw no reason to doubt the report. The same foreboding
must have been on may loftier minds these last
weeks, while the hot, dry summer, close cousin
of fire, waited with a torch ready. But what a
fool that woman must be, to attempt to besiege
the bishop in his own castle in his own city, with
the queen, every inch her match, no great distance away at the head of a strong army, and
the Londoners implacably hostile. And how ada-
mant against her, now, the bishop must be, to
venture all by defying her. And both these high

18

personages would remain strongly protected, and survive. But what of the lesser creatures they put in peril? Poor little traders and craftsmen and labourers who had no such fortresses to shelter them!

He had meditated his way from the care of horses and cattle to the tribulations of men, and was startled to hear at his back, at a moment when the traffic of the Foregate was light, the crisp, neat hooves of mules catching up on him at a steady clip. He halted at the corner of the horse-fair ground and looked back, and had not far to look, for they were close.

Two of them, a fine, tall beast almost pure white, fit for an abbot, and a smaller, lighter, fawn-brown creature stepping decorously a pace or two to the rear. But what caused Cadfael to pull up and turn fully towards them, waiting in surprised welcome for them to draw alongside, was the fact that both riders wore the Benedictine black, brothers to each other and to him. Plainly they had noted his own habit trudging before them, and made haste to overtake him, for as soon as he halted and recognised them for his like they eased to a walk, and so came gently alongside him.

'God be with you, brothers!' said Cadfael, eyeing them with interest. 'Do you come to our house here in Shrewsbury?'

'And with you, brother,' said the foremost rider, in a rich voice which yet had a slight, harsh crepitation in it, as though the cave of his breast created a grating echo. Cadfael's ears pricked at the sound. He had heard the breath of many old men, long exposed to harsh outdoor living, rasp and echo in the same way, but this man was not old. 'You belong

19

to this house of Saint Peter and Saint Paul? Yes, we are bound there with letters for the lord abbot. I take this to be his boundary wall beside us? Then it is not far to go now.'

'Very close,' said Cadfael. 'I'll walk beside you, for I'm homeward bound to that same house. Have you come far?'

He was looking up into a face gaunt and drawn, but fine-featured and commanding, with deep-set eyes very dark and tranquil. The cowl was flung back on the stranger's shoulders, and the long, fleshless head wore its rondel of straight black hair like a crown. A tall man, sinewy but emaciated. There was the fading sunburn of hotter lands than England on him, a bronze acquired over more years than one, but turned somewhat dull and sickly now, and though he held himself in the saddle like one born there, there was also a languor upon his movements, and an uncomplaining weariness in his face, a serene resignation which would better have fitted an old man. This man might have been somewhere in his mid-forties, surely not much more.

'Far enough,' he said with a thin, dark smile, 'but today only from Brigge.'

'And bound further? Or will you stay with us for a while? You'll be heartily welcome visitors, you and the young brother here.'

The younger rider hovered silently, a little apart, as a servant might have done in dutiful attendance on his master. He was surely scarcely past twenty, lissome and tall, though his companion would top him by a head if they stood together. He had the oval, smooth, boy's face of his years, but formed and firm for all its suave planes. His cowl was drawn forward over his face, perhaps against

20

the sun's glare. Large, shadowed eyes gazed out from the hood, fixed steadily upon his elder. The one glance they flashed at Cadfael was as quickly averted.

'We look to stay here for some time, if the lord abbot will give us refuge,' said the older man, 'for we have lost one roof, and must beg admittance under another.'

They had begun to move on at a leisurely walk, the dust of the Foregate powder-fine under the hooves of the mules. The young man fell in meekly behind, and let them lead. To the civil greetings that saluted them along the way, where Cadfael was well known, and these his companions matter for friendly curiosity, the older man made quiet, courteous response. The younger said never a word.

The gatehouse and the church loomed, ahead on their left, the high wall beside them reflected heat from its stones. The rider let the reins hang loose on his mule's neck, folded veined hands, long-fingered and brown, and fetched a long sigh. Cadfael held his peace.

'Forgive me that I answer almost churlishly, brother, it is not meant so. After the habit and the daily company of silence, speech comes laboriously. And after a holocaust, and the fires of destruction, the throat is too dry to manage many words. You asked if we had come far. We have been some days on the road, for I cannot ride hard these days. We are come like beggars from the south . . .'

'From Winchester!' said Cadfael with certainty, recalling the foreboding, the cloud and the fire.

'From what is left of Winchester.' The worn but muscular hands were quite still, leaving it to Cadfael to lead the mule round the west end of the church

21

and in at the arch of the gatehouse. It was not grief or passion that made it hard for the man to speak, he had surely seen worse in his time than he was now recalling. The chords of his voice creaked from under-use, and slowed upon the grating echo. A beautiful voice it must have been in its heyday, before the velvet frayed. 'Is it possible,' he said wonderingly, 'that we come the first? I had thought word would have flown thus far north almost a week ago, but true, escape this way would have been no simple matter. Have we to bring the news, then? The great ones fell out over us. Who am I to complain, who have had my part in the like, elsewhere? The empress laid siege to the bishop in his castle of Wolvesey, in the city, and the bishop rained fire-arrows down upon the roofs rather than upon his enemies. The town is laid waste. A nunnery burned to the ground, churches razed, and my priory of Hyde Mead, that Bishop Henry so desired to take into his own hands, is gone for ever, brought down in flames. We are here, we two, homeless and asking shelter. The brothers are scattered through all the Benedictine houses of the land, wherever they have ties of blood or friendship. There will never be any going home to Hyde.'

So it was true. The finger of God had pointed one poor devil out of the trap, and let him look back from a hill to see the scarlet and the black of fire and smoke devour a city. Bishop Henry's own city, to which his own hand had set light.

'God sort all!' said Cadfael.

'Doubtless he will!' The voice with its honeyed warmth and abrasive echo rang under the archway of the gatehouse. Brother Porter came out, smiling welcome, and a groom came running for the horses, sighting fraternal visitors. The great court opened serene in sunshine, crossed and re-crossed by busy, preoccupied people, brothers, lay brothers, stewards, all about their normal, mastered affairs. The child oblates and schoolboys, let loose from their studies, were tossing a ball, their shrill voices gay and piercing in the still half-hour before noon. Life here made itself heard, felt and seen, as regular as the seasons.

They halted within the gate. Cadfael held the stirrup for the stranger, though there was no need, for he lighted down as naturally as a bird settling and folding its wings; but slowly, with languid grace, and stood to unfold a long, graceful but enfeebled body, well above six feet tall, and lance-straight as it was lance-lean. The young one had leaped from the saddle in an instant, and stood baulked, circling uneasily, jealous of Cadfael's ministering hand. And still made no sound, neither of gratitude nor protest.

'I'll be your herald to Abbot Radulfus,' said Cadfael, 'if you'll permit. What shall I say to him?'

'Say that Brother Humilis and Brother Fidelis, of the sometime priory of Hyde Mead, which is laid waste, ask audience and protection of his goodness, in all submission, and in the name of the Rule.'

This man had surely known little in the past of humility, and little of submission, though he had embraced both now with a whole heart.

'I will say so,' said Cadfael, and turned for a moment to the young brother, expecting his amen. The cowled head inclined modestly, the oval face was

23

hidden in shadow, but there was no voice.

'Hold my young friend excused,' said Brother Humilis, erect by his mule's milky head, 'if he cannot speak his greeting. Brother Fidelis is dumb.'

Chapter Two

RING OUR brothers in to me,' said Abbot Radulfus, rising from his desk in surprise and concern when Cadfael had reported to him the arrivals, and the bare bones of their story. He pushed aside parchment and pen and stood erect, dark and tall against the brilliant sunlight through the parlour window. 'That this should ever be! City and church laid waste together! Certainly they are welcome here lifelong, if need be. Bring them hither, Cadfael. And remain with us. You may be their guide afterwards, and bring them to Prior Robert. We must make appropriate places for them in the dortoir.'

Cadfael went on his errand content not to be dismissed, and led the newcomers down the length of the great court to the corner where the abbot's lodging lay sheltered in its small garden. What there was to be learned from the travellers of affairs in the south he was eager to learn, and so would Hugh be, when he knew of their coming. For this time news had been unwontedly slow on the road, and matters might have been moving with considerably greater speed down in Winchester since the unlucky brothers of Hyde dispersed to seek refuge elsewhere.

'Father Abbot, here are Brother Humilis and Brother Fidelis.'

It seemed dark in the little wood-panelled parlour after the radiance without, and the two tall, masterful men stood studying each other intently in the warm, shadowy stillness. Radulfus himself had drawn forward stools for the newcomers, and with a motion of a long hand invited them to be seated, but the young one drew back deferentially into deeper shadow and remained standing. He could never be the spokesman; that might well be the reason for his self-effacement. But Radulfus, who had yet to learn of the young man's disability, certainly noted the act, and observed it without either approval or disapproval.

'Brothers, you are very welcome in our house, and all we can provide is yours. I hear you have had a long ride, and a sad loss that has driven you forth. I grieve for our brothers of Hyde. But here at least we hope to offer you tranquillity of mind, and a secure shelter. In these lamentable wars we have been fortunate. You, the elder, are Brother Humilis?'

'Yes, Father. Here I present you our prior's letter, commending us both to your kindness.' He had carried it in the breast of his habit, and now drew if forth and laid it on the abbot's desk. 'You will know, Father, that the abbey of Hyde has been an abbey without an abbot for two years now. They say commonly that Bishop Henry had it in mind to bring it into his own hands as an episcopal convent, which the brothers strongly resisted, and denying us a head may well have been a move designed to weaken us and reduce our voice. Now that is of no consequence, for the house of Hyde is gone, razed to the ground and blackened by fire.'

'Is it such entire destruction?' asked Radulfus, frowning over his linked hands.

'Utter destruction. In time to come a new house may be raised there, who knows? But of the old nothing remains.'

'You had best tell me all that you can,' said Radulfus heavily. 'Here we live far from these events, almost in peace. How did this holocaust come about?'

Brother Humilis – what could his proud name have been before he thus calmly claimed for himself humility? – folded his hands in the lap of his habit, and fixed his hollow dark eyes upon the abbot's face. There was a creased scar, long ago healed and pale, marking the left side of his tonsure, Cadfael noted, and knew, the crescent shape of a glancing stroke from a right-handed swordsman. It did not surprise him. No straight western sword, but a Seljuk scimitar. So that was where he had got the bronze that had now faded and sickened into dun.

'The empress entered Winchester towards the end of July, I do not recall the date, and took up her residence in the royal castle by the west gate. She sent to Bishop Henry in his palace to come to her, but they say he sent back word that he would come, but must a little delay, by what excuse I never heard. He delayed too long, but by what followed he made good use of such days of grace as he had, for by the time the empress lost patience and moved up her forces against him he was safely shut up in his new castle of Wolvesey, in the south-east corner of the city, backed into the wall. And the queen, or so they said in the town, was moving her Flemings up in haste to his aid. Whether or no, he had a great garrison within there, and well supplied. I ask pardon of God and

27

of you, Father,' said Brother Humilis gently, 'that I took such pains to follow these warlike reports, but my training was in arms, and a man cannot altogether forget.'

'God forbid,' said Radulfus, 'that a man should feel he need forget anything that was done in good faith and loyal service. In arms or in the cloister, we have all a score to pay to this country and this people. Closed eyes are of little use to either. Go on! Who struck the first blow?'

For they had been allies only a matter of weeks earlier!

'The empress. She moved to surround Wolvesey as soon as she knew he had shut himself in. Everything they had they used against the castle, even such engines as they were able to raise. And they pulled down any buildings, shops, houses, all that lay too close, to clear the ground. But the bishop had a strong garrison, and his walls are new. He began to build, as I hear, only ten years or so ago. It was his men who first used firebrands. Much of the city within the wall has burned, churches, a nunnery, shops – it might not have been so terrible if the season had not been high summer, and so dry.'

'And Hyde Mead?'

'There's no knowing from which side came the arrows that set us alight. The fighting had spilled outside the city walls by then, and there was looting, as always,' said Brother Humilis. 'We fought the fire as long as we could, but there was none besides to help us, and it was too fierce, we could not bring it under. Our prior ordered that we withdraw into the countryside, and so we did. Somewhat short of our number,' he said. 'There were deaths.'

Always there were deaths, and usually of the innocent and helpless. Radulfus stared with locked brows into the chalice of his linked hands, and thought.

'The prior lived to write letters. Where is he now?'

'Safe, in a manor of a kinsman, some miles from the city. He has ordered our withdrawal, dispersing the brothers wherever they might best find shelter. I asked if I might come to beg asylum here in Shrewsbury, and Brother Fidelis with me. And we are come, and are in your hands.'

'Why?' asked the abbot. 'Welcome indeed you are, I ask only, why here?'

'Father, some mile or two up-river from here, on a manor called Salton, I was born. I had a fancy to see the place again, or at least be near it, before I die.' He smiled, meeting the penetrating eyes beneath the knotted brows. 'It was the only property my father held in this shire. There I was born, as it so happened. A man displaced from his last home may well turn back to his first.'

'You say well. So far as is in us, we will supply that home. And your young brother?' Fidelis put back the cowl from his neck, bent his head reverently, and made a small outward sweep of submissive hands, but no sound.

'Father, he cannot speak for himself, I offer thanks from us both. I have not been altogether in my best health in Hyde, and Brother Fidelis, out of pure kindness, has become my faithful friend and attendant. He has no kinsfolk to whom he can go, he elects to be with me and tend me as before. If you will permit.' He waited for the acknowledging nod and smile before he added: 'Brother Fidelis will serve

29

God here with every faculty he has. I know him, and I answer for him. But one, his voice, he cannot employ. Brother Fidelis is mute.'

'He is no less welcome,' said Radulfus, 'because his prayers must be silent. His silence may be more eloquent than our spoken words.' If he had been taken aback he had mastered the check so quickly as to give no sign. It would not be so often that Abbot Radulfus would be disconcerted. 'After this journey,' he said, 'you must both be weary, and still in some distress of mind until you have again a bed, a place, and work to do. Go now with Brother Cadfael, he will take you to Prior Robert, and show you everything within the enclave, dortoir and frater and gardens and herbarium, where he rules. He will find you refreshment and rest, your first need. And at Vespers you shall join us in worship.'

Word of the arrivals from the south brought Hugh Beringar down hotfoot from the town to confer first with the abbot, and then with Brother Humilis, who repeated freely what he had already once related. When he had gleaned all he could, Hugh went to find Cadfael in the herb-garden, where he was busy watering. There was an hour yet before Vespers, the time of day when all the necessary work had been done, and even a gardener could relax and sit for a while in the shade. Cadfael put away his watering-can, leaving the open, sunlit beds until the cool of the evening, and sat down beside his friend on the bench against the high south wall.

'Well, you have a breathing-space, at least,' he said. 'They are at each other's throats, not reaching for yours. Great pity, though, that townsmen and monastics and poor nuns should be the sufferers.

30

But so it goes in this world. And the queen and her Flemings must be in the town by now, or very near. What happens next? The besiegers may very well find themselves besieged.'

'It has happened before,' agreed Hugh. 'And the bishop had fair warning he might have need of a well-stocked larder, but she may have taken her supplies for granted. If I were the queen's general, I would take time to cut all the roads into Winchester first, and make certain no food can get in. Well, we shall see. And I hear you were the first to have speech with these two brothers from Hyde.'

'They overtook me in the Foregate. And what do you make of them, now you've been closeted with them so long?'

'What should I make of them, thus at first sight? A sick man and a dumb man. More to the purpose, what do your brothers make of them?' Hugh had a sharp eye on his old friend's face, which was blunt and sleepy and private in the late afternoon heat, but was never quite closed against him. 'The elder is noble, clearly. And he is ill. I guess at a martial past, for I think he has old wounds. Did you see he goes a little sidewise, favouring his left flank? Something has never quite healed. And the young one . . . I well understand he has fallen under the spell of such a man, and idolises him. Lucky for both! He has a powerful protector, his lord has a devoted nurse. Well?' said Hugh, challenging judgement with a confident smile.

'You haven't yet divined who our new elder brother is? They may not have told you all,' admitted Cadfael tolerantly, 'for it came out almost by chance. A martial past, yes, he avowed it, though you could have guessed it no less surely. The man

31

is past forty-five, I judge, and has visible scars. He has said, also, that he was born here at Salton, then a manor of his father's. And he has a scar on his head, bared by the tonsure, that was made by a Seljuk scimitar, some years back. A mere slice, readily healed, but left its mark. Salton was held formerly by the Bishop of Chester, and granted to the church of Saint Chad, here within the walls. They let it go many years since to a noble family, the Marescots. There's a local tenant holds it under them.' He opened a levelled brown eye, beneath a bushy brow russet as autumn. 'Brother Humilis is a Marescot. I know of only one Marescot of this man's age who went to the Crusade. Sixteen or seventeen years ago it must be. I was newly monk, then, part of me still hankered, and I had one eye always on the tale of those who took the Cross. As raw and eager as I was, surely, and bound for as bitter a fall, but pure enough in their going. There was a certain Godfrid Marescot who took three score with him from his own lands. He made a notable name for valour.'

'And you think this is he? Thus fallen?'

'Why not? The great ones are open to wounds no less than the simple. All the more,' said Cadfael, 'if they lead from before, and not from behind. They say this one was never later than first.'

He had still the crusader blood quick within him, he could not choose but awake and respond, however the truth had sunk below his dreams and hopes, all those years ago. Others, no less, had believed and trusted, no less to shudder and turn aside from much of what was done in the name of the Faith.

'Prior Robert will be running through the tale of the lords of Salton this moment,' said Cadfael, 'and will not fail to find his man. He knows the pedigree of every lord of a manor in this shire and beyond, for thirty years back and more. Brother Humilis will have no trouble in establishing himself, he sheds lustre upon us by being here, he need do nothing more.'

'As well,' said Hugh wryly, 'for I think there is no more he can do, unless it be to die here, and here be buried. Come, you have a better eye than mine for mortal sickness. The man is on his way out of this world. No haste, but the end is assured.'

'So it is for you and for me,' said Cadfael sharply. 'And as for haste, it's neither you nor I that hold the measure. It will come when it will come. Until then, every day is of consequence, the last no less than the first.'

'So be it!' said Hugh, and smiled, unchidden. 'But he'll come into your hands before many days are out. And what of his youngling – the dumb boy?'

'Nothing of him! Nothing but silence and shrinking into the shadows. Give us time,' said Cadfael, 'and we shall learn to know him better.'

A man who has renounced possessions may move freely from one asylum to another, and be no less at home, make do with nothing as well in Shrewsbury as in Hyde Mead. A man who wears what every other man under the same discipline wears need not be noticeable for more than a day. Brother Humilis and Brother Fidelis resumed here in the midlands the same routine they had kept in the south, and the hours of the day enfolded them no less firmly and serenely. Yet Prior Robert had made a satisfactory end of his cogitations concerning the feudal holdings and family genealogies in the shire, and it was

33

very soon made known to all, through his reliable echo, Brother Jerome, that the abbey had acquired a most distinguished son, a crusader of acknowledged valour, who had made a name for himself in the recent contention against the rising Atabeg Zenghi of Mosul, the latest threat to the Kingdom of Jerusalem. Prior Robert's personal ambitions lay all within the cloister, but for all that he missed never a turn of the fortunes of the world without. Four years since, Jerusalem had been shaken to its foundations by the king's defeat at this Zenghi's hands, but the kingdom had survived through its alliance with the emirate of Damascus. In that unhappy battle, so Robert made known discreetly, Godfrid Marescot had played a heroic part.

'He has observed every office, and worked steadily every hour set aside for work,' said Brother Edmund the infirmarer, eyeing the new brother across the court as he trod slowly towards the church for Compline, in the radiant stillness and lingering warmth of evening. 'And he has not asked for any help of yours or mine. But I wish he had a better colour, and a morsel of flesh more on those long bones. That bronze gone dull, with no blood behind it . . .'

And there went the faithful shadow after him, young, lissome, with strong, flowing pace, and hand ever advanced a little to prop an elbow, should it flag, or encircle a lean body, should it stagger or fall.

'There goes one who knows it all,' said Cadfael, 'and cannot speak. Nor would if he could, without his lord's permission. A son of one of his tenants, would you say? Something of that kind, surely. The boy is well born and taught. He knows Latin, almost as well as his master.'

34

On reflection it seemed a liberty to speak of a man as anyone's master who called himself Humilis, and had renounced the world.

'I had in mind,' said Edmund, but hesitantly, and with reverence, 'a natural son. I may be far astray, but it is what came to mind. I take him for a man who would love and protect his seed, and the young one might well love and admire him, for that as for all else.'

And it could well be true. The tall man and the tall youth, a certain likeness, even, in the clear features – insofar, thought Cadfael, as anyone had yet looked directly at the features of young Brother Fidelis, who passed so silently and unobtrusively about the enclave, patiently finding his way in this unfamiliar place. He suffered, perhaps, more than his elder companion in the change, having less confidence and experience, and all the anxiety of youth. He clung to his lodestar, and every motion he made was oriented by its light. They had a shared carrel in the scriptorium, for Brother Humilis had need, only too clearly, of a sedentary occupation, and had proved to have a delicate hand with copying, and artistry in illumination. And since he had limited control after a period of work, and his hand was liable to shake in fine detail, Abbot Radulfus had decreed that Brother Fidelis should be present with him to assist whenever he needed relief. The one hand matched the other as if the one had taught the other, thought it might have been only emulation and love. Together, they did slow but admirable work.

'I had never considered,' said Edmund, musing aloud, 'how remote and strange a man could be who has no voice, and how hard it is to reach and touch him. I have caught myself talking of him to Brother

35

Humilis, over the lad's head, and been ashamed – as if he had neither hearing nor wits. I blushed before him. Yet how do you touch hands with such a one? I never had practice in it till now, and I am altogether astray.'

'Who is not?' said Cadfael.

It was truth, he had noted it. The silence, or rather the moderation of speech enjoined by the Rule had one quality, the hush that hung about Brother Fidelis quite another. Those who must communicate with him tended to use much gesture and few words, or none, reflecting his silence. As though, truly, he had neither hearing nor wits. But manifestly he had both, quick and delicate senses and sharp hearing, tuned to the least sound. And that was also strange. So often the dumb were dumb because they had never learned of sounds, and therefore made none. And this young man had been well taught in his letters, and knew some Latin, which argued a mind far more agile than most. Unless, thought Cadfael doubtfully, his muteness was a new-come thing in recent years, from some constriction of the cords of the tongue or the sinews of the throat? Or even if he had it from birth, might it not be caused by some strings too tightly drawn under his tongue, that could be eased by exercise or loosed by the knife?

'I meddle too much,' said Cadfael to himself crossly, shaking off the speculation that could lead nowhere. And he went to Compline in an unwontedly penitent mood, and by way of discipline observed silence himself for the rest of the evening.

They gathered the purple-black Lammas plums next day, for they were just on the right edge of ripeness. Some would be eaten at once, fresh as they were, some Brother Petrus would boil down into a preserve thick and dark as cakes of poppy-seed, and some would be laid out on racks in the drying house to wrinkle and crystallise into gummy sweetness. Cadfael had a few trees in a small orchard within the enclave, though most of the fruit-trees were in the main garden of the Gaye, the lush meadow-land along the riverside. The novices and younger brothers picked the fruit, and the oblates and schoolboys were allowed to help; and if everyone knew that a few handfuls went into the breasts of tunics rather than into the baskets, provided the depredations were reasonable Cadfael turned a blind eye.

It was too much to expect silence in such fine weather and such a holiday occupation. The voices of the boys rang merrily in Cadfael's ears as he decanted wine in his workshop, and went back and forth among his plants along the shadowed wall, weeding and watering. A pleasant sound! He could pick out known voices, the children's shrill and light, their elders in a whole range of tones. That warm, clear call, that was Brother Rhun, the youngest of the novices, sixteen years old, only two months since received into probation, and not yet tonsured, lest he should think better of his impulsive resolve to quit a world he had scarcely seen. But Rhun would not repent of his choice. He had come to the abbey for Saint Winifred's festival, a cripple and in pain, and by her grace now he went straight and tall and agile, radiating delight upon everyone who came near him. As now, surely, on whoever was his partner at the nearest of the plum-trees. Cadfael went to the edge of the orchard to see, and there was the sometime lame boy up among the branches, secure and joyous, his slim, deft hands nursing the fruit so lightly his fingers scarcely blurred the bloom, and leaning down to lay them in the basket held up to him by a tall brother whose back was turned, and whose figure was not immediately recognisable, until he moved round, the better to follow Rhun's movements, and showed the face of Brother Fidelis.

It was the first time Cadfael had seen that face so clearly, in sunlight, the cowl slung back. Rhun, it seemed, was one creature at least who found no difficulty in drawing near to the mute brother, but spoke out to him merrily and found no strangeness in his silence. Rhun leaned down laughing, and Fidelis looked up, smiling, one face reflecting the other. Their hands touched on the handle of the basket as Rhun dangled it at the full stretch of his arm while Fidelis plucked a cluster of low-growing fruit pointed out to him from above.

After all, thought Cadfael, it was to be expected that valiant innocence would stride in boldly where most of us hesitate to set foot. And besides, Rhun has gone most of his life with a cruel flaw that set him apart, and taken no bitterness from it, naturally he would advance without fear into another man's isolation. And thank God for him, and for the valour of the children!

He went back to his weeding very thoughtfully, recalling that eased and sunlit glimpse of one who habitually withdrew into shadow. An oval face, firm-featured and by nature grave, with a lofty forehead and strong cheekbones, and clear ivory skin, smooth and youthful. There in the orchard he looked scarcely older than Rhun, though there must surely be a few years between them. The halo of curling hair round his tonsure was an autumn brown, almost fiery-bright, yet not red, and his wide-set eyes, under strong, level brows, were of a luminous grey, at least

38

in that full light. A very comely young man, like a veiled reflection of Rhun's sunlit beauty. Noonday and twilight met together.

The fruit-pickers were still at work, though with most of their harvest already gleaned, when Cadfael put away his hoe and watering-can and went to prepare for Vespers. In the great court there was the usual late-afternoon bustle, brothers returning from their work along the Gaye, the stir of arrival in guesthall and stable-yard, and in the cloister the sound of Brother Anselm's little portative organ testing out a new chant. The illuminators and copiers would be putting the finishing touches to their afternoon's work, and cleaning their pens and brushes. Brother Humilis must be alone in his carrel, having sent Fidelis out to the joyous labour in the garden, for nothing less would have induced the boy to leave him. Cadfael had intended crossing the open garth to the precentor's workshop, to sit down comfortably with Anselm for a quarter of an hour, until the Vesper bell, and talk and perhaps argue about music. But the memory of the dumb youth, so kindly sent out to his brief pleasure in the orchard among his peers, stirred in him as he entered the cloister, and the gaunt visage of Brother Humilis rose before him, self-contained, uncomplaining, proudly solitary. Or should it be, rather, humbly solitary? That was the quality he had claimed for himself and by which he desired to be accepted. A large claim, for one so celebrated. There was not a soul within here now who did not know his reputation. If he longed to escape it, and be as mute as his servitor, he had been cruelly thwarted.

Cadfael veered from his intent, and turned instead along the north walk of the cloister, where the carrels

39

of the scriptorium basked in the sun, even at this hour. Humilis had been given a study midway, where the light would fall earliest and linger longest. It was quiet there, the soft tones of Anselm's organetto seemed very distant and hushed. The grass of the open garth was blanched and dry, in spite of daily watering.

'Brother Humilis. . . .' said Cadfael softly, at the opening of the carrel.

The leaf of parchment was pushed askew on the desk, a small pot of gold had spilled drops along the paving as it rolled. Brother Humilis lay forward over his desk with his right arm flung up to hold by the wood, and his left hand gripped hard into his groin, the wrist braced to press hard into his side. His head lay with the left cheek on his work, smeared with the blue and the scarlet, and his eyes were shut, but clenched shut, upon the controlled awareness of pain. He had not uttered a sound. If he had, those close by would have heard him. What he had, he had contained. So he would still.

Cadfael took him gently about the body, pinning the sustaining arm where it rested. The blue-veined eyelids lifted in their high vaults, and eyes brilliant and intelligent behind their veils of pain peered up into his face. 'Brother Cadfael . . . ?'

'Lie still a moment yet,' said Cadfael. 'I'll fetch Edmund – Brother Infirmarer. . . .'

'No! Brother, get me hence . . . to my bed . . . This will pass . . . it is not new. Only softly, softly help me away! I would not be a show. . . .'

It was quicker and more private to help him up the night stairs from the church to his own cell in the dortoir, rather than across the great court to the infirmary, and that was what he earnestly desired, that there might be no general alarm and fuss about him. He rose more by strength of will than any physical force, and with Cadfael's sturdy arm about him, and his own arm leaning heavily round Cadfael's shoulders, they passed unnoticed into the cool gloom of the church and slowly climbed the staircase. Stretched on his own bed, Humilis submitted himself with a bleakly patient smile to Cadfael's care, and made no ado when Cadfael stripped him of his habit, and uncovered the oblique stain of mingled blood and pus that slanted across the left hip of his linen drawers and down into the groin.

'It breaks,' said the calm thread of a voice from the pillow. 'Now and then it suppurates – I know. The long ride . . . Pardon brother! I know the stench offends. . . .'

'I must bring Edmund,' said Cadfael, unloosing the drawstring and freeing the shirt. He did not yet uncover what lay beneath. 'Brother Infirmarer must know.'

'Yes . . . But no other! What need for more?'

'Except Brother Fidelis? Does he know all?'

'Yes, all!' said Humilis, and faintly and fondly smiled. 'We need not fear him, even if he could speak he would not, but there's nothing of what ails me he does not know. Let him rest until Vespers is over.'

Cadfael left him lying with closed eyes, a little eased, for the lines of his face had relaxed from their tight grimace of pain, and went down to find Brother Edmund, just in time to draw him away from Vespers. The filled baskets of plums lay by the garden hedge, awaiting disposal after the office, and the gatherers were surely already within the

41

church, after hasty ablutions. Just as well! Brother Fidelis might at first be disposed to resent any other undertaking the care of his master. Let him find him recovered and well doctored, and he would accept what had been done. As good a way to his confidence as any.

'I knew we should be needed before long,' said Edmund, leading the way vigorously up the day stairs. 'Old wounds, you think? Your skills will avail more than mine, you have ploughed that field yourself.'

The bell had fallen silent. They heard the first notes of the evening office raised faintly from within the church as they entered the sick man's cell. He opened slow, heavy lids and smiled at them.

'Brothers, I grieve to be a trouble to you . . .'

The deep eyes were hooded again, but he was aware of all, and submitted meekly to all.

They drew down the linen that hid him from the waist, and uncovered the ruin of his body. A great misshapen map of scar tissue stretched from the left hip, where the bone had survived by miracle, slantwise across his belly and deep, deep into the groin. Its colouration was of limestone pallor and striation below, where he was half disembowelled but stonily healed. But towards the upper part it was reddened and empurpled, the inflamed belly burst into a wet-lipped wound that oozed a foul jelly and a faint smear of blood.

Godfrid Marsecot's crusade had left him maimed beyond repair, yet not beyond survival. The faceless, fingerless lepers who crawl into Saint Giles, thought Cadfael, have not worse to bear. Here ends his line, in a noble plant incapable of seed. But what worth is manhood, if this is not a man?

Chapter Three

DMUND RAN for soft cloths and warm water, Cadfael for draughts and oint- ments and decoctions from his workshop. Tomorrow he would pick the fresh, juicy water betony, and wintergreen and woundwort, more effective than the creams and waxes he made from them to keep in store. But for tonight these must do. Sanicle, ragwort, moneywort, adder's tongue, all cleansing and astringent, good for old, ulcerated wounds, were all to be found around the hedgerows and the meadows close by, and along the banks of the Meole Brook.

They cleaned the broken wound of its exudations with a lotion of woundwort and sanicle, and dressed it with a paste of the same herbs with betony and the chickweed wintergreen, covered it with clean linen, and swathed the patient's wasted trunk with bandages to keep the dressing in place. Cadfael had brought also a draught to soothe the pain, a syrup of woundwort and Saint John's wort in wine, with a little of the poppy syrup added. Brother Humilis lay passive under their hands, and let them do with him what they would.

'Tomorrow,' said Cadfael, 'I'll gather the same

43

herbs fresh, and bruise them for a green plaster, it works more strongly, it will draw out the evil. This has happened many times since you got the injury?'

'Not many times. But if I'm overworn, yes – it happens,' said the bluish lips, without complaint.

'Then you must not be allowed to overwear. But it has also healed before, and will again. This woundwort got its name by good right. Be ruled now, and lie still here for two days, or three, until it closes clean, for if you stand and go it will be longer in healing.'

'He should by rights be in the infirmary,' said Edmund anxiously, 'where he could be undisturbed as long as is needful.'

'So he should,' agreed Cadfael, 'but that he's now well bedded here, and the less he stirs the better. How do you feel yourself now, Brother?'

'At ease,' said Brother Humilis, and faintly smiled.

'In less pain?'

'Scarcely any. Vespers will be over,' said the faint voice, and the high-arched lids rolled back from fixed eyes. 'Don't let Fidelis fret for me . . . He has seen worse – let him come.'

'I'll fetch him to you,' said Cadfael, and went at once to do it, for in this concession to the stoic mind there was more value than in anything further he could do here for the ravaged body. Brother Edmund followed him down the stair, anxious at his shoulder.

'Will it heal? Marvel he ever lived for it to heal at all. Did you ever see a man so torn apart, and live?'

'It happens,' said Cadfael, 'though seldom. Yes, it will close again. And open again at the least strain.' Not a word was said between them to enjoin or promise secrecy. The covering Godfrid Marescot

44

had chosen for his ruin was sacred, and would be respected.

Fidelis was standing in the archway of the cloister, watching the brothers as they emerged, and looking with increasing concern for one who did not come.

Late from the orchard, the fruit-gatherers had been in haste for the evening office, and he had not looked then for Humilis, supposing him to be already in the church. But he was looking for him now. The straight, strong brows were drawn together, the long lips taut in anxiety. Cadfael approached him as the last of the brothers passed by, and the young man was turning to watch them go, almost in disbelief.

'Fidelis. . . .' The boy's cowled head swung round to him in quick hope and understanding. It was not good news he was expecting, but any was better than none. It was to be seen in the set of his face. He had experienced all this more than once before.

'Fidelis, Brother Humilis is in his own bed in the dortoir. No call for alarm now, he's resting, his trouble is tended. He's asking for you. Go to him.'

The boy looked quickly from Cadfael to Edmund, and back again, uncertain where authority lay, and already braced to go striding away. If he could ask nothing with his tongue, his eyes were eloquent enough, and Edmund understood them.

'He's easy, and he'll mend. You may go and come as you will in his service, and I will see that you are excused other duties until we're satisfied he does well, and can be left. I will make that good with Prior Robert. Fetch, carry, ask, according to need – if he has a wish, write it and it shall be fulfilled. But as for his dressings, Brother Cadfael will attend to them.'

There was yet a question, more truly a demand,

45

in the ardent eyes. Cadfael answered it in quick reassurance. 'No one else has been witness. No one else need be, but for Father Abbot, who has a right to know what ails all his sons. You may be content with that as Brother Humilis is content.'

Fidelis flushed and brightened for an instant, bowed his head, made that small open gesture of his hands in submission and acceptance, and went from them swift and silent, to climb the day stairs. How many times had he done quiet service at the same sick-bed, alone and unaided? For if he had not grudged them being the first on the scene this time, he had surely lamented it, and been uncertain at first of their discretion.

'I'll go back before Compline,' said Cadfael 'and see if he sleeps, or if he needs another draught. And whether the young one has remembered to take food for himself as well as for Humilis! Now I wonder where that boy can have learned his medicine, if he's been caring for Brother Humilis alone, down there in Hyde?' It was plain the responsibility had not daunted him, nor could he have failed in his endeavours. To have kept any life at all in that valiant wreck was achievement enough.

If the boy had studied in the art of healing, he might make a good assistant in the herbarium, and would be glad to learn more. It would be something in common, a way in through the sealed door of his silence.

Brother Fidelis fetched and carried, fed, washed, shaved his patient, tended to all his bodily needs, apparently in perfect content so to serve day and night, if Humilis had not ordered him away sometimes into the open air, or to rest in his own cell,

46

or to attend the offices of the church on behalf of both of them; as within two days of slow recovery Humilis increasingly did order, and was obeyed. The broken wound was healing, its lips no longer wet and limp, but drawing together gradually under the plasters of freshly-bruised leaves. Fidelis witnessed the slow improvement, and was glad and grateful, and assisted without revulsion as the dressings were changed. This maimed body was no secret from him.

A favoured family servant? A natural son, as Edmund had hazarded? Or simply a devout young brother of the Order who had fallen under the spell of a charm and nobility all the more irresistible because it was dying? Cadfael could not choose but speculate. The young can be wildly generous, giving away their years and their youth for love, without thought of any gain.

'You wonder about him,' said Humilis from his pillow, when Cadfael was changing his dressing in the early morning, and Fidelis had been sent down with the brothers to Prime.

'Yes,' said Cadfael honestly.

'But you don't ask. Neither have I asked anything. My future,' said Humilis reflectively, 'I left in Palestine. What remained of me I gave to God, and I trust the offering was not all worthless. My novitiate, clipped though it was because of my state, was barely ending when he entered Hyde. I have had good cause to thank God for him.'

'No easy matter,' said Cadfael, musing, 'for a dumb man to vouch for himself and make known his vocation. Had he some elder to speak for him?'

'He had written his plea, how his father was old, and would be glad to see his sons settled,

47

and while his elder brother had the lands, he, the younger, wished to choose the cloister. He brought an endowment with him, but it was his fine hand and his scholarship chiefly commended him. I know no more of him,' said Humilis, 'except what I have learned from him in silence, and that is enough, To me he has been all the sons I shall never father.'

'I have wondered,' said Cadfael, drawing the clean linen carefully over the newly-knit wound, 'about his dumbness. Is it possible that it stems only from some malformation in the tongue? For plainly he is not deaf, to blot out speech from his knowledge. He hears keenly. I have usually found the two go together, but not in him. He learns by ear, and is quick to learn. He was taught, as you say, a fine hand. If I had him with me always among the herbs I could teach him all the years have taught me.'

'I ask no questions of him, he asks none of me,' said Humilis. 'God knows I ought to send him away from me, to a better service than nursing and comforting my too early corruption. He's young, he should be in the sun. But I am too craven to do it. If he goes, I will not hold him, but I have not the courage to dismiss him. And while he stays, I never cease to thank God for him.'

August pursued its unshadowed course, without a cloud, and the harvest filled the barns. Brother Rhun missed his new companion from the gardens and the garth, where the roses burst open daily in the noon and faded by night from the heat. The grapes trained along the north wall of the enclosed garden swelled and changed colour. And far south, in ravaged Winchester, the queen's army closed round the sometime besiegers, severed the roads by

48

which supplies might come in, and began to starve the town. But news from the south was sparse, and travellers few, and here the unbiddable fruit was ripening early.

Of all the cheerful workers in that harvest, Rhun was the blithest. Less than three months ago he had been lame and in pain, now he went in joyous vigour, and could not have enough of his own happy body, or put it to sufficient labours to testify to his gratitude. He had no learning as yet, to admit him to the work of copying or study or colouring of manuscripts, he had a pleasant voice but little musical training; the tasks that fell to him were the unskilled and strenuous, and he delighted in them. There was no one who could fail to reflect the same delight in watching him stretch and lift and stride, dig and hew and carry, he who had lately dragged his own light weight along with crippled effort and constant pain. His elders beheld his beauty and vigour with fond admiration, and gave thanks to the saint who had healed him.

Beauty is a perilous gift, but Rhun had never given a thought to his own face, and would have been astonished to be told that he possessed so rare an endowment. Youth is no less vulnerable, by the very quality it has of making the heart ache that beholds and has lost it.

Brother Urien had lost more than his youth, and had not lost his youth long enough to have grown resigned to its passing. He was thirty-seven years old, and had come into the cloister barely a year past, after a ruinous marriage that had left him contorted in mind and spirit. The woman had wrung and left him, and he was not a mild man, but of strong and passionate appetites and imperious will. Desperation had driven him in to the cloister, and there he

49

found no remedy. Deprivation and rage bite just as deeply within as without.

They were working side by side over the first summer apples, at the end of August, up in the dimness of the loft over the barn, laying out the fruit in wooden trays to keep as long as it would. The hot weather had brought on the ripening by at least ten days. The light in there was faintly golden, and heady with motes of dust, they moved as through a shimmering mist. Rhun's flaxen head, as yet unshorn, might have been a fair girl's, the curve of his cheek as he stooped over the shelves was suave as a rose-leaf, and the curling lashes that shadowed his eyes were long and lustrous. Brother Urien watched him sidewise, and his heart turned in him, shrunken and wrung with pain.

Rhun had been thinking of Fidelis, how he would have enjoyed the expedition to the Gaye, and he noticed nothing amiss when his neighbour's hand brushed his as they laid out the apples, or their shoulders touched briefly by chance. But it was not by chance when the outstretched hand, instead of brushing and removing, slid long fingers over his hand and held it, stroking from fingertips to wrist, and there lingering in a palpable caress.

By all the symbols of his innocence he should not have understood, not yet, not until much more had passed. But he did understand. His very candour and purity made him wise. He did not snatch his hand away, but withdrew it very gently and kindly, and turned his fair head to look Urien full in the face with wide, wide-set eyes of the clearest blue-grey, with such comprehension and pity that the wound burned unbearably deep, corrosive with rage and shame. Urien took his hand away and turned aside from him.

50

Revulsion and shock might have left a morsel of hope that one emotion could yet, with care, be changed gradually into another, since at least he would have known he had made a sharp impression. But this open-eyed understanding and pity repelled him beyond hope. How dared a green, simple virgin, who had never become aware of his body but through his lameness and physical pain, recognise the fire when it scorched him, and respond only with compassion? No fear, no blame, and no uncertainty. Nor would he complain to confessor or superior. Brother Urien went away with grief and desire burning in his bowels, and the remembered face of the woman clear and cruel before his mind's eyes. Prayer was no cure for the memory of her.

Rhun brought away from that encounter, only a moment long and accomplished in silence, his first awareness of the tyranny of the body. Troubles from which he was secure could torture another man. His heart ached a little for Brother Urien, he would mention him in his prayers at Vespers. And so he did, and as Urien beheld still his lost wife's hostile visage, so did Rhun continue to see the dark, tense, handsome face that had winced away from his gaze with burning brow and hooded eyes, bitterly shamed where he, Rhun, had felt no blame, and no bitterness. This was indeed a dark and secret matter.

He said no word to anyone about what had happened. What had happened? Nothing! But he looked at his fellow men with changed eyes, by one dimension enlarged to take in their distresses and open his own being to their needs.

This happened to Rhun two days before he was finally acknowledged as firm in his vocation, and received the tonsure, to become the novice, Brother Rhun.

'So our little saint has made good his resolve,' said Hugh, encountering Cadfael as he came from the ceremony. 'And his cure shows no faltering! I tell you honestly, I go in awe of him. Do you think Winifred had an eye to his comeliness, when she chose to take him for her own? Welshwomen don't baulk their fancy when they see a beautiful youth.'

'You are an unregenerate heathen,' said Cadfael comfortably, 'but the lady should be used to you by now. Never think you'll shock her, there's nothing she has not seen in her time. And had I been in her reliquary I would have drawn that child to me, just as she did. She knew worth when she saw it. Why, he has almost sweetened even Brother Jerome!'

'That will never last!' said Hugh, and laughed. 'He's kept his own name – the boy?'

'It never entered his mind to change it.'

'They do not all so,' said Hugh, growing serious. 'This pair that came from Hyde – Humilis and Fidelis. They made large claims, did they not? Brother Humble we know by his former name, and he needs no other. What do we know of Brother Faithful? And I wonder which name came first?'

'The boy is a younger son,' said Cadfael. 'His elder has the lands, this one chose the cowl. With his burden, who could blame him? Humilis says his own novitiate was not yet completed when the young one came, and they drew together and became fast friends. They may well have been admitted together, and the names . . . Who knows which of them chose first?'

They had halted before the gatehouse to look

back at the church. Rhun and Fidelis had come forth together, two notably comely creatures with matched steps, not touching, but close and content. Rhun was talking with animation. Fidelis bore the traces of much watching and anxiety, but shone with a responsive glow. Rhun's new tonsure was bared to the sun, the fair hair round it roused like an aureole.

'He frequents them,' said Cadfael, watching. 'No marvel, he reaches out to every soul who has lost a piece of his being, such as a voice.' He said nothing of what the elder of that pair had lost. 'He talks for both. A pity he has small learning yet. There's neither of those two can read to Humilis, the one for want of a voice, the other for want of letters. But he studies, and he'll learn. Brother Paul thinks well of him.'

The two young men had vanished at the archway of the day stairs, plainly bound for the dortoir cell where Brother Humilis was still confined to his bed. Who would not be heartened by the vision of Brother Rhun just radiant from his admission to his heart's desire? And it was fitting, that reticent kinship between two barren bodies, the one virgin unawakened, the other hollowed out and despoiled in its prime. Two whose seed was not of this world.

It was that same afternoon that a young man in a soldier's serviceable riding gear, with rolled cloak at his saddle-bow, came in towards the town by the main London road to Saint Giles, and there asked directions to the abbey of Saint Peter and Saint Paul. He went bare-headed in the sun, and in his shirt-sleeves, with breast bared, and face and breast and naked forearms were brown as from a

53

hotter sun even than here, where the summer did but paint a further copper shade on a hide already gilded. A neatly-made young man, on a good horse, with an easy seat in the saddle and a light hand on the rein, and a bush of wiry dark hair above a bold, blunt-featured face.

Brother Oswin directed him, and with pricking curiosity watched him ride on, wondering for whom he would enquire there. Evidently a fighting man, but from which army, and from whose household troops, to be heading for Shrewsbury abbey so particularly? He had not asked for town or sheriff. His business was not concerned with the warfare in the south. Oswin went back to his work with mild regret at knowing no more, but dutifully.

The rider, assured that he was near his goal, eased to a walk along the Foregate, looking with interest at all he saw, the blanched grass of the horse-fair ground, still thirsty for rain, the leisurely traffic of porter and cart and pony in the street, the gossiping neighbours out at their gates in the sun, the high, long wall of the abbey enclave on his left hand, and the lofty roof and tower of the church looming over it. Now he knew that he was arriving. He rounded the west end of the church, with its great door ajar outside the enclosure for parish use, and turned in under the arch of the gatehouse.

The porter came amiably to greet him and ask his business. Brother Cadfael and Hugh Beringar, still at their leisurely leave-taking close by, turned to examine the newcomer, noted his business-like and well-used harness and leathern coat slung behind, and the sword he wore, and had him accurately docketed in a moment. Hugh stiffened, attentive, for a man in soldier's gear heading in from the south

54

might well have news. Moreover, one who came alone and at ease here through these shires loyal to King Stephen was likely to be of the same complexion. Hugh went forward to join the colloquy, eyeing the horseman up and down with restrained approval of his appearance.

'You're not, by chance, seeking me, friend? Hugh Beringar, at your service.'

'This is the lord sheriff,' said Brother Porter by way of introduction; and to Hugh: 'The traveller is asking for Brother Humilis – though by his former name.'

'I was some years in the service of Godfrid Marescot,' said the horseman, and slid his reins loose and lighted down to stand beside them. He was taller than Hugh by half a head, and strongly made, and his brown countenance was open and cheerful, lit by strikingly blue eyes. 'I've been hunting for him among the brothers dispersed in Winchester after Hyde burned to the ground. They told me he'd chosen to come here. I have some business in the north of the shire, and need his approval for what I intend. To tell the truth,' he said with a wry smile, 'I had clean forgotten the name he took when he entered Hyde. To me he's still my lord Godfrid.'

'So he must be to many,' said Hugh, 'who knew him aforetime. Yes, he's here. Are you from Winchester now?'

'From Andover. Where we've burned the town,' said the young man bluntly, and studied Hugh as attentively as he himself was being studied. It was plain they were of the same party.

'You're with the queen's army?'

'I am. Under FitzRobert.'

55

'Then you'll have cut the roads to the north. I hold this shire for King Stephen, as you must know. I would not keep you from your lord, but will you ride with me into Shrewsbury and sup at my house before you move on? I'll wait your convenience. You can give me what I'm hungry for, news of what goes forward there in the south. May I know your name? I've given you mine.'

'My name is Nicholas Harnage. And very heartily I'll tell you all I know, my lord, when I've done my errand here. How is it with Godfrid?' he asked earnestly, and looked from Hugh to Cadfael, who stood by watching, listening, and until now silent.

'Not in the best of health,' said Cadfael, 'but neither was he, I suppose, when you last parted from him. He has broken an old wound, but that came, I think, after his long ride here. It is mending well now, in a day or two he'll be up and back to the duties he's chosen. He is well loved, and well tended by a young brother who came here with him from Hyde, and had been his attendant there. If you'll wait but a moment I'll tell Father Prior that Brother Humilis has a visitor, and bring you to him.'

That errand he did very briskly, to leave the pair of them together for a few minutes. Hugh needed tidings, all the firsthand knowledge he could get from that distant and confused battlefield, where two factions of his enemies, by their mutual clawings, had now drawn in the whole formidable array of his friends upon one side. A shifty side at best, seeing the bishop had changed his allegiance now for the third time. But at least it held the empress's forces in a steel girdle now in the city of Winchester, and was tightening the girdle to starve them out. Cadfael's warrior blood, long since abjured, had a way of coming to the boil when he heard steel in the offing. His chief uneasiness was that he could not be truly penitent about it. His king was not of this world, but in this world he could not help having a preference.

Prior Robert was taking his afternoon rest, which was known to others as his hour of study and prayer. A good time, since he was not disposed to rouse himself and come out to view the visitor, or exert himself to be ceremoniously hospitable. Cadfael got what he had counted on, a gracious permission to conduct the guest to Brother Humilis in his cell, and attend him to provide whatever assistance he might require. In addition, of course, to Father Prior's greetings and blessing, sent from his daily retreat into meditation.

They had had time to grow familiar and animated while he had been absent, he saw it in their faces, and the easy turn of both heads, hearing his returning step. They would ride together into the town already more than comrades in arms, potential friends.

'Come with me,' said Cadfael, 'and I'll bring you to Brother Humilis.'

On the day stairs the young, earnest voice at his shoulder said quietly: 'Brother, you have been doctoring my lord since this fit came on. So the lord sheriff told me. He says you have great skills in herbs and medicine and healing.'

'The lord sheriff,' said Cadfael, 'is my good friend for some years, and thinks better of me than I deserve. But, yes, I do tend your lord, and thus far we two do well together. You need not fear he is not valued truly, we do know his worth. See him, and judge for yourself. For you must know what he suffered in the east. You were with him there?'

57

'Yes. I'm from his own lands, I sailed when he sent for a fresh force, and shipped some elders and wounded for home. And I came back with him, when he knew his usefulness there was ended.'

'Here,' said Cadfael, with his foot on the top stair, 'his usefulness is far from ended. There are young men here who live the brighter by his light – under the light by which we all live, that's understood. You may find two of them with him now. If one of them lingers, let him, he has the right. That's his companion from Hyde.'

They emerged into the corridor that ran the whole length of the dortoir, between the partitioned cells, and stood at the opening of the dim, narrow space allotted to Humilis.

'Go in,' said Cadfael. 'You do not need a herald to be welcome.'

Chapter Four

N THE cell the little lamp for reading was
not lighted, since one of the young attendants could not read, and the other could
not speak, while the incumbent himself
still lay propped up with pillows in his cot, too weak
to nurse a heavy book. But if Rhun could not read
well, he could learn by heart, and recite what he had
learned with feeling and warmth, and he was in the
middle of a prayer of Saint Augustine which Brother
Paul had taught him, when he felt suddenly that he
had an audience larger than he had bargained for,
and faltered and fell silent, turning towards the open
end of the cell.

Nicholas Harnage stood hesitant within the doorway, until his eyes grew accustomed to the dim light.
Brother Humilis had opened his eyes in wonder
when Rhun faltered. He beheld the best-loved and
most trusted of his former squires standing almost
timorously at the foot of his bed.

'Nicholas?' he ventured, doubtful and wondering,
heaving himself up to stare more intently.

Brother Fidelis stooped at once to prop and raise
him, and brace the pillows at his back, and then as
silently withdrew into the dark corner of the cell, to

59

leave the field to the visitor.

'Nicholas! It *is* you!'

The young man went forward and fell on his knee to clasp and kiss the thin hand stretched out to him.

'Nicholas, what are you doing here? You're welcome as the morning, but I never looked to see you in this place. It was kind indeed to seek me out in such a distant refuge. Come, sit by me here. Let me see you close!'

Rhun had slipped away silently. From the doorway he made a small reverence before he vanished. Fidelis took a step to follow him, but Humilis laid a hand on his arm to detain him.

'No, stay! Don't leave us! Nicholas, to this young brother I owe more than I can ever repay. He serves me as truly in this field as you did in arms.'

'All who have been your men, like me, will be grateful to him,' said Nicholas fervently, looking up into a face shadowed by the cowl, and as featureless as voiceless in this half-darkness. If he wondered at getting no answer, but only an inclination of the head by way of acknowledgement, he shrugged it off without another thought, for it was of no importance that he should reach a closer acquaintance with one he might never see again. He drew the stool close to the bedside, and sat studying the emaciated face of his lord with deep concern.

'They tell me you are mending well. But I see you leaner and more fallen than when I left you, that time in Hyde, and went to do your errand. I had a long search in Winchester to find your prior, and enquire of him where you were gone. Need you have chosen to ride so far? The bishop would have taken you into the Old Minster, and been glad of you.'

'I doubt if I should have been so glad of the

bishop,' said Brother Humilis with a wry smile. 'No, I had my reasons for coming so far north. This shire and this town I knew as a child. A few years only, but they are the years a man remembers later in life. Never trouble for me, Nick, I'm very well here, as well as any other place, and better than most. Let us speak rather of you. How have you fared in your new service, and what has brought you here to my bedside?'

'I've thrived, having your commendation. William of Ypres has mentioned me to the queen, and would have taken me among his officers, but I'd rather stay with FitzRobert's English than go to the Flemings. I have a command. It was you who taught me all I know,' he said, at once glowing and sad, 'you and the mussulmen of Mosul.'

'It was not the Atabeg Zenghi,' said Brother Humilis smiling, 'whose affairs sent you here so far to seek me out. Leave him to the King of Jerusalem, whose noble and perilous business he is. What of Winchester, since I fled from it?'

'The queen's armies have encircled it. Few men get out, and no food gets in. The empress's men are shut tight in their castle, and their stores must be running very low. We came north to straddle the road by Andover. As yet nothing moves, therefore I got leave to ride north on my own business. But they must attempt to break out soon, or starve where they are.'

'They'll try to reopen one of the roads and bring in supplies, before they abandon Winchester altogether,' said Humilis, frowning thoughtfully over the possibilities. 'If and when they do break, they'll break for Oxford first. Well, if this stalemate has sent you here to me, one good thing has come of it. And what is this business that brought you to Shrewsbury?'

'My lord,' began Nicholas, leaning forward very earnestly, 'you remember how you sent me here to the manor of Lai, three years ago, to take the word to Humphrey Cruce and his daughter that you could not keep your compact to marry her? – that you were entering the cloister at Hyde Mead?'

'It is not a thing to forget,' agreed Humilis drily.

'My lord, neither can I forget the girl! You never saw her but as a child five years old, before you went to the Crusade. But I saw her a grown lady, nearly nineteen. I did your message to her father and to her, and came away glad to have it delivered and done. But now I cannot get her out of my mind. Such grace she had, and bore the severance with such dignity and courtesy. My lord, if she is still not wed or betrothed, I want to speak for her myself. But I could not go without first asking your blessing and consent.'

'Son,' said Humilis, glowing with astonished pleasure, 'there's nothing could delight me more than to see her happy with you, since I had to fail her. The girl is free to marry whom she will, and I could wish her no better man than you. And if you succeed I shall be relieved of all my guilt towards her, for I shall know she has made a better bargain than ever I should have been to her. Only consider, boy, we who enter the cloister abjure all possessions, how then can we dare lay claim to rights of possession in another creature of God? Go, and may you get her, and my blessing on you both. But come back and tell me how you fare.'

'My lord, with all my heart! How can I fail, if you send me to her?'

62

He stooped to kiss the hand that held him warmly, and rose blithely from the stool to take his leave. The silent figure in the shadows returned to his consciousness belatedly; it was as if he had been alone with his lord all this time, yet here stood the mute witness. Nicholas turned to him with impulsive warmth.

'Brother, I do thank you for your care of my lord. For this time, farewell. I shall surely see you again on my return.'

It was disconcerting to receive by way of reply only silence, and the courteous inclination of the cowled head.

'Brother Fidelis,' said Humilis gently, 'is dumb. Only his life and works speak for him. But I dare swear his good will goes with you on this quest, like mine.'

There was silence in the cell when the last crisp, light echo had died away on the day stairs. Brother Humilis lay still thinking, it seemed, tranquil and contented thoughts, for he was smiling.

'There are parts of myself I have never given to you,' he said at last, 'things that happened before ever I knew you. There is nothing of myself I would not wish to share with you. Poor girl! What had she to hope for from me, so much her elder, even before I was broken? And I never saw her but once, a little lass with brown hair and a solemn round face. I never felt the want of a wife or children until I was thirty years old, having an elder brother to carry on my father's line after the old man died. I took the Cross, and was fitting out a company to go with me to the east, free as air, when my brother also died, and I was left to balance my vow to God and my duty to my house. I owed it to God to do as I had sworn, and go for ten years to the Holy Land, but also I owed it to my house to marry and breed sons. So I looked for a sturdy, suitable little girl who could well wait all those years for mè, and still have all her child-bearing time in its fullness when I returned. Barely six years old she was – Julian Cruce, from a family with manors in the north of this shire, and in Stafford, too.'

He stirred and sighed for the follies of men, and the presumptuous solemnity of the arrangements they made for lives they would never live. The presence beside him drew near, put back the cowl, and sat down on the stool Nicholas had vacated. They looked each other in the eyes gravely and without words, longer than most men can look each other in the eyes and not turn aside.

'God knew better, my son!' said Humilis. 'His plans for me were not as mine. I am what I am now. She is what she is. Julian Cruce . . . . I am glad she should escape me and go to a better man. I pray she has not yet given herself to any, for this Nicholas of mine would make her a fitting match, one that would set my soul at rest. Only to her do I feel myself a debtor, and forsworn.'

Brother Fidelis shook his head at him, reproachfully smiling, and leaned and laid a finger for an instant over the mouth that spoke heresy.

Cadfael had left Hugh waiting at the gatehouse, and was crossing the court to return to his duties in the herb-garden, when Nicholas Harnage emerged from the arch of the stairway, and recognising him, hailed him loudly and ran to pluck him urgently by the sleeve.

64

'Brother, a word!'

Cadfael halted and turned to face him. 'How do you find him? The long ride put him to too great a strain, and he did not seek help until his wound was broken and festering, but that's over now. All's clean, wholesome and healing. You need not fear we shall let him founder like that a second time.'

'I believe it, Brother,'said the young man earnestly. 'But I see him now for the first time after three years, and much fallen even from the man he was after he got his injuries. I knew they were grave, the doctors had him in care between life and death a long time, but when he came back to us at least he looked like the man we knew and followed. He made his plans then to come home, I know, but he had served already more years than he had promised, it was time to attend to his lands and his life here at home. I made that voyage with him, he bore it well. Now he has lost flesh, and there's a languor about him when he moves a hand. Tell me the truth of it, how bad is it with him?'

'Where did he ever get such crippling wounds?' asked Cadfael, considering scrupulously how much he could tell, and guessing at how much this boy already knew, or at least hazarded.

'In that last battle with Zenghi and the men of Mosul. He had Syrian doctors after the battle.'

That might very well be why he survived so terrible a maiming, thought Cadfael, who had learned much of his own craft from both Saracen and Syrian physicians. Aloud he asked cautiously: 'You have not seen his wounds? You don't know their whole import?'

Surprisingly, the seasoned crusader was struck silent for a moment, and a slow wave of blood crept

65

up under his golden tan, but he did not lower his eyes, very wide and direct eyes of a profound blue. 'I never saw his body, no more than when I helped him into his harness. But I could not choose but understand what I can't claim I know. It could not be otherwise, or he would never have abandoned the girl he was betrothed to. Why should he do so? A man of his word! He had nothing left to give her but a position and a parcel of dower lands. He chose rather to give her her freedom, and the residue of himself to God.'

'There was a girl?' said Cadfael.

'There *is* a girl. And I am on my way to her now,' said Nicholas, as defiantly as if his right had been challenged. 'I carried the word to her and her father that he was gone into the monastery at Hyde Mead. Now I am going to Lai to ask for her hand myself, and he has given me his consent and blessing. She was a small child when she was affianced to him, she has never seen him since. There is no reason she should not listen to my suit, and none that her kin should reject me.'

'None in the world!' agreed Cadfael heartily. 'Had I a daughter in such case, I would be glad to see the squire follow in his lord's steps. And if you must report to her of his well-being, you may say with truth that he is doing what he wishes, and enjoys content of mind. And for his body, it is cared for as well as may be. We shall not let him want for anything that can give him aid or comfort.'

'But that does not answer what I need to know,' insisted the young man. 'I have promised to come back and tell him how I've fared. Three or four days, no longer, perhaps not so long. But shall I still find him then?'

'Son,' said Cadfael patiently, 'which of us can answer that for himself or any other man? You want truth, and you deserve it. Yes, Brother Humilis is dying. He got his death-wound long ago in that last battle. Whatever has been done for him, whatever can be done, is staving off an ending. But death is not in such a hurry with him as you fear, and he is in no fear of it. You go and find your girl and bring him back good news, and he'll be here to be glad of it.'

'And so he will,' said Cadfael to Edmund, as they took the air in the garden together before Compline that evening, 'if that young fellow is brisk about his courting, and I fancy he's the kind to go straight for what he wants. But how much longer we can hold our ground with Humilis I dare not guess. This fashion of collapse we can prevent, but the old harm will devour him in the end. As he knows better than any.'

'I marvel how he lived at all,' agreed Edmund, 'let alone bore the journey home, and has survived three years or more since.'

They were private together down by the banks of the Meole Brook, or they could not have discussed the matter at all. No doubt by this hour Nicholas Harnage was well on his way to the north-east of the county, if he had not already arrived at his destination. Good weather for riding, he would be in shelter at Lai before dark. And a very well-set-up young fellow like Harnage, in a thriving way in arms by his own efforts, was not an offer to be sneezed at. He had the blessing of his lord, and needed nothing more but the girl's liking, her family's approval, and the sanction of the church.

'I have heard it argued,' said Brother Edmund,

67

'that when an affianced man enters a monastic order, the betrothed lady is not necessarily free of the compact. But it seems a selfish and greedy thing to try to have both worlds, choose the life you want, but prevent the lady from doing likewise. But I think the question seldom arises but where the man cannot bear to loose his hold of what once he called his, and himself fights to keep her in chains. And here that is not so, Brother Humilis is glad there should be so happy a solution. Though of course she may be married already.'

'The manor of Lai,' mused Cadfael. 'What do you know of it, Edmund? What family would that be?'

'Cruce had it. Humphrey Cruce, if I remember rightly, he might well be the girl's father. They hold several manors up there, Ightfeld, and Harpecote – and Prees, from the Bishop of Chester. Some lands in Staffordshire, too. They made Lai the head of their honour.'

'That's where he's bound. Now if he comes back in triumph,' said Cadfael contentedly, 'he'll have done a good day's work for Humilis. He's already given him a great heave upward by showing his honest brown face, but if he settles the girl's future for her he may have added a year or more to his lord's life, at the same time.'

They went to Compline at the first sound of the bell. The visitor had indeed given Humilis a heft forward towards health, it seemed, for here he came, habited and erect on Fidelis's arm, having asked no permission of his doctors, bent on observing the night office with the rest. But I'll hound him back as soon as the observance is over, thought Cadfael, concerned for his dressing. Let him brandish his banner this once, it speaks well for his spirit, even if his

68

flesh is drawn with effort. And who am I to say what a brother, my equal, may or may not do for his own salvation?

The evenings were already beginning to draw in, the height of the summer was over while its heat continued as if it would never break. In the dimness of the choir what light remained was coloured like irises, and faintly fragrant with the warm, heady scents of harvest and fruit. In this stall the tall, handsome, emaciated man who was old in his middle forties stood proudly, Fidelis on his left hand, and next to Fidelis, Rhun. Their youth and beauty seemed to gather to itself what light there was, so that they shone with a native radiance of their own, like lighted candles.

Across the choir from them Brother Urien stood, kneeled, genuflected and sang, with the full, assured voice of maturity, and never took his eyes from those two young, shining heads, the flaxen and the brown. Day by day those two drew steadily together, the mute one and the eloquent one, matched unfairly, unjustly, to his absolute exclusion, the one as desirable and as inviolable as the other, while his need burned in his bowels day and night, and prayer could not cool it, nor music lull it to sleep, but it ate him from within like the gnawing of wolves.

They had both begun – dreadful sign! – to look to him like the woman. When he gazed at either of these two, the boy's lineaments would dissolve and change subtly, and there would be her face, not recognising, not despising, simply staring through him to behold someone else. His heart ached beyond bearing, while he sang mellifluously in the Compline psalm.

*

69

In the twilight of the softer, more open country in the north-east of the shire, where day lingered longer than among the folded hills of the western border, Nicholas Harnage rode between flat, rich fields, unwontedly dried by the heat, into the wattled enclosure of the manor of Lai. Wrapped round on all sides by the enlarged fields of the plain, sparsely tree'd to make way for wide cultivation, the house rose long and low, a stone-built hall and chambers over a broad undercroft, with stables and barns about the interior of the fence. Fat country, good for grain and for roots, with ample grazing for any amount of cattle. The byres were vocal as Nicholas entered at the gate, the mild, contented lowing of well-fed beasts, milked and drowsy.

A groom heard the entering hooves and came forth from the stables, bared to the waist in the warm night. Seeing one young horseman alone, he was quite easy. They had had comparative peace here while Winchester burned and bled.

'Seeking whom, young sir?'

'Seeking the master, your lord, Humphrey Cruce,' said Nicholas, reining in peaceably and shaking the reins free. 'If he still keeps house here?'

'Why, the lord Humphrey's dead, sir, three years ago. His son Reginald is lord here now. Would your errand do as well to him?'

'If he'll admit me, yes, surely to him, then,' said Nicholas, and dismounted. 'Let him know, I was here some three years ago, to speak for Godfrid Marescot. It was his father I saw then, but the son will know of it.'

'Come within,' said the groom placidly, accepting the credentials without question. 'I'll have your beast seen to.'

In the smoky, wood-scented hall they were at meat, or still sitting at ease after the meal was done, but they had heard his step on the stone stairs that led to the open hall door, and Reginald Cruce rose, alert and curious, as the visitor entered. A big, black-haired man of austere features and imperious manner, but well-disposed, it seemed, towards chance travellers. His lady sat aloof and quiet, a pale-haired woman in green, with a boy of about fifteen at her side, and a younger boy and girl about nine or ten, who by their likeness might well be twins. Evidently Reginald Cruce had secured his succession with a well-filled quiver, for by the lady's swelling waist when she rose to muster the hospitality of the house, there was another sibling on the way.

Nicholas made his reverence and offered his name, a little confounded at finding Julian Cruce's brother a man surely turned forty, with a wife and growing children, where he had assumed a young fellow in his twenties, perhaps newly-married since inheriting. But he recalled that Humphrey Cruce had been an old man to have a daughter still so young. Two marriages, surely, the first blessed with an heir, the second undertaken late, when Reginald was a grown man, ready for marriage himself, or even married already to his pale, prolific wife.

'Ah, that!' said Reginald of his guest's former errand to this same house. 'I remember it, though I was not here then. My wife brought me a manor in Staffordshire, we were living there. But I know how it fell out, of course. A strange business altogether. But it happens! Men change their minds. And you were the messenger? Well, but leave it now and take some refreshment. Come to table! There'll be time to talk of all such business afterwards.'

71

He sat down and kept his visitor company while a servant brought meat and ale, and the lady, having made her grave good night, drove her younger children away to their beds, and the heir sat solemn and silent studying his elders. At last, in the deepening evening, the two men were left alone to their talk.

'So you are the squire who brought that word from Marescot. You'll have noticed there's a generation, as near as need be, between my sister and me – seventeen years. My mother died when I was nine years old, and it was another eight before my father married again. An old man's folly, she brought him nothing, and died when the girl was born, so he had little joy of her.'

At least, thought Nicholas, studying his host dispassionately, there was no second son, to threaten a division of the lands. That would be a source of satisfaction to this man, he was authentically of his class and kind, and land was his lifeblood.

'He may well have had great joy of his daughter, however,' he said firmly, 'for she is a very gracious and beautiful girl, as I well recall.'

'You'll be better informed of that than I,' said Reginald drily, 'if you saw her only three years ago. It must be eighteen or more since I set eyes on her. She was a stumbling infant then, two years old, or three, it might be. I married about that time, and settled on the lands Cecilia brought me. We exchanged couriers now and then, but I never came back here until my father was on his death-bed, and they sent for me to come to him.'

'I didn't know of his death when I set out to come here on this errand of my own,' said Nicholas. 'I heard it only from your groom at the gate. But I

72

may speak as freely with you as I should have done with him. I was so much taken with your sister's grace and dignity that I've thought of her ever since, and I've spoken with my lord Godfrid, and have his full consent to what I'm asking. As for myself,' he thrust on, leaning eagerly across the board, 'I am heir to two good manors from my father, and shall have some lands also after my mother, I stand well in the queen's armies and my lord will speak for me, that I'm in earnest in this matter, and will provide for Julian as truly as any man could, if you will . . .'

His host was gazing, astonished, smiling at his fervour, and had raised a warning hand to still the flood.

'Did you come all this way to ask me to give you my sister?'

'I did! Is that so strange? I admired her, and I'm come to speak for her. And she might have worse offers,' he added, flushing and stiffening at such a reception.

'I don't doubt it, but, man, man, you should have put in a word to give her due warning then. You come three years too late!'

'Too late?' Nicholas sat back and drew in his hands slowly, stricken. 'Then she's already married?'

'You might call it so!' Reginald hoisted wide shoulders in a helpless gesture. 'But not to any man. And you might have sped well enough if you'd made more haste, for all I know. No, this is quite a different story. There was some discussion, even, about whether she was still bound like a wife to Marescot – a great foolery, but the churchmen have to assert their authority, and my father's chaplain was prim as a virgin – thought I suspect, for all that, in private he was none! – and clutched at every point of canon law

73

that gave him power, and he took the extreme line, and would have it she was legally a wife, while the parish priest argued the opposing way, and my father, being a sensible man, took his side and insisted she was free. All this I learned by stages since. I never took part or put my head into the hornets' nest.'

Nicholas was frowning into his cupped hands, feeling the cold heaviness of disappointment drag his heart down. But still this was not a complete answer. He looked up ruefully. 'So how did this end? Why is she not here to use her freedom, if she has not yet given herself to a husband?'

'Ah, but she has! She took her own way. She said that if she was free, then she would make her own choice. And she chose to do as Marescot had done, and took a husband not of this world. She has taken the veil as a Benedictine nun.'

'And they let her?' demanded Nicholas, wrung between rage and pain. 'Then, when she was moved by this broken match, they let her go so easily, throw away her youth so unwisely?'

'They let her, yes. How do I know whether she was wise or no? If it was what she wished, why should she not have it? Since she went I've never had word from her, never has she complained or asked for anything. She must be happy in her choice. You must look elsewhere for a wife, my friend!'

Nicholas sat silent for a time, swallowing a bitterness that burned in his belly like fire. Then he asked, with careful quietness: 'How was it? When did she leave her home? How attended?'

'Very soon after your visit, I judge. It might be a month while they fought out the issue, and she said never a word. But all was done properly. Our father gave her an escort of three men-at-arms and a huntsman who had always been a favourite and made a pet of her, and a good dowry in money, and also some ornaments for her convent, silver candlesticks and a crucifix and such. He was sad to see her go, I know by what he said later, but she wanted it so, and her wants were his commands always.' A very slight chill in his brisk, decisive voice spoke of an old jealousy. The child of Humphrey's age had plainly usurped his whole heart, even though his son would inherit all when that heart no longer beat. 'He lived barely a month longer,' said Reginald. 'Only long enough to see the return of her escort, and know she was safely delivered where she wished to be. He was old and feeble, we knew it. But he should not have dwindled so soon.'

'He might well miss her,' said Nicholas, very low and hesitantly, 'about the place. She had a brightness . . . And you did not send for her, when her father died?'

'To what end? What could she do for him, or he for her? No, we let her be. If she was happy there, why trouble her?'

Nicholas gripped his hands together under the board, and wrung them hard, and asked his last question: 'Where was it she chose to go?' His own voice sounded to him hollow and distant.

'She's in the Benedictine abbey of Wherwell, close by Andover.'

So that was the end of it! All this time she had been within hail of him, the house of her refuge encircled now by armies and factions and contention. If only he had spoken out what he felt in his heart at the first sight of her, even hampered as he had been by the knowledge of the blow he was about to deal her, and gagged by that knowledge when for once he might have been eloquent. She might have listened, and at least delayed, even if she could feel nothing for him then. She might have thought again, and waited, and even remembered him. Now it was far too late, she was a bride for the second time, and even more indissolubly.

This time there was no question of argument. The betrothal vows made by or for a small girl might justifiably be dissolved, but the vocational vows of a grown woman, taken in the full knowledge of their meaning, and of her own choice, never could be undone. He had lost her.

Nicholas lay all night in the small guest-chamber prepared for him, fretting at the knot and knowing he could not untie it. He slept shallowly and uneasily, and in the morning he took his leave, and set out on the road back to Shrewsbury.

Chapter Five

T SO happened that Brother Cadfael was
private with Humilis in his cell in the
dortoir when Nicholas again rode in at
the gatehouse and asked leave to visit
his former lord, as he had promised. Humilis had
risen with the rest that morning, attended Prime
and Mass, and scrupulously performed all the duties
of the horarium, though he was not yet allowed to
exert himself by any form of labour. Fidelis attended
him everywhere, ready to support his steps if need
arose, or fetch him whatever he might want, and
had spent the afternoon completing, under his elder's approving eye, the initial letter which had been
smeared and blotted by his fall. And there they had
left the boy to finish the careful elaboration in gold,
while they repaired to the dortoir, physician and patient together.

'Well closed,' said Cadfael, content with his work,
'and firming up nicely, clean as ever. You scarcely
need the bandages, but as well keep them a day or
two yet, to guard against rubbing while the new skin
is still frail.'

They were grown quite easy together, these two,
and if both of them realised that the mere healing of

77

a broken and festered wound was no sufficient cure for what ailed Humilis, they were both courteously silent on the subject, and took their moderate pleasure in what good they had achieved.

They heard the footsteps on the stone treads of the day stairs, and knew them for booted feet, not sandalled. But there was no spring in the steps now, and no hasty eagerness, and it was a glum young man who appeared, shadowy, in the doorway of the cell. Nor had he been in any hurry on the way back from Lai, since he had nothing but disappointment to report. But he had promised, and he was here.

'Nick!' Humilis greeted him with evident pleasure and affection. 'You're soon back! Welcome as the day, but I had thought . . .' There he stopped, even in the dim interior light aware that the brightness was gone from the young man's face. 'So long a visage? I see it did not go as you would have wished.'

'No, my lord.' Nicholas came in slowly, and bent his knee to both his elders. 'I have not sped.'

'I am sorry for it, but no man can always succeed. You know Brother Cadfael? I owe the best of care to him.'

'We spoke together the last time,' said Nicholas, and found a half-hearted smile by way of acknowledgement. 'I count myself also in his debt.'

'Spoke of me, no doubt,' said Humilis, smiling and sighing. 'You trouble too much for me, I am well content here. I have found my way. Now sit down a while, and tell us what went wrong for you.'

Nicholas plumped himself down on the stool beside the bed on which Humilis was sitting, and said what he had to say in commendably few words: 'I hesitated three years too long. Barely a month after you took the cowl at Hyde, Julian Cruce took the veil at Wherwell.'

'Did she so!' said Humilis on a long breath, and sat silent to take in all that this news could mean. 'Now I wonder . . . No, why should she do such a thing unless it was truly her wish? It cannot have been because of me! No, she knew nothing of me, she had only once seen me, and must have forgotten me before my back was turned. She may even have been glad . . . It may be this is what she always wished, if she could have her way. . . .' He thought for a moment, frowning, perhaps trying to recall what that little girl looked like. 'You told me, Nick, that I do remember, how she took my message. She was not distressed, but altogether calm and courteous, and gave me her grace and pardon freely. You said so!'

'Truth, my lord,' said Nicholas earnestly, 'though she cannot have been glad.'

'Ah, but she may – she may very well have been glad. No blame to her! Willing though she may have been to accept the match made for her, yet it would have tied her to a man more than twenty years her elder, and a stranger. Why should she not be glad, when I offered her her liberty – no, urged it upon her? Surely she must have made of it the use she preferred, perhaps had longed for.'

'She was not forced,' Nicholas admitted, with somewhat reluctant certainty. 'Her brother says it was the girl's own choice, indeed her father was against it, and only gave in because she would have it so.'

'That's well,' agreed Humilis with a relieved sigh. 'Then we can but hope that she may be happy in her choice.'

79

'But so great a waste!' blurted Nicholas, grieving. 'If you had seen her, my lord, as I did! To shear such hair as she had, and hide such a form under the black habit! They should never have let her go, not so soon. How if she has regretted it long since?'

Humilis smiled, but very gently, eyeing the downcast face and hooded eyes. 'As you described her to me, so gracious and sensible, of such measured and considered speech, I don't think she will have acted without due thought. No, surely she has done what is right for her. But I'm sorry for your loss, Nick. You must bear it as gallantly as she did – if ever I was any loss!'

The Vesper bell had begun to chime. Humilis rose to go down to the church, and Nicholas rose with him, taking the summons as his dismissal.

'It's late to set out now,' suggested Cadfael, emerging from the silence and withdrawal he had observed while these two talked together. 'And it seems there's no great haste, that you need leave tonight. A bed in the guest-hall, and you could set off fresh in the morning, with the whole day before you. And spend an hour or two more with Brother Humilis this evening while you have the chance.'

To which sensible notion they both said yes, and Nicholas recovered a little of his spirits, if nothing could restore the ardour with which he had ridden north from Winchester.

What did somewhat surprise Brother Cadfael was the considerate way in which Fidelis, confronted yet again with this visitant from the time before he had known Humilis and established his own intimacy with him, withdrew himself from sight as he was withdrawn from the possibility of conversation, and left them to their shared memories of travel, Crusade and battle, things so far removed from his own experience. An affection which could so self-effacingly make room for a rival and prior affection was generous indeed.

There was a merchant of Shrewsbury who dealt in fleeces all up and down the borders, both from Wales and from such fat sheep-country as the Cotswolds, and had done an interesting side-trade in information, for Hugh's benefit, in these contrary times. His active usefulness was naturally confined to this period of high summer when the wool clip was up for sale, and many dealers had restricted their movements in these dangerous times, but he was a determined man, intrepid enough to venture well south down the border, towards territory held by the empress. His suppliers had sold to him for some years, and had sufficient confidence in him to hold their clip until he made contact. He had good trading relations as far afield as Bruges in Flanders, and was not at all averse to a large risk when calculating on a still larger profit. Moreover, he took his own risks, rather than delegating these unchancy journeys to his underlings. Possibly he even relished the challenge, for he was a stubborn and stalwart man.

Now, in early September, he was on his way home with his purchases, a train of three wagons following from Buckingham, which was as near as he could reasonably go to Oxford. For Oxford had become as alert and nervous as a town itself under siege, every day expecting that the empress must be forced by starvation to retreat from Winchester. The merchant had left his men secure on a road relatively peaceful, to bring up his wagons at leisure, and himself rode

ahead at good speed with his news to report to Hugh
Beringar in Shrewsbury, even before he went home
to his wife and family.

'My lord, things move at last. I had it from a man
who saw the end of it, and made good haste away
to a safer place. You know how they were walled
up there in their castles in Winchester, the bishop
and the empress, with the queen's armies closing all
round the city and sealing off the roads. No supplies
have gone in through that girdle for four weeks now,
and they say there's starvation in the town, though
I doubt if either empress or bishop is going short.'
He was a man who spoke his mind, and no great
respecter of high personages. 'A very different tale
for the poor townsfolk! But it's biting even the garrison within there at the royal castle, for the queen has
been supplying Wolvesey while she starves out the
opposing side. Well, they came to the point where
they must try to win a way through.'

'I've been expecting it,' said Hugh, intent. 'What
did they hit on? They could only hope to move north
or west, the queen holds all the south-east.'

'They sent out a force, three or four hundred as
I heard it, northwards, to seize on the town of
Wherwell, and try to secure a base there to open
the Andover road. Whether they were seen on the
move, or whether some townsman betrayed them
– for they're not loved in Winchester – however it
was, William of Ypres and the queen's men closed
in on them when they'd barely reached the edge of
the town, and cut them to pieces. A great killing! The
fellow who told me fled when the houses started to
burn, but he saw the remnant of the empress's men
put up a desperate fight of it and reach the great
nunnery there. And they never scrupled to use it,

either, he says. They swarmed into the church itself and turned it into a fortress, although the poor sisters had shut themselves in there for safety. The Flemings threw in firebrands after them. A hellish business it must have been. He could hear from far off as he ran, he said, the women screaming, the flames crackling and the din of fighting within there, until those who remained were forced to come out and surrender, half-scorched as they were. Not a man can have escaped either death or capture.'

'And the women?' demanded Hugh aghast. 'Do you tell me the abbey of Wherwell is burned down, like the convent in the city, like Hyde Mead after it?'

'My man never dallied to see how much was left,' said the messenger drily. 'But certainly the church burned down to the ground, with both men and women in it – the sisters cannot all have come out alive. And as for those who did, God alone knows where they will have found refuge now. Safe places are hard to find in those parts. And for the empress's garrison, I'd say there's no hope for them now but to muster every man they have, and try to burst out by force of numbers through the ring, and run for it. And poor chance for them, even so.'

A poor chance indeed, after this last loss of three or four hundred fighting men, probably hand-picked for the exploit, which must have been a desperate gamble from the first. The year only at early September, and the fortunes of war had changed and changed again, from the disastrous battle of Lincoln which had made the king prisoner and brought the empress within grasp of the crown itself, to this stranglehold drawn round the same proud lady now. Now only give us the empress herself prisoner, thought Hugh, and we shall have stalemate, recover each our sovereign, and begin this whole struggle all over again, for what sense there is in it! And at the cost of the brothers of Hyde Mead and the nuns of Wherwell. Among many others even more defenceless, like the poor of Winchester.

The name of Wherwell, as yet, meant no more to him than any other convent unlucky enough to fall into the field of battle.

'A good year for me, all the same,' said the woolmerchant, rising to make his way home to his own waiting board and bed. 'The clip measures up well, it was worth the journey.'

Hugh took the latest news down to the abbey next morning, immediately after Prime, for whatever of import came to his ears was at once conveyed to Abbot Radulfus, a service the abbot appreciated and reciprocated. The clerical and secular authorities worked well together in Shropshire, and moreover, in this case a Benedictine house had been desecrated and destroyed, and those of the Rule stood together, and helped one another where they could. Even in more peaceful times, nunneries were apt to have much narrower lands and more restricted resources than the houses of the monks, and often had to depend upon brotherly alms, even under good, shrewd government. Now here was total devastation. Bishops and abbots would be called upon to give aid.

He had come from his colloquy with Radulfus in the abbot's parlour with half an hour still before High Mass and, choosing to stay for the celebration since he was here, he did what he habitually did with time to spare within the precinct of the abbey and went looking for Brother Cadfael in his workshop in the herb-garden.

Cadfael had been up since long before Prime, inspected such wines and distillations as he had working, and done a little watering while the soil was in shade and cooled from the night. At this time of year, with the harvest in, there was little work to be done among the herbs, and he had no need as yet to ask for an assistant in place of Brother Oswin.

When Hugh came to look for Cadfael he found him sitting at ease on the bench under the north wall, which at this time of day was pleasantly warm without being too hot, contemplating between admiration and regret the roses that bloomed with such extravagant splendour and wilted so soon. Hugh sat down beside him, rightly interpreting placid silence as welcome.

'Aline says it's high time you came to see how your godson has grown.'

'I know well enough how much he will have grown,' said Giles Beringar's godfather, between complacency and awe of his formidable responsibility. 'Not two years old until Christmas, and too heavy already for an old man.'

Hugh made a derisive noise. When Cadfael claimed to be an old man he must either be up to something, or inclined to be idle, and giving fair warning.

'Every time he sees me he climbs me like a tree,' said Cadfael dreamily. 'You he daren't treat so, you are but a sapling. Give him fifteen more years, and he'll make two of you.'

'So he will,' agreed the fond father, and stretched his lithe, light body pleasurably in the strengthening sun. 'A long lad from birth – do you remember? That was a Christmas indeed, what with my son – and yours . . . I wonder where Olivier is now? Do you know?'

'How should I know? With d'Angers in Gloucester, I hope. She can't have drawn them all into Winchester with her, she must leave force enough in the west to hold on to her base there. Why, what made you think of him just now?'

'It did enter my head that he might have been among the empress's chosen at Wherwell.' He had recoiled into grim recollection, and did not at first notice how Cadfael stiffened and turned to stare. 'I pray you're right, and he's well out of it.'

'At Wherwell? Why, what of Wherwell?'

'I forgot,' said Hugh, startled, 'you don't yet know the latest news, for I've only just brought it within here, and I got it only last night. Did I not say they'd have to try to break out – the empress's men? They have tried it, Cadfael, disastrously for them. They sent a picked force to try to seize Wherwell, no doubt hoping to straddle the road and the river there, and open a way to bring in supplies. William of Ypres cut them to pieces outside the town, and the remnant fled into the nunnery and shut themselves into the church. The place burned down over them . . . God forgive them for ever violating it, but they were Maud's men who first did it, not ours. The nuns, God help them, had taken refuge there when the fight began. . . .'

Cadfael sat frozen even in the sunlight. 'Do you tell me Wherwell has gone the way of Hyde?'

'Burned to the ground. The church at least. As for the rest . . . But in so hot and dry a season. . . .'

86

Cadfael, who had gripped him hard and suddenly by the arm, as abruptly loosed him, leaped from the bench, and began to run, veritably to run, as he had not done since hurtling to get out of range from the rogue castle on Titterstone Clee, two years earlier. He had still a very respectable turn of speed when roused, but his gait was wonderful, legless under the habit, like a black ball rolling, with a slight oscillation from side to side, a seaman's walk become a headlong run. And Hugh, who loved him, and rose to pursue him with a very sharp sense of the urgency behind this flight, nevertheless could not help laughing as he ran. Viewed from behind, a Benedictine in a hurry, and a Benedictine of more than sixty years and built like a barrel, at that, may be formidably impressive to one who knows him, but must be comic.

Cadfael's purposeful flight checked in relief as he emerged into the great court; for they were there still, in no haste with their farewells, though the horse stood by with a groom at his bridle, and Brother Fidelis tightening the straps that held Nicholas Harnage's bundle and rolled cloak behind the saddle. They knew nothing yet of any need for haste. There was a whole sunlit day before the rider.

Fidelis wore the cowl always outdoors, as though to cover a personal shyness that stemmed, surely, from his mute tongue. He who would not open his mind to others shrank from claiming any privileged advance from them. Only Humilis had some manner of silent and eloquent speech with him that needed no voice. Having secured the saddle-roll the young man stepped back modestly to a little distance, and waited.

Cadfael arrived more circumspectly than he had set out from the garden. Hugh had not followed him so closely, but halted in shadow by the wall of the guest-hall.

'There's news,' said Cadfael bluntly. 'You should hear it before you leave us. The empress has made an attack on the town of Wherwell, a disastrous attack. Her force is wiped out by the queen's army. But in the fighting the abbey of Wherwell was fired, the church burned to the ground. I know no more detail, but so much is certain. The sheriff here got the word last night.'

'By a reliable man,' said Hugh, drawing close. 'It's certain.'

Nicholas stood staring, eyes and mouth wide, his golden sunburn dulling to an earthen grey as the blood drained from beneath it. He got out in a creaking whisper: 'Wherwell? They've dared . . .?'

'No daring,' said Hugh ruefully, 'but plain terror. They were men penned in, the raiding party, they sought any place of hiding they could find, surely, and slammed to the door. But the end was the same, whoever tossed in the firebrands. The abbey's laid waste. Sorry I am to say it.'

'And the women . . .? Oh, God . . . Julian's there . . . Is there any word of the women?'

'They'd taken to the church for sanctuary,' said Hugh. In such civil warfare there were no sanctuaries, not even for women and children. 'The remnant of the raiders surrendered – most may have come out alive. All, I doubt.'

Nicholas turned blindly to grope for his bridle, plucking his sleeve out of the quivering hand Humilis had laid on his arm. 'Let me away! I must go . . . I must go there and find her.' He swung back to catch again briefly at the older man's hand and wring it hard. 'I *will* find her! If she lives I'll find her, and see her safe.' He found his stirrup and heaved himself into the saddle.

'If God's with you, send me word,' said Humilis. 'Let me know that she lives and is safe.'

'I will, my lord, surely I will.'

'Don't trouble her, don't speak to her of me. No questions! All I need, all you must ask, is to know that God has preserved her, and that she has the life she wanted. There'll be a place elsewhere for her, with other sisters. If only she still lives!'

Nicholas nodded mutely, shook himself out of his daze with a great heave, wheeled his horse, and was gone, out through the gatehouse without another word or a look behind. They were left gazing after him, as the light dust of his passing shimmered and settled under the arch of the gate, where the cobbles ended, and the beaten earth of the Foregate began.

All that day Humilis seemed to Cadfael to press his own powers to the limit, as though the stress that drove Nicholas headlong south took its toll here in enforced stillness and inaction, where the heart would rather have been riding with the boy, at whatever cost. And all that day Fidelis, turning his back even on Rhun, shadowed Humilis with a special and grievous solicitude, tenderness and anxiety, as though he had just realised that death stood no great distance away, and advanced one gentle step with every hour that passed.

Humilis went to his bed immediately after Compline, and Cadfael, looking in on him ten minutes later, found him already asleep, and left him undisturbed accordingly. It was not a festering wound and a maimed body that troubled Humilis now, but an obscure feeling of guilt towards the girl who might, had he married her, have been safe in some manor far remote from Winchester and Wherwell and the clash of arms, instead of driven by fire and slaughter even out of her chosen cloister. Sleep could do more for his grieving mind than the changing of a dressing could do now for his body. Sleeping, he had the hieratic calm of a figure already carved on a tomb. He was at peace. Cadfael went quietly away and left him, as Fidelis must have left him, to rest the better alone.

In the sweet-scented twilight Cadfael went to pay his usual nightly visit to his workshop, to make sure all was well there, and stir a brew he had standing to cool overnight. Sometimes, when the nights were so fresh after the heat of the day, the skies so full of stars and so infinitely lofty, and every flower and leaf suddenly so imbued with its own lambent colour and light in despite of the light's departure, he felt it to be a great waste of the gifts of God to be going to bed and shutting his eyes to them. There had been illicit nights of venturing abroad in the past – he trusted for good enough reasons, but did not probe too deeply. Hugh had had his part in them, too. Ah, well!

Making his way back with some reluctance, he went in by the church to the night stairs. All the shapes within the vast stone ship showed dimly by the small altar lamps. Cadfael never passed through without stepping for a moment into the choir, to cast a glance and a thought towards Saint Winifred's altar, in affectionate remembrance of their first encounter, and gratitude for her forbearance. He did so now, and checked abruptly before venturing nearer. For there was one of the brothers kneeling at the foot of the altar, and the tiny red glow of the lamp showed him the uplifted face, fast-closed eyes and prayerfully folded hands of Fidelis. Showed him no less clearly, as he drew softly nearer, the tears glittering on the young man's cheeks. A perfectly still face, but for the mute lips moving soundlessly on his prayers, and the tears welling slowly from beneath his closed eyelids and spilling on to his breast. The shocks of the day might well send him here, now his charge was sleeping, to put up fervent prayers for a better ending to the story. But why should his face seem rather that of a penitent than an innocent appellant? And a penitent unsure of absolution!

Cadfael slipped away very quietly to the night stairs and left the boy the entire sheltering space of the church for his inexplicable pain.

The other figure, motionless in the darkest corner of the choir, did not stir until Cadfael had departed, and even then waited long moments before stealing forward by inches, with held breath, over the chilly paving.

A naked foot touched the hem of Fidelis's habit, and as hastily and delicately drew back again from the contact. A hand was outstretched to hover over the oblivious head, longing to touch and yet not daring until the continued silence and stillness gave it courage. Tensed fingers sank into the curling russet that ringed the tonsure, the light touch set the hand quivering, like the pricking of imminent lightning in the air before a storm. If Fidelis also sensed it, he gave no sign. Even when the fingers stirred lovingly in his hair, and stroked down into the

91

nape of his neck within the cowl he did not move but rather froze where he kneeled, and held his breath.

'Fidelis,' whispered a hushed and aching voice close at his shoulder. 'Brother, never grieve alone! Turn to me . . . I could comfort you, for everything, everything . . . whatever your need. . . .'

The stroking palm circled his neck, but before it reached his cheek Fidelis had started to his feet in one smooth movement, resolute and unalarmed, and swung out of reach. Without haste, or perhaps unwilling to show his face, even by this dim light, until he had mastered it, he turned to look upon the intruder into his solitude, for whispers have no identity, and he had never before taken any particular notice of Brother Urien. He did so now, with wide and wary grey eyes. A dark, passionate, handsome man, one who should never have shut himself in within these walls, one who burned, and might burn others before ever he grew cool at last. He stared back at Fidelis, and his face was wrung and his outstretched hand quaked, yearning towards Fidelis's sleeve, which was withdrawn from his austerely before he could grasp it.

'I've watched you,' breathed the husky, whispering voice, 'I know every motion and grace. Waste, waste of youth, waste of beauty . . . Don't go! No one sees us now. . . .'

Fidelis turned his back steadily, and walked out from the choir towards the night stairs. Silent on the tiled floor, Urien's naked feet followed him, the tormented whisper followed him.

'Why turn your back on loving kindness? You will not always do so. Think of me! I will wait. . . .'

Fidelis began to climb the stairs. The pursuer

halted at the foot, too sick with anguish to go where other men might still be wakeful. 'Unkind, unkind . . .' wailed the faintest thread of a voice, receding, and then, with barely audible but extreme bitterness: 'If not here, in another place . . . If not now, at another time!'

Chapter Six

NICHOLAS COMMANDEERED a change of horses twice on the away south, leaving those he had ridden hard to await the early return he foresaw, with the news he had promised to carry faithfully, whether good or bad. The stench of burning, old and acrid now, met him on the wind some miles from Wherwell, and when he entered what was left of the small town it was to find an almost de-peopled desolation. The few whose houses had survived unlooted and almost undamaged were sorting through their premises and salvaging their goods, but those who had lost their dwellings in the fire held off cautiously as yet from coming back to rebuild. For though the raiding party from Winchester had been either wiped out or made prisoner, and William of Ypres had withdrawn the queen's Flemings to their old positions ringing the city and the region, this place was still within the circle, and might yet be subjected to more violence.

Nicholas made his way with a cramped and anxious heart to the enclave of the nunnery, one of the three greatest in the shire, until this disaster fell upon its buildings and laid the half of them flat and the rest uninhabitable. The shell of the church stood up gaunt and blackened against the cloudless sky, the walls jagged and discoloured like decayed teeth. There were new graves in the nuns' cemetery. As for the survivors, they were gone, there was no home for them here. He looked at the newly-turned earth with a sick heart, and wondered whose daughters lay beneath. There had not yet been time to do more for them than bury them, they were nameless.

He would not let himself even consider that she might be there. He looked for the parish church and sought out the priest, who had gathered two homeless families beneath his roof and in his barn. A careworn, tired man, growing old, in a shabby gown that needed mending.

'The nuns?' he said, stepping out from his low, dark doorway. 'They're scattered, poor souls, we hardly know where. Three of them died in the fire. Three that we know of, but there may well be more, lying under the rubble there still. There was fighting all about the court and the Flemings were dragging their prisoners out of the church, but neither side cared for the women. Some are fled into Winchester, they say, though there's little safety to be found there, but the lord bishop must try to do something for them, their house was allied to the Old Minster. Others . . . I don't know! I hear the abbess is fled to a manor near Reading, where she has kin, and some she may have taken with her. But all's confusion – who can tell?'

'Where is this manor?' demanded Nicholas feverishly, and was met by a weary shake of the head.

'It was only a thing I heard – no one said where. It may not even be true.'

'And you do not know, Father, the names of those sisters who died?' He trembled as he asked it.

95

'Son,' said the priest with infinite resignation, 'what we found could not have a name. And we have yet to seek there for others, when we have found enough food to keep those alive who still live. The empress's men looted our houses first, and after them the Flemings. Those who have, here, must share with those who have nothing. And which of us has very much? God knows not I!'

Nor had he, in material things, only in tired but obstinate compassion. Nicholas had bread and meat in his saddle-bag, brought for provision on the road from his last halt to change horses. He hunted it out and put it into the old man's hands, a meagre drop in a hungry ocean, but the money in his purse could buy nothing here where there was nothing to buy. They would have to milk the countryside to feed their people. He left them to their stubborn labours, and rode slowly though the rubble of Wherwell, asking here and there if anyone had more precise information to impart. Everyone knew the sisters had dispersed, no one could say where. As for one woman's name, it meant nothing, it might not even be the name by which she had entered on her vows. Nevertheless, he continued to utter it wherever he enquired, doggedly proclaiming the irreplaceable uniqueness of Julian Cruce, separate from all other women.

From Wherwell he rode on into Winchester. A soldier of the queen could pass through the iron ring without difficulty, and in the city it was plain that the empress's faction were hard-pressed, and dared not venture far from their tight fortress in the castle. But the nuns of Winchester, themselves earlier endangered and now breathing more easily, could tell him nothing of Julian Cruce. Some sisters from Wherwell they had taken in and cherished, but she was not among them. Nicholas had speech with one of their elder members, who was kind and solicitous, but could not help him.

'Sir, it is a name I do not know. But consider, there is no reason I should know it, for surely this lady may have taken a very different name when she took her vows, and we do not ask our sisters where they came from, nor who they once were, unless they choose to tell us freely. And I had no office that should bring me knowledge of these things. Our abbess would certainly be able to answer you, but we do not know where she is now. Our prioress, also. We are as lost as you. But God will find us, and bring us together again. As he will find for you the one you seek.'

She was a shrewd, agile, withered woman, thin as a gnat but indestructible as scutch grass. She eyed him with mildly amused sympathy, and asked blandly: 'She is kin to you, this Julian?'

'No,' said Nicholas shortly, 'but I would have had her kin, and very close kin, too.'

'And now?'

'I want to know her safe, living, content. There is no more in it. If she is so, God keep her so, and I am satisfied.'

'If I were you,' said the lady, after viewing him closely for some moments in silence, 'I should go on to Romsey. It is far enough removed to be a safer place than here, and it is the greatest of our Benedictine houses in these parts. God knows which of our sisters you may find there, but surely some, and it may be, the highest.'

He was young enough and innocent enough still, for all his travels, to be strongly moved by any evidence of trust and kindness, and he caught and kissed her hand in taking leave, as though she had been his hostess somewhere in hall. She, for her part, was too old and experienced to blush or bridle, but when he was gone she sat smiling a long, quiet while, before she rejoined her sisters. He was a very personable young man.

Nicholas rode the twelve miles or so to Romsey in sobering solemnity, aware he might be drawing near to an answer possibly not to his liking. Once clear of Winchester and on his way further south-west, he was delivered from any threat, for he went through country where the queen's writ ran without challenge. Pleasant, rolling country, well tree'd even before he reached the fringes of the great forest. He came to the abbey gatehouse, in the heart of the small town, in the late evening, and rang the bell at the gate. The portress peered at him through the grille, and asked his business. He stooped entreatingly to the grid, and gazed into a pair of bright, elderly eyes in beds of wrinkles.

'Sister, have you given refuge here to some of the nuns of Wherwell? I am seeking for news of one of them, and could get no answers there.'

The portress eyed him narrowly, and saw a young face soiled and drawn with travel, a young man alone, and in dead earnest, no threat. Even here in Romsey they had learned to be cautious about opening their gates, but the road beyond him was empty and still, and the twilight folded down on the little town peacefully enough.

'The prioress and three sisters reached here,' she said, 'but I doubt if any of them can tell you much of the rest, not yet. But come within, and I'll ask if she will speak with you.'

The wicket clanked open, lock and chain, and he stepped through into the court. 'Who knows?' said the portress kindly, fastening the door again after him. 'One of our three may be the one you're seeking. At least you may try.'

She led him along dim corridors to a small, panelled parlour, lit by a tiny lamp, and there left him. The evening meal would be long over, even Compline past, it was almost time for sleeping. They would want him satisfied, if satisfaction was possible, and out of their precinct before the night.

He could not rest or sit, but was prowling the room like a caged bear when a further door opened, and the prioress Wherwell came quietly in. A short, round, rosy woman, but with a formidably strong face and exceedingly direct brown eyes, that studied her visitor from head to foot in one piercing glance as he made his reverence to her.

'You asked for me, I am told. I am here. How can I help you?'

'Madam,' said Nicholas, trembling for awe of what might come, 'I was well north, in Shropshire, when I heard of the sack of Wherwell. There was a sister there of whose vocation I had only just learned, and now all I want is to know that she lives and is safe after that outrage. Perhaps to speak with her, and see for myself that she is well, if that can be permitted. I did ask in Wherwell itself, but could get no word of her – I know only the name she had in the world.'

The prioress waved him to a seat, and herself sat down apart, where she could watch his face. 'May I know you own name, sir?'

'My name is Nicholas Harnage. I was squire to Godfrid Marescot until he took the cowl in Hyde Mead. He was formerly betrothed to this lady, and he is anxious now to know that she is safe and well.'

She nodded at that very natural desire, but nevertheless her brows had drawn together in a thoughtful and somewhat puzzled frown. 'That name I know, Hyde was proud of having gained him. But I never recall hearing . . . What is the name of this sister you seek?'

'In the world she was Julian Cruce, of a Shropshire family. The sister I spoke with in Wherwell had never heard the name, but it may well be that she chose a very different name when she took the veil. But you will know of her both before and after.'

'Julian Cruce?' she repeated, erect and intent now, her sharp eyes narrowing. 'Young, sir, are you not in some mistake? You are sure it was Wherwell she entered? Not some other house?'

'No, certainly, madam, Wherwell,' he said earnestly. 'I had it from her brother himself, he could not be mistaken.'

There was a moment of taut silence, while she considered and shook her head over him, frowning. 'When was it that she entered the Order? It cannot be long ago.'

'Three years, madam. The date I cannot tell, but it was about a month after my lord took the cowl, and that was in the middle of July.' He was frightened now by the strangeness of her reception. She was shaking her head dubiously, and regarding him with mingled sympathy and bewilderment. 'It may be that this was before you held office. . . .'

'Son,' she said ruefully, 'I have been prioress for more than seven years now, there is not a name among our sisters that I don't know, whether the world's name or the cloistered, not an entry I have not witnessed. And sorry as I am to say it, and little as I myself understand it, I cannot choose but tell you, past any doubt, that no Julian Cruce ever asked for, or received the veil at Wherwell. It is a name I never heard, and belongs to a woman of whom I know nothing.'

He could not believe it. He sat staring and passing a dazed hand once and again over his forehead. 'But . . . this is impossible! She set out from home with an escort, and a dowry intended for her convent. She declared her intent to come to Wherwell, all her household knew it, her father knew it and sanctioned it. About this, I swear to you, madam, there is no possible mistake. She set out to ride to Wherwell.'

'Then,' said the prioress gravely, 'I fear you have questions to ask elsewhere, and very serious questions. For believe me, if you are certain she set out to come to us, I am no less certain that she never reached us.'

'But what could prevent?' he asked urgently, wrenching at impossibilities. 'Between her home and Wherwell . . .'

'Between her home and Wherwell were many miles,' said the prioress. 'And many things can prevent the fulfilment of the plans of men and women in this world. The disorders of war, the accidents of travels, the malice of other men.'

'But she had an escort to bring her to her journey's end!'

'Then it's of them you should be making enquiries,' she said gently, 'for they signally failed to do so.'

No point whatever in pressing her further. He sat stunned into silence, utterly lost. She knew what she was saying, and at least she had pointed him

101

towards the only lead that remained to him. What was the use of hunting any further in these parts, until he had caught at the clue she offered him, and begun to trace that ride of Julian's from Lai, where it had begun. Three men-at-arms, Reginald had said, went with her, under a huntsman who had an affection for her from her childhood. They must still be there in Reginald's service, there to be questioned, there to be made to account for the mission that had never been completed.

The prioress had yet one more point to make, even as she rose to indicate that the interview was over, and the late visitor dismissed.

'She was carrying, you say, the dowry she intended to bring to Wherwell? I know nothing of its value, of course, but . . . The roads are not entirely free of evil customs. . . .'

'She had four men to guard her,' cried Nicholas, one last flare in desperation.

'And they knew what she carried? God knows,' said the prioress, 'I should be loth to cast suspicion on any upright man, but we live in a world, alas, where of any four men, one at least may be corruptible.'

He went away into the town still dazed, unable to think or reason, unable to grasp and understand what with all his heavy heart he believed. It was growing dark, and he was too weary to continue now without sleep, besides the care he must have for his horse. He found an alehouse that could provide him a rough bed, and stabling and fodder for his beast, and lay wakeful a long time before his own exhaustion of body and mind overcame him.

He had an answer, but what to make of it he did not know. Certain it was that she had never passed through the gates of Wherwell, and therefore had not died there in the fire. But – three years, and never a word or a sign! Her brother had not troubled himself with a half-sister he scarcely knew, believing her to be settled in life according to her own choice. And never a word had come from her. Who was there to wonder or question? Cloistered women are secure in their own community, have all their sisterhood about them, what need have they of the world, and what should the world expect from them? Three years of silence from those vowed to the cultivation of silence is natural enough; but three years without a word now became an abyss, into which Julian Cruce had fallen as into the ocean, and sunk without trace.

Now there was nothing to be done but hasten back to Shrewsbury, confess his shattering failure in his mission, and go on to Lai to tell the same dismal story to Reginald Cruce. Only there could he again hope to find a thread to follow. He set off early in the morning to ride back into Winchester.

It was mid-morning when he drew near to the city. He had left it, prudently, not by the direct way through the west gate, since the royal castle with its hostile and by this time surely desperate garrison lay so close and had complete command of the gate. But some time before he reached the spot where he should, in the name of caution, turn eastward from the Romsey road and circle round the south of the city to a safer approach, he began to be aware of a constant chaotic murmur of sound ahead, that grew from a murmur to a throbbing clamour, to a steely din of clashing and screaming that could mean nothing but battle, and a close and tangled and desperate battle at that. It seemed to centre to his left front, at some distance from the town, and the air in that direction hung hazy with the glittering dust of struggle and flight.

Nicholas abandoned all thought of turning aside towards the bishop's hospital of Saint Cross or the east gate, and rode on full tilt towards the west gate. And there before him he saw the townsfolk of Winchester boiling out into the open sunlight with shouting and excitement, and the streets within full of people, loud, exultant and fearless, all clamouring for news or imparting news at the tops of their voices, throwing off all the creeping caution that had fettered them for so long.

Nicholas caught at a tall fellow's shoulder and bellowed his own question: 'What is it? What's happened?'

'They're gone! Marched out at dawn, that woman and her royal uncle of Scotland and all her lords! Little they cared about the likes of us starving, but when the wolf bit them it was another story. Out they went, the lot of them – in good order, *then*! Now hark to them! The Flemings at least let them get clear of the town before they struck, and let us alone. There'll be pickings, over there!'

They were only waiting, these vengeful tradesmen and craftsmen of Winchester, hovering here until the din of battle moved away into the distance. There would be gleanings before the night. No man can ride his fastest loaded down with casque and coat of mail. Even their swords they might discard to lighten the weight their horses had to bear. And if they had retained enough optimism to believe they could convey their valuables away with them, there would be rich pickings indeed before the day was out.

So it had come, the expected attempt to break out of the iron circle of the queen's army, and it had come too late to have any hope of success. After the holocaust of Wherwell even the empress must have known she could hold out here no longer.

North-west along the Stockbridge road and wavering over the rising downs, the glittering halo of dust rolled and danced, spreading wider as it receded. Nicholas set off to follow it, as the boldest of the townsmen, or the greediest, or the most vindictive, were also doing afoot. He had far outridden them, and was alone in the undulating uplands, when he saw the first traces of the assault which had broken the empress's army. A single fallen body, a lamed horse straying, a heavy shield hurled aside, the first of many. A mile further on and the ground was littered with arms, pieces of armour torn off and flung aside in flight, helmets, coats of mail, saddle-bags, spilling garments and coins and ornaments of silver, fine gowns, pieces of plate from noble tables, all expendable where mere life was the one thing to be valued. Not all had preserved it, even at this cost. There were bodies, tossed and trampled among the grasses, frightened horses running in circles, some ridden almost to death and gasping on the ground. Not a battle, but a rout, a headlong flight in contagious terror.

He had halted, staring in sick wonder at such a spectacle, while the flight and pursuit span forward into the distance under its shining cloud, towards the Test at Stockbridge. He did not follow it further, but turned and rode back towards the city, wanting no part in that day's work. On his way he met the first of the gleaners, hungry and eager, gathering the spoils of victory.

*

It was three days later, in the early afternoon, when he rode again into the great court at Shrewsbury abbey, to fulfil the promise he had made. Brother Humilis was in the herb-garden with Cadfael, sitting in the shade while Fidelis chose from among the array of plants a few sprigs and tendrils he wanted for an illuminated border, bryony and centaury and bugloss, and the coiled threads of vetches, infinitely adaptable for framing initial letters. The young man had grown interested in the herbs and their uses, and sometimes helped to make the remedies Cadfael used in the treatment of Humilis, tending them with passionate, still devotion, as though his love could add the final ingredient that would make them sovereign.

The porter, knowing Nicholas well by this time, told him without question where he would find his lord. His horse he left tethered at the gatehouse, intending to ride on at once to Lai, and came striding round the clipped bulk of the tall hedge and along the gravel path to where Humilis was sitting on the stone bench against the south wall. So intent was Nicholas upon Humilis that he brushed past Fidelis with barely a glance, and the young brother, startled by his sudden and silent arrival, turned on him for once a head uncovered and a face open to the sun, but as quickly drew aside in his customary reticent manner, and held aloof from their meeting, deferring to a prior loyalty. He even drew the cowl over his head, and sank silently into its shadow.

'My lord,' said Nicholas, bending his knee to Humilis and clasping the two hands that reached to embrace him, 'your sorry servant!'

'No, never that!' said Humilis warmly, and freed his hands to draw the boy up beside him and peer searchingly into his face. 'Well,' he said with a sigh and a small, rueful smile, 'I see you have not the marks of success on you. No fault of yours, I dare swear, and no man can command success. You would not be back so soon if you had found out nothing, but I see it cannot be what you hoped for. You did not find Julian. At least,' he said, peering a little closer, and in a voice careful and low, 'not living. . . .'

'Neither living nor dead,' said Nicholas quickly, warding off the worst assumption. 'No, it's not what you think – it's not what any of us could have dreamed.' Now that it came to the telling, he could only blurt out the whole of it as baldly and honestly as possible, and be done. 'I searched in Wherwell, and in Winchester, until I found the prioress of Wherwell in refuge in Romsey abbey. She has held the office seven years, she knows every sister who has entered there in that time, and none of them is Julian Cruce. Whatever has become of Julian she never reached Wherwell, never took vows there, never lived there – and cannot have died there. A blind ending!'

'She never came there?' Humilis echoed in an astonished whisper, staring with locked brows across the sunny garden.

'She never did! Always,' said Nicholas bitterly, 'I come three years too late. Three years! And where can she have been all that time, with never a word of her here, where she left home and family, nor there, where she should have come to rest? What can have happened to her, between here and Wherwell? That region was not in turmoil then, the roads should have been safe enough. And there were four men with her, well provided.'

107

'And they came home,' said Humilis keenly. 'Surely they came home, or Cruce would have been wondering and asking long ago. In God's name, what can they have reported when they returned? No evil! None from other men, or there would have been an instant hue and cry, none of there own, or they would not have returned at all. This grows deeper and deeper.'

'I am going on to Lai,' said Nicholas, rising, 'to let Cruce know, and have him hunt out and question those who rode with her. His father's men will be his men now, whether at Lai or on some other of his manors. They can tell us, at least, where they parted from her, if she foolishly dismissed them and rode the last miles alone. I'll not rest until I find her. If she lives, I *will* find her!'

Humilis held him by the sleeve, doubtfully frowning. 'But your command . . . You cannot leave your duties for so long, surely?'

'My command,' said Nicholas, 'can do very well without me now for a while. I've left them snug enough, encamped near Andover, living off the land, and my sergeants in charge, old soldiers well able to fill my place, the way things are now. For I have not told you the half. I'm so full of my own affairs, I have no time for kings. Did we not say, last time, that the empress must try to break out from Winchester soon, or starve where she was? She has so tried. After the disaster at Wherwell they must have known they could not hold out longer. Three days ago they marched out westward, towards Stockbridge, and William de Warenne and the Flemings fell on them and broke them to pieces. It was no retreat, it was headlong flight. Everything weighty about them they threw away. If ever they do come safe back to Gloucester it will be half naked. I'll make a stay in the town and let Hugh Beringar know.'

Brother Cadfael, who had gone on with a little desultory weeding between his herb-beds, at a little distance, nevertheless heard all this with stretched ears and kindling blood, and straightened his back now to stare.

'And she – the empress? They have not taken her?' An empress for a king would be fair exchange, and almost inevitable, even if it meant not an ending, but stalemate, and a new beginning over the same exhausted and exhausting ground. Had Stephen been the one to capture the implacable lady, with his mad, endearing, chivalry he would probably have given her a fresh horse and an escort, and sent her safely to Gloucester, to her own stronghold, but the queen was no such magnanimous idiot, and would make better use of a captive enemy.

'No, not Maud, she's safely away. Her brother sped her off ahead with Brian FitzCount to watch over her, and stayed to rally the rearguard and hold off the pursuit. No, it's better than Maud! He could have gone on fighting without her, but she'll be hard put to it without him. The Flemings caught them at Stockbridge, trying to ford the river, and rounded up all those who survived. It's the king's match we've taken, the man himself, Robert of Gloucester!'

Chapter Seven

EGINALD CRUCE, whether he had, or indeed could well be expected to have any deep affection for a half-sister so many years distant from him and so seldom seen, was not the man to be tolerant of any affront or injury towards any of his house. Whatever touched a Cruce reflected upon him, and roused his hackles like those of a pointing hound. He heard the story out in stoic silence but ever-growing resentment and rage, the more formidable for being under steely control.

'And all this is certain?' he said at length. 'Yes, the woman would know her business, surely. The girl never came there. I was not in this matter at all, I was not here and did not witness either the going or the return, but now we will see! At least I know the names of those who rode with her, for my father spoke of the journey on his death-bed. He sent his closest, men he trusted – who would not, with his daughter? And he doted on her. Wait!'

He bellowed from the hall door for his steward, and in from the fading daylight, cooling now towards dusk, came a grey elder dried and tanned like old leather, but very agile and sinewy. He might have been older than the lord he had lost, and was in no awe of either father or son here, but plainly master of his own duties, and aware of his worth. He spoke as an equal, and easy in the relationship.

'Arnulf, you'll remember,' said Reginald, waving him to a seat at the table with them, as free in acknowledgement of the association as his man, 'when my sister when off to her convent, the lads my father sent off with her – the Saxon brothers, Wulfric and Renfred, and John Bonde, and the other, who was he? He went off with the draft, I know, soon after I came here . . . .'

'Adam Heriet,' said the steward readily, and drew across the board the horn his lord filled for him. 'Yes, what of them?'

'I want them, Arnulf, all of them – here.'

'Now, my lord?' If he was surprised, he took surprises in his stride.

'Now, or as soon as may be. But first, all these were of my father's close household, you knew them better than ever I did. Would you count them trustworthy.'

'Out of question,' said the steward without hesitation, in a voice as dry and tough as his hide. 'Bonde is a simpleton, or little better, but a hard worker and open as the day. The Saxon pair are clever and subtle, but clever enough to know when they have a good lord, and loyal enough to be grateful for him. Why?'

'And the other, Heriet? Him I hardly knew. That was when Earl Waleran demanded my service of men in arms, and I sent him whatever offered, and this Heriet put himself forward. They told me he was restless because my sister was gone from the manor. He was a favourite of hers, so I heard, and fretted for her.'

111

'That could be true,' said Arnulf the steward. 'Certainly he was never the same after he came back from that journey. Such girl children can worm their way into a man and get at his heart. So she may have done with him. If you've known them from the cradle, they work deep into your marrow.'

Reginald nodded dourly. 'Well, he went. Twenty men my overlord asked of me, and twenty men he got. It was about the time he had that contention of his against the bishops, and needed reinforcements. Well, wherever he may be now, Heriet is out of our reach. But the rest are all here?'

'The Saxon pair in the stable loft this minute. Bonde should be coming in about this time from the fields.'

'Bring them,' said Reginald. And to Nicholas he said, when the steward had drained his horn and departed down the stone stair into the court as nimbly and rapidly as a youth of twenty: 'Wherever I look among these four, I can see no treachery. Why should they return, if they had somehow betrayed her? And why should they do so, any man of them? Arnulf says right, they knew they had the softest of beds here, my father was of the old, paternal, household kind, easier far than I, and I am not hated.' He was well aware, to judge by the sharp smile and curl of the lip, yellow-outlined in the low lamplight, of all the tensions that still bound and burned between Saxon and Norman, and was too intelligent to strain them too far. In the countryside memories were very long, and loyalties with them, hard to displace, slow to replace.

'Your steward is Saxon,' said Nicholas drily.

'So he is! And content! Or if not content,' said Reginald, at once dour and bright in the intimate light, 'at least aware of worse, worse by far. I have benefited by my father's example, I know when to bend. But where my sister is concerned, I tell you, I feel my spine stiffen.'

So did Nicholas, as stiff as if the marrow there had petrified into stone. And he viewed the three hinds, when they came marshalled sleepily up the steps into the hall, with the same blank, opaque eyes as did their master. Two long, fair fellows surely no more than thirty years old, with all the lean grace of their northern kin and eyes that caught the light in flashes of pale, blinding blue, and a softer, squat, round-faced man perhaps a little older, bearded and brown.

It might be true enough, thought Nicholas, watching them, that they had no hate for their lord, but rather reckoned themselves lucky by comparison with many of their kind, now for the third generation subject to Norman masters. But for all that, they went in awe of Reginald, and any such summons as this, outside the common order of their labouring day, brought them to questioning alert and wary, their faces closed, like a lid shut down over a box of thoughts that might not all be acceptable to authority. But it was different when they understood the subject of their lord's enquiry. The shut faces opened and eased. It was clear to Nicholas that none of these three felt he had any reason for uneasiness concerning that journey, rather they recalled it with pleasure, as well they might, the one carefree pilgrimage, the one holiday of their lives, when they rode instead of going afoot, and went well-provided and in the pride of arms.

Yes, of course they remembered it. No, they had had no trouble by the way. A lady accompanied by two good bowmen and two swordsmen had had nothing to fear. The taller of the Saxon pair, it seemed, used the new long-bow, drawn to the shoulder, while John Bonde carried the short Welsh bow, drawn to the breast, of less range and penetration than the long-bow, but wonderfully fast and agile in use at shorter range. The other brother was a swordsman, and so had the fourth member been, the missing Adam Heriet. A good enough company to travel briskly and safely, at whatever speed the lady could maintain without fatigue.

'Three days on the way, my lord,' said the Saxon bowman, spokesman for all three, and encouraged with vehement nods, 'and then we came into Andover, and because it was already evening, we lay there overnight, meaning to finish the journey the next morning. Adam found lodging for the lady with a merchant's household there, and we lay in the stables. It was but three or four miles more to go, so they told us.'

'And my sister was then in health and spirits? Nothing had gone amiss?'

'No, my lord, we had a good journey. She was glad then to be so close to what she wished. She said so, and thanked us.'

'And in the morning? You brought her on those few miles?'

'Not we, my lord, for she chose to go the rest of the way with only Adam Heriet, and we were to wait in Andover for his return, and so we did as we were ordered. And when he came, then we set out for home.'

To this the other two nodded firm assent, satisfied that their errand had been completed in obedience to the lady's wishes. So it was only one, only her servant

114

and familiar, according to repute, who had gone the rest of the way with Julian Cruce.

'You saw them ride for Wherwell?' demanded Reginald, frowning heavily at every complexity that arose to baulk him. 'She went with him freely, content?'

'Yes, my lord, fresh and early in the morning they went. A fine morning, too. She said farewell to us, and we watched them out of sight.'

No need to doubt it. Only four miles from her goal, and yet she had never reached it. And only one man could know what had become of her in that short distance.

Reginald waved them away irritably. What more could they tell him? To the best of their knowledge she had gone where she had meant to go, and all was well with her. But as the three made for the hall door, glad to be off to their beds, Nicholas said suddenly: 'Wait!' And to his host: 'Two more questions, if I may ask them?'

'Do so, freely.'

'Was it the lady herself who told you it was her wish to go on with only Heriet, and ordered you to remain in Andover and wait for him?'

'No,' said the spokesman, after a moment's thought, 'it was Adam told us.'

'And they set out in the early morning, you said. At what hour did Heriet return?'

'Not until twilight, sir. It was getting dark when he came. Because of that we stayed the night over, to make an early start for home next day.'

'There was another question I might have added,' said Nicholas, when he was alone with his host, and the hall door stood open on the deepening dusk and

115

quiet of the yard, 'but I doubt he would have seen to his own horse, and after a night's rest there'd be no way of judging how far it had been ridden. But see how the time testifies – three or four miles to Wherwell, and he would have had no call to linger, once he had brought her there. Yet he was the whole day away, twelve hours or more. What was he about all that time? Yet he's said to have been her devoted slave from infancy.'

'It got him credit with my father, who also doted,' said Reginald sourly. 'I knew little of him. But there he is at the heart of this, and who else is there? He alone rode with her that last day. And came back here with his fellows, letting it be seen all had gone well, and the matter was finished. But between Andover and Wherwell my sister vanishes. And a month or so later, when our overlord, Earl Waleran, from whom we hold three manors, sends asking for men, who should be first to offer himself but this same man? Why so ready to seize on a way of leaving here? For fear questions should yet be asked, some day? Something untoward come to light, and start the hunt?'

'Would he have come back at all,' wondered Nicholas, 'if he had done her harm or any way betrayed her?'

'If he had wit enough, yes, and wit enough he surely had, for see how he has succeeded! If he had failed to return with the others, there would have been a hue and cry at once. They would have started it before ever they left Andover. As it is, three years are gone without a word or a shadow of doubt, and where is Heriet now?'

He had fastened on the notion now, tearing it with his teeth, savouring the inner rage he felt at any such

116

thing being dared against his house. It was for that he would want revenge, if ever it came to the proof, not for Julian's own injuries. And yet Nicholas could not but tread the same way with him. Who else was there, to have wiped out the very image and memory of that girl committed to his care? Two had ridden from Andover, one had returned. The other was gone from the face of the earth, vanished into air. It was hard to go on believing that she would ever be seen again.

A servant brought in a lamp, and refilled the pitcher of ale on the table. The lady kept her chamber with her children, and left the men to confer without interruption. The night came down almost suddenly, in the brief customary breeze that came with this hour.

'She is dead!' said Reginald abruptly, and spread a large hand flat on the table.

'No, that's not certain. And *why* should he do such a thing? He lost his security here, for he dared not stay, once the chance of leaving offered. What was there to gain that would outweigh that? Is a man-at-arms in Waleran of Meulan's service better off than your trusted people here? I think not!'

'Service for half a year? If he stayed longer it was from choice, half a year was all that was demanded. And as for what he had to gain – and by God, he was the only one of the four who could have known the worth of it – my sister had three hundred silver marks in her saddle-bags, besides a list of valuables meant for her convent. I cannot recite you the whole tally offhand, but they're listed somewhere in the manor books, the clerk can lay hands on the record. I know there was a pair of silver candle-holders. And such jewels as she had from her mother she also took in

117

gift, having no further use for them herself in this world. Enough to tempt a man – even if he had to buy in a confederate to put a better face on the deed.'

And it could be so! A woman carrying her dowry with her, with a father and household satisfied of her well-being at home, and no one to wonder at her silence . . . But no, that could not be right, Nicholas caught himself up hopefully, not if she had already sent word of her coming ahead to Wherwell. Surely a girl intending to take the veil must advance her plea and be sure of acceptance before venturing on the journey south. But if she had done so, then there would have been wonder at her failure to arrive, and rapid enquiry, and the prioress, had there ever been letters or a courier from Julian Cruce, would have known and remembered the name. No, she could not have bargained beforehand. She had taken her dowry and simply gone to knock on the door and ask admittance. He had not the experience in such matters to know if that was very unusual, nor the cynicism to reflect that it would hardly be refused if the portion brought was large enough.

'This man Heriet will have to be found,' said Nicholas, making up his mind. 'If he's still serving with Waleran of Meulan, then I may be able to find him. Waleran is the king's man. If not, he'll be far to seek, but what other choice have we? He's native in this shire, is he? If he has kin, they'll be here?'

'He's second son to a free tenant at Harpecote. Why, what are you thinking?'

'That you'd best have your clerk make two copies of the list of what your sister took with her when she left. The money can't be traced and known, but it may be the valuables can. Have him describe them

118

fully if he can. Plate meant for church use may turn up on sale or be noted somewhere, so may gems. I'll have the list circulated round Winchester – if the bishop's well rid of his empress he may know now where his interest lies! – and try to find Adam Heriet among Meulan's companies, or get word when and how he left them. You do as much here, where if he has kin he may some day visit. Can you think of anything better? Or anything more we can undertake?'

Reginald heaved himself up from the table, making the flame of the lamp gutter. A big, black-avised, affronted man, with a face grimly set. 'That's well reasoned, and we'll do it. Tomorrow I'll have him copy the items – he's a finicky little fellow who has everything at his finger-ends – and I'll ride with you to Shrewsbury and see Hugh Beringar, and have this matter in train before the day's out. If this or any villain has done murder and robbery against my house, I want justice and I want restitution.'

Nicholas rose with his host, and went to the bed prepared for him so weary that he could not fail to sleep. So did he want justice. But what was justice in this matter? He planned and thought as one following a trail. he must pursue it with all his powers, having nothing else left to attempt, but he could not and would not believe in it. What he wanted above everything else in the world was a breath of some fresh breeze, blowing from another quarter, suggesting that she was not dead, that all this coil of suspicion and cupidity and treachery was false, a mere appearance, to be blown away when the morning came. But the morning came, and nothing was new, and nothing changed.

Thus two who had only one quest in common, and nothing besides to make them allies, rode together back into Shrewsbury, armed with two well-scripted copies of the valuables and money Julian Cruce had carried with her as her dowry on entering the cloister.

Hugh had come down from the town to dine with Abbot Radulfus, and acquaint him with the latest developments in the political tangle that was England. The flight of the empress back into her western stronghold, the scattering of a great part of her forces, and the capture of Earl Robert of Gloucester, without whom she was impotent, must transform the whole pattern of events, though its first effect was to freeze them from any action at all. The abbot might not have any interest in factional strife, but he was entitled to the mitre and a place in the great council of the country, and the welfare of people and church was very much his business. They had conferred a long time over the abbot's well-furnished table, and it was mid-afternoon when Hugh came looking for Cadfael in the herb-garden.

'You'll have heard? The word that Nicholas Harnage brought me yesterday? He said he had come here first, to his lord. Robert of Gloucester is penned up in Rochester a prisoner, and everything has halted while both sides think on what comes next – we, how best to make use of him, they, how to survive without him.' Hugh sat down on the stone bench in the shade, and spread his booted feet comfortably. 'Now comes the argument. And she had better order the king loosed from his chains, or Robert may find himself tethered, too.'

'I doubt if she'll see it so,' said Cadfael, pausing to lean on his hoe and pluck out a wisp of weed from between his neat, aromatic beds. 'More than ever,

Stephen is her only weapon now. She'll try to exact the highest possible price for him, her brother will scarcely be enough to satisfy her.'

Hugh laughed. 'Robert himself takes the same line, by young Harnage's account. He refuses to consider an exchange for the king, says he's no fair match for a monarch, and to balance it fitly we must turn loose all the rearguard that were taken with him, to make up Stephen's weight in the scale. But wait a while! If the empress argues in the same way now, within a month wiser men will have shown her she can do nothing, nothing at all, without Robert. London will never let her enter again, much less get within reach of the crown, and for all she has Stephen in a dungeon, he is still king.'

'It's Robert they'll have trouble persuading,' Cadfael reasoned.

'Even he will have to see the truth in the end. If she is to continue her fight, it can only be with Robert beside her. They'll convince him. Reluctant as they all may be to loose their hold on him, we shall have Stephen back before the year's end.'

They were still there together in the garden when Nicholas and Reginald Cruce, having enquired in vain for Hugh at the castle, as they entered the town, and again at Hugh's house by Saint Mary's church, as they passed through, followed the directions given by his porter, and came purposefully hunting for him at the abbey. At the sound of their boots on the gravel, and the sight of them rounding the box hedge, Hugh rose alertly to meet them.

'You're back in good time. What news?' And to the second man he said, eyeing him with interest: 'I have not enjoyed your acquaintance until now, sir, but you are surely the lord of Lai. Nicholas here

121

has told me how things stood at Wherwell. You're welcome to whatever service I can offer. And what now?'

'My lord sheriff,' said Cruce loudly and firmly, as one accustomed to setting the pace for others to follow, 'in the matter of my sister there's ground for suspicion of robbery and murder, and I want justice.'

'So do all decent men, and so do I. Sit down here, and let me hear what grounds you have for such suspicions, and where the finger points. I grant you the matter looks ugly enough. Let me know what you've found at home to add to it.'

It was over-hot in the afternoon sun, and even in shirt-sleeves Cruce was sweating freely. They moved back into the shade, and there sat down together, and Cadfael, hospitable in his own domain, and by no means inclined to be ousted from it in the middle of his work, went instead to bring a pitcher of wine from his workshop, and beakers for their use. He served them and went aside, but not so far that he did not hear what passed. All that had gone before he already knew, and on certain points his curiosity was already pricked into wakefulness, and foresaw circumstances in which he might yet be needed. His patient fretted over the girl, and could not afford further fraying away of what little flesh he had. Cadfael clove to his fellow-crusader in a solidarity of shared experience and mutual respect. One of those few, like Guimar de Massard, who came clean and chivalrous out of a very deformed and marred holy war. And however gradually, dying of it. Whatever concerned his welfare, body or soul, Cadfael wanted to know.

'My lord,' said Nicholas earnestly, 'you'll remember

122

all I told you of the men of my lord Cruce's household who escorted his sister to Wherwell. Three of
the four we have questioned at Lai, and I am sure
they have told us truth. But the fourth . . . and he
the only one who accompanied her on the last day
of her journey, the last few miles – he is no longer
there, and him we must find.'

They told the whole story between them, at times
in chorus, very vehemently.

'He left with her from Andover early in the morning, and the other three, who had orders to remain
there, watched them away.'

'And he did not return until late evening, too late
to set out for home that night. Yet Wherwell is but
three or four miles from Andover.'

'And he, alone of those four,' said Cruce fiercely,
'was so deep in her confidence from old familiarity
that he may well have known, must have known, the
dowry she carried with her.'

'And that was?' demanded Hugh sharply. His
memory was excellent. There was nothing he needed
to be told twice.

'Three hundred marks in coin, and certain valuables for church use. My lord, we have had my clerk,
who keeps good accounts, write a list of what she
took, and here we have two copies. The one we hold
you should circulate in these parts, where the man is
native, and so was my sister, and the other Harnage
here will carry to make known round Winchester,
Wherwell and Andover, where she vanished.'

'Good!' said Hugh heartily. 'The coins can never
be certainly traced, but the pieces of church ornaments may.' He took the scroll Nicholas held out
to him, and read with lowered and frowning brows:
'Item, a pair of candlesticks of silver, made in the

123

form of tall sconces entwined with the vine, with snuffers attached by silver chains, also ornamented with grape leaves. Item, a standing cross a man's hand-length in height, on a silver pedestal of three steps, and studded with semi-precious stones of yellow pebble, amethyst and agate, together with a similar cross of the same metal and stones, a little finger's length, on a thin silver neck-chain for a priest's wear. Item, a silver pyx, small, engraved with ferns. Also certain pieces of jewellery to her belonging, as, a necklet of polished stones from the hills above Pontesbury, a bracelet of silver engraved with tendrils of vetch, and a curious ring of silver set with enamels all round, in the form of yellow and blue flowers.' He looked up. 'Surely identifiable if they can be found, almost any of these. Your clerk did well. Yes, I'll have this made known to all officers and tenants of mine here in the shire, but it seems to me that in the south they're more likely to be traced. As for the man, if he's native here he has kin, and may well keep in touch with them. You say he went to do fighting services?'

'Only a matter of weeks after he returned to my father's household, yes. My father was newly dead, and the Earl of Worcester, my overlord, demanded a draft of men, and this Adam Heriet offered himself.'

'How old?' asked Hugh.

'A year or so past fifty. A strong man with sword or bow. He had been forester and huntsman to my father, Waleran would think himself lucky to get him. The rest were younger, but raw.'

'And where did this Heriet hail from? Your father's man must belong to one of your own manors.'

'Born at Harpecote, a younger son of a free man who farmed a yardland there. His elder brother farmed it after him. A nephew has it now. They were not on good terms, or so my father said. But for all that there may be some trace of him to be picked up there.'

'Had they any other kin? And the fellow never took a wife?'

'No, he never did. I know of no others of his family, but there well may be some around Harpecote.'

'Let them be,' said Hugh decidedly. 'It had best be left to me to probe there. Though I doubt if a man with no ties here will have come back to the shire, once having taken to the fighting life. More likely to be found where you're bound for, Nicholas. Do your best!'

'I mean to,' said Nicholas grimly, and rose to be off about the work without delay. The scroll of Julian's possessions he rolled and thrust into the breast of his coat. 'I must say a word first to my lord Godfrid, and let him know I'll not abandon this hunt while there's a grain of hope left. Then I'm on the road!' And he was away at a fast stride that became a light, long-paced run before he was out of sight. Cruce rose in his turn, eyeing Hugh somewhat grudgingly, as if he doubted to find in him a sufficient force of vengeful fury for the undertaking.

'Then I may leave this with you, my lord? And you will pursue it vigorously?'

'I will,' said Hugh drily. 'And you will be at Lai? That I may know where to find you, at need?'

Cruce went away silenced, for the time being, but none too content, and looked back from the turn of the hedge dubiously, as if he felt that the lord sheriff should already have been on horseback, or at least shaping for it, in the cause of Cruce vengeance. Hugh stared him out coolly, and watched him round the thick screen of box and disappear.

'Though I had best move speedily,' he said then, wryly smiling, 'for if that one found the fellow first I would not give much for his chances of escaping a few broken bones, if not a stretched neck. And even if it may come to that in the end, it shall not be at Reginald Cruce's hands, nor without a fair trial.' He clapped Cadfael heartily on the back, and turned to go. 'Well, if it's close season for kings and empresses, at least it gives us time to hunt the smaller creatures.'

Cadfael went to Vespers with an unquiet mind, troubled by imaginings of a girl on horseback, with silver and rough gems and coin in her saddle-bags, parting from her last known companions only a few miles from her goal, and then vanishing like morning mist in the summer sun, as if she had never been. A wisp of vapour over the meadow, and then gone. If those who agonised after her, the old and the young, had known her dead and with God, they, too, could have been at peace. Now there was no peace for any man drawn into this elaborate web of uncertainty.

Among the novices and schoolboys and the child oblates, last of their kind, for Abbot Radulfus would accept no more infants into a cloistered life decreed for them by others, Rhun stood rapt and radiant, smiling as he sang. A virgin by nature and aptitude, as well as by years, untroubled by the bodily agonies that tore most men, but miraculously aware of them and tender towards them, as few are to pains that leave their own flesh unwrung.

126

Vespers at this time of year shone with filtered summer light, that showed Rhun's flaxen beauty in crystalline pallor, and flashed across into the ranks of the brothers to burn in the sullen, smouldering darkness of Brother Urien, and the dilated brilliance of his black eyes, and cool into discreet shade where Brother Fidelis stood withdrawn into the shadows of the wall, alert at his lord's elbow, with no eyes and no thought for what went on around him, as he had no voice to join in the chant. His shadowed eyes looked nowhere but at Humilis, his slight body stood braced to receive and support at any moment the even frailer form that stood lance-straight beside him.

Well, worship has its own priorities, and a duty once assumed is a duty to the end. God and Saint Benedict would understand and respect that.

Cadfael, whose mind should also have been on higher things, found himself thinking: he dwindles before our eyes. It will be even sooner than I had thought. There is nothing that can prevent, or even greatly delay it now.

Chapter Eight

F ROBERT of Gloucester had not been
trapped and captured in the waters of
the river Test, and the Empress Maud
in headlong flight with the remnant of
her army into Gloucester, by way of Ludgershall
and Devizes, the hunt for Adam Heriet might have
gone on for a much longer time. But the freezing
chill of stalemate between the two armies, each
with a king in check, had loosed many a serving
man, bored with inaction and glad of a change, to
stretch his legs and take his leisure elsewhere, while
the lull lasted and the politicians argued and bargained. And among them an ageing, experienced
practitioner of sword and bow, among the Earl of
Worcester's forces.

Hugh was a man of the northern part of the shire
himself, but from the Welsh border; and the manors to the north-east, dwindling into the plain of
Cheshire, were less familiar to him and less congen-
ial. Over in the tamer country of the hundred of
Hodnet the soil was fat and well-farmed, and the
gleaned grain-fields full of plump, contented cattle
at graze, at once making good use of what aftermath there was in a dry season, and leaving their

droppings to feed the following year's tilth. There were abbey tenants here and there in these parts, and abbey stock turned into the fields now the crop was reaped. Their treading and manuring of the ground was almost as valuable as their fleeces.

The manor of Harpecote lay in open plain, with a small coppiced woodland on the windward side, and a low ridge of common land to the south. The house was small and of timber, but the fields were extensive, and the barns and byres that clung within the boundary fence were well-kept, and probably well-filled. Cruce's steward came out into the yard to greet the sheriff and his two sergeants, and direct them to the homestead of Edric Heriet.

It was one of the more substantial cottages of the hamlet, with a kitchen-garden before it and a small orchard behind, where a tousled girl with kilted skirts was hanging out washing on the hedge. Hens ran in the orchard grass, and a she-goat was tethered to graze there. A free man, this Edric was said to be, farming a yardland as a rent-paying tenant of his lord, a dwindling phenomenon in a country where a tiller of the soil was increasingly tied to it by customary services. These Heriets must be good husbandmen and hard workers to continue to hold their land and make it provide them a living. Such families could make good use of younger sons, needing all the hands they could muster. Adam was clearly the self-willed stray who had gone to serve for pay, and cultivated the skills of arms and forestry and hunting instead of the land.

A big, tow-headed, shaggy fellow in a frayed leather coat came ducking out of the low byre as Hugh and his officers halted at the gate. He stared, stiffening, and stood fronting them with a wary face, recognising authority though he did not know the man who wore it.

'You're wanting something here, masters?' Civil but not servile, he eyed them narrowly, and straddled his own gateway like a man on guard.

Hugh gave him good-day with the special amiability he used towards uneasy poor men bitterly aware of their disadvantages. 'You'll be Edric Heriet, I'm told. We're looking for word of where to find one Adam of that name, who should be your uncle. And you're all his kin that we know of, and may be able to tell us where to seek him. And that's the whole of it, friend.'

The big young man, surely no more than thirty years old, and most likely husband to the dishevelled but comely girl in the orchard, and father to the baby that was howling somewhere within the croft, shifted uncertainly from foot to foot, made up his mind, and stood squarely, his face inclined to clear.

'I'm Edric Heriet. What is it you want with uncle of mine? What has he done?'

Hugh was not displeased with that. There might be small warmth of kinship between them, but this one was not going to open his mouth until he knew what was in the wind. Blood thickened at the hint of offence and danger.

'To the best of my knowledge, nothing amiss. But we need to have out of him as witness what he knows about a matter he had a hand in some years ago, sent by his lord on an errand from Lai. I know he is – or was – in the service of the Earl of Worcester since then, which is why he may be hard to find, the times being what they are. If you've had word from him,

130

or can tell us where to look for him, we'll be thankful to you.'

He was curious now, though still uncertain. 'I have but one uncle, and Adam he's called. Yes, he was huntsman at Lai, and I did hear from my father that he went into arms for his lord's overlord, though I never knew who that might be. But as long as I recall, he never came near us here. I never remember him but from when I was a child shooing the birds off the ploughland. They never got on well, those brothers. Sorry I am, my lord,' he said, and though it was doubtful if he felt much sorrow, it was plain he spoke truth as to his ignorance. 'I have no notion where he may be now, nor where he's been these several years.'

Hugh accepted that, perforce, and considered a moment. 'Two brothers, were they? And no more? Never a sister between them? No tie to fetch him back into the shire?'

'There's an aunt I have, sir, only the one. It was a thin family, ours, my father was hard put to it to work the land after his brother left, until I grew up, and two younger brothers after me. We do well enough now between us. Aunt Elfrid was the youngest of the three, she married a cooper, bastard Norman he was, a little dark fellow from Brigge, called Walter.' He looked up, unaware of indiscretion, at the little dark Norman lord on the tall, raw-boned dapple-grey horse, and wondered at Hugh's blazing smile. 'They're settled in Brigge, I think she has childer. She might know. They were nearer.'

'And no other beside?'

'No, my lord, that was all of them. I think,' he said, hesitant but softening, 'he was godfather to her first. He might take that to heart.'

131

'So he might,' said Hugh mildly, thinking of his own masterful heir, to whom Cadfael stood godfather, 'so he very well might. I'm obliged to you, friend. At least we'll ask there.' He wheeled his horse, without haste, to the homeward way. 'A good harvest to you!' he said over his shoulder, smiling, and chirruped to the grey and was off, with his sergeants at his heels.

Walter the cooper had a shop in the hilltop town of Brigge, in a narrow alley no great way from the shadow of the castle walls. His booth was a narrow-fronted cave that drove deep within, and backed on an open, well-lit yard smelling of cut timber, and stacked with his finished and half-finished barrels, butts and pails, and the tools and materials of his craft. Over the low wall the ground fell away by steep, grassy terraces to where the Severn coiled, almost as it coiled at Shrewsbury, close about the foot of the town, broad and placid now at low summer water, with sandy shoals breaking its surface, but ready to wake and rage if sudden rains should come.

Hugh left his sergeants in the alley, and himself dismounted and went in through the dark booth to the yard beyond. A freckled boy of about seventeen was stooped over his jointer, busy bevelling a barrel-stave, and another a year or two younger was carefully paring long bands of willow for binding the staves together when the barrel was set up in its truss hoop. Yet a third boy, perhaps ten years old, was energetically sweeping up shavings and cramming them into bags for firing. It seemed that Walter had a full quiver of helpers in his business, for they were all alike, and all plainly sons

132

of one father, and he the small, spry, dark man who straightened up from his shaving-horse, knife in hand.

'Serve you, sir?'

'Master cooper,' said Hugh, 'I'm looking for one Adam Heriet, who I'm told is brother to your wife. They know nothing of his whereabouts at his nephew's croft at Harpecote, but thought you might be in closer touch with him. If you can tell me where he's to be found, I shall be grateful.'

There was a silence, sudden and profound. Walter stood gravely staring, and the hand that held the draw-knife with its curved blade sank quite slowly to hang at his side while he thought. Manual dexterity was natural to him, but thought came with deliberation, and slowly. All three boys stood equally mute and stared as their father stared. The eldest, Hugh supposed, must be Adam's godson, if Edric had the matter aright.

'Sir,' said Walter at length, 'I don't know you. What's your will with my wife's kin?'

'You shall know me, Walter,' said Hugh easily. 'My name is Hugh Beringar, I am sheriff of this shire, and my business with Adam Heriet is to ask him some questions concerning a matter three years old now, in which I trust he'll be able to help us do right. If you can bring me to have speech with him, you may be helping him no less than me.'

Even a law-abiding man, in the circumstances, might have his doubts of that, but a law-abiding man with a decent business and a wife and a family to look after would also take a careful look all round the matter before denying the sheriff a fair answer. Walter was no fool. He shuffled his feet thoughtfully

133

in the sawdust and the small shavings his youngest son had missed in his sweeping, and said with every appearance of candour and goodwill: 'Why, my lord, Adam's been away soldiering some years, but now it seems there's almost quiet down in the southern parts, and he's free to take his pleasure for a few days. You come very apt to your time, sir, as it chances, for he's here within the house this minute.'

The eldest boy had made to start forward softly towards the house door by this, but his father plucked him unobtrusively back by the sleeve, and gave him a swift glance that froze him where he stood. 'This lad here is Adam's godson and namesake,' said Walter guilelessly, putting him forward by the hand which had restrained him. 'You show the lord sheriff into the room, boy, and I'll put on my coat and follow.'

It was not what the younger Adam had intended, but he obeyed, whether in awe of his father or trusting him to know best. But his freckled face was glum as he led the way through the door into the large single room that served as hall and sleeping-quarters for his elders. An uncovered window, open over the descent to the river, let in ample light on the centre of the room, but the corners receded into a wood-scented darkness. At a big trestle table sat a solid, brown-bearded, balding man with his elbows spread comfortably on the board, and a beaker of ale before him. He had the weathered look of a man who lives out of doors in all but the bleakest seasons, and an air of untroubled strength about his easy stillness. The woman who had just come in from her cupboard of a kitchen, ladle in hand, was built on the same generous fashion, and had the same rich brown colouring. It was from

134

their father that the boys got their wiry build and dark hair, and the fair skins that dappled in the sun.

'Mother,' said the youth, 'here's the lord sheriff asking after Uncle Adam.'

His voice was flat and loud, and he halted a moment, blocking the doorway, before he moved within and let Hugh pass by him. It was the best he could do. The unshuttered window was large enough for an active man, if he had anything on his conscience, to vault through it and make off down the slope to a river he could wade now without wetting his knees. Hugh warmed to the loyal godson, and refrained from letting him see even the trace of a smile. A dreaming soul, evidently, who saw no use in a sheriff but to bring trouble to lesser men. But Adam the elder sat attentive and interested a reasonable moment before he got to his feet and gave amiable greeting.

'My lord, you have your asking. That name and title belongs to me.'

One of Hugh's sergeants would be circling the slope below the window by now, while the other stayed with the horses. But neither the man nor the boy could have known that. Evidently Adam had seen action enough not to be easily startled or affrighted, and here had no reason he could see, so far, to be either.

'Be easy,' he said. 'If it's a matter of some of King Stephen's men quitting their service, no need to look here. I have leave to visit my sister. You may have a few strays running loose, for all I know, but I'm none.'

The woman came to his side slowly and wonderingly, bewildered but not alarmed. She had a round, wholesome, rosy face, and honest eyes.

135

'My lord, here's my good brother come so far to see me. Surely there's no wrong in that?'

'None in the world,' said Hugh, and went on without preamble, and in the same mild manner: 'I'm seeking news of a lady who vanished three years since. What do you know of Julian Cruce?'

That was sheer blank bewilderment to mother and son, and to Walter, who had just come into the room at Hugh's back, but it was plain enough vernacular to Adam Heriet. He froze where he stood, half-risen from the bench, leaning on the trestle table, and hung there staring into Hugh's face, his own countenance wary and still. He knew the name, it had flung him back through the years, every detail of that journey he was recalling now, threading them frantically through his mind like the beads of a rosary in the hands of a terrified man. But he was not terrified, only alerted to danger, to the pains of memory, to the necessity to think fast, and perhaps select between truth, partial truth and lying. Behind that firm, impenetrable face he might have been thinking anything.

'My lord,' said Adam, stirring slowly out of his stillness, 'yes, of her certainly I know. I rode with her, I and three others from her father's household, when she went to take the veil at Wherwell. And I do know, seeing I serve in those parts, I do know how the nunnery there was burned out. But vanished three years since? How is that possible, seeing it was well known to her kin where she was living? Vanished now – yes, all too certainly, for I've been asking in vain since the fire. If you know more of my lady Julian since then than I, I beg you tell me. I could get no word whether she's living or dead.'

136

It had all the ring of truth, if he had not so strongly contained himself in those few moments of silence. It might be more than half truth, even so. If he was honest, he would have looked for her there, after the holocaust. If dishonest – well, he knew and could use the recent circumstances.

'You went with her to Wherwell,' said Hugh, answering nothing and volunteering nothing. 'Did you then see her safe within the convent gates there?'

This silence was brief indeed, but pregnant. If he said yes, boldly, he lied. If not, at least he might be telling truth.

'No, my lord, I did not,' said Adam heavily. 'I wish I had, but she would not have it so. We lay the last night at Andover, and then went on with her the last few miles. When we came within a mile – but it was not within sight yet, and there were small woodlands between – she sent me back, and said she would go the end of the way alone. I did what she wished. I had done what she wished since I carried her in my arms, barely a year old,' he said, with the first flash of fire out of his dark composure, like brief lightning out of banked clouds.

'And the other three?' asked Hugh mildly.

'We left them in Andover. When I returned we set out for home all together.'

Hugh said nothing yet about the discrepancy in time. That might well be held in reserve, to be sprung on him when he was away from this family solidarity, and less sure of himself.

'And you know nothing of Julian Cruce since that day?'

'No, my lord, nothing. And if you do, for God's sake let me know of it, worst or best!'

'You were devoted to this lady?'

137

'I would have died for her. I would die for her now.'

Well, so you may yet, thought Hugh, if you turn out to be the best player of a part that ever put on a false face. He was in two minds about this man, whose brief flashes of passion had all the force of truth, and yet who picked his way among words with a rare subtlety.

Why, if he had nothing to hide?

'You have a horse here, Adam?'

The man lifted upon him a long, calculating stare, from eyes deep-set beneath bushy brows. 'I have, my lord.'

'Then I must ask you to saddle and ride with me.'

It was an asking that could not be refused, and Adam Heriet was well aware of it, but at least it was put in a fashion which enabled him to rise and go with composed dignity. He pushed back the bench and stood clear.

'Ride where, my lord?' And to the freckled boy, watching dubiously from the shadows, he said: 'Go and saddle for me, lad, make yourself useful.'

Adam the younger went, though not willingly, and with a long backward glance over his shoulder, and in a moment or two hooves thudded on the hard-beaten earth of the yard.

'You must know,' said Hugh, 'all the circumstances of the lady's decision to enter a convent. You know she was betrothed as a child to Godfrid Marescot, and that he broke off the match to become a monk at Hyde Mead.'

'Yes, I do know.'

'After the burning of Hyde, Godfrid Marescot came to Shrewsbury in the dispersal that followed. Since the sack of Wherwell, he frets for news of

138

the girl, and whether you can bring him any or no, Adam, I would have you come with me and visit him.' Not a word yet of the small matter of her non-arrival at the refuge she had chosen. Nor was there any way of knowing from this experienced and well-regulated face whether Adam knew of it or no. 'If you cannot shed light,' said Hugh amiably, 'at least you can speak to him of her, share a remembrance heavy enough, as things are now, to carry alone.'

Adam drew a long, slow, cautious breath. 'I will well, my lord. He was a fine man, so everyone reports of him. Old for her, but a fine man. It was a great pity. She used to prattle about him, proud as if he was making a queen of her. Pity such a lass should ever take to the cloister. She would have been his fair match. I knew her. I'll ride with you in goodwill.' And to the husband and wife who stood close together, wondering and distrustful, he said calmly: 'Shrewsbury is not far. You'll see me back again before you know it.'

It was a strange and yet an everyday ride back to Shrewsbury. All the way this hardened and resilient man-at-arms conducted himself as though he did not know he was a prisoner, and suspect of something not yet revealed, while very well knowing that two sergeants rode one at either quarter behind him, in case he should make a break for freedom. He rode well, and had a very decent horse beneath him, and must be a man held in good repute and trusted by his commander to be loosed as he pleased, and thus well provided. Concerning his own situation he asked nothing, and betrayed no anxiety; but three times at least before they came in sight of Saint Giles he asked:

139

'My lord, did you ever hear word of her at all, after the troubles fell on Winchester?'

'Sir, if you have made enquiries round Wherwell, did you come upon any trace? There must have been many nuns scattered there.'

And last, in abrupt pleading: 'My lord, if you do know, is she living or dead?'

To none of which could he get a direct answer, since there was none to give him. Last, as they passed the low hillock of Saint Giles, with its squat roofs and modest little turret, he said reflectively: 'That must have been a hard journey for a sick and ageing man, all this way from Hyde alone. I marvel how the lord Godfrid bore it.'

'He was not alone,' said Hugh almost absently. 'They were two who came here from Hyde Mead.'

'As well,' said Adam, nodding approval, 'for they said he was a sorely wounded man. He might have foundered on the way, without a helper.' And he drew a slow, cautious breath.

After that he went in silence, perhaps because of the looming shadow of the abbey wall on his left, that cut off the afternoon sun with a sharp black knife-stroke along the dusty road.

They rode in under the arch of the gatehouse to the usual stir of afternoon, following the half-hour or so allowed for the younger brothers to play, and the older ones to sleep after dinner. Now they were rousing and going forth to their various occupations, to their desks in the scriptorium, or their labours in the gardens along the Gaye, or at the mill or the hatcheries of the fishponds. Brother Porter came out from his lodge at sight of Hugh's gangling grey horse, observed the attendant officers, and looked with some natural curiosity at the unknown who rode with them.

'Brother Humilis? No, you won't find him in the scriptorium, nor in the dortoir, either. After Mass this morning he swooned, here crossing the court, and though the fall did him no great harm, the young one catching him in his arms and bringing him down gently, it took some time to bring him round afterwards. They've carried him to the infirmary. Brother Cadfael is there with him now.'

'I'm sorry to hear it,' said Hugh, checking in dismayed concern. 'Then I can hardly trouble him now . . .' And yet, if this was one more step towards the end which Cadfael said was inevitable and daily drawing nearer, Hugh could not afford to delay any enquiry which might shed light on the fate of Julian Cruce. Humilis himself most urgently desired knowledge.

'Oh, he's come to himself now,' said the porter, 'and as much his own master – under God, the master of us all! – as ever he was. He wants to come back to his own cell in the dortoir, and says he can still fulfil all his duties a while longer here, but they'll keep him where he is. He's in his full wits, and has all his will. If you have word for him of any import, I would at least go and see if they'll let you in to him.'

'They', when it came to authority in the infirmary, meant Brother Edmund and Brother Cadfael, and their judgement would be decisive.

'Wait here!' said Hugh, making up his mind, and swung down from the saddle to stride across the court to its north-western corner, where the infirmary stood withdrawn into the angle of the precinct wall. The two sergeants also dismounted, and stood in close and watchful attendance on their

141

charge, though it seemed that Adam was quite prepared to brazen out whatever there was to be answered, for he sat his horse stolidly for a few moments, and then lit down and freely surrendered his bridle to the groom who had come to see to Hugh's mount. They waited in silence, while Adam looked about the clustered buildings round the court with wary interest.

Hugh encountered Brother Edmund just emerging from the doorway of the infirmary, and put his question to him briskly. 'I hear you have Brother Humilis within. Is he fit to have visitors? I have the one missing man here under guard, with luck we may start something out of him between us, before he has too much time to think out his cover and make it impregnable.'

Edmund blinked at him for a moment, hard put to it to leave his own preoccupations for another man's. Then he said, after some hesitation: 'He grows daily feebler, but he's resting well now, and he has been fretting over this matter of the girl, feeling his own acts brought her to this. His mind is strong and determined. I think he would certainly wish to see you. Cadfael is there with him – his wound broke again when he fell, where it was newly healed, but it's clean. Yes, go in to him.' His face said though his lips did not utter it: 'Who knows how long his time may be? An easy mind could lengthen it.'

Hugh went back to his men. 'Come, we may go in.' And to the two sergeants he said: 'Wait outside the door.'

He heard the familiar tones of Cadfael's voice as soon as he entered the infirmary with Adam docile at his heels. They had not taken Brother Humilis into the open ward, but into one of the small, quiet cells apart, and the door stood open between. A cot, a stool and a small desk to support book or candle were all the furnishings, and wide-open door and small, unshuttered window let in light and air. Brother Fidelis was on his knees by the bed, supporting the sick man in his arm while Cadfael completed the bandaging of hip and groin where the frail new scar tissue had split slightly when Humilis fell. They had stripped him naked, and the cover was drawn back, but Cadfael's solid body blocked the view of the bed from the doorway, and at the sound of feet entering Fidelis quickly drew up the sheet to the patient's waist. So emaciated was the long body that the young man could lift it briefly on one arm, but the gaunt face showed clear and firm as ever, and the hollow eyes were bright. He submitted to being handled with a wry and patient smile, as to a salutary discipline. It was the boy who so jealously reached to conceal the ruined body from uninitiated eyes. Having drawn up the sheet, he turned to take up and shake out the clean linen shirt that lay ready, lifted it over Humulis's head, and very adroitly helped his thin arms into the sleeves, and lifted him to smooth the folds comfortably under him. Only then did he turn and look towards the doorway.

Hugh was known and accepted, even welcomed. Humilis and Fidelis as one looked beyond him to see who followed.

From behind Hugh's shoulder the taller stranger looked quickly from face to face, the mere flicker of a sharp glance that touched and took flight, a lightning assessment by way of taking stock of what he might have to deal with. Brother Cadfael, clearly, belonged here and was no threat, the sick man in the bed was known by repute, but the third

143

brother, who stood close by the cot utterly still, wide eyes gleaming within the shadow of the cowl, was perhaps not so easily placed. Adam Heriet looked last and longest at Fidelis, before he lowered his eyes and composed his face into a closed book.

'Brother Edmund said we might come in,' said Hugh, 'but if we tire you, turn us out. I am sorry to hear you are not so well.'

'It will be the best of medicines,' said Humilis, 'if you have any better news for me. Brother Cadfael will not grudge another doctor having a say. I am not so sick, it was only a faintness – the heat gets ever more oppressive.' His voice was a little less steady than usual, and slower in utterance, but he breathed evenly, and his eyes were clear and calm. 'Who is this you have brought with you?'

'Nicholas will have told you, before he left,' said Hugh, 'that we have already questioned three of the four who rode as escort to the lady Julian when she left for Wherwell. This is the fourth – Adam Heriet, who went the last part of the way with her, leaving his fellows in Andover to wait for his return.'

Brother Humilis stiffened his frail body and sat upright to gaze, and Brother Fidelis kneeled and braced an arm about him, behind the supporting pillow, stooping his head into shadow behind his lord's lean shoulder.

'Is it so? Then we know all those who guarded her now. So you,' said Humilis, urgently studying the stalwart figure and blunt, brow-bent face that stooped a sunburned forehead to him, like a challenged bull, 'you must be that one they said loved her from a child.'

'So I did,' said Adam Heriet firmly.

'Tell him,' said Hugh, 'how and when you last parted from the lady. Speak up, it is your story.'

Heriet drew breath long and deeply, but without any evidence of fear or stress, and told it again as he had told it to Hugh at Brigge. 'She bade me go and leave her. And so I did. She was my lady, to command me as she chose. What she asked of me, that I did.'

'And returned to Andover?' asked Hugh mildly.

'Yes, my lord.'

'Scarcely in haste,' said Hugh with the same deceptive gentleness. 'From Andover to Wherwell is but a few short miles, and you say you were dismissed a mile short of that. Yet you returned to Andover in the dusk, many hours later. Where were you all that time?'

There was no mistaking the icy shock that went through Adam, stopping his breath for an instant. His carefully hooded eyes rolled wide and flashed one wild glance at Hugh, then were again lowered. It took him a brief and perceptible struggle to master voice and thoughts, but he did it with heroic smoothness, and even the pause seemed too brief for the inspired concoction of lies.

'My lord, I had never been so far south before, and reckoned at that time I never should again. She dismissed me, and the city of Winchester was there close. I had heard tell of it, but never thought to see it. I know I had no right so to borrow time, but I did it. I rode into the town, and there I stayed all that day. It was peace there, then, a man could walk abroad, view the great church, eat at an alehouse, all without fear. And so I did, and went back to Andover only late in the evening. If they have told

145

you so, they tell truth. We never set out for home until next morning.'

It was Humilis, who knew the city of Winchester like his own palm, who took up the interrogation there, drily and calmly, eyes and voice again alert and vigorous. 'Who could blame you for taking a few hours to yourself, with your errand done? And what did you see and do in Winchester?'

Adam's wary breathing eased again readily. This was no problem for him. He launched into a very full and detailed account of Bishop Henry's city, from the north gate, where he had entered, to the meadows of St Cross, and from the cathedral and the castle of Wolvesey to the north-western fields of Hyde Mead. He could describe in detail the frontages of the steep High Street, the golden shrine of Saint Swithun, and the magnificent cross presented by Bishop Henry to his predecessor Bishop Walkelin's cathedral. No doubt but he had seen all he claimed to have seen. Humilis exchanged glances with Hugh and assured him of that. Neither Hugh nor Cadfael, who stood a little apart, taking note of all, had ever been in Winchester.

'So that is all you know of Julian Cruce's fate,' said Hugh at length.

'Never word of her, my lord, since we parted that day,' said Adam, with every appearance of truth. 'Unless there is something you can tell me now, as you know I have asked and asked.' But he was asking no longer, even this repetition had lost all its former urgency.

'Something I can and will tell you,' said Hugh abruptly and harshly. 'Julian Cruce never entered Wherwell. The prioress of Wherwell never heard of her. From that day she has vanished, and you

146

were the last ever to see her. What's your answer to that?'

Adam stood mute, staring, a long minute. 'Do you tell me this is true?' he said slowly.

'I do tell you so, though I think there never was any need to tell you, for you knew it, none better. As you are now left, the only one who may, who must, know where she did go, since she never reached Wherwell. Where she went and what befell her, and whether she is now on this earth or under it.'

'I swear to God,' said Adam slowly, 'that when I parted from my lady at her wish, I left her whole and well, and I pray she is now, wherever she may be.'

'You knew, did you not, what valuables she carried with her? Was that enough to tempt you? Did you, I ask you now in due form, did you rob your mistress and do her violence when she was left alone with you, and no witness by?'

Fidelis laid Humilis gently back against his pillows, and stood up tall and straight beside him. The movement drew Adam's gaze, and for a moment held it. He said loudly and clearly: 'So far from that, I would have died for her then, and so I would, gladly, now, rather than she should suffer even one moment's grief.'

'Very well!' said Hugh shortly. 'That's your plea. But I must and will keep you in hold until I know more. For I will know more, Adam, before I let go of this knot.' He went to the door, where his sergeants waited for their orders, and called them in. 'Take this man and lodge him in the castle. Securely!'

Adam went out between them without a word of surprise or protest. He had looked for nothing else, events had hedged him in too closely not to lock the door on him now. It seemed that he was not greatly discomforted or alarmed, either, though he was a stout, practised man who would not betray his thoughts. He did cast one look back from the doorway, a look that embraced them all, but said nothing and conveyed nothing to Hugh, and little enough to Cadfael. A mere spark, too small as yet to cast any light.

Chapter Nine

ROTHER HUMILIS watched the departure of prisoner and guards with a long, unwavering stare, and when they had vanished he sank back on his bed with a deep sigh, and lay gazing up into the low stone vault over him.

'We've tired you out,' said Hugh. 'We'll leave you now to rest.'

'No, wait!' There was a fine dew of sweat breaking on his high forehead. Fidelis leaned and wiped it away, and a preoccupied smile flashed up at him for a moment, and lingered to darken into a frown.

'Son, go out from here, take the sun and the air, you spend too much time caring for me, and you see I am in need of nothing now. It is not right that you should make me your only work here. In a little while I shall sleep.' It was not clear, from the serenity of his voice, weak though it was, whether he spoke of a mere restful slumber on a hot afternoon, or the last sleep of the body at the awakening of the soul. He laid his hand for a moment on the young man's hand, in the most delicate touch possible, austerely short of a caress. 'Yes, go, I wish it. Finish my work for me, your

149

touch is steadier than mine, and the detail – too fine for me now.'

Fidelis looked down at him with a composed face, looked up briefly at the two who watched, and again lowered submissively those clear grey eyes that rang so striking a contrast with the curling bronze ring of his tonsure. He went as he was bidden, perhaps gladly, certainly with a free and rapid step.

'Nicholas never stopped to tell me,' said Humilis, when silence had closed over the last light footstep, 'what these valuables were, that my affianced wife took with her. Were they so distinctive as to be recognisable, should they ever be traced?'

'I doubt if there were any two such,' said Hugh. 'Gold and silversmiths generally make to their own designs, even when they aim at pairs I wonder if they ever match exactly. These were singular enough. Once known, known for all time.'

'May I know what they were? She had coined money, I understand – that is at the service of who-ever takes it. But the rest?'

Hugh, whose memory for words was exact as a mirror, willingly described them: 'A pair of candle-sticks of silver, made in the form of tall sconces entwined with the vine, with snuffers attached by silver chains, also ornamented with grapeleaves. A standing cross a man's hand-length in height, on a silver pedestal of three steps, and studded with semi-precious stones of yellow pebble, amethyst and agate, together with a similar cross of the same metal and stones, a little finger's length, on a thin silver neck-chain for a priest's wear. Also some pieces of jewellery, a necklet of polished stones from the hills above Pontesbury, a bracelet of silver engraved with tendrils of vetch, an ' ᵃ curious ring of silver set with enamels all round, in the form of yellow and blue flowers. That's the tally. They must surely all have left this shire. They'll be found, if ever found at all, somewhere in the south, where they and she vanished.'

Humilis lay quiet, his eyelids closed, his lips moving soundlessly on the details of these chattels. 'A very small fortune,' he said in a whisper. 'But not small to some poor wretched souls. Do you truly believe she may have died for these few things?'

'Men, and women too,' said Hugh starkly, 'have died for very much less.'

'Yes, true! A small cross,' said Humilis, lips moving again upon the recollected phrases, 'the length of a little finger, set with yellow stones, and green agate and amethyst . . . Fellow to an altar cross of the same, but made for wearing. Yes, a man would know that again.'

The faint dew of weakness was budding again on his forehead, a great drop ran down into the folds of a closed eyelid. Cadfael wiped the corroding drops away, and frowned Hugh before him out at the door.

'I shall sleep . . .' said Humilis, and faintly and fleetingly smiled.

In the large room across the stone passage, where a dozen beds lay spaced in two rows, either side an open corridor, Brother Edmund and another brother, his back turned and his strong, erect figure unidentifiable from behind, were lifting a cot and the lay brother in it, to move them a short way along the wall, and make room for a new pallet and a new patient. The helper set down his end of the bed as Cadfael and Hugh passed by the open doorway. He straightened and turned, brushing his hands together

151

to rub out the dents left by the weight, and showed them the dark, level brows and burning eyes of Brother Urien. In unaccustomed content with himself and the walls and persons about him, he wore a slight, taut smile that curled his lips but never damped the smouldering of his eyes. He watched them pass as if a shadow had passed, and crossed their tracks as soon as they were by, to stack an armful of washed linen in the press that stood in the passage.

In the infirmary, by custom, all doors stood open, so that a call for help might safely reach attentive ears, and help come hurrying. Voices, the chant of the office, even birdsong, circulated freely. Only in times of storm or heavy rain or winter cold were doors closed and shutters secured, never as now, in the heat of summer.

'The man is lying,' said Hugh, pacing beside Cadfael in the great court, and worrying at the texture of truth and deceit. 'But also half the time he is telling the truth, and which half holds the lies? Tell me that!'

'If I could,' said Cadfael mildly, 'I should be more than mortal.'

'He had her trust, he knew what she was worth, he rode alone with her the last few miles, and no trace of her since,' said Hugh, gnawing the evidence savagely. 'And yet, on the road there, he asked me time and again if I knew whether she lived or was dead, and I would have sworn he was honest in asking. But now see him! Halfway through that business, he stands there unmoved as a rock, and never makes protest against being held, nor shows any further trouble over *her* fate. What's to be made of him?'

'Or of any of this,' agreed Cadfael ruefully. 'I'm of your mind, he is certainly lying. He knows what he has not declared. Yet if he has possessed himself of all she had, what has he done with it? It may not be great riches, but it would be worth more to a man than the low pay and danger and sweat of a simple soldier, yet here is he manifestly a simple soldier still, and nothing more.'

'Soldier he may be,' said Hugh wryly, 'but simple he is not. His twists and turns have me baffled. Winchester he knows well – yes, maybe, but wherever he has served the greater part of these three years, since this winter all forces have closed in on Winchester. How could he not know it? And yet I'd have sworn, at first, that he truly did not know, and longed to know, what had become of the girl. Either that, or he's the cunningest mime that ever twisted his face to deceive.'

'He did not seem to me greatly uneasy,' said Cadfael thoughtfully, 'when you brought him in. Wary, yes, and picking his words with care – and that gives them all the more meaning,' he added, brightening. 'I'll be thinking on that. But fearful or anxious, no, I would not say so.'

They had reached the gatehouse, where the groom waited with Hugh's horse. Hugh gathered the reins and set toe in stirrup, and paused there to look over his shoulder at his friend.

'I tell you what, Cadfael, the only sure way out of this tangle is for that girl to turn up somewhere, alive and well. Then we can all be easy. But there, you've had more than your fair share of miracles already this year, not even you dare ask for more.'

'And yet,' said Cadfael, fretting at the disorderly confusion of shards that would not fit together,

153

'there's something winks at me in the corner of my mind's eye, and is gone when I look towards it. A mere will-o'-wisp – not even a spark. . . .'

'Let it alone,' said Hugh, wheeling his horse towards the gate. 'Never blow on it for fear it may go out altogether. If you breathe the other way, who knows? It may grow into a candle-flame, and bring the moths in to singe their wings.'

Brother Urien lingered long over stacking the laundered linen in its press in the infirmary. He had let Fidelis pass without a sign, his mind still intent upon the three who were left within the sickroom, and the stone walls brought hollow echoes ringing across the passage, through the open doors. Brother Urien's senses were all honed into acute sensitivity by his inward anguish, to the point where his skin crawled and his short hairs stood on end at the torture of sounds which might seem soft and gentle to another ear.

He moved with precision and obedience to fulfil whatever Edmund required of him: a bed to be moved, without disturbing its occupant, who was half-paralysed and very old, a new cot to be installed ready for another sufferer. He turned to watch the departure of sheriff and herbalist brother without conceal, his mind still revolving words sharply remembered. All those artifacts of precious metal and semi-precious stones, vanished with a vanished woman. An altar cross – no, that was of no importance here. But a cross made to match, on a silver neck-chain . . . Benedictine brothers may not retain the trappings of the person, the fruit of the world, however slight, without special permission, seldom granted. Yet there are brothers who wear chains about the neck – one, at least. He had touched, once, to bitter humiliation, and he knew.

The time, too, spoke aloud, the time and the place. Those who have killed for a desperate venture, for gain, and find themselves hard pressed, may seek refuge wherever it offers. Gains may be hidden until flight is again possible and sage. But why, then, follow that broken crusader here into Shrewsbury? Flight would have been easy after Hyde burned, in that inferno who could count heads?

Yet no one knew better than he how love, or whatever the name for this torment truly is, may be generated, nursed, take tyrannical possession of a man's soul, with far greater fury and intensity here in the cloister than out in the world. If he could be made to suffer it thus, driven blind and mad, why should not another? And how could two such victims not have something to bind them together, if nothing else, their inescapable guilt and pain? And Humilis was a sick man, and could not live long. There would be room for another when he vacated his place, when the void left after him began to ache intolerably. Urien's heart melted in him like wax, thinking what Fidelis might be enduring in his impenetrable silence.

He finished the work to which he had been called in the infirmary, closed the press, glanced once round the open ward, and went out to the court. He had been a body-servant and groom in the world, and was without craft skills, and barely literate until entering the Order. He lent his sinews and strength where they were needed, indoors or out, to any labour. He did not grudge the effort such labour cost him, nor feel his unskilled aid to be menial, for the fuel that fired him within demanded a means of

155

expending itself without, or there could be no sleep for him in his bed, nor ease when he awoke. But whatever he did he could not rid himself of the too well remembered face of the woman who had spurned and left him in his insatiable hunger and thirst. He had seen again her smooth young face, the image of innocence, and her great, lucid grey eyes in the boy Rhun, until those eyes turned on him full and seared him to the bone by their sweetness and pity. But her rich, burning russet hair, not red but brown in its brightness, he had found only in Brother Fidelis, crowning and corroborating those same wide grey eyes, the pure crystals of memory. The woman's voice had been clear, high and bold. This mirror image was voiceless, and therefore could never be harsh or malicious, never condemn, never scarify. And it was male, blessedly not of the woman's cruel and treacherous clan. Once Fidelis might have recoiled from him, startled and affrighted. But he had said and believed then that it would not always be so.

He had achieved the measured monastic pace, but not the tranquillity of mind that should have gone with it. By lowering his eyes and folding his hands before him in his sheltering sleeves he could go anywhere within these walls, and pass for one among many. He went where he knew Fidelis had been sent, and where he would surely go, valuing the bench where he sat by the true tenant who should have been sitting there, and the vellum leaf on the desk before him, and the little pots of colour deployed there, by the work Humilis had begun, and bade him finish.

At the far end of the scriptorium range in the cloister, under the south wall of the church, Brother

Anselm the precentor was trying out a chant on his small hand-organ, a sequence of a half-dozen notes repeated over and over, like an inspired bird-call, sweet and sad. One of the boy pupils was there with him, lifting his childish voice unconcernedly, as gifted children will, wondering why the elders make so much fuss about what comes by nature and costs no pain. Urien knew little of music, but felt it acutely, as he felt everything, like arrows piercing his flesh. The boy rang purer and truer than any instrument, and did not know he could wring the heart. He would rather have been playing with his fellow-pupils, out in the Gaye.

The carrels of the scriptorium were deep, and the stone partitions cut off sound. Fidelis had moved his desk so that he could sit half in shade, while the full sunlight lit his leaf. His left side was turned to the sun, so that his hand cast no shadow as he worked, though the coiled tendril which was his model for the decoration of the capital letter M was wilting in the heat. He worked with a steady hand and a very fine brush, twining the delicate curls of the stem and starring them with pale, bright flowers frail as gossamer. When the singing boy, released from his schooling, passed by at a skipping run, Fidelis never raised his head. When Urien cast a long shadow and did not pass by, the hand that held the brush halted for a moment, then resumed its smooth, long strokes, but still Fidelis did not look up. By which token Brother Urien was aware that he was known. For any other this mute painter would have looked up briefly, for many among the brothers he would have smiled. And without looking, how could he know? By a silence as heavy as his own, or by some quickening that flushed his flesh and caused the hairs of his neck to rise when this one man of all men came near?

Urien stepped within the carrel, and stood close at Fidelis's shoulder, looking down at the intricate M that still lacked its touches of gold. Looking down also, with more intense awareness, at the inch or two of thin silver chain that showed within the dropped folds of collar and cowl, threading the short russet hairs on the bent neck. A cross a little finger long, on a neck-chain, and studded with yellow, green and purple stones . . . He could have inserted a finger under the chain and plucked it forth, but he did not touch. He had learned that a touch is witchcraft, instant separation, putting cold distance between.

'Fidelis,' said the softest of yearning voices at Fidelis's shoulder, 'you keep from me. Why do you so? I can be the truest friend ever you had, if you will let me. What is there I will not do for you? And you have need of a friend. One who will keep secrets and be as silent as you are. Let me in to you, Fidelis. . . .' He did not say 'brother'. 'Brother' is a title beyond desire, an easy title, no shaker of the mind or spirit. 'Let me in, and I can be to you all you need of love and loyalty. To the death!'

Fidelis laid aside his brush very slowly, and set both hands to the edge of the desk as though bracing himself to rise, and all this with rigid body and held breath. Urien pressed on in hushed haste.

'You need not fear me, I mean you only good. Don't stir, don't draw away! I know what you have done, I know what you have to hide . . . No one else will ever hear it from me, if only you'll do your part. Silence deserves a reward . . . love deserves love!'

Fidelis slid along the polished wood of the bench and stood clear, putting the desk between them. His

158

face was pale and fixed, the dilated grey eyes enormous. He shook his head vehemently, and moved round to push past Urien and quit the carrel, but Urien spread his arms and blocked the way.

'Oh, no, not this time! Not now! That's over. I've asked, I've begged, now I give you to know even asking is over.' His tight control had burned into abrupt and savage anger, his eyes flared redly. 'I have ears, I could be your ruin if I were so minded. You had best be kind to me.' His voice was still very low, no one would hear, and no one passed along the cloister flagstones to see and wonder. He moved closer, driving Fidelis deeper into shadow within the carrel. 'What is it you wear round your neck, under your habit, Fidelis? Will you show it to me? Or shall I tell you what it is? And what it means! There are those who would give a good deal to know. To your cost, Fidelis, unless you grow kind to me.'

He had backed his quarry into the deepest corner, and pinned him there with arms outspread, and a palm flattened against the wall on either side, preventing escape. Still the pale, oval face confronted him icily, even scornfully, and the grey eyes had burned into a slow blaze of anger, utterly rejecting him.

Urien struck like a snake, flashing a hand into the bosom of Fidelis's habit, down within the ample folds, to drag out of hiding the length of the silver chain, and the trophy that hung hidden upon it, warmed by the flesh and the heart beneath. Fidelis uttered a strange, breathy sound, and leaned back hard against the wall, and Urien started back from him one unsteady step, himself appalled, and echoed the gasp. For an instant there was a silence so deep that both seemed to drown in it, then

159

Fidelis gathered up the slack of the chain in his hand, and stowed his treasure away again in its hiding place. For that one moment he had closed his eyes, but instantly he opened them again and kept them fixed with a bleak, unbending stare upon his persecutor.

'Now, more than ever,' said Urien in a whisper, 'now you shall lower those proud eyes of yours, and stoop that stiff neck, and come to me pliantly, or go to whatever fate such an offence as yours brings down on the offender. But no need to threaten, if you will but listen to me. I pledge you my help, oh, yes, faithfully, with my whole heart – you have only to let me in to yours. Why not? And what choice have you, now? You need me, Fidelis, as cruelly as I need you. But we two together – and there need be no cruelty, only tenderness, only love. . . .'

Fidelis burned up abruptly like a candle-flame, and with the hand that was not clutching his profaned treasure to his breast he struck Urien in the mouth and silenced him.

For a moment they hung staring, eye to eye, with never a sound or a breath between them. Then Urien said thickly, in a grating whisper that was barely audible: 'Enough! Now you shall come to me! Now you shall be the beggar. Of your own need and your own will you shall come, and beg me for what you now refuse. Or I will tell all that I know, and what I know is enough to damn you. You shall come to me and plead, and follow me like a little dog at my heels, or else I will destroy you, as now you *know* I can. Three days I give you, Fidelis! If you do not seek me out and give yourself to me by Vespers of the third day from now, *Brother*, I will let loose hell to swallow you, and smile to watch you burn!'

160

He swung on his heel then, and flew out of the carrel. The long black shadow vanished, the afternoon light came in again placidly. Fidelis leaned in the darkness of his corner a long moment with eyes closed and breast heaving in deep, exhausted rise and fall. Then he groped his way heavily back to his bench and sat down, and took up his brush in a hand too unsteady to be able to use it. Holding it gave him a hold on normality, and presented a fitting picture of an illuminator at work, if anyone should come to witness it. Within, there was a numbed desperation past which he could not see any light or any deliverance.

It was Rhun who came to be a witness. He had met Brother Urien in the garth, and seen the set face and smouldering, wounded eyes. He had not seen from which carrel Urien had issued, but here he sensed, smelled, felt in the prickling of his own flesh where Urien in his rank rage and pain had been.

He said no word of it to Fidelis, nor remarked on the pallor of his friend's face or the strange stiffness of his movements as he greeted him. He sat down beside him on the bench, and talked of the simple matters of the day, and the pattern of the capital letter still unfinished, and took up the fine brush for the gilding and laid in carefully the gold edges of two or three leaves, the tip of his tongue arching at the corner of his mouth, like a child at his letters.

When the bell rang for Vespers they went in together, both with calm faces, neither with a quiet heart.

Rhun absented himself from supper, and went instead to the infirmary, and into the small room where

161

Brother Humilis lay sleeping. He sat beside the bed patiently for a long time, but the sick man slept on. And now, in this silence and solitude, Rhun could scan every line of the worn, ageing face, and see how the eyes were sunk deep into the skull, the cheeks fallen into gaunt hollows, and the flesh slack and grey. He was so full of life himself that he recognised with exquisite clarity the approach of another man's death. He abandoned his first purpose. For even if Humilis should awaken, and however ardently he would exert what life was left to him for the sake of Fidelis, Rhun could not now cast any part of this load upon a man already burdened with the spiritual baggage of his own departure. But he sat there still, and waited, and after supper Brother Edmund came to make the rounds of his patients before nightfall.

Rhun approached him in the stone-flagged passage.

'Brother Edmund, I'm anxious about Humilis. I've been sitting with him, and surely he grows weaker before our eyes. I know you keep good care of him always, but I thought – could not a cot be put in with him for Fidelis? It would be much to the comfort of them both. In the dortoir with the rest of us Fidelis will fret, and not sleep. And if Humilis should wake in the night, it would be a grace to see Fidelis close by him, ready to serve as he always is. They went through the fire at Hyde together. . . .' He drew breath, watching Brother Edmund's face. 'They are closer,' he said gravely, 'than ever were father and son.'

Brother Edmund went himself to look at the sleeping man. Breath came shallowly and rapidly. The single light cover lay very flat and lean over the long body.

'It might be well so,' said Edmund. 'There is an empty cot in the anteroom of the chapel, and it would go in here, though the space is a little tight for it. Come and help me to carry it, and then you may tell Brother Fidelis he can come and sleep here this night, if that's his wish.'

'He will be glad,' said Rhun with certainty.

The message was delivered to Fidelis simply as a decision by Brother Edmund, taken for the peace of mind and better care of his patient, which seemed sensible enough. And certainly Fidelis was glad. If he suspected that Rhun had had a hand in procuring the dispensation, that was acknowledged only with a fleeting smile that flashed and faded in his grave face too rapidly to be noticed. He took his breviary and went gratefully across the court, and into the room where Humilis still slept his shallow, old man's sleep, he who was barely forty-seven years old, and had lived at a gallop the foreshortened life that now crept so softly and resignedly towards death. Fidelis kneeled by the bedside to shape the night prayers with his mute lips.

It was the most sultry night of the hot, oppressive summer, a low cloud cover had veiled the stars. Even within stone walls the heat hung too heavy to bear. And here at last there was true privacy, apart from the necessities and duties of brotherhood, not low panelled partitions separating them from their chosen kin, but walls of stone, and the width of the great court, and the suffocating weight of the night. Fidelis stripped off his habit and lay down to sleep in his linen. Between the two narrow cots, on the stand beside the breviary, the little oil lamp burned all night long with a dwindling golden flame.

Chapter Ten

N HIS shallow half-sleep, half-swoon
Brother Humilis dreamed that he heard
someone weeping, very softly, almost
without sound but for the break in the
breath, the controlled but extreme weeping of a
strong being brought to a desperation from which
there was no escape. It so stirred and troubled him
that he was lifted gradually out of his dream and into
a wakeful reality, but by then there was only silence.
He knew that he was not alone in the room, though
he had not heard the second cot carried in, nor the
coming of the one who was to lie beside him. But
even before he turned his head, and saw by the faint
glimmer of lamplight the white shape stretched on
the pallet, he knew who it was. The presence or
absence of this one creature was the pulse of his
life now. If Fidelis was by, the beat of his blood
was strong and comforting, without him it flagged
and weakened.

And therefore it must be Fidelis who had grieved
alone in the night, enduring what he could not
change, whatever burden of sin or sorrow it was that
swelled in him speechless and found no remedy.

Humilis put back the single cover from over him,

and sat up, swinging his feet to the stone floor between the two beds. He had no need to stand, only to lift the little lamp carefully and lean towards the sleeper, shielding the light so that it should not fall too sharply upon the young man's face.

Seen thus, aloof and impenetrable, it was a daunting face. Under the ring of curling hair, the colour of ripe chestnuts, the forehead was both lofty and broad, ivory-smooth above level, strong brows darker than the hair. Large, arched eyelids, faintly veined like the petals of a flower, hid the clear grey eyes. An austere face, the jaw sharply outlined and resolute, the mouth fastidious, the cheekbones high and proud. If he had indeed shed tears, they were gone. There was only a fine dew of sweat on his upper lip. Humilis sat studying him steadily for a long time.

The boy had shed his habit in order to sleep in better comfort. He lay on his side, cheek pressed into the pillow, the loose linen shirt open at his throat, and the chain that he wore had slid its links down in a silver coil into the hollow of his neck, and laid bare to view on the pillow the token that hung upon it.

Not a cross studded with semi-precious stones, but a ring, a thin gold finger-ring made in the spiral form of a coiled snake, with two splinters of red for eyes. An old ring, very old, for the finer chasing of head and scales was worn smooth with time, and the coils were wafer-thin.

Humilis sat gazing at this small, significant thing, and could not turn his eyes away. The lamp shook in his hand, and he laid it back on its stand in careful haste, for fear he should spill a drop of hot oil on the naked throat or outflung arm, and startle Fidelis out of what was at least oblivion, if not genuine rest.

Now he knew everything, the best and the worst, all there was to know, except how to find a way out of this web. Not for himself – his own way out opened clear before him, and was no long journey. But for this sleeper. . . .

Humilis lay back on his bed, trembling with the knowledge of a great wonder and a great danger, and waited for morning.

Brother Cadfael rose at dawn, long before Prime, and went out into the garden, but even there there was little air to breathe. A leaden stillness hung over the world, under a thin ceiling of cloud, through which the rising sun seemed to burn unimpeded. He went down to the Meole Brook, down the bleached slopes of the pease-fields, from which the haulms had long since been sickled and taken in for stable-bedding, leaving the white stubble to be ploughed into the ground for the next year's crop. Cadfael shed his sandals and waded into the slack, shallow water that was left, and found it warm where he had hoped for a little coolness. This weather, he thought, cannot continue much longer, it must break. Some-one will get the brunt of the storm, and if it's thunder, as by the smell in the air and the prickling of my skin it surely will be, Shrewsbury will get its share. Thunder, like commerce, followed the river valleys.

Once out of his bed, he had lost the fine art of being idle. He filled in the time until Prime with some work among the herbs, and some early watering while the sun was still climbing, round and dull gold behind its veil of haze. These functions his hands and eyes could take care of, while his mind was free to fret and speculate over the complicated fortunes of people for whom he had formed a strong affection. No

166

question but Godfrid Marescot – to think of him as an affianced man was to give him his old name – was busy leaving this world at a steady, unflinching walk, and every day he quickened his pace like a man anxious to be gone, and yet every day looked back over his shoulder in case that lost bride of his might be following on his heels rather than waiting for him patiently along the road ahead. And what could any man tell him for his reassurance? And what could afford any comfort to Nicholas Harnage, who had been too slow in prizing her fitly and making his bid for her favour?

A mile from Wherwell, and never seen again. And gone with her, temptation enough for harm, the valuables and the money she carried. And one man only as visible and obvious suspect, Adam Heriet, with everything against him except for Hugh's scrupulous conviction that he had been in genuine desperation to get news of her. He had asked and asked, and never desisted until he reached Shrewsbury. Or had he simply been fishing, not for news of her so much as for a glimpse, any glimpse, into Hugh's mind, any unwary word that would tell him how much the law already knew, and what chance he still had, by silence or lies or any other means, of brazening his way safely through his present peril?

Other inconsequent questions jutted from the obscurity like the untrimmed overgrowths from the hedges of a neglected maze. Why did the girl choose Wherwell in the first place? Certainly she might have preferred it as being far from her home, no bad principle when beginning a new life. Or because it was one of the chief houses of Benedictine nuns in all the south country, with scope for a gifted sister

167

to rise to office and power. And why did she give orders to three of her escort to remain in Andover instead of accompanying her all the way? True, the one she retained was her confidant and willing slave from infancy. If that was indeed true of him? It was reputed of him, yes, but truth and reputation sometimes part company. And if true, why did she dismiss even him short of her goal? Perhaps better phrase that more carefully: *Did* she dismiss him short of her goal? Then where did he spend the lost hours before he returned to Andover? Gaping at the wonders of Winchester, as he claimed? Or attending to more sinister business? What became of the treasures she carried? No great fortune, except to a man who lacked any fortune, but to him wealth enough. And always: *What became of her?*

And through the tangle he was beginning to glimpse a possible answer, and that uncertain inkling dismayed and terrified him more than all the rest. For if he was right, there could be no good end to this that he could see, every way he probed thorns closed the path. No way out, without worse ruin. Or a miracle.

He went to Prime at last, prompt to the bell, and prayed earnestly for a beckoning light. The needy and the deserving must surely be known elsewhere even better than here, he thought, who am I to presume to fill a place far too big for me?

Brother Fidelis did not attend Prime, his empty place ached like the soreness left after a pulled tooth. Rhun shone beside his friend's vacant stall, and never once glanced at Brother Urien. Such problems must not be allowed to distract his rapt attention from the office and the liturgy. There would be a time later in the day to give some thought to Urien, whose aggression had not been absolved, but only temporarily prevented. Rhun had no fear of shouldering the responsibility for another man's soul, being still half-child, with a child's certainty and clarity. To go to his confessor and tell what he suspected and knew of Urien would be to deprive Urien of the whole value of the sacrament of confession, and to tell tales upon a comrade in travail; the former was arrogant in Rhun's eyes, a kind of spiritual theft, and the latter was despicable, a schoolboy's treachery. Yet something would have to be done, something more than merely removing Fidelis from the sphere of Urien's torment and greed. Meantime, Rhun prayed and sang and worshipped with a whole happy heart, and trusted his saint to give him guidance.

Cadfael made short work of breakfast, asked leave, and went to visit Humilis. Coming armed with clean linen pad and green healing salve, he found his patient propped up in his bed freshly washed and shaven, already fed, if indeed he had managed to swallow anything, his toilet seen to in devoted privacy, and a cup of wine and water ready to his hand. Fidelis sat on a low stool beside the bed, ready to stir at once in answer even to a guessed-at need, in any look or gesture. When Cadfael entered, Humilis smiled, though the smile was pallidly blue of lip and cheek, translucent as ice. It is true, thought Cadfael, receiving that salutation, he is fast bound out of this world. It cannot be many days. The flesh melts from his bones as you watch, into smoke, into air. His spirit outgrows his body, soon it must burst out and become visible, there is no room for it in this fragile parcel of bones.

Fidelis looked up and echoed his master's smile,

and leaned to turn back the single light cover from the shrunken shanks, then rose from the stool to give place to Cadfael, and stood ready to offer a deft, assisting hand. Those menial services he offered with so much love must be called on frequently now. It was a marvel this body could function of itself at all, but there was a will that would not let it surrender its rights – certainly not anything less than love.

'Have you slept?' asked Cadfael, smoothing his new dressing into place.

'I have, and well,' said Humilis. 'The better for having Fidelis by me. I have not deserved such privilege, but I am meek enough to entreat for it to be continued. Will you speak with Father Abott for me?'

'I would, if there was need,' said Cadfael heartily, 'but he already knows and approves.'

'Then if I'm to have my indulgence,' said Humilis, 'speak for me now to this nurse and confessor and tyrant of mine, that he use a little kindness also to himself. At least he should go now to Mass, since I cannot, and take a turn in the garden for a little while, before he shuts himself here again with me.'

Fidelis heard all this smiling, but with a smile of inexpressible sadness. The boy, thought Cadfael, knows all too well the time cannot be long, and numbers every moment, charging it with meaning. Love in ignorance squanders what love, informed, crowds and overfills with tokens of eternity.

'He says rightly,' said Cadfael. 'You go to Mass, and I'll stay here until you come again. No need to hurry, I fancy you'll find Brother Rhun waiting for you.'

Fidelis accepted what he recognised as his purposeful dismissal, and went out silently, leaving them no less silent until his slight shadow had passed from the threshold of the room and out into the open court.

Humilis lay back in his raised pillows, and drew a great breath that should have floated his diminished body into the air, like thistledown.

'Will Rhun truly be looking for him?'

'He surely will,' said Cadfael.

'That's well! Of such a one he has need. An innocent, of such native power! Oh, Cadfael, for the simplicity and the wisdom of the dove! I wish Fidelis were such a one, but he is the other, the complement, the inward one. I had to send him away, I must talk with you. Cadfael, I am troubled in my mind for Fidelis.'

It was not news. Cadfael honestly nodded, and said nothing.

'Cadfael,' said the patient voice, delivered from stress now that they were alone. 'I've grown to know you a little, in this time you have been tending me. You know as well as I that I am dying. Why should I grieve for that? I owe a death that has been all but claimed of me a hundred times already. It is not for myself I'm troubled, it is for Fidelis. I dread leaving him alone here, trapped in this life without me.'

'He will not be alone,' said Cadfael. 'He is a brother of this house. He will have the service and fellowship of all here.' The sharp, wry smile did not surprise him. 'And mine,' he said, 'if that means anything more to you. Rhun's, certainly. You have said yourself that Rhun's loyalty is not to be despised.'

'No, truly. The saints of simplicity are made of his metal. But you are not simple, Brother Cadfael. You are sometimes of frightening subtlety, and that also has its place. Moreover, I believe you understand

171

me. You understand the nature of the need. Will you take care of Fidelis for me, stand his friend, believe in him, be shield and sword to him if need be, after I am gone?'

'To the best of my power,' said Cadfael, 'yes, I will.' He leaned to wipe away a slow trickle of spittle from the corner of a mouth wearied with speaking and slack at the lip, and Humilis sighed, and let him serve, docile under the brief touch. 'You know,' said Cadfael gently, 'what I only guess at. If I have guessed right, there is here a problem beyond my wit or yours to solve. I promise my endeavour. The ending is not mine, it belongs only to God. But what I can do, I will do.'

'I would happily die,' said Humilis, 'If my death can serve and save Fidelis. But what I dread is that my death, which cannot delay long, may only aggravate his trouble and his suffering. Could I take them with me into the judgement, how gladly would I embrace them and go. God forbid he should ever be brought to shame and punishment for what he has done.'

'If God forbids, man cannot touch him,' said Cadfael. 'I see what needs to be done, but how to achieve it, God knows, I cannot see. Well, God's vision is clearer than mine, he may both see a way out of this tangle and open my eyes to it when the time is ripe. There's a path through every forest, and a safe passage somewhere through every marsh, it needs only the finding.'

A faint grey smile passed slowly over the sick man's face, and left him grave again. 'I am the marsh out of which Fidelis must find safe passage. I should have Englished that name of mine, it would have been more fitting, with more than half my blood Saxon – Godfrid of the Marsh for Godfrid de Marisco. My father and my grandfather thought best to turn fully Norman. Now it's all one, we leave here all by the same gate.' He lay still and silent for a while, visibly gathering his thoughts and such strength as he had. 'There is one other longing I have, before I die. I should like to see again the manor of Salton, where I was born. I should like to take Fidelis there, just once to be with him outside the monastery walls, in the place that saw my beginning. I ought to have asked permission earlier, but there is still time. It's only a few miles up-river from us. Will you speak for me to the lord abbot, and ask this one kindness?'

Cadfael eyed him in doubt and consternation. 'You cannot ride, that's certain. Whatever means we might take to get you there, it would be asking too much of such strength as you have left.'

'No effort on my part can now alter by more than hours what is left of my life, but it would be a happiness to exchange some part of my time remaining for a glimpse of the place where I was a child. Ask it for me, Cadfael.'

'There is the river,' said Cadfael dubiously, 'but such twists and turns, it adds double to the journey. And such low water, you'd need a boatman who knows every shoal and current.'

'You must know of such a one. I remember how we used to swim and fish off our own shore. Shrewsbury lads were watermen from birth, I could swim before I could walk. There must be many such adepts along this riverside.'

And so there were, and Cadfael knew the best of them, whose knowledge of the Severn spanned every islet, every bend and shallow, and who at any

173

season could judge accurately where anything cast into the water would again be cast ashore. Madog of the Dead Boat had earned his title through the many sad services he had rendered in his time to distracted families who had lost sons or brothers into the flood after the melting of the Welsh snows far up-river, or too venturesome infants left unguarded for a moment while their mothers spread the washing on the bushes of the shore, or fishermen fathers putting out in their coracles with too much ale already under their belts. He did not resent his title, though his preferred trade was fishing and ferrying. What he did for the dead someone had to do, in grace, and since he could do it better than any other, why should he not take pride in it? Cadfael had known him many years, an elderly Welshman like himself, and had several times had occasion to seek his help, which was never grudged.

'Even in this low water,' said Cadfael thoughtfully, 'Madog could get a coracle up the brook from the river, but a coracle wouldn't carry you and Fidelis besides. But his light skiff draws very little water, I daresay he could bring it into the mill pond, there's still depth enough that far up the brook, with the mill race fed back into it. We could carry you out by the wicket to the mill, and see you bestowed. . . .'

'That far I could walk,' said Humilis resolutely.

'You'd be wise to save your energy for Salton. Who knows?' marvelled Cadfael, noting the slight flush of blood that warmed the thin grey face at the very prospect of returning to the first remembered home of his childhood – perhaps to end where he began. 'Who knows, it may yet do you a world of good!'

'And you will ask the lord abbot?'

174

'I will,' said Cadfael. 'When Fidelis returns, I'll go to him.'

'Tell him there may be need for haste,' said Humilis, and smiled.

Abbot Radulfus listened with his usual shrewd gravity, and considered for a while in silence before making any comment. Outside the dim, wood-panelled parlour in his lodging the hot sun climbed, still veiled with a thin haze that turned it copper-colour, and made it seem to burn even more fiercely. The roses budded, flowered and fell all in one day.

'Is he strong enough to bear it?' asked the abbot at length. 'And is it not too great a load to lay upon Brother Fidelis, to bear responsibility for him all that time.'

'It's the passing of his strength that makes him ask so urgently,' said Cadfael. 'If his wish is to be granted at all, it must be now, quickly. And he says rightly, it can make very little difference to the tale of his remaining days, whether they end tomorrow or after another week. But to his peace of mind this visit might make all the difference. As for Brother Fidelis, he has never yet shrunk from any burden laid upon him for love, and will not now. And if Madog takes them, they'll be in the best of hands. No one knows the river as he does. And he is to be trusted utterly.'

'For that I take your word,' said Radulfus equably. 'But it is a desperate enterprise for so frail a man. Granted it is his heart's wish, and he has every right to advance it. But how will you get him to the boat? And at the other end, is he sure of his welcome at Salton? Will there be willing attendants there to care for him?'

175

'Salton is a part of the honour he has relinquished now to a cousin he hardly knows, Father, but tenant and servants there will remember him. We can make a sling chair for him and carry him down to the mill. The infirmary lies close to the wall there, it's no distance to the mill wicket.'

'Very well,' said the abbot. 'It had better be very soon. If you know where to find this Madog, I give you leave, seek him out today, and if he's willing this journey had better be made tomorrow.'

Cadfael thanked him and departed, well pleased on his own account. He was no longer quite as ready as he would once have been to take leave of absence without asking, unless for a life-or-death reason, but he had no objection to making the very most of official leave when it was given. The prospect of a meal with Hugh and Aline in the town, instead of the hushed austerity of the refectory, and then a leisurely hunt along the waterside for Madog or news of him, and a comradely gossip when he was found, had all the attractions of a feast-day. But he looked in again on Humilis before he left the enclave, and told him how he had fared. Fidelis was again in careful attendance at the bedside, withdrawn and unobtrusive as ever.

'Abbot Radulfus grants your wish,' said Cadfael, 'and gives me leave to go and find Madog for you this very day. If he's agreeable, you can go to Salton tomorrow.'

Hugh's house by Saint Mary's church had an enclosed garden behind it, a small central herber with grassed benches round it, and fruit trees to give shade. There Aline Beringar was sitting on

176

the clipped seat sown with close-growing, fragrant herbs, with her son playing beside her. Not two years old until Christmas, Giles stood tall and sturdy and firm on his feet, made on a bigger scale than either his dark, trim father or his slender, fair mother. He had a rich colouring somewhere between the two, light bronze hair and round brown eyes, and a will of steel inherited, perhaps, from both, but not yet disciplined. He was wearing, in this hot summer, nothing at all, and was brown as a hazel-nut from brow to toes.

He had a pair of cut-out wooden knights, garishly painted and strung by two strings through their middles, their feet weighted with little blobs of lead, their legs and sword-arms jointed so that when the cords were tweaked from both ends they flourished their weapons and danced and slashed at each other in a very bloodthirsty manner. Constance, his willing slave, had forsaken him to go and supervise the preparations for dinner, and he clamoured imperiously for his godfather to supply the vacated place. Cadfael kneeled in the turf, only mildly complaining of the creaks in his joints, and manned the cords doughtily. In these arts he was well practised since the birth of Giles. Moreover, he must be careful not to be seen to give his opponent the better of the exchange by design, or there would be a shriek of knightly outrage. The heir and pride of the Beringars knew when he was being condescended to, and wholeheartedly resented it, convinced he was any man's equal. But he was none too pleased when he was defeated, either. It was necessary to walk a mountebank's tightrope to avoid his displeasure.

'You'll be wanting Hugh,' said Aline serenely

177

through her son's squeals of delight, and drew in her feet to give them full play for their strings. 'He'll be home for dinner in a little while. There's venison – they've started the cull.'

'So have a few other law-abiding citizens of the town, I daresay,' said Cadfael, energetically manipulating the cords to make the twin wooden swords flail like windmills.

'One here and there, what does it matter? Hugh knows how long to turn a blind eye. Good meat, and enough of it – and the king with little use for it, as things are! But it may not be long now,' said Aline, and smiled over her needlework, inclining her pale gold head and fair face above her naked son, sprawled on the grass tugging his strings in two plump brown fists. 'His own friends are beginning to work upon Robert of Gloucester, urging him to agree to the exchange. He knows she can do nothing about him. He must give way.'

Cadfael sat back on his heels, letting the cords fall back. The two wooden warriors fell flat in one embrace, both slain, and Giles tugged indignantly to bring them to life again, and was left to struggle in vain for a while.

'Aline,' said Cadfael earnestly, looking up into her gentle face, 'if ever I should have need of you suddenly, and come to fetch you, or send word to come – would you come? Wherever it was? And bring whatever I asked you to bring?'

'Short of the sun or the moon,' said Aline, smiling, 'whatever you asked, I would bring, and wherever you wanted me, I would come. Why? What's in your mind? Is it secret?'

'As yet,' said Cadfael ruefully, 'it is. For I'm almost as blind as I must leave you, girl dear, until I see my way, if ever I do. But indeed, some day soon I might need you.'

The imp Giles, distracted from his game and losing interest in the inexplicable conversation of his elders, hoisted his fallen knights, and went off hopefully after the floating savour of his dinner.

Hugh came hungry and in haste from the castle, and listened to Cadfael's account of developments at the abbey with meditative interest, over the venison Aline brought to the board.

'I remember it was said when they came here – was it you who told me so? It might well be! – that Marescot was born at Salton, and had a hankering to see it again. A pity he's brought so low. It seems this matter of the girl may not be solved for him this side of death. Why should he not have what can best make his going pleasant and endurable? It can cost him nothing but a few hours or days of surely burdensome living. But I wish we could have done better for him over the girl.'

'We may yet,' said Cadfael, 'if God wills. You've had no further word from Nicholas in Winchester?'

'Nothing as yet. And small wonder, in a town and a countryside torn to pieces by fire and war. Hard to find anything among the ashes.'

'And how is it with your prisoner? He has not conveniently remembered anything more from his journey to Winchester?'

Hugh laughed. 'Heriet has the good sense to know where he's safe, and sits very contentedly in his cell, well fed, well housed and well bedded. Solitude is no hardship to him. Question him, and he says again what he has already said, and never falls foul of a detail, either, no matter how you try to trip him.

179

Not all the king's lawyers would get anything more out of him. Besides, I took care to let him know that Cruce has been here twice, thirsty for his blood. It may be necessary to put a guard on his prison to keep Cruce out, but certainly not to keep Heriet in. He sits quietly and bides his time, sure we must loose him at last for want of proof.'

'Do you believe he ever harmed the girl?' said Cadfael.

'Do you?'

'No. But he is the one man who knows what did happen to her, and if he but knew it, he would be wise to speak, but to you only. No need for any witness besides. Do you think you could bring him to speak, by giving him to understand it was between you two only?'

'No,' said Hugh simply. 'What cause has he to trust me so far, if he has gone three years without trusting any other and keeps his mouth shut still, even to his own peril? No, I think I know his mettle. He'll continue secret as the grave.'

And indeed, thought Cadfael, there are secrets which should be buried beyond discovery, things, even people, lost beyond finding, for their own sake, for all our sakes.

He took his leave, and went on through the town, and down to the waterside under the western bridge that led out towards Wales, and there was Madog of the Dead Boat working at his usual small enclosure, weaving the rim of a new coracle with intertwined hazel withies, peeled and soaked in the shallows under the bridge. A squat, square, hairy, bandy-legged Welshman of unknown age, though apparently made to last for ever, since no one could

180

remember a time when he had looked any younger, and the turning of the years did not seem to make him look any older. He squinted up at Cadfael from under thick, jutting eyebrows that had turned grey while his hair was still black, and gave leisurely greeting, his brown hands still plaiting at the wands with practised dexterity.

'Well, old friend, you've become almost a stranger this summer. What's the word with you, to bring you here looking for me – for I take it that was your purpose, this side the town? Sit down and be neighbourly for a while.'

Cadfael sat down beside him in the bleached grass, and measured the diminished level of the Severn with a considering eye.

'You'll be saying I never come near but when I want something of you. But indeed we've had a crowded year, what with one thing and another. How do you find working the water now, in this drought? There must be a deal of tricky shallows upstream, after so long without rain.'

'None that I don't know,' said Madog comfortably. 'True, the fishing's profitless, and I wouldn't say you could get a loaded barge up as far as Pool, but I can get where I want to go. Why? Have you work for me? I could do with a day's pay, easy come by.'

'Easy enough, if you can get yourself and two more up as far as Salton. Lightweights both, for the one's skin and bone, and the other young and slender.'

Madog leaned back from his work, interested, and asked simply: 'When?'

'Tomorrow, if nothing prevents.'

'It would be far shorter to ride,' Madog observed, studying his friend with kindling curiosity.

'Too late for one of these ever to ride again. He's a dying man, and wants to see again the place where he was born.'

'Salton?' Shrewd dark eyes blinked through their thick silver brows. 'That should be a de Marisco. We heard you had the last of them in your house.'

'Marescot, they're calling it now. Of the Marsh, Godfrid says it should better have been, his line being Saxon. Yes, the same. His time is not long. He wants to complete the circle of birth to death before he goes.'

'Tell me,' said Madog simply, and listened with still and serene attention as Cadfael told him the nature of his cargo, and all that was required of him.

'Now,' he said, when all was told, 'I'll tell what I think. This weather will not hold much longer, but for all that, it may still tarry a week or so. If your paladin is as set on his pilgrimage as you say, if he's willing to venture whatever comes, then I'll bring my boat into the mill-pool tomorrow after Prime. I'll have something aboard to shelter him if the rain does come. I keep a waxed sheet to cover goods that will as well cover a knight or a brother of the Benedictines at need.'

'Such a cerecloth,' said Brother Cadfael very soberly, 'may be only too fitting for Brother Humilis. And he will not despise it.'

182

Chapter Eleven

N THE streets of Winchester the stinking, blackened debris of fire was beginning to give place to the timid sparks of new hope, as those who had fled returned to pick over the remnants of their shops and households, and those who had stayed set to work briskly clearing the wreckage and carting timber to rebuild. The merchant classes of England were a tough and resilient breed, after every reverse they came back with fresh vigour, grimly determined upon restoration and willing to retrench until a profit was again possible. Warehouses were swept clear of what was spoiled, and made ready within to receive new merchandise. Shops collected what was still saleable, cleaned out ravaged rooms and set up temporary stalls. Life resumed, with astonishing speed and energy, its accustomed rhythms, with an additional beat in defiance of misfortune. As often as you fell us, said the tradesmen of the town, we will get up again and take up where we left off, and you will tire of it first.

The armies of the queen, secure in possession here and well to westward, as well as through the south-east, went leisurely about their business, consolidating what they held, and secure in the

183

knowledge that they had only to sit still and wait, and King Stephen must now be restored to them. There must have been a few shrewd captains, both English and Flemish, who saw no great reason to rejoice at the exchange of generals, for however vital Stephen might be as a figurehead to be prized and protected at all costs, and however doughty a fighter, he was no match for his valiant wife as a strategist in war. Still, his release was essential. They sat stolidly on their winnings, and wait for the enemy to surrender him, as sooner or later they must. There was a degree of boredom to be endured, while the negotiators parleyed and wrangled. The end was assured.

Nicholas Harnage, with the list of Julian Cruce's valuables in his pouch, went doggedly about the city of Winchester, enquiring wherever such articles might have surfaced, whether stolen, sold, or given in reverence. And he had begun with the highest, the Holy Father's representative in England, the Prince-Bishop of Winchester, Henry of Blois, just shaking together his violated dignity and emerging with formidable resolution into the field of discussion, as if he had never changed and rechanged his coat, nor been shut up fast in his own castle in his own city, in peril of his life. It took a deal of persistence to get admission to his lordship's presence, but Nicholas, in his present cause, had persistence enough to force his way through even these prickly defences.

'Do you trouble me with such trifles?' Bishop Henry had demanded, after perusing, with blackly frowning countenance, the list Nicholas presented to him. 'I know nothing of any such tawdry trinkets. None of these have I ever seen, none belongs to any house of worship known here to me. What is there here to concern me?'

184

'My lord, there is a lady's life,' said Nicholas, stung. 'She intended what she never achieved, a life of dedication in the abbey of Wherwell. Before ever reaching there she was lost, and what I intend is to find her, if she lives, and avenge her, if she is dead. And only by these, as you say, tawdry trinkets can I hope to trace her.'

'In that,' said the bishop shortly, 'I cannot help you. I tell you certainly, none of these things ever came into the possession of the Old Minster, nor of any church or convent under my supervision. But you may enquire where you will among other houses in this city, and say that I have sanctioned your search. That is all I can do.'

And with that Nicholas had had to be content, and indeed it did give him a considerable authority, should he be questioned as to what right he had in the matter. However eclipsed for a time, Henry of Blois would rise again like the phoenix, as formidable as ever, and the fire that had all but consumed him could be relied upon to scorch whoever dared his enmity afterwards.

From church to church and priest to priest Nicholas carried his list, and found nothing but shaken heads and helplessly knitted brows everywhere, even where there was manifest goodwill towards him. No house of religion surviving in Winchester knew anything of the twin candlesticks, the stone-studded cross or the silver pyx that had been a part of Julian Cruce's dowry. There was no reason to doubt their word, they had no reason to lie, none even to prevaricate.

There remained the streets, the shops of gold-smiths, silversmiths, even the casual market-traders who would buy and sell whatever came to hand.

Nicholas began the systematic examination of them all, and in so rich a city, with so wealthy a clientele of lofty churchmen and rich foundations, they were many.

Thus he came, on the morning of this same day when Brother Humilis entreated passage to the place of his birth, into a small, scarred shop in the High Street, close under the shadow of Saint Maurice's church. The frontage had suffered in the fires, and the silversmith had rigged a shuttered opening like a fairground booth, and drawn his work-bench close to it, to have the full daylight on his work. The raised shutter overhead protected his face from glare, but let in the morning shine to the brooch he was handling, and the fine stones he was setting in it. A man in his prime, probably well-fleshed when times were good, but now somewhat shrunken after the privations of the long siege, for his skin hung on him flaccid and greyish, like a too-large coat on a fasting man. He looked up alertly through a forelock of greying hair, and asked if he could serve the gentleman.

'I begin to think it a thin enough chance,' admitted Nicholas ruefully, 'but at least let's make the assay. I am hunting for word, any word, of certain pieces of church plate and ornaments that went astray in these parts three years ago. Do you handle such things?'

'I handle anything of gold or silver. I have made church plate in my time. But three years is a long while. What is so notable about them? Stolen, you think? I deal in no suspect goods. If there's anything dubious about what's offered, I never touch it.'

'There need not have been anything here to deter you. True enough they might have been stolen, but there need be nothing to tell you so. They belonged

186

to no southern church or convent, they were brought from Shropshire, and most likely made in that region, and to a man like you they'd be recognisable as northern work. The crosses might well be old, and Saxon.'

'And what are these items? Read me your list. My memory is not infallible, but I may recall, even after three years.'

Nicholas went through the list slowly, watching for a gleam of recognition. 'A pair of silver candlesticks with tall sconces entwined with vines, with snuffers attached by silver chains, these also decorated with vine-leaves. Two crosses made to match in silver, the larger a standing cross a man's hand in height, on a three-stepped silver pedestal, the other a small replica on a neck-chain for a priest's wear, both ornamented with semi-precious stones, yellow pebble, agate and amethyst . . . .'

'No,' said the silversmith, shaking his head decidedly, 'those I should not have forgotten. Nor the candlesticks, either.'

'. . . a small silver pyx engraved with ferns . . .'

'No. Sir, I recall none of these. If I had still my books I could look back for you. The clerk who kept them for me was always exact, he could find you every item even after years. But they're gone, every record, in the fire. It was all we could do to rescue the best of my stock, the books are all ash.'

The common fate in Winchester this summer, Nicholas thought resignedly. The most meticulous of book-keepers would abandon his records when his life was at risk, and if he had time to take anything but his life with him, he would certainly snatch up the most precious of his goods, and let the parchments go. It seemed hardly worth listing the small personal things which had belonged to Julian, for they would be less memorable. He was hesitating whether to persist when a narrow door opened and let in light from a yard behind the shop, and a woman came in.

When the outer door was closed behind her she vanished again briefly into the dimness of the interior, but once more emerged into light as she approached her husband's bench and the bright sunlight of the street, and leaned forward to set a beaker of ale ready at the silversmith's right hand. She looked up, as she did so, at Nicholas, with candid and composed interest, a good-looking woman some years younger than her husband. Her face was still shadowed by the awning that protected her husband's eyes, but her hand emerged fully into the sun as she laid the cup down, a pale, shapely hand cut off startlingly at the wrist by the black sleeve.

Nicholas stood staring in fascination at that hand, so fixedly that she remained still in wonder, and did not withdraw it from the light. On the little finger, too small, perhaps, to go over the knuckle of any other, was a ring, wider than was common, its edge showing silver, but its surface so closely patterned with coloured enamels that the metal was hidden. The design was of tiny flowers with four spread petals, the florets alternately yellow and blue, spiked between with small green leaves. Nicholas gazed at it in disbelief, as at a miraculous apparition, but it remained clear and unmistakable. There could not be two such. Its value might not be great, but the workmanship and imagination that had created it set it apart from all others.

188

'I pray your pardon, madam!' he said, stammering as he drew his wits together. 'But that ring . . . May I know where it came from?'

Both husband and wife were looking at him intently now, surprised but not troubled.

'It was come by honestly,' she said, and smiled in mild amusement at his gravity. 'It was brought in for sale some years back, and since I liked it, my husband gave it to me.'

'When was this? Believe me, I have good reasons for asking.'

'It *was* three years back,' said the silversmith readily. 'In the summer, but the date . . . that I can't be sure of now.'

'But *I* can,' said his wife, and laughed. 'And shame on you for forgetting, for it was my birthday, and that was how I wooed the ring out of you. And my birthday, sir, is the twentieth day of August. Three years I've had this pretty thing. The bailiff's wife wanted my husband to copy it for her once, but I wouldn't have it. This must still be the only one of its kind. Primrose and periwinkle . . . such soft colours!' She turned her hand in the sun to admire the glow of the enamels. 'The other pieces that came with it were sold, long ago. But they were not so fine as this.'

'There were other pieces that came with it?' demanded Nicholas.

'A necklace of polished pebbles,' said the smith, 'I remember it now. And a silver bracelet chased with tendrils of pease – or it might have been vetch.'

The ring alone would have been enough; these three together were certainty. The three small items of personal jewellery belonging to Julian Cruce had been brought into this shop for sale on the twentieth

189

of August, three years ago. The first clear echo, and its note was wholly sinister.

'Master silversmith,' said Nicholas, 'I had not completed the tale of all I sought. These three things came south, to my certain knowledge, in the keeping of a lady who was bound for Wherwell, but never reached her destination.'

'Do you tell me so?' The smith had paled, and was gazing warily and doubtfully at his visitor. 'I bought the things honestly, I've done nothing amiss, and know nothing, beyond that some fellow, decent enough to all appearance, brought them in here openly for sale. . . .'

'Oh, no, don't mistake me! I don't doubt your good faith, but see, you are the first I have found that even may help me to discover what is become of the lady. Think back, tell me, who was this man who came? What like was he? What age, what style of man? He was not known to you?'

'Never seen before nor since,' said the silversmith, cautiously relieved, but not sure that telling too much might not somehow implicate him in dangerous business. 'A man much of my years, fifty he might be. Ordinary enough, plain in his dress, I took him for what he claimed, a servant sent on an errand.'

The woman did better. She was much interested by this time, and saw no reason to fear involvement, and some sympathetic cause to help, insofar as she could. She had a sharper eye for a man than had her husband, and was disposed to approve of Nicholas and desire his goodwill.

'A solid, square-made man he was,' she said, 'brown as his leather coat. That was not a hot summer like this, his brown was the everlasting kind

190

that would only yellow a little in winter, the kind that comes with living out of doors year-round – forester or huntsman, perhaps. Brown-bearded, brown-haired but for his crown, he was balding. He had a bold, oaken face on him, and a quick eye. I should never have remembered him so well, but that he was the one who brought my ring. But I tell you what, I fancy he remembered me for a good while. He gave me long enough looks before he left the shop.'

She was used to that, being well aware that she was handsome, and it was one more reason why she had recalled the man so well. Good reason, also, for paying close attention to all she had to say of him.

Nicholas swallowed burning bitterness. It was not the fifty years, nor the beard, nor the bald crown, nor even the weathered hide that identified the man, for Nicholas had never seen Adam Heriet. It was the whole circumstance, possession of the jewellery, the evidence of the date, the fact that the other three had been left in Andover, and in any case Nicholas had seen them for himself, and none of them resembled this description. The fourth man, the devoted servant, the fifty-year-old huntsman and forester, a stout man of his hands, a man Waleran of Meulan would think himself lucky to get . . . yes, every word Nicholas had heard said of Adam Heriet fitted with what this woman had to say of the man who had sold Julian's jewels.

'I did question possession,' said the silversmith, still uneasy, 'seeing they were clearly a lady's property. I asked how he came by them, and why he was offering them for sale. He said he was simply a servant sent on an errand, his business to do as he was told, and he had too much sense to quibble over it, seeing whoever questioned the orders that man

191

gave might find himself short of his ears, or with a back striped like a tabby cat. I could well believe it, there are many such masters. He was quite easy about it, why should I be less so?'

'Why, indeed!' said Nicholas heavily. 'So you bought, and he departed. Did he argue over the price?'

'No, he said his orders were to sell, he was no valuer and was not expected to be. He took what I gave. It was a fair price.'

With room for a fair profit, no doubt, but why not? Silversmiths were not in the business to dole out charity to chance vendors.

'And was that all? He left you so?'

'He was going, when I did call after him, and asked him what was become of the lady who had worn these things, and had she no further use for them, and he turned back in the doorway and looked at me, and said no, for such she had no further use at all, for that this lady who had owned them was dead.'

The hardness of the answer, its cold force, was there in the silversmith's voice as he repeated it. Remembering had brought it back far more vividly than ever he had dreamed, it shook him as he voiced it. Even more fiercely it stabbed at Nicholas, a knife in the heart, driving the breath out of him. It rang so hideously true, and named Adam Heriet almost beyond doubt. She who had owned them was dead. Ornaments were of no further concern to her.

Out of the chill rage that consumed him he heard the woman, roused now and eager, saying: 'No, but that's not all! For it so chanced I followed the man out when he left, but softly, not to be seen too soon.' Had he given her an appraising look, smiled, flashed

192

an admiring eye, to draw her on a string? No, not if he had anything to hide, no, he would rather have slid away unobtrusively, glad to be rid of his winnings for money. No, she was female, curious, and had time on her hands to spare, she went out to see whatever was to be seen. And what was it she saw? 'He slipped along to the left here,' she said, 'and there was another man, a young fellow, pressed close against the wall there, waiting for him. Whether he gave him the money, all of it or some of it, I could not be sure, but something was handed over. And then the older one looked over his shoulder and saw me, and they slipped away very quickly round the corner into the side street by the market, and that was all I saw of them. And more than I was meant to see,' she reflected, herself surprised now that she came to see more in it than was natural.

'You're sure of that?' asked Nicholas intently. 'There was a second with him, a younger man?' For the three innocents from Lai had been left waiting in Andover. If it had not been true, one or other of them, the simpleton surely, would have given the game away at once.

'I am sure. A young fellow, neat enough but homespun, such as you might see hanging around inns or fairs or markets, the best of them hoping for work, and the worst hoping for a chance to get a hand in some other man's pouch.'

Hoping for work or hoping to thieve! Or both, if the work offered took that shape – yes, even to the point of murder.

'What was he like, this second?'

She furrowed her brow and considered, gnawing a lip. She was in strong earnest, searching her memory, which was proving tenacious and long.

'Tallish but not too tall, much the older one's height when they stood together, but half his bulk. I say young because he was slender and fast when he slipped away, and light on his feet. But I never saw his face, he had the capuchon over his head.'

'I did wonder,' said the silversmith defensively. 'But it was done, I'd paid, and I had the goods. There was no more I could do.'

'No. No, there's no blame. You could not know.' Nicholas looked again at the bright ring on the woman's finger. 'Madam, will you let me buy that ring of you? For double what your husband paid for it? Or if you will not, will you let me borrow it of you for a fee, and my promise to return it when I can? To you,' he said earnestly, 'it is dear as a gift, and prized, but I need it.'

She stared back at him wide-eyed and captivated, clasping and turning the ring on her finger. 'Why do you need it? More than I?'

'I need it to confront that man who brought it here, the man who has procured, I do believe, the death of the lady who wore it before you. Put a price on it, and you shall have it.'

She closed her free hand round it defensively, but she was flushed and bright-eyed with excitement, too. She looked at her husband, who had the merchant's calculating, far-off look in his eyes, and was surely about to fix a price that would pay the repairs of his shop for him. She tugged suddenly at the ring, twisted it briskly over her knuckle, and held it out to Nicholas.

'I lend it to you, for no fee. But bring it back to me yourself, when you have done, and tell me how this matter ends. And should you find you are mistaken, and she is still living, and wants her ring, then give

194

it back to her, and pay me for it whatever you think fair.'

The hand she had extended to him with her bounty he caught and kissed. 'Madam, I will! All you bid me, I will! I pledge you my faith!' He had nothing fit to offer her as a return pledge, she had the better of him at all points. Her husband was looking at her indulgently, as one accustomed to the whims of a very handsome wife, and made no demur, at least until the visitor was gone. 'I serve here under FitzRobert,' said Nicholas. 'Should I fail you, or you ever come to suppose that I have so failed you, complain to him, and he will show you justice. But I will not fail you!'

'Are you so ready to say farewell to my gifts?' asked the silversmith, when Nicholas was out of sight. But he sounded amused rather than offended, and had turned back to his close work on the brooch with unperturbed concentration.

'I have not said farewell to it,' she said serenely. 'I trust my judgement. He will be back, and I shall have my ring again.'

'And how if he finds the lady living, and takes you at your word? What then?'

'Why, then,' said his wife, 'I think I may earn enough out of his gratitude to buy myself all the rings I could want. And I know you have the skill to make me a copy of that one, if I so wish. Trust me, whichever way his luck runs – and I wish him better than he expects! – *we* shall not be the losers.'

Nicholas rode out of Winchester within the hour, in burning haste, by the north gate towards Hyde, passing close by the blackened ground and broken

195

toothed walls of the ill-fated abbey from which Humilis and Fidelis had fled to Shrewsbury for refuge. These witnesses to tragedy and loss fell behind him unnoticed now. His sights were set far ahead.

The inertia of despair had lasted no longer than the length of the street, and given place to the most implacable fury of rage and vengefulness. Now he had something as good as certain, a small circlet of witness, evidence of the foulest treachery and ingratitude. There could be no doubt whatever that these modest ornaments were the same that Julian had carried with her, no chance could possibly have thrown together for sale three such others. Two witnesses could tell of the disposal of that ill-gotten plunder, one could describe the seller only too well, with even more certainty once she was brought face to face with him, as, by God, she should be before all was done. Moreover, she had seen him meet with his hired assassin in the street, and pay him for his services. There was no possibility of finding the hireling, nameless and faceless as he was, except through the man who had hired him, and such enquiries as Nicholas had set in motion after Adam Heriet had so far failed to trace his present whereabouts. Only one company of Waleran's men remained near Winchester, and Heriet was not with them. But the search should go on until he was found, and when found, he had more now to explain away than a few stolen hours – possession of the lost girl's goods, the disposal of them for money, the sharing of his gains with some furtive unknown. For whatever conceivable purpose, but to pay him for his part in robbery and murder?

Once the principal villain was found, so would his tool be. And the first thing to do now was inform

Hugh Beringar, and accelerate the hunt for Adam Heriet in Shropshire as in the south, until he was run to earth at last, and confronted with the ring.

It was barely past noon when Nicholas rode out of the city. By dusk he was near Oxford, secured a remount, and rode on at a steadier and more sparing pace through the night. A hot, sultry night it was, all the more as he went north into the midlands. The sky was clear of cloud, yet without moon or stars, very black. And all about him, in the mid hours of the night, lightnings flared and instantly died again into blackness, conjuring up, for the twinkling of an eye, trees and roofs and distant hills, only to obliterate them again before the eye could truly perceive them. And all in absolute silence, with nowhere any murmur of thunder to break the leaden hush. Forewarnings of the wrath of God, or of his inscrutable mercies.

Chapter Twelve

HE MORNING came bright, veiled and still, the rising sun a disc of copper, the mill pond flat and dull like a pewter dish. The ripples evoked by Madog's oars did no more than heave sluggishly and settle again with an oily heaviness, as he brought his boat in from the river after Prime.

Brother Edmund had fussed and hesitated over the whole enterprise, unhappy at allowing the risk to his patient, but unable to prevent, since the abbot had given his permission. By way of a compromise with his conscience, he saw to it that every possible provision was made for the comfort of Humilis on the journey, but absent d himself from the embarkation to busy himself a out his other duties. It was Cadfael and Fidelis v ho carried Humilis in a simple litter out through the wicket in the enclave wall which led directly to the mill, and down to the waterside. For all his long bones, he weighed hardly as much as a half-grown boy. Madog, shorter by head and shoulders, hoisted him bodily in his arms without noticeable effort, and bade Fidelis first take his place on the thwart, so that the sick man could be settled on brychans against the young man's knees, and propped comfortably with pillows. Thus he might travel with as little fatigue as possible. Fidelis drew the thin shoulders gently back to rest against him, the tonsured head, bared to the morning air, pillowed on his knees. The ring of dark hair still showed vigorous and young where all else was enfeebled, drained and old. Only the eyes had kindled to unusual brightness in the excitement of this venture, the fulfilment of a dear wish. After all the great endeavours, all the crossing and recrossing of oceans and continents, all the battles and victories and strivings, adventure at last was a voyage of a few miles up an English river, to revisit a modest manor in a peaceful English shire.

Happiness, thought Cadfael, watching him, consists in small things, not in great. It is the small things we remember, when time and mortality close in, and by small landmarks we may make our way at last humbly into another world.

He drew Madog aside for a moment before he let them go. The two in the boat were already engrossed, the one in the open day, the sky above him, the green and brightness of the land outside the cloister, the other in his beloved charge. Neither was paying attention to anything else.

'Madog,' said Cadfael earnestly, 'if anything untoward should come to your notice – if there should be anything strange, anything to astonish you . . . for God's sake say no word to any other, only bring it to me.'

Madog looked sideways at him, blinking knowingly through the thorn-bushes of his brows, and said: 'And you, I suppose, will be no way astonished! I know you! I can see as far into a dark night as most men. If there's anything to tell, you shall be the first, and from me the only one to hear it.'

He clapped Cadfael weightily on the shoulder, slipped loose the mooring rope he had twined about a stooping willow stump, and set foot with a boy's agility on the side of the boat, at once pushing it off from the shore and sliding down to the thwart in one movement. The dull sheen of the water heaved and sank lethargically between boat and bank. Madog took the oars, and pulled the boat round easily into the outflowing current, lax and sleepy in the heat like a human creature, but still alive and in languid motion.

Cadfael stood to watch them go. The morning light, hazy though it was, shone on the faces of the two travellers as the boat swung round, the young face and the older face, the one hovering, solicitous and grave, the other upturned and pallidly smiling for pleasure in his chosen day. Both great-eyed, intent, perhaps even a little intimidated by the enterprise they had undertaken. Then the boat came round, the oars dipped, and it was on Madog's squat, capable figure the eastern light fell.

There was a ferryman called Charon, Cadfael recalled from his few forays into the writings of antiquity, who had the care of souls bound out of this world. He, too, took pay from his passengers, indeed he refused them if they had not their fare. But he did not provide rugs and pillows and cerecloth for the souls he ferried across to eternity. Nor had he ever cared to seek and salvage the forlorn bodies of those the river took as its prey. Madog of the Dead Boat was the better man.

*

There is always a degree of coolness on the water, however sultry the air and sunken the level of the stream. On the still, metallic lustre of the Severn there was at least the illusion of a breeze, and a breath from below that seemed to temper the glow from above, and Humilis could just reach a frail arm over the side and dip his fingers in the familiar waters of the river beside which he had been born. Fidelis nursed him anxiously, his hands braced to steady the pillowed head, so that it lay in a chalice of his cupped palms, quite at rest. Later he might seek to withdraw the touch of his hands, flesh against flesh, for the sake of coolness, but as yet there was no need. He hung above the upturned, dreaming face, delicately shifting his hands as Humilis turned his head from side to side, trying to take in and recall both banks as they slid by. Fidelis felt no cramp, no weariness, almost no grief. He had lived so long with one particular grief that it had settled amicably into his being, a welcome and kindly guest. Here in the boat, thus islanded together, he found also an equally profound and poignant joy.

They had circled the whole of the town in their early passage, for the Severn, upstream from the abbey, made a great moat about the walls, turning the town almost into an island, but for the neck of land covered and protected by the castle. Once under Madog's western bridge, that gave passage to the roads into Wales, the meanderings of the river grew tortuous, and turned first one cheek, then the other, to the climbing, copper sun. Here there was ample water still, though below its common summer level, and the few shoals clung inshore, and Madog was familiar with all of them, and rowed strongly and leisurely, conscious of his mastery.

'All this stretch I remember well,' said Humilis, smiling towards the Frankwell shore, as the great bend north of the town brought them back on their westward course. 'This is pure pleasure to me, friend, but I fear it must be hard labour to you.'

'No,' said Madog, taciturn in English, but able to hold his own, 'no, this water is my living and my life. I go gladly.'

'Even in wintry weather?'

'In all weathers,' said Madog, and glanced up briefly at the sky, which continued a brazen vault, cloudless but hazy.

Beyond the suburb of Frankwell, outside the town walls and the loop of the river, they were between wide stretches of water-meadows, still moist enough to be greener than the grass on high ground, and a little coolness came up from the reedy shores, as though the earth breathed here, that elsewhere seemed to hold its breath. For a while the banks rose on either side, and old, tall trees overhung the water, casting a leaden shade. Heavy willows leaned from the banks, half their roots exposed by the erosion of the soil. Then the ground levelled and opened out again on their right hand, while on the left the bank rose in low, sandy terraces below and a slope of grass above, leading up to hillocks of woodland.

'It is not far now,' said Humilis, his eyes fixed eagerly ahead. 'I remember well. Nothing here is changed.'

He had gathered a degree of strength from his pleasure in this expedition, and his voice was clear and calm, but there were beads of sweat on his brow and lip. Fidelis wiped them away, and leaned over him to give him shade without touching.

'I am a child given a holiday,' said Humilis, smiling. 'It's fitting that I should spend it where I was a child. Life is a circle, Fidelis. We go outward from our source for half our time, leave behind our kin and our familiar places, value far countries and new-made friends. But then at the furthest point we begin the roundabout return, drawing in again towards the place from which we came. When the circle joins, there is nowhere beyond to go in this world, and it's time to depart. There is nothing sad in that. It's right and good.'

He made to raise himself a little in the boat to look ahead, and Fidelis lifted and supported him under the arms. 'Yonder, behind the screen of trees, there is the manor. We're home!'

The soil was reddish and sandy here, and provided a long, narrow beach, beyond which a slope of grass climbed, and a trodden path went up through the trees. Madog ran his boat into the sand, shipped his oars, and stepped ashore to haul the boat firmly aground and moor it.

'Bide quiet here a while, and I'll go and tell them at the house.'

The tenant of Salton was a man of fifty-five, and had not forgotten the boy, nine years or so his junior, who had been born to his lord in this manor, and lived the first few years of his life there. He came himself in haste down to the river, with a pair of servants and an improvised chair to carry Godfrid up to the house. It was not the paladin of the Kingdom of Jerusalem he came hurrying to welcome, but the boy he had taught to fish and swim, and lifted on to his first pony at three years old. The early companionship had not lasted many years, and perhaps he had not given it a thought now for thirty years or more, being busy marrying and raising a family of his own, but the memories were readily reawakened. And in spite of Madog's dry warning, he checked in sharp and shocked dismay at sight of the frail spectre that awaited him in the boat. He was quick to recover and run to offer hand and knee and service, but Humilis had seen.

'You find me much changed, Aelred,' he said, fetching the name out of the well of his memory by instinct when it was needed. 'We are none of us the boys we once were. I have not worn well, but never let that trouble you. I'm well content. And glad, most glad, to see you here again on this same soil where I left you so long ago, and looking in such good heart.'

'My lord Godfrid, you do me great honour,' said Aelred. 'All here is at your service. My wife and my sons will be proud.'

He lifted his guest bodily out of the boat, startled by the light weight, and set him carefully in the sling chair. As a boy of twelve, long ago, son of his lord's steward, he had more than once carried the little boy in his arms. The elder brother, Marescot's heir, had scorned, at ten, to play nursemaid to a mere baby. Now the same arms carried the last wisp of a life, and found it scarcely heavier than the child.

'I am not come to put you to any trouble,' said Humilis, 'but only to sit here a while with you, and hear your news, and see how your fields prosper and your children grow. That will be great pleasure. And this is my good friend and helper, Brother Fidelis, who takes such good care of me that I lack nothing.'

Up the green slope and through the windbreak of trees they carried their burden, and there in the fields of the demesne, small but well husbanded, was the manor-house of Salton in its ring fence lined with byres and barns. A low, modest house, no more than a hall and one small chamber over a stone undercroft, and a separate kitchen in the yard. There was a little orchard outside the fence, and a wooden bench in the cool under the apple-trees. There they installed Humilis, with brychans and pillows to ease his sparsely covered bones, and ran busily back and forth in attendance on him with ale, fruit, new-baked bread, every gift they could offer. The wife came, fluttered and shy, dissembling startled pity as well as she could. Two big sons came, the elder about thirty, the younger surely achieved after one or two infant losses, for he was fifteen years younger. The elder son brought a young wife to make her reverence beside him, a dark, elfin girl, already pregnant.

Under the apple-trees Fidelis sat silent in the grass, leaving the bench for host and guest, while Aelred talked with sudden unwonted eloquence of days long past, and recounted all that had happened to him since those times. A quiet, settled, hard-working life, while crusaders roamed the world and came home childless, unfruitful and maimed. And Humilis listened with a faint, contented smile, his own voice used less and less, for he was tiring, and much of the stimulus of excitement was ebbing away. The sun was in the zenith, still a hazed and angry sun, but in the west swags of cloud were gathering and massing.

'Leave us now a little while,' said Humilis, 'for I tire easily, and I would not wear you out, as well. Perhaps I may sleep. Fidelis will watch by me.'

When they were alone he drew breath deep, and was silent a long time, but certainly not sleeping. He reached a lean hand to pluck Fidelis up by the sleeve, and have him sit beside him, in the place Aelred had vacated. A soft, drowsy lowing came to them from the byres, preoccupied as the humming of bees. The bees had had a hectic summer, frenziedly harvesting the flowers that bloomed so lavishly but died so soon. There were three hives at the end of the orchard. There would be honey in store.

'Fidelis. . . .' The voice that had begun to flag and fail him had recovered clarity and calm, only it sounded at a little distance, as though he had already begun to depart. 'My heart, I brought you here to be with you, you only, you of all the world, here where I began. No one but you should hear what I say now. I know you better than I know my own soul. I value you as I value my own soul and my hope of heaven. I love you above any creature on this earth. Oh, hush . . . still!'

The arm on which his hand lay so gently had jerked and stiffened, the mute throat had uttered some small sound like a sob.

'God forbid I should cause you any manner of pain, even by speaking too freely, but time is short. We both know it. And I have things to say while there's time. Fidelis . . . your sweet companionship has been the blessing, the bliss, the joy and comfort of these last years of mine. There is no way I can recompense you but by loving you as you have loved me. And so I do. There can be nothing beyond that. Remember it, when I am gone, and remember that I go exulting, knowing you now as you know me, and loving as you have loved me.'

Beside him Fidelis sat still and mute as stone, but stones do not weep, and Fidelis was weeping, for when Humilis stooped and kissed his cheek he tasted tears.

*

That was all that passed. And shortly thereafter Madog stood before them, saying practically that there was a possible storm brewing, and they had better either make up their minds to stay where they were, or else get aboard at once and make their way briskly down with what current there was in this slack water, back to Shrewsbury.

The day belonged to Humilis, and so did the decision, and Humilis looked up at the western sky, darkening into an ominous twilight, looked at his companion, who sat like one straining to prolong a dream, remote and passive, and said, smiling, that they should go.

Aelred's sons carried him down to the shore, Aelred lifted him to his place in the bottom of the boat on his bed of rugs, with Fidelis to prop and cherish him. The east was still sullenly bright, they launched towards the light. Behind them the looming clouds multiplied with black and ominous speed, dangling like overfull udders of venomous milk. Under that darkness, Wales had vanished, distance became a matter of three miles or four. Somewhere there to westward there had already been torrential rain. The first turgid impulse of storm-water, creeping insidiously, began to muddy the Severn under them, and push them purposefully downstream.

They were well down the first reach between the water-meadows when the east suddenly darkened, almost instantly, to reflect back the purple-black frown of the west, and suddenly the light died into dimness, and the rumblings of thunder began, coming from the west at speed, like rolls of drums following them, or peals of deep-mouthed hounds on their trail in a hunt by demi-gods. Madog, untroubled but

207

ready, rested on his oars to unfold the waxed cloth he used for covering goods in passage, and spread it over Humilis and across the body of the boat, making a canopy for his head, which Fidelis held over spread hands to prevent it from impeding the sick man's breathing.

Then the rain began, first great, heavy, single drops striking the stretched cloth loud as stones, then the heavens opened and let fall all the drowning accumulation of water of which the bleached earth was creditor, a downpour that set the Severn seething as if it boiled, and spat abrupt fountains of sand and soil from the banks. Fidelis covered his head, and bent to sustain the cover over Humilis. Madog made out into the centre of the stream, for the lightning, though it followed the course of the river, would strike first and most readily at whatever stood tallest along the banks.

Already soaked, he shook off water merrily as a fish, as much at home in it as beside it. He had been out in storms quite as sudden and drastic as this, and furious though it might be, he was assured it would not last very long.

But somewhere far upstream they had received this baptism several hours ago, for flood water was coming down by this time in a great, foul brown wave, sweeping them before it. Madog ran with it, using his oars only to keep his boat well out in midstream. And steadily and viciously the torrent of rain fell, and the rolls and peals and slashes of thunder hounded them down towards Shrewsbury, and the lightnings, hot on the heels of the thunder, flashed and flamed and criss-crossed their path, the only light in a howling darkness. They could barely see either bank except when the lightning flared and vanished, and the blindness after its passing made the succeeding blaze even more blinding.

Wet and streaming as a seal, Fidelis shook off water on either side, and held the cover over Humilis with braced and aching forearms. His eyes were tight-shut against the deluge of the rain, he opened them only by burdened glimpses, peering through the downpour. He did not know where they were, except by flaming visions that forced light through his very eyelids, and caused him to blink the torment away. Such a flare showed him trees leaning, gaunt and sinister, magnified by the lurid light before they were swallowed in the darkness. So they were already past the open water-meadows, surely by now morasses dimpled and pitted with heavy rain. They were being driven fast between the trees, not far now from possible shelter in Frankwell.

In spite of the covering cloth they were awash. Water swirled in the bottom of the boat, cold and sluggish, a discomfort, but not a danger. They ran with the current, fouled and littered with leaves and the debris of branches, muddied and turgid and curling in perverse eddies. But very soon now they could come ashore in Frankwell and take cover in the nearest dwelling, hardly the worse for all this turmoil and violence.

The thunder gathered and shrieked, one ear-bursting bellow. The lightning struck in time with it, a blinding glare. Fidelis opened his drowned eyes in shock at the blow, in time to see the thickest, oldest, most misshapen willow on the left bank leap, split asunder in flame, wrench out half its roots from the slithering, sodden shore, and burst into a tremendous blossom of fire, hurled into midstream over them, and blazing as it fell.

209

Madog flung himself forward over Humilis in the shell of the boat. Like a bolt from a mangonel the shattered tree crashed down upon the bow of the skiff, smashed through its sides and split it apart like a cracked egg. Trunk and boat and cargo went down deep together into the murky waters. The fire died in an immense hissing. Everything was dark, everything suddenly cold and in motion and heavier than lead, dragging body and soul down among the weed and debris of storm, turning and turning and drifting fast, drawn irresistibly towards the ease and languor of death.

Fidelis fought and kicked his way upward with bursting heart, against the comforting persuasion of despair, the cramping, crippling weight of his habit, and the swirling and battering of drifting branches and tangling weeds. He came to the surface and drew deep breath, clutching at leaves that slid through his fingers, and fastening greedily on a branch that held fast, and supported him with his head above water. Gasping, he shook off water and opened his eyes upon howling darkness. A cage of shattered branches surrounded and held him. Torn but still tenacious roots anchored the willow, heaving and plunging, against the surging current. A brychan from the boat wound itself about his arm like a snake, and almost tore him from his hold. He dragged himself along the branch, peering and straining after any glimpse of a floating hand, a pale face, phantom-like in all that chaotic gloom.

A fold of black cloth coiled past, driven through the threshing leaves. The end of a sleeve surfaced, a pallid hand trailed by and went under again. Fidelis loosed his hold, and launched himself after

210

it, clear of the tree, diving beneath the trammelling branches. The hem of the habit slid through his fingers, but he got a grip on the billowing folds of the cowl, and struck out towards the Frankwell shore to escape the trailing wreckage of the willow. Clinging desperately, he shifted to a better hold, holding the lax body of Humilis above him. Once they went down together. Then Madog was beside them, hoisting the weight of the unconscious body from arms that could not have sustained it longer.

Fidelis drifted for a moment on the edge of acceptance, in an exhaustion which rendered the idea of death perilously attractive. Better by far to let go, abandon struggle, go wherever the current might take him.

And the current took him and stranded him quite gently in the muddied grass of the shore, and laid him face-down beside the body of Brother Humilis, over which Madog of the Dead Boat was labouring all in vain.

The rain slackened suddenly, briefly, the wind, which had the whistle of anguish on its driving breath, subsided for an instant, and the demons of thunder rolled and rumbled away downstream, leaving a breath of utter silence and almost stillness, between frenzies. And piercing through the lull, a great scream of deprivation and loss and grief shrilled aloft over the Severn, startling the hunched and silent birds out of the bushes, and echoing down the flood in a long ululation from bank to bank, crying a bereavement beyond remedy.

Chapter Thirteen

ICHOLAS WAS approaching Shrewsbury when the sky began to darken ominously, and he quickened his pace in the
hope of reaching shelter in the town before the storm broke. But the first heavy drops fell
as he reached the Foregate, and before his eyes the
street was emptied of life, all its inhabitants going to
ground within their houses, and closing doors and
shutters against the rage to come. By the time he
rode past the gatehouse of the abbey, abandoning
the thought of waiting out the storm there, since he
was now so close, the sky had opened, in a downpour so opaque and blinding that he found himself
veering from side to side as he crossed the bridge,
unable to steer a straight course. It seemed he was
the only man left in a depopulated town in an empty
world, for there was not another soul stirring.

Under the arch of the town gate he halted to draw
breath and clear his eyes, shaking off the weight of
the rain. The whole width of Shrewsbury lay between
him and the castle, but Hugh's house by Saint Mary's
was no great distance, only up the curve of the Wyle
and the level street beyond. Hugh was as likely to
be there as at the castle. At least he could call in

and ask, on his way through to the High Cross, and the descent to the castle gatehouse. He could hardly get wetter than he already was. He set off up the hill. Saner folk peered out through the chinks in their shuttered windows, and watched him scurrying head-down through the deluge. Overhead the thunder rolled and rattled round a sky dark as midnight, and lightnings flickered, drawing the peals ever closer after them. The horse was unhappy but well-trained, and pressed on obedient but quivering with fear.

The gates of Hugh's courtyard stood open, there was a degree of shelter under the lee of the house, and as soon as hooves were heard on the cobbles the hall door opened, and a groom came haring across from the stables to take the horse to cover. Aline stood peering anxiously out into the murky gloom, and beckoned the traveller in.

'Before you drown, sir,' she said, all concern, as Nicholas plunged into the shelter of the doorway and let fall his streaming cloak, to avoid bringing it within. They stood looking earnestly at each other, for the light was too dim for instant recognition. Then she tilted her head, recaptured a memory, and smiled. 'You are Nicholas Harnage! You came here with Hugh, when first you came to Shrewsbury. I remember now. Forgive such a slow welcome back, but I am not used to midnight in the afternoon. Come within, and let me find you some dry clothes – though I fear Hugh's will be a tight fit for you.'

He was warmed by her candour and kindness, but it could not divert him from the black intensity of his purpose here. He looked beyond her, where Constance hovered, clutching her tyrant Giles firmly by the hand, for fear he should mistake the

213

deluge for a new amusement, and dart out into it.

'The lord sheriff is not here? I must see him as soon as may be. I bring grim news.'

'Hugh is at the castle, but he'll come by evening. Can it not wait? At least until this storm blows by. It cannot last long.'

No, he could not wait. He would go on the rest of the way, fair or foul. He thanked her, almost ungraciously in his preoccupation, swung the wet cloak about him again, took back his horse from the groom, and was off again at a trot towards the High Cross. Aline sighed, shrugged, and went in, closing the door on the chaos without. Grim news! What could that mean? Something to do with King Stephen and Robert of Gloucester? Had the attempts at an exchange foundered? Or was it something to do with that young man's personal quest? Aline knew the bare bones of the story, and felt a mild, rueful interest – a girl set free by her affianced husband, a favoured squire sent to tell her so, and too modest or too sensitive to pursue at once the attraction he felt towards her on his own account. Was the girl alive or dead? Better to know, once for all, than to go on tormented by uncertainty. But surely 'grim news' could only mean the worst.

Nicholas reached the High Cross, spectral through the streaming rain, and turned down the slight slope towards the castle, and the broad ramp to the gatehouse. Water lay ankle-deep in the outer ward, draining off far too slowly to keep pace with the flood. A sergeant leaned out from the guard-room, and called the stranger within.

'The lord sheriff? He's in the hall. If you bear round into the inner ward close to the wall you'll escape the worst. I'll have your horse stabled. Or wait a while here in the dry, if you choose, for this can't last for ever. . . .'

But no, he could not wait. The ring burned in his pouch, and the acid bitterness in his mind. He must get his tale at once to the ears of authority, and his teeth into the throat of Adam Heriet. He dared not stop hating, or the remaining grief became more than he could stand. He bore down on Hugh in the huge dark hall with the briefest of greetings and the most abrupt of challenges, an unkempt apparition, his wet brown hair plastered to forehead and temples, and water streaking his face.

'My lord, I'm back from Winchester, with plain proof Julian is dead and her goods made away with long ago. And we must leave all else and turn every man you have here and I can raise in the south, to hunt down Adam Heriet. It was his doing – Heriet and his hired murderer, some footpad paid for his work with the price of Julian's jewellery. Once we lay hands on him, he won't be able to deny it. I have proof, I have witnesses that he said himself she was dead!'

'Come, now!' said Hugh, his eyes rounding. 'That's a large enough claim. You've been a busy man in the south, I see, but so have we here. Come, sit, and let's have the full story. But first, let's have those wet clothes off you, and find you a man who matches, before you catch your death.' He shouted for the servants, and sent them running for towels and coats and hose.

'No matter for me,' protested Nicholas feverishly, catching at his arm. 'What matters is the proof I have, that fits only one man, to my mind, and he going free, and God knows where . . .'

215

'Ah, but Nicholas, if it's Adam Heriet you're after, then you need fret no longer. Adam Heriet is safe behind a locked door here in the castle, and has been for a matter of days.'

'You have him? You found Heriet? He's taken?' Nicholas drew deep and vengeful breath, and heaved a great sigh.

'We have him, and he'll keep. He has a sister married to a craftsman in Brigge, and was visiting his kin like any honest man. Now he's the sheriff's guest, and stays so until we have the rights of it, so no more sweat for him.'

'And have you got any part of it out of him? What has he said?'

'Nothing to the purpose. Nothing an honest man might not have said in his place.'

'That shall change,' said Nicholas grimly, and allowed himself to notice his own sudden condition for the first time, and to accept the use of the small chamber provided him, and the clothes put at his disposal. But he was half into his tale before he had dried his face and his tousled hair and shrugged his way into dry garments.

'. . . . never a trace anywhere of the church ornaments, which should be the most notable if ever they were marketed. And I was in two minds whether it was worth enquiring further, when the man's wife came in, and I knew the ring she was wearing for Julian's. No, that's to press it too far, I know – say rather I saw that it fitted only too well the description we had of Julian's. You remember? Enamelled all round with flowers in yellow and blue . . . .'

'I have the whole register by heart,' said Hugh drily.

'Then you'll see why I was so sure. I asked where she got it, and she said it was brought into the shop for sale along with two other pieces of jewellery, by a man about fifty years old. Three years back, on the twentieth day of August, for that was the day of her birth, and she asked the ring as a present, and got it from her husband. And the other two pieces, both sold since, they described to me as a necklace of polished stones and a silver bracelet engraved with sprays of vetch or pease. Three such, and all together! They could only be Julian's.'

Hugh nodded emphatic agreement to that. 'And the man?'

'The description the woman gave me fits what little I have been told of Adam Heriet, for till now I have not seen him. Fifty years old, tanned from living outdoor like forester or huntsman . . . You have seen him, you know more. Brown-bearded, she said, and balding, a face of oak . . . Is that in tune?'

'To the letter and the note.'

'And the ring I have. Here, see! I asked it of the woman for this need, and she trusted me with it, though she valued it and would not sell, and I must give it back – when its work is done! Could this be mistaken?'

'It could not. Cruce and all his household will confirm it, but truth, we hardly need them. Is there more?'

'There is! For the jeweller questioned the owner-ship, seeing these were all a woman's things, and asked if the lady who owned them had no further use for them. And the man said, as for the lady who had owned them, no, she had no further use for them, seeing she was dead!'

'He said so? Thus baldly?'

217

'He did. Wait, there's more! The woman was a little curious about him, and followed him out of the shop when he left. And she saw him meet with a young fellow who was lurking by the wall outside, and give something over to him – a part of the money or the whole, or so she thought. And when they were aware of her watching, they slipped away round the corner out of sight, very quickly.'

'All this she will testify to?'

'I am sure she will. And a good witness, careful and clear.'

'So it seems,' said Hugh, and shut his fingers decisively over the ring. 'Nicholas, you must take some food and wine now, while this downpour continues – for why should you drown a second time when we have our quarry already in safe hold? But as soon as it stops, you and I will go and confront Master Heriet with this pretty thing, and see if we cannot prise more out of him this time than a child's tale of gaping at the wonders of Winchester.'

Ever since dinner Brother Cadfael had been dividing his time between the mill and the gatehouse, fore-warned of possible trouble by the massing of the clouds long before the rain began. When the storm broke he took refuge in the mill, from which vantage-point he could keep an eye on both the pond and its outlet to the brook, and the road from the town, in case Madog should have found it advisable to land his charges for shelter in Frankwell, rather than com-pleting the long circuit of the town, in which case he would come afoot to report as much.

The mill's busy season was over, it was quiet and dim within, no sound but the monotonous dull drumming of the rain. It was there that Madog found

him, a drowned rat of a Madog, alone. He had come
by the path outside the abbey enclave, by which
the town customers approached with their grain to
be milled, rather than enter at the gatehouse. He
loomed shadowy against the open doorway, and
stood mute, dangling long, helpless arms. No man's
strength could fight off the powers of weather and
storm and thunder. Even his long endurance had
its limits.

'Well?' said Cadfael, chilled with foreboding.

'Not well, but very ill.' Madog came slowly within,
and what light there was showed the dour set of his
face. 'Anything to astonish me, you said! I have had
my fill of astonishment, and I bring it straight to you,
as you wished. God knows,' he said, wringing out
beard and hair, and shaking rivulets of rain from his
shoulders, 'I'm at a loss to know what to do about it.
If you had foreknowledge, you may be able to see a
way forward – I'm blind!' He drew deep breath, and
told it all in words blunt and brief. 'The rain alone
would not have troubled us. The lightning struck
a tree, heaved it at us as we passed, and split us
asunder. The boat's gone piecemeal down the river,
where the shreds will fetch up there's no guessing.
And those two brothers of yours . . . .'

'*Drowned*?' said Cadfael in a stunned whisper.

'The older one, Marescot, yes . . . Dead, at any
rate. I got him out, the young one helping, though
him I had to loose, I could not grapple with both.
But I could get no breath back into Marescot. There
was barely time for him to drown, the shock more
likely stopped his heart, frail as he was – the cold,
even the noise of the thunder. However it was, he's
dead. There's an end. As for the other – what is
there I could tell you of the other, that you do not

219

know?' He was searching Cadfael's face with close and wondering attention. 'No, there's no astonishment in it for you, is there? You knew it all before. Now what do we do?'

Cadfael stirred out of his stillness, gnawed a cautious lip, and stared out into the rain. The worst had passed, the sky was growing lighter. Far along the river valley the diminishing rolls of thunder followed the foul brown flood-water downstream.

'Where have you left them?'

'On the far side of Frankwell, not a mile from the bridge, there's a hut on the bank, the fishermen use it. We fetched up close by, and I got them into cover there. We'll need a litter to bring Marescot home, but what of the other?'

'Nothing of the other! The other's gone, drowned, the Severn has taken him. And no alarm, no litter, not yet. Bear with me, Madog, for this is a desperate business, but if we tread carefully now we may come through it unscathed. Go back to them, and wait for me there. I'm coming with you as far as the town, then you go on to the hut, and I'll come to you there as soon as I can. And never a word of this, never to any, for the sake of us all.'

The rain had stopped by the time Cadfael turned in at the gate of Hugh's house. Every roof glistened, every gutter streamed, as the grey remnants of cloud cleared from a sun now bright and benevolent, all its coppery malignancy gone down-river with the storm.

'Hugh is still at the castle,' said Aline, surprised and pleased as she rose to meet him. 'He has a visitor with him there – Nicholas Harnage is come back, he

220

says with grim news, but he did not stay to confide it to me.'

'He? He's back?' Cadfael was momentarily distracted, even alarmed. 'What can he have found, I wonder? And how wide will he have spread it already?' He shook the speculation away from him. 'Well, that makes my business all the more urgent. Girl dear, it's you I want! Had Hugh been here, I would have begged the loan of you of your lord in a proper civil fashion, but as things are . . . I need you for an hour or two. Will you ride with me in a good cause? We'll need horses – one for you to go and return, and one for me to go further still – one of Hugh's big fellows that can carry two at a pinch. Will you be my advocate, and see me back into good odour if I borrow such a horse? Trust me, the need is urgent.'

'Hugh's stables have always been open to you,' said Aline, 'since ever we got to know you. And I'll lend myself for any enterprise you tell me is urgent. How far have we to go?'

'Not far. Over the western bridge and across Frankwell. I must ask the loan of some of your possessions, too,' said Cadfael.

'Tell me what you want, and then you go and saddle the horses – Jehan is there, tell him you have my leave. And you can tell me what all this means and what I'm needed for on the way.'

Adam Heriet looked up sharply and alertly when the door of his prison was opened at an unexpected hour of the early evening. He drew himself together with composure and caution when he saw who entered. He was practised and prepared in all the questions with which he had so far had to contend, but this

221

promised or threatened something new. The bold oaken face the jeweller's wife had so shrewdly observed served him well. He rose civilly in the presence of his betters, but with a formal stiffness and a blank countenance which suggested that he did not feel himself to be in any way inferior. The door closed behind them, though the key was not turned. There was no need, there would be a guard outside.

'Sit, Adam! We have been showing some interest in your movements in Winchester, at the time you know of,' said Hugh mildly. 'Would you care to add anything to what you've already told us? Or to change anything?'

'No, my lord. I have told you what I did and where I went. There is no more to tell.'

'Your memory may be faulty. All men are fallible. Can we not remind you, for instance, of a silversmith's shop in the High Street? Where you sold three small things of value – not your property?'

Adam's face remained stonily stoical, but his eyes flickered briefly from one face to the other. 'I never sold anything in Winchester. If anyone says so, they have mistaken me for some other man.'

'You lie!' said Nicholas, flaring. 'Who else would be carrying these very three things? A necklace of polished stones, an engraved silver bracelet – and *this*!'

The ring lay in his open palm, thrust close under Adam's nose, its enamels shining with a delicate lustre, a small work of art so singular that there could not be a second like it. And he had known the girl from infancy, and must have been familiar with her trinkets long before that journey south. If he denied this, he proclaimed himself a liar, for there were plenty of others who could swear to it.

He did not deny it. He even stared at it with a well-assumed wonder and surprise, and said at once: 'That is Julian's! Where did you get it?'

'From the silversmith's wife. She kept it for her own, and she remembered very well the man who brought it, and painted as good a picture of him as the law will need to put your name to him. Yes, this is Julian's!' said Nicholas, hoarse with passion. 'That is what you did with her goods. *What did you do with her*?'

'I've told you! I parted from her a mile or more from Wherwell, at her orders, and I never saw her again.'

'You lie in your teeth! You destroyed her.'

Hugh laid a hand on the young man's arm, which started and quivered at the touch, like a pointing hound distracted from his aim.

'Adam, you waste your lying, which is worse. Here is a ring you acknowledge for your mistress's property, sold, according to two good witnesses, on the twentieth of August three years ago, in a Winchester shop, by a man whose description fits you better than your own clothes . . .'

'Then it could fit many a man of my age,' protested Adam stoutly. 'What is there singular about me? The woman has not pointed the finger at *me*, she has not seen me . . . .'

'She will, Adam, she will. We can bring her, and her husband, too, to accuse you to your face. As I accuse you,' said Hugh firmly. 'This is too much to be passed off as a children's tale, or a curious chance. We need no better case against you than this ring and those two witnesses provide – for robbery, if not for murder. Yes, murder! How else did you get possession of her jewellery? And if you did not connive at her death, then where is she now? She never reached Wherwell, nor was she expected there, it was quite safe to put her out of the world, her kin here believing her safe in a nunnery, the nunnery undisturbed by her never arriving, for she had given no forewarning. So where is she, Adam? On the earth or under it?'

'I know no more than I've told you,' said Adam, setting his teeth.

'Ah, but you do! You know how much you got from the silversmith – and how much of it you paid over to your hired assassin, outside the shop. Who was he, Adam?' demanded Hugh softly. 'The woman saw you meet him, pay him, slither away round the corner with him when you saw her standing at the door. Who was he?'

'I know nothing of any such man. It was not I who went there, I tell you.' His voice was still firm, but a shade hurried now, and had risen a tone, and he was beginning to sweat.

'The woman has described him, too. A young fellow about twenty, slender, and kept his capuchon over his head. Give him a name, Adam, and it may somewhat lighten your load. If you know a name for him? Where did you find him? In the market? Or was he bespoken well before for the work?'

'I never entered such a shop. If all this happened, it happened to other men, not to me. I was not there.'

'But Julian's possessions were, Adam! That's certain. And brought by someone who much resembled you. When the woman sees you in the flesh, then I may say, brought by *you*. Better to tell us, Adam. Spare yourself a long uncovering, make your

224

confession of your own will, and be done. Spare the silversmith's wife a long journey. For she *will* point the finger, Adam. This, she will say when she sets eyes on you, *this* is the man.'

'I have nothing to confess. I've done no wrong.'

'Why did you choose that particular shop, Adam?'

'I was never in the shop. I had nothing to sell. I was not there . . . .'

'But this ring was, Adam. How did it get there? And with necklace and bracelet, too? Chance? How far can chance stretch?'

'I left her a mile from Wherwell . . . .'

'Dead, Adam?'

'I parted from her living, I swear it!'

'Yet you told the silversmith that the lady who had owned these gems was dead. Why did you so?'

'I told you, it was not I, I was never in the shop.'

'Some other man, was it? A stranger, and yet he had those ornaments, all three, and he resembled you, and he knew and said that the lady was dead. Here are so many miraculous chances, Adam, how do you account for them?'

The prisoner let his head fall back against the wall. His face was grey. 'I never laid hand on her. I loved her!'

'And this is not her ring?'

'It *is* her ring. Anyone at Lai will tell you so.'

'Yes, they will, Adam, they will! They will tell the court so, when your time comes. But only you can tell us how it came into your possession, unless by murder. Who was the man you paid?'

'There was none. I was not there. It was not I . . . .'

The pace had steadily increased, the questions coming thick as arrows and as deadly. Round and

225

round, over and over the same ground, and the man was tiring at last. If he was breakable at all, he must break soon.

They were so intent, and strung so taut, like overtuned instruments, that they all three started violently when there was a knock at the door of the cell, and a sergeant put his head in, visibly agape with sensational news. 'My lord, pardon, but they thought you should know at once . . . There's word in town that a boat sank today in the storm. Two brothers from the abbey drowned in Severn, they're saying, and Madog's boat smashed to flinders by a tree the lightning fetched down. They're searching downstream for one of the pair . . . .'

Hugh was on his feet, aghast. '*Madog*'s boat? That must be the hiring Cadfael told me of . . . Drowned? Are they sure of their tale? Madog never lost man nor cargo till now.'

'My lord, who can argue with lightning? The tree crashed full on them. Someone in Frankwell saw the bolt fall. The lord abbot may not even know of it yet, but they're all in the same story in the town.'

'I'll come!' said Hugh, and swung hurriedly on Nicholas. 'God knows I'm sorry, Nick, if this is true. Brother Humilis – your Godfrid – had a longing to see his birthplace at Salton again, and set out with Madog this morning, or so he intended – he and Fidelis. Come with me! We'd best go find out the truth of it. Pray God they've made much of little, as usual, and they've come by nothing worse than a ducking . . . Madog can outswim most fish. But let's go and make sure.'

Nicholas had risen with him, startled and slow to take it in. 'My lord? And he so sick? Oh, God, he

226

could not live through such a shock. Yes, I'll come
. . . I must know!'

And they were away, abandoning their prisoner. The door closed briskly between, and the key turned in the lock. No one had given another look or thought to Adam Heriet, who sank back slowly on his hard bed, and bowed himself into his cupped hands, a demoralised hulk of a man, worn out and emptied at heart. Gradually slow tears began to seep between his braced fingers and fall upon his pillow, but there was no one there to see and wonder, and no one to interpret.

They took horse in haste through the town, through streets astonishingly drying out already in the gentle warmth after the deluge. It was still broad day and late sunlight, and the roofs and walls and roads steamed, so that the horses waded a shallow, frail sea of vapour. They passed by Hugh's house without halting. As well, for they would have found no Aline there to greet them.

People were emerging into the streets again wherever they passed, gathering in twos and threes, heads together and chins earnestly wagging. The word of tragedy had gone round rapidly, once it was whispered. Nor was it any false alarm this time. Out through the eastern gate and crossing the bridge towards the abbey, Hugh and Nicholas drew rein at sight of a small, melancholy procession crossing ahead of them. Four men carried an improvised litter, an outhouse door taken from its hinges in some Frankwell householder's yard, and draped decently with rugs to carry the corpse of one victim, at least, of the storm. One only, for it was a narrow door, and the four bearers handled it as if the weight was light, though the swathed body lay long and large-boned on its bier.

They fell in reverently behind, as many of the townsfolk afoot were also doing, swelling the solemn progress like a funeral cortège. Nicholas stared and strained ahead, measuring the mute and motionless body. So long and yet so light, fallen away into age before age was due, this could be no other but Godfrid Marescot, the maimed and dwindling flesh at last shed by its immaculate spirit. He stared through a mist, trying impatiently to clear his eyes.

'That is this Madog, that man who leads them?'

Hugh nodded silently, yes. No doubt but Madog had recruited friends from the suburb, part Welsh, as he was wholly Welsh, to help him bring the dead man home. He commanded his helpers decorously, dolorously, with great dignity.

'The other one – Fidelis?' wondered Nicholas, recalling the retiring anonymous figure forever shrinking into shadow, yet instant in service. He felt a pang of self-reproach that he grieved so much for Godfrid, and so little for the young man who had made himself a willing slave to Godfrid's nobility.

Hugh shook his head. There was but one here.

They were across the bridge and moving along the approach to the Foregate, between the Gaye on the left hand and the mill and mill-pool on the right, and so to the gatehouse of the abbey. There the bearers turned in to the right with their burden, under the arch, into the great court, where a silent, solemn assembly had massed to wait for them, and there they set down their charge, and stood in silent attendance.

The news had reached the abbey as the brothers came from Vespers. They gathered in a stunned

228

circle, abbot, prior, obedientiaries, monks and novices, brought thus abruptly to the contemplation of mortality. The townspeople who had followed the procession to its destination hovered within the gate, somewhat apart, and gazed in awed silence.

Madog approached the abbot with the Welshman's unservile readiness to accept all men as equals, and told his story simply. Radulfus acknowledged the will of God and the helplessness of man with an absolving motion of his hand, and stood looking down at the swathed body a long moment, before he stooped and drew back the covering from the face.

Humilis in dying had shed all but his proper years. Death could not restore the lost and fallen flesh, but it had relaxed the sharp, gaunt lines, and smoothed away the engraved hollows of pain. Hugh and Nicholas, standing aloof at the corner of the cloister, caught a brief glimpse of Humilis translated, removed into superhuman serenity and repose, before Radulfus lowered the cloth again, blessed the bier and the bearers, and motioned to his obedientiaries to take up the body and carry it into the mortuary chapel.

Only then, when Brother Edmund, reminded of old reticences those two lost brothers had shared, and manifestly deprived of Fidelis, looked round for the one other man who was in the intimate secrets of Humilis's broken body, and failed to find him – only then did Hugh realise that Brother Cadfael was the one man missing from this gathering. He, who of all men should have been ready and dutiful in whatever concerned Humilis, to be elsewhere at this moment! The dereliction stuck fast in Hugh's mind, until he made sense of it later. It was, after all, possible that a dead man should have urgent unfinished business

229

elsewhere, even more dear to him than the last devotions paid to his body.

They extended their respects and condolences to Abbott Radulfus, with the promise that search should be made downstream for the body of Brother Fidelis, as long as any hope remained of finding him, and then they rode back at a walking pace into the town, host and guest together. The dusk was closing gently in, the sky clear, bland, innocent of evil, the air suddenly cool and kind. Aline was waiting with the evening meal ready to be served, and welcomed two men returning as graciously as one. And if there was still a horse missing from the stables, Hugh did not linger to discover it, but left the horses to the grooms, and devoted his own attention to Nicholas.

'You must stay with us,' he said over supper, 'until his burial. I'll send word to Cruce, he'll want to pay the last honours to one who once meant to become his brother by law, and he has a right to know how things stand now with Heriet.'

That caused Aline to prick up her ears. 'And how do things stand now with Heriet? So much has happened today, I seem to have missed at least the half of it. Nicholas did say he brought grim news, but even the downpour couldn't delay him long enough to say more. What has happened?'

They told her, between them, all that had passed, from the dogged search in Winchester to the point where news of Madog's disaster had interrupted the questioning of Adam Heriet, and sent them out in consternation to find out the truth of the report. Aline listened with a slight, anxious frown.

'He burst in crying that two brothers from the abbey were dead, drowned in the river? Named

230

names, did he? There in the cell, in front of your prisoner?'

'I think it was I who named names,' said Hugh. 'It came at the right moment for Heriet, I fancy he was nearing the end of his tether. Now he can draw breath for the next bout, though I doubt if it will save him.'

Aline said no more on that score until Nicholas, short of sleep after his long ride and the shocks of this day, took himself off to his bed. When he was gone, she laid by the embroidery on which she had been working, and went and sat down beside Hugh on the cushioned bench beside the empty hearth, and wound a persuasive arm about his neck.

'Hugh, love – there's something you must hear – and Nicholas must *not* hear, not yet, not until all's over and safe and calm. It might be best if he never does hear it, though perhaps he'll divine at least half of it for himself in the end. But *you* we need now.'

'*We?*' said Hugh, not too greatly surprised, and turned to wind an arm comfortably about her waist and draw her closer to his side.

'Cadfael and I. Who else?'

'So I supposed,' said Hugh, sighing and smiling. 'I did wonder at his abandoning the disastrous end of a venture he himself helped to launch.'

'But he did not abandon it, he's about resolving it this moment. And if you should hear someone about the stables, a little later, no need for alarm, it will only be Cadfael bringing back your horse, and you know he can be trusted to see to his horse's comfort before he gives a thought to his own.'

'I foresee a long story,' said Hugh. 'It had better be interesting.' Her fair hair was soft and sweet against

231

his cheek. He turned to touch his lips to hers, very softly and briefly.

'It is. As any matter of life and death must be. You'll see! And since it was blurted out in front of poor Adam Heriet that two brothers have drowned, you ought to pay him a visit as soon as you can, tomorrow, and tell him he need not fret, that things are nor always what they seem.'

'Then tell me,' said Hugh, 'what they really are.'

She settled herself warmly into the circle of his arm, and very gravely told him.

The search for the body of Brother Fidelis was pursued diligently from both banks of the river, at every spot where floating debris commonly came ashore, for more than two days, but all that came to light was one of his sandals, torn from his foot by the river and cast up in the sandy shoals near Atcham. Most bodies that went into the Severn were also put ashore by the Severn, sooner or later. This one never would be. Shrewsbury and the world had seen the last of Brother Fidelis.

Chapter Fourteen

HE BURIAL of Brother Humilis brought together in the abbey guest-hall representatives of all the small nobility of the shire, and most of the Benedictine foundations within the region. Sheriff and town provost would certainly attend and so would many of the elders and merchants of Shrewsbury, more by reason of the dramatic and tragic nature of the dead man's departure than for any real knowledge they had had of him in his short sojourn in the town. Most had never seen him, but knew his reputation before he took the cowl, and felt that his birth and death here in their midst gave them some title in him. It would be a great occasion, befitting an entombment within the church itself, a rare honour.

Reginald Cruce came down from Lai a day in advance of the ceremony, malevolently gratified at all that Nicholas had to report, and taking vengeful pleasure in having the miscreant who had dared do violence to a member of the Cruce family securely in prison and tacitly acknowledged as guilty, even if trial had to await the legal formalities. Hugh did nothing to cast doubts on his satisfaction.

Reginald held the enamelled ring in a broad palm, and studied the intricate decoration with interest. 'Yes, I remember it. Strange it should be this small thing that condemns him. She had another ring, I recall, that she valued, perhaps all the more because it was given to her as a child, when her fingers were far too small to retain it. Marescot sent it to her when the contract of betrothal was concluded, it was old, one that had been handed down bride to bride in his family. She used to wear it on a chain round her neck because it was too big for her fingers. I'm sure she would not leave that behind.'

'This was the only ring listed in the valuables she took with her,' said Nicholas, taking back the little jewel. 'I'm pledged to return it to the silversmith's wife in Winchester.'

'The list was of the things intended for her dowry. The ring Marescot sent her she probably meant to keep. It was gold, a snake with red eyes making two coils about the finger. Very old, the scales were worn smooth. I wonder,' said Reginald, 'where it is now. There are no more Marescots left, not of that branch, to give it to their brides.'

No more Marescots, thought Nicholas, and no more Julians. A double, grievous loss, for which revenge, now that he seemed to have it securely in his hands, was no compensation at all. 'Should you be mistaken, and she is still living,' the silversmith's wife had said, 'and wants her ring, then give it back to her, and pay me for it whatever you think fair.' If I had more gold than king and empress put together, thought Nicholas, nursing the ache he carried within him, it would not be enough to pay for so inexpressible a blessing.

*

234

Brother Cadfael had behaved himself extremely modestly and circumspectly these last days, strict to every scruple of the horarium, prompt in every service, trying, he admitted to himself ruefully, to deserve success, and disarm whatever disapproval the heavens might be harbouring against him. The end in view, he was certain, was not only good but vitally necessary, for the sake of the abbey and the church, and the peace of mind of all those whose fate it was to live on now that Humilis was delivered out of the body, and safe for ever. But the means – he was less certain that the means were above reproach. But what can a man do, or a woman either, but use what comes to hand?

He rose early on the funeral day, to have a little time for his private and vehement prayers before Prime. Much depended on this day, he had good reason to be uneasy, and to turn to Saint Winifred for indulgence, pardon and aid. She had forgiven him, before this, for very irregular means towards desirable ends, and shown him humouring kindness when sterner patrons might have frowned.

But this morning she had another petitioner before him. Someone was crouched almost prostrate on the three steps leading up to her altar. The rigid lines of body and limbs, the convulsive knot of the linked hands contorted on the highest step, spoke of a need at least as extreme as his own. Cadfael drew back silently into shadow, and waited, and after what seemed a long anguished time the petitioner gathered himself stiffly and slowly, like a man crippled, rose from his knees, and slipped away towards the south door into the cloister. It came as a surprise and a wonder that Brother Urien should be tearing out his heart thus alone in the early morning.

235

Cadfael had never paid, perhaps, sufficient attention to Brother Urien. Who did? Who talked with him, who was familiar with him? The man elected himself into solitude.

Cadfael made his prayers. He had done what seemed best, he had had loyal and ingenious helpers, now he could only plump the whole matter confidingly into Saint Winifred's tolerant Welsh arms, remind her he was her distant kin, and leave the rest to her.

In the morning of a mild, clear day, with all due ceremony and every honour, Brother Humilis, Godfrid Marescot, was buried in the transept of the abbey church of Saint Peter and Saint Paul.

Cadfael had been looking in vain for one particular mourner, and had not found her, but having rested his case with the saint he left the church not greatly troubled. And as the brothers emerged into the great court, Abbot Radulfus leading, there she was, neat and competent and comely as ever, waiting near the gatehouse to advance to meet the concourse, like a lone knight venturing undeterred against an army. She had a gift for timing, she had conjured up for herself a great cloud of witnesses. Let the revelation be public and wonderful.

Sister Magdalen, of the Benedictine cell of Godric's Ford, a few miles distant towards the Welsh border, had been both beautiful and worldly in her youth, a baron's mistress by choice, and honest and loyal to her bargain at that. True to her word and bond then, so she was now in her new vocation. If she had bought as escort some of her devoted army of countrymen from the western forests on this occasion, she had discreetly removed them from sight at this moment. She had the field to herself.

A plump, rosy, middle-aged lady, bright-eyed and brisk, the remnant of her beauty wisely tempered by the austere whiteness of her wimple and blackness of her habit into something homely and comfortable, at least until her indomitable dimple plunged dazzlingly in her cheek, like the twinkling dive of a small golden fish, and again smoothed out as rapidly and demurely as the water of a stream resuming its sunny level. Cadfael had known her for a few years now, and had had occasion to rely on her more than once in complex matters. His trust in her was absolute.

She advanced decorously upon the abbot, glanced aside and veered slightly towards Hugh, and succeeded in halting them both, arresting sacred and secular authority together. All the remaining mourners, monks and laymen, flooded out from the church and stood waiting respectfully for the nobility to disperse unimpeded.

'My lords,' said Sister Magdalen, dividing a reverence between church and state, 'I pray your pardon that I come so late, but the recent rains have flooded some parts of the way, and I did not allow enough time for the delays. *Mea culpa*! I shall make my prayers for our brothers in private, and hope to attend the Mass for them here, to make amends for today's failing.'

'Late or early, sister, you have a welcome assured,' said the abbot. 'You should stay a day or two, until the ways are clear again. And certainly you must be my guest at dinner now you are here.'

'You are very gracious, Father,' she said. 'Having failed of my time, I would not have ventured to

237

trouble you now, but that I am the bearer of a letter, to the lord sheriff.' She turned and looked full at Hugh, very gravely. She had the rolled and sealed parchment leaf in her hand. 'I must tell you how this came to Godric's Ford. Mother Mariana regularly receives letters from the prioress of our mother house at Polesworth. In the most recent, which came only yesterday, this other letter was enclosed, from a lady just arrived with a company of other travellers, and now resting after her journey. It is superscribed to the lord sheriff of Shropshire, and sealed with the seal of Polesworth. I brought it with me at this opportunity, seeing it may be important. With your leave, Father, here I deliver it.'

How it was done remained her secret, but she had a way of holding people so that they felt they might miss some prodigy if they went away from her. No one had moved, no one had slipped into casual talk, all the movement there was in the court was of those still making their way out to join the press, and sliding softly round the periphery to find a place where they might see and hear better. There was only the softest rustling of garments and shuffling of feet as Hugh took the scroll. The seal would be immaculate, for it was also the seal of Polesworth's daughter cell at Godric's Ford.

'Have I your leave, Father? It may well be something of importance.'

'By all means, read,' said the abbot.

Hugh broke the seal and unrolled the leaf. He read with brows drawn close in fixed attention. Round the great court men held their breath, or drew it very softly and cautiously. There was tension in the air, after all that had passed.

238

'Father,' said Hugh, looking up abruptly, 'there is matter here that concerns more than me. Others here have much more to do in this, and deserve and need to know at once what is set down here. It is a marvel! O such weight, I should have had to issue its purport as a public proclamation. With your leave I'll do so here and now, before all this company.'

There was no need to raise his voice, every ear was strained to attend on every word as he read clearly:

'"My lord Sheriff,
It is come to my ears, to my great dismay, that in my own shire I am rumoured to be dead, robbed and done to death for gain. Wherefore I send in haste this present witness that I am not so wronged, but declare myself alive and well, here arrived into the hospitality of the house of sisters at Polesworth. I repent me that lives and honours may have been put in peril mistakenly on my account, some, perhaps, who have been good friends and servants to me. And I ask pardon if I have been the means of disruption and distress to any, unknown to me but through my silence. There shall be amends made.

'"As to my living heretofore, I confess with all humility that I came to doubt whether I had the nun's true vocation before ever I reached my goal, and therefore I have been living retired and serviceable, but have taken no vows as a nun. At Sopwell Priory by Saint Albans a devout woman may live a life of holiness and service short of the veil, through the charity of Prior Geoffrey. Now, being advised I am sought as one dead, I desire to show myself to all those who know me, that no one may go any longer in grief or peril because of me.

"'I entreat you, my lord, make this known to my good brother and all my kin, and send some trustworthy man to bring me safe to Shrewsbury, and I shall rest your lordship's grateful debtor.
Julian Cruce.'"

Long before he had reached the end there had begun a stirring, a murmur, an eddy that shook its way like a sudden rising wind through the ranks of the listeners, and then a roused humming like bees in swarm, and suddenly Reginald's stunned silence broke in a bellow of wonder, bewilderment and delight all mingled:

'My sister *living*? She's alive! By God, we have been wildly astray . . .'

'Alive!' echoed Nicholas in a dazed whisper. 'Julian is alive . . . alive and well . . . .'

The murmur grew to a throbbing chorus of wonder and excitement, and above it the voice of Abbot Radulfus soared exultantly: 'God's mercies are infinite. Out of the shadow of death he demonstrates his miraculous goodness.'

'We have wronged an honest man!' cried Reginald, as vehement in amends as in accusation. 'He was as truly her man as ever he claimed! Now it comes clear to me – all that he sold he sold for her, surely for her! Only those woman's trinkets that were hers in the world – she had the right to what they would fetch . . .'

'I'll bring her from Polesworth myself, along with you,' said Hugh, 'and Adam Heriet shall be hauled out of his prison a free man, and go along with us. Who has a better right?'

240

The burial of Brother Humilis had become in a moment the resurrection of Julian Cruce, from a mourning into a celebration, from Good Friday to Easter. 'A life taken from us and a life restored,' said Abbot Radulfus, 'is perfect balance, that we may fear neither living nor dying.'

Brother Rhun came from the refectory with his mind full of a strange blend of pleasure and sorrow, and took them with him into the quietness and solitude of the abbey orchards along the Gaye. There would be no one there at this hour of this season if he left the kitchen garden and the fields behind, and went on to the very edge of abbey ground. Beyond, trees came right down to the waterside, overhanging the river. There he halted, and stood gazing downstream, where Fidelis was gone.

The water was still turgid and dark, but the level had subsided slightly, though it still lay in silvery shallows over hollows in the water-meadows on the far shore. Rhun thought of his friend's body being swept down beneath that opaque surface, lost beyond recovery. The morning had seen a woman supposed dead restored to life, and there was gladness in that, but it did not balance the grief he felt over the loss of Fidelis. He missed him with an aching intensity, though he had said no word of his pain to anyone, nor responded when others found the words he could not find to give expression to sorrow.

He crossed the boundary of abbey land, and threaded a way through the belt of trees, to have a view down the next long reach. And there suddenly he stopped and drew back a pace, for someone else was there before him, some creature even more unhappy than himself. Brother Urien sat huddled in the muddy grass among the bushes at the edge of the water, and stared at the rapid eddies as they coiled and sped by. Downstream from here the dull mirrors of water dappling the far meadows had been fed, since the storm, by two nights of gentler rain, and once filled could not drain away, they could only dry up slowly. Their stillness and tranquillity, reflecting back the pale blue of sky and fleeting white of clouds, made the demonic speed of the main stream seem more than a mere aspect of nature, rather a live, malignant force that gulped down men.

Rhun had made no noise in his approach, yet Urien grew aware that he was not alone, and turned a defensive face, hollow-eyed and hostile.

'You, too?' he said dully. 'Why you? It was I destroyed Fidelis.'

'No, you did no such thing!' protested Rhun, and came out of the bushes to stand beside him. 'You must not say or think it.'

'Fool, you know what I did, why deny it? You know it, you did what you could to undo it,' said Urien bleakly. 'I drove, I threatened – I destroyed Fidelis. If I had the courage I would go after him by the same way, but I have not the courage.'

Rhun sat down beside him in the grass, close but not touching him, and earnestly studied the drawn and embittered face. 'You have not slept,' he said gently.

'How should I sleep, knowing what I know? Not slept, no, nor eaten, either, but it takes a long time to die of not eating. A man can go on water alone for many weeks. And I am neither patient nor brave. There's only one way for me, and that is full confession. Oh, not for absolution, no – for retribution. I

242

have been sitting here preparing for it. Soon I will go and get it over.'

'No!' said Rhun, with sudden, fierce authority. 'That you must not do.' He was not entirely clear himself why this was so urgent a matter, but there was something pricking at his mind, some truth deep within him that he could glimpse only by sidelong flashes, out of the corner of his mind's eye. When he turned to pursue it directly, it vanished. Life and death were both mysteries. A life taken from us and a life restored, Abbot Radulfus had said, is perfect balance. A life taken, and a life restored, almost in the same moment . . .

He had it, then. Light opened brilliantly before him, the load on his heart was lifted away. A perfect balance, yes! He sat entranced, so filled and overfilled with enlightenment that all his senses were turned inward to the glow, like cold hands spread blissfully at a bright fire, and he scarcely heard Urien saying savagely: 'That I must and will do. How can I bear this longer alone?'

Rhun stirred and awakened from his trance of bliss. 'You need not be alone,' he said. 'You are not alone now. I am here. Say what you choose to me, but never to any other. Even the confessional might not be secret enough. Then you would indeed have destroyed all that Fidelis was, all that Fidelis did, fouled and muddied it into a byword, a scandal that would cast a shadow on us all, on the Order, most of all on his memory . . . .' He caught himself up there, smiling. 'See how strong is habit! But I do know – I know now what you could tell, and for the sake of Fidelis it must never be told. Surely you see that, as clearly as I now see it. Do no more harm! Bear what you have to bear, and be as silent as Fidelis was.'

Urien's stony face quivered and melted suddenly like wax. He clenched his arms fiercely over his eyes and bowed himself into the long, wet grass, and shook with a terrible storm of dry and silent sobbing. Rhun leaned down and confidently embraced the heaving shoulders. At the touch a great, soft groan passed through Urien's body and ebbed out of him, leaving him limp and still. Once it had been Urien who touched, and Rhun who looked him mildly in the eyes and filled him with rage and shame. Now Rhun touched Urien, laid an arm about him and let it lie quiet there, and all the rage and shame sighed out of him and left him clean.

'Keep the secret. You must, if you loved him.'

'Yes – yes,' said Urien brokenly out of his sheltering arms.

'For his sake . . . .' This time Rhun turned back, smiling, to set right what he had said. 'For her sake!'

'Yes, yes – to the grave. Stay with me!'

'I'm here. When we go, we'll go together. Who knows? Even the harm already done may not be incurable.'

'Can the dead live again?' demanded Urien bitterly.

'If God pleases!' said Rhun, who had his own good reasons for believing in miracles.

Julian Cruce arrived at the abbey of Saint Peter and Saint Paul just in time to attend the Mass for the souls of Brother Humilis and Brother Fidelis, drowned together in the great storm. It was the second day after the burial of Humilis, a fresh, cool day of soft blue sky and soft green earth, the gloss of summer briefly restored. By that time every soul

244

in and around Shrewsbury had heard the story of the woman come back from the dead, and everyone was curious to witness her return. There was a great crowd in the court to watch her ride in, her brother at her side and Hugh Beringar and Adam Heriet following. Within the gates they dismounted, and the horses were led away. Reginald took his sister by the hand, and brought her between the eager watchers to the church door.

Cadfael had had some qualms about this moment, and had taken his stand close beside Nicholas Harnage, where he could pluck at his sleeve in sharp warning should he be startled into some indiscreet utterance. It might have been better to warn him beforehand, and forestall the danger. But on the other hand, it must be gain if the young man never did make the connection, and it seemed worth taking the risk. If he was never forced to consider how formidable a rival was gone before him, and how indelible must be the memory of a devotion unlikely ever to be matched, there would be less of a barrier to his own courtship. If he approached her in innocence he came with strong advantages, having had the trust and affection of Godfrid Marescot, as well as amply proving his concern for the girl herself. There was every ground for kindness there. If he recognised her, and saw in a moment the whole pattern of events, he might be too discouraged ever to approach her at all, for who could follow Humilis and not be diminished? But he might – it was just possible – he might even be large enough to accept all the disadvantages, hold his tongue, and still put his fortune to the test. There was promise in him. Still, Cadfael stood alerted and anxious, his hand hovering at the young man's elbow.

She came through the crowd on her brother's arm, no great beauty, simply a tall girl in a dark cloak and gown, with a grave oval face austerely framed in a white wimple and a dark blue hood. Sister Magdalen and Aline between them had done well by her. The general mourning forbade bright colours, but Aline had carefully avoided providing anything that could recall the rusty monastic black. They were of much the same build, tall and slender, the gown fitted well. The tonsure would take some time to grow out, but hiding the ring of chestnut hair completely and covering half the lofty brow did much to change the shape of the serious face. She had darkened her lashes, which gave a changed value and an iris shade to the clear grey of her eyes. She held up her head and walked slowly past men who had lived side by side with Brother Fidelis for many weeks now, and they saw no one but Julian Cruce, nothing to do with the abbey of Shrewsbury, simply a nine days' wonder from the outer world, interesting now but soon to be forgotten.

Nicholas watched her draw near, and was filled with deep, glowing gratitude, simply that she was alive. Her life might have no place for him, but at least it was hers, all the years he had thought stolen from her by a cruel crime, while here, it seemed, was no crime at all. He could, he would, make the assay, but not yet. Let her have time to know him, for she knew nothing of him yet, and he had no claim on her, unless, perhaps, Hugh Beringar had told her of his part in the search for her. Even that gave him no rights. Those he would have to earn.

But as she drew level with him she turned head and looked him in the eyes. An instant only, but it was enough.

Cadfael saw him start and quiver, saw him open his lips, perhaps to cry out in the sheer shock of recognition. But he made no sound, after all. Cadfael had gripped him by the arm, but released him at once, for there had been no need. Nicholas turned on him face of starry brightness, dazzled and dazzling, and said in a rapid whisper: 'Never fret! I am the dumb one now!'

So quick and agile a mind, thought Cadfael approvingly, would not be put off by difficulties. And the girl was still barely twenty-three. They had time. Why should a girl who had had the devoted company of one fine man therefore fail to appreciate the value of a second? I wonder, he thought, what Humilis said to her at Salton that last day? Did he know, in the end, what and who she was? I hope he did. Certainly he knew the candlesticks and the cross, once Hugh described them to him, for of course she took them with her into Hyde, and with Hyde they must have gone to dust. But then, I think, he was in two minds, half afraid his Fidelis had been mixed up in Julian's death, half wondering . . . By the end, however the light came, surely he knew the truth.

In his chosen stall next to Brother Urien, Rhun leaned close to whisper: 'Look! Look at the lady! This is she who should have been wife to Brother Humilis.'

Urien looked, but with listless eyes that saw only what they expected to see. He shook his head.

'You know her,' said Rhun. 'Look again!'

He looked again, and he knew her. The load of guilt and grief and penitence lifted from him like a lark rising. He ceased to sing, for his throat was constricted and his tongue mute. He stood lost between knowledge and wonder, the inheritor of her silence.

Julian emerged from the church into the temperate sunlight with the blankness of wonder, endurance and loss still in her face. Watching her from the shadow of the cloister, Nicholas abandoned all thought of approaching her yet. Now that he understood at last the magnitude of what she had done, it became impossible to offer her an ordinary marriage and a customary love. Not yet, not for a long while yet. But he could bide his time, keep touch with her brother, make his way to her by delicate degrees, open his heart to her only when hers was reconciled and at peace.

She had halted, looking about her, withdrawing her hand from her brother's as if she sought someone to whom recognition was due. The palest of smiles touched her face. She came towards Nicholas with hand extended. About the middle finger the little golden serpent twined in a double coil, he caught the tiny glitter of its ruby eyes.

'Sir,' said Julian, in a voice pitched almost childishly high, but very soft and sweet, 'the lord sheriff has told me of all the pains you have been spending for me. I am sorry I have caused you and others so much needless trouble and care. Thanks are poor recompense for so much kindness.'

Her hand lay firm and cool in his. Her smile was still faint and remote, acknowledging nothing of any other identity but that of Julian Cruce. He might have thought she was denying her other self, but for the clear, straight gaze of her grey eyes, opened wide to admit him into a shared knowledge where words were unnecessary. Nothing need ever be said where everything was known and understood.

'Madam,' said Nicholas, 'to see you here alive and well is all the recompense I need or want.'

'But I hope you will come soon to visit us at Lai,' she said. 'It would be a kindness. I should like to make better amends.'

And that was all. He kissed the hand he held, and she turned and went away from him. And surely this was nothing more than paying a due of gratitude, as she paid all her dues, to the last scruple of pain, devotion and love. But she had asked, and she was not one of those women who ask without meaning. And he would go to Lai, soon, yes, very soon. To make do with the touch of her hand and her pale smile and the undoubted trust she had just placed in him, until it was fair and honourable to hope for more.

They sat in Cadfael's workshop in the herb-garden, in the after-dinner hush, Sister Magdalen, Hugh Beringar and Cadfael together. It was all over, the curious all gone home, the brothers innocent of all ill except the loss of two of their number, and two who had been with them only a short time, and somewhat withdrawn from the common view, at that. They would soon become but very dim figures, to be remembered by name in prayer while their faces faded from memory.

'There could still be some awkward questions asked,' admitted Cadfael, 'if anyone went to the trouble to probe deeper, but now no one ever will. The Order can breathe again. There'll be no scandal, no aspersions cast on either Hyde or Shrewsbury, no legatine muck-raking, no ballad-makers running off

249

dirty rhymes about monks and their women, and hawking them round the markets, no bishops bearing down on us with damning visitations, no carping white monks fulminating about the laxity and lechery of the Benedictines . . . And no foul blight clinging round that poor girl's name and blackening her for life. Thank God!' he concluded fervently.

He had broached one of his best flasks of wine. He felt they deserved it as much as they needed it.

'Adam was in her confidence throughout,' said Hugh. 'It was he who got her the clothes to turn her into a young man, he who cut her hair, and sold for her the few things she considered her own, to pay her lodging until she presented herself at Hyde. When he said she was dead, he spoke in the bitterness of his heart, for she was indeed dead to the world, by her own choice. And when I brought him from Brigge, he was frantic to get news of her, for he'd given her up for lost after Hyde burned, but when I told him there was a second brother come from Hyde with Godfrid, then he was easy, for he knew who the second must be. He would have died rather than betray her. He knew the ugliness of which men are capable, as well as we.'

'And she, I hope and think,' said Cadfael, 'must know the loyalty and devotion of which one man, at least, was capable. She should, seeing it is the mirror of her own. No, there was no other solution possible but for Fidelis to die and vanish without trace, before Julian could come back to life. But I never thought the chance would come as it did . . . .'

'You took it nimbly enough,' said Hugh.

'It was then or never. It would have come out else. Madog would never have said anything, but she had stopped caring when Humilis died.' He had

had her in his arms, herself half-dead, on that ride to Godric's Ford to commit her to Sister Magdalen's care, the russet tonsure wet and draggled on his shoulder, the pale, soiled face stricken into ice, the grey eyes wide open, seeing nothing. 'It was as much as we could do to get him out of her arms. Without Aline we should have been lost. I almost feared we might lose the girl as well as the man. But Sister Magdalen is a powerful physician.'

'That letter I composed for her,' said Sister Magdalen, looking back on it with a critical but satisfied eye, 'was the hardest ever I had to write. And not a lie from start to finish! Not one in the whole of it. A little mild deception, but no lies. That was important, you understand. Do you know why she chose to be mute? Well, there is the matter of her voice, of course, a woman's if ever there was. The face – it's a good face, clear and strong and delicate, one that could as well belong to a boy as to a girl, but not the voice. But beyond that,' said Sister Magdalen, 'she had two good reasons for being dumb. First, she was resolute she would never ask anything of him, never make any woman's appeal, for she held he owed her nothing, no privilege, no consideration. What she got of him she had to earn. And second, she was absolute she would never lie to him. Who cannot speak cannot plead or cajole, and cannot lie.'

'So he owed her nothing, and she owed him all,' said Hugh, shaking his head over the unfathomable strangeness of women.

'Ah, but she also had her due,' said Cadfael. 'What she wanted and held to be hers she took, the whole of it, to the end, to the last moment. His company, the care of him, the secrets of his body, as intimate as

251

ever was marriage – his love, far beyond the common claims of marriage. No use any man telling her she was free, when she *knew* she was a wife. I wonder is she free even now.'

'Not yet, but she will be,' Sister Magdalen assured them. 'She has too much courage to give over living. And if that young man who fancies her has courage enough not to give over loving, he may do very well in the end. He starts with a strong advantage, having loved the same idol. Besides,' she added, viewing a future that held a certain promise even for some who felt just now that they had only a past, 'I doubt if that household of her brother's, with a wife in possession, and three children, not to speak of another on the way – no, I doubt if an unwed sister's part in Lai will have much lasting attraction for a woman like Julian Cruce.'

The half-hour of rest after dinner had passed, the brothers stirred again to their work, and so did Cadfael, parting from his friends at the turn of the box hedge. Sister Magdalen and her two stout woodsmen would be off back to Godric's Ford by the westward track, and Hugh was heading thankfully for home. Cadfael passed through the herb-garden into the small plot where he had a couple of apple trees and a pear tree of his own growing, just old enough to crop. He surveyed the scene with deep content. Everything was greening afresh where it had been pale as straw. The Meole Brook had still a few visible shoals, but was no longer a mere sad, sluggish network of rivulets struggling through pebble and sand. September was again September, mellowed and fruitful after the summer heat and drought. Much of the abundant weight of fruit had fallen unplumped by reason of the dryness, but even so there would still be harvest enough for thanksgiving. After every extreme the seasons righted themselves, and won back the half at least of what was lost. So might the seasons of men right themselves, with a little help by way of rain from heaven.

* * *

O God, who hast consecrated the state of Matrimony to such an excellent mystery . . . Look mercifully upon these thy servants.

from 'The form of Solemnization of Matrimony' in *The Book of Common Prayer*